"W.E.B. Griffin is the ... ever to put pen to paper—and rates among the best storytellers in any genre."

—*The Phoenix Gazette*

Praise for
THE HOSTAGE

"IS GRIFFIN OUR HOMER OR TACITUS? Those military experts wrote about real soldiers and what the world needs now is a real-life Charley Castillo, Griffin's smart and efficient Department of Homeland Security agent . . . Castillo and his team of tough and shrewd experts are just the kind of believable people we want in these situations. And if it takes a novelist like Griffin, who has honed his skills and weapons in five previous series, to bring them to life, at least their real counterparts will have some fictional role models to live up to." —*Publishers Weekly*

"WILL APPEAL TO THRILLER READERS, especially Griffin's many fans . . . [*The Hostage* has] fast pacing and the relevance of the story to today's events and headlines."

—*Booklist*

BY ORDER OF THE PRESIDENT

"CUTTING-EDGE MILITARY MATERIAL . . . Those who love Griffin's stories of past wars will take to this new series based on present and future conflicts."

—*Publishers Weekly*

"PLENTY OF ACTION, HIGH-LEVEL INTRIGUE, interesting characters, flip dialogue, romance, and a whole lot of drinking and other carrying on." —*Library Journal*

RETREAT, HELL!

"LOVERS OF MILITARY YARNS WILL GRAB THIS BOOK." —*The Columbus Dispatch*

"GRIFFIN . . . STICKS MORE CLOSELY TO THE ACTION AND MOVES AHEAD WITH GALVANIZED SELF-ASSURANCE." —*Kirkus Reviews*

continued . . .

"ANOTHER SOLID ENTRY . . . Veterans of the series will enjoy finding old comrades caught up in fresh adventures, while new-guy readers can easily enter here and pick up the ongoing story." —*Publishers Weekly*

W.E.B. GRIFFIN'S CLASSIC SERIES

THE CORPS

The bestselling saga of the heroes we call Marines . . .

"GREAT READING. A superb job of mingling fact and fiction . . . [Griffin's] characters come to life."
—*The Sunday Oklahoman*

"THIS MAN HAS REALLY DONE HIS HOME-WORK . . . I confess to impatiently awaiting the appearance of succeeding books in the series." —*The Washington Post*

"ACTION-PACKED . . . DIFFICULT TO PUT DOWN."
—*Marine Corps Gazette*

HONOR BOUND

The high drama and real heroes of World War II . . .

"ROUSING . . . AN IMMENSELY ENTERTAINING ADVENTURE." —*Kirkus Reviews*

"A TAUTLY WRITTEN STORY whose twists and turns will keep readers guessing until the last page."
—*Publishers Weekly*

"A SUPERIOR WAR STORY." —*Library Journal*

BROTHERHOOD OF WAR

The series that launched W.E.B. Griffin's phenomenal career . . .

"AN AMERICAN EPIC." —Tom Clancy

"FIRST-RATE. Griffin, a former soldier, skillfully sets the stage, melding credible characters, a good eye for detail, and colorful gritty dialogue into a readable and entertaining story." —*The Washington Post Book World*

"ABSORBING, salted-peanuts reading filled with detailed and fascinating descriptions of weapons, tactics, Green Beret training, army life, and battle."
—*The New York Times Book Review*

"A CRACKLING GOOD STORY. It gets into the hearts and minds of those who by choice or circumstance are called upon to fight our nation's wars."
—William R. Corson, Lt. Col. [Ret.], U.S.M.C., author of
The Betrayal and *The Armies of Ignorance*

"A MAJOR WORK . . . MAGNIFICENT . . . POWER-FUL . . . If books about warriors and the women who love them were given medals for authenticity, insight, and honesty, Brotherhood of War would be covered with them."
—William Bradford Huie, author of *The Klansman*
and *The Execution of Private Slovik*

BADGE OF HONOR

Griffin's electrifying epic series of a big-city police force . . .

"DAMN EFFECTIVE . . . He captivates you with characters the way few authors can." —Tom Clancy

"TOUGH, AUTHENTIC . . . POLICE DRAMA AT ITS BEST . . . Readers will feel as if they're part of the investigation, and the true-to-life characters will soon feel like old friends. Excellent reading." —Dale Brown

"COLORFUL . . . GRITTY . . . TENSE."
—*The Philadelphia Inquirer*

"A REAL WINNER." —*New York Daily News*

MEN AT WAR

The legendary OSS—fighting a silent war of spies and assassins in the shadows of World War II . . .

"WRITTEN WITH A SPECIAL FLAIR for the military heart and mind." —*Winfield Daily Courier* (KS)

"SHREWD, SHARP, ROUSING ENTERTAINMENT."
—*Kirkus Reviews*

ALSO BY W.E.B. GRIFFIN

HONOR BOUND
HONOR BOUND
BLOOD AND HONOR
SECRET HONOR

BROTHERHOOD OF WAR
BOOK I: THE LIEUTENANTS
BOOK II: THE CAPTAINS
BOOK III: THE MAJORS
BOOK IV: THE COLONELS
BOOK V: THE BERETS
BOOK VI: THE GENERALS
BOOK VII: THE NEW BREED
BOOK VIII: THE AVIATORS
BOOK IX: SPECIAL OPS

THE CORPS
BOOK I: SEMPER FI
BOOK II: CALL TO ARMS
BOOK III: COUNTERATTACK
BOOK IV: BATTLEGROUND
BOOK V: LINE OF FIRE
BOOK VI: CLOSE COMBAT
BOOK VII: BEHIND THE LINES
BOOK VIII: IN DANGER'S PATH
BOOK IX: UNDER FIRE
BOOK X: RETREAT, HELL!

BADGE OF HONOR
BOOK I: MEN IN BLUE
BOOK II: SPECIAL OPERATIONS
BOOK III: THE VICTIM
BOOK IV: THE WITNESS
BOOK V: THE ASSASSIN
BOOK VI: THE MURDERERS
BOOK VII: THE INVESTIGATORS
BOOK VIII: FINAL JUSTICE

MEN AT WAR
BOOK I: THE LAST HEROES
BOOK II: THE SECRET WARRIORS
BOOK III: THE SOLDIER SPIES
BOOK IV: THE FIGHTING AGENTS
BOOK V: THE SABOTEURS
(with William E. Butterworth IV)

PRESIDENTIAL AGENT
BOOK I: BY ORDER OF THE PRESIDENT
BOOK II: THE HOSTAGE
BOOK III: THE HUNTERS

THE HOSTAGE

★ ★ ★

W.E.B. GRIFFIN

JOVE BOOKS, NEW YORK

THE BERKLEY PUBLISHING GROUP
Published by the Penguin Group
Penguin Group (USA) Inc.
375 Hudson Street, New York, New York 10014, USA
Penguin Group (Canada), 90 Eglinton Avenue East, Suite 700, Toronto, Ontario M4P 2Y3, Canada
(a division of Pearson Penguin Canada Inc.)
Penguin Books Ltd., 80 Strand, London WC2R 0RL, England
Penguin Group Ireland, 25 St. Stephen's Green, Dublin 2, Ireland (a division of Penguin Books Ltd.)
Penguin Group (Australia), 250 Camberwell Road, Camberwell, Victoria 3124, Australia
(a division of Pearson Australia Group Pty. Ltd.)
Penguin Books India Pvt. Ltd., 11 Community Centre, Panchsheel Park, New Delhi—110 017, India
Penguin Group (NZ), Cnr. Airborne and Rosedale Roads, Albany, Auckland 1310, New Zealand
(a division of Pearson New Zealand Ltd.)
Penguin Books (South Africa) (Pty.) Ltd., 24 Sturdee Avenue, Rosebank, Johannesburg 2196,
South Africa

Penguin Books Ltd., Registered Offices: 80 Strand, London WC2R 0RL, England

This is a work of fiction. Names, characters, places, and incidents either are the product of the author's imagination or are used fictitiously, and any resemblance to actual persons, living or dead, business establishments, events, or locales is entirely coincidental. The publisher does not have any control over and does not assume any responsibility for author or third-party websites or their content.

THE HOSTAGE

A Jove Book / published by arrangement with the author

PRINTING HISTORY
G. P. Putnam's Sons hardcover edition / January 2006
Jove premium edition / January 2007

ISBN: 978-0-515-14240-2

JOVE®
Jove Books are published by The Berkley Publishing Group,
a division of Penguin Group (USA) Inc.,
375 Hudson Street, New York, New York 10014.
JOVE is a registered trademark of Penguin Group (USA) Inc.
The "J" design is a trademark belonging to Penguin Group (USA) Inc.

PRINTED IN THE UNITED STATES OF AMERICA

10 9 8 7 6 5 4 3 2 1

26 July 1777

The necessity of procuring good intelligence is apparent and need not be further urged.

George Washington
General and Commander in Chief
The Continental Army

FOR THE LATE

WILLIAM E. COLBY
An OSS Jedburgh first lieutenant
who became director of the Central Intelligence Agency.

AARON BANK
An OSS Jedburgh first lieutenant
who became a colonel and the father of Special Forces.

WILLIAM R. CORSON
A legendary Marine intelligence officer
whom the KGB hated more than any other U.S. Intelligence
officer—and not only because he wrote the definitive
work on them.

FOR THE LIVING

BILLY WAUGH
A legendary Special Forces command sergeant major
who retired and then went on to hunt down the infamous
Carlos the Jackal.
Billy could have terminated Osama bin Laden
in the early 1990s but could not get permission to do so.
After fifty years in the business, Billy
is still going after the bad guys.

RENÉ J. DÉFOURNEAUX
A U.S. Army OSS second lieutenant attached to the British
SOE who jumped into Occupied France alone and later
became a legendary U.S. Army counterintelligence officer.

JOHNNY REITZEL
An Army special operations officer who could have
terminated the head terrorist of the seized cruise ship
Achille Lauro but could not get permission to do so.

RALPH PETERS
An Army intelligence officer
who has written the best analysis of our war against
terrorists and of our enemy that I have ever seen.

AND FOR THE NEW BREED

MARC L.
A senior intelligence officer despite his youth
who reminds me of Bill Colby more and more each day.

FRANK L.
A legendary Defense Intelligence Agency officer
who retired and now follows in Billy Waugh's footsteps.

OUR NATION OWES THESE PATRIOTS
A DEBT BEYOND REPAYMENT.

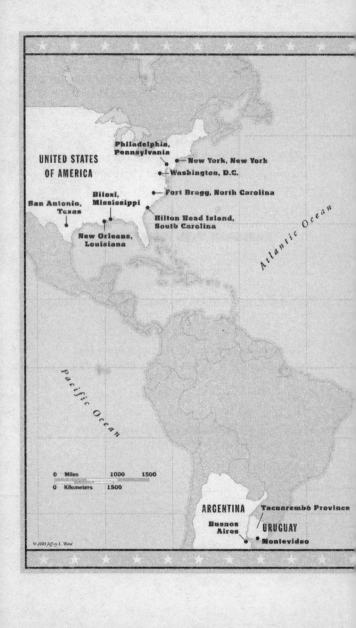

UNITED STATES
OF AMERICA

Philadelphia,
Pennsylvania

New York, New York

Washington, D.C.

Fort Bragg, North Carolina

San Antonio,
Texas

Biloxi,
Mississippi

Hilton Head Island,
South Carolina

New Orleans,
Louisiana

Atlantic Ocean

Pacific Ocean

0   Miles   1000   1500
0   Kilometers   1500

ARGENTINA

Tacuarembó Province

Buenos
Aires

URUGUAY

Montevideo

© 2005 Jeffrey L. Ward

I

As an American, Jean-Paul Lorimer was always annoyed or embarrassed, or both, every time he arrived at Vienna's international airport. The first thing one saw when entering the terminal was a Starbucks kiosk.

The arrogance of Americans to sell coffee in Vienna! With such a lurid red neon sign!

Dr. Jean-Paul Lorimer, Ph.D.—a very black man of forty-six who was somewhat squat, completely bald, spoke in a nasal tone, and wore the latest in European fashion, including tiny black-framed glasses and Italian loafers in which he more waddled than walked—had written his doctoral thesis on Central European history. He knew there had been coffee in Europe as early as 1600.

Dr. Lorimer also knew that after the siege of Vienna in 1683, the fleeing Turkish Army left behind bags of "black fodder." Franz Georg Kolschitzky, a Viennese who had lived in Turkey, recognized it as coffee. Kolschitzky promptly opened the first coffeehouse. It offered free newspapers for his customers to read while they were drinking his coffee, which he refined by straining out the grounds and adding milk and sugar.

It was an immediate success, and coffee almost immediately became a part of cultured society in the Austro-Hungarian Empire. And spread from there around the world.

Dr. Lorimer waddled past the line of travelers at the kiosk, shaking his head in disgust. *And now the Americans are bringing it, as if they invented it, like Coca-Cola, to the world? Spreading American culture? Good God! Outrageous!*

Dr. Jean-Paul Lorimer no longer thought of himself as an American. For the past twenty-two years, he had been a career professional employee of the United Nations, with the personal rank of minister for the past five.

His title was chief, European directorate of interagency coordination. It had its headquarters in Paris, and thus he had lived there nearly a quarter-century. He had purchased an apartment several years ago on Rue Monsieur in the VII Arrondissement and planned—when the time was right—to buy a little house somewhere on the Côte d'Azur. He hadn't even considered, until recently, ever returning to the United States to live.

Dr. Lorimer's blue, gold-stamped United Nations diplomatic passport saw him waved quickly past the immigration officer on duty.

He got in the taxi line, watched as the driver put his small, take-aboard suitcase into the trunk of a Mercedes, got in the back and told the driver, in German, to take him to an address on Cobenzlgasse.

Lorimer had mixed feelings, most of them bad, about

Vienna, starting with the fact that it was difficult to get here from Paris by air. There was no direct service. One had to go to either London or Brussels first to catch a plane. Today, because he had to get here as quickly as possible, he'd come via London. An extra hour and a half of travel time that got him here two hours earlier than going through Brussels would have.

There was the train, of course, *The Mozart,* but that took forever. Whenever he could, Lorimer dispatched one of his people to deal with things in Vienna.

It was a beautiful city, of course. Lorimer thought of it as the capital city of a nonexistent empire. But it was very expensive—not that that mattered to him anymore—and there was a certain racist ambience. There was practically none of that in Paris, which was one of the reasons Lorimer loved France generally and Paris in particular.

He changed his line of thought from the unpleasant to the pleasant. While there was nothing at all wrong with the women in Paris, a little variety was always pleasant. You could have a buxom blond from Poland or Russia here in Vienna, and that wasn't always the case in Paris.

Jean-Paul Lorimer had never married. When he'd been working his way up, there just hadn't been the time or the money, and when he reached a position where he could afford to marry, there still hadn't been the time.

There had been a film about ten years ago in which the actor Michael Caine had played a senior diplomat who similarly simply didn't have the time to take a wife, and had found his sexual release with top-notch hookers. Jean-Paul reluctantly had identified with Caine's character.

The apartment Lorimer was going to was the Viennese pied-à-terre of Henri Douchon, a Lebanese business associate. Henri, as Lorimer, was of Negroid ancestry—with some Arab, of course, but a black-skinned man, taller and more slender—who also had never married and who enjoyed buxom blond women.

Henri also liked lithe blond young men—that sort of thing was common in the Middle East—but he sensed that Jean-Paul was made uncomfortable in that ambience, and ran them off from the apartment when Jean-Paul was in town, replacing them with the buxom blond Poles or whatever they both liked. Sometimes four or even six of them.

I might as well enjoy myself; God only knows what will happen tomorrow.

There was no response to the doorbell of the apartment when Jean-Paul rang it.

Henri had not answered his phone, either, when Jean-Paul called that morning from Paris to tell him he was coming. He had called from one of the directorate's phones—not his—so the call couldn't be traced to him, and he hadn't left a message on the answering machine, either, for the same reason.

But he knew Henri was in town because when he was not, he unplugged his telephone, which caused the number to "ring" forever without activating the answering machine.

Jean-Paul waited exactly ninety seconds—timing it

with his Omega chronometer as he looked back onto Cobenzlgasse, the cobblestone street that he knew led up the hill to the position where Field Marshal Radetsky had his headquarters when the Turks were at the gates of Vienna—before putting his key in the lock.

There was no telling what Henri might be doing, and might be unwilling to immediately interrupt. It was simply good manners to give him ninety seconds.

When he pushed the door open, he could hear music—Bartók, Jean-Paul decided—which suggested Henri was at home.

"Henri," he called. "*C'est moi*, Jean-Paul!"

There was no answer.

As he walked into the apartment, there was an odor he could not immediately identify. The door from the sitting room to Henri's bedroom was open. The bed was mussed but empty.

Jean-Paul found Henri in the small office, which Henri somewhat vainly called the study.

He was sitting in the leather-upholstered, high-back desk chair. His arms were tied to the arms with leather belts. He was naked. His throat had been cut—cut through almost to the point of decapitation.

His hairy, somewhat flabby chest was blood-soaked, and blood had run down from his mouth over his chin.

There was a bloody kitchen knife on the desk, and a bloody pair of pliers. Jean-Paul was made uncomfortable by the sight, of course, but he was never anywhere close to panic or nausea or anything like that.

He had spent a good deal of time, as he worked his

way up in the United Nations, in places like the Congo, and had grown accustomed to the sight and smell of mutilated bodies.

He looked again at the body and at the desk and concluded that before they'd cut his throat, they had torn out two fingernails and then—probably later—half a dozen of his teeth. The torso and upper thighs had also been slashed in many places, probably with the knife.

I knew something like this would probably happen, but not this soon. I thought at the minimum we would have another two weeks or so.

Did anyone see me come in?

No.

I gave the cabdriver the address of a house six up Cobenzlgasse from this one, and made sure that he saw me walking up the walk to it before he drove off.

Is there anything incriminating in the apartment?

Probably after what they did to him, there is nothing of interest or value left.

And it doesn't matter, anyway. It's time for me to go.

The only question seems to be whether they will be waiting for me in Paris.

It is possible this is only a warning to me.

But certainly, I can't operate on that assumption.

Dr. Jean-Paul Lorimer walked calmly out of the study, reclaimed his carry-on suitcase where he'd left it when coming in, paused thoughtfully a moment, then took the key to the apartment from his pocket and laid it on the table by the door.

Then he walked out of the apartment and onto

Cobenzlgasse, dragging his suitcase behind him. He walked down the hill to the streetcar loop, and when one came, got on it.

When the streetcar reached the Vienna Opera on Karnter Ring, he got off and then boarded a streetcar that carried him to the Vienna West railroad station on Mariahilferstrasse.

He bought a ticket for a private single room on train EN 262, charging it to his United Nations Platinum American Express card.

Then, seeing that he had enough time before the train would leave for Paris's Gare de l'Est at eight thirty-four, he walked out of the station, found a coffeehouse and ordered a double coffee *mit Schlagobers* and took a copy of the *Wiener Kurier* from the rack to read while he drank his coffee.

[TWO]
7, Rue Monsieur
Paris VII, France
1205 13 July 2005

Dr. Jean-Paul Lorimer took a last sad look around his apartment. He knew he was going to miss so many of his things—and not only the exquisite antiques he had been able to afford in recent years—but there was simply nothing that could be done about it.

He also had second thoughts about leaving nearly seven thousand euros in the safe. Seven thousand euros was right at eight thousand U.S. dollars. But leaving just about everything—including money in the safe—would almost certainly confuse, at least for a while, anyone looking for him.

And it wasn't as if he would be going to Shangri-La without adequate financial resources. Spread more or less equally between the Banco Central, the Banco CO-FAC, the Banco de Crédito, and the Banco Hipotecario were sixteen million dollars, more money than Jean-Paul could have imagined having ten years before.

And in Shangri-La, there was both a luxury apartment overlooking a white sand beach of the Atlantic Ocean and, a hundred or so miles farther north, in San José, an isolated two-thousand-hectare *estancia* on which cattle were being profitably raised.

All of the property and bank accounts were in the name of Jean-Paul Bertrand, whose Lebanese passport, issued by the Lebanese foreign ministry, carried Jean-Paul Lorimer's photograph and thumbprint. Getting the passport had cost a fortune, but it was now obvious that it was money well spent.

Jean-Paul was taking with him only two medium-sized suitcases, plus the take-aboard suitcase he'd had with him in Vienna. Spread between the three was one hundred thousand U.S. dollars in neat little packs of five thousand dollars each. It was more or less concealed in shoes, socks, inner suit jacket pockets, and so on. He had already steeled himself to throwing away the cash if it developed he could not travel to Shangri-La without passing through a luggage inspection.

He also had five thousand dollars—in five packets of a

thousand each—in various pockets of his suit and four passports, all bearing his likeness, but none of them issued by any government.

Jean-Paul had some trouble with the two suitcases and the carry-aboard until he managed to flag down a taxi, but after that things went smoothly.

From Charles de Gaulle International, he flew on Royal Air Maroc as Omar del Danti, a Moroccan national, to Mohamed V International in Casablanca. Two hours later, he boarded, as Maurice LeLand, a French national, an Air France flight to Dakar's Yoff International Airport in Senegal. Still as LeLand, at nine-thirty that night he boarded the Al Italia flight to São Paolo, Brazil. There he boarded a twin-turboprop aircraft belonging to Nordeste Linhas Aéreas, a Brazilian regional airline, and flew to Santa Maria.

In Santa Maria, after calling his estancia manager, he got on an enormous intercity bus—nicer, he thought, than any Greyhound he'd ever been on. There was a television screen for each seat; a cold buffet; and even some rather nice, if generic, red wine—and rode it for about two hundred miles to Jaguarao, a farming town straddling the Brazil-Uruguay border.

Ricardo, his estancia manager, was waiting for him there with a Toyota Land Cruiser. They had a glass of a much better red, a local merlot, in a decent if somewhat primitive restaurant, and then drove out of town. Which also meant into Uruguay. If there was some sort of passport control on either side of the border, Dr. Lorimer didn't see it. Two hours later, the Land Cruiser turned off a well-maintained gravel road and passed under a wrought-iron sign reading SHANGRI-LA.

"Welcome home, Doctor," Ricardo said.

"Thank you, Ricardo," Jean-Paul said, and then, "I'm going to be here for a while. The fewer people who know that, the better."

"I understand, Doctor."

"And I think, man-to-man, Ricardo, that you will understand I'll more than likely be in need of a little company."

"Tonight, Doctor? You must be tired from your travel."

"Well, let's see if you can come up with something that will rekindle my energy."

"There are one or two maids, young girls," Ricardo said, "that you may find interesting."

"Good," Dr. Lorimer said.

Ten minutes later the Land Cruiser pulled up before a rambling one-story white-painted masonry house.

Half a dozen servants came quickly out of the house to welcome *El Patrón* home. One of them, a light-skinned girl who appeared to be about sixteen, did indeed look interesting.

Dr. Lorimer smiled at her as he walked into the house.

[THREE]
The United States Embassy
Avenida Colombia 4300
Palermo, Buenos Aires, Argentina
1825 20 July 2005

J. Winslow Masterson, a very tall, well-dressed, very black African American of forty-two, who was almost belligerently American and loathed most things French, stood leaning on the frame of his office window looking at the demonstration outside.

Masterson's office was on the second floor of the embassy building, just down the hall from that of the ambassador. Masterson was deputy chief of mission—read number two, or executive officer, or deputy ambassador—and at the moment was the acting minister extraordinary and plenipotentiary of the President of the United States to the Republic of Argentina.

The ambassador, Juan Manuel Silvio, was "across the river"—in Montevideo, Uruguay—having taken a more or less working lunch with Michael A. McGrory, the minister extraordinary and plenipotentiary of the President of the United States to the Republic of Uruguay. The two ambassadors or their chiefs of mission got together regularly, every two weeks, either in Buenos Aires or Montevideo.

Silvio had taken the red-eye, the first flight from Jorge Newbery airport in downtown Buenos Aires, which departed on the twenty-six-minute flight to Montevideo at 7:05 A.M., and he would return on the 3:10 P.M. Busquebus. The high-speed catamaran ferry made the trip in just over three hours. The ambassador said that much time allowed him to deal uninterrupted in the comfortable first-class cabin with at least some of the bureaucratic papers that accumulated on his desk.

There were, Masterson guessed, maybe three hundred demonstrators today, banging pots and pans, held back by fences and maybe fifty cops of the Mounted Police, half of them actually on horseback.

The demonstrators waved—at least when they thought the TV cameras were rolling—banners protesting the International Money Fund, the United States' role therein, American fiscal policy, and America generally. There were at least a half dozen banners displaying the likeness of Ernesto "Che" Guevara.

The Argentine adulation of Guevara both surprised and annoyed Masterson. He admitted a grudging admiration for Fidel Castro, who had taken a handful of men into the mountains of Cuba for training, then overthrown the Cuban government, and had been giving the finger to the world's most powerful nation ever since.

But Guevara was another story. Guevara, an Argentine who was a doctor, had been Castro's medic. But as far as Masterson knew that was all he had ever done to successfully further the cause of communism. As a revolutionary, he had been a spectacular failure. His attempt to communize Africa had been a disaster. All it had taken to see him flee the African continent with his tail between his legs was a hundred-odd-man covert detachment of African American Special Forces soldiers. And when he'd moved to Bolivia, an even smaller covert group of Green Berets, this one mostly made up of Cuban-Americans, had been waiting for him, not so much to frustrate his revolutionary ambitions as to make him a laughingstock all over Latin America.

The Green Berets had almost succeeded. For example, they had almost gleefully reported that Guevara had taken a detachment of his grandly named Revolutionary Army on an overnight training exercise, promptly gotten lost in the boonies, drowned four of his men trying to cross a river, and taken two weeks to get back to his base, barely surviving on a diet of monkeys and other small but edible jungle animals. And when he got back to his base, Guevara found that it was under surveillance by the Bolivian Army. A farmer had reported the Revolutionary Army to the Bolivian government, in the belief they were drug smugglers.

The President of Bolivia, however, was not amused, nor receptive to the idea that the best way to deal with Dr. Guevara was to publicly humiliate him. He ordered a quick summary court-martial—the bearing of arms with the intent of overthrowing a government by force and violence being punishable by death under international law—followed by a quick execution, and Guevara became a legend instead of a joke.

"Lost in thought, Jack?" a familiar voice, that of Alexander B. Darby, asked behind him. Darby's official title was embassy commercial attaché, but among the senior officers it wasn't exactly a closely guarded secret that he actually was the CIA's station chief.

Masterson turned and smiled at the small, plump man with a pencil-line mustache.

"My usual unkind thoughts about Che Guevara."

"They're still out there?"

Masterson nodded.

"It looked like rain. I hoped it would, and they would go away."

"No such luck."

"You about ready?"

"At your disposal, sir," Masterson said, and started for the door.

Masterson was bumming a ride home with Darby, who lived near him in the suburb of San Isidro. His own embassy car had been in a fender bender—the second this month—and was in the shop.

"The boss back?" Darby asked, as they got on the elevator that would take them to the basement.

"He should be shortly; he took the Busquebus," Masterson replied.

"Maybe he was hoping it would rain, too," Darby said.

Masterson chuckled.

If the demonstrations outside the embassy did nothing else, they made getting into and out of the embassy grounds a royal pain in the ass. The demonstrators, sure that the TV cameras would follow them, rushed to surround embassy cars. Beyond thumping on the roofs and shaking their fists at those inside the car—they could see only the drivers clearly; the windows in the rear were heavily darkened—they didn't do much damage. But it took the Mounted Police some time to break their ranks so that the cars could pass, and there was always the risk of running over one of them. Or, more likely, that a demonstrator—who hadn't been touched—would suddenly start howling for the cameras, loudly complaining the gringo imperialists had run over his foot with malicious intent. That was an almost sure way to get on the evening news and in *Clarín*, Buenos Aires's tabloid newspaper.

The elevator took them to the basement, a dimly lit area against one wall of which was a line of cars. Most of them were the privately owned vehicles of secondary embassy personnel, not senior enough to have an official embassy car and driver, but ranking high enough to qualify for a parking slot in the basement. There was a reserved area on the curb outside the embassy grounds for the overflow.

Closest to the ramp leading up from the basement were parking spaces for the embassy's vehicles, the Jeep Wagoneers and such used for taxi service, and for the half dozen nearly identical "embassy cars." These were new, or nearly new, BMWs. They were either dark blue or black 5- and 7-series models, and they were all armored. They all carried diplomat license plates.

There were five of these vehicles lined up as Masterson and Darby crossed the basement. The big black 760Li reserved for the ambassador was there, and its spare, and Darby's car, and the consul general's, and Ken Lowery's. Lowery was the embassy's security officer. The military attaché's car was gone—he had a tendency to go home early—and Masterson's was in the shop getting the right front fender replaced.

Darby's driver, who had been sitting on a folding chair at the foot of the ramp with the other drivers, got up when he saw them coming and had both rear doors open for them by the time they reached Darby's car.

One of the many reasons it wasn't much of a secret that Alex Darby was the CIA station chief was that he had a personal embassy car. None of the other attachés did.

All the drivers were employees of the private security service that guarded the embassy. They were all supposed to be retired policemen, which permitted them the right to carry a gun. It wasn't much of a secret, either, that all of them were really in the employ of Argentina's intelligence service, called SIDE, which was sort of an Argentine version of the CIA, the Secret Service, and the FBI combined.

"We'll be dropping Mr. Masterson at his house," Darby announced when they were in the car. "Go there first."

"Actually, Betsy's going to be waiting for me—is, in fact, probably already waiting for me—at the Kansas," Masterson said. "Drop me there, please."

The Kansas was a widely popular restaurant on Avenida Libertador in a classy section of Buenos Aires called San Isidro. Getting out of the embassy grounds was not simple. First, the security people checked the identity of the driver, and then the passengers, and then logged their Time Out on the appropriate form. Then, for reasons Masterson didn't pretend to understand, the car was searched, starting with the trunk and ending with the undercarriage being carefully examined using a large round mirror on a pole.

Only then was the car permitted to approach the gate. When that happened, three three-foot-in-diameter barriers were lowered into the pavement. By the time that happened, the lookout stationed at the gate by the demonstrators had time to summon the protestors, and one of the Mounted Police sergeants had time to summon reinforcements, two dozen of whom either ran up on foot or trotted up on horseback, to force the passage of the car through the demonstrators.

Then the double gates were opened, the car left the embassy grounds, and the demonstrators began to do their thing.

No real damage was done, but the thumping on the roof of the BMW was unnerving, and so were the hateful faces of some of the demonstrators. Only some. From what Masterson could see, most of the demonstrators just seemed to be having a good time.

In a minute or so, they were through the demonstrators and, finding a hole in the fast-moving traffic, headed for Avenida Libertador.

Alex Darby gestured in the general direction of the Residence—the ambassador's home, a huge stone mansion—which faced on Avenida Libertador about five hundred yards from the embassy.

Masterson looked and saw a pack of demonstrators running from the embassy to the residence.

"No wonder he's taking his time getting back on the

Busquebus," Darby said. "If he'd been at the embassy, he'd have had to run the gauntlet twice, once to get out of the embassy, and again to get in the residence."

A hundred yards past the residence, there was no sign whatever of the howling mob at the embassy. There was a large park on their right, with joggers and people walking dogs, and rows of elegant apartment buildings on their left until they came to the railroad bridge. On the far side of the bridge they had the Army's polo fields to their left, and the racetrack, the Hipódromo, on their right. There was nothing going on at the polo fields, but the horse fanciers were already lining up for the evening's races.

Then there were more rows of tall apartment buildings on both sides of the street.

They passed under an elevated highway, which meant they were passing from the City of Buenos Aires into the Province of Buenos Aires. The City of Buenos Aires, Masterson often thought, was like the District of Columbia, and the province a state, like Maryland or Virginia.

"It looks like traffic's not so bad," Alex said.

Masterson leaned forward to look out the windshield.

They were passing a Carrefour, a French-owned supermarket chain. Masterson, who had served a tour as a junior consular officer in the Paris embassy, and thought he had learned something of the French, refused to shop there.

"You're right," Masterson said, just as the driver laid heavily on the horn.

There came a violent push to the side of the BMW,

immediately followed by the sound of tearing and cru__
ing metal. The impact threw Darby and Masterson vio-
lently against their seat belts.

There came another crash, this one from the rear, and
again they felt the painful pressure of the restraints.

The driver swore in rapid-fire Spanish.

"Jesus Christ!" Masterson exploded, as he tried to sit
straight in his seat.

"You all right, Jack?" Darby asked.

"Yeah, I think so," Masterson said. "Jesus Christ!
Again! These goddamn crazy Argentine drivers!"

"Take it easy," Darby said, quickly scanning the situation outside their windows with the practiced eye of a
spook.

Masterson tried to open the door. It wouldn't budge.

"We'll have to get out your side, Alex," he said.

"That's not going to be easy," Darby said, gesturing
toward the flow of traffic on the street.

The driver got out of the car, stepped into the flow of
traffic, and held up his hand like a policeman. Masterson
thought idly that the driver had probably started his career as a traffic cop.

A policeman ran up. The driver snapped something at
him, and the policeman took over the job of directing
traffic. The driver came back to the car, and Darby and
Masterson got out.

Masterson saw the pickup that had first struck them
was backing away from them. It was a four-door Ford
F-250 pickup with a massive set of stainless steel tubes
mounted in front of the radiator. He thought first that
the tubes—which were common on pickup trucks to

…es out of the mud on country roads—
…oing to have a minor scratch or two and
…probably going to need a new door and a
new rear … panel.

Then he saw the car, a Volkswagen Golf, that had hit them from the rear. The right side of the windshield was shattered. He went quickly to the passenger door and pulled it open. A young man, well-dressed, was sitting there, looking dazed, holding his fingers to his bloody forehead.

Masterson had an unkind thought: *If you didn't think seat belts were for sissies, you macho sonofabitch, your head wouldn't have tried to go through the windshield.*

He waved his fingers before the man's eyes. The man looked at him with mingled curiosity and annoyance.

"Let's get you out of there, señor," Masterson said in fluent Spanish. "I think it would be better for you to lie down."

He saw that the driver was an attractive young woman—*probably Señor Macho's wife; Argentine men don't let their girlfriends drive their cars for fear it will make them look unmanly*—who looked dazed but didn't seem to be hurt. She was wearing her seat belt, and the airbag on the steering wheel had deployed.

"Alex," Masterson called, "get this lady out of here."

Then he pulled his cloth handkerchief from his pants pocket, pressed it to the man's bleeding forehead, and placed the man's right hand to hold it.

"Keep pressure on it," Masterson said as he helped the man out of the Volkswagen and to the curb. He got him to sit, then asked, "Need to lie down?"

"I'm all right," the man said. *"Muchas gracias."*

"You're sure? Nothing's broken?"

The man moved his torso as if testing for broken bones, and then smiled wanly.

Alex Darby led the young woman to the curb. She saw the man and the bloody handkerchief, sucked in her breath audibly, and dropped to her knees to comfort him.

It was an intimate moment. Masterson looked away.

The big Ford truck that had crashed into them was disappearing into the Carrefour parking lot.

The sonofabitch is running away!

Masterson shouted at the policeman directing traffic, finally caught his attention, and, pointing at the pickup, shouted that he was running away.

The policeman gestured that he understood, but as he was occupied directing traffic, there wasn't much that he could do.

Goddammit to hell!

Masterson took his cellular telephone from his inside pocket and punched an autodial number. When there was no response, he looked at the screen.

No bars! I am in the only fucking place in Buenos Aires where there's no cellular signal!

Darby saw the cellular in Masterson's hand and asked, "You're calling the embassy?"

"No goddamn signal."

Darby took his cellular out and confirmed that.

"I'll call it in with the radio," he said, and walked quickly to the BMW.

A minute later he came back.

"Lowery asked if we're all right," he said. "I told him

yes. He's sending an Automobile Club wrecker and a car. It'll probably take a little while for the car. The demonstrators are still at it."

"The sonofabitch who hit us took off," Masterson said.

"Really? You're sure?"

"Yes, goddammit, I'm sure."

"Take it easy, Jack. These things happen. Nobody's hurt."

"He is," Masterson said, nodding at Señor Macho.

"The cops and an ambulance will be here soon, I'm sure."

"Betsy's going to shit a brick when I'm late," Masterson said. "And I can't call her."

"Get on the radio and have the guard at Post One call her at the Kansas."

Masterson considered that.

"No," he decided aloud. "She'll just have to be pissed. I don't want the guard calling her and telling her I've been in another wreck."

[FOUR]
Restaurant Kansas
Avenida Libertador
San Isidro
Buenos Aires Province, Argentina
1925 20 July 2005

Elizabeth "Betsy" Masterson, a tall, slim, well-groomed thirty-seven-year-old, with the sharp features and brownish black skin that made her think her ancestors had been of the Watusi tribe, was seated alone at the bar of Kansas—the only place smoking was permitted in the elegant steakhouse. She looked at her watch for the fifth time in the past ten minutes, exhaled audibly, had unkind thoughts about the opposite sex generally and Jack, her husband, specifically, and then signaled to the bartender for another Lagarde merlot, and lit another cigarette.

Goddamn him! He knows that I hate to sit at the bar alone, as if I'm looking for a man. And he said he'd be here between quarter to seven and seven!

Jack's embassy car had been in a fender bender—another fender bender, the second this month—and was in the shop, and he had caught a ride to work, and was catching a ride home, with Alex Darby, the embassy's commercial attaché. Jack had called her and asked if she could pick him up at Kansas, as for some reason it would be inconvenient for Alex to drop him at the house.

The Mastersons and the Darbys, both on their second tours in Buenos Aires, had opted for embassy houses in San Isidro, rather than for apartments in Palermo or Belgrano.

Their first tours had taught them there was a downside to the elegant apartments the embassy leased in the city. They were of course closer to the embassy, but they were noisy, sometimes the elevators and the air-conditioning didn't work, and parking required negotiating a narrow access road to a crowded garage sometimes two floors below street level. And they had communal swimming pools, if they had swimming pools at all.

The houses the embassy leased in San Isidro were

nice, and came with a garden, a *quincho*—outdoor barbecue—and a swimming pool. This was important if you had kids, and the Mastersons had three. The schools were better in San Isidro, and the shopping, and Avenida Libertador was lined with nice shops and lots of good restaurants. And of course there were easy-access garages for what the State Department called Privately Owned Vehicles.

The Masterson POV was a dark green 2004 Chrysler Town & Country van. With three kids, all with bicycles, you needed something that large. But it was big, and Betsy didn't even like to think about trying to park what the Mastersons called "the Bus" in an underground garage in the city.

When she went to Buenos Aires, to have lunch with Jack or whatever, she never used a garage. The Bus had diplomat license plates, and that meant you could park anywhere you wanted. You couldn't be ticketed or towed. Or even stopped for speeding. Diplomatic immunity.

The price for the house and the nice shops, good restaurants, and better schools of San Isidro was the twice-a-day thirty—sometimes forty-five—minute ride through the insane traffic on Libertador to the embassy. But Jack paid that.

Her bartender—one of four tending the oval bar island—came up with a bottle of Lagarde in one hand and a fresh glass in the other. He asked with a raised eyebrow if she wanted the new glass.

"This is fine, thank you," Betsy said in Spanish.

The bartender filled her glass almost to the brim.

I probably shouldn't have done that, she thought. *The*

way they pour in here, two glasses is half a bottle, and with half a bottle in me I'm probably going to say something—however well deserved—to Jack that I'll regret later.

But she picked the glass up carefully and took a good swallow from it.

She looked up at the two enormous television screens mounted high on the wall for the bar patrons. One of them showed a soccer game—what Argentines, as well as most of the world, called "football"—and the other was tuned to a news channel.

There was no sound that she could hear.

Typical Argentina, she thought unkindly. *Rather than make a decision to provide the audio to one channel, which would annoy the watchers of the other, compromise by turning both off. That way, nobody should be annoyed.*

She didn't really understand the football, so she turned her attention to the news. There was another demonstration at the American embassy. Hordes of people banging on drums and kitchen pots, and waving banners, including several of Che Guevara—which for some reason really annoyed Jack—being held behind barriers by the Mounted Police.

That's probably why Jack's late. He couldn't get out of the embassy. But he could have called.

The image of a distinguished-looking, gray-bearded man in a business suit standing before a microphone came on the screen. Betsy recognized him as the prominent businessman whose college-aged son had been a high-profile kidnapping victim. As the demands for ransom went higher and higher, the kidnappers had cut off the boy's fingers, one by one, and sent them to his father to prove he was still alive. Shortly after the father paid, the boy's body—shot in the head—was found. The father was now one of the biggest thorns in the side of the President and his administration.

Kidnapping—sometimes with the participation of the cops—was big business in Argentina. The *Buenos Aires Herald,* the American-owned English-language newspaper, had that morning run the story of the kidnapping of a thirteen-year-old girl, thought to be sold into prostitution.

Such a beautiful country with such ugly problems.

The image shifted to one of a second-rate American movie star being herded through a horde of fans at the Ezeiza airport.

Betsy took a healthy swallow of the merlot, checked the entrance again for signs of her husband, and returned her attention to the TV screen.

Ten minutes later—*well, enough's enough. To hell with him. Let him stand on the curb and try to flag a taxi down. I'm sorry it's not raining*—she laid her American Express card on the bar, caught the bartender's eye, and pointed at the card. He smiled, and nodded, and walked to the cash register.

When he laid the tab on the bar before her, she saw that the two glasses of the really nice merlot and the very nice plate of mixed cheeses and crackers came to $24.50 in Argentine pesos. Or eight bucks U.S.

She felt a twinge of guilt. The Mastersons had lived well enough on their first tour, when the peso equaled the dollar. Now, with the dramatic devaluation of the peso, they lived like kings. It was indeed nice, but also it was difficult to completely enjoy with so many suffering so visibly.

She nodded, and he picked up the tab and her credit card and went back to the cash register. Betsy went in her purse and took out a wad of pesos and pulled a five-peso note from it. For some reason, you couldn't put the tip on a credit card. Five pesos was about twenty percent, and Jack was always telling her that the Argentines were grateful for ten percent. But the bartender was a nice young man who always took good care of her, and he probably didn't make much money. Five pesos was a buck sixty.

When the bartender came back with the American Express form, she signed it, took the carbon, laid the five-peso note on the original, and pushed it across the bar to him.

"Muchas gracias, señora."

"You're welcome," Betsy said in Spanish.

She put the credit card in her wallet, and then the wallet in her purse, and closed it. She slipped off the bar stool and walked toward the entrance. This gave her a view of the kitchen, intentionally on display behind a plate-glass wall. She was always fascinated at what, in a sense, was really a feeding frenzy. She thought there must be twenty men in chef's whites tending a half-dozen stainless steel stoves, a huge, wood-fired *parrilla* grill, and other kitchen equipment. All busy as hell. The no-smoking dining room of the Kansas was enormous and usually full.

The entrance foyer was crowded with people giving their names to the greeter-girls to get on the get-seated roster. One of the greeters saw Betsy coming and walked quickly to hold open the door for her.

Betsy went out onto Avenida Libertador, and looked up and down the street; no husband. She turned right on the sidewalk toward what she thought of as the Park-Yourself entrance to the Kansas parking lot. There were two entrances to the large parking area behind the restaurant. The other provided valet parking.

Betsy never used it. She had decided long ago, when they had first started coming to the Kansas, that it was really a pain in the you-know-where. The valet parkers were young kids who opened the door for you, handed you a claim check, and then hopped behind the wheel and took off with a squeal of tires into the parking lot, where they proved their manhood by coming as close to other cars as they could without taking off a fender.

And then when you left, you had to find the claim check, and stand outside waiting for a parker to show up so you could give it to him. He then took off at a run into the parking lot. A couple of minutes later, the Bus would arrive with a squeal of tires, and the parker would jump out with a big smile and a hand out for his tip.

It was easier and quicker to park the Bus yourself. And when you were finished with dinner—*or waiting for a husband who didn't show the simple courtesy of calling and saying he was delayed, and who didn't answer his cellular*—all you had to do was walk into the parking lot, get in the Bus, and drive off.

When she'd come in today, the parking lot had been nearly full, and she'd had to drive almost to the rear of it to find a home for the Bus. But no problem. It wasn't that far, and the lot was well lit, with bright lights on tall poles on the little grassy-garden islands between the rows of parked cars.

She was a little surprised and annoyed when she saw that the light shining down on the Bus had burned out. Things like that happened, of course, but she thought she was going to have a hell of a hard time finding the keyhole in the door.

When she actually got to the Bus, it was worse. Some sonofabitch—one of the valet parkers, probably—had parked a Peugeot sedan so close to the left side of the van that there was no way she could get to the door without scraping her rear and/or her boobs on either the dirty Peugeot or the Bus, which also needed a bath.

She walked around to the right side of the Bus and with some difficulty—for a while she thought she was going to have to light her lighter—managed to get the key in the lock and open the door.

She was wearing a tight skirt, and the only way she was going to be able to crawl over the passenger seat and the whatever-it-was-called thing between the seats to get behind the wheel was to hike the skirt up to her crotch.

First things first. Get rid of the purse, then hike skirt.

She opened the sliding door and tossed her purse on the seat.

The front door suddenly slammed shut.

What the hell?

She looked to see what had happened.

There was a man coming toward her between the cars. He had something in his hand.

What the hell is that, a hypodermic needle?

She first felt arms wrap around her from behind, then a hand over her mouth.

She started to struggle. She tried to bite at the hand over her mouth as the man coming toward her sort of embraced her. She felt a sting on her buttocks.

Oh, Jesus Chri . . .

Four minutes later, a dark blue BMW 545i with heavily darkened windows and a Corps Diplomatique license plate pulled out of the flow of traffic on Avenida Libertador and stopped at the curb. It was a clearly marked NO PARKING NO STOPPING zone, but usually, as now, there were two or three cars with CD tags parked there.

In the rear seat of the BMW, Jack Masterson turned to Alex Darby.

"Now that your car has joined mine in the shop, how are you going to get to work in the morning?"

"I can have one of my guys pick me up," Alex replied.

"Wouldn't you rather I did?"

"I was hoping you'd ask."

"Eight-fifteen?"

"Fine. You want me to send this one back here after he drops me off?"

"No. Betsy has the Bus. Send this one back to the embassy." He raised his voice and switched to Spanish. "Make sure the dispatcher knows I need a car at my house at eight tomorrow morning."

"*Sí, señor,*" the driver replied.

"That presumes," Masterson said to Darby, "that I'm still alive in the morning. She who hates to wait is going to be highly pissed."

Darby chuckled.

Masterson got out of the car and half-trotted across the sidewalk to the Kansas entrance. He pushed his way through the crowd of people waiting to be seated and went up the shallow three-step stairs to the bar.

Betsy was nowhere in sight, either at the bar or in one of the half dozen booths.

Shit!

One of the bartenders caught his eye and held up his hands in a helpless gesture. Jack walked to him.

"You just missed her, señor," the bartender said. "Not two minutes ago, she left."

Shit!

Maybe I can catch her in the parking lot!

"*Muchas gracias,*" he said, and then hurriedly went back through the entrance foyer and left through the door leading to the valet parking entrance.

If she used valet parking, she might still be waiting.

Betsy was nowhere in sight.

Shit!

Jack trotted into the parking lot and looked around.

He didn't see the Bus anywhere at first, and then he did, in the back of the lot. The interior lights were on, which meant she'd just gotten to the car.

He took off at a dead run for the Bus.

I don't have any idea what she's doing with the door open, but it means I probably can get there before she drives off.

"Sweetheart, I'm sorry!" he called when he got to the Bus.

Where the hell is she?

There was no room to get to the driver's door, and when he got to the passenger side, he saw that it wasn't open, just not fully closed. That explained the interior lights being on.

Where the hell is she?

He slid the sliding door open enough so that he could slam it shut. He saw the purse on the seat.

"Oh, Jesus H. Christ!" he said softly.

He took his cellular from his shirt pocket and pushed an autodial button.

Answer the fucking phone, Alex!

"Alex Darby."

"Alex, I think you'd better come back here. Come to the rear of the parking lot."

Darby heard the tone of Masterson's voice.

"Jesus, what's up?"

"The Bus is here. The door was half open. Betsy's purse is on the backseat. No Betsy. I don't like the looks of this."

"On my way, Jack."

"Hand me the microphone and turn the speaker up," Alex Darby said to his driver. "And then head back to the Kansas. Fast."

"*Sí, señor,*" the driver said, and took the shortwave radio microphone from where it lay on the passenger seat and handed it to Darby. The shortwave net provided encrypted voice communication.

Allegedly, the encryption was unbreakable. Very few people believed this.

Alex keyed the mic. "Darby to Lowery."

Almost instantly, the speaker came to life. "Yeah, Alex. What's up?"

"I just had a call from Jack Masterson. Something very unusual is going on at the Kansas on Aven—"

"In San Isidro?" Lowery cut him off. "That Kansas?"

"Right. His van is there, and his wife's purse, but no wife. Jack sounds very concerned."

"I'll call the San Isidro cops," Lowery said. "I'm in Belgrano; ten, twelve minutes out. On my way."

"Thanks, Ken."

"Let's hope she's in the can, powdering her nose," Lowery said. "See you there. Lowery out."

Jack Masterson, scanning the parking lot and making mental notes of what and who were in the immediate area, pushed another autodial button on his cellular phone.

"Post One, Staff Sergeant Taylor," the Marine guard on duty at the embassy said, as he answered the unlisted telephone.

"This is Masterson. I need to speak to Ken Lowery now."

"Sir, Mr. Lowery has left the embassy. May I suggest you try to get him on the radio?"

"I don't have a goddamn radio. You contact him, and tell him to call me on my cellular. Tell him it's an emergency."

"Yes, sir."

[FIVE]
The Residence
Avenida Libertador y Calle John F. Kennedy
Palermo, Buenos Aires, Argentina
2110 20 July 2005

"¿Hola?" Ambassador Juan Manuel Silvio said, picking up the telephone beside his armchair in the sitting room of the ambassadorial apartment on the third floor of the residence.

"Alex, Mr. Ambassador. We have a problem."

"Tell me."

"Everything points to Betsy Masterson having been kidnapped from the parking lot of the Kansas in San Isidro about an hour ago."

For a long moment, the ambassador didn't reply. He was always careful with his words.

"Ken Lowery is aware of this?" he asked, finally.

"Yes, sir. I'm in Ken's car, headed downtown from the Kansas."

"Jack?"

"I talked him into going home, sir. My wife is on her way over there."

"Why don't you and Ken come here, Alex?" Silvio asked. "And I think it might be useful if Tony Santini came, too. I could call him."

Anthony J. Santini, listed in the embassy telephone directory as the assistant financial attaché, was in fact a Secret Service agent dispatched to Buenos Aires to, as he put it, "look for funny money." That meant both counterfeit currency and illegally acquired money being laundered.

"I'll call him, sir."

"Then I'll see you here in a few minutes, Alex. Thank you," the ambassador said, and hung up.

"You'll call who?" Ken Lowery inquired.

"Tony Santini," Alex Darby replied. "The ambassador wants him there, too."

"The residence or the embassy?"

"Residence," Darby replied, then added, "I guess he figures Tony is the closest thing we have to the FBI."

There were no "legal attachés"—FBI agents—at the embassy at the moment. There were a half dozen "across the river" looking for money-laundering operations. Money laundering in Argentina had just about dried up after the Argentine government had, without warning several years before, forcibly converted dollar deposits to pesos at an unfavorable rate and then sequestered the pesos. International drug dealers didn't trust Argentine banks any more than industry did and moved their laundering to Uruguay and elsewhere.

Darby punched an autodial button on his cellular to call Santini.

• • •

Ambassador Juan Manuel Silvio was a tall, lithe, fair-skinned, well-tailored man, with an erect carriage and an aristocratic manner, and when he opened the door to the ambassadorial apartment Alex Darby thought again that Silvio looked like the models in advertisements for twelve-year-old scotch or ten-thousand-dollar wristwatches.

He was a Cuban-American, brought from Castro's Cuba as a child. His family had arrived in Miami, he said, on their forty-six-foot Chris-Craft sportfisherman with nothing but the clothing on their backs and a large cigar humidor stuffed with his mother's jewelry and hundred-dollar bills.

"My father was one of the few who recognized Castro as more than a joke," he had once told Darby. "What he didn't get quite right was how quickly Castro would march into Havana."

Darby knew he wasn't boasting, but the opposite. Silvio was proud of—and greatly admired—his fellow Cubans who had arrived in Miami "with nothing but the clothes on their backs" and subsequently prospered. He simply wanted to make it plain that it had been much easier for his family than it had been for other refugees.

Silvio graduated from his father's alma mater, Spring Hill College, a Jesuit institution in Mobile, Alabama, with a long history of educating the children of upper-class Latin Americans, took a law degree at Harvard, and then a doctorate in political science at the University of Alabama.

He joined the State Department on graduation.

He joked, "My father decided that the family owed one son to the service of the United States. I am the youngest son, so, to my brothers' delight, here I am, while they bask in the Miami sun."

Alex Darby liked the ambassador both personally and professionally. He had served in other American embassies where the ambassadors—career State Department and political appointees alike—had demonstrated an appalling lack of knowledge of geopolitics and history, and had regarded the CIA especially, and the other embassy "outsiders"—the FBI and the Drug Enforcement Administration (DEA) and the Secret Service and even the military attachés who worked under the Defense Intelligence Agency (DIA)—as dangerous nuisances who had to be kept on a very tight leash lest they disrupt the amiable ambience of diplomatic cocktail parties.

It was a given to Ambassador Silvio that communism in Latin America was not dead; that it posed a genuine threat to the United States; that Islamic fascism was present in Latin America and growing stronger, and posed an even greater threat to the United States; and that the drug trade financed both.

His attitude toward and support of Darby and the other outsiders made their work easier, even if it did tend to annoy the "real" Foreign Service staff at the embassy.

The ambassador heard out Darby's report of what had happened, considered what he had heard for a long moment, and then asked Lowery and Santini if either had anything to add.

Lowery said, "No, sir," and Santini shook his head.

"The priorities, as I see them," the ambassador said,

"are to get Betsy back to her family, and then to help Jack through this. Any comments on that?"

All three men shook their heads. Lowery said, "No, sir," again.

"The Policía Federal are in on this, I presume?"

"Yes, sir," Lowery said.

"Were you considering involving SIDE, Alex?"

"I think SIDE already knows what's happened, sir," Darby replied. "But I can make a call or two if—"

"Let's hold off on that for a while. Do you think SIDE has informed the Foreign Ministry?"

"I think we have to assume they will, sir. The Policía Federal probably already have."

"Do you think this is politically motivated? Do we have any reason to suspect this is a terrorist act?"

"It may be, of course," Darby said. "But we've always thought that if the rag-heads were going to do anything, it would be a violent act, either a bomb at the embassy or here, or a drive-by assassination attempt on you—"

"You think it may be a run-of-the-mill kidnapping?" Silvio interrupted.

"Sir, I don't know what to think. But if I had to make a choice, that seems most likely."

"But kidnapping not only an American, but one with diplomatic status . . . that doesn't strike me as being smart."

"It will certainly get SIDE and the police off their a— Get them moving," Lowery said. "This is really going to embarrass the government."

"Mr. Santini? You have any thoughts?"

"Not many, sir. But my experience with what the sociologists call the 'criminal element' has been that they often do stupid things because they're usually stupid. I wouldn't be surprised if these guys missed the diplomat tag on the car."

"And when they learn who Mrs. Masterson is? You think they may let her go?"

"I hate to say this, sir," Santini replied, "but I think it's better than fifty-fifty that they won't. She can identify them."

"Jesus Christ!" Lowery said.

"Another scenario," Santini said, "is that they won't care about her diplomatic status, and may just demand a ransom, and if paid, let her go. We can assume only that they're willing to break the law, not that they are going to act rationally."

The ambassador asked, "Is this going to be on television tonight, and on the front page of *Clarín* in the morning?"

"Very possibly," Darby said. "Unless there is strong pressure from the government—the foreign minister or maybe the President or one of his cronies—to keep it quiet."

"That would be—pressure from on high—more effective in keeping this out of the press than anything we could do, wouldn't it?"

"Yes, it would," Darby said, simply.

"I'll call the foreign minister right now," the ambassador said. "Before I call Washington."

"I think that's a good idea, sir," Lowery said.

"Alex, why don't you stop by Jack's house? Tell him that everything that can be done is being done? And that he's in my prayers?"

"Yes, sir."

"I'll call him myself just as soon as I get off the phone—I may even go out there—but . . ."

"I understand, Mr. Ambassador," Darby said.

"I don't think it needs to be said, does it, that I want to know of any development right away? No matter what the hour?"

[SIX]

"Reynolds," the man answering the telephone announced.

"This is the Southern Cone desk?" Ambassador Silvio asked.

There was a more formal title, of course, for that section of the State Department charged with diplomatic affairs in the republics of Chile, Uruguay, and Argentina, but "Southern Cone" fit to describe the three nations at the southern tip of South America and was commonly used.

"Yes, it is. Who is this, please?"

"My name is Silvio. I'm the ambassador in Buenos Aires."

"How may I be of service, Mr. Ambassador?" Reynolds inquired. His voice sounded considerably more interested than it had been when he answered the telephone.

"I want you to prepare a memorandum of this call for

the secretary of state. If she is available, get it to her now. I want her to have it, in any event, first thing in the morning. Is that going to pose any problems for you?"

"None at all, Mr. Ambassador."

"We have strong reason to believe that Mrs. Elizabeth Masterson, the wife of my chief of mission, J. Winslow Masterson, was kidnapped at approximately eight P.M., Buenos Aires time. Beyond that, little is known."

"My recorder is on, Mr. Ambassador," Reynolds interrupted. "I should have told you. Would you like me to turn it off and erase what it has?"

"No. A recording should help you prepare the memorandum."

"Yes, sir, it will. Thank you, sir."

"The federal police are aware of the situation," Silvio went on. "So it must be presumed that the minister of the interior and the foreign minister have been told. However, when—just now—I attempted to telephone the foreign minister to inform him officially, he was not available. His office told me they will have him call me as soon as he is available, but that I should not expect this to happen until tomorrow morning.

"I interpret this to mean that he does not feel he should discuss the situation with me until he learns more about it and/or discusses it with the President.

"All of my staff concerned with intelligence and legal matters are aware of the situation. Their consensus, with which I am in agreement, is that there is not presently enough intelligence to form a reasonable opinion as to motive. In other words, we do not know enough at this time to think that this is, or is not, a terrorist act, or that it is, or is not, an ordinary kidnapping, or may have some political implications.

"Mr. Kenneth Lowery, my security chief, has been directed to compile a report of what we know to this point, and that will be sent to Washington by satburst almost certainly within the hour.

"I will furnish the department either by telephone or by satburst with whatever information is developed as soon as it comes to me.

"I have spoken with Ambassador McGrory in Montevideo. He is presently determining if any of the FBI agents attached to his embassy have experience with kidnappings, etcetera, and if any of them do, he will immediately send them here."

He paused, then said, "I think that covers everything. Unless you can think of anything, Mr. Reynolds?"

"No, sir, Mr. Ambassador. I think you have everything in there. I'll get this to the secretary as soon as possible."

"In that connection, Mr. Reynolds, while I have no objection to an appropriate dissemination of what I'm reporting, I want your memorandum of this call to go directly to the secretary. You understand what I'm saying?"

"Yes, sir. Directly to the secretary. Not through channels."

"Thank you, Mr. Reynolds."

Ambassador Silvio hung up the secure telephone and picked up the one connected to the embassy switchboard. He punched one of the buttons.

"Silvio here. Will you have a car for me at the residence immediately, please? And inform Mr. Lowery that I will be going to Mr. Masterson's home?"

[SEVEN]
The Breakfast Room
The Presidential Apartment
The White House
1600 Pennsylvania Avenue, NW
Washington, D.C.
0815 21 July 2005

"Let me have that business about the diplomat's wife again, please," the President of the United States said to the deputy director of Central Intelligence, who had just finished delivering the Daily Intelligence Summary.

The DDCI read again the paragraph of the DIS reporting the kidnapping of Mrs. Masterson. It was essentially a condensation of the memorandum prepared by the Southern Cone desk officer for the secretary of state.

When he had finished, the President asked, "That's all we have?"

"We have just a little more, Mr. President, not in the DIS."

The President gestured, somewhat impatiently, with the fingers of his left hand, that he wanted to hear it.

"When I was at Langley earlier, Mr. President, our station chief in B.A. called. Five-thirty our time, six-thirty in B.A. I talked to him myself. He said that the Argentine cops were really active—the phrase he used was they 'had rounded up all the usual suspects'—and that there had been no word from the kidnappers, and that two FBI agents from the Montevideo embassy had been on the first flight."

"What's that about?"

"Apparently there are no FBI agents in the B.A. embassy, Mr. President. There's half a dozen in Montevideo."

"What the hell is this all about, Ted?" the President asked.

"I just don't know, Mr. President. But I'm sure there will be more details very soon."

"My curiosity is in high gear," the President said.

"Mine, too, Mr. President. It sounds wacko, frankly. If you'd like, I can call you whenever I hear something else."

"Do that, Ted, please."

"Yes, sir. Will that be all, Mr. President?"

"Unless you'd like another cup of coffee."

"I'll pass, thank you just the same, Mr. President."

"Thanks, Ted," the President said.

The President watched as the DDCI left the room, and then—almost visibly making a decision as he did so—topped off his coffee cup.

"What the hell, why not?" he asked aloud, and picked up the telephone.

"Will you get me the secretary of state, please?"

"Good morning, Mr. President," Dr. Natalie Cohen answered her phone.

"Natalie, you want to give me your take on that diplomat's wife who got kidnapped in Argentina?"

"That made the DIS, did it?"

"Uh-huh. What's going on?"

"I talked to the ambassador late last night, Mr. President. He—I guess I should say 'they'—don't know very much. He said kidnapping down there is a cottage industry, and he hopes that's all it is. I told him to call me with any developments, but so far he hasn't."

"At the risk of sounding insensitive, I could understand some lunatic trying to assassinate the ambassador, or this woman's husband, but . . ."

"The ambassador said just about the same thing, Mr. President. He can't understand it, either."

"Ted Sawyer said the CIA guy down there called this morning and said the embassy in Uruguay had sent a couple of FBI agents from the embassy there. How come we don't have FBI agents in Buenos Aires? That embassy is bigger than the one in Uruguay, right?"

"The money laundering takes place in Uruguay; that's where they need the FBI."

"He also said the Argentines had really mobilized their police."

"The ambassador told me that, too. It's embarrassing for them, Mr. President."

"I had an unpleasant thought just before I called you. We don't pay ransom, do we?"

"No, sir, we don't. That's a Presidential Order. Goes back to Nixon, I think."

"So the best we can hope for—presuming that this is just a kidnapping, and not a political slash terrorist act—is that once these people realize they've kidnapped a diplomat's wife and the heat is really going to be on, that they'll let her go?"

"That's one possibility, Mr. President, that they'll let her go."

He took her meaning.

"Jesus Christ, Natalie, you think they'd . . ."

"I'm afraid that's also a possibility, Mr. President," she said.

"What odds are you giving?"

"Fifty-fifty. That's for their turning her loose unharmed. I would give seventy-thirty that the cops will catch them."

"I told Sawyer I want to be in the loop. Will you keep me advised?"

"Yes, sir. Of course."

"Among other things we don't need is terrorists deciding that kidnapping our diplomats' wives is a good—and probably easy—thing to be doing."

"That thought ran through my head, too, Mr. President. But I don't think we can do anything beyond waiting to see what happens. I just don't see what else anyone can do right now."

"Keep me in the loop, please, Natalie. Thank you."

"Yes, sir, I will."

The President broke the connection with his finger.

"I just thought what else I can do," he said aloud, and took his finger off the telephone switch.

"Get me the secretary of Homeland Security," he said into the receiver to a White House operator.

II

Office of the Secretary
Department of Homeland Security
Nebraska Avenue Complex
Washington, D.C.
0840 21 July 2005

In the federal government, the secretary is not that person who answers the telephone, takes dictation, makes appointments, and brings the boss coffee. In Washington, the secretary is someone as high in the bureaucracy as one can rise without being elected President, and is therefore the boss.

In Washington, therefore, those individuals who answer the secretary's telephone, bring the coffee, make appointments, et cetera, have titles like "executive assistant."

The Honorable Matthew Hall, secretary of Homeland Security, had three executive assistants.

The first of these was Mrs. Mary-Ellen Kensington, who was fifty, gray-haired, and slim. She was a GS-15, the highest grade in the career Civil Service. She maintained Hall's small and unpretentious suite of offices in the Old Executive Office Building, near the White

House. Secretary Hall and the President were close friends, which meant that the President liked to have him around more than he did some other members of his cabinet. When Hall was in Washington he could usually be found in his OEOB office, so that he was readily available to the President.

The second was Mrs. Agnes Forbison, who was forty-nine, gray-haired, and getting just a little chubby. She was also a GS-15. She reigned over the secretary's office staff in his formal office, a suite of well-furnished rooms in the Nebraska Avenue Complex, which is just off Ward Circle in the northwest of the District of Columbia. The complex had once belonged to the Navy, but it had been turned over in 2004 by an act of Congress to the Department of Homeland Security when that agency had been formed after 9/11.

When the red telephone on the coffee table in the secretary's private office in the complex buzzed, and a red light on it flashed—signaling an incoming call from either the President himself, but more than likely from one of the other members of the President's cabinet; or the directors of either the FBI or the CIA; or the chairman of the Joint Chiefs of Staff; or the commander-in-chief of Central Command—Mrs. Forbison was in the process of pouring a cup of coffee for the secretary's third executive assistant, C. G. Castillo.

Castillo, who was thirty-six, a shade over six feet tall, and weighed 190 pounds, was lying on the secretary's not-quite-long-enough-for-him red leather couch with his stockinged feet hanging over the end of it.

Castillo looked at the red telephone, saw that Agnes was holding the coffeepot, and reached for the telephone.

"Secretary Hall's line. Castillo speaking."

"Charley," the caller said, "I was hoping to speak to your boss."

Castillo sat up abruptly, spilling a stack of papers onto the floor.

"Mr. President, the secretary's en route from Chicago. He should be landing at Andrews in about an hour."

"Aha! The infallible White House switchboard apparently is not so infallible. I can't wait to tell them. Nice to talk to you, Charley."

"Thank you, sir."

The line went dead. Charley, as he put the phone back in its cradle, exchanged *I wonder what that was all about?* looks with Agnes.

The phone buzzed again.

"Secretary Hall's line. Castillo speaking."

"What I was going to ask your boss, Charley, is if there is some good reason you can't go to Buenos Aires right now."

Buenos Aires? What the hell is going on in Argentina?

"Sir, I'm sure the secretary would tell you that I'm at your disposal."

"Well, I'll ask him anyway. But you might want to start packing. I've just been told the wife of our deputy chief of mission was kidnapped early last night. I want to know how and why that happened, and I want to know now, and I don't want to wait until whoever's in charge down there has time to write a cover-his-ass report. Getting the picture?"

"Yes, Mr. President."

After a moment, Charley realized the President had hung up.

Agnes waited for a report.

"He wants me to go to Buenos Aires," Charley replied, obviously thinking that over. "It seems somebody kidnapped the deputy chief of mission's wife. He wants me to find out about it. He's apparently laboring under the misconception that I'm some kind of a detective."

"You're not bad at finding missing airplanes, Sherlock."

"Jesus, Agnes, that's a big embassy. They probably have ten FBI agents, plus CIA spooks, plus Drug Enforcement guys . . . not to mention the State Department's own security people."

"But the President doesn't know any of them, Charley. And he knows you. Trusts you," Agnes said, and then added, "But to buttress your argument, there's also a heavy hitter Secret Service guy in Buenos Aires. Name of Tony Santini. He's an old pal of Joel's. The reason I know is that once a month or so he sends Joel twenty, twenty-five pounds of filet mignon steaks on the courier plane. They're in a box marked TISSUE SAMPLES."

"Maybe I can tell the boss that, and get Joel's pal to find out what happened. I really don't want to go down there."

What I really want to do is go to Glynco, Georgia—wherever the hell that is—and see how ex-Sergeant Betty Schneider is doing in Secret Service school.

• • •

"I understand, Mr. President," the secretary of Homeland Security said into the red phone. "Consider Charley gone." He laid the telephone back in the cradle and turned to Castillo.

Matthew Hall was a large man—his Secret Service code name was "Big Boy"—with a full head of hair. While he usually presented the image of a dignified senior government officer with the means to employ a good tailor, right now he looked a little rumpled.

His necktie was pulled down, and his collar button open. His suit needed pressing, and his beard was starting to show.

His appearance was temporary. As soon as the Citation had landed at Andrews Air Force Base, he had come to the Nebraska Complex to check on what was going on before going home. An hour from now, he would be freshly shaven, in a crisply starched white shirt and a freshly pressed suit.

"No go, Charley," Hall said. "He doesn't want it to get out that he's taking a personal interest."

"Yes, sir."

"Sir, what about Tony Santini?" Joel Isaacson asked. "He could probably be helpful as hell to Charley. You want me to give him a heads-up?"

Hall had told the President that Isaacson—a tall, slim, forty-year-old very senior Secret Service agent who was head of Hall's security detail and had once been number two on the presidential detail—had said he had a good friend in Buenos Aires, a Secret Service agent who could probably report on the kidnapping more quickly than Castillo possibly could. The President had been unimpressed.

"Santini?" Hall asked. "That's your friend's name?"

Isaacson nodded. "He and I—and Tom—go way, way back. Tony's down there working funny money."

Secret Service agent Tom McGuire, a large, red-haired Irishman, had also come from the presidential detail to protect Hall.

"You trust him to keep his mouth shut?"

Isaacson raised his hands in a gesture suggesting "dumb question."

"Sorry, Joel," Hall said. "Okay, give him a heads-up. And find out how Charley can quietly get in touch with him."

"If I'm to do this quietly, sir," Charley asked, "can I go as Gossinger?"

Hall considered that a moment, too, before replying.

"Your call, Charley."

Secretary Hall had decided about six months earlier—political correctness be damned—that he needed a male assistant, preferably unmarried. He was constantly on the move all over the country and sometimes outside it. He almost always flew on a Cessna Citation X. The airplane belonged to the Secret Service, which had been transferred from the Treasury Department to Homeland Security after 9/11.

Hall almost always traveled with Joel Isaacson and Tom McGuire. They often left for where they were going in the wee hours of the morning, and/or came back to Washington at the same ungodly hour.

Both Mrs. Kensington and Mrs. Forbison were married and not thrilled with the idea of flying on half an hour's notice to, say, Spokane, Washington, at half past five in the morning with no hint of when they'd be coming back to feed their husbands or play with their grandchildren.

Moving down the staff structure, Hall had taken maybe a dozen female administrative types with him on thirty or more trips, women with job titles like "senior administrative assistant." While all had been initially thrilled with the prospect of personally working for the secretary, none of them had kept at it for long.

Primarily, the ones who weren't married had boyfriends, and they all had grown accustomed to the federal government's eight-to-five, Monday-to-Friday workweek, and its generous day-off recognition of holidays. Hall worked a seven-day week, with an exception for, say, Christmas.

Moreover, having some female in the confines of the Citation X cabin posed problems. For one thing, Matt Hall believed with entertainer Ed McMahon that alcohol—especially good scotch—was God's payment for hard work. With a female in the cabin, that meant he had to drink alone, and he didn't like that.

Joel Isaacson and Tom McGuire couldn't drink with him if a senior administrative assistant—or someone of that ilk—was on the plane. Both were fully prepared to lay down their lives for the secretary, both as a professional duty and because they had come to deeply admire

Hall. But as a practical matter, once the local security detail had loaded them on the Citation and they'd gotten off the ground and were on their way home, having a belt—or two—with the secretary in no way reduced—in their judgment and the secretary's—the protection they were sworn to provide.

But what they could not afford was Miss Whateverhername rushing home to her boyfriend's pillow to regale him with tales of the secretary and his security detail sucking scotch all the way across the country while they exchanged politically incorrect and often ribald jokes.

When General Allan Naylor, the Central Command commander-in-chief, had been a captain in Vietnam, Matt Hall had been one of his sergeants. They had remained friends as Naylor had risen in the Army hierarchy and Hall had become first a congressman and then governor of North Carolina and then secretary of Homeland Security.

Their relationship was now professional as well. Central Command, *de facto* if not *de jure*, was the most important operational headquarters in the Defense Department. It controlled Special Operations, among many other things. The President had made it clear that whatever the secretary of Homeland Security wanted from Central Command he was to have, and if that violated procedure or regulations, either change the procedures or regulations, or work around them.

Hall and Naylor talked at least once a day on a secure communications link—sometimes a half dozen times a day when world events dictated—and they met as often as that worked out.

At a mixed business and social meeting, over drinks in the bar of the Army-Navy Club in Washington, Hall had confided in Naylor his problem traveling with females, and almost jokingly asked if Naylor happened to know of some young officer—male and unmarried—he could borrow as an assistant.

"Aside from carrying your suitcase and answering your phone, what else would he have to do?"

"It would help if he could type, and had decent table manners."

"Anything else?"

"Seriously?" Hall asked, and Naylor nodded.

"Handle his booze, know how to keep his mouth shut," Hall furnished. "And since this is a wish list, maybe speak a foreign language or two. Especially Spanish."

"How about one who speaks Spanish like a Spaniard?"

"You've got somebody?"

Naylor nodded. "Just back from Afghanistan. He's on the five-percent list for lieutenant colonel. They've been wondering where to assign him."

"How come you know a lowly major?"

"I've known this fellow a long time. West Pointer. Green Beret. About as bright as they come."

"And I can have him?"

Naylor nodded.

"Why?"

"Maybe because I like you, and maybe because I think he'd learn something working for you. If he doesn't work out, you can send him back."

Major Carlos Guillermo Castillo, Special Forces, had shown up at the Nebraska Complex three days later. In uniform, which displayed an impressive row of decorations and I-Was-There ribbons, plus a Combat Infantry Badge and a set of Senior Army Aviator wings. The latter surprised Hall, as Naylor hadn't mentioned that Castillo was a pilot.

He was also surprised at his appearance. He didn't look Latin. He was blue-eyed, fair-skinned, and Hall suspected his light brown hair had once been blond.

Hall, who had a CIB of his own, liked what he saw.

"Major, would it offend you if I called you 'Carlos'?"

"Not at all, sir. But I'd prefer 'Charley,' sir."

" 'Charley' it is. And—so people don't start asking 'who's that Army officer working for Hall?'—I'd like you to wear civvies. A suit, or a sports coat with a shirt and tie. Is that going to pose a problem?"

"No, sir."

Hall had stopped himself just in time from saying, "Don't go out and spend a lot of money on civvies; this may not work out."

Instead, he asked, "You're going to try to get in the BOQ at Fort Myer?"

"Sir, I'm on per diem, and I've spent more than my

fair share of time in BOQs. I thought I'd look for a hotel, or an apartment."

"Up to you," Hall had said, "but—frankly, this may not work out for either of us—I wouldn't sign a lease on an apartment right away."

"Yes, sir. A hotel."

"If such a thing exists, try to find a reasonably priced hotel near the White House—you might try the Hotel Washington. I spend most of my time in the OEOB, which means you will, too."

"Yes, sir."

Hall had risen and put out his hand.

"Welcome aboard, Charley. You come recommended by General Naylor, and with that in mind, and from what I've seen, I think you're going to fit in very well around here. Get yourself settled—take your time, do it right—and when you're finished, come to work."

"Yes, sir. Thank you, sir."

When Hall went to his OEOB office at nine the next morning, Castillo was there, waiting for him. In a gray suit, black wingtip shoes, a crisp white button-down shirt, and a red-striped necktie, none of which, Hall knew, had come off the racks at Sears, Roebuck.

Good, he looks like a typical bureaucrat, Hall thought, and then changed that assessment. *No. Like a successful Capitol Hill lobbyist or lawyer.*

Castillo said he'd found a hotel not far from the White House and the OEOB.

"One you can afford?" Hall asked, with a smile.

"Yes, sir."

"Well, then, if you're ready to go to work, I'll have Mrs. Kensington show you how we throw away the tax-payers' money."

Three days later, when Hall was dictating to Mary-Ellen, Castillo appeared at the door and said he had a little problem.

"What's that?"

"I need some kind of a title, sir. I got the feeling you didn't want the military connection, so I don't say 'Major.' When somebody asks me what I do here, I've been saying, 'I work in Secretary Hall's office.'"

"That makes you sound like a clerk," Mary-Ellen said. "Nobody will pay any attention to you."

Hall smiled at her. He had noticed that Mary-Ellen had liked Charley from the first day.

"Okay, Mary-Ellen, what do you suggest?"

"Executive assistant," Executive Assistant Kensington replied immediately. "That has a certain *je ne sais quoi* in the upper echelons of the Washington bureaucracy."

"But he's not an executive assistant," Hall had protested.

"He is if you say so, boss. And who's to know?"

"By the power invested in me by myself," Hall said, "you are decreed to be my executive assistant. Go forth and do good work."

"Yes, sir. Thank you, sir," Castillo replied to Hall. He turned to Mary-Ellen and added, *"Et merci mille fois, madame."*

Hall had picked up on that.

"You speak French, do you, Charley?"

"Yes, sir."

"Any other languages?"

"Yes, sir."

Hall made a come-on gesture.

Charley hesitated, and Hall added, "Modesty does not befit an executive assistant. Which ones?"

"Russian, sir. And Hungarian. German. Some Arabic. Several others."

"Jesus Christ!"

"Languages come easy to me, sir."

"They don't to me," Hall confessed. "You have plans for the evening, Charley?"

"No, sir."

"You have a dinner jacket?"

"Yes, sir."

"Your bluff is called. We are going to a reception at the Hungarian embassy. Whenever I ask the ambassador a question he doesn't want to answer, he forgets how to speak English. Getting the picture?"

"Yes, sir."

"How'd you learn to speak Hungarian?"

"When I was a kid, sir, my mother's aunt, who was Hungarian, lived with us. She taught me."

"Nice for you. Okay, Charley, I'll have Joel pick you up on his way here to get me. Where are you living?"

"I can meet you here, sir."

"Joel will pick you up. Where did you find a hotel?"

"I'm in the Mayflower, sir."

"The Mayflower?" Hall asked. "Isn't that kind of expensive on a major's pay, including per diem?"

"Yes, sir, it is."

"Joel will pick you up just before seven," Hall said, deciding it best not now to pursue the question of affordable housing with Castillo. "Wait for him on the street."

"Yes, sir."

The moment Castillo had closed the door, Hall reached for the red phone on his desk and pressed the button that would connect him over a secure line with the commander-in-chief, Central Command.

"Hey, Matt," Naylor said, answering almost immediately. "What's up?"

"I just found out my newly appointed executive assistant, Major Castillo, has taken a room in the Mayflower. How's he going to pay for that?"

"Would you be satisfied with 'no problem'?"

"No."

"Well, Charley told me that he'd taken a small apartment in the Mayflower," Naylor said. "The bill will probably be paid by Castillo Enterprises of San Antonio. Or maybe by the *Tages Zeitung*."

"The what?"

"It's a newspaper—actually a chain of newspapers—Charley owns in Germany."

"You didn't tell me much about this guy, did you, Allan?"

"You didn't ask. All you wanted was somebody who would carry your suitcase and who spoke Spanish. That's what I gave you."

"What's your connection with Charley, Allan? Other

than the usual relationship between a four-star general and one of his five thousand majors?"

"Elaine thinks of him—and I do, too, truth to tell—as the third son. We've known him since he was a twelve-year-old orphan."

"You didn't mention that, either."

"You didn't ask, Matt," Naylor said. "What do you want to do with him? Send him back?"

"No," Hall had said. "Presuming there is no further deep dark secret you're leaving for me to discover, I think he's going to be pretty useful around here."

Major/Executive Assistant Castillo did, in fact, and quickly, prove himself useful to the secretary of Homeland Security. And he fit in. Both Mary-Ellen Kensington and Agnes Forbison were clearly taken with him. Hall kindly ascribed this to maternal instincts, but he confided to his wife that he suspected both had amorous fantasies about Castillo.

"He's one of those guys women are drawn to like moths to a candle."

"I hate men to whom women are drawn like moths to a candle," Janice Hall had said.

The day Janice came to the office and met Castillo, she suggested to her husband that they have him to dinner.

"He's probably lonely living in a hotel," Janice said, "and would really appreciate a home-cooked meal."

"I thought you hated men to whom women were drawn like moths to a candle."

"That's not his fault, and he's obviously a nice guy. Ask him."

Castillo also got along from the start with Joel Isaacson and Tom McGuire. Hall had worried a little about that; Secret Service guys aren't impressed with most anyone. But Joel and Tom—both excellent judges of character—seemed to sense that Special Forces Major C. G. Castillo wasn't most anyone. Isaacson had even gone to Hall and suggested that Castillo be given credentials as a Secret Service agent.

"He could get through airport security that way. And carry a gun. I'll handle the credentials guys at Secret Service, if you like."

What really moved Castillo from being sort of a male secretary cum interpreter in whose presence it was possible to imbibe intoxicants and relate ribald stories to being a heavy hitter in Hall's office was a fey notion of the President of the United States.

In May 2005, an old Boeing 727 that had been sitting at the airport at Luanda, Angola, waiting for parts for more than a year, suddenly took off without permission and disappeared. No one really thought it had been stolen by terrorists and was going to be flown into some American landmark in a repeat of 9/11—that had quickly become regarded as a ridiculous notion at the highest levels; for one thing, the aged bird didn't have the range to fly to the United States—but no agency in what the President described as "our enormous and enormously expensive intelligence community" seemed to be able to learn what had happened to it.

The President was annoyed. At a private dinner—really private, just the President, the first lady, and Secretary and Mrs. Hall—the President said that he had been talking to Natalie Cohen—then his national security advisor, and now the secretary of state—and they had come up with an idea.

Hall understood that "they had come up with an idea" meant it was the President's idea. If it had been Natalie's, the President would have said so. What had probably happened was that he had proposed the idea, she had first argued against it, but then had given in to the President's logic, and the idea had become "their" idea. If she hadn't given in, and he had decided to go ahead anyhow, he would have claimed the idea as his own.

"You're the only department without an in-house intelligence operation," the President had said. "So this will work. Natalie will send everybody in the intelligence community a memo saying that since this stolen airliner poses a potential threat to the homeland, you are to be furnished, immediately, all the intelligence they've developed about this missing airplane.

"That will give us who knew what and when they knew it. Then, very quietly, we send somebody—just one man—to go over the scene quietly, very quietly, and see if he can find out why the CIA, for instance, knew something on Tuesday that the DIA didn't find out until Thursday. Or why the FBI didn't find out at all. You with me?"

"Yes, sir, Mr. President."

"The question is: Who can we send to do this without setting off a turf war?"

After meeting Major Carlos G. Castillo, the President decided he was just the man to very quietly, without setting off a turf war, find out which intelligence agencies were running with the ball; or had fumbled the ball; or had just sat on it, waiting for another agency to do the work.

Castillo went to Luanda, Angola, where the whole thing had started, and immediately ignited a turf war that had very nearly cost Secretary Hall his job.

He not only learned that the missing 727 had been stolen by Somalian terrorists, who planned to crash it into the Liberty Bell in Philadelphia, but with the help of Aleksandr Pevsner, an infamous Russian arms dealer, located the airplane no one else could find, and then with the help of the ultrasecret Gray Fox unit of Delta Force, stole the missing airplane back from the terrorists. With Castillo flying as copilot, Air Commando Colonel Jake Torine had flown the airplane from Costa Rica to Central Command headquarters at MacDill Air Force Base in Florida.

When the President had authorized the Gray Fox mission he had done so fully prepared to pay the price of an outraged Costa Rica—for that matter, the outraged membership of the United Nations—for launching a military operation without warning on a peaceful country that didn't even have an army.

With his imagination seeing the world's television screens lit up with CNN's—and Deutsche Welle's, and the BBC's, and everybody else's—report of the shocking, unilateral American incursion of poor little Costa Rica, with pictures of the flaming hulk of the airplane surrounded by dead Costa Ricans, the President was understandably delighted to hear that the only loss in Costa Rica was a fuel truck.

True to its professionalism, Gray Fox had left behind no bodies—American or Costa Rican—and no 727 gloriously in flames, and no traceable evidence that could place them ever at the scene.

Dissuaded by General Naylor from awarding Torine and Castillo medals for valor—which would have necessarily entailed detailing the valor—the President settled for awarding them Distinguished Flying Crosses "for superb airmanship in extremely difficult circumstances." It was Colonel Torine's thirteenth DFC and Castillo's third.

The President also had them down to the Carolina White House for a weekend.

There was a downside to this happy ending, of course. The director of Central Intelligence and the director of the Federal Bureau of Investigation were unhappy with the secretary of Homeland Security and his goddamn executive assistant for a number of reasons.

The DCI was of course smarting because Castillo had found the missing airplane before the agency could. And because Castillo had been able to talk the CIA station chief in Angola out of CIA intelligence files.

The director of the FBI was smarting because after the special agent in charge of the bureau's Philadelphia office had reported to him his belief that the missing airplane almost certainly had been "stolen" by its owners, a small-time aircraft leasing company on the edge of bankruptcy, so they could collect the insurance, and he had reported this to the President, Castillo had gone to Philadelphia and learned that the airplane had indeed not only been stolen, but stolen by Somalian terrorists whose names—as possible terrorists—had been provided to the FBI by the Philadelphia police some time before. The FBI had told the cops that the Somalians were okay, just some African airline pilots in the United States for training.

And because when an FBI inspector had been sent to Major/Executive Assistant Castillo to tell him he was confident that whenever Castillo heard from Alex Pevsner or his assistant, a former FBI agent named Howard Kennedy, again, Castillo would immediately notify the FBI, Castillo had told him not to hold his breath.

But since it had to be admitted by both the FBI and the CIA that they had not, in fact, furnished to the secretary of Homeland Security all the material they had been directed to furnish by then National Security Advisor Natalie Cohen, the directors vowed this would never happen again.

From this moment on, Homeland Security would get copies of every bit of intelligence generated that had, even remotely, to do with Homeland Security.

And if it kept that goddamn Castillo up all night reading it, and if he went blind reading it, so much the better.

• • •

When the red telephone on the coffee table buzzed, Charley Castillo was working his way through that day's intelligence—everything that had come in since five the previous afternoon—graciously furnished by the FBI and the CIA. He had been at this task since half past six.

The secretary hadn't made up his mind how to deal with the wealth of intelligence—most of it useless—that they were getting from the FBI and the CIA every day, but he and Charley and Joel and Tom were agreed that it had to be read.

Joel Isaacson said—only half jokingly—that both directors were entirely capable of sending over hard intel that a nuclear device in a container was about to arrive in Baltimore harbor, sandwiched between intel about two suspicious-looking Moroccan grandmothers, and an overheard and unsubstantiated rumor that the bishop of Sioux Falls, South Dakota, was a crossdresser, and that therefore it had to be read.

What would seem to be the obvious solution to the problem—Hall calling the directors of the CIA and FBI and saying, "Okay, enough is enough, stop sending the garbage"—almost certainly wouldn't work. It was possible—maybe even more than likely—that the directors, with straight faces, would tell the secretary they had no idea what he was talking about. And that would mean Hall would have to go to the President. He didn't want to do that; he was trying to spread oil on the troubled waters, not onto the smoldering fire.

One possible solution—which Agnes thought the

most likely—was to bring into the office two Secret Service agents-in-training now going through the Federal Law Enforcement Training Center in Glynco, Georgia, just as soon as they were, as Joel put it, "credentialed."

Both were experienced police officers, recruited at the suggestion of Secretary Hall from the Philadelphia Police Department as a result of his and Castillo's experience with them looking for the 727. One had been a sergeant in the intelligence unit, and the other a detective in the counterterrorism division, who had worked for years undercover infiltrating Muslim communities considered potentially dangerous. Both would be able to sort through the stacks of intel reports knowing what to look for, and what was garbage.

But this would mean they would be working directly for the secretary, instead of just—Hall's original idea—becoming Secret Service agents with far more experience and knowledge than the usual rookies, and being assigned to a field office somewhere.

Agnes knew that Hall was reluctant to have his own in-house intelligence unit, but she thought sooner or later—probably sooner, since while Charley was sifting through the garbage he was not available to him; he had not gone with Hall to Chicago last night because he had to read the overnight files—he was going to have to face the facts.

The secretary of Homeland Security picked up the red handset and punched one of the buttons on the base.

"Natalie Cohen."

"Good morning, Mademoiselle Secretary," Hall said.

"Goddammit, Matt, you know I don't think that's funny," the secretary of state said.

"It makes more sense than a female lawyer calling herself 'Esquire,'" Hall went on, undaunted. "I learned in school that 'madam' is a married lady and an unmarried one a 'mademoiselle'—"

"Is there something on your sophomoric mind, Matt? Or are you just seeing what happens when you push the buttons on your red phone?"

"The President, Mizz Secretary . . ."

She chuckled. "Better. Not good. But better."

". . . is sending Charley to Buenos Aires. I guess you can figure out why."

There was a perceptible pause before the secretary of state replied.

"To find out who knew what, and when they knew it," she said, just a little bitterly. Those had been the President's instructions to Castillo when the President had sent him off to learn what he could about the missing airliner. "I should have seen this coming, I suppose."

"I tried to talk him out of it. You want to try?"

"(A) I don't think he wants me to know that he's sending Charley down there, and (b) I think the reason he didn't tell me was because he knew I would argue against it, and (c) if I happened to mention this to him, he'd know I heard it from you, and we both would be on the bad-guy list."

"It wasn't my idea, Nat."

"I know," she said. "Actually, now that I've had thirty whole seconds to think about it, I'm not nearly as livid as

I was. Maybe Charley will come up with something the ambassador down there would rather that I didn't hear. You will . . ."

"Give you what he gets? Absolutely."

"Thanks for the heads-up, Matt."

"Do you know something about the ambassador that Charley should?"

"I never met him. I talked to him last night on the telephone, and I was favorably impressed. And everything I hear about him is that he's first-rate. He's a Cuban. You might tell Charley that, so he'll expect a Cuban temper if the ambassador finds out he's snooping around down there."

"I'll do it."

"Tell Charley to be careful. We don't need a war with Argentina," the secretary of state said, and hung up before Hall could reply.

[TWO]
Room 404
The Mayflower Hotel
1127 Connecticut Avenue, NW
Washington, D.C.
1120 21 July 2005

Room 404—which was actually what the hotel called an "executive suite" and consisted of a living room, a large bedroom, a small dining room, and a second bedroom, which held a desk and could be used as an office—was registered to Karl W. Gossinger on a long-term basis.

The bill for the suite was sent once every two weeks by fax to the *Tages Zeitung* in Fulda, Germany, and payment was made, usually the next day, by wire transfer to the hotel's account in the Riggs National Bank.

When he took the room, Herr Gossinger told the hotel he would need two outside telephone lines. One of these would be listed under his name and that of the *Tages Zeitung*. The second, which would not be listed, would be a fax line. He also told the hotel that Mr. C. G. Castillo, whom he described as an American associate, would be staying in the suite whenever he was in town, and the hotel should be prepared to take telephone calls, accept packages, and so forth for Mr. Castillo.

Karl Wilhelm von und zu Gossinger had been born out of wedlock in Bad Hersfeld, Germany, to an eighteen-year-old German girl and a nineteen-year-old American warrant officer helicopter pilot. The Huey pilot had gone to Vietnam shortly after their three-day-and-two-night affair.

When Jorge Castillo never wrote as he had promised, Erika von und zu Gossinger tried to put him out of her mind, and when the baby was born, she christened him Karl Wilhelm, after her father and brother.

Frau Erika—she never married; "Frau" was honorific—turned to the U.S. Army for help in finding the father of her only child only after she was diagnosed with terminal pancreatic cancer. Karl was twelve at the time. His grandfather and uncle, the only known relatives, had been killed in an autobahn accident some months before. Frau Erika reasoned that any family would be better for Karl than leaving him an orphan in Germany. Even an orphan with vast family wealth.

Largely through the efforts of then-Major Allan Naylor of the 11th Armored Cavalry, which was stationed on the East German border near Fulda, WOJG Jorge Alejandro Castillo of San Antonio, Texas, was located. He was interred in San Antonio's National Cemetery. A representation of the Medal of Honor was chiseled into his tombstone. He had died a hero in Vietnam, apparently without ever suspecting that when he had sown his seed it had been fertile.

Once it was realized they were dealing with the love child of an officer whose courage had seen him posthumously awarded the nation's highest recognition of valor, the Army shifted into high gear to make sure that everything possible would be done for the boy.

Major Naylor was rushed to San Antonio to first find and then as gently as possible inform the late WOJG Castillo's family about the boy.

A pragmatist, Naylor had considered several unpleasant possibilities. One was that Mr. Castillo's parents might not be overjoyed to learn that their son had left an illegitimate child in Germany, at least until they heard of his coming inheritance. That would put a new—and possibly unpleasant—light on the subject.

Senior Army lawyers were looking into setting up a trust for the benefit of the boy—and only the boy.

His concern proved to be without basis in fact. General Amory T. Stevens, the Fort Sam Houston commander, who had been Major Naylor's father's roommate at West Point, and was Naylor's godfather, quickly told him that he knew the late Mr. Castillo's parents.

"They are Fernando and Alicia Castillo," Stevens said. "Well known in Texas society as Don Fernando and Doña Alicia. The Don and Doña business isn't only because they own much of downtown San Antonio; plus large chunks of land outside the city; plus, among others, a large ranch near Midland, under which is the Permian basin, but because of something of far more importance to Texans.

"Doña Alicia is the great-, great-, whatever grand-daughter of a fellow named Manuel Martinez. Don Fernando is similarly directly descended from a fellow named Guillermo de Castillo. Manuel and Guillermo both fell in noble battle beside Jim Bowie, William Travis, and Davy Crockett at the Alamo.

"What I'm saying, Allan, is that if this boy in Germany needed help, Don Fernando would quickly cut a check for whatever it would cost. What I'm not sure about is whether he—or, especially, Doña Alicia—is going to be willing to take the love child of their son and a German—probably Protestant—gringo into the family. The Castillos can give lessons in snobbery to the Queen of England."

Twenty-two hours after the late WOJG Castillo's mother was informed, very delicately, that she had an illegitimate grandson, Doña Alicia was at the door of the von und zu Gossinger mansion in Bad Hersfeld. Don Fernando arrived nine hours later.

Two weeks after that, the United States Consulate in

Frankfurt am Main issued a passport to Carlos Guillermo Castillo. Don Fernando was not without influence in Washington. The same day—Frau Erika, then in hospital, having decided she didn't want her son's last memory of her to be of a pain-racked terminally ill woman in a drug-induced stupor—Carlos boarded a Pan American Airlines 747 for the United States. Frau Erika died five days later.

On her death, as far as the government of the Federal Republic of Germany was concerned, American citizen with a new name or not, Karl Wilhelm von und zu Gossinger, native-born son, had become the last of the von und zu Gossinger line.

At twenty-one, just before C. G. Castillo graduated from West Point, Karl Wilhelm von und zu Gossinger came into his German inheritance, which included the *Tages Zeitung* newspaper chain, two breweries, vast—for Germany—farmlands, and other assets.

A second identity, as Herr Karl Gossinger, foreign correspondent of the *Tages Zeitung,* had proved very useful to Major C. G. Castillo, U.S. Army Special Forces, in the past, and it probably would again in Argentina.

In his suite at the Mayflower, C. G. Castillo was nearly finished with packing his luggage. He had carefully packed his small, guaranteed-to-fit-in-any-airplane-overhead-bin suitcase-on-wheels with enough winter clothing to last three or four days. When it was mid-summer in Washington, it was midwinter in Buenos Aires. He didn't think he'd be down there longer than that.

All that remained was to pack his briefcase, which also came with wheels and was large enough for his laptop computer. This was somewhat more difficult as it required carefully separating a section of the padding from the frame. Inside was a ten-by-thirteen-inch plastic folder. There was a sticky surface to keep things from sliding around, and the folder material itself was designed to confuse X-ray machines. Castillo carefully arranged his American passport; his U.S. Army identification card; C. G. Castillo's Gold American Express and Gold Visa credit cards; his Texas driver's license; and credentials identifying him as a supervisory special agent of the U.S. Secret Service on the sticky surface, closed the folder, and then replaced the padding.

He then went into the small dining area, and from a small refrigerator concealed in a credenza, took out a bottle of Dos Equis beer, popped the top, took a healthy swallow from the neck, burped, and then went into the living room, where he sat down in a red leather recliner—his, not the hotel's—shifted his weight so that it opened, and reached for the telephone.

He punched in a number from memory, took another sip of the Dos Equis, and then lay back in the chair as he waited for the call to be completed.

The general director of Gossinger Beteiligungsgesellschaft, G.m.b.H., who was also the editor-in-chief of one of its holdings, the *Tages Zeitung* newspapers, answered his private line twenty seconds later.

"Göerner."

"Wie geht's, Otto?" Castillo said.

"Ach, der verlorene Sohn."

"Well, you may think of me as the prodigal son," Castillo said, switching to English, "but I like to think of myself as one of your more distinguished foreign correspondents."

"Distinguished, I don't know. But I'll go with most expensive."

Castillo thought of Otto Göerner as his oldest friend, and he certainly was that. Otto had been at Philipps University in Marburg an der Lahn with Wilhelm von und zu Gossinger, Karl's uncle, and had been with the *Tages Zeitung* since their graduation. He had been around *der Haus im Wald* in Bad Hersfeld, as Uncle Otto, as far back as Castillo could remember. He remembered, too, the very early morning when Otto had brought the news of her father's and brother's death to his mother.

And how, when his mother had told him they had located his father's family and he would probably— "after"—be going to them in the United States, he had thrown a hysterical fit, demanding that he be allowed— "after"—to live with Uncle Otto.

And how, at the airport in Frankfurt, tears had run unashamedly down Otto's cheeks when he'd seen him off to the States. And how he had been a friend ever since.

"How's ol' Whatsername and the kids?"

"Ol' Whatsername and your godchildren are doing very well, thank you for asking. To what do I owe the honor?"

"I'm off to Buenos Aires on a story, and I thought I'd

see if there was anything else you wanted me to do down there."

"Can't think of anything, Karl," Otto said.

Göerner didn't ask what story Castillo would be pursuing in Argentina.

He's the opposite of a fool, Charley thought for the hundredth time, *and without any question knows what I do for a living. But he never asks and I never tell him. All he does is give me what I ask for.*

"I won't be gone long," Charley said. "Probably less—"

"Yeah, come to think of it, Karl, I do," Göerner interrupted.

"Okay, shoot."

Karl Gossinger, the *Tages Zeitung*'s Washington-based foreign correspondent, usually had a bylined story in the paper once a week. These were generally paraphrased—stolen—from the *American Conservative* magazine. There was a dual purpose. First, if someone checked on Gossinger, there was his picture, beside his latest story from Washington. And if they looked closer, the masthead said the *Tages Zeitung* was founded by Hermann von und zu Gossinger in 1817. Using material from the *American Conservative,* moreover, gave Charley Castillo a chance to put before German readers what some Americans—including Charley—thought about the Germans turning their backs on America when the United States asked for their help in the Iraq war.

Editing only for grammar, Otto printed whatever

Charley sent him without comment. Charley didn't know, or ask, whether this was because Otto agreed the Germans had behaved badly, or because the bottom line was that Charley owned the newspapers.

"The *Graf Spee*," Göerner said.

Charley knew the story of the *Graf Spee*: The German pocket battleship, named after a World War I German hero, was scuttled just outside the harbor of Montevideo, Uruguay, in 1939, to keep her from being sunk by three British cruisers waiting for her to come out. Her crew went to Buenos Aires. Her captain, Hans von Langsdorff, put on his dress uniform, laid her battle ensign on the floor of his hotel room, positioned himself so that his body would fall on it, and shot himself in the temple. He was buried in Buenos Aires.

The crew was interned in Argentina. When the war was over, many of her crew declined repatriation. And many of those who did return to the fatherland took one look at the destroyed remnants of the Thousand Year Reich and went back to Argentina as quickly as they could.

"What about the *Graf Spee*?" Charley asked.

"A fellow named Bardo—a young and very rich financier from Hamburg—has raised the money to salvage her and turn her into a museum in Montevideo. I could use a human-interest piece on the survivors, if any—they'd all be in their eighties. And most of them would be in Argentina."

Finding the survivors—if any—shouldn't be hard. And

neither would taking some pictures and writing a feature story. And it would give journalist Gossinger a credible excuse to be in Argentina.

"I'll have a shot at it," Charley said. "Anything else?"

Göerner hesitated before replying.

"Karl, I'm a little reluctant to get into this . . ."

"Into what?"

"I went over to Marburg an der Lahn a couple of weeks ago. They were doing a fund-raiser for the library at the university. All *Alte Marburgers* were invited. I overheard parts of a conversation between some of the big shots. What caught my attention was a line, something about 'Der Führer was the first to come up with that idea. Ha, ha!' "

"You've lost me."

"You remember that during World War Two, Hitler—the top Nazi—sent a lot of money to Argentina to buy themselves a sanctuary when they lost the war?"

"Uh-huh."

"These guys were talking about moving money to Argentina."

"To buy sanctuary? Sanctuary from what? You're talking about drug money?"

"What I'm thinking about is Iraqi oil-for-food money bribes that may have wound up in the pockets of these guys."

"Jesus!"

"Yeah, Jesus. Anyway, I've got people looking into it here, and the idea I had—probably not a good one—was that maybe you would hear something in Argentina."

"I'll keep my ears open," Charley said.

"Just that, Karl," Göerner said seriously. "If you hear something, anything, pass it to me. But stop there. You understand me?"

That's as close as he's ever come to saying, "You and I know you're not really a journalist."

"I take your point."

"I also have people looking into the mysterious deaths of people who knew about these oil-for-food bribes."

"I take your point, Otto."

"Aside from that, have a good steak and a bottle of wine for me, and don't try to spread your pollen on more than ten or twelve of those lovely Argentine señoritas."

"Didn't I tell you? I have taken a vow of chastity. Celibacy is supposed to increase your mental powers."

"Ach, Gott, Karlchen," Göerner laughed. "Keep in touch."

"Kiss my godchildren, and say hello to Ol' Whatsername."

"My regards to Fernando and your grandmother. *Auf wiedersehen!*"

The line went dead.

Castillo hung up, shifted his weight in the chair so the back came up, and then got out of it. He finished the bottle of Dos Equis as he looked around the apartment to see if he had forgotten anything, and then put on the jacket to his seersucker suit.

He looked at himself in the mirror.

I am probably going to freeze my ass off in Buenos Aires

until I can get to the Hyatt, but on the other hand, I won't have to go through Reagan and Miami International wearing a woolen sports coat.

[THREE]
Miami International Airport
Miami, Florida
1850 21 July 2005

As Castillo stood before the luggage carousel waiting for his suitcase, he had very unkind thoughts about Delta Airlines, on whose flight 431 he had just arrived.

When he boarded the airplane at Ronald Reagan Washington National, he had had the suitcase in hand. All of the overhead luggage bins in the first-class section were full. The first-class section itself had not been any-where near full—probably because Delta's DCA-MIA first-class fare bordered on the rapacious—which sug-gested, *ergo sum,* that the luggage in the first-class bins had been placed there by people traveling economy class as they passed through the first-class section en route to the rear of the aircraft.

"I'm afraid you'll have to check that," the stewardess told him.

"Why do I suspect that all the luggage in the bins does not belong to first-class passengers?"

"I'm afraid you'll have to check that," the stewardess repeated.

"I don't suppose that since I thought I would have space in the first-class bins, and find that I don't, you could put this in with the coats and jackets? I really hate to check it."

"I'm afraid you'll have to check it," the stewardess said firmly.

It would also seem to logically follow, Castillo thought, watching the luggage carousel rotate at MIA, *that since my suitcase was loaded, if not last, then close to last, it would be unloaded first. That obviously is not the case.*

The suitcase finally showed up. Castillo pulled out the handle and dragged it from luggage recovery. Surprising him not at all, the map in the entrance foyer showed him that Aerolíneas Argentinas was at the other end of the airport, almost in Key West. It was a long walk through the crowded airport, which reminded him of his cousin Fernando Lopez's appraisal of Miami International: "It is the United States' token third world airport."

That reminded him, *Jesus Christ, I almost forgot!* that he would have to call Fernando and/or *Abuela,* their grandmother, and tell them he would not be able to come home for the weekend, even if Fernando flew up to pick him up.

He finally reached the Aerolíneas Argentinas counter. There was a long line of people in the first-class line, all of whom seemed to have extra, overweight, or oversize luggage. There were far more such people than there were seats in the first-class compartment of either a 747 or a 767, which suggested that they were economy-class passengers who had taken advantage of there being no one in the first-class line.

Twenty minutes later, he reached the head of the line and was given permission to approach the counter by the clerk, who beckoned to him with her index finger like the Queen of Spain summoning a footman.

He laid a passport issued by the German Federal Republic and an American Express corporate credit card issued to the *Tages Zeitung* on the counter.

"My name is Gossinger," he said. "I have an electronic ticket, I believe."

Getting through airport security was—if possible—more harassing than usual. Castillo was randomly selected for close examination. Not only did the security people make him take his shoes off, but their pawing through his luggage effectively nullified his careful packing. And he was concerned about the detailed examination of his briefcase cum laptop carrier that was to come.

They made him turn the laptop on to prove that it indeed was not an explosive device, but they didn't show much interest in the briefcase itself. That was a relief. Herr Gossinger did not want to have to explain what he was doing with C. G. Castillo's passport and Secret Service credentials.

Finally they were through with him, and he went to the Club of the Americas, the first- and business-class lounge that served Aerolíneas Argentinas and other South American airlines that did not have their own lounges.

He fixed himself a double scotch on the rocks, then found a secluded corner and sat down. He took his cellular telephone from his pocket and punched an auto-dial key.

"Hello?"

"And how is my favorite girl?"

"Your favorite girl is wondering if you're calling to tell me you're not coming home for the weekend."

"*Abuela*, I'm in the airport in Miami, waiting to get on a plane for Buenos Aires."

"Well, I'll give you this. Your excuses are out of the ordinary. Darling, I was so looking forward—"

"*Abuela*, this wasn't my idea."

"What are you going to do in Argentina? Am I allowed to ask?"

No, you're not.

"I should be back within the week."

"Buenos Aires?"

"Uh-huh."

"It's winter down there now. You did think to pack warm clothing?"

"Yes, ma'am."

"If it's convenient, Carlos, I'm almost out of brandy. You know the kind."

"I'll get you a case."

"I think you're limited to six liters."

"I'll find out."

"Be careful. I talked to Jeanine Winters just this morning, and she said kidnapping is now the cottage industry down there."

Jeanine Winters was a very old friend of Doña Alicia. The Winters family, Texans, had been operating an enormous cattle operation in Entre Ríos province and a vineyard in Mendoza Province for generations.

Jesus, has she heard about this diplomat's wife? Did Mrs. Winters hear about it already, and tell her?

"*Abuela,* nobody's going to kidnap me."

"Just be careful, Carlos, is all I'm saying."

"*Sí, Abuela.*"

"I'll say a prayer for you."

"Thank you."

"*Vaya con Dios, mi amor,*" Doña Alicia said, and hung up.

[ONE]
**Aeropuerto Internacional Ministro Pistarini de
   Ezeiza**
Buenos Aires, Argentina
0615 22 July 2005

Aerolíneas Argentinas proved to be much more accommodating about luggage than Delta had been. Just as soon as Castillo had stepped aboard through the main cabin door, a steward had offered to take his briefcase on wheels from him.

"I can store it with the coats, sir," the steward said. "Save you from having to hoist it into the overhead bin."

This courtesy was followed as soon as he took his seat

in the first-class compartment of the Boeing 767; a stewardess appeared with a tray of champagne glasses.

He took one, even though he told himself he didn't need it after the three drinks he'd had in the Club of the Americas.

He hadn't needed the glass of merlot that came with the appetizers just as soon as they reached cruising altitude, either, but he took that, and a second glass with the entrée—a nice little filet mignon, served with roasted potatoes. And the glass of brandy he had with the camembert and crackers dessert wasn't needed, either.

When the movie came on, he thought the odds were that in a couple of minutes he would doze off and sleep the sleep of the Half-Crocked and More or Less Innocent most of the way across the Southern Hemisphere.

Nothing wrong with that. Unless you're sitting in the left seat in the cockpit, that's the only way to fly: unconscious.

He didn't fall asleep. It was a Mel Gibson movie; Gibson was playing the role of a prosperous businessman whose kid was kidnapped.

Well, let's see how he handles this; maybe I'll learn something, Castillo thought as he pushed the overhead button to summon a stewardess to order another brandy.

Castillo thought Gibson was a fine actor. He had played, very credibly, the role of light colonel Hal Moore in the movie version of the book *We Were Soldiers Once . . . and Young,* written by Moore and Joe Galloway.

Castillo had read the book, the story of what had happened to one of the first battalions of paratroopers who had been converted to air assault—helicopter inserted—troops at Fort Benning, and then followed them to Vietnam, where some nitwit in the First Cav had inserted them in the wrong place and almost gotten them wiped out.

It was nonfiction, and he'd bought the book because he'd heard that Galloway—who had been at Fort Benning and then gone to Vietnam with the battalion—had done a good job describing the early days of Army aviation, and he thought it might tell him something about what the late WOJG Jorge Alejandro Castillo, boy chopper jockey, had gone through before he bought the farm. And because he knew the light bird battalion commander Galloway had written about—Moore—had wound up with three stars; there had to be a lesson in that alone.

He'd really liked the book, and had taken a chance and gone to see the movie. He almost never went to war movies; most of them were awful. The ones that didn't make you laugh made you sick.

The *Soldiers* movie had been as good as the book. He thought it was just about as realistic as the movie version of *Black Hawk Down*, Mark Bowden's book on the disaster that hit the special operators in Mogadishu in 1993, and he had viewed that one with the expert eye of someone who'd been flying a Blackhawk in Somalia at the time.

And Castillo thought that Gibson's portrayal of the battalion commander was right on the money.

● ● ●

Gibson's portrayal of the distressed father was very credible, too. Gibson was being forced to make the very tough call between not paying the ransom, or following the advice of the FBI and the cops—and his hysterical wife, the mother of the child—to pay it.

When a stewardess gently woke him to offer orange juice, Castillo was more than a little annoyed—if not very surprised—to realize that he had fallen asleep before Gibson had made the tough call.

That last glass of brandy did you in. Now you'll never know what Gibson decided.

I wonder what he did decide?

What the hell would I do in his shoes?

Jesus, it's only a movie.

But you're about to get close to a real kidnapping.

Let this missing the end of the movie be a lesson to you, Charley me boy.

Now you're working. Lay off the booze.

Except maybe for a glass or two of wine.

Breakfast was nice, too: grapefruit juice that tasted like freshly squeezed, a mushroom omelet, and hard-crusted rolls served with large pats of unsalted butter.

He remembered Don Fernando—Grandpa—saying, "The only thing the Argentines do well consistently is eat."

Five minutes after a stewardess served a second cup of coffee, Castillo sensed that the pilot had retarded the throttles a tad, and two minutes after that a steward announced—in Spanish, English, and German, which Herr Gossinger thought was a nice touch—that they were beginning their approach to Buenos Aires, where the local time was five-thirty and the temperature was three degrees Celsius.

I really am going to freeze my ass in this seersucker.

·

As the 767 taxied up to the terminal, another 767 caught his eye. It was parked on the tarmac, not at one of the terminal's airways. The legend painted in Arabic and English on its glistening white fuselage read "Pan Arabic."

Good ol' Alex Pevsner told me one of the reasons he hadn't stolen that 727 was that he didn't need an old airplane. And then he had added, "I just bought a nearly new 767 from an airline that went belly up in Argentina."

I wonder if that's it.

Probably not. But you never know with Pevsner.

Castillo was the third person to get off the 767—after a portly housewife towing a howling five-year-old—and when he rolled his bags into the terminal, he thought for a moment that he had inadvertently gone through a door that should have been locked.

He hadn't. He was in a duty-free store, and a young woman—*Jesus, I like that; long legs, dark eyes, and a splendid bosom*—handed him a flyer announcing both that day's bargains and that he could take three hundred

U.S. dollars' worth of goods duty-free into Argentina in addition to what was already permitted.

The duty-free store people have solved their problem of getting travelers into their emporium by making it impossible to get to Immigration and Customs without passing through the store; they've built it on both sides of the corridor.

Clever.

But screw them. I don't need anything.

When he got to the Immigration window, a large bag containing a double-box of Famous Grouse scotch, a half-pound bag of M&M's, and two eight-ounce cans of cashews was hanging from the handle of the wheeled briefcase.

My intentions were noble. I thought I would see if they had any of Abuela's Reserva San Juan Extra Añejo, so that I would be sure to remember to bring her some. They didn't, but they did have a damned good price on the Famous Grouse. And the cashews and M&M's were certainly a hell of a lot cheaper than the ten-bucks-a-can cashews and five-dollar one-ounce packages of nuts Hyatt offers in their minibars.

You're rationalizing again, Charley. The truth is you have no strength of character. If the duty-free-store spending spree isn't enough proof of that, note the way you lusted after the señorita passing out the flyers. You promised yourself you would be faithful to your Secret Service trainee—is that what they're calling her? Maybe cadet?—Betty Schneider, even though she professes not to want to get to know you better than she does now, which is to say, hardly at all. And absolutely not at all in the biblical sense.

• • •

"And are you in Argentina on business or pleasure, Señor Gossinger?"

"Business and pleasure."

"What's the nature of your business?"

"I'm a journalist, here on a story."

"You understand that as a journalist, you will have to register with the Ministry of Information?"

"I'm only going to be here for a few days. Just to do a story on the survivors of the *Graf Spee*."

"The law is the law, señor."

This guy never heard of the Graf Spee.

"I certainly understand, and I'll register just as soon as I can. Probably later today."

That was pretty stupid, Inspector Clouseau. You didn't have to tell him you were a journalist. You could have told him you were a used-car salesman on vacation.

How come James Bond never gets asked what he's doing when he goes through Immigration?

Customs didn't give him any trouble. The customs officers pushed a button for each traveler, which randomly flashed a red and a green light. If it came up red, your bags went through the X-ray machine. If it came up green, they waved you through. Castillo won the push of the button.

He pushed through the doors to the arrival lobby.

There was a stocky man holding a crudely lettered sign with GOSSINGER on it.

"My name is Gossinger."

A balding, short, heavyset man in his forties standing next to the man with the sign put out his hand.

"Mr. Gossinger, my name is Santini. Mr. Isaacson asked me to meet you. Welcome to Argentina."

Castillo picked up on the "Mr. Isaacson." Not Joel. Not Agent. And responded accordingly.

"That was very kind of him. And kind of you. How do you do?"

"Some of the taxi drivers here at the airport tend to take advantage of unwary visitors."

"That happens at a lot of airports," Charley replied. "La Guardia comes immediately to mind."

Santini smiled, and then said: "We have a remise— you know what a remise is?"

Charley nodded.

". . . with an honest driver," Santini finished, then gestured toward the doors. "Shall we go?"

When the man with the sign got two steps ahead of him, Santini quickly gestured—his index finger across his lips—for Castillo to say nothing important in the presence of the driver. Castillo quickly nodded his head.

They stood for a couple of minutes on the curb while the driver went for the car. Santini didn't say a word. Castillo, feeling colder by the second in his summer suit, silently hoped the driver hurried.

The car was a large, black Volkswagen with heavily tinted glass. As the driver bent to put Castillo's luggage in the trunk, Castillo saw that he had a pistol—it looked like a Beretta 9mm—in a belt holster.

Santini opened the rear door and motioned for Castillo to get in. When he had, Santini slid in beside him. When the driver got behind the wheel, Santini asked, "You don't speak Spanish, do you?"

Castillo asked with a raised eyebrow how he should reply. Santini, just perceptibly, shook his head.

"I'm afraid not," Castillo said.

"Pity," Santini said. "Mr. Isaacson didn't say where you would be staying."

"The Hyatt."

"It's now the Four Seasons, formerly Hyatt Park. They sold it."

"I guess nobody told my travel agent," Castillo said.

"You heard that, Antonio?" Santini asked. "The Four Seasons?"

"Sí, señor."

The Volkswagen started off.

It was a thirty-minute drive from the airport to the hotel. First down the crowded but nonetheless high-speed autopista toll road, and then onto Avenida 9 Julio, which Castillo remembered was supposed to be the widest avenue in the world.

As they came close to the Four Seasons, formerly Hyatt Park, Castillo saw that it was next to the French embassy, an enormous turn-of-the-century mansion. He'd forgotten that.

A top-hatted doorman welcomed him to the Four Seasons and blew a whistle, which caused a bellman to appear.

"Find somewhere to park," Santini ordered Antonio. "I'll see that Señor Gossinger gets settled."

• • •

Room 1550 in the Four Seasons was a small suite, a comfortable sitting room and a large bedroom, both facing toward the Main Railroad Station—which Castillo remembered was called "El Retiro"—and the docks and the River Plate beyond. There was something faint on the far horizon.

Castillo wondered aloud if they were high enough so that he was looking at the shore of Uruguay.

"Clear day," Santini replied. "Could be. Why don't we go out on the balcony and have a good look?"

"Why not?"

When they were out on the small balcony, Santini took a small, flat metal box from his pocket and ran it over the walls, then over the tiny table and two chairs, and finally over the floor.

"Clean," he announced. "But it never hurts to check."

Castillo smiled at him.

"Joel tells me there's a warrant out for you in Costa Rica," Santini said with a smile. "Grand Theft, Airplane."

"Joel's mistaken. The name on the warrant is 'Party or Parties Unknown.' "

Santini chuckled, then asked, "What's going on with you here?"

"I was sent to find out about our diplomat's wife who got herself kidnapped."

"When did kidnapping start to interest Special Forces?"

"Joel told you about that, too, huh? To look at him, you wouldn't think he talks too much."

"Your shameful secret is safe with me, Herr Gossinger."

"I guess you know I'm on loan from the Army to Matt Hall?" Santini nodded. "The President told him to send me down here to, quote, find out what happened and how it happened before anybody down there has time to write a cover-his-ass report, end quote."

Santini nodded, then offered:

"Mrs. Elizabeth Masterson, nice lady, wife of J. Winslow Masterson, our chief of mission. Nice guy. She was apparently snatched from the parking lot of a restaurant called Kansas, nice place, in San Isidro, which is an upscale suburb. So far, no communication from the kidnappers. I'm thinking that they may have been very disappointed to find the lady has a diplomatic passport; I wouldn't be surprised if they turn her loose. On the other hand, they may decide that a dead woman can't identify anybody."

"You give it good odds that they'd kill her?"

"They kidnapped a kid not so long ago—not a kid. He was twenty-three. In San Isidro, where they grabbed Mrs. Masterson. He was the son of a rich businessman. They cut off his fingers, one at a time, and sent them to Poppa, together with rising demands for ransom. Poppa finally paid, three hundred thousand American. That's roughly nine hundred thousand pesos, a fortune in a poor country. And shortly thereafter, they found the kid's body, shot in the head."

"Why'd they kill him?"

"Dead men tell no tales," Santini said, mockingly. "Hadn't you heard?"

"Wouldn't that discourage other people from paying ransom?"

"When they've got junior or the missus, you pay and hope you get them back alive. The only thing that may keep Mrs. Masterson alive is if the bad guys are smart enough to realize that killing her would really turn the heat up. That would embarrass the government." He paused, and then, mimicking the sonorous tone of a condescending professor, added, "My experience with the criminal element, lamentably, suggests that very few of them are mentally qualified to be able to modify their antisocial behavior and become nuclear physicists."

Castillo chuckled. "I don't know why I'm laughing," he said, then asked, "What did you say about the Kansas?"

"It's a nice restaurant. She was snatched from the parking lot in back of it. If you want, I'll take you out there for lunch, and you can have a look-see for yourself."

"Thank you. I'd like that. I won't know what I'm looking at, but I have to start somewhere."

"Pardon my ignorance, but why can't you just walk into the embassy and tell the security guy, Ken Lowery, nice guy, what you're doing down here?"

"That would put me in the system. The whole idea is for me not to be in the system."

"Nobody knows you've been sent down here? Not even the agency?"

"Especially the agency. I'm on their bad-guy list. Theirs and the FBI's."

Santini thoughtfully considered that.

"But I'd like to know about them. Or is that putting you on the spot?"

"You're okay with Joel. That's good enough for me. Anyway, there's not much to tell. The CIA station chief—his cover, so called, is commercial attaché—is a good guy by the name of Alex Darby. From what I've seen, he's okay. There's no FBI at the embassy, but they sent a couple agents over yesterday from Montevideo to see if they could be useful. I just barely know them. Typical FBI agents."

"You think—what did you say his name is? Darby?—you think Darby's in tight with SIDE and/or the local cops?"

"You know what SIDE is?"

"The Argentine versions of the CIA and the FBI combined in one, right?"

Santini nodded, then asked, "You've been here before?"

"Yeah."

"Nobody at the embassy knows you?"

"I don't think so. I've never actually been inside the place."

Santini nodded, accepting that, and then answered the question:

"I would say Darby's tight with SIDE and Lowery's tight with the cops." He paused, and then asked, "What's going to happen if—when—they find out you're down here? Nosing around down here? I'm not going to say anything, but . . ."

"I really hope they don't. It would put Natalie Cohen

on the spot with the ambassador for not telling him. She knows I'm down here, and why."

"You call the secretary of state by her first name?"

"No. I call her 'ma'am,'" Castillo said, but then added, smiling: "But she calls me Charley."

"Speaking of names, Joel said Gossinger's a beard."

"My name is really Castillo. Charley Castillo."

He put out his hand. Santini took it.

"Tony," he said, and then in Italian, "You don't look Italian."

Charley shook his head and replied, in Italian, "Half German and half Texan, heavy on the Hispanic heritage."

"You speak good Italian."

"Languages come pretty easy to me."

Santini nodded his acceptance of this, then asked, "How good a cover? If SIDE develops an interest in you, they'll check. They're pretty good at that."

"It'll hold up. Gossinger, who works for a German newspaper, the *Tages Zeitung*, is here to do a human-interest story on the survivors of the *Graf Spee*. If my editor at the *Tages Zeitung* hasn't already told the German embassy I'm here and said I would appreciate all courtesies, he will soon."

Santini looked at him a moment.

"Okay, so you speak Spanish, you've been here, you've got what sounds like a pretty good cover. But I still don't know how you can do what you're supposed to do without going to the embassy."

"I didn't say I wasn't going to go to the embassy. *Charley Castillo's* not going to the embassy."

"You're pretty good at this undercover business? Playing make-believe? You could get away with playing Gossinger at the embassy?"

"Why not?"

"Can I make a suggestion?"

"I'm wide open."

"Even if they swallow you whole at the embassy as Herr Gossinger, they're not going to tell you anything. For one thing, it hasn't been in the papers or on the tube. The Argentines are embarrassed, and they put a lid on the story. We're not talking about it to the Americans—not the newspaper, not the *New York Times,* nobody. The Argentines are hoping that when the bad guys find out they've got a dip's wife they'll turn her loose, and the whole thing can be forgotten. Personally, I think they're pissing in the wind, but that's where it is right now. So if Herr Gossinger goes to the embassy and starts answering questions, Lowery and everybody else are going to wonder how the hell Herr Gossinger heard about it."

"I hope Joel told you I wasn't sent here because I was the best-qualified man all around to conduct an under-cover kidnapping investigation."

"Joel said you had two skills: you were one hell of a swordsman and pretty good about stealing stolen air-liners back from the bad guys."

"He didn't mention my poker playing?"

"No," Santini said, smiling. "But figure that out. If he told me that, he would be admitting you took him."

"Joel has one flaw in his character," Charley said. "He actually thinks he can play poker."

"He also thinks he can actually play gin," Santini said.

"When we were on the presidential detail, waiting, we got to play a hell of a lot of gin. I took a lot of his money."

They smiled at each other.

"But we digress, Herr Gossinger," Santini said. "We were talking about my little suggestion."

"Let's hear it."

"If, say," Santini began, "a fellow Secret Service agent just happened to be passing through Buenos Aires, and checked in with me at the embassy, and he and I just happened to bump into Ken Lowery, and I told Lowery, 'I was just telling Agent Whatsisname here about Mrs. Masterson,' Lowery would understand that—he's always making reference to 'we federal agents' as if he were one—and would probably stumble over his tongue to tell you how he's dealing with the problem."

"Am I detecting you don't think too much of this guy's ability as an investigator?"

"He's a good guy, like I said, but how many times do you think he's had a chance to investigate anything more serious than some dip diddling another dip's wife? Such conduct being detrimental to the foreign service of the United States."

Castillo chuckled, then asked, "What would happen to you if they found out you'd set this up? And they probably would, sooner or later."

"Maybe they would send me home in disgrace," Santini said. "And I could go back to being a real Secret Service agent. Coming down here wasn't my idea. Or maybe you could have told me, as the Presidential Agent, what you were doing and ordered me to keep my mouth shut."

"Consider yourself so ordered," Castillo said. "But I

have to tell you the last time I did that—to a guy who had some information I needed—the DCI wasn't impressed and relieved him for cause. He finally wound up with a letter of commendation from the President, but he had a very uncomfortable couple of days before that happened."

"What'll happen will happen," Santini said.

"How come they sent you down here?"

"I hurt myself, and was placed on limited duty, so they sent me down here to look for funny money."

"How'd you hurt yourself?"

"Joel didn't tell you?"

Castillo shook his head.

"If you laugh, I'll break both your arms," Santini said, conversationally. "I fell off the Vice President's limo bumper, and the trailing Yukon ran over my foot."

"I won't laugh, but can I smile broadly?"

"Fuck you, Herr Gossinger," Santini said, smiling.

"What would another Secret Service agent be doing, passing through Argentina?"

"Any one of fifty things, it happens all the time, at least once a month. Usually, it's a supervisory special agent bitching about my expenses; crap like that. The only problem I can see would be if somebody asked you to prove who you were."

"Wait one," Charley said.

Less than two minutes later, he handed his Secret Service credentials to Santini.

"Hall got you these?" he asked when he'd examined them.

Castillo shook his head.

"Joel went to Hall and got them for me."

"These would work, I think. Your call."

"It looks to me like a winner," Castillo said. "Thanks, Tony."

Santini made a deprecating gesture.

"The dips don't go to work until nine," he said. "So why don't you get yourself settled, and then about nine, take a taxi to the embassy?"

"Okay."

"Facing the embassy, to the right is the gate for employees. Use that one. The guards are Argentines. Flash the tin at one of them, and they'll escort you into the building, to Post One, where there's a Marine guard. Flash the tin at him, tell him you want to see me. I will appear and profess surprise at seeing Supervisory Special Agent Castillo, and get you a visitor's badge. Then we will arrange to bump into Lowery."

"Sounds good. A taxi? Not a remise?"

"A taxi to the embassy. There's no sense in letting SIDE know you went right from your hotel to the embassy."

Castillo asked for an explanation with a raised eyebrow.

"For a little background," Santini said, "the drivers of Palermo Remise are off-duty cops. That means they can carry guns. That's useful; there's a lot of bad guys here. The problem is I suspect the off-duty cops they send me are SIDE agents. If my cynicism is on the money, I've worked out an unspoken agreement with SIDE. I use their remises, the drivers report to SIDE where I go, and who I talk to. That way they don't have to put a tail on me. I just don't talk business in a remise."

"Understood," Castillo said.

"But generally—unless you don't want SIDE to know where you're going—Palermo Remise is a good idea," Santini said, and handed him a business card. "It never takes them much longer than ten minutes to pick you up, no matter where you are. They use cellulars."

Castillo nodded.

"Thanks, Tony."

Santini handed him a Motorola cellular telephone and a charger. Again, Castillo asked about it with a raised eyebrow.

"My personal cell number is Auto Four," Santini said. "My personal—unlisted—number is Five, and my office is Six. I've got a good Argentine administrative assistant, Daniel. *As far as I know,* he's not working for SIDE."

Castillo nodded his understanding.

"You can call the States with that, but it's about nine dollars a second, so don't spend hours chatting up your girlfriend."

"Who pays the bills for this? The Secret Service or the embassy?"

"The Secret Service. Which means me. Which means, I guess, Supervisory Agent Castillo, you can talk to your girlfriend as long as you want to."

Hi there, Betty. Charley Castillo. I was just sitting here in my hotel room in Buenos Aires wondering how things are going up there in Georgia, and thought I'd give you a call.

Yeah, I know they must be keeping you pretty busy there in agent school, or whatever the hell they call it.

Sorry to bother you.

"Thanks, Tony."

Santini touched his arm.

"See you a little after nine," he said, and walked from the balcony, through the room, and out the door.

Charley took a shower. The only word to describe the bathroom was *sumptuous*. Except for the ceiling, everything was marble. There was both a Jacuzzi and a large shower stall, and a heated chrome rack on one wall held enough thick towels to dry an elephant.

He put on what he thought of as his "bureaucrat's uniform," a dark gray single-breasted suit with a white button-down shirt and a striped necktie.

He looked at his watch and saw that it was five minutes past eight, which meant it was five minutes past seven in Washington. Calling Joel Isaacson to thank him for Santini would have to wait. And it didn't make sense to send an e-mail. For one thing, he didn't have much to say, except what Santini had told him. Maybe after he talked to the security guy at the embassy he would know more. And if by twelve—eleven in D.C.—he didn't know more, then he would send an e-mail saying just that: *Nothing yet. Working on it. Best wishes. Sherlock Holmes.*

He reached for the telephone to call room service and then changed his mind. He would have coffee in the lobby. If there was nothing else to attract his attention— and he thought there was a good chance there would be; the only other place he knew where there were so many good-looking women was Budapest—he'd have a look at the *Buenos Aires Herald*.

He thought for a moment about what to do with Gossinger's passport and credit cards, and then put them in the padding of the laptop case. It was always awkward to be found with two sets of identification.

He walked down the corridor to the bank of elevators and pushed the down-arrow button. The door opened almost immediately, and he found himself looking at a slim man in his early forties, with shortly cropped, thinning hair. He wore a light brown single-breasted suit and a subdued necktie. He would not stand out in a crowd.

"Either you're a much better actor than I've previously given you credit for being, or that startled look is genuine," the man said.

So it was Pevsner's 767 at Ezeiza. I wonder what the hell they're doing in Buenos Aires?

"Good morning, Howard," Castillo said.

"I would say, 'How are you?'" Howard Kennedy said. "But I think the more important question is 'Who are you today?'"

"Today my name is Castillo," Charley said. "How about you?"

"Charley Castillo, intrepid Green Beret? Or Charley Castillo of the Secret Service?"

It was a high-speed elevator. The door opened onto the lobby as Castillo's mouth opened. There were people—a family, husband, wife, and two teenaged boys—waiting to get on the elevator.

"The latter, Howard," Castillo said as he got off the elevator.

Kennedy waited until no one was within hearing.

"So what brings you to Gaucho Land, Charley?" he asked.

"I'll tell you what I'm doing here if you tell me what you are."

"Over a cup of coffee? I'll buy. I know from painful experience how little the government pays its law enforcement agents, even the very good ones."

"Flattery, and the offer of a free cup of coffee, will get you everywhere."

Kennedy smiled and touched Castillo's arm.

"This is probably very foolish of me, but I'm really glad to see you."

Castillo smiled at him.

"I'm not sure if I'm glad to see you, or just overwhelmed with curiosity."

Kennedy chuckled and led the way to the nice restaurant set for breakfast and lunch, an open area furnished with low tables and leather-and-chrome armchairs.

A waitress—a stunning young woman with long legs and large dark eyes—appeared almost immediately. They ordered coffee.

"And bring some pastry, please," Kennedy added. When she had gone, he said, "Very nice. I envy you your bachelor status."

"I saw the Pan Arabic 767 at Ezeiza," Charley said. "I wondered if it was yours."

"My, you are observant, aren't you? It got in at an obscene hour, and I came here to take a shower and a nap. And then, surprise, surprise!"

"You were going to tell me what you're doing here."

"We brought a load of tapestries and other decorations from Riyadh for the King Faisal Islamic Center, and we're going to take back two dozen polo ponies, and cases of boots and saddles and other accoutrements, for the game of kings."

"So you're now a horse trader?"

"Your turn, Charley."

"There's a personnel problem at the embassy. They sent me down to see what it really is."

"Instead of what the ambassador is saying it is?"

Castillo nodded. "Something like that."

The waitress appeared with coffee and pastry.

"That was quick," Kennedy said.

He reached for a *petit four*.

Castillo said, "My grandfather used to say the only things the Argentines do consistently well is eat."

Kennedy chuckled. "You going to tell me the nature of the personnel problem at the embassy?"

"Just as soon as you tell me what you're really doing here."

Kennedy smiled at him. "Now that I think about it, I really don't give much of a damn about personnel problems in the embassy."

"On the other hand, I'd really like to know what you're really doing here."

"I'm sure you would. But you're going to have to be satisfied with that it is neither illegal nor inimical to the interests of the United States."

"I could ask for no more," Castillo said, and then asked, "You ever see that Mel Gibson movie where they kidnap his kid?"

"No. I can't say that I have. I'd love to know why you're asking."

"It was the in-flight movie. I fell asleep in the middle,

and I've been wondering how it turned out."

"I think you're serious."

"They kidnapped his kid, and he had to decide to pay the ransom, which his wife and the FBI wanted him to do, or not pay."

Kennedy shook his head.

"In a previous employment," Kennedy said, "I worked a half dozen big-dollar kidnappings. Big-dollar kidnappings are usually either inside jobs, in which case a couple of good interrogators can usually find out who done it in a matter of hours. Or they're professional jobs, in which case the victim is kept alive only long enough for them to collect the ransom. Phrased somewhat indelicately, if you pay the ransom, you lose the victim *and* the money. Does that satisfy your curiosity, Charley? What did Gibson do?"

"I told you I fell asleep before that happened."

"And now you'll lie awake nights wondering about it," Kennedy said sarcastically, and then asked, "How long are you going to be here, Charley?"

Castillo raised both hands in a *Who the hell knows?* gesture.

"Maybe we can have dinner," Kennedy said, "or drinks."

"I'd like that."

"How do I get in touch with you?"

"Here, I suppose."

"You don't have a cellular? Or you're not going to give me the number? Which?"

"You show me yours and I'll show you mine."

"Deal."

They exchanged cellular phones.

I know how come I have a cellular, even though I just got here.

So where did you get yours, Howard? Maybe you didn't just arrive in the obscene hours of the morning?

"Rushed right from the plane to the cellular store, did you, Charley?"

"Howard, it's not nice—didn't your mommy tell you?—to read other people's minds. But, to satisfy your curiosity, I got mine from the Secret Service guy here. The Secret Service takes care of its own. Where did you get yours?"

"I borrowed it from a friend."

"Sure."

Kennedy looked at him and smiled, but didn't respond directly. He handed Charley's cellular back to him.

"I'd love to push the autodial buttons on that, and see who answers."

"Who do you think might answer?"

"They call the FBI guys in embassies 'legal attachés,' I guess you know."

"Cross my heart and hope to die," Castillo responded, "none of the autodial buttons will call the FBI. I don't even know anybody in the FBI here. As a matter of fact, I just learned they don't even have an FBI detachment, or whatever, at the embassy. What about your buttons?"

Kennedy didn't reply directly to that, either. Instead, he said, "So what's on your agenda right now? Can I drop you someplace?"

"I'm going to the embassy."

"It's right on my way. I'll drop you."

"On your way to where?"

"The King Faisal Islamic Center. It's just a couple of blocks from the embassy."

"I have a hard time picturing you touching your forehead to the floor in prayer."

"It's business, Charley. Just business."

"Isn't that the line the Mafia uses, just before they shoot people?"

"Would that the Arabs were as easy to deal with as the Mafia," Kennedy said, and stood up. He took a wad of money from his pocket and dropped several bills on the table. "You want a ride or not?"

A black Mercedes-Benz S500 with heavily darkened windows was waiting for Kennedy when he came through the revolving door. A large man who looked vaguely familiar got quickly out of the front passenger seat and opened the rear door.

"You remember Herr Gossinger, don't you, Frederic?" Kennedy said.

"Guten morgen, Herr Gossinger," the man said without expression.

The last time I saw you was in Vienna. I pegged you as either Hungarian or Czech, but what the hell. It all used to be Austria.

"Grüss Gott!" Charley said, trying to sound as Viennese as possible.

Kennedy got quickly in the backseat, and Charley slid in after him.

[TWO]
The United States Embassy
Avenida Colombia 4300
Buenos Aires, Argentina
0905 22 July 2005

As Kennedy's Mercedes turned off Avenida Libertador, Castillo could see both the American embassy and the ambassador's residence, a large, vaguely European-looking mansion fronting on Libertador. A large, armored, blue Policía Federal van was parked on the street across from it, but Charley couldn't see any police.

The embassy sat a block away, overlooking a park, behind both a steel picket fence and a half circle of highway-divider concrete barricades. It was unquestionably American, he thought somewhat unpatriotically.

Another building—the embassies in London and Montevideo come to mind—built to the pattern that should have won the architect the opposite of the Pritzker Prize: one for designing the Ugliest Office Buildings of the Century.

The only thing that keeps people from confusing that drab concrete oblong with a misplaced airport warehouse is that the gray walls are perforated with neat rows of square inset windows.

There are probably a thousand roadside Marriott or Hilton motels that are better-looking and look American. Why the hell couldn't they have used brick, and thrown in a couple of columns? Made it look a little like Monticello, or even the White House?

The intensity of his reaction surprised him.

Why am I pissed?

Fatigue? Hangover?

Being sent down here to do something I have no idea how to do?

Maybe that. Okay, certainly that. But really, it's Howard Kennedy.

What the hell is he doing here? It's no coincidence. Or is it?

I don't know—have no way of knowing—and that disturbs me.

And why is he absolutely unable to believe that I have no intention of flipping him to the FBI? Goddammit, by now he should know he can trust me. Which of course makes me unable to trust him . . .

"The entrance is way down on the left," Kennedy said. "And it looks like there's a line of people ahead of you."

"Probably people applying for visas," Castillo replied. "There's supposed to be an employee entrance on the right. Just drop me anywhere along here."

A moment later the Mercedes pulled to the curb. Charley saw the man in the front jump out to open the door for him. He turned to Kennedy and offered his hand.

"Thanks, Howard," he said.

"I have every confidence you're not going to tell the legal attaché how you got here."

"Oh, goddammit, Howard! I told you, there's no FBI here."

"So you said."

"Fuck you, Howard."

"Hey, Charley, I'm just pulling your chain."

"No, you're not."

"Let's try to have a drink and/or dinner," Kennedy said.

"Yeah. Give me a call."

He got out of the Mercedes and walked quickly across the street. There was a gap wide enough to walk through between the wedges of the concrete barrier. Once through that, he could see a gate, with a guard shack and a revolving barrier, in the steel picket fence.

There were three men in the guard shack, wearing police-style uniforms with embroidered patches of some security service on the sleeves. What looked like Smith & Wesson .357 Magnum revolvers hung in open holsters from Sam Browne belts.

He extended the leather folder holding his Secret Service credentials to one of the guards.

"I'm here to see Mr. Santini," he said in English.

"This gate is for embassy personnel only," the security guard said, more than a little arrogantly, and pointed to the far side of the embassy.

You sonofabitch, you didn't even look at my credentials!

An Argentine rent-a-cop is denying a Secret Service agent access to an American embassy? No fucking way!

"You get on that goddamn telephone and tell the Marine guard that a United States Secret Service officer is here at the gate," Castillo snapped, in Spanish.

Looking a little surprised at the fluent Spanish, as well as the tone, the guard gestured for Castillo to show him his credentials again. Another security guard picked up the telephone.

Castillo turned his back on them.

That little display of anger was uncalled for. What the hell is the matter with me?

But on the other hand, I think that would have been the reaction of a bona fide Secret Service agent. Maybe not Joel, but Tom McGuire certainly would not put up with any crap from a rent-a-cop.

He saw the Mercedes had not moved.

Trying to see if I'm really going in, are you, Howard?

No. What you're trying to do is see whether I am immediately passed in, which would mean I'm known here, or whether I'm being subjected to this rent-a-cop bullshit because they don't know me.

He smiled and waved cheerfully, and the Mercedes started to move.

"If you will come with me, please, señor?" the rent-a-cop who had been on the telephone said in English.

Castillo turned and saw that the revolving barrier was moving. He went through it, and the security cop was waiting for him.

"Do you have a cellular telephone or other electronic device, sir?"

"I have a cellular," Castillo said in Spanish.

"You'll have to leave it with me, sir. It will be returned when you leave."

"We will talk to the Marine guard about that," Castillo snapped in Spanish, and started walking to the embassy building.

After a moment's hesitation, the security guard walked after him.

There were maybe fifteen people standing outside the glass entrance walls. They were all smoking.

I doubt the you-can't-smoke-in-a-U.S.-government-building zealots have ever wondered how much time is lost by all these people taking a smoke break. What's that cost the taxpayer?

Okay, Charley. Tantrum time is over. Be nice.

Inside the lobby there was a row of chrome-and-leather benches—like the seats in an airport—against the wall, portraits of the President, the Vice President, and the secretary of state on the walls, and, behind a glass-walled counter, a Marine guard—a sergeant—wearing a khaki shirt, dress blue trousers, and a white Sam Browne belt.

"May I help you, sir?" the Marine guard asked.

Charley handed him the credentials folder, which the sergeant examined carefully.

"I'm here to see Mr. Santini."

"He has a cellular," the security guard accused.

The sergeant picked up a telephone and punched a button.

"Sergeant Volkmann at Post One," he said. "There's a Mr. Castillo to see you, sir." There was a pause, and then the sergeant said, "Yes, sir," and looked at Castillo.

"Mr. Santini will be right down, sir," the Marine sergeant said. "Please have a seat."

He pointed to the benches.

"He has a cellular," the security guard said again.

"Excuse me, sir," the Marine sergeant said.

Castillo looked at him.

"Are you armed, sir?" the Marine sergeant asked, pointing to a metal-detector arch in front of the door leading inside.

Castillo shook his head.

"Thank you, sir."

Castillo sat down on one of the benches.

The secretary of state, unsmiling, looked down at him from the wall.

Natalie, I really wish you had been able to talk the President out of sending me down here.

The security guard flashed Castillo a dirty look as he walked out of the lobby.

Santini came through the metal detector arch a minute later.

"Good morning, sir," he said, putting out his hand. "I just learned that you were coming."

"How are you, Santini?" Castillo said as he shook the hand.

Santini turned to the Marine guard.

"Can I get Supervisory Special Agent Castillo a frequent visitor badge, or am I going to have to run that through Lowery?"

"Sorry, sir," the Marine said. "Mr. Lowery runs a tight ship."

"Well, then, give him a regular visitor badge."

"Yes, sir. I'll have to have his passport, Mr. Santini."

"Jesus Christ!" Castillo said, and then smiled at the sergeant as he handed him his passport. "Sergeant, that 'Jesus Christ' was directed at whoever made a dumb rule, not you."

"No problem, sir," the Marine said, with a hint of a smile.

He handed Castillo a plastic yellow visitor's pass on what looked like a dog tag chain, and pushed a clipboard to him.

"If you'll sign that, please, sir."

"And if you'll follow me, sir," Santini said, "we'll see if we can't straighten this out with Mr. Lowery."

"He the security guy?" Castillo asked.

"Yes, sir, he is."

Castillo hung the visitor's badge around his neck and followed Santini through the metal detector.

Inside, behind the Marine guard post enclosure, was a foyer. In the center of it were two elevator doors, one of them open. Santini waved Castillo through it and pushed a floor button.

"I would say that we are about to corner the security lion in his lair," Santini said, when the door had closed and they were alone, "except that he's more of a pussy-cat."

The door from the third-floor corridor to the embassy security officer's office was open. Kenneth W. Lowery—*he looks a hell of a lot like Howard Kennedy*—was sitting at his desk, talking on the telephone.

When he saw Santini, he smiled and waved him in.

"I'll get back to you," Lowery said, and hung up the telephone.

"Good morning, Tony," he said.

"Say hello to Supervisory Secret Service Agent Castillo," Santini said. "He's in town to complain about my expense sheet."

"Having seen your lifestyle, I can see where that would be entirely possible," Lowery said, getting up and extending his hand across his desk. "Nice to meet you."

"How are you?" Castillo said.

"What are the chances of getting Mr. Castillo a frequent visitor badge? He's going to be in and out."

"How long are you going to be here, Mr. Castillo?"

"Call me 'Charley,' please," Castillo said. "As long as it takes to get Santini to admit he's been robbing the service blind. That shouldn't take more than a week or so."

"Could I see your credentials, please? And your travel orders?"

"Credentials, yes," Castillo said. "Travel orders, no."

"You don't have travel orders?" Lowery asked.

"Blanket," Castillo said.

Lowery examined the credentials carefully.

"I don't think I've ever met a supervisory special agent before," he said, making it a question.

How the hell do I respond to that?

"I wasn't notified that you were coming," Lowery said.

Another question, not a statement.

"That's why they call it the Secret Service," Santini said. "What we do is secret; we don't tell anyone."

Lowery did not find that amusing.

"Except for having a couple of chats with Santini, I have no business with the embassy," Castillo said. "If there's a problem with this frequent visitor badge he thinks I should have, forget it." He paused and added: "There's a number you can call to verify my bona fides on the back side of the photo ID."

"Oh, no. No problem at all," Lowery said quickly. "Can I borrow these for a moment? I'll have my secretary make up the badge."

"Sure," Castillo said.

Lowery went through a side door and came back a moment later.

"Take just a couple of minutes. She'll type it out and then plasticize it. I told her to make it out for two weeks. That be long enough?"

"More than long enough," Castillo said. "Thank you."

"Can I offer you a cup of coffee while we're waiting?"

"Yes, thank you."

Lowery went through the door again, and returned shortly with three china mugs.

"I know Tony takes his black," Lowery said. "But there's . . ."

"He takes it black? Then what's that thirty-eight-dollar item for cream and sugar, Santini?"

Lowery looked at him, then laughed.

"Tony's been telling me about your problem," Castillo said.

"What problem is that?" Lowery asked warily.

"The missing wife," Castillo said.

Lowery flashed Santini a dirty look.

Santini rose to it.

"Come on, Ken, it's not as if Mr. Castillo works for the *New York Times*."

Lowery considered that for a moment.

"Actually, just before you came in, I was wondering how long it will be before the *Times* guy hears about it." He paused, then added: "What did Tony tell you?"

"Just that the wife of the chief of mission is missing under mysterious circumstances."

"The husband's climbing the walls, understandably," Lowery said. "She was waiting for him in a restaurant in San Isidro. When he got there, her purse and car were there, and she wasn't."

"And you think she was kidnapped?"

Lowery hesitated before replying, then asked, "Have you got much experience with this sort of thing, Mr. Castillo?"

"A little."

Once, for example, I helped snatch two Iraqi generals, one Russian general, one Russian colonel, and half a dozen other non-Iraqis from a Scud site in the Iraqi desert. I don't think that's what you have in mind, but let's see where this goes.

"Frankly, I don't," Lowery said. "Let me tell you what I've got, and you tell me what you think."

"Sure."

"I don't think these people were just hanging around the Kansas parking lot to grab the first woman they thought looked as if someone would pay to get her back. Too many well-heeled folks pass through that parking lot on any given night, and never a nab. They were looking for Mrs. Masterson."

"That suggests they think the government would pay

to get her back. Don't they know that we don't pay ransom to turn people loose?"

"Jack Masterson has money," Lowery said. "Lots of money. You don't know who he is?"

Castillo shook his head.

" 'Jack the Stack'?" Lowery asked.

Castillo shook his head again.

"The basketball player?"

That didn't ring a bell, but there was a very slight tinkle. "Oh."

"In the fourth month of his professional basketball career," Lowery explained, "for which, over a five-year period, Jack the Stack was to be paid ten million dollars . . ."

Castillo's eyebrows went up. *Christ, now I know!* "But he was run over by a beer truck when leaving the stadium," Castillo said.

"Driven by a guy who had been sampling his product," Lowery finished. "He had twice as much alcohol in his blood than necessary to be considered legally under the influence."

"And there was a settlement," Castillo said.

"One hell of a settlement. Without even going to court. Jack wasn't badly injured, but enough so that he would never be able to play professional ball again. The brewery didn't want to go to court because not only were they going to lose—they were responsible and knew it; the truck driver was their agent—but there would be all sorts of the wrong kind of publicity. They paid not only the ten million he would have earned under his contract, but also what he could reasonably have expected to earn in the rest of his professional career. It came to sixty million, not counting the money he could have made with endorsements."

"I always wondered what happened to him after he left the game," Castillo said.

My thoughts were unkind. I wondered how long it would take him—like the winners of a lottery or heavyweight champions—to piss away all that money and wind up broke, reduced to greeting people in the lobby of some casino in Las Vegas.

And he wound up a diplomat?

Oh, you are a fine judge of character, Charley Castillo!

"Jack could have, of course, bought an island in the Bahamas and spent the rest of his life fishing, but he's not that kind of guy. He wanted to do something with his life, and he had an education."

"The foreign service seems a long way from a basketball court," Castillo said.

"Not if your wife is the daughter of an ambassador—and, for that matter, your brother-in-law a pretty highly placed guy in the United Nations. Jack had a degree—cum laude—in political science, so when he took the foreign service examination and passed it with flying colors, no one was really surprised."

"You don't think of pro athletes having cum laude degrees in anything," Castillo said.

Do I believe that?

No. I know better. There have been exceptions.

But the accusation has been made, justifiably, that C. G. Castillo has a tendency toward political incorrectness.

"Once Jack was in the foreign service, he started working his way up. Quickly working his way up. He's good at what he does. After this tour, they'll probably make him an ambassador."

"And you think the people who grabbed his wife knew this story?"

"Hell, this is the age of satellite television. The average Argentine twenty-year-old knows more about American professional basketball than I do."

Certainly more than I do. I have never understood why people stay glued to a television screen watching outsized mature adults in baggy shorts try to throw a basketball through a hoop.

"There aren't very many African Americans in Argentina," Lowery said. "Even fewer who stand six-feet-eight and get their pictures on the TV and in *La Nación* and *Clarín* when they're standing in for the ambassador, or explaining a change in visa policy. *'Who is that huge black guy? Looks like a basketball player. Why, that's Jack the Stack, that's who he is, the guy who got all those millions when the* cerveza *truck ran over him.'"*

"That makes sense."

"'Let's snatch his wife,'" Lowery concluded.

"Yeah," Castillo agreed.

"So far, not a word from the kidnappers," Lowery said.

"Is that unusual?"

"The Policía Federal tell me they usually call within hours just to tell the family not to contact the police, and make their first demands either then, or within twenty-four hours. It's been—my God, it will be forty-eight hours at seven tonight."

"How good are the police?"

"The ones that aren't kidnappers themselves are very good."

"Really?"

"They fired the whole San Isidro police commissariat—like a precinct—a while back on suspicion of being involved in kidnappings there."

"Were they?"

"Probably," Lowery said.

He looked thoughtfully at Castillo for a moment.

"Have I made it clear that I like Jack Masterson? Personally and professionally?"

Castillo nodded.

"I'm worried about him, both personally and professionally," Lowery said.

"How so?"

"The policy of never dealing with terrorists or kidnappers makes a lot of sense intellectually," Lowery said. "But emotionally? My wife hasn't been kidnapped, and I don't have the money to pay any ransom."

"You think if they contact him, he'll pay?"

"I don't know. If he did, he might get his wife back, and he might not. These people have . . . Just a couple of months ago, after a rich Argentine businessman paid an enormous ransom . . . after the kidnappers sent him his son's amputated fingers . . ."

"Santini told me that story," Castillo interrupted.

". . . they found the boy's body. They'd shot him in the head."

"Nice people," Castillo said.

"Who are entirely capable of doing the same thing to Betsy Masterson," Lowery went on. "Worst-case scenario, Jack doesn't get Betsy back, and it comes out that he paid a ransom. In violation of strict policy with which he is familiar. That'd mean he would have lost both his wife and his career in the State Department. Or he does get her back, and they find out he's paid the ransom, and that would end his career."

A price any reasonable man would be happy to pay, I think. Wives are more important than money or careers.

I wonder if Mel Gibson came to that conclusion?

"You do have somebody sitting on him?" Castillo asked.

"Excuse me?"

It's cop talk. The first time I heard it was in the Counterintelligence Bureau of the Philadelphia Police Department. Captain O'Brien ordered Sergeant Schneider to sit on Dick Miller and me until further orders. I was more than a little disappointed to realize he only meant that she was to be helpful, while not letting us out of her sight, and ensuring that we didn't do anything we should not be doing.

"Keeping him company," Castillo said.

"Interesting term," Lowery said. "No. I mean, I try to stay in contact with him. But I couldn't assign a guard to him, or anything like that. He has a driver, of course, one of those Argentine security people in civilian clothes. And armed. But he does what Jack tells him, not the other way around. But for one thing, Jack wouldn't permit being followed around by one of my guys, and for another, I don't have much of a staff."

Castillo grunted, then asked, "Is he coming into work?"

"Yes and no. He comes in, but then he leaves. I know that yesterday he took their kids to school and picked them up. And he called in this morning to say he was taking them to school again."

"There's adequate security at the school? He's not worried about something happening to the kids?"

"It's the Lincoln School," Lowery said. "It's an accredited K-through-twelve American school. Many non-American diplomats send their kids there, and a lot of Argentines. Not only does the school have its own security people—the same company we use at the embassy, as a matter of fact—but a lot of the parents station their own security people outside when school is in session. It's one of the safest places in town."

I don't know what I'm talking about, of course, but if my wife was kidnapped, and I knew their school was safe, I'd send them—or take them. Make their life, at least, as normal as possible. Take their minds off Mommy.

A very tall African American in a very well-tailored suit walked into Lowery's office without knocking, followed by a small, plump man with a pencil-line mustache in a rumpled suit.

That has to be Masterson. I wonder who the bureaucrat with him is?

Chief of Mission J. Winslow Masterson smiled absently at Castillo and Santini, and then looked at Kenneth Lowery.

"Anything, Ken?" he asked.

"Not a word, Jack," Lowery said.

"I just dropped the kids at school," Masterson said. "It looked to me like there were more Policía Federal there than usual."

"Could be, Jack," Lowery said.

Masterson looked at Santini.

"Good morning, Tony."

"Good morning, sir. Mr. Masterson, this is Supervisory Special Agent Castillo."

Masterson smiled and put out his hand.

"FBI? From Montevideo? I was just about to go looking for you."

"I'm with the Secret Service, Mr. Masterson," Castillo said. "Just passing through. I just now heard what's happened."

Masterson shook his head but said nothing for a moment. Then he said, "It's the not knowing that's getting to me. What do these bastards want? Why haven't we heard anything from them?"

You poor bastard.

"I was going to suggest, Jack—even before Mr. Castillo showed up—that Tony get together with those FBI people," Lowery said. "If you wouldn't mind, Mr. Castillo. Maybe you and Tony—"

"I think that's a very good idea," Masterson said. "What's that phrase they use in the advertising business? 'Brainstorm'? Where are they?"

"They're using the DEA office," Lowery said.

"We could use my office," Masterson said. "But it would probably be better if we went there."

Lowery stood up. He looked at Castillo. "I'll have my secretary bring your frequent visitor badge up there."

Castillo smiled at him and nodded.

"Excuse me," Masterson said. "Mr. Castillo . . . or do I call you 'Agent Castillo'?"

"Mister's fine, sir. Charley's better."

Masterson smiled at him.

"Okay, Charley. This is Alex Darby, our commercial attaché. More important, my friend."

Darby offered Castillo his hand. There was curiosity in his eyes.

Is the friend-the-commercial-attaché curious about the Secret Service being here? Or the CIA station chief?

"Hello, Mr. Castillo," Darby said.

"How do you do?" Charley replied.

Now there was the hint of a smile on Darby's thin lips.

What the hell does that mean?

The Drug Enforcement Administration office—a large room with a dozen desks, and a large conference table, plus three smaller glass-walled offices—was on the third floor of the embassy.

The seven men seated around the conference table stood up when they saw Masterson come in.

Three of them are wearing shoulder holsters. Probably the DEA agents.

"Keep your seats," Masterson said with a wave and a smile.

There was a chorus of "Good morning, sir."

"I thought maybe if we all put our heads together," Masterson said, "and brainstorm the situation, we might be able to make some sense out of it. Is that all right with everybody?"

Another chorus, this time of "Yes, sir."

The man at the head of the table, one of those wearing a shoulder holster, stood up, clearly offering Masterson his seat. Masterson took it.

"This gentleman is Supervisory Special Agent Castillo, of the Secret Service," Masterson said, gesturing at Castillo and then offering his hand to one of the other men. "I'm presuming you're one of the FBI agents from Montevideo?"

"Yes, sir," the man said. "Special Agent Dorman, sir. And this is Special Agent Yung."

Special Agent Yung was Oriental.

Not Korean, Castillo judged. *Or Japanese. Most likely Chinese.*

Yung looked at Castillo with far greater interest than Dorman did.

"I'm presuming you know Mr. Santini, our resident Secret Service agent?" Masterson asked. Both FBI agents nodded.

"Well, I suppose the best place to start is at the beginning," Masterson went on. "And two things, gentlemen: One is that you're the experts. I have no experience with this sort of thing. And second, this will only work if you say almost anything that comes to mind. Okay, let's start with what I sort of suspect may be the beginning. Does anyone think there's anything but unfortunate coincidence in the three automobile accidents—the third on my way to meet my wife—I've been involved in in the past month or five weeks?"

He looked at Yung. "Why don't we start with you, Mr. Yung?"

Two hours and some minutes later, Masterson himself finally called off the brainstorming session. Everyone had really run out of ideas—wild and reasonable—thirty minutes before, but no one seemed to be willing to suggest they stop. Masterson was no better off than when they had started, and everyone felt sorry for him and a little guilty that they and he knew now exactly what they had known when they started: nothing.

As Masterson, Lowery, Santini, Darby, and Castillo were standing waiting for the elevator, and Castillo was wondering why they didn't just walk down the stairs, Darby broke the silence.

"I just had a thought," he announced, and looked at his wristwatch. "It's a couple of minutes to twelve. I thought maybe Mr. Castillo would be able to see something at the Kansas that the rest of us have missed. Would you be all right, Jack, if I took him out there for lunch? Maybe you could have lunch with Tony and Ken?"

Castillo saw that Masterson was as obviously surprised at the suggestion as he was. Masterson looked like he was going to object to at least parts of it, but finally— *clutching at straws?*—said, "Good idea, Alex."

"We can walk over to the Rio Alba," Tony Santini said. "And Ken can buy."

"I'll come back for you, Jack, in time to pick up the kids after school," Darby said.

When the elevator stopped at the second floor, Darby touched Castillo's arm, as a signal they weren't getting off. The others did.

When they got off in the basement, Darby picked up a telephone, punched a button, and delivered a cryptic message/order: "I'm taking your car; don't take mine. I'll be back a little after two."

When they walked down the row of cars, and Darby pointed to a Volkswagen Golf and got behind the wheel, Castillo thought he understood. Darby didn't want an embassy car with a driver. The Golf had ordinary Argentine license plates. For some reason, Darby didn't want to be seen at the restaurant in an embassy car.

It wasn't until the security guard at the gate asked for Castillo's identification that Castillo realized Lowery's secretary still had them.

"Don't give me any trouble about this," Darby said, not pleasantly, in fluent Spanish. "All you have to know is that this gentleman is with me."

Reluctantly, the security guard passed them out of the embassy grounds.

"About half of them are really nice guys," Darby said. "The other half are like that. They love to show their authority."

"I had a little trouble getting into the embassy myself," Castillo said.

"So, from what you've seen so far, Castillo, how do you like Buenos Aires?"

Castillo was about to reply when he belatedly realized Darby had switched from English to Pashtu, one of the two major languages of Afghanistan, the other being Afghan Persian.

Darby saw the surprise on Castillo's face and laughed.

"You really don't remember me, do you?" he asked, still in Pashtu.

Castillo shook his head.

"The last time I saw you was in Zaranj," Darby said. "There were several high-ranking Army officers who couldn't seem to make up their minds whether to court-martial you and send you home in chains, or give you a medal. Something about a stolen Blackhawk, I seem to recall."

"Well, so much for my cover," Castillo said, in Pashtu. "What were you doing in Zaranj?"

Zaranj was a city on the border of Iran and Afghanistan.

"I ran the agency there. Whatever happened to that black guy whose knee was really all fucked up?"

"If you mean, did he make it, yeah, he made it."

"Thanks to you. I was there when you brought the chopper back. He wouldn't have made it—probably none of them would—if you hadn't gone after them."

"He would have done the same thing for me," Castillo said. "As to what happened to him, truth being stranger than fiction, he was—at least for a while—station chief in Luanda, Angola."

"I thought it probably was you two," Darby said.

"Thought what was?"

"I hate to think how many man-hours and how much money I pissed away here looking for that stolen 727," Darby said. "Langley was hysterical when they couldn't find it. And then the search was called off without explanation. I was curious, so when I was in Langley a month ago, I asked. Strictly out of school, an old pal told me that some hotshot named Castillo had put his nose into agency affairs, and found it, and stole it back, said action seriously pissing off the DCI. I figured that had to be you, particularly after he also told me the DCI had tried to crucify the Luanda station chief, who just happened to be an ex–Special Forces officer with a bad knee from Afghanistan, for giving intel to said Castillo."

"I'm not too popular with the FBI, either," Castillo said.

"So now what I'm wondering is what the hell you're doing here, waving a Secret Service badge around."

"The badge is legitimate."

"I figured that. Santini would spot a phony right away. Or would have been told to ask no questions."

"I don't think I could talk you into asking no questions?"

"Not a chance."

"The President sent me down here to find out what's going on with Masterson's wife."

"The way you said that, it sounds as if the President himself said, 'Castillo, go to Buenos Aires'; that it didn't come down through channels."

"What the President said was, 'I want to know how and why that happened, and I don't want to wait until whoever's in charge down there has time to write a cover-his-ass report.'"

"He said that to you?"

Castillo nodded.

"Is that what you think I'm going to do, write a cover-my-ass report?"

"No. I think what you want to do is whatever it takes to get that poor bastard's wife back to him alive."

"Thank you," Darby said.

There was a long silence, and then Darby said, "What we're going to do now is have a nice lunch, during which I will make up my mind what I'm going to tell who about you and when."

"You'll tell me what you decide?"

"Yeah, I'll tell you."

"Thank you," Castillo said.

IV

Restaurant Kansas
Avenida Libertador
San Isidro
Buenos Aires Province, Argentina
1315 22 July 2005

"How much of that sixty million did he actually get, do you think?" Castillo asked Darby.

They were sitting at a table in the crowded bar of the Kansas, smoking cigars with their coffee.

They had been sitting for several minutes without speaking, lost in their own thoughts, and the question came out of the blue. It took Darby a moment to come back from wherever he had been.

"I'm going to give you the benefit of the doubt, Charley, that that's not curiosity."

"I was wondering if there is a ransom demand, and he says, 'Fuck the rules, I want my wife back, I'll pay,' where would he get the money, how would he get it down here?"

"What is that line, 'Great minds run on parallel paths'?"

"Something like that."

"The answer to the first part of the question is that the IRS took their bite—at his level, right at half, counting Louisiana state income tax—out of the lost-wages part of the settlement. In other words, he got something like eight and a half million, and taxes ate half of that. The rest of the settlement was compensation for pain and suffering, et cetera. That's tax free."

"You're talking more than forty million dollars. Where is it?"

"It's more than that now. There's a guy—he and Jack went to some private high school together—in the Hibernia National Bank and Trust in New Orleans who's been managing it for him. Managing it very well."

"He's from New Orleans?"

Darby shook his head. "Just across the border in Mississippi, a place called Pass Christian, on the gulf. Betsy's from New Orleans; her father, who's a retired ambassador, lives there."

"You checked Masterson out, I guess?"

"No. He told me. I met Jack when we were both in Paris, years ago. We're close. I'm the successor executor—after his father—of his will. So he figured I should know what I was letting myself in for."

Castillo nodded and they fell silent for a moment.

"That's another problem the poor bastard has, telling Betsy's family," Darby said.

"You think he's told his?"

"I don't think he'd want to tell his father without telling Betsy's, and Betsy's father's likely to have a heart attack. Literally. He's got a really bad heart condition."

"Somebody said something about a brother-in-law?"

"Works for the UN. Jack doesn't like him."

"Why not?"

Darby shrugged. "He never told me. But it was pretty evident."

Then Darby changed the subject: "To answer your first question: What I would do if I were Jack Masterson—what I'm half afraid he's already done—is get on the phone to his money guy at Hibernia: 'Get me a million dollars, get on the next plane down here with it, and don't tell anyone.'"

"It might not be that easy," Castillo said. "Rich people don't keep much cash around, either cash-cash, or in a checking account. Even a banker would have trouble coming up with a million in cash without somebody asking some hard questions."

"You sound like you're speaking from experience," Darby said.

Castillo ignored him.

"And a million dollars in hundreds takes up a lot of space. A hundred thousand right from the Federal Reserve makes a bundle about this big."

He demonstrated with his hands.

"You really live in an apartment in the Mayflower, Charley?" Darby asked.

Castillo decided to ignore that, too, but then changed his mind.

"Where'd you hear that?"

"From the same guy who told me about you and the DCI. I won't tell you who he is, but you know him. He was in Afghanistan when we were. Not to worry; he likes you."

"What else did my friend with the big mouth tell you about me?"

"That you're Texas oil money."

"I'm from Texas and I can afford to live in the Mayflower. Can we leave it at that?"

"Okay."

"There's also some sort of a law," Castillo said, "that when you take ten thousand, or more, in cash from a bank, the bank has to tell somebody. I don't know who, maybe the IRS, but somebody. And I don't know what I'm talking about here, but I think there's another law that says you have to declare it if you're taking ten thousand—maybe five thousand—in cash out of the country."

"I'll ask Tony. He'd know. Or one of those FBI guys from Montevideo. They would know . . ."

There was the buzzing of a cellular phone. Both men took theirs out.

"Hey, Charley," Howard Kennedy's voice came somewhat metallically over Castillo's cellular. "How's things going?"

Darby put his cellular away and looked with interest at Castillo.

"What's new, Howard?" Castillo asked.

"A mutual friend would like to see you."

"Really?"

"He's quite anxious you meet."

Why do I find that menacing?

"That's very flattering. Why?"

"I have no idea. What are you doing now? Where are you?"

"I'm drinking a cup of coffee in a restaurant in San Isidro."

"It would just take a couple of hours, Charley. Can I pick you up? What restaurant?"

"Hold one, Howard," Castillo said, and took the cellular from his ear.

Painful experience had taught him that cellular microphones were very sensitive. He hit a series of keys with his thumb to select the MUTE function, then, for insurance, raised his right buttock, shoved the cellular under, and sat on it. His buttocks was the only object he knew for sure would effectively cover the cellular's mic.

Darby had apparently come to the same conclusion, because he smiled understandingly. Castillo smiled back.

"This is a guy I really should see," Castillo explained.

"I was hoping it was Tony saying they'd heard something."

"Me, too," Castillo said. "Is there some reason you think I should go back to the embassy?"

Darby shook his head. "But I have to get back. I told Jack I'd go with him to pick up his kids at school. You'll be all right to get to your hotel?"

"I'll be fine."

Castillo lifted his rump, reclaimed the phone, and keyed UNMUTE.

"You still there, Howard?"

"What the hell was that all about?"

"I'm in the Kansas restaurant, on Libertador."

"I know where it is. I'll be there in ten, fifteen minutes. Same car. Can I get you to wait on the street?"

"Why don't you go into the parking lot? That will make it easier for the FBI."

"That's not funny, goddammit!"

"Just pulling your chain, Howard."

"Ten minutes, out in front," Kennedy said, and the connection went dead.

Darby looked at him curiously.

"Private joke," Castillo explained. "Somebody else the FBI doesn't like."

Darby nodded. "There's a lot of people like that. Why don't we put our numbers in each other's cellular?"

"If you're going to tell Lowery—or Masterson or the ambassador—what I'm doing down here, that would be a waste of time."

"Not tonight. Maybe tomorrow. But I'm not going to say anything tonight, and then not until I give you warning. And who knows what's liable to happen tonight?"

"Thanks," Castillo said, and handed him his cellular for Darby to punch in his number.

[TWO]

The black Mercedes-Benz S500 appeared in the flow of westbound traffic on Avenida Libertador, and Castillo stepped off the curb so they would see him. The car pulled to the curb and the rear door was opened from the inside. He saw Kennedy inside.

"Get in, Charley," Kennedy said.

The car started the moment Castillo had pulled the door closed.

"Grüss Gott," Castillo said, speaking the Viennese greeting in as thick an accent as he could muster.

"Grüss Gott, Herr Gossinger," Frederic replied from behind the wheel.

That's not a Viennese accent. Not even Czech. Good ol' Frederic's probably a Hungarian.

Why did I do that? Why do I care?

The Mercedes made the next left turn. They were moving through a residential area, looking much, Castillo thought, like one of the better neighborhoods of San Antonio, except that all the houses here were behind walls—some of them topped with razor wire—and almost all of them had bars on the windows.

Kennedy touched his arm and handed him something. It looked like a black velvet bag.

"What's this?"

"It's a velvet bag," Kennedy said. "It goes over your head."

Now I know why I felt menaced. They call it "intuition."

"You're kidding, right?"

"Not at all. You know my boss. He pays a good deal of consideration to his privacy."

"Fuck you, Howard, and fuck your boss!" Castillo said evenly. Then he raised his voice for the benefit of Frederic. "Stop the car!"

"Jesus Christ, Charley, there's nothing personal in this!"

"Stop the car before I have to hurt you, Howard."

"Take us back to the restaurant," Kennedy ordered in German, and then added, to Castillo, "You know he's not going to like this."

"Make sure you tell him I said, 'Go fuck yourself, Alex.' Now stop the goddamn car."

Kennedy hesitated a moment, then ordered Frederic to pull to the curb.

Castillo got out, slammed the door, and started to walk toward Avenida Libertador. He heard the Mercedes drive off.

It was a three-block-long walk to Libertador, and he was half a block away when he saw the Mercedes. It was stopped at the curb, facing him, and Kennedy was standing on the sidewalk beside it. He was holding something in his left hand.

I don't think he's stupid enough to pull a gun and force me into the car, but there's no telling.

When Castillo got closer, he saw that what Kennedy had in his hand was a cell phone.

"You have a call, Herr Gossinger," Kennedy said jokingly. He was wearing an uncomfortable smile.

"If Frederic looks like he's even thinking of getting out of the car, you're going to either the hospital or the morgue," Castillo said.

Kennedy handed Castillo the telephone, and then took three steps backward and raised his open hands to show he had no intention of doing anything.

Castillo, maintaining eye contact, said into the phone, "Hello?"

"If Howard offended you in any way, my friend," Alex Pevsner said in Russian, "you have my apology."

"Howard was doing what you told him to do. And don't call me your friend," Castillo replied in Russian. "Where I come from, friends trust friends; friends don't ask friends to put bags over their heads."

"When you get here, my friend, you will understand why I was trying to be a little more cautious than I usually am. And you will understand that I really consider you a trustworthy friend."

"Why should I go anywhere?"

"Because I am asking you as a friend."

"I don't want to have to hurt Howard."

"There will be no need to even consider something like that. Please give me just a few hours of your time."

Whatever this is about, it's important to him. He doesn't ask people to do things; he tells them, and, it is credibly alleged, has them killed if they don't do what he says.

"Okay," Castillo said, after a just perceptible hesitation.

"Thank you, Charley," Pevsner said, and there was a click as the connection was broken.

Castillo looked at Kennedy and then tossed the phone to him.

"Get in the car, Howard, and put the bag over your head," Castillo said.

He took pity on Kennedy when he saw the look on his face.

"Just pulling your chain, Howard."

[THREE]

Their route took them through the residential district of San Isidro, and then past a long line of interesting-looking restaurants facing the San Isidro Jockey Club. He thought he more or less knew where he was. His grandfather had taken him and Charley's cousin Fernando here a half dozen or more times when they were in high school.

Then quickly they were on a wide superhighway—six lanes in each direction—and although this was new to him, Castillo was pretty sure that it was the old Pan Americana Highway. The Argentines had been expanding it for years, and they had apparently finally finished what they called an *autopista*.

After six or seven kilometers at what Castillo decided was at least twenty klicks above the posted 130-kilometers-per-hour speed limit—meaning they were going ninety-plus miles per hour—the road split, and Frederic took the left fork. Signs said that the right fork was the highway to Uruguay and that they were now headed for Pilar.

They went through a tollbooth without stopping, just slowing enough for a machine to read a device that opened the barrier, and then Frederic quickly accelerated back to their way-above-the-speed-limit velocity.

On the left was a large factory, a long rectangular building three stories high and three hundred meters long, connected to four enormous round concrete silos with a rat's nest of conveyors.

LUCCETTI, LA PASTA DE MAMA was lettered in thirty-foot-tall letters across the silos.

Castillo chuckled. Kennedy looked at him.

"Mama's family obviously eats a lot of pasta," Charley said.

Kennedy smiled and said, "There are more Italians here than Spanish."

The autopista here was narrower—three lanes in each direction—but the speed limit was still 130 kph, and Frederic was still driving much faster than that.

Outside the autopista fence there were now large, attractive restaurants and what looked like recently constructed showrooms for Audi, BMW, and other European and Japanese automobiles. Charley saw only a Ford showroom to represent American manufacturers, and wondered idly where Mercedes-Benz had their showroom.

He had been out this way as a kid, too, but then there had been only a two-lane highway leading from Buenos Aires to the estancias in the country.

The area around Pilar was obviously now an upscale residential area—somebody had to be buying the Audis and BMWs—but there were no houses visible from the highway, just businesses catering to people with money.

Frederic took an exit ramp off the highway, and there was the missing Mercedes showroom, a typically elegant affair across the road from a large shopping center anchored by a Jumbo supermarket.

And then they were in the country again.

Three klicks or so down a two-lane highway—which slowed Frederic down to no more than, say, sixty-five or seventy mph—the car braked suddenly and turned off the road and slowed as they approached a two-story red-tiled-roof gatehouse.

A sign carved from wood read BUENA VISTA COUNTRY CLUB.

There were four uniformed guards at the gatehouse, two of whom looked into the Mercedes carefully before a heavy, red-and-white steel barrier pole was raised. All the guards were armed, and inside the gatehouse Charley saw a rack holding a half-dozen riot guns. They looked like American Ithaca pump shotguns.

Now this, Castillo thought, *is what you call a "gated community."*

Once inside the property, there were signs announcing a thirty-kph speed limit, and these were reinforced with speed bumps on the macadam road every two hundred meters or so. Frederic now obeyed the speed limit.

And then, far enough into the property so they would not be visible from the road outside, the first houses came into view.

The Mercedes rolled slowly down a curving road past long rows of upscale houses set on well-manicured hectare lots. There were no barred windows, as there had been on the upscale houses in San Isidro. They passed a polo field—lined with the same quality houses—and then another, and then came to several greens and then the clubhouse of a well-maintained golf course. There were thirty or so cars in the parking lot.

And then more houses on the winding road. The houses and the lots in this area were larger. Some— perhaps most—of them were ringed with shrubbery, tall enough so that only the upper floors of the houses were visible. Castillo saw that the shrubbery also concealed fences.

Frederic turned off the road and stopped before a ten-foot-high gate. After a moment, the gate rolled open to the right. Charley saw a workman at what was probably the gate control. He had a pistol under his loose denim jacket. Once they were inside, Charley saw a man in a golf cart rolling along the perimeter of the property. There was a golf bag mounted on the cart that did not completely conceal the butt stock of a shotgun.

This is obviously a double-gated community, a gated community within a gated community, as opposed to a double-gaited community, which is one whose inhabitants are a little vague about their sexual preferences.

He saw first a Bell Ranger helicopter sitting on what looked like a putting green, and then the house, an English-looking near mansion of red brick with casement windows. As they approached, the main door of the house opened and a tall man who appeared to be in his late thirties walked out and down a shallow flight of steps to the cobblestone driveway.

Aleksandr Pevsner—also known as Vasily Respin and Alex Dondiemo and a half dozen other names, an international dealer in arms and, it was often and credibly alleged, head of at least a dozen other enterprises of very questionable legality, and for whom arrest warrants had been issued at one time or another by at least thirteen governments—was wearing gray flannel slacks, a white button-down shirt (in the open neck of which, in the Argentine manner, was a silk scarf held in place by a sterling silver ring), a powder blue pullover sweater, and highly polished brown shoes with thick rubber cushion soles.

He folded his arms over his chest, smiled, and waited for the Mercedes to stop and for Frederic to quickly run around the front of the car to open the rear door.

"Ah, Charley," Pevsner called in Russian as Castillo got out. "Thank you for coming. It's a delight to see you."

"Frankly, I didn't think much of the first invitation, Alex," Castillo replied, also in Russian, offering Pevsner his hand.

"For which I have already apologized, and will apologize again now, if you wish."

"Once is enough, Alex," Castillo said, adding, "Nice house."

Pevsner broke the handshake and put his hands firmly on Castillo's upper arms and looked into his eyes. Pevsner's eyes were large and blue and extraordinarily bright. The first time Charley had met him, he had unkindly wondered if Pevsner had been inhaling controlled substances through his nose.

"I must ask you two questions, my friend," Pevsner said. "In a moment, you will understand why."

"Ask."

"What are you doing in Argentina? Why are you here?"

This is one of those times when telling the truth and only the truth is the smart thing to do. Charley immediately answered, "The wife of the chief of mission at our embassy here has disappeared under circumstances which look like kidnapping. The President sent me down here to see what's going on."

Castillo saw that his answer surprised Pevsner, but he didn't pursue it directly.

"Your being here has nothing to do with me?"

Castillo shook his head.

"Not a thing. I had no idea you—or Howard—were anywhere near Argentina."

Pevsner looked into Castillo's eyes for a long moment.

Alex, I don't care how long you look for signs of me lying. You won't find any. And if I have any luck at all, you won't see signs indicating that I'm more than a little afraid of you.

Pevsner finally squeezed Castillo's arms in a friendly gesture and let him go.

"Thank you for your honesty, my friend," he said. "Now, why don't we go in the house, have a glass of wine, and let me introduce you to my family?"

"Your family?" Castillo blurted.

"Yes. My family. My wife and children."

I'll be goddamned! Well, that explains all the concern. But what the hell are they doing here?

Castillo, after meeting Aleksandr Pevsner for the first time in Vienna, had reported to Secretary of Homeland Security Matt Hall that Pevsner had told him the missing 727 had been stolen by Somalian terrorists who intended to crash it into the Liberty Bell. Pevsner had said he would do whatever he could to help locate it because he was against Muslim terrorists for many reasons, the primary one being he was a family man who adored his wife and three children. He didn't want them hurt by Muslim fanatics. Pevsner had then produced a photograph of him with what he said was his family: a very attractive blond wife and three blond children who looked straight from a Clairol advertisement. Castillo knew it sounded incredible, and that Hall was going to have a hard time believing any of it.

He was not prepared, however, for the look of unabashed incredulity on Hall's face—and on Joel Isaacson's and Tom McGuire's. Clearly, they not only believed zero, zilch, nada of what he was telling them, but were also—worse—now questioning his reputation as a hard-ass special operator for wasting his and their time relating it.

"Charley, I've seen his dossier," Isaacson said. "It's this thick." He held his hands eighteen inches apart. "There's a lot in there about murder, extortion, bribery, smuggling, arms-dealing, you name it, but not one line about his being a devoted husband and loving daddy."

"I believed him," Castillo had replied.

"About what part?" Hall asked.

"Most of it," Charley said. "The family photograph looked too cozy not to have been staged."

"You actually think the airplane was stolen by Somalians? Who plan to crash it into the Liberty Bell? Because of what this international thug told you?" Hall asked, more sadly than angrily.

"Sir, you told me that one of the major problems in intelligence is with people at my level telling their superiors what they think the superiors want to hear, instead of what they believe. What I told you just now is what I believe."

"That wasn't me who told you that," Hall said after a long pause. "That was the President."

"Charley, do you know how close you came to having this guy take you out?" Joel Isaacson asked.

"Yeah, I do, Joel. He said he was glad he didn't have to give me an 'Indian beauty spot'—a small-caliber bullet in the forehead—and I believed that, too."

[FOUR]

Pevsner led Castillo into the house, through a two-story entrance foyer to a sitting room. With the exception of what was probably an antique samovar sitting on a table, the furnishings of the sitting room gave it a British feeling. Two walls were lined with books and oil paintings, and there was a red-leather couch with matching armchairs.

The windows offered a view of a large swimming pool under a curved plastic roof, something like a Quonset hut. Vapor rose from the pool.

Well, they don't have many heated swimming pools in Merry Old England, but this place still feels English.

A middle-aged woman in a maid's uniform came into the sitting room from a side door as the three men entered.

"Would you please ask Madam Pevsner if it is convenient for her and the children to join us?" Pevsner ordered in Russian.

The woman, unsmiling, nodded but didn't say anything. She left the sitting room by the door Pevsner, Kennedy, and Castillo had come in.

"Howard, see if you can find someone in the kitchen who can bring wine, and so forth," Pevsner ordered in English.

"Red, right, Charley?" Kennedy asked. "A cabernet?"

"Please," Castillo said, as he walked to the samovar for a closer look. He had just decided that it was a bona fide antique Russian kettle when Pevsner said in Russian, "Ah, Anna, come and welcome Charley to our home!"

Castillo turned and saw the wife and kiddies from the

Clairol commercial walking into the room. They were all almost startlingly blond and fair-skinned. The mother looked to be in her late twenties, but Charley decided she had to be older than that to be the mother of the girl, who was thirteen or fourteen. There were two boys, one who Charley guessed was ten or so, and another about six. Everyone was wearing a thick white terry cloth robe.

Madam Pevsner smiled and put out her hand to Castillo and said in Russian, "I'm happy to meet you. My husband has told me so much about you."

The maid was now in the room.

"Olga, would you bring some wine?" Madam Pevsner ordered, and the maid walked to what was apparently the kitchen door.

"Howard's getting the wine," Pevsner said in Russian, and then switched to English. "Greet our guest in English," he said to the children. "Charley, this is Elena. Darling, this is Mr. Castillo."

Elena, shyly, almost blushing, curtsied and said, "How do you do, Mr. Castillo?" in a pronounced British accent.

"I'm very pleased to meet you, Elena."

The ten-year-old was even more shy. The six-year-old was not. He walked past his brother, put out his hand, and announced, "I am Sergei and I am happy to make your acquaintance, sir."

"And I'm pleased to meet you."

"Aleksandr!" Pevsner said, propelling the ten-year-old into action.

The ten-year-old, squirming, finally offered his hand and mumbled something unintelligible.

Pevsner beamed proudly.

"You'll have to excuse the robes, Mr. Castillo," Anna Pevsner said. "But my husband said he wasn't sure if you could come, and the children like to have a swim when they come from school."

"Well, I certainly don't want to interfere with that," Castillo said.

The six-year-old, Sergei, beamed at Castillo.

"I really hate to leave them alone in the pool," Anna said.

"Howard can watch them for a few minutes, darling," Pevsner said.

Kennedy came into the room.

"Howard, would you mind watching the children in the pool for a few minutes?"

"Not at all."

Howard is being banished from the conversation I'm about to have with Pevsner and his wife. What's going on?

The older two children, trailed by Kennedy, went out of the sitting room. Sergei marched up to Castillo, shook his hand, and ran after them.

"Nice kids, Alex," Castillo said.

"Thank you, Charley," Pevsner said, and then, as a younger maid—this one looked Argentine—came in with a tray holding glasses, a bottle of wine, and a large chrome corkscrew, said, "Ah, finally, the wine!"

"Why don't we sit down?" Anna asked, gesturing at the red-leather couch and armchairs.

Castillo sat in one of the armchairs. Anna sat on the couch, and Pevsner, after gesturing for the maid to put the tray on the coffee table, sat beside her and reached for the wine and corkscrew.

"Local wine," Pevsner said, "from a bodega near Mendoza, in the foothills of the Andes. Ever been to Mendoza, Charley?"

"Uh-huh. We have some friends there."

Pevsner poured the wine into enormous crystal glasses, handed one first to his wife, then one to Charley. Then he tapped his glass against Charley's.

"Welcome to our home, Charley," he said.

"Thank you."

Charley took a sip, and expressed his appreciation with a smile.

"Why do I think, Charley, that your curiosity is about to bubble over? 'What in hell is Alex doing here?' "

"Maybe you're reading my mind again," Castillo said.

"What we're doing, Charley, is hiding in the open," Pevsner said. "Aleksandr Pevsner, a Hungarian whose estates were seized by the communists, got everything back when freedom came, and then, having enough of both Hungarian winters and oppressive governments, sold everything and came to the New World to start life again. He invested his money in land and vineyards. Including this one, as a matter of fact." He tapped the wine bottle.

"Very clever," Castillo said.

"There's a tradition of that, you know, of people running from what's going on in Europe to find peace in Argentina. There's a bona fide grand duke of the Austro-Hungarian empire—actually, his grandson, but he has taken the title and is pleased when I call him 'Your Grace'—in a little town called Maschwitz near here. He teases me that I have the same name as an infamous Russian scoundrel."

"Very clever," Castillo repeated.

"Think about it, Charley. Where could we live? In Russia? Russia is now not far from where it was before the 1917 revolution. Crime and corruption are rampant, and I wouldn't be at all surprised if communism—under another name, of course—came back. Anywhere in a Muslim country? I do business there, of course, but can you imagine Anna in an environment like that, not even allowed to drive a car? Living in constant fear that some Muslim fanatic will machine-gun her car because she's obviously an infidel? And while this may surprise you, there are people in Prague and Vienna and Budapest and Bucharest who don't like me."

"I'm shocked," Castillo said.

"There is corruption here, of course. And crime. The newspapers are full of stories of robbery and kidnapping. The result of that has been the development of what I call the country club culture. The upper classes live in places like this, and when they go to Buenos Aires, they frequently are accompanied by bodyguards—called 'security'—which raises no eyebrows whatever."

"I saw the guy in the golf cart with the shotgun," Castillo said.

"I have a few of my own people, of course, but most of my security is Argentine. There is golf here. . . . Do you play, Charley?"

Castillo shook his head.

"And polo. I don't play, but Aleksandr and Sergei are

taking lessons, and Anna and Elena are taking courses in horse riding . . . what's that called?"

"Equestrianism," Anna furnished.

". . . *equestrianism* at the stables here. And, of course, the schools are good. The better ones, like Saint Agnes in the Hills, are a British legacy."

"Your kids go to a school called 'Saint Agnes in the Hills'?" Castillo asked, smiling.

Pevsner smiled back. "Which has an Anglican priest for a headmaster. There being no Russian Orthodox church to speak of in Argentina, and since the Anglicans and the Russian Orthodox recognize each other's priesthood and liturgy, Elena was last year confirmed into the Anglican church."

"Well, you seem to have everything under control, Alex," Castillo said. "Good for you."

"I thought so, Charley, until Howard came here this morning and asked me, 'Guess who got onto my elevator in the Four Seasons just now?'"

"At the risk of repeating myself, I had no idea until today that either you or Howard had ever been near Argentina. And if you're worried that I'm going to tell anyone we bumped into each other, don't."

"You said something about a kidnapping?"

"The wife of the chief of mission at the American embassy is missing under circumstances that suggest kidnapping," Castillo said.

"Kidnapping is common here," Pevsner said. "Didn't she have security?"

"Why would anyone kidnap a diplomat's wife?" Anna asked. "Does he have money?"

"A lot of money," Charley said.

"I didn't see anything in the paper," Pevsner said, as he leaned forward to pour wine into Charley's glass.

"They're trying to keep it quiet. They hope that maybe when the kidnappers find out she's a diplomat's wife, they'll turn her loose."

"That's not what they're liable to do," Pevsner said. "I can make a couple of calls for you, if you'd like."

"All contributions gratefully received," Castillo said. "So far there's been no contact. I really feel sorry for the husband. They have three kids, and they want to know when Mother's coming home."

"Oh, God!" Anna said. "How awful!"

"Yeah," Castillo said.

"Where did they take her?" Anna asked. "Not from their home?"

"From the parking lot of the Kansas restaurant in San Isidro."

"Alex and I eat there often," Anna said, then, a touch of horror in her voice: "Not right in front of her children?"

Castillo shook his head. "She was waiting for her husband to pick her up after work. The kids were at home."

"And the President sent you down here to do what?" Pevsner asked.

"Find out what happened and report to him."

"Speaking of the President, and before I make those calls, did you ever have a chance to mention to him that I was helpful in getting that airplane back for you?"

"Yes, I did."

The President's diary for that weekend read, in part:

```
Friday 17 June 2005 7:55 PM: Arrival at
President's Residence.
Saturday 18 June 2005 through Sunday 19
June 2005 8:25 PM:
No official events or guests or visitors.
Sunday 19 June 2005 8:25 PM: Departure for
The White House.
```

That was not exactly the truth. The President believed both that what he did in the privacy of his home was nobody's business but his own, and furthermore, that he had the right to decree what was an official event and what was not.

The diaries of the secretary of Homeland Security, the director of Central Intelligence, the director of the Federal Bureau of Investigation, and the commander in chief of U.S. Central Command for the same period, however, all reported they had spent periods of from two to five hours on Saturday 18 June at a location variously described as the "Carolina White House"; the "Presidential Residence"; or "Hilton Head."

All but Secretary Hall of Homeland Security were sitting in upholstered white wicker armchairs drinking beer with the President when the first of the helicopters, a glistening blue twin-engine Air Force Huey, made its approach to the lawn between the house and the Atlantic Ocean and fluttered down.

John Powell, the DCI, and Mark Schmidt, the director of the FBI, were in business suits, and General Allan Naylor, C-in-C Central Command, was in uniform. The Pres-

ident was wearing a white shirt with the cuffs turned up, a necktie pulled down, khaki trousers, and loafers.

An Air Force colonel in a summer-weight uniform got out of the helicopter, reached back inside to pick up a small soft-sided suitcase, and then followed one of the Secret Service Presidential Detail agents to the awning-shaded verandah of the house.

The President shook the hand of Colonel Jacob D. Torine, USAF, then handed him a bottle of beer. Then they watched as another Huey—this one a single-engine Army helicopter painted a dull olive drab—made its approach over the sea and landed.

A large man in a business suit and an Army officer, a major in a summer-weight uniform, got out and followed another Secret Service agent to the verandah.

"Better late than never, right, Tom?" the President greeted Secretary Hall.

"Mr. President, we're ten minutes early," Hall said.

"How are you, Charley?" the President said to Major (Promotable) C. G. Castillo, Special Forces, USA, offering him his hand.

"Good afternoon, Mr. President," Castillo said.

"Well, let's get this over with," the President said. "Then you two can get out of those uniforms."

He turned to look at a door of the house. Three men were already coming onto the verandah. One held two blue leather-covered boxes about eight inches by three. The second held a Nikon digital camera, and the third a suit jacket.

The President folded down his cuffs, buttoned them, buttoned his collar, pulled the necktie into place, and then put his arms into the suit jacket.

"Do not get the khaki pants in the picture," the President said to the photographer, then asked, "Where do you want us?"

"Against the wall would be fine, Mr. President."

"You're about to be decorated," the President said. "You've heard I've had a problem with this?"

"Yes, sir," Torine and Castillo said, almost in chorus.

"Well, let me tell the story again, for the benefit of Director Schmidt and Director Powell. There is no question in my mind that what these two officers did merits a higher decoration than the Distinguished Flying Cross. When they found that 727 that no one else seemed to be able to find, and then stole it back, they saved the lives of God only knows how many people, and prevented chaos and panic in Philadelphia and across the nation. Not quite as important, but nearly so, they sent a message to like-minded lunatics that the United States possesses military force and intelligence resources that can stop what we have to admit was a pretty clever plan.

"Unfortunately, to award them a medal for valor—my initial thought was the Distinguished Service Cross—there has to be a citation to accompany the decoration. Since their activities were of a covert nature, acting on a Presidential Finding that certain actions were necessary, a citation describing what they have done would make that Presidential Finding public. That's not in the best interests of the nation. General Naylor pointed out to me, too, that a citation saying nothing more specific than 'actions of a classified and covert nature' would come to the attention of one or more Congressional oversight committees who would *demand to know just what the hell was going on. The result would be the same. The story would be all over the* Washington Post *and the* New York Times.

"*So they don't get the decoration they deserve and I would really like to see them have. General Naylor also suggested that what they did could honestly be described as 'participating with the highest degree of professionalism in aerial flight under exceedingly hazardous conditions.' So that's what the citations on the DFCs say.*"

He looked at the directors of the FBI and the CIA.

"*These pictures will not be released to the press, but when Charley and Colonel Torine look at them in years to come, I'd like them to be able to recall the award was made with you two—and you, too, Tom, of course—looking on.*

"*Come on, up against the wall. General, will you read the orders, please?*"

The FBI director and the DCI with absolutely no enthusiasm got out of their white wicker armchairs.

General Naylor waited until the photographer had lined everybody up, and then began to read: "*Attention to orders. Headquarters, Department of the Air Force, Washington, D.C. 18 June 2005. Subject: Award of the Distinguished Flying Cross. The Distinguished Flying Cross, thirteenth award, is awarded to Colonel Jacob . . .*"

"*Much better, Charley,*" *the President said, in reference to what Castillo was now wearing, a polo shirt, khaki trousers, and boat shoes.* "*Now sit down, have a beer, and tell me what I can do for you.*"

The President saw the look on Castillo's face.

"Why do I think I'm going to regret that offer?" the President asked.

Castillo didn't reply.

"Come on, Charley, what's on your mind?" the President pursued.

General Naylor's face was frozen.

"There's two things, Mr. President," Castillo said. "We would never have located that airplane without Mr. Pevsner."

"That's the Russian gangster?"

"Yes, sir."

"What do you want me to do, Charley?" the President asked, more than a little sarcastically. "Pardon him? I don't think I can do that. I think we're the only country in the Western world who doesn't have a warrant out for him."

"Sir, he has intelligence sources we, self-evidently, don't have. I'd really like to . . . to suggest that the government should maintain a relationship with him."

"For God's sake, Castillo," FBI Director Mark Schmidt exploded, "that Russian bastard's got a record that makes John Gotti look like a Boy Scout."

"And he has intelligence sources we just don't have," Castillo repeated evenly. "And which he has proved willing to make available to us."

"He's got a point, Mark," the President said. "How would we do what you suggest, Charley? What does this guy want?"

"He wants the CIA off his back, sir. Right or wrong, he suspects that since they have stopped using him, they—"

"Hold it right there," the President interrupted.

"'Stopped using him'? The CIA's been using him?" He looked at the DCI. "Tell me about that, John."

The DCI looked uncomfortable.

"On several occasions, Mr. President," he said, "Operations has covertly dealt with Pevsner, chartered his aircraft to deliver certain things where they were needed—"

"How about 'frequently dealt' with him?" Castillo interrupted, earning an immediate glower from the DCI.

"To deliver the weapons and other goodies they bought from him?" Castillo went on.

The President looked at Castillo, and then at the DCI and waited for him to go on.

"There were some transactions of that nature, Mr. President," the DCI admitted. "But that's in the past. I've ordered that all connections with this character be severed."

"And now he believes, rightly or wrongly," Castillo said, "that since the agency has stopped using him, they've been trying to arrange his arrest—or worse—by the governments the agency hired him to work against."

"You don't know that, Castillo!" the DCI snapped.

"I said that's what he believes," Castillo said.

"Why?" the President asked, softly.

"Because if he's in some jail in a remote area of the Congo—or dead—there's no trail back to the agency, sir."

The President sat back in his chair and looked out across the Atlantic. He took a long and thoughtful pull at the neck of his beer bottle.

After a moment, he turned to Charley and said carefully, "I want you to tell Mr. Pevsner that while I find it difficult to believe that anything like that could be happening—it sounds more than a little paranoiac—I have, as a token of

*my gratitude for his valuable assistance vis-à-vis locating
that 727, directed the DCI to look into the matter, and if
anything like that is going on, to stop it immediately."*

"Thank you, sir," Castillo said.

"You have any questions about that, John?" the President
asked.

"No, sir," the DCI said.

*"And that I have told the director of the FBI that I
want to be informed of the details of any investigation of
Mr. Pevsner now under way in the United States, or which
may be begun in the States. Make sure he understands that
if he violates any of our laws, he will be prosecuted."*

"Yes, sir."

"You understand what I've just said, Mark?"

"Yes, sir," the director of the FBI said.

*Castillo happened to look at General Naylor, who was
shaking his head as if in disbelief.*

"Okay, Charley," the President asked, jocularly. "What
else can I do for you?"

*"I don't suppose you would let me go back to being a
simple soldier, would you, Mr. President?"*

General Naylor's eyebrows rose.

"From what I have seen, Charley," the President said,
"I doubt if you were ever a simple soldier. But to answer
your question, no, I would not. That's out of the question."

"And what was the President's reaction?" Alex Pevsner
asked.

"He said that if he finds out you're breaking any laws

in the United States, he will cheerfully throw you in jail. But he told the director of Central Intelligence that if he's running any sort of operation to tip you to anybody to stop it."

"And you believe he really said that to the CIA?"

"I was there when he said it. He appreciates what you did helping us find that airplane."

Pevsner looked with his brilliant blue eyes into Castillo's face for a long moment. "I was about to say that I will show my appreciation for the President's appreciation by seeing what I can find out about the diplomat's wife . . ."

"Thank you," Castillo said.

"Let me finish, please," Pevsner said sharply. "But, obviously, if you reported to him that I had told you thus and so, that would locate me here, and I don't want that. So I will make inquiries with the understanding that if I am able to learn anything, you will tell no one the source of your information. Okay?"

"Understood. Thank you, Alex."

"Anna, why don't you get a pair of my swimming trunks for Charley? Then you can have a swim while I'm on the phone."

"I should be getting back to Buenos Aires," Castillo said.

"I think your time would be more profitably spent waiting for me to find out what I can," Pevsner said, somewhat sharply, and then added, far more charmingly: "And Anna and I would really like you to stay for dinner."

"Thank you," Castillo said.

"If there were developments, someone from the embassy would call you, right?"

"Uh-huh."

"Then have a swim, and later we'll have some more wine and I will personally prepare an Argentine pizza for you."

You will personally prepare an Argentine pizza?

"Sounds fine, Alex. Thank you."

[FIVE]

The pizza oven, a wood-fired, six-foot-wide, clay-covered brick dome, was about twenty feet from the swimming pool in front of a thatch-roofed *quincho*, which was a building devoted to the broiling of food over a wood-fired *parrilla*, and then eating it picnic-style.

There were fires—tended by a young Argentine man—blazing in both the *parrilla* and the oven when Castillo followed Anna and the children through a flap in the heavy plastic swimming pool enclosure to walk to the *quincho*, where more enormous crystal glasses and a half dozen bottles of wine awaited them.

There was also a wooden table, near the oven, covered with a tablecloth, at which two young Argentine maids, under the stern supervision of the middle-aged Russian-speaking maid, were kneading pizza dough and chopping tomatoes and other pizza toppings.

Castillo felt a tug at his sleeve and looked down to see that Sergei was smilingly offering him a plate of *empanadas*, a deep-fried meat-filled dumpling.

"Muchas gracias," Castillo said, taking one.

"De nada," Sergei said.

"It would appear Sergei is taken with you," Pevsner said. Castillo hadn't seen him come into the *quincho*.

"At least one member of your family is a good judge of character."

"Unfair, Charley," Pevsner said. "I'm an excellent judge of character, and Anna is even better."

Castillo smiled but didn't reply.

Pevsner handed him a glass of wine.

"Come with me and watch as I personally prepare your pizza," Pevsner said.

"I wouldn't miss that for the world."

"The secret is the oven temperature," Pevsner said as he walked up to the domed oven. "And this is the way you test that."

He walked to the table, behind which the three maids and the young man were lined up, and picked from it a page from a newspaper. He crumpled it in his hands and walked back to the oven.

The young man trotted over and raised its iron door with a wrought-iron rod. Pevsner tossed the balled-up paper into the oven and signaled to the young man that he should lower the door.

"One, two, three, four, five, six," Pevsner counted aloud, then gestured for the door to be raised.

The newspaper was blazing merrily.

"If it doesn't ignite in six seconds, it's not hot enough," Pevsner announced very seriously, gesturing for the door to be closed again.

"Fascinating," Castillo said.

Pevsner gestured for him to go with him to the table.

The Russian-speaking maid came around with a two-foot-wide pizza dough on a large wooden paddle. She held it between Pevsner and the maids, who stood waiting behind the table with large serving spoons. With his index finger, Pevsner directed one maid to spoon tomato sauce onto the dough, and kept pointing the finger until he decided there was a sufficiency.

He repeated the process with red and green peppers, then with several kinds of salami and pieces of bacon and chicken, finally concluding the process by supervising the spread of what looked like Parmesan cheese over the whole thing.

Then he marched back to the oven with the maid holding the pizza on a paddle trailing him, gestured to the young man to raise the door, and then gestured for the maid to slide the pizza into the oven, and finally for the young man to close the door.

Charley had a hard time keeping a smile off his face.

So far, he hasn't touched the pizza he's personally preparing for me with so much as his pinkie!

"I will now prepare another," Pevsner announced and marched back to the table, where he repeated the process twice more. This time, however, the prepared but unbaked pizzas on paddles were laid on the table.

"I can usually trust them," Pevsner said, "once I've made sure the temperature is right, to put them into the oven and take them out, but I like to prepare them myself."

"If you want something done right, do it yourself," Charley heard himself saying solemnly.

"Exactly," Pevsner said.

It's not fair of me to make fun of him. What's the matter with me? He's being nice, this whole thing is nice, the little kid, Sergei, handing me an empanada is nice. The whole family thing is nice. It reminds me of Grandpa dodging Abuela to slip Fernando and me a couple of slugs of wine at the ranch in Midland while he was roasting a pig over an open fire for the family. Except, of course, that Grandpa did everything but butcher the pig and crank the spit.

This is family. This is nice.

I think Betty Schneider would like this. Not the guy with the shotgun in his golf cart, but Anna and the three kids, and proud Papa preparing a pizza for everybody with his own unsullied hands.

I wonder what the Masterson kids are going to have for supper tonight?

I wonder what that poor bastard has told them, is telling them?

Is he pretending everything is going to be all right?

Preparing them for the worst?

Jesus, when you hear somebody's been snatched, you never think of the kids! What a rotten fucking way to make an easy buck, grabbing a kid's mother!

And here I am making nice watching Alex looking into his pizza oven.

There's nothing I could do in Buenos Aires, so why am I feeling guilty?

"Lost in thought, Charley?"

Castillo turned to see Howard Kennedy holding a glass of wine.

He had disappeared from the swimming pool when

Castillo and Anna Pevsner had gone out to it, and he hadn't been around since.

"I was wondering what the Masterson kids are having for supper tonight," Castillo said.

"The kids of the wom . . . ?"

Castillo nodded.

"Alex is working on it," Kennedy said. "There should be something soon."

"Jesus, I hope so. What's the penalty for kidnapping here? Do you know?"

"Not for sure, but I do know there's no death penalty period, and the average sentence for murder is fifteen years, which means they're on the street in seven-to-ten."

The Russian-speaking maid marched into the *quincho* with the now-baked pizza, and Alex Pevsner supervised her slicing of it with an enormous butcher knife.

Pevsner was called to the telephone three times as they ate their supper—the pizza was followed by steaks and foil-wrapped potatoes from the *parrilla;* Castillo was stuffed—each time taking the call in a small closet with a small window through which Castillo could see him talking.

It reminded Charley of the "phone booth" off General Naylor's conference room at CentCom headquarters in Tampa, where the secure telephone was located.

Pevsner returned to the table without saying anything the first two times, but when he came out of the closet the third time, he signaled for Charley to come with him.

They walked thirty feet or so away from the *quincho*.

"I don't have anything for you, Charley, I'm sorry. This last call was from someone who knows the important people at SIDE . . . you know SIDE?"

Charley nodded.

"And if anybody knew anything, SIDE would. And they're looking hard. The pressure is on them."

"Well, thanks for the effort," Charley said.

"I'll keep trying," Pevsner said, then, "All of my sources believe this is not an ordinary kidnapping. My source with connections to the Policía Federal and the Gendarmeria said that they've hauled in for questioning everybody even suspected of being involved in kidnappings, and they came up with nothing." He paused and then asked, "Did this fellow actually get fifty million dollars after a truck ran over him?"

"Sixty million," Charley said.

"The kidnappers may not be Argentine. They might even be American."

"Yeah," Charley agreed, thoughtfully.

I'll put that thought in my e-mail to Hall. It's the only wild idea about this that didn't come up in that brainstorming session at the embassy.

Why e-mail? I'll be up all night if I start swapping e-mails with Hall. And Darby made it clear that he's going to blow my cover to the ambassador tomorrow anyway. It'd be better to get on the horn.

He took his cellular out and pressed an autodial number. He had the phone to his ear before he considered the genuine possibility that there might not be cellular service out here in the country.

"Darby."

"Charley Castillo. I want to get on a secure line to Washington. Can you do that for me?"

"I can, but there's the problem of you being just a Secret Service agent, and there would be questions."

"Go ahead and tell the ambassador. Why not?"

"Okay. I think that's probably the best thing to do. I'll set up things at the embassy. Where are you?"

Castillo was aware that Pevsner was trying to make sense of his call.

"Ever hear of a little town called Maschwitz?"

"Yeah. I won't ask what the hell you're doing way out there."

"Don't. There's one more thing, Alex. It was suggested to me that the kidnappers might not be Argentine, that they might even be American."

"That was very delicately suggested to the FBI by the Policía Federal. If you notice a lot of activity in the commo center, it's the transmission of the names of every American who's come to Argentina in the past thirty days to the NCIC—the National Crime Information Center—to see if they come up with a hit."

"Well, somebody's done this, Alex."

"Some sonsofbitches."

"One more thing, Alex. Lowery took my Secret Service credentials to get me a visitor's badge, and we left the embassy before I got them back."

"I'll take care of it," Darby said. "We'll be in touch."

The connection was broken.

"Thank you," Pevsner said.

"For what?"

"For Maschwitz."

"If I think anyone is unusually curious about where I've been, or with whom, I'll drop your Austro-Hungarian grand duke into the conversation," Castillo said. "That'll lead them on an interesting expedition."

Pevsner smiled.

"Alex, I have to get back to Buenos Aires."

"I understand. You want me to send Howard with you?"

"That's not necessary. I just need a ride to the embassy."

Charley's cellular buzzed as they approached Buenos Aires.

"Hello?"

"Mr. Castillo?"

Castillo recognized Darby's voice.

"Alexander Darby here, Mr. Castillo."

"What can I do for you?"

"Mr. Castillo, Ambassador Silvio wonders if you would be free to come to his office at nine-thirty tomorrow morning."

"I'll be there."

"Thank you. I'll see you then."

The connection was broken.

It didn't take you long to tell the ambassador about me, did it, Alex?

And why do I suspect you made that call in his presence?

And that you told him simply that I had identified myself to you, and not that we knew each other in Afghanistan?

• • •

An American who did not identify himself in any way—making Castillo reasonably confident that he was a CIA agent who worked for Darby—was waiting just outside the fence at the employee entrance to the embassy grounds with Castillo's visitor's pass and Secret Service credentials.

"If you'll come with me, please, Mr. Castillo?"

[SIX]
The Communications Center
The United States Embassy
Avenida Colombia 4300
Buenos Aires, Argentina
2230 22 July 2005

There was a "phone booth" in the embassy communications room, too. As the man Castillo now thought of as "Darby's guy" led him to it, most of the eight or ten people in the room looked at him with frank curiosity. One of them was the Oriental FBI agent, Yung.

The guy who looked at me in the brainstorming center with what I thought was a little too much interest. He's either fascinated with my good looks and manly charm, or the Secret Service, or he knows something about me. Or suspects something.

Oh, Jesus! Has there been an FBI back-channel, no copies, burn before reading, "Let us know if a guy named Castillo shows up anywhere and what he's doing. He has embarrassed the director and we would really like to burn his ass"?

Castillo closed the door of the phone booth and sat down before a tiny desk, more of a shelf built into the wall, on which sat the secure telephone. It looked— except for the much thicker than usual cords to the wall, and from the base to the handset—like an ordinary phone. There was also a lined notepad, which had a sheet of aluminum under the top page to keep whatever was written from making an impression on the pages beneath, two sharpened pencils in a water glass, and a red- striped Burn Bag hanging from the wall.

Castillo picked up the telephone.

"Operator," a male voice said.

He sounds young. Probably a soldier.

"My name is Castillo. I need a verified secure line."

"Yes, sir. You have been cleared. The number, please?"

It's a little after ten-thirty here; half past nine in Wash- ington. Hall may or may not be in the office. I'll let the switchboard find him.

Castillo gave the White House switchboard number to the operator.

"Sir, that's the White House," the operator said.

"Yeah, I know."

"Sir, you're not cleared to call the White House."

"Who has to clear me?" Castillo asked, and at the last split second added, "Sergeant."

"Either the ambassador or Mr. Masterson, sir."

Well, he took the Sergeant without any reaction. That may be helpful.

"Well, I don't want to bother Mr. Masterson, Sergeant, so I suppose you'd better get the ambassador on the horn. I need to put this call through."

"Sir, Mr. Darby has the authority to clear calls to the White House. Would he know if you're authorized?"

"Yes, he would. Give him a yell, Sergeant."

Thirty seconds later, "Commercial Attaché" Darby gave the operator permission to put Mr. Castillo's call through to the White House switchboard.

"White House."

"This is the U.S. Embassy, Buenos Aires," the operator said. "Would you verify the line is secure, please?"

That took about fifteen seconds.

"The line is secure," the White House operator announced.

"This is C. G. Castillo. I need to speak with Secretary Hall. I have no idea where he is."

"Oh, I think we can find him for you. Hold one."

"Hall."

"I have a secure call for you, Mr. Secretary, from Mr. Castillo in Buenos Aires."

"Put Mr. Castillo through, please," Hall said.

In the presidential apartment in the White House, the President looked across the table in the breakfast room at his wife, and Matt Hall's wife, and made a decision.

"Put that on the speakerphone, Matt," he ordered, "but don't tell him."

• • •

"You there, Charley?"

"Yes, sir."

"We've been expecting to hear from you before this."

"Sir, there's not much to report that you probably haven't heard already."

"Well, take it from the top, Charley. You never know."

"Yes, sir. Joel's pal Tony Santini met me at the airport. Really good guy, sharp as a tack. Tony took me to the hotel, the Hyatt—which is now the Four Seasons, by the way. He told me what he knew, essentially that Mrs. Masterson was grabbed in the parking lot of a restaurant called Kansas in an upscale neighborhood called San Isidro. She was waiting for her husband, and when he didn't show went to her car and was grabbed.

"He said there had been no word from the kidnappers—this was at maybe seven this morning, and there still has been no word, as of now. Tony said the Argentines were keeping it out of the papers, so if I went there as Gossinger, they would (a) wonder how I heard about it, and (b) tell me zilch.

"So I went there as a Secret Service agent who just happened to be in town. Apparently that happens all the time. Tony introduced me to the embassy security guy, Lowery, nice guy, but a lightweight—"

"Why do you say that, Charley?" Hall interrupted.

"The way Tony Santini put it, most of his investigations have been of some diplomat fooling around with some other diplomat's wife. Nothing like this."

"Okay," Hall said.

"While I was in his office, Masterson came in. A really nice guy, and really upset. You know the story of his getting run over and—"

"Getting a fifty-million-dollar settlement? Yeah, I know it."

"The figure I heard was sixty million. Anyway, I was introduced to him as a Secret Service agent, and he asked me to go to a brainstorming session with all the players. The CIA station chief—more about him in a moment—the DEA people, and two FBI guys from Montevideo who are supposed to have some experience with kidnappings. One of them looked at me strangely. Then, and just now when I came in the commo room."

"What do you mean by that?"

"If I were paranoid, and I am, I would suspect that there's been a deniable bulletin from the J. Edgar Hoover Building telling everybody to keep an eye open for that sonofabitch Castillo."

"You really think that, Charley?"

"I can't prove it, but I got the same look from the CIA station chief, a guy named Darby—he's as sharp as a tack, too—and I know he knew who I was. Am."

"How do you know that?"

"After the brainstorming session—which came up with nothing—he offered to show me the restaurant, and when we got in his car, he told me the last time he'd seen me was in Zaranj, Afghanistan—he was station chief there—and that he'd put two and two together and concluded I was the guy involved in getting the 727 back."

"So is he going to tell the ambassador? Or anyone else?"

"For auld lang syne he said he would wait until tomorrow morning, but that he would have to tell him. About two hours ago, I told him to go ahead and tell him. I wanted to get on a secure line, rather than screw around with e-mails. So he knows. As I was coming into town, Darby relayed a very polite request from the ambassador that I come to his office at half past nine in the morning."

"What about the ambassador?"

"Both Santini and Darby think he's first class. Anyway, after having a very nice lunch in the Kansas which really made me feel guilty, I went nosing around by myself, and came up with zilch, except the possibility that the kidnappers are American. When I passed this on to Darby, he said the Argentine cops had already—'delicately,' he said—offered this possibility. Outside this phone booth, the FBI—including Yung, the FBI guy I think has made me—is sending the names of all Americans who've come down here in the past thirty days to the NCIC."

"What about the local authorities?"

"From everything I've been able to pick up, they're really doing their best, and with the same result, zilch. So what everybody is doing is waiting for the other shoe to drop."

"And that's about it?"

"Yes, sir. I feel about as useless as teats on a boar hog. Jesus, I wish the President hadn't come up with the nutty idea that I'm Sherlock Holmes. I'd really like to help, and I'm in way over my head."

"Hold one, Charley."

"Sherlock, this is the President."

"Jesus Christ!" Castillo blurted.

"No. Just the President," the President chuckled. "And I'm glad I did, Sherlock. I could not have asked for a more succinct and comprehensive report, and I know that any report that came close to being as good as the one you just gave Secretary Hall would have taken a lot more time to reach me."

"Sir, I'm sorry—"

"No need to be, Charley. I have just one question."

"Sir?"

"What about Mr. Masterson? Is he—and their children—being protected?"

"Yes, sir. Mr. Darby—he and Mr. Masterson are close—told me that he's having some of his people sit on Mr. Masterson, hopefully without his being aware that this is going on. And there's Argentine cops and SIDE people all over, too."

"Their FBI?"

"Yes, sir. Much like it. Both Mr. Santini and Mr. Darby tell me they're good at what they do."

"When you see Ambassador Silvio in the morning, you might tell him of my concern."

"Yes, sir, I will."

"Well, I guess that's it," the President said. "You're doing what I sent you down there to do, Charley, and doing it well."

"Thank you, sir."

"Mrs. Hall wants me to pass on her regards, and I'm sure my wife would like to add hers."

"Yes, sir."

"Goodnight, Charley," the President said.

"Interesting guy," the President observed.

"And a very nice one," Mrs. Janice Hall said. "You could hear his concern for that poor woman and the family in his voice."

"Until she actually met him, Janice could not stand men to whom women are drawn like moths to a candle."

"You can go to hell, Matt," Mrs. Hall said.

"I think sending him down there was one of my better ideas," the President said, and then added, "As was leaving him with Matt."

"Excuse me?" the first lady asked.

"When he got that airplane back, my first thought was to bring him into the White House. Then I realized that wouldn't be smart. Can you imagine what pressure would be on him if he worked here? Everybody in this building would be trying to (a) control him, and (b) keep him off my phone and out of the Oval Office. Having him working for Matt fixes all of that."

[SEVEN]
Room 1550
The Four Seasons Hotel
Cerrito 1433
Buenos Aires, Argentina
0625 23 July 2005

Castillo had left a call for seven—which would give him two hours to get dressed, have breakfast, and get to the embassy by half past nine—and when he glanced at his watch as he reached for the ringing telephone and saw what time it was, he felt a chill. It was too much to hope this call was going to be good news.

"¿Hola?"

"Castillo?" It was Darby's voice, not at all charming.

"Yes."

"You didn't answer your cellular," Darby accused.

"What's up?"

"There will be a car waiting for you by the time you can get downstairs."

"What's up?"

"Well, I'll tell you it's not good news," Darby said, and hung up.

V

[ONE]
Avenida Tomas Edison
Buenos Aires, Argentina
0640 23 July 2005

There had been a small gray Alfa Romeo—as far as Castillo could tell, they were identical to Fiats, except for the nameplates—with Argentine civilian license plates waiting on the drive outside the Four Seasons hotel when Castillo pushed through the revolving door.

As Castillo looked at it, wondering if it was meant for him, the driver pushed open the passenger door. "Señor Castillo?"

Castillo walked quickly to the car and got in. The car took off with a squeal of its tires before Castillo had time to fasten the seat belt.

"You speak Spanish, Mr. Castillo?" the driver asked in American English.

Castillo took a good look at him. He was an olive-skinned, dark-haired man in his thirties in a business suit who could, Castillo decided, easily pass for a *porteño,* a native of Buenos Aires.

"Sí," Castillo said.

"Say hello to Colonel Alfredo Munz of SIDE," the driver said, in fluent *porteño* Spanish.

The windows of the Alfa Romeo were heavily darkened; Castillo had not seen anyone in the backseat. He
turned on his seat and saw a stocky blond man in his forties. Castillo put out his hand.

"Mucho gusto, mi coronel."

Munz's grip was firm.

"Mucho gusto," he replied, adding, "Señor Darby has
told me about you, señor."

I wonder what he told you?

The car was now passing the French embassy, its horn
blowing steadily in short beeps. The driver ran the red
light and nearly got clipped by a Fiat delivery truck going
up Avenida 9 Julio. The Alfa Romeo made a squealing left
turn onto 9 Julio, and then raced down the autopista in
the extreme right lane, reserved for emergency vehicles.

"What's happened?" Castillo asked. "Where are we
going?"

"The cocksuckers shot Masterson," the driver said.

What did he say? They shot her? Oh, Jesus H. Christ!
But that sounded as if he meant him.

"Mrs. Masterson, you mean?"

"No. Masterson."

What the hell?

"I thought Darby had somebody sitting on him."

"Yeah, he did. Me. I fucked up big time."

They came to a row of tollbooths. Without slowing,
still blowing the horn, the driver went through the right
lane, despite the furious arm-waving of a policeman who
saw him coming. The policeman jumped out of the way
at the last minute and reached for his pistol.

"SIDE! SIDE! SIDE!" Colonel Munz shouted out his open window.

Christ, I hope that cop believes him!

There was no shot.

At least none that I can hear.

They came to a T in the road. Running another red light, the driver turned left, dodging between two enormous over-the-road tractor-trailers and then rapidly accelerating.

Castillo saw they were now on Avenida Presidente Castillo.

This is not a very elegant street to be named after a Castillo, El Presidente, or even one from San Antonio.

It was apparently the main route to the docks, and the roadway showed the effects of heavy—most probably grossly overloaded—trucks. The Alfa bottomed out every thirty seconds or so.

It was too noisy in the car to ask questions, and it would not have been wise to distract the driver's attention from the traffic.

Avenida Presidente Castillo took a bend to the left, then came to a stop sign, which the driver ignored, which almost saw them hit head-on by an enormous Scania tractor pulling a trailer with two containers on it.

Then another left, and another, and Castillo saw they were now on Avenida Tomas Edison. This was even rougher looking than Avenida Presidente Castillo. It was a two-lane road where the macadam had been mostly worn away from the cobblestones it had at one time covered. On their left were deserted warehouses, and on their right a decrepit port area, lined with rusting, derelict, and half-sunk riverboats.

And then there was a sea of flashing red-and-blue lights.

Four Policía Federal stood in the middle of the street, all of them with their hands up to stop them. Castillo saw a half dozen other cops taking barriers from the back of a truck.

The driver slammed on the brakes, slowing but not stopping.

Colonel Munz was now halfway out the rear window, waving his credentials and shouting, "SIDE! SIDE! SIDE!"

The policemen got out of the way; two of them saluted.

Fifty meters farther down the street an enormous— and enormously confident—Policía Federal sergeant held up his hand in casual arrogance to stop them.

The arrogance disappeared immediately when he recognized Munz.

"In there, *mi coronel*," he said, pointing to the shell of a deserted warehouse, the entire front of which was open, another thirty meters distant.

There were three police cars: one Policía Federal; a second from the Naval Prefecture, which has police power in the port; and a third from the Gendarmeria National. There were several unmarked cars, with flashing blue lights on their dashboards, and two ambulances, one from the German Hospital, the second from the Naval Prefecture.

Fifty yards past them, a huge tractor-trailer with a single, enormous container on it was stopped in the middle of the road, its stop and parking lights flashing.

When the driver slammed the brakes on and the Alfa Romeo screeched to a stop before the deserted warehouse, Castillo could see a taxicab parked nose-in against the rear wall of the building. There was a knot of seven or eight men, most of them in uniforms carrying the symbols of senior police officers, between the taxi and the front of the building.

Munz erupted from the backseat of the Alfa and marched purposefully toward them. Castillo and the driver got out and followed. The knot of police all turned to face him. Several of the senior police officers saluted.

"I sent word that nothing was to be touched until I got here," Munz announced. "I presume nothing has?"

"Mi coronel," a man in a navy uniform with the sleeve stripes of a commander said, "one of my men was first on the scene. Aside from reaching into the victim's pockets looking for identification, he touched nothing else."

"Looking into his pockets to see if he had any money is more like it," the driver of the Alfa Romeo said softly, behind his hand, to Castillo.

One of the senior police officers said something to Munz that Castillo couldn't hear.

Colonel Munz's eyebrows went up in surprise.

"Where is he?" Munz demanded.

The Navy officer indicated a man in a khaki uniform standing uncomfortably near the street.

"Get him over here," Munz ordered. He pointed to a spot on the ground.

The command to have the Naval Prefecture policeman come over worked its way down the hierarchy of police officers, and finally one of them walked quickly toward the policeman.

Munz walked toward the taxi. Castillo started after him, and then the driver, and that started the police officers moving. Munz sensed this. He turned and held out his hand to stop them, then pointed at Castillo and the driver, signaling them they should—or were permitted to—go with him.

The right rear door of the taxi was open.

Munz stuck his head inside, looked around for a moment, and then pulled it out. He signaled that it was permitted for the driver and Castillo to have a look.

Castillo was closest and went first.

There was the smell of blood and the buzzing of flies.

J. Winslow Masterson was leaning against the far door, half sitting up. His eyes and mouth were open. There was one entrance wound in his temple, and to judge from the now dried blood on his neck, another entrance wound under the hair behind his ear.

The taxi driver was slumped over the wheel. The silver gray hair at the back of his skull was heavily matted with blood, and the back of his jacket was black with dried blood.

Castillo pulled his head out of the cab, met the Alfa driver's eyes, and said, "Sonofabitch!"

He heard another squeal of tires near the opening of the building, and when he looked saw Alex Darby open the door of an embassy BMW and get out.

Several policemen tried to stop him.

"Pass him!" Colonel Munz shouted in a voice that

would have done credit to a drill sergeant. Then he started walking toward him.

Castillo heard Darby ask, "It's him?"

"I'm afraid it is," Munz said.

"And he's dead?"

Munz nodded. "Shot twice in the head."

"Where's Mrs. Masterson?" Darby asked.

Christ, I didn't even think of her!

Munz gestured toward the German Hospital ambulance.

Darby started toward the ambulance. Munz caught up with him.

"Alex, I think she's drugged," Munz said.

"Dammit! Who authorized that?" Darby demanded furiously.

"According to the first policeman on the scene, she was drugged when he got here."

"Presumably, there's a doctor with her?" Darby said.

"I think there's three doctors," Munz said. "I called the German Hospital myself."

Darby went to the ambulance, a large Mercedes van, pulled the door open, and climbed inside.

Castillo became aware the driver was now standing beside him.

"Darby's in the ambulance with Mrs. Masterson," Castillo said. "I heard Munz tell him she's drugged, was drugged when the Navy cop got here."

"Shit!" the driver said. "I make it two shots to the heads."

"I saw only one entrance wound in the cabdriver's head," Castillo said.

"I think there's two," the driver said, not argumentatively.

Darby came out of the ambulance and walked with Munz toward the taxi.

"Alex," the driver said, "I'm sorry."

"We're all sorry, Paul," Darby said.

Darby walked to the taxicab, looked inside for a long moment, and then walked back to where Munz, the driver, and Castillo were standing.

"Alex," Munz said, "I think she should be taken to the hospital. They can't determine what they gave her here."

"They told me," Darby said. "But I think the ambassador would want to see her here. He's on the way."

"Of course," Munz said.

Darby looked at the driver.

"Paul?"

"It looks to me like an assassination," the driver said.

"You agree with that, Charley?" Darby asked.

"Could be. I don't know."

Another embassy BMW pulled up, and then a second. A tall, lithe, well-tailored man got out of the backseat, and another man got out of the front passenger seat.

That has to be the ambassador, Castillo decided. *And the other guy his bodyguard.*

"Well, here comes the ambassador," the driver confirmed.

Ken Lowery, the embassy security officer, and three other men got out of the second BMW. One of the men was a burly Scandinavian type with a nearly shaven head.

Castillo decided he was one of the embassy's Marine guards.

Ambassador Silvio and Lowery walked past the outer line of Argentine police. No one tried to stop them.

They must recognize them.

All the others stopped at the line of policemen.

Silvio walked up to them.

"Good morning," he said. "Bring me up to speed."

"Jack is in the taxi, Mr. Ambassador," Darby said. "He has been shot twice in the head."

Silvio looked at Castillo but didn't say anything to him.

"Excellency," Munz said, "permit me to be the first to express my most profound regrets."

"Thank you, Colonel," Silvio said in Spanish. "Does anyone know what's happened?"

Before anyone could form a reply, Silvio went on, "Mrs. Masterson?"

"She's in the German Hospital ambulance, Your Excellency," Munz said. "She has apparently been drugged. By the villains."

Silvio's eyebrows rose, but he didn't speak. He started for the ambulance. Munz, Darby, and Lowery walked after him. After a moment—*what the hell, I'm supposed to find out what's going on*—Castillo walked after them.

As they reached the ambulance, Silvio turned to Castillo.

"You're Mr. Castillo?" he asked.

"Yes, sir."

Silvio knocked at the rear door of the ambulance, and then pulled it open and climbed in.

• • •

There in the van were two men and a woman, all wearing thin blue hospital coats, all of which carried nameplates with their names, followed by "M.D."

Mrs. Elizabeth Masterson was sitting on a chair against the far interior wall of the roomy ambulance. There was a plastic oxygen mask over her nose and mouth, and a blood pressure device wrapped around one arm. The female doctor was taking her pulse.

Silvio went to Mrs. Masterson, dropped to his knees, and took her hand.

"Elizabeth," he said softly in English, "I am so very sorry."

She looked at him, visibly confused, and then looked away.

"She has apparently been drugged," the female doctor said.

"What are you doing about it?" Silvio asked.

"There's not much we can do until we know what drug was used. We suspect a couple, but can't be sure until we get a blood sample to the laboratory."

"Why hasn't she been taken to the hospital?" Silvio asked, and then, without waiting for a response, said, "Please take her there now."

He turned and looked at Lowery.

"Go with her, please, Mr. Lowery. Make sure she is all right."

"Yes, sir," Lowery said.

"Take as many people as you think will be necessary."

"Yes, sir."

As Silvio started to leave the ambulance, Munz shouted, in a parade-ground bellow, "Captain Jiminez!"

One of the men in civilian clothing in the knot of police officers came running over.

"Eight men, two cars," Munz ordered. "One car to precede the ambulance, one to trail. There will be Americans. Make sure of Señora Masterson's safety. Report when she is safely in the hospital. And do not allow the press anywhere near her or the medicos."

"*Sí, mi coronel.*" Captain Jiminez turned and ran off, shouting orders as he ran. Lowery ran after him.

"Thank you, Colonel," Silvio said to Munz. "Now, what do we know about what happened?"

"We were about to find out, Excellency, just before you arrived," Munz said. "If you will come with me, Excellency?"

Munz led them to the policeman from the Naval Prefecture.

"You were the first officer on the scene?" Munz asked.

"*Sí, mi coronel.*"

That cop's about to piss his pants. He's terrified of Munz.

Ambassador Silvio saw this, too. He smiled at the policeman and put out his hand.

"Good morning," he said, in what Castillo now recognized as a good *porteño* Spanish accent. "My name is Silvio. I'm the United States ambassador, and we're trying to find out what happened here."

"*Sí, señor.*"

"Well?" Munz demanded.

"*Mi coronel,* I was patrolling in Puerto Madero when I got the call to come here."

"What did the call say?"

"Investigate a possible robbery murder," the policeman said, and added, reluctantly, "and a crazy woman."

"Do we know where that call came from?" Munz asked, looking over Castillo's shoulder. Castillo turned and saw that the Navy commander who had spoken to Munz earlier had come up.

"The truck driver, *mi coronel*," the commander said.

"Where is he? Get him over here."

When two Naval Prefecture policemen started to hustle the truck driver, a burly, visibly nervous man in his late forties, over toward them, Munz signaled them to stop and walked over to them. The ambassador, Castillo, Darby, and the driver followed. The Navy officer started to, but was ordered with a wave of Munz's hand to stay where he was. Then Munz dismissed the policemen with an impatient wave of his fingers.

"Would you please tell us what you know of this, señor?" Munz asked.

The man nodded, and then turned and gestured toward the street.

"I was coming down Edison," the truck driver began, "toward Jorge Newbery, when I saw the woman. She was staggering in the street. I thought she was drunk."

He stopped, having considered that he might have said something he should not have said.

I don't think he knows who Munz is, beyond being someone of importance to the other police, but he's afraid of him.

"And?" Munz prodded.

"I felt sorry for her and stopped," the driver said, not

too convincingly, and then added, "She was in the middle of the street, and I didn't want to run over her."

He waited for a response.

"And?" Munz prodded again.

"So I got out of my truck and she sort of dragged me in here," the driver said. "And I saw the taxi, what was in it—they were both dead—and I got on my phone and called—"

There seemed to be more flashing red-and-blue lights, and now sirens. Castillo saw that a little convoy had been formed and was apparently waiting for the ambulance. Then the flashing lights on the ambulance began to blaze, and its siren started screaming. It backed up, and then left the building. A policeman directed it into the column of lined-up vehicles. Castillo saw that the embassy car had been placed into the convoy behind the ambulance.

Then the whole convoy took off.

When the sound of the sirens had diminished to the point where he could be heard, Munz again said, "And?"

"Yes, sir," the truck driver said. "The lady fell down."

"What?"

"She fell down," the truck driver said. "She didn't pass out, but she couldn't stand up and she didn't understand what I was saying to her."

"What were you saying to her?"

"That the police were coming, and it would be better if she got out of the middle of the street. I tried to pick her up, but she screamed, so I just waited."

"And what happened between then and when the policeman came?"

"Nothing," the truck driver said, and then corrected himself: "What happened was she crawled out of the street—maybe she wanted to go back to the taxicab—"

"Maybe?"

"She was only as far as the curb when the policeman came," the truck driver said. "He said to leave her where she was, and he went and looked into the cab, and came out with the man's wallet—"

"How much money, would you say, was in the wallet?" Munz interrupted.

"I didn't see any money," the truck driver said. "And then he called for an ambulance and an officer, and picked her up and put her in the front seat of the police car. And he told me that the man in the back was a *norteamericano* diplomat, and to leave my truck where it was, and we waited for the others."

"Who came first?" Munz asked.

"I don't remember," the truck driver said.

Munz looked at him for a moment, then at the ambassador, and then at Darby, Castillo, and the driver, as if asking them if they had any questions. No one did.

"Thank you, señor," Munz said. "What's going to happen now is that as soon as the technicians get here, they will take some photographs of your truck, and otherwise examine it, and then we'll move it out of the middle of the road. Then you will be taken to the Naval Prefecture, where other officers will take a statement from you, and probably your photograph and fingerprints. I will issue orders that your truck will be guarded while you are gone, and that you be allowed to telephone your employer and your wife, if you want. You will tell them that you witnessed an accident, and that the police are taking your statement, nothing more. Nothing about the taxicab. You understand me?"

"*Sí, señor.*"

"Thank you," Munz said, and offered the man his hand. And then Ambassador Silvio offered his and said, "Thank you." Darby and then the driver and finally Castillo shook hands with the driver.

Then everybody followed Munz back to where the Navy commander stood with the policeman.

Another embassy car drove up. The two FBI agents from Montevideo got out.

Special Agent Yung looks more than a little surprised to see me.

"Colonel," Ambassador Silvio said, "those are two FBI agents I borrowed from Montevideo. If at all possible, I would like them to be able to witness your investiga—"

"Pass them!" Munz bellowed.

The two FBI agents trotted over.

Munz turned to the Navy commander. "I want the truck driver taken to the prefecture. Get a statement, take his photograph and his fingerprints. Let him call his employer and his wife, but make sure that he says nothing more than that he witnessed an accident and is giving a statement. Treat him well—my first reaction is that he's a good Samaritan—but keep him there until you hear from me."

"*Sí, señor.*"

"All right," Munz said to the Naval Prefecture policeman. "Tell me what happened from the moment you arrived on the scene."

His story neatly dovetailed with what the truck driver had told them.

Munz looked at the two FBI agents.

"I will issue orders that you are to have access to all facets of this investigation."

"Thank you," Ambassador Silvio said.

"Is there anything else, Your Excellency?" Munz asked.

Silvio responded, but to Darby.

"The children," he said.

"My wife is at the Masterson house," Darby replied.

"I will send my wife over there as soon as I can get on the phone," Silvio said. And then he asked, "Presumably, you've taken steps to guard it?"

"Yes, sir."

"Your Excellency, Señora Masterson and the children will not be out of sight of my best men," Munz said. "I realize that's not much you can put confidence in."

"Why do you say that, Colonel?" Silvio asked, courteously.

"Señor Sieno and I were sitting in his car outside the Masterson home from eleven P.M. onward, and Señor Masterson got away from us."

So that's his name. Sieno. Paul Sieno.

"Is that how you think of it, 'He got away from you'?"

"From Señor Sieno and me, and from Señor Sieno's men and mine. There were eight people watching his house, Your Excellency."

"Why would he want to 'get away from you,' do you think?"

"I think he was contacted by the villains, who told him where to meet them, and threatened his wife's well-being if he didn't come alone. So he went alone. How, I don't know, but he was desperate, and he got away from us, and made it to somewhere where he could find a taxi—the San Isidro railroad station, probably—and took it to wherever he was told to meet them. Did Your Excellency notice the taxi is not a Buenos Aires city taxi?"

"Yes, I did, as a matter of fact," Ambassador Silvio said. "And I was thinking that's what probably happened."

"I am both deeply sorry and grossly embarrassed, Your Excellency, that I have failed my duty," Munz said.

"If you and Sieno were sitting up all night in Paul's car, Colonel," Silvio said, "I don't think anyone can fairly accuse you of being derelict in your duties."

"I fucked up big time, Mr. Ambassador, that's the bottom line," Paul Sieno said.

"I don't feel that you did, Paul," Silvio said kindly, then turned to Alex Darby. "Alex, will you stay here to learn what you can? And at the hospital?"

"Yes, sir."

"Mr. Castillo, can I see you for a moment?"

"Yes, sir, of course."

Silvio took Castillo's arm and led him out of earshot.

"We're going to have to talk, Mr. Castillo," the ambassador said. "Is there some reason we can't do that now? Would you ride to the embassy with me?"

"Yes, sir, of course."

"Do you have any idea what's going on here, Mr. Castillo?" Ambassador Silvio asked when they were in the ambassador's big BMW. "Is there something I should know?"

"Sir, I have no idea what's going on," Castillo said, and then blurted, "except that it's a fucking outrage."

"I'm a diplomat, I'm not supposed to use language like that, but I quite agree."

"Sorry, sir. That slipped out. He was such a nice guy!"

"Yes, he was," Silvio agreed. Then he said, "Excuse me," and took out his cellular telephone and pushed an autodial number.

"Jack has been murdered, my love," he said in Spanish. "At the moment, that's all I know. Betsy, who has been drugged, has been taken to the German Hospital—

"No. Drugged. Not sedated—

"I was going to suggest that you go to the hospital, but until they bring her out of it, I can't see what good that would do. Alex Darby's wife is with the Masterson children—

"Thank you. Make sure you have at least one of Lowery's people with you, and that the Policía Federal are following you—

"None of us would have believed what just happened, my love. Do what I tell you. I'll call you shortly."

[TWO]
The Office of the Ambassador
The United States Embassy
Avenida Colombia 4300
Palermo, Buenos Aires, Argentina
0635 23 July 2005

"I expect that you will want to make a report to your superiors, Mr. Castillo," Ambassador Silvio said as he led Castillo into his office.

"Yes, sir."

"You might as well do that from here," Silvio said.

"That's very kind of you, sir, but I don't mind—"

"We really haven't finished our conversation, have we?" Silvio interrupted him. "Just as soon as I speak with the secretary of state, I'll have them put you through."

Is he doing that to be a nice guy—which he certainly seems to be—or so that he can hear my report?

"Thank you very much, sir."

"Having said what I just said, I realize that I have no idea how to get through to the secretary at this hour of the morning—it's what, half past five in Washington? And I think she would want to hear this directly from me."

"Sir, I know how to do that," Castillo said.

The ambassador indicated the secure telephone on his desk.

Castillo put the receiver to his ear and heard, "Operator."

"My name is Castillo. I need a secure line to the White House. The ambassador's here to clear it, if you need that."

Silvio took the phone from Castillo.

"This is Ambassador Silvio. Mr. Castillo is cleared to call the White House now and at any time in the future."

"Thank you," Castillo said as he took the handset back.

"White House."

"This is the United States Embassy, Buenos Aires. Please verify this line is secure."

Ten seconds later the White House operator said, "This line is secure."

"This is C. G. Castillo. I need the secretary of state on a secure line, please."

This took a little longer. It was thirty-five seconds before a male voice said, "This is the secretary of state's secure line."

"C. G. Castillo for the secretary of state."

"The secretary is asleep, Mr. Castillo."

"I thought she might be. Put me through, please."

Another forty-five seconds passed.

"Put him through, please," Natalie Cohen said.

"Castillo, Madam Secretary."

"Charley, do you realize what time it is here in Washington?"

"Yes, ma'am. Hold one for Ambassador Silvio."

He heard the secretary of state mutter, "Oh, God!" as he handed the ambassador the telephone.

Then he started for the door. The ambassador waved his hand to signal him to stay.

"Ambassador Silvio, Madam Secretary," Silvio said. "I have the sad duty to inform you that the body of Chief of Mission J. Winslow Masterson was found an hour and a half ago. He had been shot twice in the head. . . ."

"The secretary wishes to speak to you, Mr. Castillo," Silvio said, and handed him the telephone.

"Yes, ma'am?"

"How come you placed the call, Charley?"

"I knew how to get through to you without going through layers of bureaucrats."

"Do you know anything the ambassador doesn't?"

"No, ma'am. Nobody has any idea what's going on."

"Presumably you've told Matt Hall?"

"No, ma'am. That's next."

"You want me to give him a heads-up?"

"Thank you, but I don't think that'll be necessary."

"I'm going to have to wake the President up with this. He finally told me, last night, that he'd sent you down there. And of what you found out, Sherlock."

"Yes, ma'am."

"I'm sure we'll be talking, Charley."

"Yes, ma'am."

There was a series of clicks on the line, then:

"White House. Are you through?"

"Castillo again. Now I need Secretary Hall on a secure line."

"Hold, please."

"Secretary Hall's secure line," said a new voice.

"Tom?"

"This is Special Agent Dinsler. Who is this, please?"

"Is either Tom McGuire or Joel Isaacson around there?"

"No."

"My name is Castillo. Will you put me through to Secretary Hall, please."

"The secretary is asleep, sir."

He called me "sir," which means he doesn't know Castillo from Adam's off ox.

"Wake him, please."

"May I ask what this concerns, sir?"

"Get him on the goddamn phone, now!"

There was no reply, but fifteen seconds later Secretary of Homeland Security Matthew Hall came on the line.

"All you had to do was tell Dinsler who you are, Charley. You didn't have to swear at him," Hall said, his voice annoyed.

"Yes, sir. Sir, Mr. Masterson, *Mr. Masterson,* the chief of mission, has been murdered."

"Jesus Christ!" Hall said. "And his wife?"

"She's in the German Hospital, surrounded by eight SIDE agents, and four of ours. The bastards drugged her. She woke up—more accurately, came half out of it— in the backseat of a taxicab and found her husband slumped beside her with two bullets in his brain."

"My God, Charley!"

"Yeah, and he was a really nice guy, too."

"When did this happen?"

"Sometime after midnight. He got away from the people sitting on him at his house—a CIA guy and a big shot, a colonel from SIDE, plus half a dozen others—

and apparently took a taxicab to meet somebody. Probably to pay ransom, or to arrange to pay it."

"Give me all the details, and slowly. I'm going to have to tell the President and Natalie."

"Natalie already knows. Ambassador Silvio just talked to her, and she said she would tell the President."

"Okay. Now you tell me what you know."

"Yes, sir. There's not much beyond what I already have told you. A truck driver found Mrs. Masterson wandering dazed on a street in the port. She had been drugged. He called the cops, the cops found Masterson's body, searched it enough to find his diplomat's carnet, and called SIDE. The colonel from SIDE, a heavy hitter, was sitting outside Masterson's house with one of Darby's guys.

"Darby's guy called Darby, Darby called the ambassador, and then called me and said he was sending a car for me. The SIDE colonel, his name is Munz, was in Darby's guy's car. When we got there, Mrs. Masterson was already in an ambulance, with an oxygen mask, and there were cops all over the place.

"Darby, the ambassador, and the embassy security guy, Lowery, and some of his guys showed up moments later. Once the ambassador had seen Mrs. Masterson, they took her to the hospital. The SIDE colonel sent two cars and eight of his men with the ambulance, and Lowery and some of our people went with them."

"How is Mrs. Masterson?"

"She's still pretty much out of it, but once they get her to the hospital—"

"What the hell is going on, Charley? Who the hell is doing this? Why?"

"Nobody has a clue, and every time I think maybe this, or maybe that, it doesn't wash."

"For example?"

"A bungled kidnapping. Why did they kill Masterson if he paid the ransom? Why didn't they kill her, too? They killed the cabdriver, maybe—probably—because he saw them. So why let her live? She certainly saw something. I just wish the President had sent somebody who knows what he's doing down here."

"He didn't. He sent you," Hall said, and then asked, "You think Masterson was trying to pay the ransom? Where would he get the money? I thought you said there had been no contact with the kidnappers?"

"Somebody contacted Masterson last night. Maybe before. Otherwise, why would he have gotten away from the agency guys—and SIDE—watching his house?"

"Okay."

"And as far as getting money to pay the ransom, all that would take is a telephone call, telling somebody—his financial guy, probably; they're old friends—to get five hundred thousand, or a million, in cash and get it down here as quickly as possible. A courier could have been on the same plane I was on, for that matter, and there's a direct American Airlines flight from Dallas. Or he could have hired a Citation or something like it. He has—had—the money, and he was desperate."

"Yeah," Hall agreed thoughtfully, and then asked, "Where are you?"

"I'm with Ambassador Silvio. In his office."

"He knows you were sent down there by the President?"

"Yes, sir."

"What's your next step? You know he's going to ask."

"I'm going to go to the hospital. Maybe, when she comes out of it . . ."

"How am I going to be able to get in touch with you?"

"Santini, Joel's buddy, loaned me a cellular. I don't know if you can call it, but I know I can call the States with it."

"Give me the number."

Ninety seconds later, as Castillo held it in his hand, the cellular rang.

"Castillo."

"It works, apparently," Hall said. "I'm going back to the secure line."

Two seconds later, Hall said, "I could have said this on the cellular. Keep in touch, Charley. Let me know anything you find out."

"Yes, sir."

Hall broke the connection without saying anything else.

"White House. Are you through?"

"Shut it down, please," Castillo said, and replaced the handset in its cradle. He sensed Silvio's eyes on him.

"You think Jack Masterson was trying to pay ransom?" Silvio asked.

"Sir, that's one—"

A female voice came over an intercom loudspeaker.

"Mr. Ambassador, the foreign secretary is on two."

Silvio reached for the telephone.

"Good morning, Osvaldo.

"Osvaldo, I'm always happy to receive you at your convenience.

"That will be fine. I will be expecting you.

"I appreciate that, Osvaldo. And I agree, this is a genuine tragedy. I will be waiting for you."

Silvio broke the connection with his finger, but kept the handset in his hand.

"The foreign minister officially requests an immediate audience," Silvio said. "And personally, he said he's heartbroken. I think he means that; he got along very well with Jack."

Castillo nodded, but didn't say anything.

Silvio took his finger off the switch, then pressed a button on his telephone.

"Oh, Sylvia. I'm glad you're in. Could you come in right away, please? Thank you."

He hung up the telephone and looked at Castillo again.

"The foreign minister, sometime during our audience, is going to ask me how I intend to deal with the press. To avoid hurting his feelings by having some doubts about his suggestions along that line, I'm going to show him what I have already released to the press."

A moment later, a slightly chubby woman in her late forties put her head into Silvio's office. She had heavily rimmed spectacles sticking out of her salt-and-pepper—and somewhat unkempt—hair. Silvio waved her in.

"Good morning, Sylvia," Silvio said.

"With all due respect, Mr. Ambassador, what's good

about it? Jack was one of the good guys. And those poor kids!"

"Sylvia, this is Mr. Castillo. Mr. Castillo, this is Mizz Sylvia Grunblatt, our public affairs officer."

Ms. Grunblatt's offered handshake suggested that while she considered it a strange custom and a complete waste of her time, she resigned herself to the act.

"How much have you heard, Sylvia?"

She looked at Castillo as if wondering what she could say before a man she didn't know.

"Ken Lowery gave me a heads-up earlier," she said finally. "And then he called and told me he was at the German Hospital, and I went there on my way here. He pretty much filled me in."

"The foreign minister is on his way here. When he gets here I want to be able to tell him what we have released to the press."

"Which is?"

"In the opening lines, I'd like something to the effect that we are grateful to the Argentine government—on whom we have been relying to get to the bottom of this tragic event since it developed—for their great efforts, in which we have complete confidence."

Ms. Grunblatt considered that for about fifteen seconds.

"Okay. And what else?"

"Sylvia, I learned from you that when all else fails, tell the truth."

"And the truth is?"

"All we know is that Mrs. Masterson disappeared under circumstances that suggested she had been kidnapped, and that Mr. Masterson was murdered, probably by the abductors, as she was left in the taxicab with him."

"Okay," she said. "I'll get right on it."

"It will take him, say, fifteen minutes to get here."

"You'll have it, Mr. Ambassador."

"I'd like a look at what Miss Grunblatt comes up with, please," Castillo said.

That earned him a frosty glance. She said, "It's Mizz Grunblatt, Mr. Costello."

"It's Castillo, Mizz Grunblatt."

"You think you might wish to add something, Mr. Castillo?" Silvio asked.

"Oh, no, sir. I'd just like to know what we're saying."

"Am I allowed to ask who Mr. Castillo is?" she asked.

"He works for the President, Sylvia, which means we tell him anything he wants to know."

"Is that for dissemination?" she asked.

"Absolutely not," Castillo said.

She held up both hands, palms out, to indicate that that information could not be torn from her under any conditions.

He smiled at her.

"Do you kill people who look over your shoulder while you work?" Castillo asked.

"Only if they're looking down my dress," Ms. Grunblatt said. "You that hot to see what I come up with?"

"I'd like to see it before I go to the German Hospital," he said.

"Sure, why not?" she said.

"I'll see that you have a car and driver, Mr. Castillo," the ambassador said.

"I can take a taxi, sir."

"Indulge me," the ambassador said.

"Thank you, sir."

[THREE]

"So what do you think?" Ms. Grunblatt asked.

"I think it's just what the ambassador wants," Castillo replied. "Who gets this?"

"Once the boss approves it, I'll e-mail it first to the *Herald*—that's the English-language paper here—and then AP, then the *New York Times*. Then I'll call them to let them know I sent it. After that, everybody else—the local media."

"Fax one to a man named Karl Gossinger at the Four Seasons."

"Who is he?"

"He works for a German newspaper called the *Tages Zeitung*."

And he will shamelessly paraphrase your very well-written yarn and send it off as his own.

She looked at him curiously but said only, "Consider it done."

The door to her office opened and a large and muscular young man in civilian clothing came in. His tweed jacket didn't do much to conceal the large revolver on his belt. Castillo was sure he was one of the Marine guards.

"Mr. Castillo?"

"Right."

"Sir, I've got your car anytime you're ready to go."

"I'm ready," Castillo said. He looked at Ms. Grunblatt. "Thanks."

"If you find out anything over there, you'll keep it to yourself, right?"

"You will be the second to know."

The Marine led him to an embassy BMW in the embassy basement and held the rear door open for him.

"Would it be all right with you if I rode up front?" Castillo asked.

"Yes, sir. Whatever you want, sir."

Castillo walked around the front of the car and pulled the passenger door open. There was a leather toilet kit on the seat.

"There's a toilet kit on the seat," Castillo announced. "Yours?"

"No, sir. That's for you, sir."

"The ambassador thought I needed a shave?"

"It's a weapon, sir. A pistol."

"Really?"

Castillo unzipped the bag. It held a GI 9mm Beretta semiautomatic pistol.

That was a damned nice thing for Silvio to do for me.

Castillo took the pistol from the bag and pressed the magazine release button. The magazine did not slip out. He looked. There was no magazine.

"Sir, that's a Beretta Model 92 semiautomatic pistol, caliber nine millimeter."

"I'll be damned."

"Yes, sir. It will fire fifteen rounds just as fast as you can pull the trigger."

"This one won't."

"Sir?"

"There's no whatchacallems? 'Bullets'?"

"Sir, the *cartridges* are held in a magazine."

He held up a full magazine for Castillo's edification, and only then began to understand his chain was being pulled.

"What is it, 'Sergeant'?" Castillo asked, reaching for the magazine.

"Staff Sergeant, sir."

He more than reluctantly let go of the magazine. Castillo took it, checked to see there was no round chambered in the pistol, and then slid the magazine into its place in the handle.

"I don't want this to get any further than it has to, Sergeant, which means that was the last time you call me 'sir,' but the cold and unvarnished truth is that I'm a soldier."

"Sir, the ambassador didn't say anything—"

"What part of don't-call-me-'sir' didn't you understand?"

"Sorry, s—"

"I don't think the ambassador knows I'm a soldier. Actually—the reason I can give you orders—I'm a major."

"Yes, s—" the sergeant said, and then, "Major, it comes automatically. I say 'sir' to civilians all the time."

"Well, try not to say it to me, okay?"

"Yes, sir. Oh, shit."

"I'm sorry I brought the subject up," Castillo said, chuckling. "Let's go, Sergeant."

[FOUR]
Room 677
The German Hospital
Avenida Pueyrredón
Buenos Aires, Argentina
0940 23 July 2005

There were half a dozen uniformed Policía Federal in the lobby of the hospital, and when Castillo asked for Mrs. Masterson, one of them, a sergeant, walked up to him somewhat menacingly.

"Señor," he began.

A tall, well-dressed man walked up.

"Señor Castillo?"

Charley nodded.

"Come with me, please, señor."

"Get yourself a cup of coffee," Castillo said to the Marine.

"The ambassador said I'm not to let you out of my sight."

"Good, no 'sir,'" Charley said. "Tell the ambassador I was difficult. Not to worry."

Almost biting his lip not to say "sir," the Marine said, "I'll be right here."

The tall man waved Castillo onto an elevator, nodding at another well-dressed man already on it as they entered. The man pushed the button for the sixth floor.

There was a sign saying Seimens had built the elevator.

And the lobby was spotless, waxed, and shiny. And that RAUCHEN VERBOTEN! *sign in black and red!*

When they say "German Hospital," they mean German hospital.

When the door opened, Castillo saw more uniformed police and several other well-dressed men who he decided were almost certainly SIDE agents.

The tall man led him down a corridor to a door, opened it, and waved Castillo in.

Colonel Munz was in the room, which was some sort of monitoring center. There was a row of television sets—all of German manufacture—on the wall.

"I thought it would be best if Señor Darby and Señor Lowery spoke with Mrs. Masterson," Munz greeted him, "as I don't think she feels kindly about anything Argentine right now."

He dismissed the tall man with a wave of his hand, and then pointed to the television monitors. On two of them Castillo could see Mrs. Masterson. She was in a hospital gown, sitting up in a bed. Lowery was on one side of her and Darby on the other. Something from a limp plastic bottle was dripping into her arm. He could hear Darby talking to her, but he couldn't make out what he was saying.

"How long has she been out of it?" Castillo asked.

"About ten minutes," Munz replied. "They found a drug in her blood. They're giving her something to neutralize it. It's obviously working."

"I can't hear what they're saying."

Munz walked to one of the monitors and increased the volume.

Darby was assuring her that the children were all right, that they were under the protection of both Argentine police and security people from the embassy.

Castillo got the feeling that Darby was repeating his assurances, meaning she had not yet completely come out from under the effects of the narcotic.

He heard Munz's cellular buzz.

Munz said, "*¿Hola?*" but then switched to German.

It soon became obvious that he was speaking with someone who was not overly impressed with Colonel Munz of SIDE, or more likely not impressed at all. His explanations that something had happened that had kept him from coming home as promised, and from at least calling, apparently were not falling on appreciative ears. The odds were that El Coronel Munz was speaking with Señora Munz.

He turned his attention back to Darby's gentle interrogation of Mrs. Masterson.

She didn't have much to tell him. From the time she was grabbed and felt what was the prick of a hypodermic needle in her buttocks, she remembered practically nothing until she had woken up in the taxicab sitting beside her dead husband.

She did not get a good look at her abductors; she didn't even know how many of them there had been. She had no idea where she had been taken. She could not describe the room in which she had been held.

Castillo had just had an uncomfortable thought, one that shamed him—*Jesus, she's still probably full of that drug*—when Munz spoke to him, in German.

"Why do I suspect you speak German, Herr Castillo?"

Castillo turned to look at him.

"While I was talking to my wife, in a thick Hessian accent, I saw your reflection on one of the monitors. You were smiling."

Why the hell is she lying? And to Darby, who is an old and close friend?

"Guilty," Castillo said, speaking German. "My mother was German. A Hessian, as a matter of fact."

And I've got to get an e-mail off to the Tages Zeitung, *which I don't think I'll mention to Munz.*

And I want to call Pevsner.

I should have gotten his phone number; all I have is Kennedy's cellular number.

Well, he can either give me the number or have Pevsner call me.

Maybe she's just scared. She has every right to be.

She must know that Darby's the resident spook, and that she is now safely in his hands.

"Really?" Munz said. "Where in Hesse was your mother from?"

Jesus, is he onto something? Has he connected me with Gossinger at the Four Seasons? Both Santini and Darby said SIDE is good.

"A little town called Bad Hersfeld."

"I know it. My father's family was from Giessen, and my wife's family from Kassel."

"How'd you wind up here?"

"I was born here. One day, maybe, I'll tell you how my mother and father got here. And my wife's parents."

"Okay."

She's not drugged. She's making decisions. She's lying.

Munz changed his mind.

"You ever hear of the Gehlen Organization?"

Castillo nodded.

Immediately after World War II, a German general staff officer, Reinhardt Gehlen, who had been in charge of "Eastern Intelligence," had gone to the Americans and offered to turn over not only his files, but his entire intelligence network—which included, among other things of great intelligence value, in-place spies in the Soviet Army and in Moscow.

His price was that none of his officers be tried as Nazis, and that the Americans arrange to get their families out of Germany to somewhere safe—like South America, Argentina being preferred—with their husbands to join them later.

The deal was struck.

When Castillo had first heard the story, as a West Point cadet, he had been fascinated. He had wondered then who had made the decision to deal with Gehlen; it had to have been someone really senior. If the story had gotten out, there would have been a political eruption.

He had been trying ever since—and for years he had held security clearances that gave him access to a great deal of heavily classified files—to find out more. He hadn't learned much. The conclusion he had drawn, without any proof whatsoever, was that the decision to deal with Gehlen had been made by President Harry S Truman himself, probably at the recommendation of General Eisenhower, who at the time was commander in chief in Europe. Almost as soon as Roosevelt had died, and Truman had started dealing with the Soviet Union, he had recognized the Soviet threat.

"My mother came here in 1946, and my father in 1950," Munz went on. "He became one of the few civilian instructors at the military academy. When he died several years ago, he was buried here quite close to a man named Hans von Langsdorff. That name ring a bell?"

"The *Graf Spee* captain," Castillo said.

Why is he telling me this?

To let me know he's one of the good guys?

Maybe Darby has him in his pocket, and he wants me to know?

Or maybe he wants me to think that he's muy simpatico, and I will thereafter regard him as a pal and tell him things I shouldn't.

Well, I don't have time to stay here and play games with him.

"When Mr. Darby comes out of there, would you ask him to give me a call? I don't see any point in hanging around here."

"Certainly," Munz said.

[FIVE]
Room 1550
The Four Seasons Hotel
Cerrito 1433
Buenos Aires, Argentina
1035 23 July 2005

"Why don't we go in the bar and get you a cup of coffee while you're waiting for me?" Castillo said to the sergeant as they entered the hotel lobby.

"We're back to the ambassador saying I'm not supposed to let you out of my sight."

"I need thirty minutes out of your sight," Castillo said. "If you think you have to, Sergeant, call the ambassador and tell him I said that. Otherwise, your waiting in the bar will be our little secret."

"I would say, 'Yes, sir,' but you told me not to. Just don't take off on me, please? That would put my ass in a crack."

"I'll be down in thirty minutes, maybe a little less," Castillo said.

He walked the sergeant into the bar, got a bar tab, signed it—making sure the sergeant didn't see the Gossinger signature—and then rode the elevator to his room.

There was no fax press release from the embassy for Herr Gossinger waiting in his room; nor, when he called, was it waiting downstairs to be delivered. He wondered if Ms. Sylvia Grunblatt had overlooked sending it, or had intentionally not done so. Castillo knew that that didn't matter right now. He got out his laptop computer, and, working from his memory of the press release, wrote the story of the murdered diplomat, and then e-mailed it to Otto Göerner at the *Tages Zeitung*. He thought about calling him immediately, but decided that he might not read it right away, and that he would call him after he talked to Pevsner.

Alex Pevsner answered Kennedy's cellular on the second buzz.

"*¿Hola?*"

"That you, Alex?"

"I heard what happened about thirty minutes ago. I thought you would call, and I knew you didn't have the number here, so I asked Howard for his cellular. I should have given the number to you. How is Mrs. Masterson?"

"You heard about that, too?" Castillo replied, and then went on without waiting for an answer. "They doped her—bupivacaine, I'm told—and she doesn't seem to remember much of what happened."

"But she'll be all right?"

"I think so. Yes."

"Anna was concerned."

"I don't suppose you've heard anything?"

"My source—and he's close to a man named Munz, who is the power at SIDE—tells me he doesn't think this is a kidnapping for ransom."

"He say what he thinks it is?"

"He doesn't have any idea, and neither, apparently, does Colonel Munz. If I hear anything, I'll let you know. Is it all right if I call your cellular number?"

"Of course."

"Let me give you the numbers here," Pevsner said, and did so.

"Göerner."

"Did you get my Masterson story?"

"I'm fine, Karl. And how are you? I've been a little concerned."

"About what?"

"I got your story. Very interesting. So far, there's nothing on the wires or CNN."

"There will be shortly."

"I'm impressed with your—what do they say in the States? Your 'scoop.'"

"Well, I try to earn my keep."

"I hope you haven't had time to work on the oil-for-food scandal I mentioned."

"I haven't. Why do you ask?"

"I got a story from our guy in Vienna yesterday. I would have called to tell you about it, but, as usual, I didn't know where to find you. If you check your e-mail, you'll find a rather anxious message from me. There's also a rather pointed message on your voice mail at the Mayflower in Washington."

"What sort of a story?"

"The Vienna police were called to an apartment on the Cobenzlgasse to investigate a terrible odor. It came from the decomposing corpse—he'd apparently been dead for ten days or so—of a Lebanese man named Henri Douchon."

A mental image of the Cobenzlgasse, the cobblestone

street in Grinzing leading up the hill to the Vienna Woods, popped into Castillo's mind. He had met Alex Pevsner for the first time at the top of the hill.

"Who's he?"

"From what I've been told, he was a middleman, a very important middleman, in the oil-for-food arrangement; the illegal part."

"What's that got to do with me?"

"According to my man, before they cut Herr Douchon's throat—almost decapitating him—they pulled several of his fingernails out, and several of his teeth. He was strapped into a chair."

"Jesus!"

"I don't want anyone pulling your teeth out with a pair of pliers, Karlchen, much less cutting your throat. I want you to forget everything I told you about there possibly being an Argentine connection."

"That cow is out of the barn, Otto."

"If I had known how to reach you yesterday, I was going to tell you not to make inquiries, discreet or otherwise, about Oil for Food, moving money to Argentina, or anything remotely connected with either."

"Not to worry, I won't have time now. I'm on the kidnapping story."

"Yes, I'm sure you are," Göerner said.

That was a not-very-well-veiled reference to what he knows I do for a living.

"One of the reasons I called was to ask what—off the top of your head—you think might entice someone to kidnap a diplomat's wife?"

"When I gave your story to the foreign news editor—

it will run in all the papers, with your byline and photograph—he asked me, 'Isn't Masterson that football player who got seventy-five million dollars after he was run over by a coal truck?' "

"Basketball, sixty million, and a beer truck," Castillo said.

"That wasn't in your story, Karlchen," Göerner said. "We're going to see if the AP or CNN or BBC mentions it. Then we'll either quote them in our wrap-up, or run it as a sidebar."

Why the hell didn't I mention it? I was writing a news story, not an embassy press release.

Because you are not a bona fide journalist, that's why.

"It should have been in the story," Castillo said.

"What did you say, sixty million? That would inspire a kidnapper, I'm sure."

"One of my sources, a good one"—*you know who he is, Otto. Alex Pevsner*—"just told me there is some doubt in the minds of the senior cops here—they're called SIDE, sort of a combined CIA and FBI—that the abduction and the murder had anything to do with collecting a ransom."

"Even more reason that you not ask penetrating questions when you are far from home. There are some very unpleasant people in the world, Karlchen. People who are willing to attract all the attention that kidnapping an American diplomat's wife, and then killing the diplomat, would bring to them would not hesitate before killing a journalist from a not very important German newspaper if they thought he was asking impertinent questions."

"Hey, I'm a big boy, Otto."

"Who has always been too big for his pants," Göerner said. "There was something else I found missing in your story, Karl. What happens now?"

"I don't know what you mean."

"'Ambassador Joe Blow said the remains of Masterson will be flown to the United States for burial in Arlington National Cemetery.' Something like that."

"I don't know, Otto. But I'll find out and send it to you."

"Your editor would like you, if possible, to accompany the remains to the United States, and provide the full story of the funeral."

"I'm not sure that will be possible."

"I'm not sure you would go if it was possible. But I am a foolish old man who worries about the godfather of his children, and thought I should ask."

"Otto . . ."

"Hold it a minute," Göerner said, and a moment later, "It just came in on Agence France Press," he said. "They say seventy million and baseball player."

"Trust me, it's sixty million and basketball."

Castillo's cellular buzzed.

"My cellular just went off. I have to go, Otto. I'll keep you up to speed."

"After you give me that cellular number and where you're staying," Göerner said.

"Hold one," Castillo said to the cellular, then gave Otto the cellular number and his room number in the Four Seasons.

"Please, Karlchen, be very careful," Otto said.

"I will. Thanks, Otto."

"*Auf wiedersehen*, Karlchen."

"Sorry," Castillo said into the cellular. "I was on the other line."

"How long will it take you to get to a secure line, Charley?" the secretary of Homeland Security asked.

"Ten, fifteen minutes."

"The sooner the better," Hall said. "I'll be waiting. He's gone ballistic."

The line went dead.

Castillo had no doubt that he who had gone ballistic was the President of the United States.

VI

[ONE]
Communications Center
The United States Embassy
Avenida Colombia 4300
Palermo, Buenos Aires, Argentina
1100 23 July 2005

The slender, trim man sitting behind the desk rose when Castillo walked in. The man was wearing a suit and a crisp white shirt, but there was something about him—carriage, short haircut, attitude—that made Charley sure he was a soldier.

"Mr. Castillo?"

"Right. I need a secure line to the White House. It's been cleared."

"Sir, the ambassador left word that if you came in, he wanted to see you right away."

Shit!

This situation wasn't covered in Obeying Orders 101 at The Point. The rule there was simple: you obey your last lawful order. My last order was to get on the horn as quickly as possible. And technically, Ambassador Silvio can't even legally issue me orders.

Or can he? He's the ambassador extraordinary and plenipotentiary of the President of the United States.

And Major C. G. Castillo is not about to tell Ambassador Silvio, in his embassy, that I don't have time for him right now, but I will try to fit him into my busy schedule just as soon as I can.

"Thank you," Castillo said, and headed for the ambassador's office.

"You wanted to see me, sir?" Castillo asked, when Silvio's secretary ushered him into the ambassador's office.

"Yes, I did. Thank you for coming so quickly. I just wanted to tell you that the security staff has been alerted and are holding themselves ready for your instructions."

What the hell is he talking about?

"Sir?"

"You don't have any idea what I'm talking about, do you?"

"No, sir. I don't."

"I thought you might not. May I ask what you're doing in the embassy?"

"Sir, I got word to get on a secure line to my boss . . . to Secretary Hall . . . as quickly as possible."

"I just had a very interesting conversation with my boss, as a matter of fact. Well, why don't you speak with your boss, and when you're finished, we can compare notes, so to speak."

"Sir, I have the uncomfortable feeling that I've done something to displease you."

"I'm displeased, frankly, but it's nothing you've done, Mr. Castillo," Silvio said. "In a manner of speaking, I would say that you and I are leaves being blown about by the winds of a storm."

Charley couldn't think of anything to say.

"Why don't you speak with Secretary Hall? And then come see me?" Silvio said.

"Yes, sir."

"Hall."

"Charley, sir."

"Let me get right to it," Secretary Hall said. "By direction of the President, Major Castillo, you are directed and empowered (a) to take whatever action you deem necessary to protect the family of the late J. Winslow Masterson while they are in Argentina, and (b) to ensure their safe return—"

"Jesus Christ!"

"Let me finish, Charley. By direction of the President, I have written all this down."

"Sorry, sir."

"And (b) to ensure their safe return to the United States; and you are (c) directed and empowered to assume responsibility for the investigation of the kidnapping of Mrs. Elizabeth Masterson and the murder of Mr. Masterson." He paused. "You understand me so far?"

"Yes, sir."

"The U.S. ambassador in Buenos Aires has been advised of this Presidential Directive and directed to provide you with whatever you feel you need to accomplish your duties. The directors of the CIA and the FBI have similarly been notified of this directive and directed to furnish you with whatever support you feel you may need to carry out your duties."

"My God!"

"I told you he went ballistic. It began with him banging his fist on the desk and declaring, 'The assassination of a U.S. embassy official will not stand,' and got more heated from there. I don't think I've seen him so angry since we were under fire in 'Nam."

"Sir, you know I'm not qualified to do anything like this."

"The President apparently feels you are."

"From what I've seen, everybody from the ambassador on down has done everything possible . . . and is still doing everything possible."

"Apparently, the President doesn't think so. This is not open to debate, Charley. That's another quote."

"Yes, sir."

"To assist you in the accomplishment of your duties, the DCI has notified the CIA station chief that he is to place himself under your orders, and the director of the FBI has been ordered to send a team of FBI experts down there to assist you in your investigation, and the commander in chief CentCom has been ordered to dispatch an aircraft, together with adequate security personnel, to return the remains of Mr. Masterson, and his family, to the United States. I understand from General Naylor that that aircraft will be wheels-up within the hour—which means it's probably already in the air—and the senior officer aboard has been placed under your orders."

"Sir—"

"What part of 'this is not open to debate' did you miss, Charley?"

"I understand, sir."

"The only thing I need to hear from you—in addition to 'timely reports of any and all developments,' of course—is what assistance you think you need."

Castillo exhaled audibly.

"How are the FBI experts going to come down here? On the Air Force transport?"

"They have their own plane."

"Is there any chance you could send Jack Britton and Betty Schneider down here on either airplane?"

"Odd that you should ask, Charley. Just after the fireworks started, Joel told me that since he thought they were both spinning their wheels in the training academy, he had asked the superintendent of the school if he could get them out early to come here and take over your reading of the daily intel reports. I don't suppose you knew anything about this?"

"No, sir, I did not."

"The objections the superintendent had were twofold. It would set a bad precedent, and he had planned to ask for both to serve as instructors."

"Sir, I really—"

"By now both have been sworn in, issued credentials, and are probably already on their way here, if they haven't landed already. Joel can be very persuasive, if you hadn't noticed."

"I've noticed, sir."

"Why do you want them down there?"

"Because they're both cops, and I'm not, and Betty's a woman, and I'm not, and Jack is black, and I'm not."

" 'Welcome to the Secret Service. Don't unpack; go back to the airport, where an FBI plane is waiting for you. Castillo will explain everything when you get to Argentina.' "

"Can you do that, sir?"

"The truth is, Charley, that I can't *not* do it. I don't want to explain to the President why I didn't give you something you asked for."

"Sir, how about getting Dick Miller out of the hospital and having him vet the daily intel reports?"

"Charley, you know as well as I do that he just had yet another operation on his knee."

"Sir, he told me that just as soon as he can get out of bed, he's going on recuperative leave."

"And instead you want him to come over here with his knee in a cast and go through the daily intels?"

"I think he'd rather do that than lie in a bed at Walter Reed or go home."

"I'll see what I can find out, but refusing you that would be something I might be able to justify to the President. Even in his present state of mind, I think he might be sympathetic to my explanation, 'Sir, Major Miller is in Walter Reed, recovering from an operation on his knee.'"

"Yes, sir."

"I'll call you when I have ETAs on both planes."

"Thank you, sir."

"Charley, did you ever hear that 'no good deed goes unpunished'?"

"Yes, sir."

"I'm almost sorry—operative word *almost*—that you found the goddamn 727."

"Yes, sir."

[TWO]

"Doctor," the secretary of Homeland Security said into the phone to the chief, orthopedic surgery division, the Walter Reed Army Medical Center, at the other end of the line, "let me be sure I understand you. Presuming he keeps his leg as immobile as reasonably possible, there is no reason Major Miller has to stay in Walter Reed while waiting for his cast to be removed, and that will not be for fifteen days?

"And you have advised him of this and that he's free to go on recuperative leave?"

Hall looked at Joel Isaacson sitting in an office chair on the other side of the desk as Hall parroted the doctor:

"You have *strongly recommended personally* that he go

home and get TLC from his mother, whom you have known all of Major Miller's life.

"And you think I should know that Major Miller is at least as stubborn and hardheaded as his father, whom you have known even longer than you have his mother, as he has declined to take the recuperative leave despite your strong personal recommendation."

Isaacson smiled and shook his head.

"With your permission, Doctor, I'm going to ask Major Miller if he would like to perform some limited duty—administrative—in my office. If he agrees, I have a place—with room service—for him to stay, and can get a Yukon to haul him back and forth—"

"Just keep him off his leg? I can do that, sir."

"Joel, you call him," Secretary Hall directed. "If I call, he'll consider it an order."

Isaacson nodded and reached for Hall's telephone. Hall slid a yellow stick-'em note with the Walter Reed telephone number on it, and Isaacson punched it in.

"Put it on the speakerphone," Hall ordered.

"Dick, Joel Isaacson. Am I calling at a good time?"

"A good time for what?"

"For you to tell me how you're doing, for example?"

"I'm up to my ass, literally, in about thirty pounds of plaster of paris."

"How do you feel?"

"How would you feel, Joel, if you were up to your ass, literally, in thirty pounds of plaster of paris?"

"I thought they might let you go home on recuperative leave."

"They are trying to make me go home on recuperative leave."

"You don't want to go?"

"Tell me, Joel, if you were up to your ass in thirty pounds of plaster of paris, would you want to spend your days taking the correspondence courses offered by the Command and General Staff College?"

"I don't follow you."

"That is what Major General Miller has in mind for his beloved son to do. He has this thing about using one's time profitably, and never wasting a second."

"So what are you doing with your time?"

"Watching reruns of *Hollywood Squares* and *M*A*S*H* on the tube. I haven't been too successful in enticing any of the nurses to hop in bed with me."

"We need some help in the office. Couple of hours a day. Interested?"

"Joel, when was the last time you were kissed by a six-foot-two black man? When do you want me?"

"You didn't even ask what we need you to do."

"Quoting Clark Gable in *Gone With the Wind*, which I have seen two more times since I have been in here, 'Frankly, my dear, I don't give a damn!' "

"What if I came over in the morning and picked you up? You're still welcome in Charley's apartment, I guess?"

"What if you come over right now and pick me up? And where is that sonofabitch? He was supposed to bring me a bottle the day before yesterday and never showed up."

"He's in Argentina."

"I just saw that on Fox News. The bad guys blew Jack the Stack away. What's Charley got to do with that?"

"I'll tell you when you get here."

"And, back to that question, when will that be?"

"Hold one, Dick," Isaacson said, punched off the speakerphone, covered the microphone with his hand, and looked at Secretary Hall.

"Go get him," Hall ordered.

"Dick, I'll be over there in, say, half an hour," Isaacson said.

"Well, if that's the best you can do," Miller said, and hung up.

[THREE]

Castillo came out of the phone booth and smiled at the guy in charge of the communications room.

"Thank you," he said, and then, pointing at a coffeemaker, "What are my chances of getting a cup of that?"

"Couldn't be better, sir," the man said, and handed Castillo a china mug.

"Soldier or Marine?" Castillo asked.

"Soldier, sir. Sergeant First Class."

"Do you ever yearn for simple soldiering?" Castillo asked. "Nothing to worry about except maybe an IG inspection?"

"Sometimes, sir. But this is pretty interesting, and the life here is good."

"Did you know Mr. Masterson?"

"Yes, sir. One of the good guys. What the hell is going on?"

"Right now, nobody knows," Castillo said.

Including, or maybe especially, the guy who by direction of the President is now in charge of the investigation.

And who is about to become the most unpopular sonofabitch in the embassy, with everybody from the ambassador on down pissed at him.

And with cause.

They have done their very best, from a sense of duty plus their feelings of admiration for Masterson and his wife, and it hasn't been good enough.

They're probably thinking, Some hotshot who's been in Buenos Aires for two days is now in charge. God only knows what that sonofabitch said about us when he got on a secure line to Washington.

He took a sip of the coffee, burned his lip, and said, "Shit!"

"I should have warned you it was hot," the commo sergeant said.

"My fault," Castillo said.

Well, at least I learned how to handle a situation like this at The Point.

It's essentially a matter of what not to do.

You don't line the troops up and say, "Jesus, guys, wait until you hear what a dumb order we just got."

When you get a lawful order, no matter how dumb— and with all due respect, Mr. President, this decision of yours is about as dumb as orders get—you either refuse to obey it or you obey it.

And since this order cannot be refused—it's "not open for debate" and I have sworn a solemn oath, without any mental reservations whatsoever to cheerfully obey the orders of officers appointed over me, which would certainly include the President—that means I will have to go before the troops bubbling over with enthusiasm to carry out the brilliant order I have just received. And then do my goddamnedest to execute it.

"Can I take this with me? The ambassador wants to see me ten minutes ago."

"Sure," the sergeant said.

[FOUR]

"Sir, I just spoke with Secretary Hall, who told me what the President has ordered."

"The President made it crystal clear what he wishes done; what he wants you to do," Ambassador Silvio said.

"For your ears only, sir, I'm way out of my depth."

"The President doesn't seem to think so," Silvio said, "and that's all that really matters, isn't it?"

"Yes, sir, I guess it is."

"I've asked everybody with a role in this to come to the conference room. They're in there now."

"Have you said anything to them, sir?"

"I thought I would ask you what you would like me to say before I said anything."

"Sir, I think the simple facts—that the President told you he has given me the responsibility to get Mrs. Masterson and the children, and Mr. Masterson's body, safely out of the country, and that I am now in charge of the investigation—would be the best way to handle it."

"That's about what I was thinking," Silvio said. "Just before the President called me, I made a decision that I don't think is going to please the FBI team that's coming down."

"Yes, sir?"

"Colonel Munz asked for permission to perform the autopsy on Mr. Masterson's body and I gave that permission. It was a tough call."

"I'm not sure I follow you, sir."

"We get into a somewhat hazy area of law and diplomacy here," Silvio said. "A murder and an abduction have occurred. Those are violations of Argentine law. The murder of an official of the U.S. government, no matter where it occurs, is a violation of the United States Code, one of the few offenses for which the death penalty may be applied. . . ."

Castillo thought, *If I needed another proof that I don't know what the hell I'm doing, I never thought about any of this.*

". . . And in theory at least, the government can demand that the perpetrators be extradited to the United States for trial. I don't know—I just haven't had the time to look into it—where Mrs. Masterson's abduction fits into this, but her abduction violates Argentine law."

"I never even thought about this," Castillo confessed.

"I've given it some thought," Silvio said. "Now, presuming that the people who did this are apprehended, they would be arrested by the Argentines, and tried in an Argentine court. The problem I have with that is that if found guilty, the maximum penalty is twenty or twenty-five years' imprisonment."

"No death penalty," Castillo said.

"And, for your ears only, Mr. Castillo, while I would dearly love to see these people—what is that lovely phrase?—'hung by the neck until dead, dead, dead,' that's just not going to happen.

"Furthermore, extradition poses some problems. Unfortunately, a number of Argentine officials and more important legislators oppose anything we *norteamericanos* ask for—probably a vestige of Juan Domingo Perón—as a Pavlovian reflex. While I'm fairly certain that extradition would ultimately be approved, I'm not certain.

"Our death penalty enters into the equation. When I was a young consular officer in Paris, there was a terrible man from Philadelphia who stuffed his girlfriend in a trunk and let her petrify there. When this was finally discovered and he was arrested, his attorney—now Senator Arlen Specter, as a matter of interest—got him out on bail, which he promptly jumped. We finally located him in France. When we tried to have him extradited, French officials and legislators, who seem to share the Argentine fondness for denying anything we Americans ask, were more than a little difficult.

"One of the reasons they cited for denying extradition was that we have the death penalty, and they don't. There were other reasons, but that was one of their major moral arguments. It took us about twenty years to get this chap extradited from France. That took place just a couple of years ago. And I feel sure that our death penalty would be advanced as a reason for the Argentines to deny extradition."

"I heard that story," Castillo said. "I have some friends in the Philadelphia Police Department."

Including a former sergeant named Betty Schneider, who at this very moment is on her way down here. And who may not be nearly as delighted to see me as I will be to see her.

"Two of whom, sir," Castillo went on, "have become Secret Service agents. I asked that they be sent here to assist me. One of them is a woman, whom I intend to assign to Mrs. Masterson's security detail. The other is a very bright detective, who will keep his eyes on the investigation for me. He's a black guy, which I thought might be useful."

"So you do have some ideas what to do?" Silvio said. "I suspect you're not nearly as far out of your depth as you say you are."

Oh, yes I am. And did I ask for Sergeant Schneider because I wanted her to sit on Mrs. Masterson, or because I can't get her out of my mind? How does Dick Miller so cleverly phrase it? That I have the lamentable tendency to think with my dick?

"With all of these things in mind," Silvio said, "it seemed to me that justice—as much of it as can be expected in this circumstance—would best be served to have these scum tried and convicted in an Argentine court."

"Yes, sir. I understand."

"Which means, of course, that all evidence gathered will be retained by the Argentine judicial system; that extradition of these people, even if finally approved, would be futile. Even if we could get around the double jeopardy business, we would have no evidence to present. Plus, the very act—justified, legally permissible, or not—of asking for extradition would certainly offend Argentine pride. It would be tantamount to saying we don't trust their judicial system."

"Did you tell the President what you had decided, Mr. Ambassador?"

"The conversation, Mr. Castillo, was rather one-sided," Silvio said. "Is there anything else we should talk over before we go into the conference room, do you think?"

"I can't think of anything, sir."

[FIVE]

Everyone sitting at the long conference table stopped talking and rose to their feet as Ambassador Silvio and Castillo entered the room.

Alex Darby was at the foot of the table. Kenneth Lowery sat on his right, and Tony Santini on his left. The two FBI agents from Montevideo sat together. There were a dozen other men around the table. Castillo didn't know any by name, but some of them, the DEA people, he recognized from the brainstorming session Masterson had organized the day before. There were three people in uniform: an Air Force colonel, an Army colonel, and a Marine gunnery sergeant.

Castillo pegged them as the defense attaché, the military mission commander, and the NCO in charge of the

Marine guards. Everybody looked at Castillo with unabashed curiosity.

"Keep your seats, please, gentlemen," Silvio ordered,
as he walked to the head of the table. He put his hands
on the back of the chair there.

"For those of you who haven't had the opportunity to
meet him, this gentleman is Mr. C. G. Castillo, who is in
Argentina as the President's agent. A short time ago, the
President conveyed to me his decision to place Mr.
Castillo in charge of dealing with all aspects of the unfortunate situation we find ourselves in vis-à-vis Chief of
Mission J. Winslow Masterson and his family. The President further informed me that the secretary of state, the
secretary of defense, and the directors of the Central Intelligence Agency and the Federal Bureau of Investigation have been informed of his decision."

The ambassador looked at Castillo, said, "Mr.
Castillo, you have the floor," and sat in the first chair at
the side of the table.

Castillo looked around the room.

*There's not a hell of a lot of friendly faces looking at me.
As a matter of fact, none.*

Well, here goes.

"Good morning, gentlemen," Castillo began. "Our
priorities are these. First, the protection of Mrs. Masterson and her children. Second, the protection of all embassy personnel. Third, to cooperate with the Argentine
authorities in their investigation of what has happened.

"In regard to the last, after consulting with Ambassador Silvio, I have decided that we will proceed on the
assumption that the Argentine government will find out

who committed these crimes, arrest the culprits, and subject them to trial in Argentine courts."

"We're not even going to try to extradite these scumbags?" FBI agent Yung asked.

"That is what, after consultation with Ambassador Silvio, I have decided. And please don't interrupt me again until I open the floor for comments and questions," Castillo said.

There was some murmuring, but nothing more.

Well, I got away with that. Let's see what else I can get away with.

"With regard to Priority One: Mr. Santini, who has had extensive experience with the Secret Service Presidential Protection Detail, will assume responsibility for the protection of the Masterson family until we can get them safely out of the country. An Air Force transport is already in the air on its way down here to transport Mr. Masterson's body and his family to the United States.

"With regard to Priority Two: Mr. Lowery will put in place whatever heightened security measures he deems necessary for the protection of all other embassy personnel. I know the President has a deep interest in this, so I'd like, within the hour, a rough game plan from you, Mr. Lowery, so that after Ambassador Silvio approves it—or modifies it—I can send it to Washington."

Castillo looked at Lowery, who said, "Yes, sir. Within the hour."

Two down.

"With regard to Priority Three: Mr. Darby will handle all arrangements to cooperate with the Argentine authorities in their investigation of this situation, and, coordinating with Mr. Santini and Mr. Lowery, the incorporation of what security personnel the Argentine government provides into our own security arrangements.

"Further, the FBI is sending a team of investigators down here. They will report to Mr. Darby. Mr. . . . Yung, is it?"

"Yung," he confirmed.

"You will be responsible for the logistic support of the FBI team. Find them someplace to live, to operate, automobiles, whatever they need, and also keep Ambassador Silvio, Mr. Darby, Mr. Lowery, Mr. Santini, and myself advised on a timely basis of whatever their investigation develops.

"The Secret Service is sending two special agents down here. One, Special Agent Schneider, will report to Mr. Santini to assist in the protection of the Masterson family. Special Agent Britton will monitor both the Argentine's and our investigation—including, of course, the FBI's—and report to the ambassador and me what information he comes up with. I will, since both special agents will be working for me, handle their logistic requirements."

Now how the hell are you going to do that?

"Finally, to ensure everyone's working on the same page, and to ensure that someone sitting behind a desk in Washington doesn't start to try to micromanage what we're going to do here, there will be no communication by any means—radio, e-mail, or telephone—with any agency in Washington unless it has been first vetted by the ambassador or myself."

"You're telling me, sir, that I'm forbidden to communicate with the bureau?" Yung demanded.

"Thank you for the opportunity to make myself perfectly clear, Agent Yung, as apparently my request to finish without interruption also went unheard," Castillo said icily. "You are forbidden to communicate with the bureau—or anyone else—absent the approval of the ambassador or myself in every instance. Got it?"

There was a moment's hesitation. Then a cold, "I've got it."

"Now, are there any questions or comments?"

There were far fewer questions and comments than Castillo expected.

There is, however, a sullen, bubbling resentment toward Presidential Agent Castillo that can be cut with a knife.

But I think trying to be a nice guy would have made things even worse.

"Well, if that's it, gentlemen, thank you for your time and attention. Now let's get to work. Mr. Darby and Mr. Santini, will you remain behind, please?"

"Will you be needing me for anything else, Mr. Castillo?" Ambassador Silvio asked, when everyone but Darby and Santini had left the room.

"If you would, sir. Give me another minute."

"Of course."

"Tony, Alex, that commo block doesn't apply to either of you. But I couldn't keep just the FBI off the horn. And I really didn't want some hotshot second-guessing what we're going to try to do here." He looked at Darby. "Remember the Langley hotshots with access to a satellite phone in Afghanistan, Alex?"

"Painfully," Darby chuckled.

"Joel said you were really a hardnose," Santini said. "You did very well in here just now, Ace."

"I wish I thought so."

"I thought so, too," Ambassador Silvio said. "I did wonder, however, why you claimed my decision not to go for extradition as your own?"

"We had a saying in Afghanistan, sir, when we did something we suspected might get us in hot water. 'Screw it. What are they going to do, send me to Afghanistan?' "

Silvio chuckled.

"There's also an expression, 'If you can't stand the heat, get out of the kitchen.' But that was gracious of you, Mr. Castillo. I'm grateful."

"Sir, do you think you could bring yourself to call me 'Charley'?"

"Of course. Thank you. My first name is Juan. My friends usually call me John."

"My real first name is Carlos, sir, and with your permission, I will continue to call you 'sir' and 'Mr. Ambassador.' "

"Charley, who are these two agents they're sending down?" Santini asked.

"They're both ex–Philadelphia cops. We worked with them when we were looking for the 727. The lady was a sergeant in intelligence, and the guy worked deep cover for years for counterterrorism. Hall was impressed with both of them, and told Joel to recruit them. Joel just got them out of the training academy early to work in Hall's office. So they were available."

"What are you going to do with them?"

Well, as far as the sergeant is concerned, I am going to look passionately into her beautiful eyes and get as much cabernet sauvignon down her lovely throat as possible.

"This is why I asked you to stay, Mr. Ambassador," Castillo said. "Alex, I was at the hospital when you and Lowery were talking with her—"

"Munz told me you were there," Darby interrupted.

"—and I had the feeling, Alex, that you weren't getting the truth, the whole truth, and nothing but."

Darby's eyes first registered surprise, and then hardened.

"Charley, she was coming out of the drug; she didn't know what she was saying."

"She knew enough to be very concerned about her kids," Castillo said. "But when it came to any detail of her abduction, she drew a blank. Not a partial blank, Alex, a blanket blank."

"That was not the feeling I had," Darby said.

"Well, what we're going to do now is go over to the hospital so that you—and if you can spare the time, Mr. Ambassador, you, too—can introduce her to Tony and me. At which time, Tony will ask her what happened, and what she remembers."

Darby shook his head.

"Why would she lie? About what?" he asked.

"I think Mr. Cast—Charley—is suggesting that her abductors told her to tell you—us—as little as possible, and threatened her," Silvio said.

"Yes, sir," Castillo said. "And we need all the information we can get."

"After they blew Jack away," Darby pursued, "it seems to me she would want to tell us anything we wanted to know."

"Unless they threatened her children," Castillo said. "If they were willing to blow her husband away, she knew they'd be willing to hurt the kids. Kill the kids. Or maybe her family. Her father and the brother."

"I think you're really reaching, Charley," Darby said.

"What brother?" Santini asked.

"He works for the UN," Castillo said. "That's about all I know, except what Alex told me about his not getting along with Masterson."

"I met him once, years ago," Silvio said. "He has some sort of liaison, coordination-of-agencies job in Paris. I was thinking of perhaps trying to get in touch with him, so that he could break this news to his father, who has some sort of heart problem."

"Sir—Alex, do you know his name?"

"Lorimer," Alex said. "Jean-Pierre, Jean-Paul, something like that. French. The ambassador's—Betsy's father's—first name is Philippe."

"They're French?"

"Maybe way back, way way back, like Jack's family," Darby said. "Jack used to delight in telling people who hated the South that there were three Mastersons—'free men of color'—who were Confederate officers, two in the navy and one in the army. If he was really pulling their chain, he'd say the family had made its money in the slave trade."

Silvio chuckled.

"Was there money, Alex?" Castillo asked. "Before he was run over by the beer truck?"

"Not that kind of money, but yeah. Both families are more than—what's the word?—'comfortable.' Sugar, I think, and cotton. Growing it and dealing in it."

"Mr. Ambassador," Charley said, "I was going to suggest that you get in touch with the State Department and see if we can get a location, maybe even a telephone number, on the brother. In case we can't get that information from Mrs. Masterson."

"I'll get right on it," Silvio said, "and if you'd like, I'll go to the German Hospital with you and introduce you and Tony to Mrs. Masterson."

"Thank you, sir. That will be very helpful."

[SIX]
The German Hospital
Avenida Pueyrredón
Buenos Aires, Argentina
1305 23 July 2005

El Coronel Alfredo Munz of SIDE walked up to them as they entered the lobby of the hospital.

"Your Excellency, gentlemen," he said in Spanish. "What a fortunate happenstance. I was about to call Señor Castillo and ask if he could spare me a moment of his time."

"Fortunate happenstance," my ass. Munz wasn't surprised at all to see us. He was waiting for us, which means he knew we were coming here.

How did he do that?

He's got somebody inside the embassy, more than likely, to keep an eye on things generally and the ambassador in particular. Somebody who heard the ambassador call for his car to bring us here, or someone listening to that allegedly encrypted radio in his car, or Darby's, or maybe hearing the Marine guard calling Lowery to update him on the ambassador's location.

Why am I surprised? Both Darby and Santini told me SIDE's good, and with this business going on, they've got their act in high gear.

But what does he want with me?

"*Mi coronel,* I am at your disposal," Castillo said, and then, to the ambassador, "Sir, why don't you go up to Mrs. Masterson's room? I know where it is and I can catch up with you."

Munz led Castillo to a corner of the lobby.

"You have at once greatly disappointed several important people in the Ministry of Information, Herr Gossinger," Munz said in German, "and added a little excitement to what I'm sure you and I would both regard as their rather boring and mundane lives."

Oh, shit. He found out I entered the country as Gossinger.

And I never went to the Ministry of Information to register as a journalist.

Castillo smiled at him.

"How is that, *Herr Oberst?*" he replied in German.

Munz handed him a sheet of paper. It was a copy of

the immigration form Castillo had filled out on the airplane and handed to the immigration officer at the airport. It also had his photograph, obviously taken by a good and unobtrusive camera as he stood at the immigration booth.

"They so wanted to explain to a prominent German journalist how concerned the Argentine government is with this sad situation, and then, when you failed to show up at the Ministry of Information, as you promised to do, they thought that perhaps this German fellow had something to do with the villains we're looking for."

"Actually, my name is Gossinger," Charley began.

"I know. I took the trouble to find out. The German embassy told me you are not only a distinguished foreign correspondent for the *Tages Zeitung,* but the great-great-grandson of the founder. What a wonderful cover! A second persona that is real."

"I feel like a kid caught with my hand in the cookie jar. What happens now?"

"I've assured them that not only have I informed you of our efforts to get to the bottom of this situation, but also that I told you it would be unnecessary to register with the Ministry of Information. There is no longer a problem."

"Thank you."

"And I have this for you, too."

He handed him a small, plastic-covered card. It read "Corps Diplomatique" and had his photograph and Gossinger's name on it.

"A diplomatic carnet, in case one of our ever-alert police would ask why you're carrying a pistol."

"A pistol?"

"Actually, it was my intention to loan you one, but I see under your suit coat that you're already carrying one in the small of your back."

"The ambassador lent it to me."

"Karl—you don't mind if I call you 'Karl,' do you?"

"Herr Oberst, you may call me anything you wish."

"There are some very dangerous people here in Argentina, I'm afraid, and I'm not talking about our cottage kidnapping industry. I haven't been able to come up with any connection between Herr Masterson and them—from what I have, he's, in that charming North American phrase, 'Mr. Clean'—but that doesn't mean there isn't one. And these people have proven that murder is just part of their game. I would be very sorry if they decided to eliminate you."

"You don't think this is a kidnapping, do you?"

"Do you?"

"Well, they abducted her, so that's a kidnapping. But it smells."

"Yes, it does. You have no ideas whatever?"

"None."

"If you did, would you tell me?"

Castillo met his eyes.

"Yes, I would. Between us, what did you think when Mrs. Masterson was being . . . I guess the word is 'interrogated' by Darby and Lowery?"

"I would not describe her responses as fully forthcoming."

"What do you think she's hiding?"

"There may be more to it than this, but the first thing that came to my mind was that they threatened her—probably her children—if she revealed anything she had learned about them."

"Why didn't they kill her?"

"They want something from her. Maybe Masterson didn't bring the ransom with him. And they are threatening to kill the children if she doesn't get it to them. I just don't know."

"Tony Santini is an experienced Secret Service agent—"

"I know. Did he really injure himself falling off the President's limousine?"

Castillo thought a moment before replying, "The *Vice* President's limousine."

"How embarrassing for him!"

"Anyway," Charley said, ignoring the subject, "the ambassador's going to introduce him as the Secret Service man assigned to protect her and the children, and he's going to use that to see what he can get out of her."

"And is he going to tell her of your appointment as the generalissimo in charge?"

"You heard about that, too, did you, Alfredo?"

"Like yourself, Karl, I'm sure, I like to keep my ear to the grindstone."

"*Nose* to the grindstone, ear to the *ground*," Castillo smilingly corrected him.

"Thank you," Munz said.

"There's a planeload of FBI agents on their way down here to assist in the investigation. And two Secret Service agents to assist me. One is a really bright female with a good deal of experience in intelligence. I'm going to put her on the protection detail, hoping she'll be able to get to Mrs. Masterson. The other one is a very good, street-smart cop who worked under deep cover in really bad situations for years. I'm going to have him look at what the FBI comes up with, and I would be grateful if you would let him see what you've come up with."

"Certainly, but there's not much."

"There's also an Air Force transport on its way to transport Masterson's body and his family home."

"Are you going with them?"

Jesus, I never thought about that!

"Maybe. But if I do, I have the feeling that I'll be coming back."

Munz nodded, then put out his hand.

"I'm glad we had this chance to chat, Karl."

"Thank you for everything, Alfredo."

[SEVEN]

Mrs. Elizabeth Masterson was not in the intensive care room where she had first been placed, but Castillo had no trouble in finding the room to which she had been moved. There were four uniformed Policía Federal, un-der the command of a sergeant, and two men in civilian clothing—one of them Paul Sieno, the CIA agent—hovering around a door near the end of the corridor.

Sieno nodded at Castillo, who then knocked on the door. A moment later, Ambassador Silvio opened it a crack, and then all the way.

"Come in, Mr. Castillo," he said, and as Castillo went through the door, the ambassador went on, "Betsy, here's Mr. Castillo."

Mrs. Masterson was sitting up in a hospital bed. She was in a nightgown that had to be hers from home, and Castillo saw there were two other women in the room, almost certainly Darby's wife and the ambassador's. They were sitting in chairs along the wall, and Darby and Santini were leaning on the wall next to them.

Castillo walked up to the bed.

"The President has asked me to tell you how terribly sorry he is, Mrs. Masterson."

That little lie came quickly to my lips, didn't it?

Well, if the President had thought about it, he would have.

"That's very kind of him," Mrs. Masterson said. She did not offer her hand and her smile was visibly an effort.

"And if I may, I would like to offer my own condolences."

When there was no response to this except the frozen smile, Castillo went on, "My orders, ma'am, are first to absolutely guarantee your safety, and that of your children, and then to get you to the United States just as quickly and as safely as possible."

The smile remained fixed, and she said nothing.

"Has Ambassador Silvio told you that Mr. Santini has many years' experience on the Secret Service Presidential Protection Detail?"

"Yes, he has."

"And the Argentine authorities have provided us with some of their very best men to help Mr. Santini."

"So the ambassador has told me."

"We hope to have word very soon about the arrival of the aircraft the President has sent down here. One of them is a transport, which will carry you and your family to the United States just as soon as you feel up to it, and the other is bringing both a team of FBI experts to assist in the investigation, and two Secret Service agents for your protection detail. One of them is a female agent."

Mrs. Masterson nodded.

"I'm very much aware, Mrs. Masterson, that this is a difficult time for you . . ."

Mrs. Masterson snorted.

". . . but I hope you'll understand that certain plans have to be made."

"Such as?"

"Where in the United States would you like to go?"

"Keesler," she said. "Keesler Air Force Base in Biloxi is closest to Jack's parents' home. In Pass Christian."

"Pass Chris-tee-ann"? That's the French pronunciation. And while I'm on that subject . . . what about her brother, who's supposed to be in France?

"Is there someone there, in Pass Christian, who we can contact? Your father?"

"My father lives in Metairie—New Orleans. And he has a heart condition. My father-in-law lives in Pass Christian. I really think he'd be the man to break this to my father. I was just talking about that, frankly, with Mrs. Silvio when you came in, Mr. Castillo. She's going to call Jack's father, or the ambassador is, just as soon as they can get to a phone. I hope they can get through to him before he sees it on CNN or Fox. And then I'll call him, of course, when they let me out of here."

"Have they told you when that's going to be?"

"They want to keep me overnight for observation," she said, then turned to the ambassador. "Juan, can't you do something about that? I want to be with the children."

"I understand," Silvio said. "But they really want to look for signs of whatever that drug might have done to you. If you'd like, we can bring the kids here to see you."

"No. I don't want them to see me like this. They're better off with Julia."

Julia, presumably, is Darby's wife.

"They're in school now?" Castillo asked.

"Their father has just been murdered," she snapped. "Of course they're not in school."

"Forgive me," Castillo said.

Then the other woman is Lowery's wife; Darby's wife—Julia, the old friend of the family—is with the kids.

"Is there anyone else, ma'am, that we should contact?"

"No. I'll notify everyone just as soon as I'm out of here."

That "no" came really quick. Wouldn't she want to tell her brother, even if he didn't get along with her husband?

"Mrs. Masterson, I won't intrude on your grief anymore. If there's anything you need, all you'll have to do is tell Mr. Santini."

"Thank you."

Castillo nodded at the people in the room and walked out.

He had taken half a dozen steps to the elevator when

Ambassador Silvio caught up with him. Santini was on the ambassador's heels.

"I'm forced to agree with you, Mr. Cas—Charley," Silvio said. "She's concealing something."

"I got nowhere with her, either," Santini said.

"Mr. Ambassador, she didn't even mention her brother," Castillo said. "Would you be willing to try to get him on the telephone?"

"I thought that was odd, too," Silvio agreed. "I'll put a call in to him just as soon as I get back to the embassy. Where will you be?"

"At the embassy, sir. I want to get the ETAs of the airplanes."

"Then I'll see you there."

[EIGHT]
The United States Embassy
Avenida Colombia 4300
Palermo, Buenos Aires, Argentina
1450 23 July 2005

It was a frustrating forty-five minutes on the telephone.

Even getting the number of the United Nations European directorate of interagency coordination was frustrating. The Buenos Aires international operator had trouble first connecting to and then communicating with the Paris information operator.

Silvio gave up on that and called the American embassy in Paris. The political attaché had somewhat reluctantly—and only after Silvio had proven to him who he was—provided a listing for the directorate, but said he had neither an address nor a number for a Jean-Paul Lorimer.

A somewhat nasal-voiced French woman at the directorate told Silvio—whose French was fluent—that M'sieu Lorimer was out of the office, that she had no number at which he could be reached, and that any further inquiries should be directed to the director of information. She was unmoved by Silvio's announcement that he was the United States ambassador to Argentina, and was trying to contact Lorimer because there had been a death in the family.

The only address and telephone number the State Department in Washington and the United States Mission to the United Nations in New York City had for Lorimer was his office.

"Let me see what the Secret Service can do, sir," Castillo said, finally, and started to punch in Isaacson's number in Washington on his cell phone.

"You don't want to get a secure line?"

"What's classified?" Castillo said, and immediately added, "I didn't mean to sound flip, sir. Sorry."

"I didn't think you were being flip," Silvio said. "It was a dumb question."

"Isaacson."

"Charley, Joel."

"I see we're being telepathic again," Isaacson replied. "I was just about to call you about the FBI plane—on which, I'm sure you'll be thrilled to hear, Casanova, is the beauteous Agent Schneider—and the C-17."

"You didn't say something allegedly witty to her, did you, Joel?"

"No, but I was sorely tempted. She really is a delight to the eyes, and I felt duty-bound to warn her about you."

"Tell me about the airplanes."

"She and Jack Britton are on a Gulfstream Five, which left here at eleven-oh-five local time. They make about four hundred sixty knots, and it's about fifty-two hundred miles from here to there, so you figure it out."

Without asking permission, Castillo snatched a pencil from a mug on Silvio's desk. Silvio quickly handed him a yellow lined pad.

"The call sign is Air Force Zero-Four-Seven-Seven. They're bound for an airport called Jorge Newbery, which I presume is somewhere near Buenos Aires. Also on the plane are six somewhat annoyed FBI agents, pissed not only because they were told to report to you—as Secret Service, not Presidential Hotshot—but because two of their number got bumped because Schneider and Britton got on."

"Jorge Newbery is the downtown airport in Buenos Aires."

"The C-17—tail number Air Force Zero-Three-Eight-One—left Charleston Air Force Base, South Carolina, an hour earlier, but it's going to—probably already has—made a stop at Hurlburt, where it picked up a dozen Air Commandos ready to go to war, and a ten-man spit-and-polish detail from the Old Guard under a lieutenant for the burial party, who were conveniently in Florida burying some retired general."

"Jesus."

"I think you can guess where that order originated,"

Isaacson added. "Anyway, the C-17 will be landing at an airfield called Ezeiza—"

"That's the main international field."

"I guess they couldn't get that big airplane into the little airport."

"You can sit a Globemaster down in your backyard, Joel."

"No kidding. Well, for some reason, that's where it's going. And it will take however long after it leaves Hurlburt to go forty-two hundred nautical miles at four hundred fifty knots."

Castillo scribbled down those numbers.

"Okay. Got it. Now I need something from you."

"Shoot."

"The widow's brother, Jean-Paul Lorimer, works for the UN in Paris. The ambassador has been trying for forty-five minutes to get him on the phone without any luck. Have we got anybody in Paris who can help?"

"I'll get right on it."

"Call the embassy here and leave the numbers and address with the ambassador's secretary."

"Done. You got anything else you want me to tell the boss?"

"I put Tony Santini in charge of the Mastersons' security. She came out of the drug they gave her all right, but they're keeping her in the hospital overnight. I don't know when she'll want to leave here, but when she does, she wants to go to Keesler Air Force Base in Mississippi, near where he lived."

"She wants to bury him there?"

"Apparently."

"I know the President was thinking of Arlington . . ."

"I think she wants the family plot in Mississippi, Joel."

"That's going to pose a little problem. I also know the President wants Walter Reed to do the autopsy."

"The Argentines are already doing the autopsy. And they're going to prosecute these bastards, presuming we can catch them, in Argentine courts."

"Who decided that?"

"I did," Charley said. He met Silvio's eyes, and added, "The ambassador concurs."

"I think that may cause more than a little pique at the highest level, Charley."

"There was considerable doubt that we could extradite the doers. And the crime occurred here. And it's a done deed. The ambassador has already told the Foreign Ministry."

"I think the boss will more than likely want to talk to you about that, Charley. Or maybe his boss will."

"I thought that might happen."

"We'll be in touch, Charley. Watch your back."

Castillo pushed the disconnect button, and then did the calculation of the arrival times.

"Both planes will probably arrive here between eleven and midnight tonight," he announced to Ambassador Silvio, "the Gulfstream to Jorge Newbery, and the C-17 at Ezeiza. There's an honor guard from the Third Infantry Regiment—'the Old Guard'—on the Globemaster, plus a detail of Air Commandos."

"As a suggestion, if you want to meet your agents and the FBI, I can have the defense attaché meet the transport."

"Thank you."

"He'll have to arrange transportation for them, and a place to live. I think the best thing to do with the military personnel is move them in with the Marines. And you told that FBI agent Yung to arrange to take care of the FBI. What about your agents?"

"I'll take care of them. But I am going to need wheels. Can I rent cars for them?"

"You could, but the rentals here are generally small and not always reliable. And they don't have radios. I'll have Ken Lowery deal with it. How many are you going to need?"

"If I can keep the one I have, one more. I really don't need a driver."

"You never know," the ambassador said. "I'll tell Ken to get you another car and a driver. Tonight?"

"First thing in the morning."

"And what are you going to do now?"

"Sir?"

"What are your immediate plans? For the next forty-five minutes or an hour?"

"I don't have any, sir. I thought I might go have a look at the Masterson house."

"Have you had breakfast?"

"No, sir."

"Neither have I, and it's now after three. Fortunately, right around the corner from here is a restaurant—the Rio Alba—that serves what I believe are the finest steaks in the world. Why don't we go have one while we wait to hear from your friend in the Secret Service?"

"I think that's a splendid idea, sir."

VII

The Marine guard—who Castillo had learned was Staff Sergeant Roger Markham, twenty years old, of Des Moines, Iowa, who had been a seventeen-year-old fresh from Parris Island when he had been on the Marine March to Baghdad before being assigned to the Marine Embassy Guard battalion—pulled the embassy BMW 545i to a smooth stop in front of the Four Seasons and started to open his door.

Castillo caught his arm.

"If you try to rush around and open my door, Roger, I swear to God you'll regret it."

Markham looked at him sheepishly.

"It's now a little after nine," Castillo said. "The plane's due at eleven-thirty, give or take, which means we should leave here around eleven. What are your plans for those two hours?"

"Wait."

"Here?"

"Right here."

"Can you leave the car here?"

"Dip plates. I can leave it anywhere."

"What you are going to do, Roger, is park it. The driveway is right there." Castillo pointed to the entrance of the hotel's basement garage. "And then you're going to come to my room, where we will try to get a little shut-eye."

"Whatever you say, s—"

"There you go again," Castillo said. "What do they do to you at Parris Island, give you fifty push-ups every time you to forget to say 'sir'?"

"Fifty, sometimes a hundred. Sorry."

"Not really a problem, but try, huh?"

Markham nodded.

"Go park the car," Castillo said, and got out.

As he walked through the lobby Castillo remembered that he had not gotten rooms for Betty Schneider and Jack Britton.

That proved to be more of a problem than he anticipated.

The house was nearly full, the assistant manager on duty told him. After ten minutes of consulting the computer, it was decided that Herr Gossinger would move from his suite—1550—into 1500. Fifteen hundred was far grander than Castillo needed, and consequently far more expensive.

He toyed with the idea of putting Betty into 1500, but decided against it.

She would almost certainly decide that I was plying her with luxurious accommodation as part of my wicked and devious plan to get into her pants.

If I thought that would work, I'd rent the whole god-damn floor.

Vacating 1550 made it available to someone else, and somehow that freed up 1510 and 1518, both very nice single rooms with views of Avenida 9 Julio and the port. Both were equipped with two queen-sized beds. Castillo asked the assistant manager which was farthest from 1500 and was told 1518.

"Put Señorita Schneider in fifteen-eighteen, please."

"Would you like to have a bottle of champagne and some flowers—roses, perhaps?—waiting for the young lady, Señor Gossinger?"

"I don't think that would be a very good idea, thank you."

As far as the young lady is concerned, our relationship is—and will remain—professional and platonic.

There wasn't much that had to be moved from 1550 to 1500, and there were two bellmen and Sergeant Markham to help him, but it was after nine-thirty before the process was completed.

"I am now going to drink one of these," Castillo said, holding up two bottles of Quilmes beer from the in-room bar, "and then make a valiant attempt to catch a few winks." He extended a bottle to Markham, and added, "I suggest you do the same."

"I'm not sure I should be drinking," Markham said.

"Trust me, Roger, you should drink that beer."

• • •

With Sergeant Markham stretched out on the couch in the sitting room of suite 1500, Castillo lay down on the super-king-sized bed in the bedroom. The first thing that came to mind were mental images, not all of which could honestly be deemed lewd and obscene, of Special Agent Schneider.

He finally chased them away with images of Jack the Stack Masterson in the taxicab.

Jesus, was that only this morning?

When his cellular telephone buzzed, he was dreaming. In his dream, Sergeant Schneider was being much, much more affectionate than she had ever been in his waking hours.

He looked at his watch. He had been asleep for fifteen minutes.

"Castillo."

"I really hope I either woke you up or interrupted something really indecent," Major H. Richard Miller's very familiar voice announced.

You have no idea, you sonofabitch!

How did he get this number?

"How's the knee?"

"How do you think it is? After every sonofabitch and his brother has been digging around in it for a month with the very latest in shiny sharp instruments of torture?"

"What's up, Dick?"

"We can't find this Lorimer guy in Paris, and God knows I've tried. You are going to have one hell of a phone bill, old pal."

"You sound as if you're not calling from your Walter Reed bed of pain."

"Actually, having accepted your kind invitation to share your pad," Miller said, "I'm lying on your couch in the Mayflower as we speak. In the morning they will roll me into your office at the Nebraska complex, where I will lie on your couch there."

"What about Lorimer?"

"Well, we finally got an address for him, seven Rue Monsieur, and a phone number. No answer on the phone. Isaacson called some Secret Service guy he knows in Paris. The guy went there. The concierge said she had no idea where Lorimer was, but that he was often gone for a week or two. His car is in the garage. Isaacson said that he's going to ask Secretary Hall to ask Secretary Cohen to lean on the UN to find out where he is. And Isaacson said for me to call you and bring you up to speed."

"Thanks, Dick. Are you sure you're all right to work?"

"I'm fine. I presume the love of your life has not yet arrived?"

"Screw you. And if you're referring to Betty Schneider, the ETA is twenty-three-thirty local."

"An hour difference between here and there, huh?"

"It's almost ten here."

"As a friendly word of advice I'm almost positive you will ignore, try to think with your upper brain for a change, before you do something stupid with that woman."

"Jesus Christ!" Castillo heard himself flare. "She's no longer a cop that I can make a pass at. She's now in the

Secret Service and she works for me. I still like to think of myself as an officer and a gentleman. So fuck you, Dick!"

There was a moment's silence, and then Miller said, "Charley, ol' buddy, you have no idea how happy that outburst made me. I'll be in touch."

The line went dead.

Castillo sat up in the bed and turned the light on.

I don't know where that outburst came from, either, but it was right on the money. I can't make a pass at Special Agent Schneider. I shouldn't even be fantasizing about her.

Moot point. She has made it as clear as humanly possible that she has no interest in me at all.

But I'm glad Dick brought it up.

I am entirely capable of doing the wrong thing, and probably would have.

What the hell is the matter with me?

In one movement, he laid the cellular on the bedside table and fell back on the bed.

Then, a moment later, he sat up again, picked up the phone, and punched the autodial button for Howard Kennedy.

Kennedy answered on the third ring.

"Hello?"

"Did I wake you up, Howard?"

"As a matter of fact, no."

"Are you in the hotel?"

"Why?"

"I thought we might have a drink. There's a jazz quartet in the bar."

"Very kind of you, but what I'm doing is standing in

the rain at Ezeiza watching ground handlers in whom I have no confidence whatsoever loading very expensive— and very nervous—horses onto an airplane. I'll take a rain check, though."

"Are you going with the horses wherever they're going?"

"As a matter of fact, yes."

"But you'll be coming back soon?"

Kennedy's silence indicated he wasn't going to answer the question.

"Pity," Castillo went on, "some old friends of yours are coming to town."

There was another silence long enough to make Castillo think Kennedy was not going to respond when he did:

"The major crime investigation team from Quantico?"

"I don't know where they're from, but they're coming from Washington."

"Have you got their names?"

This time Castillo hesitated before replying.

Why the hell not get him the names? What harm can it do?

"I can get them as soon as they get off the Gulfstream."

"When will that be?"

"Eleven-thirty, give or take. I told another of your former associates to meet the plane and find them someplace to sleep."

"What's his name?"

"Yung. He's stationed in Montevideo—"

"Chinese? Feisty little bastard? Round face, five-eight, one-fifty?"

"Yeah. You know him?"

"Very well. What did he tell you he's doing in Montevideo?"

"He didn't tell me he's doing anything. I have the impression he's just one more of your former associates looking into money laundering. The ambassador asked the ambassador in Montevideo if any of them had kidnapping experience, and he sent Yung and another guy here."

"His name?"

"I don't have it handy. But I can get it."

"Where are they landing? Here?"

"Jorge Newbery. There's a transport on the way that should land at Ezeiza at about the same time."

"I just saw an Air Force colonel in full uniform surrounded by Argentine Air Force brass; I wondered what he was up to."

"I'm going to get the family—and the body—out of here just as soon as I can."

"What were you planning to chat about, Charley, while we were listening to the jazz quartet?"

"I thought I might idly inquire if you had ever heard of a fellow named Jean-Paul Lorimer."

Kennedy replied by spelling Lorimer in the phonetic alphabet.

"Correct."

"Never heard of him, but if you get me those names, I'll be happy to ask around."

"Deal. How do I get them to you?"

"On the phone. How else?"

"I thought you were about to leave."

"I'll leave after I have those names."

"Done."

"Here's a freebie, Charley. Whatever David William Yung, Jr., is doing in Montevideo, it almost certainly has very little to do with examining bank statements."

"You mean he's looking for you?"

"That, too, of course. But that's not what I meant. He's a real hotshot; they don't waste people like David looking for dirty money."

"You sound as if you know him well."

"I told you I did. We used to work together."

"Can you give me a hint?"

"I just did. I'll be waiting for your call, Charley."

The line went dead.

[TWO]
Aeropuerto Internacional Jorge Newbery
Buenos Aires, Argentina
2305 23 July 2005

Sergeant Roger Markham had just turned the embassy BMW 545i onto Avenida 9 Julio near the Four Seasons hotel when the radio went off.

"Yung for Castillo."

Castillo was looking around for a microphone when Markham put one in his hand. Castillo took it and pushed the PRESS TO TALK button.

"Go."

"Sir, the aircraft will be parked on the private aviation side of the field."

"Got it. Thank you."

"Sir, ETA is forty-five minutes."

"Got it. Thank you. We're on the way."

"Out."

Well, he not only told me where the airplane will be parked, which he didn't have to do, but he called me "sir." Maybe he's resigned to me being in charge and decided he might as well go along; but on the other hand, it's equally likely, considering that everybody in the FBI got the Castillo-knows-Kennedy memo, he thinks that if we can become pals, I just might let something slip that would put him onto Howard Kennedy.

What the hell did Kennedy mean when he said, "Whatever Yung's doing he's not looking for dirty money"?

"You might as well slow down, Roger. They're forty-five minutes out."

"Am I driving too fast, sir?"

"I wish there was someplace we could get a cup of coffee," Castillo said. "Back to the hotel?"

"There's all kinds of restaurants on the river near the airport."

"Pick one."

"Yes, s— I'll do that."

"Don't let this go to your head, Roger, but maybe there's some hope for you after all."

• • •

It was raining hard when they got to the civilian side of Jorge Newbery airfield, so hard that Castillo wondered if the Gulfstream was going to be able to land.

There was only one runway, paralleling the bank of the Río de la Plata, and it didn't look like a fun place to try to land in a driving rain with gusting winds.

On the tarmac in front of a Southern Winds hangar, he saw a BMW with diplomat plates, two small white Mercedes-Benz buses, called *Traffiks,* each of which had a cardboard sign with CD lettered on it taped to the windshield, and a Peugeot sedan with Argentine plates.

When Sergeant Markham pulled in beside the buses, Castillo saw that the interior lights of one of the buses were on and saw Special Agent Yung, holding a newspaper, looking out at them. There was an Air Force major on the bus.

If I sit here, eventually Yung will come here, establishing me as King of the Hill. But he will get drenched and make the seats here wet. And I can get a much better look at him in the bus than I can here. I want to see his eyes.

Castillo turned to Markham.

"I suppose it's too much to expect you to have an umbrella?" The sergeant produced one instantly, seemingly out of thin air. Castillo chuckled appreciatively. "Thank you, Roger, for the umbrella."

As Castillo reached the bus, and the door swung open inwardly with a *whoosh,* two men got out of the Peugeot and, holding newspapers over their heads, half ran toward it.

"Well, what do you think, Yung? Are they going to be able to get in?"

"Señor Castillo?" one of the Argentine men said, and when Castillo turned, he was handed a small, handheld transceiver. He saw that it was lit up and tuned to what he presumed was the Jorge Newbery tower frequency.

He put it to his ear. There was the to-be-expected hissing, which suddenly cleared.

"Jorge Newbery, this is United States Air Force Zero-Four-Seven-Seven. I have your runway in sight," a cheerful, confident American voice announced.

Castillo handed the Argentine the radio.

"Thank you," he said, and then to Yung: "Talk about timing!"

He sat down so that he could see out the windshield.

For a moment he could see nothing, and then, a second after he spotted first a Grimes light, and then the navigation lights, a very bright landing light suddenly blazed.

The glistening white Gulfstream—a U.S. Air Force C-37A—came in low and touched down immediately after the threshold. The words UNITED STATES OF AMERICA were lettered boldly down the side of the fuselage. They were illuminated so the legend couldn't be missed, telling Castillo the airplane belonged to the 89th Presidential Airlift Group at Andrews Air Force Base, Maryland. Only their airplanes had the classy paint jobs.

Castillo felt a lump in his throat. It was like seeing the colors flying somewhere very foreign. Which indeed was the case now.

"Jesus, that's a pretty bird!" the Air Force major said, softly.

"My sentiments exactly, Major," Castillo said, smiled, and offered the major his hand. "My name is Castillo."

"Yes, sir, I know. My name is Jossman, sir."

"You're going to take care of the crew?"

"The embassy administrative officer put everyone in the Las Pampas Aparthotel, Mr. Castillo," Yung answered for him. "I presumed he had checked with you. Is that all right?"

You are a clever sonofabitch, aren't you, Yung?

"He obviously did so with the ambassador's blessing," Castillo said. "Are you satisfied with them?"

"Yes, sir."

"Yung, I'm going to need a list of the FBI people," Castillo said. "Put your name and the other FBI agent from Montevideo on it. Just the names, and what they do if they're not special agents. And while you're at it, you might as well list the FBI personnel in Uruguay."

"I'll get it to you first thing in the morning."

"Is there some reason I can't have it right now? I'm going to give one copy to these gentlemen for Colonel Munz." He paused, and then asked, in Spanish, "You do work with *El Coronel* Munz?"

The man nodded.

"Thank you, Señor Castillo," he said. "I was about to ask. If I have the names, there will be no problem with Immigration."

"There you go, Yung," Castillo said, with a smile he really hoped would burn Yung. "Have at it."

"Yes, sir."

He is not used to being ordered around. Like Howard Kennedy, another, if former, FBI hotshot. What the hell is he doing in Uruguay?

"Here it comes," Air Force Major Jossman said, gesturing out the window.

Castillo looked and saw the Gulfstream coming down the taxiway.

"Do I have the only umbrella?" he asked.

"I've got some," Major Jossman said.

As the Gulfstream rolled onto the tarmac before the Southern Winds hangar, floodlights in the hangar came on, and a stream of Gendarmeria National men, most of them carrying submachine guns, came out of the hangar, formed a line, and came to attention, ignoring the rain. The officer in charge saluted.

Major Jossman took two umbrellas, opened one inside the bus, and then tried and failed to get it through the door. He gave up, collapsed it, stepped into the rain, and then opened it.

"Major," Castillo ordered. "Everybody in here. They can deal with the luggage later."

The major nodded and walked to the now-stopped Gulfstream, its engines winding down.

The door opened, and a stocky man in a business suit appeared in the doorway. The major handed him the second umbrella. The major pointed to the bus, and the man nodded, opened the umbrella, and started toward the bus.

Special Agent Elizabeth Schneider appeared next in the doorway.

Major Castillo's heart jumped.

Special Agent Schneider looked around, saw the bus, saw Major Castillo in it, smiled, and gave a little wave.

Major Castillo's heart jumped again. Harder.

Jossman held the umbrella for Special Agent Schneider and walked with her to the bus. They got there as the stocky man came through the door.

"My name is . . ." he started to say, but then noticed Agent Yung. "Well, hello, Dave."

Yung looked up from his lined yellow pad.

"Hey, Paul," he said, then, "Mr. Castillo, this is Special Agent Paul Holtzman."

"I'm supposed to report to you, sir," Holtzman said. "I'm the senior agent."

He didn't offer his hand.

"Hand your umbrella to the major, please," Castillo said. "And take a seat. I'll save what I have until everyone's on board."

It had been Major Castillo's firm intention to greet Special Agent Schneider formally.

She blew this plan out of the water by smiling at him again, then sitting down next to him, innocently resting her hand on his shoulder in the process, and saying, "Hello, Charley," so close to him that he could smell her breath.

Peppermint. They had apparently issued chewing gum to counter the pressure differential that occurs when an aircraft makes a rapid descent from cruising to approach altitude.

So the plan to greet Special Agent Schneider with "Good to see you again, Schneider," or words to that effect, was replaced with, "Jesus, I'm glad to see you."

As he also became aware of Special Agent Schneider's

perfume, he became simultaneously aware that Special Agent Yung hadn't missed a thing.

It took several minutes for the umbrella shuttle to get everybody off the Gulfstream into the bus, including the crew. Special Agent Jack Britton was about the fifth man to climb onto the bus, and for a moment Castillo didn't recognize him. The last time Castillo had seen him, Britton had been wearing a somewhat straggly beard and the Philadelphia conception of Arabic robes, and his hair had been both cornrowed and embedded with beadery.

Now his hair was neatly cut. He wore a well-fitted suit. He looked, Castillo thought, like Colin Powell.

Britton's grip was firm.

"I don't know the protocol—am I supposed to call you 'sir'?—but it's good to see you."

"Charley's fine, Jack. It's good to see you, too. Ready to go to work?"

"I would like to visit a gentleman's rest facility first; the one on the airplane went on the fritz somewhere over Brazil. And if possible, I'd like to get something to eat."

"There's probably a men's room in the hangar. You want to take a chance? What's going to happen here won't take long. And then it's about ten minutes to the hotel."

Britton looked at the driving rain and said, "I think I'll wait."

While this was going on, Castillo was more than a little aware that Special Agent Schneider's upper leg was pressed against his, no doubt only because the seats in the Mercedes *Traffik* seemed to have been designed for midgets.

Finally, everyone was aboard.

Castillo stood up and faced the rear of the bus.

"May I have your attention, please?" he began, and when he had it, went on: "My name is Castillo. As I understand you have been informed, I have been placed in charge of the American investigation into Mr. Masterson's murder, and the abduction of Mrs. Masterson. Additionally, I have been given responsibility for the safety of the Masterson family while they are in Argentina.

"The investigation itself is being conducted by Argentine authorities, under the overall control of SIDE, and I think you all know what SIDE is."

There was a tug on his jacket, and he looked down and saw first that Agent Schneider's eyes were even deeper and more lovely than he had remembered, and also that she was shaking her head just enough to indicate she didn't know what SIDE was.

"I'll brief you and Agent Britton separately later, Agent Schneider," he said, and then went on. "It has been decided that this investigation, and any prosecution resulting from it, will be done by the Argentine authorities."

"Who the hell decided that?" Special Agent Holtzman demanded.

"I did, and Ambassador Silvio concurred," Castillo replied. "And let me bring you up to speed on what else the ambassador and I have decided. There will be no communication of any sort by any means with any federal agency in Washington or elsewhere without the prior approval of Ambassador Silvio or myself. I want that clearly understood. Are there any questions about it?"

An agent in the back said, "You mean I can't call my wife and tell her I got down here all right?"

"You can call anyone you wish, as long as there is no reference to the situation here. Clear?"

There were murmurs.

"Nothing is going to happen tonight. Special Agent Yung will take you to your hotel and get you fed, et cetera. In the morning, I will inform him, or you, Agent Holtzman, your call, where you can meet with the Argentine authorities. They have agreed to make you privy to what they have learned so far, but I want it kept in mind this is their investigation, and things will be done their way. We're here to help, that's all.

"So far as interviewing Mrs. Masterson is concerned, for a number of reasons, including that she was drugged by her abductors and is still in the hospital, unless there is some overriding reason for the FBI to question her, all interviews of her will be conducted by Special Agent Santini of the Secret Service, and Special Agent Schneider. If she is interviewed by the FBI, it will be in the presence of one of them, or of Mr. Alex Darby."

"Who's he?" Holtzman asked.

"He's the commercial attaché of the embassy. He has the complete confidence of the ambassador, Mrs. Masterson, and myself."

"What the hell are we doing down here, then? If we can't even—"

"You're here, Agent Holtzman," Castillo interrupted, "for the same reason I am. The President has ordered it."

"May I ask a question, sir?" a man in an Air Force

flight suit with the insignia of command pilot and the silver leaf of a lieutenant colonel asked.

I wonder how long it will be before Yung confides in the lieutenant colonel that the hotshot in charge is really a lowly Army major?

"Yes, sir, of course."

"How long are you going to need the C-37?"

"I'll be able to answer that better in the morning, Colonel. After I get my orders. That's the best I can give you right now."

"Fine. How's the security here?"

"That platoon of men in the brown uniforms—the ones with the submachine guns—will guard the Gulfstream, Colonel. They're Gendarmeria National."

"You think that's enough?"

Castillo felt the eyes of the SIDE agents on him.

"I have no problem with them at all, Colonel."

"Good enough. Thank you, sir."

"That's all I have. I'll give Agent Yung my cellular number in case anything comes up, but please don't call it unless it's really necessary. I've been up since half past six, and I want to go to bed."

"I'll bet," Special Agent Yung said softly, with a knowing smile.

You sonofabitch!

"You have that list of names for me, Agent Yung?" Castillo asked, smiling at him warmly.

[THREE]

The rain, if anything, was heavier, and Castillo thought that if the Gulfstream had come in ten minutes later there would have been a real problem.

Where, other than Ezeiza, was the alternate field? And how much fuel was remaining? It was a long flight nonstop from Andrews.

Sergeant Roger Markham got himself soaking wet first getting into the bus from the BMW, and then, now armed with a description of it, getting Betty and Jack's luggage from the other bus into the BMW.

Betty's umbrella was blown inside out as she ran for the BMW—Castillo wondered how she had managed to hang on to it at all—and she was soaked, too, when Castillo and Britton made their dash from the bus to the BMW. Britton got in the front seat.

I didn't elbow Jack out of the way. This time the fickle finger of fate got me the backseat next to her.

Hey, stop! An officer and a gentleman does not make passes at his subordinates.

For Christ's sake, remember that!

Major Castillo smiled at Special Agent Schneider. She appeared to be shivering.

"Cold, Schneider?" he asked.

"Freezing," she admitted. "What is it, winter down here?"

"Yes, it is. They should have told you. Here, let me give you my jacket."

The first duty of an officer is to take care of his men.

And that's what she is, one of your men. Remember that!

"Thanks," she said.

It was a ten-minute drive from the airport to the Four Seasons. Halfway there the rain seemed to slacken. By the time they rolled up to the Four Seasons it had stopped completely.

Bellmen appeared and took care of the luggage.

"Roger, are you hungry?" Castillo asked.

"No, s— No. I'm not."

"Go home, get a hot shower, and be here at half past seven."

Sergeant Markham nodded and got back in the car.

"Very nice," Jack Britton said about the hotel.

"I didn't want him to catch pneumonia," Castillo said, gesturing at the departing BMW.

"Who's he?" Special Agent Schneider asked.

"One of the Marine guards."

"I noticed the haircut," she said.

"So we don't have wheels to go out to a restaurant—"

"Can we go inside, please?" Special Agent Schneider said. "It's cold out here."

"Sorry," he said, and motioned her ahead of him through the door. He saw that water was dripping from the hem of her skirt onto the polished marble floor.

She found her way to the reception desk by herself, and they handed her her key.

"So, about dinner," Castillo said.

"It's midnight. Is anything open?" Jack Britton interrupted.

"This is Argentina. They go to dinner starting at ten,"

Castillo said. "There's the hotel restaurant."

"I don't want to get dressed up enough to go to a restaurant," Britton said. "You, Betty?"

"I want to get out of these clothes," Special Agent Schneider said, triggering mental images in Major Castillo's mind, "and into a hot shower," she concluded, triggering additional mental images. "But I'm starved."

"What about room service?" Britton asked.

"Sure. Is that what you want to do?"

"Are the rooms big enough for all three of us to have dinner?" Special Agent Schneider asked. "I don't like to eat sitting on a bed."

"Mine is," Castillo said.

"Why don't we do that?" Britton asked. "Could you order dinner for us while we shower? Neither of us speaks Spanish that well."

"What do you want?"

"Anything, as long as it's warm and comes with a double Jack Daniel's," he said.

Special Agent Schneider laughed and got onto the elevator.

"Make that two," she said, and handed Castillo his jacket.

Major Castillo happened to notice that with the jacket no longer covering her, Special Agent Schneider's rain-soaked dress now clung to her body like a coat of varnish. He averted his eyes.

"I'm in fifteen-hundred," he announced as they got off the elevator. "At the far end of the corridor. I'll order us something to eat."

The elevator triggered a memory of Howard Kennedy.

Shit, I didn't call him with the names.

He felt in his jacket for the sheet of lined paper Yung had given him. It was soaked, but it was legible.

He carefully laid the soggy sheet of paper on the glass-topped coffee table in the sitting room, then went into his bedroom and stripped off his clothing.

Four years of practicing West Point Class 202—Personal Hygiene, or How to Take a Shower in No Time at All—paid off. Five minutes after entering his bedroom he came out of it, showered and dressed in slacks and a shirt.

First he called room service and ordered dinner, plus a bottle of Jack Daniel's and, after a moment's thought, a bottle of Famous Grouse and two bottles of Senetín cabernet sauvignon. He had shared a bottle of that with Ambassador Silvio at lunch, and, as the ambassador had said, it was really first class.

Then he called the valet and told him he had a soaking wet suit that he absolutely had to have dried and pressed and back by six-thirty in the morning. That posed no problem for the valet, which made Castillo suspect the drying and pressing service of the Four Seasons was probably going to cost as much as the suit had when he'd bought it at the annual Brooks Brothers sale at thirty-five percent off the tag price.

Finally, he sat down on the couch and punched Kennedy's autodial button on his cellular.

They could barely hear each other, which was explained when Kennedy said he'd never seen so much goddamn rain in his life. The rainstorm had apparently moved the fifteen miles or so between Jorge Newbery and Aeropuerto Internacional Ministro Pistarini de Ezeiza and was interfering with the cellular signals.

He was down to the last name on the list of FBI agents—he'd had to spell each one phonetically, sometimes twice—when the doorbell chimes bonged.

When he opened it, Special Agent Schneider, a lady who was probably from the valet service, and a man in a bartender's white jacket pushing a rolling table with the whiskey, wine, and the accoutrements were standing there.

Special Agent Schneider was wearing blue jeans and a sweater. Her hair looked damp.

He motioned them all into the room.

"Fix yourself a drink," he said. "Food's on the way."

He signed the bill for the drinks, then motioned the lady from the valet service into the bedroom and pointed out the waterlogged suit to her.

All of this while simultaneously spelling Daniel T. Westerly's name phonetically to Howard Kennedy for the third or fourth time, and being very much aware that Special Agent Schneider filled out both her sweater and her blue jeans in an incredibly delightful way. She wasn't wearing makeup, not even lipstick, and Castillo thought she looked fine without it.

Kennedy finally could hear Westerly's name spelled out phonetically.

"*Westerly.* Okay. He's a fingerprint guy. Damned good at it, too. He once lifted two eight-point digits from a used condom."

"That's it, Howard, that's the last of the names."

"All of them are on the major crimes team."

"Should any of them be of special interest to me?"

"No. Yung's the one who interests me. Watch yourself with him, Charley."

"I will. And you will inquire about Mr. Lorimer for me, right? Just as soon as you get where you're going?"

"The way it's raining, Charley, I may never get out of here."

That's two—no, four—sentences that came through intact.

"Howard, I like you. I'm going to make the rain stop."

"What?"

"Trust me, Howard, in ten minutes, fifteen tops, it will stop raining. I have issued the order. Have a nice flight, and remember to call."

He pushed the END button and laid down the cellular.

"What was that all about?" Special Agent Schneider asked.

"Not that I'm not delighted to see you, but I thought women took longer to shower and dress than men."

"That means you're not going to tell me, right?" Betty replied. "To answer the second question, Jack's calling his wife."

"You really don't want to know," Castillo said.

She raised her glass of bourbon.

"You're not drinking?"

"I'm going to have the wine."

"On your good behavior, are you?"

"Yes, ma'am."

"This quote room unquote looks like a set for a movie," she said. "And mine's not exactly a slum, either. The whole bathroom is marble. Which raises the question, how do we pay for all this?"

"Wait until you see the view," he said and went to the windows and found the switch for the opening mechanism.

"That's beautiful!" she said and walked and stood beside him. "But it doesn't answer the question about the bill."

"When we get back to Washington, Agnes—Mrs. Forbison, who runs things in the Nebraska complex— will show you how to fill out the forms for travel expenses outside the country. When you get the check, sign it over to me."

"What I think that means is that you intend to pick up the difference between what the Secret Service will pay and what you will."

"I wanted to keep you and Jack separate from the FBI," Castillo said. "This is the only answer I could come up with on short notice."

The chimes bonged again.

This time it was Jack Britton and two waiters pushing two room-service carts loaded with food covered by stainless-steel domes. Britton was wearing a sports jacket, slacks, and a shirt and tie.

"I thought you didn't want to get dressed up for dinner," Castillo said.

"I changed my mind when I saw my room. Do you always live this good?"

"Whenever I can. Fix yourself a drink, Jack. And as soon as they've set up the food, I'll tell you what's going on."

"Just out of idle curiosity, what does this place cost by the night?"

"I really have no idea," Castillo said.

"Why am I not surprised?" Betty said, and there was an unpleasant sarcastic tone in her voice.

"I really don't know how this works in the Secret Service," Castillo said. "But I don't think the presidential protection detail people stay in the economy motel ten blocks from where the President is staying to save the government money. I intend to find out. I don't want to spend my money to buy things I've bought to carry out what I've been ordered to do. The government is not on my list of favorite charities."

Britton nodded.

"I wanted to keep you two away from the FBI," Castillo said.

"They don't like you much, either," Britton said. "I picked that up on the airplane."

Castillo found an excuse not to get into that when he saw one of the waiters opening a bottle of the cabernet.

"I'll do that, thank you," he said in Spanish. "And we'll serve ourselves."

By the time Castillo had finished relating what had happened, and why he had asked that they be sent to Argentina, and what he expected of them, they had finished what had turned out to be an enormous meal.

And as they talked, Castillo had the feeling that his moral dilemma had solved itself. Special Agent Schneider was in fact a cop, and a smart one, and this was business, not romantic fantasy. And there was no question in his mind that if he made the first preliminary pass at Schneider, she would turn it down. Gently and kindly, probably, because Schneider was a good guy, but turn it down.

And it was after two A.M.

"Let's knock it off," he said. "I want to get started early in the morning. You want to eat here—we may think of something we missed—or do you want to meet in the restaurant downstairs at, say, quarter to seven?"

"If you don't mind, here," Special Agent Schneider said. "For personal reasons: I want to look out your windows in the daylight."

"Okay, here at quarter to seven," Britton said. "My ass is dragging."

He got up from the table and walked to the door. Special Agent Schneider followed. Both waved a goodnight, but neither said anything.

Three minutes after they had gone, Castillo was in bed.

And then—he had no idea how much later—the door chimes bonged.

Oh, shit! The floor waiter wants to get the goddamn dishes!

Not quite knowing why he did so, he picked up the Beretta from the bedside table and held it behind his back as he stormed out of the bedroom and across the sitting room to the door and jerked it open.

Special Agent Schneider was standing in the corridor.

"I seem to have dropped my handkerchief," she said.

He didn't reply.

"May I come in?"

He stepped out of the way.

"I thought it was the floor waiter," he said.

"Were you going to shoot him?" Special Agent Schneider asked.

He held up both hands—one of them holding the Beretta—helplessly.

She walked to the table and poured wine into a glass.

"I'm not sure this is a very good idea," he said.

She walked to him and handed him the glass and smiled.

"There stands the legendary Charley Castillo, in his underwear with a gun in one hand and a glass of wine in the other," she said, and shook her head, and then went back to the table and poured another glass of wine.

With her back to him, she said, "I thought of you all the way down here on the airplane. I thought of you at other times, of course, but I thought of you all the god-damned time I was on the airplane."

Castillo saw her take a healthy swallow of the cabernet.

"One of the things I thought about," she went on, speaking softly, "was how I was going to handle the pass the man whose Secret Service code name is Don Juan was certainly going to make at me."

"I wouldn't dare make a pass at you," Castillo said, jocularly. "Not only would your brother break both my legs—"

"Let me finish, please, Charley," she interrupted firmly.

"Sorry."

"I had to be very careful, so as not to hurt your feelings—which I didn't want to do—or to piss you off, because you might get your masculine ego in an uproar and do something crappy and screw me up with the Secret Service. From what I've seen so far, I like the Secret Service, and when I took the appointment, I burned my bridges with the department in Philadelphia."

"Christ, I wouldn't—"

"Goddamn you, Charley, let me finish."

She turned to glare at him. He nodded, and she turned her back to him again.

She took another swallow of the cabernet, shook her head, and went on: "So then what happened was that you didn't make a pass at me, and my initial reaction to that was, 'Thank God!' and then I realized that you were being responsible, you were being the upstanding guy who would never make a pass at somebody who worked for him.

"And my reaction to that was, what the hell is the difference? He's not going to make a pass at you, so that's it. Relax.

"And then when I left here and I saw you sitting at the table, I thought that's the loneliest guy in the world. And then I got in bed and faced the facts. The truth."

"Which is?" he asked softly.

"That what I really wanted to do was come back," she said, and turned her head to look at him, and then quickly looked away.

He didn't move or say anything.

"Which, obviously, was a pretty dumb thing," she said. "Sorry."

She turned and walked quickly toward the door.

He caught her arm and she tried to break loose, but he held on.

"What?" she asked.

"I don't think you've been out of my mind for more than thirty consecutive minutes since the last time I saw you in Philadelphia."

She turned to face him and looked up into his eyes.

"Oh, Jesus, Charley!"

"Oh, Jesus!" Presidential Agent Castillo said to Special Agent Schneider.

He had just rolled onto his back, breathing heavily, and put his arm over his eyes.

"Yeah," Betty said. After a moment, she shifted around on the bed so that she could rest her head on his chest.

He put his arm around her and ran the balls of his fingers gently up and down her spine.

"What happens now?" Charley asked. "Your brother comes in and breaks both my legs?"

"Well, he'd have no trouble finding us," Betty said. "We left a trail of my clothes from the living room into here."

He chuckled.

"What are you thinking now, Charley? 'I knew all along she'd be easy'?"

"Worse than that. I think—ignore that—I *know* I'm in love with you."

"You're under no obligation to say something like that."

" 'Ye shall know the truth and the truth shall make you free,' " Castillo quoted. "I think John Lennon said that."

She tweaked his nipple.

"That's from the *Bible*," she said, chuckling.

"Well?"

"Well what?"

"No response? In other words, are my feelings for you reciprocated? Partially reciprocated? Or reciprocated not at all?"

She raised her head and looked down at him.

"My God, couldn't you tell?" she asked, then: "You want me to say it, don't you?"

He nodded.

"Okay. I love you. I guess I knew that when I walked into Counterterrorism and saw the guy who'd thought I was a hooker in the Warwick bar and my heart jumped."

"Oh, boy!"

[FOUR]
The Buenos Aires Herald
Azopardo 455
Buenos Aires, Argentina
0327 24 July 2005

At almost exactly this time—although neither of them cared a whit what hour it was, or even what day, as Charley reached down to pull Betty onto him—a small white Fiat van pulled away from the loading dock at the *Buenos Aires Herald* building in downtown Buenos Aires.

It drove to the Austral Air Cargo building at Jorge Newbery airfield, where the driver handed over approximately six hundred copies of the *Herald,* so fresh from the press that the ink had not had time to completely dry.

The newspapers were tied together in sixteen packages, each with a simple address. Most were in fifty-copy packages, but some of the packages contained far fewer—in three instances, only five.

The Austral people put all of them into three large blue plastic shipping containers, and then put the containers on a baggage cart. After all other cargo and passenger luggage had been loaded aboard Austral Flight 622, the containers would be loaded aboard—last on, first off.

Flight 622 would depart Jorge Newbery at 0705 and land in Montevideo twenty-five minutes later. The blue plastic containers would be off-loaded first, and turned over to a representative of the *Herald,* who would arrange for their further distribution.

He would load two hundred copies in his car. They were destined for downtown Montevideo (150) and for Carrasco, a suburb through which he would pass on his way downtown.

The others he took to the airport's bus terminal, where they were stacked according to their destination. The Route 9 stack would be placed aboard the first morning bus to San Carlos, Maldonado, and Punta del Este, the posh seaside resort on the Atlantic Ocean. The Route 8 stack would see stacks of the newspaper dropped off at Treinta y Tres, Melo, and Jaguarão. The Route 5 bus would drop off newspapers at Canelones, Florida, and then continue across the dam holding back the Lago Artificial de Rincon Del Bonete to Tacuarembó, where it would drop off the last stack. There were just three copies of the *Herald* in the last stack.

The manager of the Tacuarembó Bus Terminal—he was paid to do so—would then telephone the manager of a remote estancia to tell him the *Herald* had arrived. Sometimes it didn't—things happened—and telephoning the estancia manager to tell him that the newspapers had, or had not, arrived saved the manager an hour-long ride down an unpaved highway.

All of this took time, of course, and it was almost three in the afternoon before the *Herald* was delivered to Estancia Shangri-La and another half hour before it was in the hands of El Patron, who was taking an afternoon siesta with Juanita, a sixteen-year-old maid.

Jean-Paul Lorimer, sitting up in bed, read the front-page banner headline with dismay, and muttered, "*¡Merde!*"

The banner headline read: AMERICAN DIPLOMAT MUR-
DERED IN PORT AREA and showed a photograph of the
late J. Winslow Masterson.

Lorimer was of course disturbed and at first frightened. Jack was, after all, his brother-in-law, and this had
to be very difficult on poor Betsy.

But there was no reason, to judge from the *Herald*'s
rather extensive coverage of the matter, for Jean-Paul
Lorimer to think it had anything to do with him.

Jack and his family had been ripe for something like
this to happen for years, ever since he had been given
that obscenely generous payment for being run over by
the beer truck.

And Argentina certainly was the place for it to have
happened. Kidnapping there had replaced schools that
taught English as the national cottage industry.

He would not—could not—allow what had happened
to Jack to force him to change his plans. All this really
meant was that it would soon be discovered that Jean-
Paul Lorimer was missing in Paris—and that might have
already happened.

If he called Betsy to express his condolences, even if
he didn't tell her where he was calling from, that would
mean that although he had been missing since the thirteenth of July—in other words, for ten days—he'd been
alive on the twenty-third.

That didn't even get into the matter of traceable telephone records, which would locate him.

And his expression of condolences would, after all, be
hypocritical.

I never liked the arrogant sonofabitch, and am not at

all sorry that he got knocked off his high horse with two bullets in the brain.

There was even an upside to this.

The attention by the press would be to the murder of Jack the Stack Masterson, who despite his Phi Beta Kappa key didn't have enough brains to get out of the way of a beer truck, and no one would pay much, if any, attention to the disappearance of his brother-in-law in France.

He dropped the *Herald* onto the floor beside the bed and turned to Maria del Juanita.

"Darling, put some clothes on, and tell Señora Sanchez I will have my coffee in the library."

VIII

[ONE]
El Presidente de la Rua Suite
The Four Seasons Hotel
Cerrito 1433
Buenos Aires, Argentina
0647 24 July 2005

A full minute after Special Agent Jack Britton lifted the brass knocker on the door of suite 1500—which was actually a switch triggering the door chimes—Major C. G. Castillo pulled the door open to him.

Castillo was wearing a plush white ankle-length terry cloth robe adorned with the crest of the Four Seasons hotel. He needed a shave, his hair wasn't combed, and it wasn't wet, either.

Britton thought, *I got here even before he got into the shower,* then said: "Schneider's not up yet, either. Or she's in the shower. She didn't answer when I knocked. But your driver is. They put him through to me by mistake. I told him I'd tell you he was here."

"Come on in, Jack," Castillo said. "We're running a little late. They haven't even taken the dishes away from last night."

Castillo walked to the telephone on the coffee table, punched a number, and in Spanish asked the concierge to send up his driver with copies of *La Nación, Clarín,* and the *Herald;* to check on his suit with the valet; and to immediately send up two large pots of coffee.

Britton listened and watched intently, trying to understand what was being said.

And then his interest really perked up.

The bedroom door opened and Special Agent Schneider came out, dressed as she had been the night before in blue jeans and a sweater.

"Good morning, Jack," she said, matter-of-factly.

She had her voice under control but not her blush mechanism.

"If you're going to order breakfast," she said, "order a big one for me."

She then walked out of the El Presidente de la Rua Suite, calling over her shoulder, "I won't be long."

The door closed, and Britton and Castillo looked at each other.

"I think, Jack," Castillo said finally, "that this is one of those times when silence would be golden."

Britton nodded, then said, "Sorry. I have to say this. From the way you looked at her just now, I could tell that you're not fooling around with her, that it's something more serious. So good for you. I know she's nuts about you."

"How the hell could you know that?"

"When we were in G-Man School, the subject of our conversations always seemed to wind up with you. And the proof came last night when we were eating. Both of you looked at everything but each other. And then, just now, the two of you looked like Adam and Eve in the garden before Eve started fooling around with the snake. She's a good lady. You're lucky."

Because he could think of nothing else to say, Castillo asked, "Is that what you call it, 'G-Man School'?"

"Yeah. Actually, it wasn't too bad." He grinned. "Betty was a laugh when they finally put us on the range. She had kept her mouth shut and her face straight when they were explaining how to *squeeze* the trigger and telling her not to let the recoil throw her, after a while she'd get used to it, but I could tell she didn't like being patronized.

"Anyway, there we are on the pistol range, two lowly candidates and the instructor. I'm standing behind her. So she gets the 'open fire' order, and her Glock sounds like an Uzi.

"'This was timed fire, Candidate Schneider. *One aimed shot* at a time.'

" 'That's what I did, sir,' Schneider says, all sweet and feminine. 'I aimed each time, sir.'

" 'Well,' the instructor adds, 'as you will see, you'll never hit anything firing that rapidly. Roll back number seven.'

"So they rolled the target back to us and she'd put all fourteen rounds into the bad guy's face.

"The instructor didn't like being duped but couldn't let it go. 'It would seem, Candidate Schneider, that you have had some previous marksmanship experience. If you're trying to make me look foolish or whatever, it won't work.' "

Castillo chuckled.

The door chimes went off. It was the lady from the valet service with Castillo's suit.

"There's a room-service menu in the drawer of that desk," Castillo said, and pointed. "When Roger gets up here, find out what he wants, and then order for everybody. I'm going to get dressed."

[TWO]

Special Agent Schneider sat across the breakfast table from Major Castillo, which position precluded Major Castillo from surreptitiously holding her hand—or perhaps touching her knee—beneath the table, but did not, he soon learned, prohibit Special Agent Schneider from rubbing the ball of her foot against his calf.

They were almost finished eating when the chimes sounded again.

Roger Markham rushed to the door, and Castillo was wondering what the hell it could be now when he heard a familiar voice: "You're American, right? Maybe a Marine?"

"Yes, sir," Markham replied.

"Go back in there, throw Major Castillo and whoever's with him out of bed, and tell him Colonel Jake Torine, USAF, wishes a moment of his valuable time."

Castillo, laughing, started to get out of his chair. As he did, he saw from Special Agent Schneider's face that she failed to see what was amusing.

Colonel Torine, a tall, somewhat bony man in a sports jacket and slacks, marched into the sitting room and saw the people at the table in the dining alcove.

"Oops!" he said. "Sorry, Charley. I didn't know you had people in here."

"Good morning, sir," Castillo said. "I should have contacted you last night."

"No. It's the other way around. I should have *reported to you* when we got in last night. Those were my orders, from General Allan Naylor himself. But it was late, and raining like hell, and I figured I'd wait until morning. The defense attaché told me where I could find you."

"Great!" Castillo began.

Torine silenced him with an upraised palm and went on: "Then I got here, and the hotel had never heard of you. So I stood there in the lobby for a couple of minutes, wondering why the attaché had sent me to the wrong hotel, and then I decided that there are two Four

Seasons hotels, and I was in the wrong one, so I went back to the desk and asked the guy where the other one was."

Castillo laughed.

"At that point, I remembered your alter ego, asked for Herr Gossinger, and here I am."

Castillo saw from their faces that Betty had some idea what was going on, and Jack Britton and Roger Markham none at all.

"Guys, I sometimes use the name Gossinger when I'm working," he explained. "That's how I'm registered here."

Britton, who had worked deep undercover for years as Ali Abid Ar-Raziq, nodded his understanding. Roger Markham's face registered what could have been awe.

My God, he's a real intel operator with a phony ID and all!

"Colonel," Castillo said, "remember when the Philadelphia cops turned up the intel that the guy who owned our 727 had sold another one to Costa Rica?"

"Oh, yeah."

"There they are," Charley said.

"No," Britton said. "There *she* is. Betty put that together. I had nothing to do with it."

"Betty Schneider and Jack Britton, now of the Secret Service," Castillo went on. "This is Colonel Jake Torine, who flew the 727 home from Costa Rica."

They shook hands.

"No, I haven't had breakfast, and yes, thank you, I could eat a bite," Torine said.

"I don't know how warm it still is," Castillo said, lifting a stainless-steel dome and revealing a pile of still-steaming scrambled eggs.

"Warm enough," Torine said and sat down.

He started spooning eggs onto a plate.

"So what's going on, Charley?" Torine asked.

Castillo handed him the *Buenos Aires Herald*.

"This is what's been given out," he said. "Most of it's pretty accurate. I'll fill you in on what's not."

Torine took the newspaper and started to read.

Shaking his head as he swallowed his last bite of breakfast, Torine handed the *Herald* back to Castillo.

"There's an editorial, too," Castillo said. "Headlined THE NATION IS SHAMED."

"Should they be?" Torine asked.

"Embarrassed, sure," Castillo said. "A diplomat's wife is kidnapped and then the diplomat gets blown away. That's not supposed to happen in a civilized nation. This isn't the Congo. But 'shamed' is a little strong. And God knows, they got their act in high gear the minute this happened to find out who did it.

"What we think happened is that Mrs. Masterson's kidnappers got in touch with him, set up a meeting, and he sneaked out of his house and went to meet them. And got himself blown away."

"Weren't they watching the house?" Torine asked, incredulously.

"They had cops and SIDE agents—you know what SIDE is?"

Torine nodded.

"So, not only cops and SIDE agents all over the place, but sitting in a car in front of his house at two in the morning when Masterson sneaked out was a CIA spook named Paul Sieno and Colonel Alfredo Munz, the head of SIDE."

"You think Masterson went to pay the ransom and something went wrong?"

"I just don't know. All I know is that Alex Darby, the station chief, Sieno—good guy, I knew him in Afghanistan; his cover is commercial attaché and Alex says he's his best man—and Munz did the best they know how to make sure something like this didn't happen. And it did. I should throw in that Masterson was Darby's best friend."

"Jesus, what the hell is this all about?"

"I wish to hell I knew," Castillo said. "And one more thing, Colonel: These bastards have something on Mrs. Masterson—maybe a threat to kill the kids, maybe something else—that's got her terrified."

"That's understandable, isn't it?"

"Surrounded by the embassy's security people, plus the CIA, the Secret Service, and SIDE, you'd think she'd feel protected enough to at least come up with a description of who grabbed her," Castillo said. "If we are to believe her, and I don't, she doesn't remember anything. That's one of the reasons I had them send Betty down here"—*one of them, anyway*—"to see if she can get close to her and come up with something."

Special Agent Schneider's mind apparently ran on a parallel path with *one of them, anyway*. Castillo felt the ball of her foot on his calf again, and when he looked at her, there was a hint of a smile on her lips and a naughty look in her eyes.

"The one question in my mind, ever since I heard about this, was whether it is terrorist-connected," Torine said.

"If it had just been assassinating Masterson, maybe. But if terrorists did it, they would have been boasting about it an hour after it happened. And I don't think they would have passed up the opportunity to kill Mrs. Masterson when they had the chance."

Torine nodded his understanding.

"So what happens now?" he asked.

"We get her and the children out of Argentina just as soon as we can get her on your airplane. Have you got approach charts for Keesler Air Force Base?"

"Of course. Why Keesler?"

"Mrs. Masterson wants him buried in Mississippi. That's where he's from. The Mississippi Gulf Coast."

"General Naylor told me the President wants Mr. Masterson buried in Arlington."

"It's her call, isn't it?"

"Obviously. When do you think she'll be ready to leave?"

"I think—*think,* don't know—that they're going to release her from the hospital this morning. If I had my way, she'd go directly from the hospital to the airport. But I doubt that's going to happen. Maybe late tonight, which would put us into Keesler in the morning. But probably sometime tomorrow."

"The defense attaché told me the Argentines want to put the casket in the Catedral Metropolitana, so they can pay their respects," Torine said. "What's that?"

"I hadn't heard that," Castillo replied. "And I have no idea."

"It's like their national cathedral," Sergeant Roger Markham furnished. "Not far from the Casa Rosada, which is like their White House. Except it's pink. The Casa Rosada, I mean. The cathedral looks like what the Parthenon must have looked like before it fell down. Marble, I think."

"The Marines to the rescue," Castillo said. "Keep going, Roger."

"Well, it's their big-time church. San Martín—that general they call 'the Great Liberator'? He was a pal of Thomas Jefferson. Avenida Libertador is really named after him, like if we named Washington Square 'Father of Our Country Square.'"

"Fascinating," Colonel Torine said, managing to keep a straight face.

"They guard his tomb inside like we do the Unknown Soldier, twenty-four/seven. If they want to put Mr. Masterson's body in there, it's really an honor."

"You're right, Roger. And I can see why they'd want to do it, but I don't know how that's going to go down with Mrs. Masterson, not to mention my orders to get her and the kids out of here as quickly as possible."

He looked at Torine.

"What we're going to do now is go to the hospital and introduce Betty and Jack to her. I told you, she's frightened. It might be useful if you went along, if you'd be willing. Tell her the travel plans, you know, whatever might make her feel better."

"You don't have to ask, Charley," Colonel Torine said. "About that or anything else. General Naylor didn't like it much, I don't think, but he made it very clear that you're running this exercise."

"I hear a cell phone ringing," Betty announced.

Castillo patted his clothing as he remembered his was in the bedroom, then quickly got up and went to get it. That took some time, as it was in the pocket of the pants he had been wearing when Betty had come looking for her lost handkerchief, and had been kicked out of sight when Jack Britton had rung the door chimes.

As had, Castillo learned when he reached under the bed for them, Betty's brassiere and underpants.

That means when she walked out of here, she wasn't wearing anything under her blue jeans and sweater!

A series of mental images flooded his mind.

Goddammit, what's the matter with you? Answer the goddamn cellular!

By the time he'd gotten the telephone from his pocket, it was too late.

The phone, however, had captured the caller's number. He pushed the MISSED CALL key, then the DIAL key.

"Sylvia Grunblatt."

The embassy public information officer. What the hell does she want?

"C. G. Castillo, Ms. Grunblatt. Were you trying to reach me?"

"Where are you?"

Not that it's any of your business, but—

"I'm in the Four Seasons."

"According to them, they don't have anybody named Castillo registered. You want to tell me what that's all about?"

"How'd you get my cellular number?"

"Ambassador Silvio gave it to me."

"How can I help you, Ms. Grunblatt?"

"The shoe's on the other foot. The press is onto you. Somebody around here has a big mouth."

"You want to explain that?"

"The *New York Times* guy wants to know about the President's agent, starting with his name, and so do CNN and AP and *La Nación,* ad infinitum. What do I tell them?"

"You have no idea what they're talking about."

"They're not going to believe that, and they're not going to like it."

"Ambassador Silvio told me you're a first-class press officer. You'll think of something."

"I can hear them now," she said. " 'Are you trying to tell me, Sylvia, that my source was lying to me?' "

"To which you respond, 'I cannot vouch for your unnamed sources. I can only tell you what I have been told.' "

"To which they will respond, 'Oh, bovine excreta, Sylvia,' or words to that effect."

"Sylvia, I'm sorry, but your splendid relations with the press are going to have to be sacrificed for operational requirements."

"I was afraid of that," she said. "The ambassador said I was to handle this any way you wanted."

"The one thing I don't need is my name, picture, or the words 'Presidential Agent' in the newspapers or on the tube."

"Okay, you got it. But be warned, they'll be looking for you. Since there are—with one exception—no other developments in the story, you—the President's agent—are the story."

"What's the one exception?"

"Presuming the ambassador can get Mrs. Masterson to go along—he hasn't asked her yet—the Argentines want to pin the Grand Cross of the Great Liberator on Jack's casket, which at the time will be lying in state in the Catedral Metropolitana. If she goes along—and she might not; if I were her I think I'd tell the Argentines to go piss up a rope—that will be a spectacle. The press—especially TV—likes spectacles, and that may get some of the heat off you."

"I was about to go to the German Hospital," Castillo said.

"You got somebody from SIDE with you who can get you in the back door? Otherwise be prepared for celebrity."

"How will they know what I look like?"

"The leak about the President's agent was intentional. I think it follows they would have also leaked a description."

"You have any idea who the leaker is?"

"If I had to bet, I'd bet it was one of the law enforcement types . . ."

Yeah, Castillo thought, *and I'll bet the bastard's name is Yung.*

". . . but nothing more specific than that. If I can get the name, you want it?"

"Indeed I do."

"I was hoping you would."

"Why?"

"Because I ran out of imagination after I thought castration would be a suitable punishment for the sonofabitch, and I'm sure you can think of something more exquisitely painful."

"Indeed I can."

"Stay in touch, please, Mr. X."

"Thanks, Sylvia."

Castillo put the cellular in his trousers pocket, whereupon it immediately rang again.

Now what the hell does she want?

"Yes, Sylvia?"

"Actually, this is Juan Silvio."

"Good morning, sir."

"Before I get into this, I presume Ms. Grunblatt did get in touch with you?"

"Yes, sir. I just got off the line with her."

"I guess she told you there's been a leak?"

"Yes, sir."

"I'm sorry. I'd really like to know who did it."

"So would I."

"Did Sylvia also tell you the Argentine government wants to honor Mr. Masterson both by having him lie in state in the cathedral, and by posthumously decorating him with the Grand Cross of the Great Liberator?"

"Yes, sir."

"I didn't think I had the right to agree to either without talking to both you and Mrs. Masterson. And I think we should talk this over before I broach the subject to her."

"Sir, I was just about to go to the hospital. I want to introduce Special Agent Schneider to Mrs. Masterson. She's the female agent I asked be sent down here. And I have Colonel Torine, who flew the C-17 down here, with me. I thought he might be able to reassure Mrs. Masterson about the travel arrangements. Which brings up something else, sir. Colonel Torine informed me the President wants to inter Mr. Masterson at Arlington, and—"

"All of which suggests that we should talk, and not on the telephone, as soon as possible."

"I'm at your disposal, sir."

"Since we both are going to the hospital, why not there? I'm sure we could find someplace there to talk."

"You tell me when and where, sir."

"The hospital in thirty, thirty-five minutes. Can you do that?"

"I'll see you there, sir."

"Thank you."

Castillo broke the connection, looked at the cellular for a moment, and then pushed an autodial button.

"¿*Sí*?"

"Alfredo?"

"*Sí.*"

"Karl, Alfredo. I need a service."

"Whatever I can do, Karl."

"I'm on my way to the German Hospital. Someone at

the American embassy not only got the crazy idea that there is some sort of White House agent down here, and that I am that agent, but he told the press."

"Herr Gossinger, you mean?"

"Probably Castillo. Anyway, I understand that the press is all over the hospital . . ."

"Then, my friend, I suggest you stay away from the hospital."

"I have to see Mrs. Masterson; and the ambassador's going to meet me there."

There was just a moment's hesitation.

"You're at the Four Seasons, right?"

"Yes."

"You have an embassy car?"

"Right."

"I have a car in the basement garage."

"The embassy car is there."

"Very well. Go to the basement and get in your car. My man will make himself known to you. Follow him to the hospital. I will arrange for you to enter via their service basement."

"Thank you."

"When you finish your business with Mrs. Masterson—I presume you heard about the lying in state and the decoration?"

"I'm not sure Mrs. Masterson wants to go along with that. That's one of the reasons I have to see her."

"May I ask the others?"

"I want to introduce her to the female agent I had sent from Washington, and I want to confirm her travel plans. And if you're going to be there, I want to introduce the other Secret Service agent to you."

"I'll see you here shortly, then."

"You're at the hospital?"

"I thought your security man would like to hear our security plans for the Catedral Metropolitana."

"And so would I. I'd also like a look at the place."

"I'll see you here, then, shortly."

Was that tone of voice a "yeah, sure"? Or an "I don't know about that"?

"Thank you, Alfredo."

[THREE]
The German Hospital
Avenida Pueyrredón
Buenos Aires, Argentina
0930 24 July 2005

The embassy BMW had been crowded. Colonel Torine had claimed the front passenger seat because of his long legs. Special Agent Schneider rode in the middle of the backseat, between Castillo and Britton.

While Special Agent Schneider's right calf did come in contact with that of Castillo, what he had been most aware of was something hard and sharp-edged pressing against his lower left rib cage. He endured the discomfort, deciding that saying, "Schneider, your Glock is stabbing me in the ribs" would not only provoke mirth from the other passengers, but probably result in Betty sitting so far away from him that the calf-to-calf contact would be lost.

The SIDE car—two burly men in a Peugeot—had taken a fairly circuitous route from the Four Seasons, and had turned off Avenida Pueyrredón two blocks before they had reached the German Hospital. As they followed, Castillo could see that the street and sidewalk at the hospital were crowded with television vans with satellite link dishes and journalists of one kind or another festooned with microphones, and still and video cameras.

The SIDE car led them to the basement of the hospital, past doors that opened as they approached, and closed the moment they were inside.

Gendarmeria National troops guarding the elevator passed them through somewhat reluctantly, and only after the SIDE agents had vouched for them.

The corridor outside Mrs. Masterson's room was crowded with more uniformed and plainclothes security personnel, Argentine and American, and the walls were lined with floral displays. Two of them—the ones on each side of the door—were enormous.

"Is Mr. Santini in there?" Castillo asked one of the Americans. He didn't know his name, but he had been in the brainstorming session.

"Yes, sir."

"Would you tell him I'm here, please?"

The man went into the room and Castillo bent over the largest of the floral displays to get a look at the card.

I wonder if anyone took a look at this to make sure it won't blow up?

Of course they did. Munz wouldn't let it into the building, much less up here, without checking.

The card was impressive. It had a gold-embossed

representation of the seal of the Republic of Argentina at the top, under which it had the name of the President.

The message was handwritten: "With my profound condolences for your loss and my prayers for your rapid recovery."

Just as Santini came through the door, Charley looked at the card on the other floral display. This one carried the gold seal of the foreign minister, who also offered his condolences and prayers.

Can I read anything of significance in them being outside her room, instead of inside?

"Good morning," Santini said, and then saw Colonel Torine and Jack Britton and Betty Schneider.

"This is Colonel Torine, who's flying the C-17," Castillo said. "And Special Agents Britton and Schneider."

Santini smiled at Betty Schneider.

"Did you really put all fourteen rounds in the bad guy's face?" he asked.

"Thirteen," Betty said. "One went in his ear."

"You have an admirer in Joel Isaacson," Santini said. "He told me. When this business is over, I think they're going to want you on the protection detail."

When this business is over, Tony, Special Agent Schneider is going to give all this fun up, and come live with me in a rose-covered cottage by the side of the road.

Or maybe on the ranch in Midland.

I wonder if she's ever been on a horse?

Santini shook Britton's and Torine's hands, and then, gesturing down the corridor, said, "Come on. They gave me a room to use. The ambassador's waiting for you."

Castillo wondered about the security of the room, and looked with a raised eyebrow at Santini. When Charley mouthed *swept?* Santini blinked once slowly and made a slight nod.

"You must be Miss Schneider," Ambassador Silvio said, offering his hand with a smile.

"Yes, sir."

"I'm very glad you're here. Mrs. Masterson will probably be delighted to see a feminine face in the sea of men around her."

"Let's hope so, sir," Betty said.

"You all might as well hear this," Silvio said. "I'm torn between my sense of duty as a diplomat and my personal feelings. The Argentines are determined to go ahead with this business of having Mr. Masterson's casket lying in state in the Catedral Metropolitana and awarding him the medal—the Grand Cross of the Great Liberator. Officially, I am delighted. Personally, and not only because I knew Jack well enough to know that his reaction would be, 'A medal? For what? Getting shot?' I wish the Argentines hadn't had the idea. I also don't like the idea of exposing Mrs. Masterson and the children to any possible danger."

"Colonel Munz assures me, sir," Santini said, "that the level of protection being established at the cathedral will be as good, if not better, than that provided to the President. I almost asked him when was the last time someone took a shot at his President, then realized that with the country's economy still in dire straits, there likely have been some serious threats. The bottom line, sir, is that I really can't fault Munz's plans. And I'll be with her, and Special Agent Schneider and some other of our people."

"And the government would be—perhaps understandably—upset if I just told them, 'Thank you, but no thank you,'" Silvio said, and then looked at Castillo. "Charley?"

"Sir, isn't it her call?" Castillo asked. "If she doesn't want to go to the cathedral, we can say, truthfully, that she's just too grief-stricken. I think the Argentines would understand that."

"You mean, have the casket lie in state, but not have Mrs. Masterson participate in the decoration ceremony?"

"Yes, sir."

"That's a good thought."

"Sir, I'd like to get the Mastersons out of the country as soon as possible. When are they going to let her leave here?"

"She can leave anytime," Santini answered. "They did another blood workup first thing this morning. She's clean."

"When do the Argentines want to start the show?" Castillo asked.

"They want to move the body to the cathedral this afternoon," Silvio said. "Then, they will permit the public to pay its respects from six until ten tonight, and from eight to ten in the morning. They're going to provide an honor guard, and I've asked the Marines to be ready to do the same. They've scheduled the award ceremony for ten, starting with a mass, which will be celebrated by the papal nuncio. Fortunately, Jack was a Roman Catholic."

"As opposed to being a Southern Baptist, you mean?" Santini said, and immediately added, "I didn't mean to be flippant."

"If Jack had been a Southern Baptist, or Jewish, or a Mormon," the ambassador said, "that probably *would* pose a problem."

"How's the security at her house?" Castillo asked.

"I went out there in the wee hours," Santini replied. "It looked fine to me."

"And if she leaves the hospital in, say, an hour, how long is it going to take to set up a secure motorcade?"

"Munz says give him thirty minutes' notice. He has people standing by."

"Will the motorcade be secure?" Ambassador Silvio asked.

"Actually, sir, there will be three motorcades," Santini said, "each consisting of a Gendarmeria National lead car, followed by a Policía Federal car, followed by two armored embassy cars with blacked-out windows, followed by another Policía Federal car and an ambulance and a Gendarmeria chase car. They will go to the house in San Isidro by three different routes. The embassy cars will have security personnel in both. Mrs. Masterson will be in one of them."

"Which one?" Castillo asked.

"I'll decide that just before we leave the hospital," Santini said.

Castillo had just thought, *That three-motorcade business is really clever; thank God Santini really knows how to handle things like this*, when the ambassador asked,

"Sound good to you, Charley?" which brought on the sobering realization, *Jesus Christ, Santini may be good, but this is my responsibility.*

"It sounds fine to me, sir," Castillo said.

"Well, let's go see how Mrs. Masterson feels about all this," Ambassador Silvio said. "As Charley says, it's her call."

No, Castillo thought, *it's not. It's mine. I have both the responsibility for her safety, and the authority to say, "No way are we going to put her in the line of fire again. I don't care if the Argentines like it or not."*

The roll-down metal shutters over the windows of Elizabeth Masterson's room were closed. The fluorescent lights in the room were harsh.

She was sitting in an armchair, wearing a dressing gown. The ashtray on the small table beside her was full of butts. Most of them were long, as if she'd taken just a few puffs before putting them out.

"Good morning, Betsy," Ambassador Silvio said, taking the dirty ashtray from the table and handing it to one of the guards at the door with the unspoken order to bring a clean one. "How are you?"

"How would you suppose I am, Mr. Ambassador?" she asked, sarcastically.

"I hoped I was Juan to you, Betsy," Silvio said. "You remember Mr. Castillo from yesterday?"

"Good morning," Castillo said.

She acknowledged his presence with a slight inclination of her head and the faintest of smiles.

Yesterday she looked sick. Today she looks bitter. And more than a little wary. She obviously would prefer that I not be here. What the hell is she hiding?

"Mrs. Masterson," Castillo said, "this is Special Agent Schneider of the Secret Service. If you have no objection, she'll be with you and the children."

"Hello," Mrs. Masterson said, with a smile that looked genuine. She put out her hand.

"I'm very sorry about your husband, Mrs. Masterson," Special Agent Schneider said.

"Thank you. Would you be offended— What do I call you?"

"Betty would be fine, ma'am."

"Would you be offended, Betty, if I said you're not what comes to mind when you hear 'Secret Service'?"

"Not at all."

Betsy Masterson turned to Silvio.

"I heard a doctor tell a nurse—I guess they think I don't speak Spanish—something about a ceremony at the Catedral Metropolitana. What's that all about?"

"Actually, it's the reason I'm here, Betsy," Silvio replied. "What the Argentine government wants to do is to place Jack's casket in the cathedral—to have him lie in state, in other words, with an honor guard—let the public pay their respects tonight and tomorrow morning, and then, in connection with a memorial mass to be celebrated by the papal nuncio, to award Jack the Grand Cross of the Great Liberator. Either the President or the foreign minister—probably the President—will do that. It's quite an honor."

"Jack didn't like either one of them," she said, then

immediately added, "I shouldn't have said that."

"You can say anything you want to say," Silvio said.

"Am I expected to participate in this?"

"All you would have to do is be there, and that's entirely up to you, Betsy. Mr. Castillo and I are agreed that it's your decision. The entire diplomatic corps will be there."

"In other words, it would be what Jack would call a command performance?" she asked, but it was a statement, not a question.

"Jack had a good many friends in the diplomatic corps," Silvio said.

"When Jack thought it was in the interests of the United States, he could make the devil himself think they were close friends," she said.

"That's true," Silvio said, with a smile.

"Jack would want me to participate in something like this, so okay."

"To repeat myself, Betsy, that's entirely up to you."

"Not really," she said. "My father would not understand my not participating. It's always been duty first with him, too. He used to say—and I don't think he was joking—that a diplomat should be like a Jesuit priest, who gives up his personal life and comfort to serve something far more important. And we both know Jack went along with that notion. Which brings me to my family. Have they been told what's happened?"

"I spoke with Ambassador Lorimer shortly after I saw you yesterday," Silvio said. "I didn't get into your abduction, just . . . what happened to Jack."

"What exactly did you tell him?"

"That Jack had been assassinated by parties un-known," Silvio said. "I'm aware of Ambassador Lorimer's physical condition—"

"That was the right thing to do. Thank you."

"He wanted to telephone, but I told him—I guess this is a diplomatic obfuscation; I really believed it was in a good cause—that you had been sedated, and it proba-bly would be best to wait until you felt yourself again, at which time you would call him."

"Again, Juan, that was the right thing to do. And thank you again. Well, I feel myself again. When do I get out of here?"

"An hour after you say the word, Mrs. Masterson," Castillo said. "It will take us about that long to arrange your transportation."

She looked at him, and not with gratitude.

I don't think I've done anything to annoy her—except maybe being an intruder into the diplomatic community—so that leaves her being afraid of me.

What the hell is that all about?

And how come her brother, the UN diplomat—Jean-Paul Lorimer—wasn't in the conversation? She didn't ask if he'd been notified, and he wasn't mentioned in that diplomatic holy orders speech she gave.

"What's the word?" she asked, almost belligerently. "I want to get out of here and be with my children."

"You just said it, Mrs. Lorimer. I'll tell Mr. Santini to get things rolling."

"Good."

"Mrs. Masterson," Castillo went on, "Colonel

Torine, the pilot of the C-17—the Globemaster III that the President sent down here—is outside. I thought perhaps he could tell you about what's planned to get you and the children out of here and back to the States. And that you could tell him what you require."

She looked at him and nodded, then turned to Betty Schneider.

"Would my children be safe at the ceremony in the cathedral?"

"The head of SIDE, Mrs. Masterson—" Castillo began.

"If you don't mind, Mr. Castillo, I asked her."

"Excuse me."

Betty exchanged a glance with Charley, who nodded, and turned to Mrs. Masterson. "Mr. Santini and Mr. Castillo are better equipped to answer that, Mrs. Masterson, than I am."

"Still, I'd like to hear what you think, please."

Betty nodded, and then after a just-perceptible hesitation said, "The Secret Service is pretty good at protecting people, Mrs. Masterson, but it's not perfect. President Reagan was shot. A crazy woman shot at President Ford twice."

"Let me put it this way: If they were your children, would you take them to the cathedral?"

"Fortunately for me, I don't have to make that choice. And I certainly wouldn't presume to advise you what to do."

"Thank you. I appreciate your honesty," Mrs. Masterson said, and then looked at Castillo. "My children and I will attend the ceremony at the cathedral. I want them to have that memory, of their father being honored. And Jack—and my father—would see it as my duty."

Castillo nodded.

And again, no mention of the brother.

"Send in your colonel, please, Mr. Castillo," Mrs. Masterson said. "I'd like to be able to tell my children what's the agenda."

Castillo nodded again, and left the room.

El Coronel Alfredo Munz was standing in the corridor with Colonel Torine, Jack Britton, and Tony Santini.

"She has decided to attend the ceremony, with the children," Castillo announced. "And she wants to go home."

"Give me thirty minutes," Santini said.

"I told her an hour," Castillo said. "Which will give me a chance to take a look at her house before we send her out there."

"Everything's in place, Charley," Santini said evenly.

"I'd like a fresh look myself," Munz said. "I directed some modifications to the plan."

Well, maybe that got me off the hook with Santini, who understandably wonders who the hell I think I am to be checking his work.

"Tony, what this probably is is me covering my ass, but I want to see for myself the arrangements at the house and at the cathedral," Castillo said.

"Your call, Charley."

"And I want you to get Schneider a cell phone. I want the number of mine on an autodial button on it, and I want the number of her phone on mine."

Santini reached in his pocket and came out with a cellular telephone.

"I already gave one to Jack and one to Colonel Torine," he said. "And if you'll give me yours, I'll put their numbers in it."

Castillo handed him his telephone and then looked at Britton. "I'm presuming you've met Colonel Munz."

"Yes, sir. He's offered, when you're finished with me here, to send me to his headquarters and show me the investigation so far."

Castillo turned to Munz. "Thank you, Alfredo. Will it be possible for us to get a copy of the investigation report?"

"Of course. It may take some time to get it translated."

"You give me the report, I'll translate it."

Munz nodded.

"Colonel, why don't you go in there and tell Mrs. Masterson about the travel plans?"

"When do you want to go wheels-up, Charley?"

"What I'd like to do is go directly from the cathedral to Ezeiza," Castillo said. "I haven't asked her—or the ambassador—but shoot for that."

"You're not going in there with me?" Torine asked.

"I have the feeling she'd rather I just went away," Castillo said. "But yeah, just as soon as Tony gives me my cellular back, I'm going in there. I've got to get you some wheels."

[FOUR]

Dr. Jose Arribena 25
San Isidro
Buenos Aires Province, Argentina
1035 24 July 2005

Major C. G. Castillo stood in the middle of the residential street in front of the Mastersons' property in the upscale San Isidro neighborhood. He pulled out his cell phone, punched an autodial button, and Special Agent Schneider answered on the second ring.

"Schneider."

"Hello, baby."

"Yes, Mr. Castillo?"

"I love you."

"So I have been led to believe."

"And vice versa?"

"That is my understanding of the situation. Where did you say you were, sir?"

"I'm standing on the street in front of the Masterson house."

"And you're satisfied with the security arrangements, sir?"

"I'd like to have a couple of Abrams tanks and a couple of twenty-millimeter Gatlings, but yeah, I am. Since you're all business, I'll let you know what to expect."

"Please."

"The whole area—maybe ten blocks on a side—is cordoned off. Provincial cops stop everybody trying to get in. They demand identification and want to know where everyone is going. Then they search the car.

There's a second ring inside the outer one, this one manned by the Gendarmeria National. More military than cops. They're armed with submachine guns. Same routine, more thorough. This is an upscale residential neighborhood, people have to get to—and out of—their houses."

"And the house itself, sir?"

"I'm not finished, Special Agent Schneider."

"Sorry, sir."

"On the block the Masterson house is on—it's in the middle of the block—the street is blocked off with barriers, cars, and whatever they call those strips with steel points on them to blow tires."

"I know what you mean, sir."

"Plus more Gendarmeria National and SIDE people and our guys. Now the house itself sits behind an eight-foot brick wall topped with razor wire. The wall completely surrounds the property. In the rear, there is a service road—for deliveries, garbage, et cetera. That's been blocked off.

"The house is three stories, masonry, and all the windows except two in the attic are barred. Heavily barred, and they don't open. The front door looks like a bank vault, and the rear door is steel. The gates in the fence—two in the front, one vehicular, one for people, and two in the back, ditto—are steel, decorative but heavy-duty. The vehicular gate in the front slides on tracks when a switch inside the front door is pushed. The one in the back has to be moved by hand. Closed, it's locked with a huge padlock, keys kept in the kitchen. The people gates are opened with a solenoid, switches by the front door and in the kitchen. The front and back yards are illuminated by floodlights, triggered by motion sensors, or they can be turned on and left on.

"We have two of our guys and two SIDE guys inside the house. There are two telephone lines, plus a dedicated line for the burglar alarm. And everybody has cellulars. I can't think of a thing to add, except maybe the Abrams tanks I mentioned."

"That sounds pretty secure, sir."

"When are you going to leave the hospital?"

"In the next couple of minutes."

"If you tell me you love me, I'll tell you where I'm going from here."

"That would be very difficult at this time, sir."

"Well, if somebody's listening to us, then why don't you say 'Wiener schnitzel' and I'll understand."

She giggled, then said, "Wiener schnitzel."

"And same to you, love of my life."

"Where will you be, sir?"

"We—Munz, Jack, and me—are going from here to the cathedral. After that we're going to SIDE headquarters. I'll call again. Better yet, when you've got Mrs. Masterson in her house, call me."

"Yes, sir."

"And be prepared to say, 'Wiener schnitzel.'"

"Whatever you say, sir."

"Wiener schnitzel, baby."

[FIVE]
Catedral Metropolitana
Plaza de Mayo
Buenos Aires, Argentina
1130 24 July 2005

C. G. Castillo answered his cellular telephone on the second buzz.

"Castillo."

"Schneider, sir."

" 'Wiener schnitzel Schneider,' that Schneider?"

"Yes. sir. I called to tell you we're in the house in San Isidro."

"No problems?"

"No, sir. Went off like clockwork."

"I've just had a tour of the cathedral, led by Sergeant Roger Markham. He dazzled Colonel Munz; he knew more about the cathedral than Munz did."

Betty chuckled. "He's a really nice kid."

"Anyway, no problems that I can see. It's right down the street from the Casa Rosada. The cops around here have a lot of experience dealing with angry mobs, and they keep a cache of barriers handy. Munz offered a helicopter to fly the family from the racetrack—the Jockey Club—in San Isidro. After they put the barriers up, there's room to sit one down. But I turned him down."

"May I ask why, sir?"

"Two reasons—and you may ask me anything you want to, Wiener schnitzel. The first is—I thought you knew this—that I am one of the best—if not *the* best—

chopper pilots in the world, and I don't trust any other chopper jockey unless I've flown with him—"

"Jesus, Charley!"

"I guess no one can hear this conversation?"

"No. I'm in the kitchen, having a cup of coffee."

"In that case, can we dispense with the Wiener schnitzel nonsense and come right out with 'I love you, Charley'?"

"You said there were two reasons, sir?"

"And I'll tell you the other one if you tell me you love me."

Betty hesitated a moment, and then said, chuckling, "Wiener schnitzel, okay?"

"Close enough. Okay, what Munz offered was a French Alouette III, the SA 316A. It's an old one. That bothered me, as I don't know what kind of maintenance it gets here. And they replaced the tail and main rotors—they had problems with them not being strong enough—on the B model, and this is the A model."

"You do know about helicopters, don't you?"

"Therefore, Special Agent Wiener schnitzel, after carefully weighing the pros and cons of the matter, I decided it would be more prudent to have the Alouette fly roof cover than to utilize it for personnel transport."

"You're really hooked on that Wiener schnitzel nonsense, aren't you? And what's roof cover?"

"First of all, it's not nonsense, and second, you might say that I'm in love with Wiener schnitzel. And roof cover, Special Agent Wiener schnitzel, is when a rotary wing aircraft flies low over an urban area, carefully observing rooftops to make sure there are no bad guys with sniper rifles, mortars, or other lethal weaponry on them."

"And he's going to do that? Colonel Munz?"

"Yeah. And this way, the Frog bird will also be available as emergency transport if we need it."

"You think that's liable to happen?"

"No. I don't. The cathedral looks as safe to me as the house. The family will arrive by car, enter the cathedral by a side door, make a brief appearance at the casket, then take seats in an alcove. There's two alcoves, near the altar. The President, probably, and the foreign minister for certain, plus assorted bigwigs, including Ambassador Silvio, will be in the one on the left—on the left, facing the altar—and the family, two guys from SIDE, and you, Special Agent Wiener schnitzel . . ."

"Enough already with the Wiener schnitzel, Charley."

". . . will be in the one on the right. At the appointed hour—ten—the prime minister or the President will approach the casket, drop to his knees for a moment on the prie-dieu—"

"The what?"

"A thing you kneel on. It means *pray God* in French. I suppose that identifies you as a non-Catholic?"

"I'm Lutheran, as a matter of fact."

"Wonderful. So am I."

"Why do I suspect that if I said I was Catholic, you would have said the same thing."

"I would have, and with a clear conscience. My mother was *Evangelische*, which is just about the same thing as Lutheran, and until I was twelve, I even went to an Evangelische school. Then I moved to Texas, where my Texican family is all Roman Catholic. I am a multi-faith sinner, in other words. May I continue?"

"You're a lunatic."

"And is that why you Wiener schnitzel me, Special Agent Wiener schnitzel?"

"God!"

"As I was saying, after whoever does this rises from the prie-dieu, one of his staff will hand him the Grand Cross the Great Liberator, which he will then pin to the flag on the casket. He will then return to his alcove. The Mass will start. Communion will be served to the family in their alcove. As soon as the papal nuncio moves across the aisle to do the same for the President, the family will leave their alcove, get back in the motorcade, and head for the airport. This motorcade will not have flashing lights or a motorcycle escort, but it will have lead and chase cars, three of each.

"At the airport, the Mastersons will immediately board the Globemaster III. Meantime, Mass will be offered to the bigwigs and diplomatic corps only—the first four rows of reserved seats. As soon as that's done, the casket will be taken out a side door and loaded into one of the embassy's Yukons, and taken under heavy escort to Ezeiza. As soon as it's on the Globemaster, we go wheels-up for Keesler."

"I'm going to need clothing," Betty said. "Something for the cathedral. And how am I going to get my things from the hotel?"

"You'll be at the hotel tonight," Castillo said.

"Not here?"

"I want you bright-eyed and bushy-tailed for the cathedral and the flight tomorrow." *And for tonight, too, as a matter of fact. Bright-eyed, bushy-tailed, and naked.* "All you could do at the Masterson place is doze in an armchair." *While I tossed, sexually frustrated and miserable, alone in my bed.*

"I suppose," she said.

"I'll call after I've been to SIDE with Jack and Munz. Then I'm going to see the ambassador and (a) sell him on my plan to get out of here, and (b) get him to sell Mrs. Masterson. I have the feeling if I suggested it, she'd be against it."

"She doesn't like you, that's pretty obvious," Betty said.

"I'll call you later, sweetheart."

"Charley?"

"Yeah?"

"Wiener schnitzel."

[SIX]
The American Club of Buenos Aires
Viamonte 1133
Buenos Aires, Argentina
1430 24 July 2005

SIDE headquarters was not at all like the J. Edgar Hoover Building, which is the FBI headquarters in Washington, or like the CIA complex in Langley, Virginia. It was housed in a nondescript office building half a block off Avenida 9 Julio and two blocks away from the Colon Opera House. As they followed Colonel Munz's

Peugeot past the opera house, Sergeant Roger Markham matter-of-factly informed them the opera house had been built in the heyday of Argentina wealth with the primary architectural concern that it be larger and more elegant than the opera houses of Vienna, Paris, and Rome.

There was no sign identifying the building's purpose, and entrance to SIDE headquarters was through a truck loading dock and then onto a freight elevator operated by a man with an Uzi submachine gun hanging from his neck.

Special Agents David William Yung, Jr., and Paul Holtzman of the FBI had been given a small glass-walled office in which to review the reports of the SIDE and other law enforcement investigations. Neither seemed either surprised or pleased to see Castillo and Markham.

And, since those reports are all written in Spanish, it can logically be assumed that they both read and write Spanish.

Colonel Munz announced he had "a few calls to make," and Castillo and Markham sat down at a table beside Yung and Holtzman and started reading the reports.

Alex Darby walked into the small office about an hour later, and a moment later Munz came in.

"I just came from the embassy," Darby announced, "where there are now two demonstrations, one to express sympathy and the other protesting the price of milk or something in Patagonia. There was a third, which seemed to approve of what happened to Jack. That was ended in front of the TV news cameras of the world by twenty guys on horses from the Corps of Mounted Police. There were no flashing sabers, but just about everything else, including Mace. Sylvia Grunblatt's nearly hysterical."

He paused, and looked at Castillo.

"And a guy from your office called. Miller. He said either your cellular doesn't work or you talk a lot. He couldn't get through to you. The message is you're to call your boss on a secure line at four Washington time. Five here."

"Got it."

"And the ambassador wants to be brought up to speed. To avoid the circus at the embassy, he suggests lunch at the American Club. I reserved a private room. He especially hopes you can be there, Alfredo."

"Of course," Munz said.

"Does that include us?" Holtzman asked.

After a moment, Castillo said, "Yes, of course."

The American Club was on the eleventh floor of an office building across the street from the Colon Opera House. The first thing Castillo saw when they got off the elevator was a huge American flag which had been flown from a warship off Normandy on D-Day, 1944. It was framed and hung on the wall.

Castillo was a little surprised that Sergeant Roger Markham—who he insisted eat with them—did not deliver a little historical lecture on D-Day activities and World War II in general.

There was a good-looking oak bar with a very appealing display of various spirits.

"Me for one of those," Darby said, heading for the bar. "Possibly two. I have earned it."

So have I, Castillo thought. *But I better not.*

C. G. Castillo and Sergeant Markham were the only two teetotalers, and Castillo suspected that was because Markham was following his noble example.

The meeting went well.

Ambassador Silvio solved the problem of whether Mrs. Masterson would be willing to leave for the United States immediately after the ceremony in the Catedral Metropolitana by calling her, suggesting that was what he thought to be the best idea, and getting her approval.

As they waited for the elevator Castillo had an unpleasant thought.

Everything is going very well. Too well. What the hell am I missing? When does the other shoe drop?

[SEVEN]
The United States Embassy
Avenida Colombia 4300
Palermo, Buenos Aires, Argentina
1705 24 July 2005

"My name is C. G. Castillo. I need Secretary Hall on a secure line, please."

"We've been expecting your call, Mr. Castillo. Hold one, please.

"Mr. Castillo is on a secure line, Madam Secretary.

"Mr. Castillo is on a secure line, Mr. Secretary.

"I have Secretary Cohen, Secretary Hall, and Mr. Castillo for you, Mr. President."

Oh, shit!

"Good afternoon, Charley," the President said. "How are things going down there?"

"Good afternoon, Mr. President. Sir, I'm calling from Ambassador Silvio's office. I thought I should tell you he can—"

"You're on a speakerphone, Charley?"

"Yes, sir."

"Good afternoon, Mr. Ambassador," the President said. "Your boss and Charley's are in on this. You all right with that?"

"Yes, of course, Mr. President. Good afternoon, Madam Secretary, Mr. Secretary."

"Let's have it, Charley," the President said.

"Well, sir, to get to the bottom line, Mrs. Masterson and the children will be wheels-up probably no later than noon, local time, tomorrow."

"She's still okay with that medal business in the cathedral?"

"Yes, sir."

"Is she—are they—going to be safe, Charley?"

"Yes, sir. I believe they will be safe. The ambassador and I just came from a meeting with the head of SIDE, and the Argentine government is taking every possible measure to ensure their safety."

"Our people—you—presumably are in on that?"

"Yes, sir."

"Is that right, Mr. Ambassador?"

"Yes, sir. I agree with Mr. Castillo."

"And the investigation, how's that going?"

"Sir, we also met with Special Agent Holtzman, the agent in charge of the FBI team, and . . ."

"Okay, Charley, that seems to be about it," the President said. "If everything continues on track, I'll see you tomorrow night in Mississippi. Natalie and I will. You, too, Matt?"

"If you wish me to be there, yes, sir," Hall said.

That's the first time he's opened his mouth.

"I think it would be a good idea, Matt," the President said.

"Then I'll be there, sir."

"And you, Mr. Ambassador, presumably we'll see you there, too?"

"Sir, I thought I would ask Secretary Cohen's guidance."

"About what?" the President asked, sounding impatient.

"Sir, Mr. Masterson was our chief of mission. If I came along, and my wife and I would personally very much like to come, direction of the mission would fall on the shoulders of Mr. Darby, our commercial attaché . . ."

"Juan," Secretary of State Cohen said, "I know how you feel, but I think it would be best if you remained in Buenos Aires. We don't want to make it appear as if we're recalling you for consultation."

And that's the first time she's opened her mouth.

"Yes, ma'am," the ambassador replied.

"Your call, Natalie," the President said. "Anything else from anybody?" There was a moment's silence, then the President said, "Thank you, Charley. Thank you, both."

[EIGHT]

"Schneider."

"Don Juan for Agent Wiener schnitzel."

"I don't think you're funny, Charley."

"Why do I suspect no one can overhear this conversation?"

"As a matter of fact, I'm in the restroom."

"You want me to call you back in a couple of minutes?"

"No. What's on your mind?"

"Roger and I just escaped from the embassy," Castillo said. "It's a circus. Anyway, we're on Avenida Libertador. Roger is going to drop me at the Kansas, go where you are, pick you up, and bring you to the Kansas."

"What's that all about?"

"I want you to see the place, for one thing; and I want to be with you and have a drink, for another; and I thought it would look better if your boyfriend didn't pick you up at work."

"Is that what you are, my boyfriend?"

"I was getting that impression, frankly."

"Okay. You're sure you don't want me to spend the night here? Roger could drive me to the hotel—"

"I'm sure I don't want you to spend the night there."

I want you to spend it with me, frolicking in the nude.

"Getting back to business," Betty said, "I may be able to get to her."

"How so?"

"She's really nice, and we talked some, and then she asked me if I would do her a personal favor, so I said sure, and then she asked me to find the best private security business in Mississippi—she thought the gambling places along the coast would probably have some good ones—or in New Orleans. She said she wanted the best she could get."

"I would, too, in her shoes. So what did you tell her?"

"That I would look into it."

"I'll get on the horn to Joel Isaacson and see what he can come up with."

"Thank you."

"I'll see you in just a little while, baby. We can talk about it."

"How soon will Roger be here?"

"No more than twenty minutes."

"Okay, I'll be ready."

[NINE]
Restaurant Kansas
Avenida Libertador
San Isidro
Buenos Aires Province, Argentina
1810 24 July 2005

Charley's glass of Senetín cabernet sauvignon was just about empty and he was getting just a little concerned— *Jesus, Betty should have been here by now*—when his cellular buzzed.

"Castillo."

"Wo bist du, Karl?"

Munz, and using the intimate form of address, as if we're pals.

"Between us, man-to-man, I'm sitting in the bar of the Kansas, waiting for my lady love."

"At the bar? You're sitting at the bar?"

"Yes, I am. And no, I don't want any more comp—"

"Listen to me, Karl, carefully. This instant, get away from the bar and into a booth. Keep your head down."

He's serious. What the hell is going on? Charley thought, then said, *"Was ist los?"*

"Do what I tell you, for God's sake! I'm trying to keep you alive! I'll have cars there in a couple of minutes."

The line went dead.

Shit!

Castillo got off the bar stool, signaled to the bartender that he was moving to a banquette, and did so.

As surreptitiously as he could, he took the Beretta from the small of his back and worked the action. He didn't think anyone saw what he did.

A minute or so later, he heard the wail of a siren, and then realized it was sirens, plural.

A minute after that, there was the screech of brakes outside, and first two members of the Gendarmeria Nacional burst into the restaurant, their hands on Uzis. And on their heels came two men in civilian clothing, also carrying Uzis.

Smart. If they'd come in first, instead of the uniforms, after Munz's warning, I might have decided to shoot first and sort it out later.

One of the men he was sure were SIDE agents half trotted into the bar, saw him, and walked quickly to the table.

"If you'll come with us, please, Mr. Castillo?"

"What the hell is going on?"

"If you'll come with us, please, Mr. Castillo?" he repeated. "Colonel Munz will explain everything when we get there."

It was a short ride, actually. The narrow streets and the high speed made it seem longer.

He saw first the flashing lights of police cars, and then the ambulances, and then the embassy car.

The embassy car—the windows looked as if someone had attacked them with a baseball bat—*Jesus Christ, somebody shot the shit out of the car!*—was backed into a sidewalk café at the traffic circle at the southeast corner of the San Isidro Jockey Club property. Tables and chairs had been scattered, and there were people sitting in chairs and lying on the ground who had either been run over or shot.

Castillo was out of the car before it stopped moving.

Munz was standing by the embassy car.

"Karl, I'm sorry!" Munz said.

Castillo started for the car. Munz tried to stop him. Castillo evaded him. Three other men rushed to stop him.

Munz ordered the men to let Castillo pass.

The front passenger window was gone.

Castillo stuck his head in.

Sergeant Roger Markham, USMC, was lying across the front seats. His head looked as if it had exploded.

Castillo couldn't see in the backseat, so he pulled open the rear door.

Where the hell is Betty?

There was a lot of blood on the leather upholstery.

Castillo ran to Colonel Munz.

"Where is she?"

"I sent her by ambulance to the racetrack," Munz said. "A helicopter will take her to the German Hospital."

"How bad?" Castillo asked.

"Multiple gunshot wounds. At least one to the face."

"What the hell happened?"

"First scenario, fragmentary witness reports," Munz said, professionally. "The car was making the circle. At that point it stopped. For some reason, the driver—"

"His name was Roger. He was twenty years old," Castillo blurted.

"*Roger* lowered the window. Then he apparently saw what was happening . . ."

"Which was?"

"A Madsen submachine gun," Munz said. "It's still in the window. Roger didn't get it closed in time, but the window closed. The Madsen's still there. . . ." He pointed.

Castillo looked. A Madsen's barrel was pinned between the driver's-side window and the window frame.

"They go all the way up automatically," Castillo said.

"And he put the car in reverse and tried to get away. Which is why the car is where it is."

Jesus H. Christ!

"So the villain held on to the trigger as long as he could," Munz said. "And then ran away."

"Did you catch him?"

Munz shook his head, and then made a gesture. One of his men walked up with a resealable plastic bag. Munz took it and then extended it to Castillo.

It held a Glock semiautomatic pistol. The inside of the bag was heavily smeared with blood that had come off the pistol.

"Your agent got one shot off," Munz said.

"She's not my fucking agent." He handled the weapon through the bag with disbelief. "She's my . . . my . . . my love."

"I know, Karl," Munz said. "I saw your eyes."

There was the sound of rotor blades and Castillo looked in the direction in time to see an Alouette III, the SA 316A, the one with the weak main and tail rotors, struggling for altitude.

"I'll go with you to the hospital, Karl," El Coronel Munz said.

IX

[ONE]
Autopista Del Sol
Accesso Norte
San Isidro
Buenos Aires Province, Argentina
1850 24 July 2005

El Coronel Alfredo Munz leaned forward, tapped the driver of the Jeep Grand Cherokee on the shoulder, and told him to slow down, turn off the siren, and take the flashing blue light from the roof.

Castillo looked at him in surprise, then anger, then horror as it occurred to him the probable reason it was no longer necessary to speed.

Jesus Christ, did somebody call him to tell him she's dead, and I missed it?

Munz read his mind.

"If you and I wind up in hospital beds beside *Fräulein* Schneider because we ran into a gasoline truck, that won't do her any good, will it, Karl?"

Castillo didn't reply.

"What will happen at the hospital is that they will check her vital signs, type her blood—"

"Her blood type's on her credentials," Castillo interrupted.

"If they were in her purse, that's on the way to my laboratory. I don't think they'll find any prints of use on it, but I don't want to omit anything."

Munz waited until that had sunk in, then went on: "And even if the hospital had something alleging to give her blood type, they would make their own examination unless her condition was really critical. Giving transfusions of the wrong type of blood can be fatal."

"Not critical? Christ, Alfredo, there was blood all over the backseat!"

"Not all of it, I don't think, was hers," Munz said. "And you know how heavily any wound to the head bleeds."

Yeah, I do. I'm a soldier.

So start thinking like one, Charley, for Christ's sake!

This damn situation is my fault, no question about that, but it's done.

Evaluate the damage, and decide on a course of action!

Fighting to keep control of his voice, Castillo said, "You didn't tell me where she was hit."

Munz tapped his right cheek, just above his mouth.

"And in the body, the upper leg, and here in the side. That's all I saw." He pointed to both locations.

"Three wounds from . . . what was that Madsen firing?"

"I don't know; I saw some nine-millimeter casings."

"Well, maybe we got lucky and it wasn't one of the Madsen .45s."

"I don't think it was .45 ACP," Munz said, noting that Castillo knew of the Brazilian-made model. "And we may be even luckier."

"What do you mean?"

"I didn't see an exit wound on her face. That makes me think maybe it was bounced bullets."

"What?"

"Bounced bullets."

"You mean ricochets?"

"Exactly. Those marvelous windshields on that armored BMW, designed to keep bullets out, in this case may unfortunately have kept them in as well."

"Jesus, I didn't think about that."

"We'll find out when we get to the hospital."

And there's something else I didn't think about, either!

He took out his cellular and punched an autodial button.

Alex Darby answered on the second buzz.

"Darby."

"Castillo. There's been an ambush. My car, at the Sante Fe Circle in San Isidro. They got Sergeant Markham, and Betty Schneider is in a chopper on the way to the German Hospital."

"Are you all right, Charley?"

"I don't know if 'all right' is the phrase, but I wasn't in the car. I was drinking wine in a bar."

"Where are you now?"

"In Colonel Munz's car, on the Accesso Norte, on the way to the hospital."

"So the Argentines know."

"They told me . . . me, the guy who's supposed to be on top of things."

"Charley, you can't blame yourself for not being in the car."

"Who do you think these bastards were trying to hit? Me, or a female Secret Service agent and a Marine driver?"

"I'll have people at the hospital in ten minutes. Don't move from there until they get there."

"If you have anybody to spare, send them to the Masterson house. Tell them not to let Mrs. Masterson hear what happened."

"Charley, it'll be all over the television and the radio."

"Then make sure she doesn't watch TV or listen to the radio. I want her to hear about this from the ambassador. As soon as I get off this with you, I'm going to call him."

"Okay, Charley. Anything else?"

"Find Tony Santini, tell him to get Jack Britton something heavier than his Glock, then get him a car and send him to the hospital."

"Done."

"I'll be in touch, Alex," Castillo said, pushed the END key and then the autodial key for Ambassador Silvio. Then he pushed the END key again and turned to Munz.

"Alfredo. Sergeant Markham's body. What's going to happen to it?"

"When my people have finished doing their work at the Sante Fe Circle, it will be taken to the German Hospital for an autopsy."

"Is an autopsy necessary? We know what killed him. 'At least one gunshot wound to the cranium, causing severe trauma to the brain.'"

"We will need the bullets in his body as evidence when we catch the villains and bring them to trial," Munz said, matter-of-factly.

"Yeah, right," Castillo said, and put his finger back on the autodial key that would connect him with Ambassador Silvio.

"Is that about it, Charley?" Silvio asked. "I'll go to San Isidro and ask Mrs. Masterson what she wants to do about the ceremony tomorrow and call you and let you know."

"One more thing, sir. I would—"

"Let me interrupt," Silvio said. "Forgive me. How do you want to handle telling Washington? Would you like to do that yourself? I'll have to call the State Department, obviously. Would you like to meet me at the embassy after I speak with Mrs. Masterson?"

"I'm going to call Washington as soon as I can, reporting what happened . . ."

"From the embassy?"

"On this phone."

"Not on a secure line?"

"If they want me on a secure line, I'll tell them I'll go to the embassy as soon as I can. Which will be after I learn Betty Schneider's condition."

"I understand how you feel," Silvio said. "But I really think they're going to want you on a secure line as soon as possible."

"And as soon as possible, I'll get on a secure line," Castillo said simply.

There was a perceptible hesitation before Silvio went on: "You said there was one more thing?"

"Two, now that I think about it. I would be personally grateful if you could send one or more Marines right now to the Sante Fe Circle to be with, and stay with, Sergeant Markham's body. If it's gone when they get there, tell them to go to the German Hospital. The Marines take pride in never leaving anybody behind, and Roger was one hell of a Marine."

"I'll take care of that right away," Silvio said.

"And get a casket and a flag to the German Hospital. Roger will be on the Globemaster when it goes wheels-up tomorrow."

"I'll see that that's done."

"Thank you, sir."

"Let me know about Miss Schneider's condition as soon as you learn anything, will you, please?"

"Yes, sir. I will."

"We'll be talking, Charley."

"Yes, sir."

Castillo pressed the END key and then punched in a long series of numbers from memory.

"Department of Homeland Security. How may I direct your call?"

"Five, please."

"Secretary Hall's office. Mrs. Kensington."

"This is Charley, Mrs. K."

"Well, how are you?"

"Lousy. Is the boss there?"

"You just missed him, Charley."

"Good, I really didn't want to talk to him."

"Excuse me?"

"What about Dick Miller?"

"He's here. What's going on, Charley?"

"Get him on, please. Listen in. If you can, record it, so that you can play it back for the boss."

"Give me thirty seconds," Mrs. Kensington said.

Twenty-one seconds later Mrs. Kensington announced, "This telecon at five-ten P.M. Washington time July twenty-four, 2005, between C. G. Castillo, H. R. Miller, and Mary-Ellen Kensington, all of the Office of the Secretary of Homeland Security, is being recorded with the permission and knowledge of all parties thereto."

Major H. Richard Miller, Jr., came on the line. "What's going on, Charley?"

"You remember telling me not to do anything stupid with Betty Schneider?"

"Yeah. Why?"

"Well, I exceeded your expectations. I'm in a SIDE car on the outskirts of Buenos Aires, on my way to the German Hospital, to which Betty was medevaced suffering from multiple gunshot wounds to the head and body."

"Jesus H. Christ!" Major Miller said.

"Oh, my God!" Mrs. Kensington exclaimed.

"What the hell happened?" Miller asked.

"To spare Special Agent Schneider any possible embarrassment that might ensue from the hotshot in overall charge of this operation picking her up at work himself—people might get the idea she was emotionally involved with her boss, and we couldn't have that—her boss had himself dropped off at a bar, and sent his car and driver to pick up said Special Agent Schneider.

"As Sergeant Roger Markham, USMC, was navigating the Sante Fe traffic circle in San Isidro en route to the bar, where the hotshot in overall charge of this operation was sipping wine, the car was bushwhacked by parties unknown. The bastards managed to get a Madsen through Roger's window, and damned near emptied the magazine.

"Roger took several hits in the head, which just about exploded it, and the projectiles from the Madsen ricocheted off the bulletproof glass inside the car. At least three of them wound up in Betty."

"Jesus H. Christ!" Miller said.

"You already said that, Dick," Castillo said. "Now, while Mrs. K. is reporting this to the boss—tell him, please, Mrs. K., that Ambassador Silvio is going to get on a secure line to report this just as soon as he tells Mrs. Masterson about this, and sees what she wants to do about the medal ceremony tomorrow, and that I will do the same as soon as I can, which means after I find out about Betty."

"Of course," Mrs. Kensington said. "Oh, Charley, I'm so sorry—"

"You, Dick," Castillo interrupted her, "get on the horn to the police commissioner in Philadelphia. What's his name?"

"Kellogg," Miller furnished.

"Better yet, what was the name of the counterterrorism guy, the one that had been in the Tenth Special Forces Group? Fritz something?"

"Chief Inspector F. W. 'Fritz' Kramer," Miller furnished, softly.

"That's the guy. Call him. Give him a heads-up. Tell him you don't know much more than she has been hurt—don't tell him she was shot, just hurt—and that we're going to send her to Philadelphia just as soon as possible. Ask him to make the call whether to tell her family or not. Tell him as soon as you know more, you'll pass it on."

"Got it."

"And then get with Joel Isaacson and ask him what to do about Roger Markham. . . ."

"He's the Marine driver who bought the farm?" Miller interrupted.

"Yeah. The ambassador's going to call the State Department, but I don't know what they'll do about notifying the Marine Corps, or the next of kin, and I don't want that fucked up . . . sorry, Mrs. K."

"I'll handle that, Charley," Mrs. Mary-Ellen Kensington said. "What about you? Are you all right? Safe?"

"I'm sitting next to the guy who runs SIDE. In Argentina, it don't get no safer than that."

"You will call when you know something about Betty?" Mrs. Kensington asked.

"I will. Now I have to break off. We're nearly at the hospital."

"Watch your back, buddy," Major H. Richard Miller said.

Castillo pushed the END key, slipped the telephone in his pocket, and looked at Munz.

"May I suggest, Karl, that before we enter the hospital, it might be a good idea to take the round out of the chamber of your pistol?"

"Jesus Christ, I forgot about that! How did you know?"

"I saw the pistol at Sante Fe Circle," Munz said.

When I looked in the window of the BMW.

Castillo took the Beretta from the small of his back, removed the magazine, ejected the round from its chamber, put the round in the magazine, and then put the magazine back in the pistol.

[TWO]
The German Hospital
Avenida Pueyrredón
Buenos Aires, Argentina
1920 24 July 2005

Castillo got to the intensive care unit of the hospital just as Special Agent Schneider was being wheeled on a gurney out of one of the glass-walled treatment units. There were so many hospital personnel around the gurney that Castillo had trouble getting a good look.

One of the medical people was pushing what looked like a clothes tree on wheels. There were three plastic bags hanging from it, with clear plastic tubing leading from them to under the blue sheets. One of the bags contained human blood.

Charley could only guess what the other two bags held.

Betty was wrapped in pale blue sheets. They were

fresh and crisp but bloodstained near the groin and in the side. Her head was swaddled in white bandage, also bloodstained. Her eyes were open, but there was no reaction when, as the gurney was rolled out of intensive care toward a bank of elevators, he pushed one of the nurses aside to look down at her.

"I don't see any reaction," Charley said.

"I don't speak English," a man in surgical greens answered in broken English.

Charley repeated the question in Spanish.

"She has been sedated," the man answered.

They reached the elevator bank. A button was pushed and eventually a door whooshed open.

"We are taking the patient to the operation theater," the man in surgical greens said. "You are forbidden."

Charley was about to say, "Fuck you and your forbidden!" when he felt Munz's hand firmly on his shoulder.

"The chief of surgical staff will explain what's going to happen to her, Karl," Munz said gently. "You just can't go into the operation theater with her."

The chief of surgical staff looked like Santa Claus with a shave. His more than ample belly strained the buttons of his white nylon jacket. His name tag read JOSE P. ROMMINE, M.D.

There was an X-ray viewing device on one wall of his office, holding so many large X-ray films that in places three and four were pinned by the same stainless-steel clip.

"I regret my English is not good," Dr. Rommine said, as he shook Castillo's hand.

"Herr Castillo speaks German," Munz said in German.

"That would be easier," Rommine replied in German. "I took my university in Germany. First at Philipps, in Marburg an der Lahn, then at Heidelberg."

"I know the schools," Castillo said.

German doctors—and I'm sure she had the best— couldn't keep my mother alive. I hope you can do better for Betty, Herr Doktor Santa Claus.

Please, God, let him do better!

"We're interested in your diagnosis, Herr Doktor," Munz said.

"Of course," the doctor said, turning to the X-rays and picking up a pointer. "As you can see from this, the wound to the leg, while it has of course done some muscle damage—and there will be more as the projectile is removed—could have been much worse."

Yeah, sure, those bastards could have used a 20mm and blown it off.

Jesus, if they wanted to whack me, and they obviously have access to weapons, why didn't they use a hand grenade? Once they got Roger to lower the window, all they would have had to do was drop it inside the car. Heroic stories to the contrary, when a grenade lands close, very few people have ever been able to toss it back.

Castillo had an unpleasant image of Roger Markham desperately searching for a grenade on the floorboard, and then finding it just before it went off. Grenade shards would have gone through the upholstery and thin sheet metal of the seats without trouble. And of course probably bounced off that wonderful bullet-resistant glass.

Dr. Rommine's learned lecture concerning Betty's leg wound, illustrated with half a dozen X-rays, took at least three minutes.

So did Part II, the wound in the groin area, which was also serious but not as serious as it could have been. The X-rays revealed no damage to the reproductive organs, except for the sympathetic trauma—

Whatever the hell that means.

—and the surgery to remove that projectile would of course clear up the questions unanswered by the X-rays.

"I think the wound to the face is going to cause the greatest difficulty," Dr. Rommine said, turning to the X-rays of the patient's cranium with emphasis on the mandible area.

"As you can see, the projectile is rather deeply embedded in the bone here." He used the pointer, and then turned to first one, and then a second, and then a third X-ray, covering the mandible area from all angles. "There is a fracture and some to-be-expected splintering. Removing the projectile will be somewhat difficult. We don't do much oral surgery here, and I attempted to locate a good man I know, but he's skiing in Bariloche and he won't be available for several days."

I hope the bastard breaks both his legs.

Castillo asked, "Are you saying you're going to leave the bullet in her jaw until you can get this guy back from Bariloche?"

"Dr. Koos is his name. Oh, no. The projectile will be removed now. But the restorative surgery—her jaw will of course have to be wired closed—is quite important, and should be placed in the hands of the best man available."

Jesus, that's Betty's skull I'm looking at.

Castillo suddenly felt light-headed, then dizzy.

What am I going to do, pass out? Throw up on Santa Claus's shiny floor?

No, goddammit, I will not lose control of myself!

He steadied himself with a hand on the X-ray display rack.

"Doctor, how soon can she be moved?"

"I beg your pardon?"

"How soon could I fly her to the United States?"

"Oh, I see what you're thinking." He thought the question over and then continued: "That would depend in large measure on what sort of support you could provide, in terms of oxygen, blood—in case of unexpected bleeding—et cetera, on the aircraft. And there would have to be provision to feed her. Liquids, of course. Her jaw, as I say, will be immobilized for at least two weeks. She would have to be accompanied by a physician and a nurse. I'm speaking of moving her soon—say, tomorrow or the day after. If you were willing to wait, say, seventy-two or ninety-six hours—three or four days—while she would be in some discomfort, she could travel far more easily. With medical personnel in attendance, of course."

"How long is she going to be in the operating room now?"

"Oh, I would say . . ." Dr. Rommine began, then thought that over for a good twenty seconds before finishing: "Two hours, perhaps a little longer. And I'd better get scrubbed. They almost certainly have the patient prepared by now."

"You're going to operate?"

"Of course. El Coronel Munz has explained the situation to me. It will be my privilege."

Dr. Rommine then walked out of his office without saying another word. He left so quickly that Castillo doubted Dr. Santa Claus had heard his somewhat belatedly expressed thanks.

"You all right, Karl?" Munz asked.

Castillo nodded.

"You looked a little pale there for a while."

"I'm all right. Thank you for everything."

"Let's see if we can find a cup of coffee," Munz said. "And we'd better start thinking about getting a little something to eat."

"Alfredo, I'm not hungry."

"If people don't eat, their blood sugar drops, especially after they have been subjected to stress, and they pass out," Munz said.

Castillo looked at him a moment, realized reluctantly that he was right, and nodded his thanks.

"Okay," Castillo said, starting for the door, "let's go."

"Sit down, Karl," Munz said. "I'll have something sent up."

"Alfredo, do you really think these bastards would try to whack me in a hospital cafeteria?"

"That seems to be the problem, doesn't it? If you don't have any idea who the villains are, then it's rather difficult to assess their plans or their capabilities."

Munz punched an autodial key on his cellular and told someone to go to the cafeteria and bring up some sandwiches—*lomo* sandwiches, if they had them, otherwise ham and cheese—coffee, and some very sweet pastry.

Castillo sat in Dr. Santa Claus's chair and looked at the bullet lodged in Betty's jaw.

Jack Britton showed up at the same time as the sandwiches. He had a Madsen submachine gun under his arm, hanging from a web strap around his shoulder.

"She's in the operating room," Castillo told him without waiting to be asked. He pointed to the X-ray films and then the weapon. "Three wounds from one of those."

"From one of these?" Britton asked, incredulously.

"Yeah, from one of those. Where'd you get that?"

"Darby," Britton said. "He asked me if I could handle it, and I lied. I never saw one before. They hit Betty with one of these?"

"Yeah, a nine-millimeter model. And blew Sergeant Markham away."

"I heard that," Britton said. "What the fuck is going on, Charley?"

"I have no goddamn idea," Castillo confessed, and extended his hands for the Madsen. "Let me have that. I'll show you how it works."

Britton handed Castillo the submachine gun. He removed the magazine and checked to see that there was no cartridge left in the mechanism.

"Pay attention, Jack. You may have to use this," Castillo said.

"I'm all ears," Britton said.

"This is a Madsen M53," Castillo began, "caliber nine-millimeter Parabellum. This has a curved thirty-round magazine; the earlier models have a stick. It fires from an open chamber; in other words, to fire it, you pull the operating lever on the top to the rear. . . ."

He demonstrated by pulling the operating lever back. It caught in place with a firm click.

"The first thing you do is take the safety off. In other words, move this thing to 'F' . . ."

He demonstrated the functioning of the safety control.

"Then you select auto or single-shot mode. This is the selector lever for that; 'A' stands for automatic. . . ."

He demonstrated the function of the selector switch.

"Then you pull the trigger."

He pulled the trigger. The bolt slammed into the battery position.

"If there had been a loaded magazine in there, the bolt would have stripped off the top cartridge, shoved it in the action, and it would have gone *bang*. Then the bolt would return to the rear position. If you were in single-shot mode, to fire again, you would have to release your finger on the trigger and then pull it again. If you were in auto mode—your finger still holding the trigger to the rear—it would go *bang-bang-bang* at a rate of six hundred and fifty rounds per minute until you ran out of ammo. We try to teach people to try to get off three-shot bursts—it takes some practice—because otherwise, as when firing any other submachine gun, the muscles of the shooter tend to involuntarily contract, raising the muzzle, and you miss what you wanted to shoot."

He looked at Britton. "I hope you took notes. There will be a quiz."

"When you said 'we try to teach people,' you meant Special Forces, didn't you?"

Castillo nodded. "You've fired submachine guns, right?"

"Yeah. But not this one."

"A lot of people like the Madsen," Castillo said.

He handed the weapon back to Britton.

"The bolt is forward," he said. "Put the safety lever on 'S' and the rate of fire selector on 'A,'" he said, and when Britton looked at him, added, "Yeah, now, please, Jack."

Britton did as he was told.

"Okay. It is now safe to load the magazine." He handed it to him, watched as Britton inserted it, and then went on. "Okay, all you have to do now is pull the action lever back, take off the safety, and pull the trigger."

"Got it," Britton said.

"Good," Castillo said. "Now, carefully lay it down on that shelf. I don't think you're going to need it in here right now, and I want to eat my sandwich. Are you hungry, Jack?"

"No. Thanks."

"You sure? These look good," Castillo said and reached for one.

Castillo was finishing a generous slice of incredibly good *apfelstrudel*—*why I am surprised? This is the German Hospital*—when there was a knock on the office door. A large man in civilian clothing came in and offered Colonel Munz a small, resealable plastic bag.

"And, *mi coronel,* there are Americans here for Señor Castillo."

Munz didn't reply directly. He held up the bag. Castillo saw that it held two fired cartridge cases.

"There are others, right? We won't need these in court?"

"There are twenty-four in all, *mi coronel.* We are still looking. It is possible that some spectators took some others as souvenirs."

Munz opened the bag and took out a brass cartridge case, examined it carefully, and then handed it to Castillo.

"Israeli," he said. "Same year stamp as the ones we found on Avenida Tomas Edison in the taxicab."

Castillo took the case and handed it to Britton.

"We now have conclusive proof that in 1999 Israel made nine-millimeter ammunition," he said.

Munz smiled at him.

"Don't smile," Castillo said. "I can't think of anything else we have conclusive proof of." He looked at Britton. "Just to satisfy my curiosity, what's in the embassy Madsen?"

Britton took a curved magazine from his pocket, thumbed a cartridge loose, and examined its base.

"Israeli, 1992," he said.

"And conclusive proof that the bad guys have fresher ammo than the good guys," Castillo said. "Not that it matters, as I'm beginning to wonder if we'll ever get a chance to shoot back."

"You want these?" Munz nodded.

"Yes, thank you," Castillo said, and took the plastic

bag, put the cartridge Britton held out to him in it, zipped it shut, and dropped it in his pocket.

"Americans for me?" he asked Munz's man.

"*Sí, señor.*"

Castillo gestured for them to be brought in.

A civilian—Castillo recognized his face from the brainstorming session but couldn't come up with a name—and a Marine. The man, in his middle twenties, was olive-skinned, and Castillo decided he was probably one of the Drug Enforcement Administration agents. He was carrying an M-16 rifle.

The Marine, who was in greens and had a Beretta in a field holster hanging from a web belt, was a corporal.

"I'm Castillo. You're looking for me?"

"Solez, Mr. Castillo. DEA. I was told to report to you and do whatever you told me to do."

"Do you speak Spanish, Mr. Solez?" Castillo said in Spanish.

"I spoke it before I learned to speak English," Solez replied in Spanish.

Castillo picked up on the accent.

"And where are you from in Texas?" Castillo asked, still in Spanish.

"San Antone, señor."

"Me, too."

"Yes, sir, I know."

"How do you know?"

"My father is Antonio Solez, sir. I think you know him."

Antonio Solez had been one of Castillo's grandfather's cronies, a familiar face around both the offices and the ranches, and a pallbearer at the funeral of Don Juan Fernando Castillo. A mental image of him, a large swarthy man, standing across the open grave with his chest heaving and tears running unashamedly down his cheeks, leaped into Castillo's mind.

"Indeed I do. How is he?"

"Still taking care of Don Fernando," Solez said, with a smile. It took a moment for Charley to take his meaning. He smiled back.

"When did my fat and ugly cousin start calling himself 'Don Fernando'?"

"People started calling him that after Don Fernando passed. I think he likes it. Doña Alicia does, I know."

"You're Ricardo, right? The last I heard you were at College Station."

"*Sí, señor.* I graduated in 2001, and went right into the DEA."

"You don't have to call me 'sir.' And please don't."

Solez nodded.

"Why didn't you say something when we were at that brainstorming thing?" Castillo asked.

Solez shrugged. "I wasn't sure you would remember me."

"I should have recognized you. I'm sorry."

Solez shrugged again. "No problem. You had other things on your mind. We're both a long way from San Antonio."

"I'm really happy to see you, Ricardo," Castillo said. "You heard what happened?"

Solez nodded.

"She's in the operating room now," Castillo said.

"She'll be in there for probably another two hours. From the moment she gets off the elevator until I get out of here, I want you or Special Agent Britton—you know each other?"

"We met."

"Since you're talking about me, I wish you'd do it in English, Charley," Britton said.

"Sorry," Charley said, now in English. "It seems that Special Agent Solez is not only a fellow Texican, but his family and mine have been friends for generations."

"My dad is chief engineer for Castillo Properties," Solez said with pride. "Everything but the petroleum side."

Britton looked at him and nodded.

"Okay," Castillo went on, "from the time Special Agent Schneider gets out of the operating room until I can get her the hell out of here, I want one or the other, preferably both, sitting on her."

"You got it," Britton said. Solez nodded.

"There will be SIDE people with you, of course," Munz said.

Both Britton and Solez nodded.

Castillo turned to the Marine corporal and looked closely at him for the first time. He was no more than five feet four or five and weighed no more than one-forty. He looked to be about seventeen years old.

I thought Marines on embassy duty had to be five-eleven and one-eighty or better. Where did this little guy come from?

Oh, yeah. Rule of War Thirteen B: "Every military organization with an authorized strength of two or more men will have a designated paper pusher."

This little guy is the Marine guard detachment clerk, pressed into duty as a driver.

"You're the driver, right, Corporal?"

The corporal came to attention.

"No, sir. The driver is with the car, sir. The gunny instructed me to tell you, sir, that an armored car was not immediately available, and to suggest you take appropriate precautions until one can be found for you."

"Okay."

"My name is Corporal Lester Bradley, sir. I am your bodyguard, sir."

For a moment there was silence, and then Jack Britton was suddenly overwhelmed with a coughing fit. Colonel Munz, his face turned red, and DEA Special Agent Solez became suddenly fascinated with the X-rays on display.

Major C. G. Castillo—after covering his mouth with his hand so it would not be obvious he was biting his lip as hard as he could; one chuckle, the hint of a giggle, from him, or anyone else, would trigger something close to hysterics in everybody—finally decided he could trust his voice.

"Well, I'm glad to have you, Corporal," he said. "I know how reliable the Marines are."

"*Semper fi,* sir," Corporal Lester Bradley said sincerely.

Colonel Munz turned from his examination of the X-rays, and probably not trusting himself to speak, signaled with a nod of his head toward the door that he wanted a private word with Castillo.

"Excuse me a minute, guys. I'll be right back," Castillo said, and followed Munz into the corridor.

Munz put his hand on Castillo's arm.

"Now that you're under the protection of the U.S. Corps of Marines, Karl, would you mind if I left you?"

"Don't underestimate the Marines, Alfredo. They're nice people to have in your corner."

"Are they all like that boy?"

"They are not often troubled with self-doubt," Charley said.

"And neither should you be, Karl," Munz said seriously. "I've been practicing our trade for a while, and I have met very few people with your natural talent for it."

"I take that as a great compliment, Alfredo."

"It was meant as one. Listen to me, Karl. Don't let what happened in there bother you. . . ."

He means my almost taking a dive.

". . . There would be something wrong with a man who, looking at a bullet in the skull of the woman he loves—a bullet which, but for God's mercy, would have taken her life—was not affected as you were."

Castillo met his eyes but said nothing.

Munz squeezed his arm.

"And pay attention to what your bodyguard said about your not having an armored car," Munz said with a smile. "I presume you'll be going to your embassy?"

Why not? Dr. Santa Claus said Betty'll be in there two hours. And I'm going to have to talk to Washington on a secure line.

Castillo nodded. "I took that to heart."

"There will be a SIDE car with you," Munz said, and then offered Castillo his hand. "Goodbye, Karl."

Goodbye? What does he mean by that?

"Thanks for everything, Alfredo."

"I will pray for your lady, Karl," Munz said, touched Castillo's shoulder, then walked quickly down the corridor to the elevator.

Charley went back in the office, told Britton and Solez he was going to the embassy and to call him if there was any word at all, and then—under the careful watch of Corporal Bradley, his bodyguard—went to the basement and got in the unarmored embassy car.

On the way, his cellular went off, and he answered it with his heart in his throat. It was Ambassador Silvio, who told him that Mrs. Masterson wished to go ahead with the ceremony at the Catedral Metropolitana.

"I'm on the way to the embassy, sir. To get on the horn to Washington. Would you like me to wait until you get there?"

"Please, Charley. I'll be there in thirty minutes."

[THREE]
The United States Embassy
Avenida Colombia 4300
Buenos Aires, Argentina
2040 24 July 2005

"White House."

"This is C. G. Castillo. I need to speak on a secure—"

"We've been waiting for your call, sir. Hold one, please."

• • •

"Secretary Hall's office. Mrs. Kensington speaking."

"We have Mr. Castillo for Secretary Hall, Mrs. Kensington. This line is secure."

Mrs. Kensington pushed her intercom button, said, "Pick up, boss. It's Charley on a secure line," then dialed another number on the secure phone.

Charley listened as she said, "We have Secretary Hall and Mr. Castillo on a secure line for a conference call with Director Montvale."

Oh shit!

Charles W. Montvale, former deputy secretary of state, former secretary of the treasury, and former ambassador to the European Union, was the recently appointed United States director of national intelligence. The press had immediately dubbed him the "intel czar."

"Charles Montvale."

Oh, shit, again! He sounds like he's got his teeth clenched.

"Are you okay, Charley?" Secretary Hall asked as he came on the line.

"I'm well, thank you, Matt. And yourself?" Director Montvale said, a touch of condescending amusement in his voice.

"Castillo, are you on?" Hall asked. There was a touch of impatience in his voice.

"Yes, sir."

"Are you all right, Charley?"

"Yes, sir. I'm fine."

"And the girl?"

"She's in surgery now at the German Hospital. She took three hits—"

"Am I correct in assuming the third party to this call

is Major Castillo?" Director Montvale interrupted. He still sounded amused.

"Yes, sir," Castillo said.

"I am Charles Montvale, Major. Do you know who I am?" Now his voice was serious.

"Yes, sir."

"The President has asked me to take your call, Major. Do you understand?"

"Yes, sir."

"This call is being recorded. You may proceed."

"Hold off, Charley," Matt Hall said icily. "Mr. Montvale, let's get some things clear between us before anyone says another word."

"Is there a problem?"

"Several, I'm afraid. For one thing, I don't like being informed that my call is being recorded. You said nothing about that when you told my executive assistant you wanted to listen to this call."

"Actually, it was my executive assistant who spoke with your executive assistant," Montvale said. "And recording my calls—especially calls of this nature—is standard procedure."

"It's not my standard procedure. I would like your assurance that the recording device has been turned off, that what has been recorded so far will be erased, and that there is no one privy to this call but the three of us."

"I intend to have the tape of this conversation available should the President ask for it when I report this telecom to him."

"Do I understand I don't have your assurance the recorder is being turned off?"

"I frankly don't understand your attitude, Secretary Hall."

"Is that a yes or a no, Mr. Montvale?"

"Jo-Anne, turn off the recorder," Montvale said after a moment.

"And erase anything that's been recorded," Hall insisted.

"Erase what has been recorded so far, please, Jo-Anne."

"Thank you."

"You said there were several problems, Secretary Hall?"

"Major Castillo works for me. I will tell him when to proceed or when not to. Is that clear?"

"May I point out, Mr. Secretary, that we all work for the President? And that it is at the President's order that I am taking the call?"

"Major Castillo," Hall said. "You understand that you take your orders from either the President or me? And only the President and me?"

"Yes, sir."

"I will, of course, seek clarification of this from the President," Montvale said.

"We both will, Mr. Montvale," Hall said, and then, when there was no response from Montvale, went on: "Okay, Charley, go on."

"Sir, Ambassador Silvio is with me. We're in his office in the embassy. The call is on the speakerphone."

"Good evening, Mr. Ambassador," Hall said. "You've heard what's been said so far?"

"Yes, I have, Mr. Secretary," Silvio said.

"Do you know the director of national intelligence, Mr. Montvale?"

"Yes, sir. I know the ambassador. Good evening, sir."

"How are you, Silvio?"

"Very well, sir. Thank you."

"I attempted to call you, Silvio, earlier, when the President brought me in on this. You were not available."

"When was that, sir?"

"Forty-five minutes ago, an hour. I'm curious why you weren't available."

"I was with Mrs. Masterson at that time, sir."

"And they didn't tell you I was calling?"

"I left instructions that I was not to be disturbed when I was with her, Mr. Montvale."

"Even for a call from me?"

"From anyone, sir. It was my intention, sir, to return your call when Mr. Castillo had completed his call to Secretary Hall."

"I must say that's an odd priority. But why don't you tell me about Mrs. Masterson? The President is deeply concerned."

"Yes, sir."

"Mr. Montvale," Hall said. "May I respectfully suggest that you telephone Ambassador Silvio when Major Castillo has finished his report to me?"

"You don't seem to understand, do you, Hall, that I am acting at the orders of the President?"

"From the tone of your voice, Charles, and if I didn't know better, I might think that two of my most senior staff are having a little tiff over turf," the President of the United States said. "You fellows don't mind if I join the conversation, do you?"

"Of course not, Mr. President," Montvale said.

"Good evening, sir," Hall said.

"You on here, Charley?" the President asked.

"Yes, sir," Castillo replied. "And so is Ambassador Silvio, sir."

"How much did I miss? I hate to make you go over it all again, but I just couldn't get the goddamn . . . get my distinguished visitor to leave."

"I was just about to start, Mr. President."

"Start with the condition of the female agent," the President said.

"Yes, sir. Special Agent Schneider is in surgery. She suffered three gunshot wounds from a nine-millimeter Madsen submachine gun. . . ."

It took Castillo perhaps five minutes to report what had happened, and what was planned. The President had interrupted him three times, once to ask where the Argentine police were when the embassy car had been attacked, a second time to ask what Castillo thought about the quality of the medical treatment Special Agent Schneider was getting, and a third time to ask what had been done about notifying Schneider's family, and that of Sergeant Roger Markham.

"That's about it, sir," Castillo concluded.

There was a ten-second silence, and then the President said: "You haven't had much to say, Mr. Ambassador. Can I take that to mean you and Charley are on the same page?"

"Yes, sir," Silvio said, simply. "We pretty much see things the same way."

"And would you tell me if you didn't?"

"Yes, sir, I would," Silvio said.

There was another long pause, and then the President said, "You ever hear that story about the people who went to President Lincoln to tell him General Grant was a drunk? Lincoln was pretty fed up with people around him bickering, and history tells us he had one hell of a temper. But this time he kept it in check. What President Lincoln said was, 'Well, find out what General Grant is drinking and I'll see that my other generals get some of it.'"

The President paused. "Now, Mr. Ambassador, changing the subject, I wonder if you would be good enough to send me, via Major Castillo, a bottle of whatever you two have been drinking? I'll share it with Secretary Hall and Director Montvale."

"It would be my pleasure, Mr. President," Silvio said, a smile in his voice.

"Just idle curiosity," the President asked, "what will it be?"

"Major Castillo, sir, shares my appreciation of a local wine, a cabernet sauvignon from the Sentenir bodega in Mendoza."

"I'll look forward to it," the President said. "Maybe two bottles would be better than one. Better yet, make it a case."

"Yes, sir."

"One more thing," the President said. "Charley, are you watching your back?"

"Yes, sir."

"I guess what I really meant to ask is who's helping you watch your back?"

"Sir, as we speak, my Marine bodyguard is standing outside the ambassador's door."

"Well, do what he says, Charley. Too many people are getting shot down there."

"Yes, sir, I will."

"Unless someone has something else, that would seem to be it."

No one said anything.

"Okay. I'll see you sometime late tomorrow, Charley. And, *Charles,* I think it would be a good idea if you went down to Mississippi with us, too."

"Of course, Mr. President," Director of National Intelligence Montvale said.

[FOUR]

As Castillo came out of Ambassador Silvio's office, Corporal Lester Bradley, USMC, popped to attention and said, "There are two Air Force officers to see you, sir. I asked them to wait in the outer office."

"Thank you, Corporal," Castillo said and went into the outer office, where he found Colonel Jake Torine and the light bird pilot of the Gulfstream—if he had ever heard his name, Castillo couldn't remember it now—sitting in the row of chairs against the wall. Both were in civilian clothing: sports jackets and slacks.

"I was just about to call you," Castillo said, shaking Torine's hand.

"We heard what happened," Torine said. "How's that female Secret Service agent doing? Betty?"

"Betty took three hits. She's in surgery now."

"Nice girl," Torine said. "Is she going to be all right?"

"Jesus Christ, I hope so," Castillo said. "I'm going to the German Hospital from here."

"Any change in the plan for tomorrow?"

"No. Mrs. Masterson has decided she's going ahead with the whole dog-and-pony show. Jake, just now I remembered, or think I did, something about an ambulance configuration for the Gulfstream."

Torine shrugged, indicating he didn't know either, and then asked, "Walter?"

"Yes, there is an emergency ambulance configuration for the C-37," the lieutenant colonel confirmed.

"Installed on the one you're flying, Colonel?" Charley asked.

"Yes, there is."

"Tell me about it, please."

"May I ask why you're asking?"

"What, is it classified or something, Walter?" Torine asked, sarcastically.

"Yes, sir, as a matter of fact it is. The configuration of all Eighty-ninth Presidential Airlift Group aircraft is classified—"

"Jesus Christ!" Torine exploded. "And you're worried Castillo doesn't have the proper clearance—or maybe it's me?"

For a moment, Charley thought the light bird was going to say just that. But then, as Castillo studied him, he thought, *This chicken-shit light bird has only now decided that a full bird colonel sent on Presidential Orders as pilot in command of a Globemaster more than likely has the proper security clearances, and since he was senior, if he said it was all right to describe the configuration of the Gulfstream, any breach of security would fall on his shoulders.*

"Three of the seats on the left side of the cabin can be placed in a horizontal position," the light bird began. "There is a mattress and sheets—rubber and the ordinary kind—stored behind the galley. Behind the paneling by the sheets is some other medical equipment. A blood pressure device, things like that. And an oxygen feed, connected to the aircraft's main oxygen supply."

"What's on your mind, Charley?" Torine asked.

Castillo didn't reply directly.

"Colonel, you came direct from Washington," Castillo said. "Can I extrapolate that to mean you can go direct Jorge Newbery–Philadelphia?"

"Are you a pilot, Major Castillo?"

Aha! Somebody's tipped him—and I think I know who—that he's dealing with a lowly major. That's why he doesn't want me to know the secrets of the Gulfstream.

"Yes, I am," Castillo said.

"With some experience in long-distance, jet-long-distance, flight?"

"I know for a fact that he flew the right seat of a 727 from Costa Rica to MacDill, and worked the radios and everything," Torine said, smiling at Charley. "What's with all the questions, Walter?"

"Sir, it would be easier if the major were conversant with the problems involved in a flight of that distance."

"Can your fancy little bird make it from here to Philadelphia nonstop, or not, Walter? Jesus Christ!" Torine exploded.

"Theoretically, yes. But it would be prudent to think of somewhere to refuel if fuel consumption turned out to be greater for one reason or another than planned for."

"Worst fuel-consumption scenario, Colonel. Can you make it from here to Miami?"

"Very probably. There are never any guarantees."

"What about MacDill?" Castillo asked. "As a refueling stop?"

"Very probably," the lieutenant colonel said, after considering it for a moment.

"Thank you," Castillo said.

"But speaking hypothetically, MacDill requires advance notice—twelve hours, I believe, I'd have to check—to refuel transient aircraft."

"I'm not being hypothetical, Colonel," Castillo said. "What's going to happen is this: Ambassador Silvio at this moment is arranging for an American physician . . ."

He paused and looked at Torine.

". . . who fortunately (a) is a fellow Miami Cuban, and (b) is in town conducting a seminar at the University of Belgrano, and a nurse or maybe two."

Torine nodded his understanding, and Castillo looked back at the lieutenant colonel.

"You are going to fly Special Agent Schneider, the doctor, and the nurses from here to Philadelphia just as soon—maybe tomorrow, maybe the day after tomorrow—as they say she's up to the trip."

"On whose authority, Major?"

"On mine," Castillo said softly.

"I'm afraid I can't do that, Major. My orders were to fly the FBI team down here, and then to return them to Washington."

"Listen to me very carefully, Colonel Newley," Colonel Torine said, icily. "I am telling you that Major Castillo has all the authority he needs to tell you to do anything. Now you can accept that, and cheerfully and willingly comply with any orders he may give you, or I will get on the horn to General McFadden at CentCom and inform him that after relieving you for obstructing a presidential mission, I am placing your copilot in command of the Gulfstream, assigning one of my backup crew as copilot, and returning you to Andrews by commercial air."

General Albert McFadden, U.S. Air Force, was the CentCom deputy commander.

Lieutenant Colonel Walter Newley's face paled. He swallowed, then said, "Yes, sir," very softly.

"Does that mean you understand you're under Major Castillo's orders?"

"Yes, sir," Lieutenant Colonel Newley said softly.

"What? I didn't hear that. You're supposed to sound like an Air Force officer, not some faggot wearing the wings of an Air Chad cabin attendant."

"Yes, sir," Lieutenant Colonel Newley said, much louder.

"Wait in the corridor for me, please, Colonel," Torine said, in a normal voice.

"Yes, sir," Lieutenant Colonel Newley said, somewhat loudly.

Torine waited until the door closed, then turned to Castillo.

"Charley," he began, and then saw that Corporal Lester Bradley, USMC, had heard the exchange.

"Son," Torine asked, "I don't think you heard much of that little conversation, did you?"

"What conversation is that, sir?" Corporal Bradley asked.

"The only thing I like better than a Marine is a selectively deaf Marine," Torine said.

"Permission to speak, sir?"

"Granted."

"During our training at Quantico, sir, we are told we will hear things we will immediately forget we heard."

"Thank you," Torine said. "Now, son, please go into the corridor for a moment so that it won't be necessary for you to forget what Major Castillo and I are going to discuss."

"Yes, sir," Corporal Bradley said, and went into the corridor.

When the door had closed, Torine said, "I have no idea what that nonsense with Newley was all about, but I have the feeling there's something more to it than him being a by-the-book asshole."

"He knew I'm a major. I never said I was. So somebody told him. I think I know who."

Torine made a give-it-to-me gesture with his hands.

"There's an FBI agent, assigned to the embassy in Montevideo. Name of Yung. I think he's made me."

"I don't think I understand."

"Howard Kennedy told me he's one of their hot-shots—"

"Kennedy is here?" Torine asked, visibly surprised.

"He was. Kennedy said he used to work with this guy, and that whatever he's doing in Montevideo—he's sup-posed to be working on money laundering—isn't what he's really doing."

"I'll try to figure this out as you continue, Charley."

"I suspect there's still an FBI interest in Charley Castillo. What the cops would call a 'locate but do not detain.' Kennedy is still very worried about what he calls his 'former associates,' and he's not a fool. The FBI thinks I can lead them to Pevsner and/or Kennedy."

"Charley, I was there, with you, when the President told the DCI and director of the FBI to lay off Pevsner. I interpreted that to mean lay off Pevsner and the people who work for him."

"That's the primary reason I'm telling you this now, Jake. Somebody told the *New York Times* guy here—and some others—that the President's agent is down here, and somebody told Colonel Newley that I'm a major. And probably a troublemaker. 'Watch out for that son-ofabitch, he can get you in trouble.' Am I being para-noid, or is it possible the FBI is ignoring what you and I would call a direct order from the President?"

Colonel Torine considered that for a moment, then said, "Well, you know what they say, Charley."

"No, what do they say?"

"Just because you're paranoid doesn't mean that little green men aren't trying to castrate you with machetes."

"Shit," Castillo chuckled.

"What are you going to do about it?" Torine asked.

"I have a gut feeling I should do nothing about it now. Maybe because I'm a little afraid of the clout they've given me, and I don't want to burn the bastard until I'm sure he is a bastard. And I also want to find out what Howard Kennedy meant when he said whatever Yung is doing in Montevideo, it's not reading bank statements."

"What else could he be doing?"

"I have no idea, but I do know that the minute the FBI finds out I've fingered him, he'll stop doing it, and then I'll never know."

Torine shrugged. "It's your call, Charley. I can't fault it. What do you want me to do with Newley?"

"See that he gets the airplane ready. Have him hang around here until we can get this doctor to look at the airplane and see what else he will need."

"Done," Torine said. "Charley, I've got a guy at Ezeiza who can fly that Gulfstream. Redundancy was one of the reasons I brought him along. Say the word and I'll have him fly it."

"No, I don't want to do that. If you relieve Newley, there goes his career. He was doing what he thought was the right thing to do, and I think you made a Christian out of him."

"Your call. What are you going to do now?"

"I'm going back to the hospital and wait for Betty to come out of the operating room."

"Want some company? After I make sure I've made a true Christian out of Newley? One who won't go back to his wicked ways the minute we get off the ground?"

"Thanks but no thanks, Jake."

X

[ONE]
The German Hospital
Avenida Pueyrredón
Buenos Aires, Argentina
2135 24 July 2005

There were two men Castillo suspected were SIDE agents in the lobby of the hospital when he and Corporal Bradley walked in. Confirmation came when one of them walked up to them and told Castillo "your agent" was in room 677.

It was the room where Mrs. Masterson had been placed. Castillo wondered whether it was coincidence or whether the ever-resourceful Colonel Munz had an arrangement with the hospital for really secure rooms for patients in whom SIDE had an interest.

When he got to the sixth floor, Castillo found Jack Britton sitting in a folding metal chair outside the room, holding a Madsen on his lap.

"Betty's still in the operating room, Charley," Britton said. "Solez talked somebody into letting him wait outside the operating room. Apparently, they're going to bring her here instead of to a recovery room. They've been taking all sorts of equipment in there. And there's a couple of guys with Uzis down the hall."

Castillo looked, and then said, "I just made arrangements for Betty to be flown—on the Gulfstream that brought you down here—to Philadelphia when she's up to traveling. I want you to go with her."

Britton nodded.

"I had Dick Miller call Chief Inspector Kramer to give him a heads-up. When we know something, I'll call him and bring him up to speed. Unless I'm gone before that happens, then you'll have to do it."

Britton nodded again.

Castillo looked into the room and saw that it was prepared to treat someone just out of an operating room.

"I hope there's a john in there," Castillo said. "I really need to take a leak."

He saw on Corporal Lester Bradley's face that a visit to a toilet was high on his agenda, as well. Clearly uncomfortably, perhaps even painfully high.

"Corporal, there are two things that a warrior must always remember," Castillo said sternly. "The first is to void one's bladder at every opportunity, because one never knows when there will be another opportunity to do so."

"Yes, sir."

"The second is RHIP."

"Rank Has Its Privileges, yes, sir."

"Which in this case means I get to go in there before you do."

"Yes, sir."

"Just kidding. Go on, Bradley," Castillo said. "I can wait."

"You go ahead, sir."

"You have your orders, Corporal! This is your opportunity, maybe your only opportunity. Take it!"

"Yes, sir."

Britton chuckled. "Nice kid," he said, when Bradley had gone into the room.

"Yeah. And so was Sergeant Roger Markham," Castillo said, and then went on, bitterly, " 'The secretary of the Navy regrets to inform you that your son, Staff Sergeant Roger Markham, was killed in the line of duty. What he was doing was chauffeuring a Secret Service agent to a bar, where she was to meet her boyfriend.' "

"First I'll tell you about Markham," Britton said.

"Tell me about Markham?"

"The gunnery sergeant came looking for you—the guy in charge of the Marine guards?"

"I know who he is."

"He brought a casket for Markham's body, and a flag. They've got him in a cooler in the morgue here in the hospital, and they're going to take him out to Ezeiza first thing in the morning. He said that if he didn't get a chance to see you, to tell you thanks for making sure Markham had a Marine escort—there's two Marines in the morgue with the body—and for sending him home in a military aircraft, instead of like one more piece of luggage on Delta or American."

"Well, you know me, Jack. 'Charley Castillo, always looking out for his men. He's not very good at it, and some of them get blown away, but what the hell, Castillo means well.' "

"Oh, bullshit, Charley. That's the second thing I'm

going to tell you: What happened to Markham and Betty is not your fault."

"I should have been in that car, Jack, and you know it."

"No. That's bullshit. If you had been in that car, one of two things would have happened. You'd either be in the cooler with Markham, or you'd be in a hospital bed like Betty."

"Maybe I could have gotten one of the bastards."

"More bullshit and you should know it. Face the facts, Charley."

"What are the facts?"

"I don't *know* how it is with the Secret Service, but I suspect it's just like on the cops."

"I don't follow you, Jack."

"On the cops, when something like this happens— your partner gets shot, or whacked—they won't let you near the investigation. You're too emotionally involved. I'm afraid if you keep up this 'it's all my fault' bullshit somebody important's going to hear you and they'll keep you off the investigation. And I wouldn't like that."

"Why not?"

"Because the only way a brand-new Secret Service agent like me is going to be allowed to try to find the bastards who whacked Masterson, Markham, and almost whacked Betty is if you can fix it. And I really want those bastards, Charley."

For a moment, Castillo couldn't find his voice. Then he said, "For however long I'm on this, Jack, if I have anything to say about it, you will be, too."

"You'll be on it a lot longer if you get your act to-gether. Starting with nobody has to know about you and Betty. Can you get that Air Force colonel to keep his mouth shut?"

"Yeah."

"Okay. It was just the four of us in the hotel room, and Markham's dead, you say the Air Force guy will keep his mouth shut, and if you and I play it cool, no one has to know about you and Betty."

"That'll be tough for me to fake, Jack."

"You're supposed to be a hard-ass. Fake it."

Corporal Bradley returned to the corridor.

Castillo touched Britton's shoulder and went into room 677.

When he came out of the toilet, there was a large, well-dressed man with a full, neatly trimmed mustache standing with his hands folded in front of him, by the door, which was closed.

Castillo was startled, but quickly recovered.

If this guy wasn't supposed to be in here, Britton wouldn't have let him in. Maybe he's a doctor, or something.

No, he's not, unless the doctors around here wear shoulder holsters.

Conclusion: One more guy from SIDE. A senior guy from SIDE.

"Señor?" Castillo asked.

"Señor Castillo?"

"Sí."

"I am el Coronel Alejandro Gellini of SIDE, Señor Castillo."

Castillo crossed the room to him and put out his hand.

"Mucho gusto, mi coronel," Castillo said.

"I have just seen Ambassador Silvio, señor. I conveyed to him, on behalf of the President of the Nation, our profound regret for what has happened to the female Secret Service agent and the Corps of Marines sergeant."

"That was very good of you, of the President, *mi coronel,*" Castillo said.

"Ambassador Silvio told me that you are in charge of security for Señora Masterson and her children, in fact of everybody."

"That's true," Castillo said.

"And I have come to personally assure you that all the resources of SIDE will be used for the protection of Señora Masterson and her children and of course the female agent and yourself while you are in Argentina. I give you my personal guarantee that nothing like this will happen again."

"Mi coronel, that's very kind, but I have to say that el Coronel Munz is already doing everything possible."

"I have replaced el Coronel Munz as director of SIDE, señor."

"Excuse me?"

"El Coronel Munz has been relieved of his duties, señor. A board will be convened to look into allegations of his dereliction of his duties."

Oh, shit!

And Munz knew this was coming.

That's why I got the little pep talk and the "Goodbye, Charley" when he left.

These bastards needed a scapegoat—this had to be someone's fault; anybody's but some bureaucrat's—and they're hanging Alfredo out to flap around in the wind.

Sonofabitch, that's rotten!

· "*Mi coronel,* if there will be witnesses before the board you speak of, I would like to appear, to testify for the defense."

"Señor Castillo, forgive me, but this is an internal Argentine matter."

I better shut up right now. Whatever I say next will be the wrong thing.

Fuck it!

"Forgive me, *mi coronel,* but any dereliction of el Coronel Munz would obviously have to do with what has happened to Americans, and I, as the American officer charged with the security of those Americans, am probably better qualified than anyone else to judge how well el Coronel Munz discharged his responsibilities."

"I repeat, Señor Castillo, that this is an internal Argentine matter."

"It stinks, *mi coronel,* and you may quote me."

"I regret you feel that way, señor," Colonel Gellini said. "If you have some question, my men know how to contact me. Good evening, señor."

He put out his hand. Castillo looked at for a long moment, and then turned his back.

That wasn't too smart, Charley.

Fuck it!

He heard the door close and took out his cellular and pushed an autodial button. Ambassador Silvio answered on the second buzz.

"Silvio."

"Castillo, sir. Colonel Munz's replacement just came to see me."

"He came to see me. I wondered if sending him to see you was the wise thing to do."

"Probably not. That's a rotten thing to do to Munz."

"Jack Masterson used to say that it took him a long time to figure out the Argentines, but he finally had: Anything that goes wrong is always somebody else's fault. In this case, somebody is Colonel Munz."

"Is there anything we can do for Munz?"

"I've been thinking of writing a letter expressing our appreciation of Colonel Munz's services, and sending it to the newspapers. But it probably wouldn't do much good."

"Why not? Munz is out there hanging in the breeze. And God knows, he's done everything possible."

"They probably wouldn't print the letter, and if they did it would be regarded as an unwelcome meddling by the *norteamericanos* in Argentina's affairs. And following that, it would start being bandied about that the whole affair was really our fault; we shouldn't have sent Jack down here, knowing that a very wealthy man like Jack would almost certainly be a target for kidnappers."

"I don't think what's happened has anything to do with kidnapping," Castillo said.

"The trouble is we don't *know* what this is all about," the ambassador said. "How undiplomatic were you, Charley?"

"Not as undiplomatic as I would have liked to have been," Castillo replied. "I told him I would like to be a witness in Munz's defense, and then, after he told me twice that it was an internal matter, I told him it stinks, and he knows it, and that he can quote me."

"Oh, how I sometimes yearn to be free of diplomatic restraints," Silvio said. "You may not quote me, of course, but I couldn't have said it any better myself."

Charley chuckled. "Thank you, sir."

"I expect you're still waiting for the young lady to come out of the operating room?"

"Yes, sir."

"Please let me know as soon as you know something," Silvio said. "I just sent a car to pick up Dr. Mellener to take him to Jorge Newbery to meet the pilot and see what medical equipment is on the Gulfstream."

"Thank you."

[TWO]

After talking to the ambassador, Castillo had just enough time to see that the battery on his cellular was running low and to slip it in his pocket when the door to room 677 swung inward and two somewhat burly nurses in operating-room-blue uniforms pushed in a gurney.

A good deal less gently than Charley would have preferred, they transferred the body on the gurney to the hospital bed, and connected it to an array of wires and clear plastic tubing. It was only after the heavier of the two nurses had settled in a chair by the side of the bed—it looked as if she planned to be there for a while—that Charley could get close enough to the bed to get a look at Betty.

All of Betty's body but her face and one arm was wrapped in pale blue sheets, and most of her face was hidden under bandages. What he could see of it was grayish and looked distorted.

He felt woozy again.

The door swung open and Dr. Santa Claus waddled into the room. His surgical mask was hanging from his neck and his surgical blues were blood-spotted.

He smiled at Charley and held up both hands, balled into fists with the thumbs extended.

Then he saw Charley's face.

"Get out of that chair," he ordered the nurse, as he quickly and firmly led Charley to her chair and sat him down in it. "Put your head between your knees," he ordered, as he firmly shoved Charley's head into that position.

Charley had no idea how long he was in that position, for the next thing he became aware of was a vial of aromatic spirits of ammonia under his nose.

He pushed it away and sat up.

"Usually," Dr. Santa Claus observed dryly, his German accent subtle yet clearly evident, "I have to do that to husbands who insist on seeing the miracle of birth themselves. Are you all right?"

Charley felt Dr. Santa Claus's hands on his face, and then became aware that the surgeon was holding his eyes open, apparently to examine them. Then he answered his own question. "You're all right."

"Thank you," Castillo said, then: "How did the operation go?"

"Procedures, plural," the surgeon said. "The trauma

to the wound in the patient's leg was far less severe than it could have been. There was some musculature damage, and she will find walking painful for some time.

"Vis-à-vis the wound in the groin area: I saw no damage of any consequence to the reproductive organs . . ."

What the fuck does that mean? *"No damage of any consequence"?*

". . . and while the area will likely be quite painful for some time—contributing to the discomfort when the patient moves—I can see no indication that the patient will not fully recover."

Well, thank you, God, for that!

"The trauma to the patient's jaw is problematical. The initial trauma, plus the trauma caused by the removal of the projectile, which was rather deeply embedded, caused both fracturing and splintering. I have immobilized her jaw, which means she will not be able to take solid food for some time. Just as soon as Dr. Koos is available—"

"He's the fellow who's skiing?"

"Right. I'd like him to look at the patient."

"Doctor, I've arranged for an airplane to fly her to the United States as soon as she is able to travel. Can you tell me when that will be?"

The surgeon did not reply directly.

"There's a very good orthognathic surgeon at the University of Pennsylvania Hospital," he said. "Chap by the name of Rieger. William Rieger."

"What kind of a surgeon?"

"Orthognathic," the surgeon repeated. "Actually, something like this requires three specialists, an orthog-

nathicist, a plastic reconstructive surgeon, and an ortho-
dontist."

"May I have that doctor's name again? And would
you spell 'orthognathic' for me?"

The surgeon corrected Castillo's botched pronunciation of the term, and then spelled it and the name of the
physician at the University of Pennsylvania. Castillo
wrote it down.

"She should be able to travel, presuming she will be
accompanied by a physician and a nurse, sometime tomorrow. I will prepare a package—her X-rays, a report of
the procedures she has undergone, a record of her pharmacology, et cetera—and have it available for you."

"Thank you."

"I presume you intend to stay with her until she
wakes up?"

"Yes, I do."

"It will be some time before she wakes up at all, and
when she does, the drugs I have prescribed for the pain
will be having their effect. I don't suppose you'd listen to
my suggestion that you go home and get a good night's
rest yourself, and come back in the morning? I doubt if
she'll even recognize you tonight."

"I'll stay."

"I'll check in on her later," Dr. Santa Claus said, and
walked out of the room.

Castillo followed him out.

Corporal Lester Bradley, USMC, had acquired a second folding chair somewhere and was sitting beside Jack
Britton.

"Betty's going to live," Castillo told them, "but the sooner we get her to Philadelphia, the better. Dr. Whatsisname . . ."

He gestured at the surgeon, who had just reached the elevator bank.

". . . gave me the name of a good doctor in Philadelphia, at the University Hospital. Rieger. Ever hear of him?"

Britton shook his head.

"I need to get on the phone, but my battery's about dead," Castillo said. He looked at Corporal Bradley. "Bradley, go get me a battery charger. This is a Motorola, I think." He checked, then extended the telephone to Bradley. "Take a look. Make sure you get a charger that'll fit."

"With respect, sir. I don't like leaving you."

"I'll be all right for a few minutes," Castillo said, as he reached into his pocket for money. "Not only are SIDE agents controlling who can come onto this floor, but Special Agent Britton is here."

Corporal Bradley looked doubtful, and then on the edge of saying something.

Jesus Christ, he's working up the courage to ask me why Britton can't go buy a charger!

"Bradley, all you have is your pistol. Special Agent Britton has the Madsen and"—*to keep you from letting me know you shot Expert with the Madsen*—"is generally acknowledged to be the best Madsen marksman in the Secret Service."

"Aye, aye, sir," Corporal Bradley said reluctantly, as he examined the cell phone.

He handed it back to Castillo.

"I'll be as quick as I can, sir," Bradley said, and trotted off toward the elevators.

"Best Madsen marksman in the Secret Service, my ass," Britton chuckled.

"To the best of my knowledge you're the only Madsen marksman in the Secret Service, making you ipso facto its best." Castillo smiled at him and went back into room 677.

The plump nurse had made herself comfortable in a metal folding chair by the window. She had her feet resting on an overturned wastebasket, and was reading a magazine with a picture of the king of Spain on the cover. What looked like a kitchen timer was clicking away on the windowsill.

I guess when that goes off, she goes and checks on Betty.

Castillo went to the bed and looked down at Betty. After a couple of moments, he gently rested the balls of his fingers on Betty's wrist, just above the needle that had been inserted in the back of her hand and was dripping something into her vein.

Charley was still there when Corporal Bradley came quietly into the room and offered whispered apologies for having taken so long.

Then Bradley searched the room for a socket into which the cellular charger could be plugged. He found one behind the bedside table, plugged in the charger, and connected it to Castillo's cellular, which chirped encouragingly.

"There you are, sir," he said.

"Good man," Castillo said, and reached for the cellular.

When connected to the cellular, the cord was not long enough for Castillo to use it standing up, or, he immediately learned, even when he was sitting in a folding metal chair.

He sat on the floor next to the bedside table and punched in a long string of numbers from memory.

There was not an immediate answer, and he had just decided it was seven o'clock—supper time—in San Antonio and the kids were making so much noise the phone couldn't be heard, or that the El Patron of the Casa Lopez was watching O'Reilly on Fox and didn't want to be disturbed, when a voice impatiently snarled, "What?"

"Don Fernando?"

"*Sí.*"

"This is Don Carlos."

Castillo heard Fernando Lopez, his cousin, exhale in exasperation. Then Fernando said, "I wondered when you were going to check in, Gringo. You're all over television."

"Excuse me?"

" 'Live from our Fox man in Buenos Aires. Long lines of Argentines wait patiently outside the National Cathedral to pay their last respects to J. Winslow Masterson. . . .' "

"Jesus!"

"And since you're *el jefe* of what's going on down there, we've all been sitting here hoping to catch a glimpse of Uncle Gringo on the tube."

Castillo heard, faintly but clearly, two female voices.

One said, "Don't call him that in front of the children, for God's sake." Castillo recognized the voice as that of Maria, Fernando's wife.

The second said, "Fernando!" in a tone suggesting both annoyance and sadness. Castillo recognized that voice, too. It was that of his—and Fernando's—grandmother, Doña Alicia Castillo.

"As you walk out of the room, Fernando, so *Abuela* can't hear this conversation, answer this question carefully: Was my name or picture or the phrase 'President's agent' or anything like that on the tube?"

Castillo heard Fernando say, "I can't hear him. I'll go in the library."

A moment later, Fernando said, "Okay."

"Answer the goddamn question."

"No."

"Then how the hell did you know about me being *el jefe?*"

Fernando hesitated, long enough for Castillo to find the answer to his own question.

"I'm going to burn that bigmouthed sonofabitch a new anal orifice."

"Calm down, Gringo," Fernando said.

"Fuck you, too."

"When you're through with your tantrum, let me know."

"Jesus Christ, he's a federal agent! He should know better than to run off at the mouth!"

"Let's start with why he's in the DEA."

"I don't give a goddamn!"

"Ricardo originally wanted to be an Army aviator. Like the family heroes, Jorge Castillo and his son, Carlos. When he couldn't pass that physical, he was willing to become an ordinary Armor officer, like me. And when he couldn't pass that physical, either, and filled with a noble desire to serve his country, he settled for the DEA. All they wanted was somebody with a college degree who could speak Spanish."

"You seem to know a lot about the sonofabitch."

"Of course I do."

"What the hell does that mean?"

"You don't know, do you?" Fernando asked, incredulously.

"Know what, for Christ's sake?"

"If you had more than a passing interest in the family, Carlos, maybe you would."

Fernando only calls me "Carlos" when he's really pissed at me.

"Get to the goddamn point!"

"*Abuela* is Ricardo's godmother."

"I didn't know that."

"I figured you didn't. And when Ricardo's mother died—he was thirteen at the time. How old were you when your mother died?"

"Twelve."

"Three guesses, Gringo, which really nice old lady who took her godmother vows seriously just about raised Ricardo Solez?"

"I didn't know that," Castillo admitted, softly. "And he didn't say anything."

"So what happened is *Abuela* called Ricardo—they have this thing, Gringo, called the telephone, which some people use just to say 'Hello, how are you?' and not only when they're in trouble and want something—and he said, 'Hey, Doña Alicia, guess who's *el jefe* in charge of finding out who killed Jack the Stack and protecting his family?' Or words to that effect. And our *Abuela,* who really is always running off at the mouth, called me, and said, 'Hey, Fernando, guess who's *el jefe. . . .*'"

"Okay, okay, I'm sorry. I didn't know."

"Which had the whole family sitting in front of the tube hoping to see—what is it Otto calls you?—'the prodigal son' in action."

Castillo didn't reply.

"So what kind of trouble are you in now, Gringo? And how can the family help?"

"You're right," Castillo said.

"Does that mean you agree that you're a sonofabitch or that you're in trouble?"

"Both."

"What kind of trouble, Gringo?" Fernando said. There was now concern in his voice.

"I'm sitting on the floor of a room in the German Hospital. In the bed next to me is Betty Schneider—"

"What? What the hell is she doing in Argentina?"

"Right now, she just came out of the operating room, where they took three nine-millimeter bullets from a Madsen out of her . . ."

"*¡Madre de Dios!*"

". . . one from the leg, one from the jaw, and one from what the doctor euphemistically refers to as 'the groin area.' "

"Is she going to be all right?"

"She's going to live."

"Thank God!"

"Yeah, I did that. At the time Special Agent Schneider suffered her wounds, she was being transported in my car from her place of duty—the Masterson house—to a bar called the Kansas, where her boyfriend was waiting for her. The most likely scenario is that the bastards who whacked Masterson attacked said car in the belief that I was in it. I wasn't, but what the hell, since they were there, they stuck a Madsen through the driver's window, emptied the magazine, and succeeded in blowing away the driver, a really nice, twenty-year-old Marine named Staff Sergeant Roger Markham, by putting two, maybe three, rounds in his head, and getting Betty three times."

"They didn't get the boyfriend?" Fernando asked. "And who the hell is he?"

Castillo didn't reply. After a moment Fernando understood.

"No shit? When did that happen?"

"Last night. Right after she got here."

"Wow!" Fernando said. "You have been busy." He paused, and then went on: "So what do you need? Before you answer that: What about you? Who's covering your back?"

"I've got a Marine bodyguard," Castillo said. "And Ricardo and Jack Britton—remember him?"

"The black undercover cop from Philadelphia?"

"Yeah. Ricardo and Jack are sitting on Betty. Tomorrow—or no later than the day after tomorrow— she'll be on a plane to Philadelphia. She's going to need more surgery for her face and jaw. I've got the name of a good doctor at the University of Pennsylvania Hospital."

"Gringo, you don't want to send her commercial. If I leave at first light tomorrow in the Lear—"

"I thought about the Lear. You'd have to refuel at least twice."

"So what?"

"I've got an Air Force Gulfstream that can make it to Philadelphia with only one stop for fuel. It also has a hospital configuration. What I want you to do is send the Lear to Keesler Air Force Base in Mississippi."

"Why there?"

"Because that's where I'm taking Masterson's body and his wife and kids. And I think I will probably need some fast transportation."

"Okay."

"We're going to be wheels-up here no later than noon tomorrow, Buenos Aires time. In a Globemaster, it's about ten hours. There's a two-hour time difference, so we'll probably be on the ground there at eight, eight-thirty tomorrow night."

"I'll be there."

"I said, 'Send the Lear.'"

"And I said, 'I'll be there.' Anything else, Gringo?"

"Yeah, don't call me that when your kids are listening."

Fernando chuckled. "I'll say a prayer for your girl-friend, Gringo."

"Have *Abuela* say one. She's probably got more influence than you do."

"Watch your back."

Castillo got off the floor, stood by the bed, looked down at Special Agent Schneider for a long minute. Then he put his back to the wall, slid down, and punched another long series of numbers into the cellular.

Supervisory Special Agent Thomas McGuire of the United States Secret Service answered on the second ring: "Four-Zero-Seven-Seven."

"Tom?"

"Is that you, Charley?"

"Yeah."

"How's Schneider?"

"She's out of surgery. She's going to be all right. But she was pretty badly hurt. As soon as she can travel—tomorrow or the next day—I'm going to send her to Philadelphia. On that Air Force Gulfstream. That's one of the reasons I'm calling."

"Before we get into that—how are you?"

"I'm all right."

"What do you need?"

"Can you arrange for somebody to meet the airplane? The surgeon who treated her—"

"Hey, Charley. She's Secret Service. We take care of our own." He paused, and then asked, incredulously, "You're not sending her alone?"

"Jack Britton will be with her. And a doctor and a nurse. The surgeon who treated her here has a packet of

records—X-rays, her pharmacology, et cetera. Jack will
have that. I want to make sure he's able to get it to—"

"There will be people at the airport. They'll do whatever has to be done. Have the pilot send an in-flight advisory as soon as he enters American airspace. Okay?"

"I've got the name of a doctor at the University of
Pennsylvania who's supposed to be very good."

"Give me his name. I'll check him out."

"William Rieger, M.D."

"What does Schneider need?"

"She took a nine-millimeter bullet in the jaw. Plus two
others in the body. But the problem is the jaw. The medical specialty is—you better write this down."

"Ballpoint in hand."

"I don't even know how to say this. She needs an or-
thognathicist. I'll spell that." He did.

"Got it. Anything else?"

"A plastic reconstructive surgeon and an orthodon-
tist," Castillo finished.

"She'll have them."

"Thanks."

"What happened, Charley? All we got is that she was
shot and her driver got killed."

"They ambushed my car. . . ." In the back of his
mind, he heard Jack Britton's warning: *"If you keep up
this 'it's all my fault' bullshit somebody important's going
to hear you and they'll keep you off the investigation."*
Castillo stopped himself.

"And?" McGuire pursued.

Castillo stuck to the basics. "It was stopped at a traffic
circle near Masterson's house. Somebody got the driver

to lower his window, stuck a Madsen in it, and emptied the magazine. The driver, a Marine sergeant named Markham, took at least two hits in the head as he was trying to back off. The doctor thinks what hit Schneider were ricochets off the bulletproof glass."

Did that sound professionally dispassionate enough? Or is McGuire going to see right through it?

"It's 'projectile resistant,' not 'bulletproof,'" McGuire corrected him absently. "You said it was your car. You think they were trying to get you?"

"I don't know, Tom."

"Just an ordinary 'let's whack an American, any American' assassination? I don't think so. These people are obviously professionals. Why would they risk something like this going sour for them just to take out a Secret Service agent? Unless maybe (a) they expected you to be in the car, and (b) they know that you're not just a Secret Service agent but the President's agent. That would put you in the same category as Masterson, somebody important enough to whack—for whatever reason."

"That brings us back to: Why did they kill Masterson? And not Mrs. Masterson when they had the chance?"

McGuire didn't reply for a moment, then he said, mockingly solemn, "If you would be interested in the opinion of a lowly but old, balding, and wise Secret Service agent, there is something rotten in the state of Denmark. I just wish to hell I knew what it is."

"Me, too, Tom."

"What else can I do for you?"

"Two things. Ask Dick Miller to take my Officer's

Model .45—which is cleverly concealed behind the books on the bookshelf behind my bed—and put it and enough summer clothes for a couple of days in Mississippi into one of the carry-on bags in the closet and somehow get it down to me in Mississippi."

"I'll get it for you, Charley. Joel and I are going down there on Air Force One with the boss."

"Thanks."

"Anything else?"

"I asked my cousin Fernando to bring his airplane to Keesler. I'm not sure they'll let him land there. Can you fix it?"

"I don't think it'll be a problem. If there is, I'll call him and tell him where to take it."

"Thanks again."

"Charley, would you take some straight advice from the old Irishman?"

"I'm all ears for anything you have to say."

"One scenario that came to my mind is that we're dealing with a lunatic or lunatics—not necessarily ragheads; maybe even American—who get off by whacking important people. Masterson qualified as a diplomat and as Jack the Stack. That may explain both why they kidnapped the wife and why they didn't kill her. They just used her to get to him."

Castillo grunted.

"And it may explain why they tried to whack you. The President's agent is in the same league as a diplomat. Maybe even more important. How much of a secret is that down there?"

"Somebody tipped the *New York Times* that there is a Presidential Agent. And some other members of the press. I don't think my name came out."

"Well, that might explain the ambush. Do you know who had the big mouth?"

"I've got my suspicions."

"Have you got a name?"

"I'm not sure about this, Tom."

"When people are trying to whack you, Charley, an overdose of decency can be lethal."

"There's an FBI agent down here who I think made me."

"Made you how?"

"Do you think—despite the President personally ordering the director to lay off Pevsner—that they still have a 'locate but do not detain' out on me?"

"It would be stupid of them, but it wouldn't surprise me. They really want Kennedy."

"This guy's name is Yung. He's attached to the embassy in Montevideo, supposedly working on money laundering."

"Supposedly?"

"I ran into Howard Kennedy—"

"He's down there?" McGuire interrupted. His surprise was evident in his voice.

"He was."

"Doing what?"

"He said he had brought an airplane load of *objets d'art* to the King Faisal Islamic Center and was going to take a load of polo ponies back to Arabia."

"Oddly enough, that sounds legitimate."

"I think that's what he was doing. Anyway, he's gone, and I don't think he or Pevsner has anything to do with this. Pevsner wants to be invisible, what Kennedy wants is what Pevsner wants, and whacking an American diplomat does not seem to be a good way to be invisible."

"With Pevsner, you never know."

"Anyway, Kennedy said he knows this guy Yung, says that he's a hotshot, and whatever Yung's doing in Montevideo has nothing to do with money laundering."

"That's interesting. Let me see what I can find out about this guy."

"Thanks again, Tom."

"I was about to offer you some serious advice."

"Shoot."

"Tell me it's okay for me to call Tony Santini and tell him to sit on you until you get out of there."

"Tony's with the Mastersons. I think he should stay there. And I have a Marine bodyguard who won't let me out of his sight."

"Your call, Charley. But the more I think about it, I think these people are trying to whack you, so be careful."

"I will."

"I just had another thought," McGuire said. "Off the wall."

"Let's hear it."

"The whackers—of Schneider, if they weren't specifically after you—are sending a message."

"What kind of a message?"

"I haven't figured that out yet. But part of it could be, 'We can get to you if we want to, Secret Service protection or not.'"

"I don't know, Tom."

"I said it was off the wall," McGuire said. "That doesn't mean it's not possible."

"It brings up something else, Tom. What about protection for the Mastersons in Mississippi?"

"Charley, the President's going to be in Mississippi. The Secret Service will be all over Keesler. And the head of the protection detail has to know how pissed off he is about Masterson getting whacked."

"The President's not going to stay in Mississippi."

"Good point. I'll talk to Joel and see what he says. Anything else?"

"Can't think of anything."

"Okay, I'll see you down there."

Castillo called Ambassador Silvio and told him that Betty was out of the operating room but still unconscious, and that her doctor had said she could travel either the next day or the day following.

Then he got off the floor and looked down at Betty again. She was still out.

Castillo turned to the heavyset nurse.

"How long will she be like this?" he asked.

"Probably for at least an hour, señor."

"If she wakes before I get back, tell her I'll be back," Castillo ordered.

"I will."

Castillo unplugged the cellular from the charger, saw that he now had enough battery remaining to get to the Four Seasons, then unplugged the charger from the wall and put both devices in his pocket. Then he walked out of the room.

Corporal Lester Bradley, USMC, who was sitting beside Jack Britton, got quickly to his feet when he saw Castillo.

Castillo met Britton's eyes.

"She's still out. The nurse says she'll be out for an hour or more. So Corporal Bradley and I are going to go pack. I'll have them move your stuff and hers into my room and settle those bills. After we're gone tomorrow, there will be people to relieve you and Solez and—"

"Got it," Britton said.

"While I'm dealing with the hotel, Bradley will go where his billet is and pack enough clothing—including his dress blues—for a week. Then he will go back to the hotel, pick me up, and we'll come back here."

"Sir?" Bradley said.

"What?"

"My orders are that I'm not to leave you. And . . . why do I need my dress blues?"

"Because you have the sad duty, Corporal, of taking Sergeant Markham home and burying him."

"The gunny didn't say anything about that, sir."

"The gunny doesn't know about it yet."

"Sir, I can't go without orders."

"You just got your orders," Castillo said. "If it makes

you feel better, call your gunny and tell him what I have ordered."

"Yes, sir," Corporal Bradley said, doubtfully.

One of the SIDE agents in the corridor followed Castillo and Bradley onto the elevator, and when the elevator door opened in the basement, two more men, obviously SIDE agents also, were waiting for them.

Castillo wondered how they had been notified; he hadn't seen the SIDE man use a cellular.

Obviously, stupid, one of the other SIDE agents called and said we were getting on the elevator.

And since it took you some time to figure that out, it means you're tired and not thinking clearly.

"Sir, I am the Major Querrina of the SIDE, with the honor of having your security—"

"I speak Spanish, Major," Charley interrupted him.

Major Querrina's relief was visible.

"You're going someplace, sir?"

"First to the Four Seasons. And while I am in there, my bodyguard here is going to the Marine barracks, or whatever it's called, to quickly pack a suitcase."

Major Querrina looked dubiously at Corporal Bradley but didn't say anything.

"When he's done that," Castillo went on, "he's going to go back to the Four Seasons and pick me up, and we're coming back here." He turned to Bradley. "Where is this place, Corporal?"

"Just off Libertador—" Bradley started.

"I know where it is," Querrina interrupted. "It's a

twenty- to thirty-minute drive from the Four Seasons. Is time important?"

"I want to get back here as quickly as I can."

"May I suggest, sir, that we send the corporal to the Marine House in one of my cars? That will save time, and so far as security for yourself is concerned, there will be two SIDE cars with you."

Or I could ride with SIDE, and send Bradley in the embassy car.

But if I do that, and these bastards want to—what did Tom McGuire say?—"send a message" by taking me out, then I might have two dead Marines on my conscience. And, God, I don't want that.

"Major Querrina has kindly offered one of his cars to take you to the Marine House." He saw Bradley's face drop. "Corporal, you will go in one of their cars, which will bring you back here to the hospital. That's not open for discussion."

"Aye, aye, sir," Bradley said, with a visible lack of enthusiasm.

[THREE]
El Presidente de la Rua Suite
The Four Seasons Hotel
Cerrito 1433
Buenos Aires, Argentina
2240 24 July 2005

"Why don't you fix yourself a drink, Major?" Castillo said to Querrina as they came into the sitting room of the suite. "I won't be long."

"Very kind of you, sir. But no thank you. I have the duty."

"I have it, too," Castillo said. "But there are exceptions to every rule, and I have just decided this is one of those times."

He walked to the bar and poured an inch and a half of Famous Grouse into a glass. He took a sip, and then held the glass up in a second invitation.

"As you say, sir, there are always exceptions," Querrina said.

"Help yourself, I won't be long," Castillo said, and carried his glass into the bedroom and closed the door.

He found a socket for the cellular charger behind the bedside table and plugged it in. When he connected his cellular to it, he found that he wasn't going to have to sit on the floor. He laid the charging cellular on the bed, and then started to pack.

It didn't take him long, and he was just about to zip the bag closed when he remembered the bill he'd gotten at the desk. There was no sense carrying that around in his pocket for God knows how long, and he couldn't just toss it, because the Teutonically efficient financial department of the *Tages Zeitung* demanded a copy of his bills to compare with what American Express said he had spent.

He patted his pockets, found the bill, and started to put it in his laptop briefcase when a warning light lit up in the back of his brain.

What the hell is wrong?

He looked at the bill carefully.

Well, the Four Seasons doesn't give its accommodations away. But there's nothing on here out of the ordinary—

Except that it's made out to Karl Gossinger.

There's nothing wrong with that, either, except that Gossinger entered the country, which means Castillo didn't, and Castillo's going to leave tomorrow. All sorts of questions would be asked about the German national getting on the USAF Globemaster with the Widow Masterson and her husband's body.

Shit!

You fucked up again, Inspector Clouseau!

As a practical matter, however, when Argentine Immigration shows up at Ezeiza, I don't think they are going to peer suspiciously at C. G. Castillo's passport to see if he entered the country legally, especially since C. G. Castillo will be surrounded by SIDE agents.

So what I'll do is hand them my American passport, hope they don't look closely, and worry about Gossinger's immigration problems later.

He put the Four Seasons bill in the briefcase and checked to make sure Gossinger's passport was concealed in the lid with his other alter ego identification.

Then he sat on the bed and pushed an autodial number.

A deep-voiced male answered, *"¿Hola?"*

"My name is Castillo," he said in Spanish. "May I speak with Señor Pevsner, please?"

"One moment, señor."

Castillo glanced around the room and saw something he hadn't seen before. On the bedside table on the other side of the bed was some sort of package. Whatever it was, it was wrapped in tissue, and a rose lay across it.

What the hell is that?

"Charley? I was hoping you would call," Aleksandr Pevsner said in Russian.

"Were you? Why?"

"To learn that you're all right. I heard what happened to your driver and agent."

"Well, if you heard that from somebody close to Colonel Munz, Alex, you better get a new source. They fired Munz."

"I heard that, too. I'm sorry about your people, Charley."

"Alex, I want the bastards who did that."

"I understand."

"This is personal, Alex."

There was a moment's hesitation before Pevsner replied.

"I would expect nothing less of you as an officer. Or do you really mean personal?"

"I mean really personal, Alex."

"Oh, then I really am sorry, my friend."

"I spoke with Howard just before he left."

"He didn't mention that."

"I asked him to find out what he could about a man named Jean-Paul Lorimer, a UN diplomat in Paris. The next time you speak with him, would you tell him that I now really want to know about this man?"

"I'll have Howard contact you. Where will you be?"

"Here until about noon tomorrow. That's when we leave with Masterson's family. And his body."

"I doubt if I'll hear from him before that. Then you'll be in Washington?"

"First Mississippi, then Washington. Tell him to call my cellular or the hotel."

"I will. And I will also see what I can learn about this Lorimer person. Jean-Paul Lorimer, you said?"

"Right. I would really be grateful."

"I hesitate to say this to someone of your background, but are you adequately protecting yourself?"

"I have two SIDE cars, four SIDE agents—including a major—and, far more reassuring, an American Marine I'm not sure is old enough to vote."

Pevsner chuckled, then said, seriously: "There are some very dangerous people—obviously professionals—involved in whatever's going on. I'm sure you appreciate that."

"I do. You haven't had any fresh ideas about what this is all about, have you?"

"No. And no one I've talked to—people one would think would have at least an idea—have any idea, either."

"Keep asking, will you?"

"Of course. And Anna will pray for you—and yours—my friend."

"Thank you."

"Friends take care of friends, my friend. We'll be in touch, Charley. Be careful."

"Goodbye, Alex."

Pevsner switched to German: "Not goodbye. *Auf wiedersehen.*"

Castillo broke the connection, then looked at the cellular.

Flash! CNN and the New York Times *have learned*

that C. G. Castillo, the President's not-so-secret agent, is a close personal friend of Aleksandr Pevsner, the infamous Russian arms dealer and all-around bad guy. Their source is an unnamed FBI agent whose reports have been reliable in the past.

Shit!

He put the cellular in his pocket.

What the hell is in that tissue-wrapped package?

He walked around the bed, pushed the rose on top of the package out of the way, and untied the bow that held the tissue paper in place.

The package contained the freshly laundered brassiere and underpants of Special Agent Elizabeth Schneider, which the room maid had apparently found where they had been kicked under the bed.

"Oh, Jesus!" Castillo breathed.

With some difficulty—his eyes were watering—Castillo rewrapped the intimate apparel and put it in his laptop briefcase, in the space beside the extendable handle.

Then he swallowed hard, breathed deeply, and picked up his bag and the briefcase and went into the sitting room.

"Okay, Major," he said. "All done. Let's go."

[FOUR]
Room 677
The German Hospital
Avenida Pueyrredón
Buenos Aires, Argentina
2340 24 July 2005

Corporal Lester Bradley, USMC, was visibly relieved to see Castillo when he got off the elevator.

"All packed, Corporal?" Castillo asked.

"Yes, sir," Bradley replied. "Sir, the gunny said, in case he misses you tomorrow, to tell you thanks."

"For what?"

"For sending me with Sergeant Markham."

Castillo nodded but didn't reply. He turned to Jack Britton. "The hotel's moved your stuff and Betty's to my room, Jack. The bill's taken care of. Tom McGuire said to tell you to send an in-flight advisory as soon as the Gulfstream enters American airspace, giving your ETA in Philadelphia. The Secret Service will meet the plane."

Britton nodded. "Send it to who?"

Shit! Castillo thought. He said, "That little detail got overlooked. Send it to Philadelphia Approach Control, with a copy to the office of the secretary of Homeland Security, personal attention Secretary Hall. That ought to get their attention. You're also probably going to re-fuel at MacDill Air Force Base. There's Secret Service people there. Find them, and tell them."

"Got it."

Castillo nodded and then slowly opened the door to room 677.

There wasn't much light, just a small lamp on the bedside table, over which the stout nurse had draped a blue cloth.

"Did she wake up?" Castillo asked softly.

"She's starting to," the nurse said.

Castillo walked to the bed and looked down at Betty. She looked gray.

The stout nurse tugged at his arm, and he turned to look at her.

She had a cheap white stackable plastic chair in her hands. Charley had heard—he didn't know if it was true—that they were molded from the recycled plastic of milk cartons and Coke bottles.

"You can't just stand there until she wakes up, señor," the nurse said. "Sit down, put your feet on this, and try to get a little sleep."

How the hell am I going to be able to sleep?

"Muchas gracias."

He sat in the folding chair, put his feet on the plastic chair, and when he was reasonably sure the nurse wasn't watching, put his hand up so that he could touch Betty's shoulder.

Castillo opened his eyes.

Jack Britton was standing beside him, extending a coffee mug.

Castillo took the mug as a reflex action.

"What time is it?" he asked.

"Quarter to nine," Britton said. "Time for you to change shirts, shave, and head for the cathedral."

"Jesus Christ! I should be in San Isidro. Why the hell didn't you wake me?"

"All you were going to do, Charley, was get in the way in San Isidro," Britton said. "I talked to Santini. He said to let you sleep."

Castillo got up, knocking the plastic chair over as he did.

"Your electric razor and a clean shirt's in the bathroom," Britton said, and walked out of the room.

Castillo looked down at Betty.

Her eyes were open, and she was pale but no longer gray.

"Hello, baby," Castillo said.

Betty made a grunt that could have meant, "Hi."

"How do you feel?"

Betty rolled her eyes, and then touched the bandages on her face and then made grunting sounds that after a moment he understood meant, "Can't talk."

"Sweetheart, you're going to be all right."

Betty pointed to the chair and grunted. When he looked confused, she repeated the grunts.

"I snore?" he asked.

She nodded.

"I love you," Charley said.

Betty nodded.

He bent over her and very gently kissed her on the lips.

More grunts, but this time he easily made the translation: "Wiener schnitzel."

"You took three hits," Castillo said. "You're going to be all right. Either tomorrow or the next day, you're going to Philadelphia on the Gulfstream. Jack will be with you."

She nodded, then grunted, "Roger?"

"He didn't make it, baby. He went out quick."

Tears ran down her cheeks into the bandages.

Betty pointed to herself, then mimed firing a pistol, and grunted, "Get bastards?"

He shook his head.

She grunted, "Damn!"

"I have to go with the Mastersons," Charley said.

She nodded.

"I don't want to leave you."

She nodded again, then mimed something that after a moment he understood was shaving.

She's telling me to go shave.

He nodded, and walked to the bathroom. As he started to pull the door closed, she made a loud sound, and he quickly turned and looked at her.

She shook her head and pointed to her eyes.

He nodded, not trusting himself to speak. As he shaved, he could see her watching him in the mirror.

When he'd finished, and had changed his shirt, he went to the bed and looked down at her and ran his fingertips over her forehead.

She raised her balled hand with the thumb extended.

"Oh, Jesus!" he said softly.

She pointed to the door.

He kissed her once more and then turned and walked quickly out of the room.

XI

When the three-car convoy carrying Castillo and Corporal Lester Bradley—a leading SIDE car, the embassy BMW, and a trailing SIDE car—approached the rear of the cathedral, Castillo saw that the entire block was ringed with brown-uniformed Gendarmeria National troops armed with submachine guns.

When he and Bradley got out of the embassy car and started for the side door of the church, they were stopped, and it was only after Major Querrina more than a little arrogantly flashed his SIDE credentials at the Gendarmeria major in charge that they were passed inside.

In the corridor just inside the door, there were uniformed Policía Federal officers and men in civilian clothing who Castillo presumed were SIDE agents. They guarded the door to the alcove in which the Mastersons would be seated.

With Bradley on his heels he went through the door to the alcove. Once inside, he could see Masterson's casket, covered by an American flag. At each corner of the casket, two soldiers, one Argentine and the other American, stood facing outward, at Parade Rest, their rifles resting on the ground.

There were people seated in the alcove across the nave, obviously Argentine dignitaries. There were four empty chairs in the front row, which suggested that the President and the foreign minister and their wives—or two other dignitaries—had not yet arrived.

El Coronel Alejandro Gellini of SIDE was standing to one side of the alcove, with another burly, mustachioed man Castillo guessed was one more SIDE officer. Gellini met Castillo's eyes, but there was no nod or other sign of recognition.

Castillo looked again at the absolutely rigid soldiers at the corners of the casket. The Argentines were in a dress uniform that looked as if it dated back to the early nineteenth century. They wore black silk top hats with a ten-inch black brush on the side. They were armed with what looked like Model 98 Mausers, which had been chrome-plated. The Americans were in class A uniforms with white pistol belts. They were holding chrome-plated M-14 rifles on which chrome-plated bayonets had been mounted. The U.S. Army had stopped using the M-14 during the Vietnam war. But the M-16, which replaced it, did not lend itself to the ballet-like Manual of Arms practiced by the Old Guard.

Castillo had the unkind thought that whatever kind of soldiering they had done before they had been assigned to the 3rd Infantry—and to judge from the medals glistening on their tunics, they had heard shots fired in anger—what they were now were actors in a pageant.

He turned and for the first time saw a first lieutenant in an incredibly crisp and precise Old Guard uniform standing stiffly, almost at Parade Rest, in a corner of the alcove.

That beret he's wearing looks like those molded leather hats the Spanish Guardia Civil wear. What did he do, soak it in wax?

And it's not a green beret, or even a tan Ranger beret. Anybody who can stumble through basic training gets to wear what he has on, thanks to the remarkably stupid idea of the chief of staff that putting a beret on any soldier's head turns him into a warrior.

The lieutenant looked at Castillo, but there was no nod nor a hint of a smile.

And all of those medals glistening on his chest are I-Wuz-There medals. Plus, of course, the Expert Infantry badge, which means he's never been in combat. And—why I am not surprised?—he's wearing the ring identifying him as a graduate of the United States Military Academy at West Point.

More important—he's the officer in charge of a guard detail—why the hell didn't he ask me who I am? Or, if he knows who I am, why didn't he say, "Good morning, sir"?

Castillo walked over to him.

"Good morning, Lieutenant."

"Good morning, sir."

"I was wondering how much ammunition your men have."

The question surprised the lieutenant.

"Actually, none, sir."

"Why is that?"

"Sir, we're a ceremonial unit."

"You are aware, aren't you, that the man in the casket was murdered?"

"Yes, sir."

"And that last night, the bad guys—presumably the same ones—murdered a Marine sergeant and seriously wounded a Secret Service agent?"

"Yes, sir."

"Under those circumstances, Lieutenant, don't you think it behooved you to acquire enough ammunition for your men so that they could at least defend themselves?"

The lieutenant didn't reply.

"And possibly even be in a position to contribute to the defense of Mrs. Masterson and her children should that situation arise?"

The lieutenant colored but did not reply.

"To answer the unspoken question in your eyes, Lieutenant—to wit, *'Who the fuck is this civilian questioning the behavior of a professional officer such as myself?'*—I'm Major C. G. Castillo, U.S. Army, charged with the security of this operation."

"Permission to speak, sir?"

"Granted."

"Sir, I have been taking my direction from the defense attaché."

"And?"

"Sir, I can only presume that if he wanted my men to have live ammunition, he would have issued live ammunition."

"Lieutenant, I was a Boy Scout. Therefore, even before I was told by my tactical officer at that school on the

Hudson River of which we are both graduates that the second great commandment for any officer—right after Take Care of Your Men—is that he be prepared for the unexpected, I knew that Be Prepared is a commendable philosophy to follow. Since you were apparently asleep when your tac officer tried to impart that philosophy to you, I suggest you write it down so you won't forget it."

"Yes, sir."

Castillo heard the door to the alcove open, and turned.

Ambassador Silvio and Alex Darby came through the door.

Jesus! Castillo suddenly thought. *What was that all about?*

Why did I jump all over that guy?

Not that he didn't deserve it.

Because you're angry with the world, and want to vent it on somebody and he was there.

But it wasn't smart.

"Good morning, sir," Castillo said. "Alex."

"The Mastersons are three minutes out," the ambassador said. "We just got a call from Mr. Santini."

"Yes, sir."

"What I would like to do," Silvio went on, "if it's all right with you, is stay behind when the Mastersons go to Ezeiza, then go out there with the casket."

"Anything you want to do, sir, is fine with me."

"Tony needs to know, Charley, if you're going to go out there with the Mastersons," Darby said.

"Tony has more experience than I do," Castillo said. "I don't want to get in his way."

"Then I'll go with the family," Darby said, "my wife and I will."

"Fine. And I'll go out there with the ambassador."

"Okay," the ambassador said. "Let's go find our seats, Alex."

A moment after they had left, Castillo decided he should be outside when the Mastersons arrived, and walked out of the alcove. Corporal Lester Bradley followed on his heels.

They found themselves standing alone in the narrow street outside the church.

I wonder where the hell the gendarmes are?

Then he saw. There were gendarmes at either end of the street. Some were blocking the street where it entered Plaza de Mayo. At the other end, a gendarme was making policeman-like traffic-control gestures, and a moment later a Peugeot sedan started backing into the street. An embassy BMW followed, then a GMC Yukon XL.

"I guess they're backing the convoy in so they can get out quick," Lester said.

"My thoughts exactly, Corporal Bradley."

"Permission to speak, sir?"

"Granted."

"You really ate that lieutenant a new asshole, didn't you, sir?" Bradley said, admiringly.

"You weren't supposed to hear that, Corporal."

"Hear what, sir?"

Castillo smiled at him and shook his head.

Bradley pointed up the street.

Tony Santini and two other Americans whose faces Castillo recognized but whose names he didn't know were walking quickly down the street to them. Both were wearing topcoats Castillo knew concealed submachine guns.

"How's Schneider?" Santini greeted him.

"Awake and hurting. She was really unhappy that she didn't hit one of the bastards with the one shot she got off. Britton and a DEA agent named Ricardo Solez are with her."

"You checked inside?" Santini asked, nodding toward the cathedral.

Two embassy Yukons had now backed down the street to where they were standing. One of them discharged six Americans, three armed with M-16 rifles, two with Uzi submachine guns, and one with a Madsen. Santini motioned one of the men with an Uzi to them, and then looked at Castillo.

"You checked inside?" he repeated.

Castillo nodded. "Argentine VIPs, but neither the President nor the foreign minister is across the aisle."

"They probably want to come in last, for the show," Santini said.

"The ambassador and Darby and wives are here," Castillo went on. "Darby and his wife want to go to Ezeiza with you and the Mastersons. The ambassador wants to go with the casket."

"And you?"

"I thought that's what I'd do."

Santini nodded. "Scenario," he said, "Masterson family convoy leaves. We head for Ezeiza via Avenida 9 Julio and the autopista. As soon as the street is clear, the ambassador's car, the embassy Yukons—three, one for the casket, two for the honor guard—plus a bus for the Argentine soldiers, back in here with the SIDE tail vehicles. Mass is over, honor guard moves casket to Yukons, that convoy takes same route to Ezeiza. Okay with you?"

"Fine."

"Where's your car?"

"Around the corner," Castillo said, gesturing. "With two SIDE cars."

"I'd say go with the ambassador, but these SIDE people are not going to like it if they're not in the parade. Your call."

"I'd say screw them, but they're liable to insist and cause trouble."

"I agree. I'll have your car and theirs lined up back there," Santini said, pointing to the rear of the cathedral. "When the SIDE and embassy lead cars pull out of the street, the ambassador's car will get in the line, and then after the Yukon with the casket passes, you'll get in the line with your SIDE cars, then everybody else. Okay?"

"Tony, you know what you're doing. We'll do whatever you think we should."

Santini nodded, then turned to the man with the Uzi.

"You heard that?"

"Yes, sir."

"Set it up."

"Yes, sir."

Santini raised his voice for the benefit of those out of earshot: "I'm going to check inside. If everything looks all right, we take the Mastersons in."

"You want me to go inside with you?" Castillo asked.

"Your call, Charley."

"I'll follow the Mastersons in," Castillo said.

Santini nodded and entered the cathedral. Ninety seconds later, he came out again.

"Okay, we move them!" he ordered, and walked quickly to the closest Yukon and opened the rear side door.

A very tall slim girl of thirteen or so got out first. Santini smiled at her, then showed her the door to the cathedral. Then a ten-year-old boy got out and followed his sister into the cathedral, and then Mrs. Masterson climbed down from the Yukon. She looked at Castillo, and then turned back to the truck.

"Just climb over the seat, Jim," she ordered, and then a six-year-old appeared in the open door.

Mrs. Masterson put her arm around his shoulders and led him toward the door in the cathedral wall.

As she passed Castillo, she said: "I can't tell you how sorry I am about Betty and the Marine."

Castillo didn't reply.

The only difference between the Masterson kids and Pevsner's kids is the color of their skin. Same sexes, same ages, same intelligent eyes.

Wrong. There's one more difference: Some sonofabitch shot the Masterson kids' daddy.

Castillo followed Mrs. Masterson and the six-year-old into the cathedral.

The President of the Republic of Argentina, whose face Castillo recognized, was now sitting across the nave of the cathedral with another man and two women, who Castillo guessed were the foreign minister and the appropriate wives. Colonel Gellini stood behind the President.

The organ, which had been playing softly, suddenly changed pitch and volume, and Castillo heard the scuffling of feet as people stood up.

Thirty seconds later a crucifer appeared in the nave, carrying an enormous golden cross and leading a long procession of richly garbed clergy, in two parallel columns, which split to go around the flag-draped casket of the late J. Winslow Masterson.

[TWO]
Estancia Shangri-La
Tacuarembó Province
República Oriental del Uruguay
1045 25 July 2005

Jean-Paul Bertrand had been sitting in his silk Sulka dressing robe before the wide, flat-screen Sony television in his bedroom since nine o'clock, watching the ceremonies marking the departure of J. Winslow Masterson from Argentina, first on Argentina's Channel Nine, and then on BBC, CNN, and Deutsche Welle, and now on Channel Nine again.

Jean-Paul Lorimer had acquired a Uruguayan immigration stamp on Jean-Paul Bertrand's Lebanese passport indicating Bertrand had legally entered Uruguay on July fourth, and another document dated the next day attesting to his legal residence in that country as an immigrant.

July fourth, of course, predated by nine days Jean-

Paul Lorimer's having gone missing from his apartment in Paris. It was unlikely that any party attempting to find Lorimer would be interested in anyone crossing any border on a date prior to a date Lorimer was known to have been in Paris.

He could, of course, have picked any date to be placed on the passport—the immigration stamp and the Certificate of Legal Residence had cost him ten thousand U.S. dollars in cash—but he had picked, as a fey notion, July fourth because it was now his, as well as the United States', independence day.

Once Jean-Paul Bertrand had the documents in his safe at Shangri-La, Jean-Paul Lorimer had ceased to exist, and Jean-Paul Bertrand could—after a suitable period, of course, of at least eighteen months, probably two years during which he would be very discreet—get on with his life.

Bertrand had been a little surprised at the amount of attention Jack Masterson's murder had caused around the world. He would not have thought the BBC or Deutsche Welle would have had nearly the interest in the murder of a relatively unimportant American diplomat that they showed. Jack had been the chief of mission, not the ambassador, and Buenos Aires was not really a major capital city of the world, although, in honesty, it had to be admitted that its restaurants did approach the level of those in Paris.

He was not surprised by the attention being paid by Argentine and American television. Jack had been shot in Argentina, which explained the Argentine interest. In all the time Jean-Paul had been coming to Uruguay, and especially since satellite television had become available, he had seen, with mingled amusement and disgust, that Argentine television was even more devoted to mindless game shows and gore than American television, which was really saying something.

The coverage of the murder—and today's events—by American television seemed to be based more on Jack's fame as the basketball player who had been paid sixty million dollars for getting himself run over by a beer truck than on his status as a diplomat. They had even sought out and placed the driver of the truck on the screen, asking his opinion of the murder of the man obviously destined for basketball greatness before the unfortunate accident.

And of course his fellow players, both from Notre Dame and the Boston Celtics, had been asked for their opinions of what had happened to Jack the Stack and what effect it would have on basketball and the nation generally. Jean-Paul had always been amused and a little disgusted that a basketball team whose name proclaimed Celtic heritage had been willing to pay an obscene amount of money to an obvious descendant of the Tutsi tribes of Rwanda and Burundi for his skill in being able to put an inflated leather sphere through a hoop.

From the comments of some of Jack's former playmates, Jean-Paul was forced to conclude that many of them had no idea where Argentina was or what Jack the Stack was doing there at the time of his demise. One of them, who had apparently heard that Jack was "chief of mission," extrapolated this to conclude that Jack was a missionary bringing Christianity to the savage pagans of

Argentina and expressed his happiness that Jack had found Jesus before going to meet his maker.

Jean-Paul had also been surprised by the long lines of Argentines who had filed into the Catedral Metropolitana to pass by Jack's casket. He wondered if it was idle curiosity, or had something to do with the funeral of Pope John Paul—also splendidly covered on television—or had been arranged by the Argentine government. He suspected it was a combination of all three factors.

He had hoped to see more of Betsy and the children—they were, after all, his sister and niece and nephews, and God alone knew when, or if, he would see them again. He didn't see them at all at the cathedral. There had been a shot from a helicopter of a convoy of vehicles racing on the autopista toward the Ezeiza airport that was described as the one carrying the Masterson family, but that might have been journalistic license, and anyway, nothing could be seen of the inside of the three large sport utility trucks in the convoy.

There was a very quick glimpse of them at the airfield, obviously taken with a camera kept some distance from the huge U.S. Air Force transport onto which they were rushed, surrounded by perhaps a dozen, probably more, heavily armed U.S. soldiers.

That whole scene offended, but did not surprise, Jean-Paul Bertrand. It was another manifestation of American arrogance. The thing to do diplomatically—using the term correctly—would be for the U.S. government to have sent a civilian airliner to transport Jack's body and his family home, not a menacing military transport painted in camouflage colors that more than likely had landed in Iraq or Afghanistan—or some other place where the United States was flexing its military muscles in flagrant disregard of the wishes of the United Nations—within the past week. And if it was necessary to "provide security"—which in itself was insulting to Argentina—to do it with some discretion. Guards in civilian clothing, with their weapons concealed, would have been appropriate. Soldiers armed with machine guns were not.

Jean-Paul corrected himself. *Those aren't soldiers. They're something else: Air Force special operators wearing those funny hats with one side pinned up, like the Australians. They're—what do they call them?—Air Commandos.*

That distinction is almost certainly lost on the Argentines.

What they see is heavily armed norteamericanos *and a North American warplane sitting on their soil as if they own it.*

Will the Americans ever learn?

Probably, almost certainly not.

I have seen this sort of thing countless times before.

The only difference is this time I have no reason to be shamed and embarrassed by the arrogance of my fellow Americans, for I am now Jean-Paul Bertrand, Lebanese citizen, currently resident in Uruguay.

Nothing much happened on the television screen for the next couple of minutes—replays of the activity at the cathedral, the convoy on the way to the airport, and the far too brief glimpse of his sister and niece and nephews being herded onto the Air Force transport—and Jean-

Paul had just stood up, intending to go into his toilet, when another convoy racing down the autopista came onto the screen.

This convoy, the announcer solemnly intoned, carried the last remains of J. Winslow Masterson, now the posthumous recipient of Argentina's Grand Cross of the Great Liberator.

Jean-Paul Bertrand sat back down and watched as the convoy approached the airfield and was waved through a heavily guarded gate and onto the tarmac before the terminal where the enormous transport waited for it.

The soldiers—he corrected himself again—*the machine gun–armed Air Commandos* were out again protecting the airplane as if they expected Iraqi terrorists to attempt to seize it at any moment.

Now more soldiers appeared. These were really soldiers, wearing their dress uniforms. Some of them lined up at the rear ramp of the airplane, and half a dozen of them went to the rear of one of the sport utility trucks, opened the door, and started to remove a flag-draped casket.

When they had it out, they hoisted it onto their shoulders and started, at a stiff and incredibly slow pace, to carry it up the ramp and into the airplane.

The Air Commandos gave the hand salute.

Some other people got out of the trucks. Jean-Paul had no idea who they were. They went into the airplane. A minute or so later, four people, two men and two women, came back out. They were followed by eight or ten other people, some of them—including two Marines—in uniform. They all headed for the

Yukons and got into them. The remaining soldiers and the Air Commandos went quickly up the ramp and into the airplane.

The four people who had come out of it watched as the ramp of the airplane began to close, and then got in two of the trucks.

The huge transport began to move.

Jean-Paul Bertrand watched his television until it showed the airplane racing down the runway and lifting off.

And then he went to the toilet.

[THREE]
Aeropuerto Internacional Ministro Pistarini de
Ezeiza
Buenos Aires, Argentina
1110 25 July 2005

Colonel Jacob D. Torine, USAF, who was wearing a flight suit, had been standing on the tarmac beside the open ramp of the Globemaster III when the first convoy had arrived.

He had saluted when Mrs. Masterson and her children, surrounded by the protection detail, approached the ramp.

"My name is Torine, Mrs. Masterson. I'm your pilot. If you'll follow me, please?"

She smiled at him but said nothing.

He led them down the cavernous cargo area of the aircraft, past the strapped-down, flag-covered casket of Sergeant Roger Markham, USMC. A Marine sergeant standing at the head of the casket softly called "Aten-hut," and he and a second Marine, who was standing at the foot of the casket, saluted.

Torine led the Mastersons up a shallow flight of stairs to an area immediately behind the flight deck. Here there was seating for the backup flight crew: two rows of airline seats, eight in all, which often doubled, with the armrests removed, as beds.

Torine installed the Mastersons in the front row, where the kids would be able to see the cockpit, pointed out the toilet, and offered them coffee or a Coke. There were no takers.

"I'll be with you in a moment," Torine said. "Just as soon as everybody's aboard."

Mrs. Masterson nodded, made a thin smile, but again said nothing.

Torine went back to the ramp, where the loadmaster, a gray-haired Air Force chief master sergeant, was waiting for him.

"How we doing?" Torine asked.

"There was an unexpected bonus," the chief master sergeant said. "The caterers' lunch *and* dinner came with wine."

"Which you, of course, declined with thanks, knowing that consumption of intoxicants aboard USAF aircraft is strictly forbidden."

The chief master sergeant chuckled. "Nice food," he said. "Chicken and pasta for lunch, filet mignon and broiled salmon for dinner. And very cheap."

"And the headset?"

The chief master sergeant held up a wireless headset.

"Thank you," Torine said.

The chief master sergeant gestured toward the terminal. A second convoy of Yukons and security vehicles was approaching the Globemaster.

C. G. Castillo got out of an embassy BMW and walked to the ramp. A Marine corporal went to the trunk of the BMW and took luggage from it, then followed Castillo to the ramp.

"Put that inside, Corporal, and then find yourself a seat," Castillo ordered, and then turned to Torine. "Good morning, sir."

"How is she, Charley?"

"Her jaw is wired shut," Castillo said. "But she was awake and reasonably comfortable when I left her."

Torine shook his head sympathetically, and then said, "I spoke with Colonel Newley a few minutes ago. He assured me that the Gulfstream has been placed in the ambulance configuration and is ready to go wheels-up on thirty minutes' notice."

"Thank you."

"Chief Master Sergeant Dotterman, this is Major Castillo."

Sergeant Dotterman saluted. "The colonel's told me a good deal about you, sir."

He held out the wireless headset.

"Intercom is up," he said, indicating a switch. "Down is whatever radio the pilot is using."

Castillo examined the headset and then put it on.

"Voice-activated," Sergeant Dotterman said.

Castillo blew into the small microphone and then

nodded, signifying both that he understood and that the device was working.

The flag-draped casket of J. Winslow Masterson, on the shoulders of the honor guard of the Old Guard, was now very slowly approaching the ramp.

"I better go up front, Charley," Torine said. "Dotterman will let me know when everybody's onboard."

"Yes, sir," Castillo and Dotterman said, almost in chorus.

The honor guard pallbearers slow-marched up the ramp and into the airplane with the casket.

Dotterman followed them inside to supervise its placement and tie-down. Castillo turned to watch and saw that Dotterman was placing it aft of Sergeant Markham's casket, and decided that meant they were going to unload Masterson first.

"How's Special Agent Schneider?" Ambassador Silvio asked, startling Castillo.

When he turned to look at him, he saw that Mrs. Silvio, Alex Darby, and another woman, probably Mrs. Darby, were also standing at the bottom of the ramp.

"She was awake when I left the hospital. Her jaw is wired shut."

The ambassador introduced Mrs. Darby, then said, "My wife and Mrs. Darby, if you think it's a good idea, will go to the hospital from here to let her know she's not alone."

"I think that's a wonderful idea. Thank you," Castillo said, and then had a sudden thought. "Where's Santini?"

Darby pointed.

Tony Santini, an M-16 rifle cradled in his arms like a hunter, was standing on the cab of an enormous yellow fire engine.

When he saw Castillo looking, Santini waved.

"Alex," Castillo said, returning the wave, "tell him thanks and that I'll be in touch, please."

"We'll tell the Mastersons goodbye and then let you get out of here," Ambassador Silvio said.

Castillo nodded.

As soon as they had moved into the fuselage, the Old Guard lieutenant walked—more accurately, marched— down the ramp to Castillo, came to attention, and saluted.

"Good morning, Lieutenant," Castillo said. "That was well done. At the cathedral and here."

"Thank you, sir," the lieutenant replied and then handed Castillo a handful of ribbon and a gold medal.

"Mr. Masterson's Grand Cross of the Great Liberator, sir. I took the liberty of removing it from the colors."

"Good thinking, Lieutenant. Thank you. No presentation box, I gather?"

"None that I saw, sir."

Castillo looked around to make sure no one was watching, then put the medal in his trousers pocket.

"I'll see that Mrs. Masterson gets this. Thank you."

"Yes, sir," the lieutenant said, saluted again, did a crisp about-face movement, and marched back up the ramp.

Castillo watched as he went. *The difference between me and that natty young officer—when I was out of Hudson*

High as long as he's been out—was that I had already
fallen under the mentorship—General Naylor called it
"the corrupting influence"—of General Bruce J. McNab,
and had already acquired at least some of his contempt for
the spit-and-polish Army and a devout belief in the Scotty
McNab Definition of an Officer's Duty: Get the job done
and take care of your men, and if the rules get in the way,
screw the rules.

Ambassador Silvio, Alex Darby, and their wives came
back through the fuselage.

Darby wordlessly offered his hand, and then, after the
wives had done the same, started to help the high-heeled
women down the ramp. Ambassador Silvio put out his
hand.

"I expect we'll be seeing more of one another?" he
asked.

"Yes, sir, I'm sure we will," Castillo said, and then remembered something. "I won't be needing this anymore, sir. Thank you."

He took the 9mm Beretta from the small of his back,
cleared its action, and handed it to the ambassador, who
matter-of-factly stuck it in his waistband.

"Muchas gracias, mi amigo," Silvio said. "And I don't
mean only for the pistol."

Then he touched Castillo's shoulder and walked
quickly down the ramp. The moment he had cleared it,
the Air Commandos who had been on perimeter guard
came trotting up to it. The moment the last of them had
cleared the door, there was the whine of an electric mo-
tor and the ramp started to retract.

Castillo saw Chief Master Sergeant Dotterman with his hand on the ramp control, and then a moment later heard his voice on the headset.

"All aboard and closing the door, Colonel."

"Roger that," Torine's voice came over the headset. "Starting Number Three."

Five seconds after that, Dotterman reported. "All closed, Colonel."

"Roger that. Starting Number Two."

Castillo looked at Dotterman.

Dotterman, smiling, was bowing him into the fuselage in an "After you, Gaston!" gesture.

Castillo smiled back.

What I should do now is give Mrs. Masterson her husband's medal.

Fuck it. I don't want to see her right now.

Castillo sat down in the nearest aluminum pipe–framed nylon seat, next to one of the Air Commandos, and fastened the seat harness. Then he moved the switch on the headseat to the RADIO position.

"Ezeiza, U.S. Air Force Zero-Three-Eight-One," Torine's voice called. "Ready to taxi."

Ten seconds later, the Globemaster III began to move.

They were still climbing to cruise altitude when Castillo unfastened his harness and made his way through the fuselage and up the stairs to the airliner seats. He stopped, took the Grand Cross of the Great Liberator from his pocket, folded the silk ribbon as best he could, and then walked to Mrs. Elizabeth Masterson.

"Mrs. Masterson," he said, extending it to her. "The officer in charge of the honor guard unpinned this from the colors and asked me to give it to you."

She took it from him, looked at it for a long moment, softly said, "Thank you," then put the medal in her purse.

When she looked up again, Castillo had moved to the head of the stairs.

"Mr. Castillo!" she called.

He stopped. When she realized that he was not going to come to her, she unfastened her seat belt and walked to him.

"I wanted to thank you for everything you've done," she said. "And to tell you how sorry I am about Miss Schneider and the sergeant."

Castillo didn't reply. He looked past her for a long moment, told himself to keep his thoughts private. But when he looked back at Mrs. Masterson, the scene of the shot-up embassy BMW fresh in his mind, he said, "His name was Sergeant Roger Markham, Mrs. Masterson. He was twenty years old. And in my judgment, that very nice young man would still be alive and Special Agent Schneider would not be in a hospital bed with three bullet wounds—and her jaw wired shut—if you had been truthful about the people who abducted you."

"How dare you talk to me in that manner?"

"My orders are to protect you and your children, Mrs. Masterson. I have done that to the best of my ability—

and will continue to do so—until I am relieved of the responsibility. But there is nothing in my orders requiring me to politely pretend I think you were telling the truth to the officers investigating your abduction and your husband's murder when you and I both know you were lying."

He met her eyes for a moment, then nodded, and went down the stairs to the cargo section of the fuselage.

Twenty minutes later, Chief Master Sergeant Dotterman walked up to Castillo, who was sitting on the floor of the fuselage—a good deal of experience in riding Globemasters had taught him the floor was far more comfortable than the aluminum pipe–supported nylon seats—and mimed that Castillo should put the headset back on.

When he had done so, Dotterman leaned over him and flipped the switch on the headset to INTERCOM.

"Castillo, you on?" Torine's voice asked.

"Yes, sir."

"You want to come up here, please?"

"Yes, sir."

Well, I put Jake Torine on the spot, didn't I?

In addition to flying the airplane and his other worries, he's had to contend with a furious female who didn't like being called a liar and wasted no time whatever to complain to the most senior officer she could find.

And he didn't need that. Torine is one of the good guys.

But am I sorry I told her what I thought?

Not one goddamn little bit!

Castillo pulled himself to his feet and went through

the fuselage again and up to the cockpit. There was no way he could avoid seeing Mrs. Masterson, but if she saw him, she gave no sign.

He walked between the pilot's and copilot's seats, and when Colonel Torine didn't seem to be aware of his presence, leaned down and touched his shoulder.

Torine turned and looked up at him, smiling.

"Dotterman told me you were on the floor back there," Torine said. "If you want to lay down, Charley, and God knows you have every reason to be tired, just pull the armrests out from one of the seats. I've even got a blanket and pillow I'll loan you."

He's neither pissed nor embarrassed, which he would be if the Widow Masterson had complained to him about me.

Well, maybe she's waiting to tell the President what a cold-hearted bastard I am.

And I really don't care if she does.

"Thanks, but I'm not sleepy, sir."

"Well, then, maybe you'd like to sit in the right seat for a while and see how real pilots aerial navigate over the Amazon jungle?"

"Is that where we are, over the Amazon jungle?"

"I don't know where we are," Torine said. He nodded at the copilot. "I'm relying on him, and my painful experience with him has been that he often gets lost in a closet. How about getting out of there, Bill, and we'll see if this Army aviator can find out where we are?"

The copilot smiled and unfastened his harness.

When Castillo had taken his seat and strapped himself in, the copilot leaned over him and pointed out a screen on which their location was shown. A well-detailed electronic map showed that they were about two hundred miles from Buenos Aires, a few miles north of Rosario. The screen also showed their altitude, airspeed, course, and the distance and time to alternate airfields. Castillo was familiar with the equipment. There was a civilian version of it in the Lear Bombardier. Guided by data from three—or more—satellites fed through a computer, the location and ground speed provided on the screen was accurate within six feet and three miles per hour.

I wonder if Tom got Fernando permission to land at Keesler?

"That gadget takes all the fun out of flying," Colonel Torine said. "It was much more fun when you could stick your head out into the slipstream and see if the highway was still under you."

[FOUR]
Keesler Air Force Base
Biloxi, Mississippi
2035 25 July 2005

As Castillo sat in the jump seat while Torine lined the Globemaster up with the Keesler runway and then smoothly sat the huge airplane down, he could see, bathed in the light of maybe a dozen pole-mounted banks of high-intensity floodlights, the Boeing 747—the Air Force called it the VC-25A, which when the President of the United States was aboard became Air Force One—parked at the end of the taxiway paralleling the runway. It was being protected not only by sentries but also by a half dozen Humvees with .50 caliber machine guns.

"Three-Zero-One on the ground at three five past the hour," Torine said into his microphone. "Close me out, please. And taxi instructions, please."

"Air Force Three-Zero-One, this is Keesler Ground Control. Halt in place at the termination of your landing roll. Be advised that you will be met by a follow-me vehicle. Be advised that you will be met by a vehicle which will take Major C. Castillo from the aircraft to his ground destination. Acknowledge."

"Keesler," Torine responded, "Three-Zero-One understands halt in place at termination of landing roll. Further understand follow-me vehicle will be there. Further understand Major Castillo will be taken by a second vehicle to his ground destination."

"That is correct, Three-Zero-One."

The copilot touched Torine's shoulder and then pointed out the window. An Air Force blue pickup truck with a FOLLOW ME sign mounted on the bed and a GMC Yukon were sitting side by side on a taxiway access ramp.

"Dotterman, you heard that?" Torine asked.

"I'm by the side door, Colonel."

Torine turned to Castillo.

"Why do I think your ground destination is that 747?"

"Keesler," the copilot said into his microphone. "Three-Zero-One is halted on the runway."

"We have you in sight, Three-Zero-One," ground control replied.

"Colonel," Dotterman announced, "here comes a

Suburban and a Follow-Me. The Suburban sees me. He's coming up this side of the fuselage."

"That's probably a Yukon, Dotterman," Torine said.

"What's the difference?"

"I don't know," Torine confessed.

"People getting out of the whatever-the-hell-it-is," Chief Master Sergeant Dotterman reported.

When Colonel Torine started to unfasten his harness with the obvious intention of leaving his seat, Castillo got off the jump seat, folded it out of the way, and stood in the cockpit door. He felt Mrs. Masterson's eyes on him. He met them for a moment, and then looked away.

Thirty seconds later a tall, slim, Marine lieutenant colonel in dress blues, to which splendor had been added the golden aiguillettes worn by aides to the commander in chief, appeared at the head of the stairs.

He glanced at Castillo then headed straight for Mrs. Masterson.

"Mrs. Masterson, I'm Lieutenant Colonel McElroy, an aide to the President. What's going to happen next is the aircraft will taxi to a hangar. Ambassador and Mrs. Lorimer will come onboard at that time . . ."

"I'm Special Agent Willkie of the Secret Service," a stocky man announced in Castillo's ear. "Are you Mr. Castillo?"

Castillo was annoyed at the interruption. Mrs. Masterson had locked eyes with him again, and had been paying far more attention to him than to the President's aide.

And she wasn't angry. It wasn't a "Now you're going to get yours, you sonofabitch" look.

It was an "I need your help" look. Or a "We have to talk" look.

Or both.

What's going on?

And now this sonofabitch is in the way!

Castillo stopped himself at the last split second from pushing the Secret Service agent out of the way.

"I'm Castillo."

"Will you come with me, please, sir? The President would like a word with you."

Castillo nodded.

Special Agent Willkie started down the stairs. As Castillo turned to follow him he looked at Mrs. Masterson again. Their eyes locked again.

She looks distressed, almost frightened.

She doesn't want me to leave.

Mrs. Masterson stood up and pushed Lieutenant Colonel McElroy to one side and called, "Mr. Castillo!"

"Yes, ma'am?"

"May I have a moment alone with you, please?"

"Yes, ma'am. Of course."

She brushed past McElroy and walked up to the cockpit opening. She got so close that Castillo backed up, which pushed him right up against Torine.

"What can I do for you, ma'am?" Castillo asked. "Is something wrong?"

She looked up at him. He saw tears forming.

"I was afraid to say anything in Buenos Aires, Mr. Castillo," she said. "My priority was keeping my children safe."

He nodded.

Elizabeth Masterson took a deep breath.

"But now we're out of Argentina. We're here." She paused, and then went on, slowly and carefully, as if she had rehearsed what she was going to say: "The people who abducted me wanted me to tell them where my brother is. They said that unless I told them, they would kill my children, one at a time. And they said they would kill my children and my parents if I said anything about it. And then they killed Jac—" Her voice caught. She swallowed and went on, "Then they killed my husband to show me they mean what they say."

"And you don't know where your brother is, do you?" Castillo asked, gently.

She shook her head.

Castillo put his hands on her arms.

"Listen to me, Mrs. Masterson. You have my word that no one is going to hurt your children. Or your parents. Or you . . ."

"I just didn't know what to do. That's why I didn't—"

"Mr. Castillo, the President is waiting!" Secret Service Special Agent Willkie impatiently announced.

"He's just going to have to wait," Castillo snapped, and then looked down at Mrs. Masterson again.

She was shaking her head and smiling through her tears.

He looked at her quizzically.

"I knew I was going to have to tell somebody," she said. "And I guess I was right in choosing you."

"I don't under—"

"How many people do you think there are who, on being told the President of the United States is waiting for them, would say, 'He's just going to have to wait'?"

"That just may be an indication that I act impulsively," Castillo said.

"No, Mr. Castillo. What it is is that you're what Alex Darby told me you are."

He looked at her quizzically again.

She explained: "One really tough sonofabitch, and just the guy you need in your corner when you're really in trouble."

"Well, if you believe that, ma'am, please believe I'm in your corner."

"Mr. Castillo, for God's sake, the President is waiting!" Special Agent Willkie called.

"I'll be back as soon as I can," Castillo said.

She reached up and kissed his cheek, said, "Thank you," and went back to her seat.

Castillo looked at Colonel Torine.

"You heard all that, right?"

Torine, his face stern, nodded.

"Would you come with me, please? I may need a witness."

"Sure," Torine said, turned his head and raised his voice. "Bill, I'm leaving the aircraft. It's now yours."

"Yes, sir."

When Special Agent Willkie saw Colonel Torine follow Castillo down the stairs, he looked at him in surprise, and then announced, "The President said nothing about wanting to see anyone but you, Mr. Castillo."

"Well, then I guess he'll be surprised when he sees Colonel Torine, won't he?"

As soon as they were standing on the runway beside the Globemaster, Special Agent Willkie spoke to his lapel microphone.

"Mr. Castillo insists on bringing the pilot with him."

"Not 'the pilot,' my friend," Torine said, not very pleasantly. "Colonel Jake Torine, U.S. Air Force."

"He says his name is Torine," Special Agent Willkie said to his lapel microphone.

Thirty seconds later, Special Agent Willkie said, "If you'll get in the Yukon, please, gentlemen, I will escort you to the President."

They had been in the backseat of the Yukon about thirty seconds when Torine touched Castillo's shoulder and pointed out the window.

Castillo looked and saw soldiers armed with Car 16 rifles forming a perimeter guard around the Globemaster.

"I didn't know they trusted Air Force guys with loaded guns," Castillo said.

Torine smirked. "Those aren't Air Force guys, wiseass. They're soldiers, almost certainly Special Forces and probably Delta Force. And at least one of them is Gray Fox. That is Sergeant Orson, isn't it?"

Castillo looked. One of the soldiers was a tall, blond sergeant first class named Orson. The last time Castillo had seen the Gray Fox communicator/sniper was in

Costa Rica, where Orson had very professionally taken out two of the terrorists who had stolen the 727.

"I'll be damned, that's Orson all right."

What the hell is going on?

The Yukon stopped in front of the wide flight of stairs that had been rolled up to the huge Boeing, and Castillo and Torine got out. There was a knot of people guarding access to the stairs, including two females who were obviously Secret Service agents.

One of them spoke to her lapel microphone, and then turned to Castillo and Torine.

"You may board, gentlemen," she said. "The President is expecting you."

XII

[ONE]
Aboard Air Force One
Keesler Air Force Base
Biloxi, Mississippi
2050 25 July 2005

Although he'd seen the presidential aircraft before, and had been closer to both of them than most people ever get, Castillo had never actually been inside one of them.

The first thing he noticed when he stepped through the door was that the interior was unlike any other that he'd ever seen on any Boeing 747 or, for that matter, on any airliner. Instead of row after row of seats, he found himself looking at the seal of the President of the United States mounted on a cream-colored wall running as far as he could see—fifty feet or so—along the left side of the aircraft, down to where there was a bend in the corridor that the wall formed.

The second thing he noticed was a Secret Service agent standing in the short section of corridor to his left. Castillo had heard that the presidential apartment was in the nose of the aircraft, under the flight deck, and had just decided the Secret Service agent was guarding the President when a second Secret Service agent spoke to him. This one he knew.

"Down the corridor to the door," Joel Isaacson said, pointing. And then he added: "Good to see you, Charley."

Castillo shook Isaacson's hand as he walked past him, but didn't speak.

The door Isaacson made reference to was in the bend of the corridor. As Castillo got close to it, a Secret Service agent appeared and pushed the door inward.

Castillo stepped through it and found himself in a decent-sized conference room. There was a large table, with eight leather-upholstered armchairs around it. They all had seat belts.

Seated at the table were the secretary of state, Dr. Natalie Cohen; the secretary of Homeland Security, the Honorable Matthew Hall; the director of national intelligence, Ambassador Charles Montvale; and General Allan Naylor, commander in chief of CentCom. The President of the United States was sprawled on a leather sectional couch against the interior wall, talking on the telephone.

When he saw Castillo, he smiled and signaled for him to come in and to take one of the unoccupied armchairs at the table. Then, when he saw Colonel Torine, he signaled for him to come in and to take another of the armchairs.

Castillo got a smile from the secretary of state and the secretary of Homeland Security. General Naylor nodded at him, and the director of national intelligence looked at him in what Castillo thought was both curiosity and disapproval.

Then the President said into the phone, "Sweetheart, Charley Castillo just walked in the door. I'll have to call you later."

With a little bit of difficulty, the President replaced the handset in a wall rack, then stood up and walked to Castillo. As Castillo started to get up, the President waved his right hand to order him to stay seated, and then offered the hand to him.

"Good to see you, Charley," he said, and then turned to Torine. "And you, too, Colonel. I was a little surprised to hear you'd flown the Globemaster down there, but then I realized I shouldn't have been. You and Charley are sort of a team, aren't you?"

"Yes, sir. I suppose we are."

"Is it still hot outside?" the President asked, as he walked to the head of the conference table and sat down.

"Hot and humid, sir," Torine said.

"Wise people don't come to Mississippi in the middle of the summer," the President lightly proclaimed, "or go to Minnesota in the middle of the winter. Wise people go to South Carolina during any season and never leave."

There was dutiful laughter.

"Two things are going to happen right away," the President quickly said next, his tone now serious. "The first, because I simply can't stay here for the funeral as much as I would like to, is that we're making a photo-op ceremony of taking Mr. Masterson's casket from the airplane. Including a band. They're setting that up now. I understand we'll have about fifteen minutes. Which is time enough to set the second thing that's going to happen in motion."

He reached under the table and came up with a well-worn leather attaché case. He opened it and took out two sheets of paper and handed them to General Naylor.

"Would you please read that aloud, General?"

"Yes, sir."

Naylor took the sheets of paper, glanced at them a moment, then began to read.

"Top Secret–Presidential.

"The White House, Washington, D.C. July 25, 2005.

"Presidential Finding.

"It has been found that the assassination of J. Winslow Masterson, chief of mission of the United States embassy in Buenos Aires, Argentina; the abduction of Mr. Masterson's wife, Mrs. Elizabeth Lorimer Masterson; the assassination of Sergeant Roger Markham, USMC; and the attempted assassination of

Secret Service Special Agent Elizabeth T. Schneider indicate beyond any reasonable doubt the existence of a continuing plot or plots by terrorists, or terrorist organizations, to cause serious damage to the interests of the United States, its diplomatic officers, and its citizens, and that this situation cannot be tolerated.

"It is further found that the efforts and actions taken and to be taken by the several branches of the United States government to detect and apprehend those individuals who committed the terrorist acts previously described, and to prevent similar such acts in the future, are being and will be hampered and rendered less effective by strict adherence to applicable laws and regulations.

"It is therefore found that clandestine and covert action under the sole supervision of the President is necessary.

"It is directed and ordered that there be immediately established a clandestine and covert organization with the mission of determining the identity of the terrorists involved in the assassinations, abduction, and attempted assassination previously described and to render them harmless. And to perform such other covert and clandestine activities as the President may elect to assign.

"For purposes of concealment, the aforementioned clandestine and covert organization will be known as the Office of Organizational Analysis, within the Department of Homeland Security. Funding will initially be from discretional funds of the office of the President. The manning of the organization will be decided by the President acting on the advice of the chief, Office of Organizational Analysis.

"Major Carlos G. Castillo, Special Forces, U.S. Army, is herewith appointed chief, Office of Organizational Analysis, with immediate effect."

General Naylor stopped reading and looked at the President.

"The finding is witnessed by Miss Cohen as secretary of state, Mr. President."

The only sound in the room was that of cold air flowing through ports in the ceiling.

"That deafening silence we're hearing, Major Castillo," the President said softly, after a moment, "suggests to me that everyone is trying to come up with good and solid reasons why I should tear that finding up, and how these objections can be brought diplomatically to my attention. So let me save everybody the effort. This finding is not open for debate."

The President looked around the table as he let that sink in, then continued:

"I not only want the bastards who murdered Masterson and Sergeant Markham brought down, but I want to send a message to whoever is behind them, and to anyone else who thinks they can get away with murdering an American diplomat, that this President will be as ruthless as necessary to keep this from ever happening again, and this is how I've decided is the best way to do that."

"Mr. President," Ambassador Montvale asked, "may I ask what my relationship to the major will be?"

"I'm glad you asked, Charles," the President said. "Let's make sure everyone understands this. It also applies to Natalie and Tom, of course, and to the other secretaries and the attorney general. You, and they, will provide to him whatever he feels is necessary to carry out the mission I have given to him. But he answers only to me. Everyone clear on that?"

"There are some potential problems that immediately come—"

"Charles, you can discuss those with Major Castillo," the President interrupted. "You did hear me say, didn't you, that this is not open for debate?"

"Yes, I did, Mr. President."

"Okay, this is Ground Zero," the President said. "What I would like now is for Major Castillo to tell us where he believes we are, and where he's going from here." He looked at Castillo. "Okay, Charley, go ahead."

Castillo realized that he was sitting erectly on the edge of the armchair seat, like any other junior determined not to miss a word of what would be said by the President or any of the others so vastly senior to a major.

As a Pavlovian reflex he started to stand up as a mark of respect and subordination to those seniors.

Wait a minute!

If I do that, it will signal that a lowly major is delivering a report to his seniors that they can consider with their greater wisdom and accept or reject.

I don't think the President wants me to do that.

Instead of standing up he slumped back in the chair and crossed his interlocked hands on his chest, as if gathering his thoughts, which happened to be true.

He saw that General Naylor and Colonel Torine were looking at him incredulously.

Well, let's see if I can get away with this.

"Mr. President," he began, sitting up, "when Mrs. Masterson was being interviewed at the German Hospital by Mr. Darby, who is the CIA station chief in Argentina and was a close friend of the Mastersons, she professed to know absolutely nothing about her abductors. I thought she was lying—"

"*You* decided, Major, that she was lying?" Montvale interrupted incredulously.

"Yes, Ambassador Montvale, I did," Charley said, meeting his eyes. "And later, both Mr. Darby and Ambassador Silvio agreed with that judgment."

"Lying about what, Charley?" the President asked.

"More of an omission, sir, than a mistruth. She said she could recall no details whatever of her abduction. I didn't believe that."

"The woman," Montvale said, "was obviously under the most severe—"

The President held up his hand to silence Montvale.

Castillo looked at the President, then continued: "Just before we took off from Ezeiza—the Buenos Aires airport—I gave Mrs. Masterson the medal, the Grand Cross of the Great Liberator, which had been pinned to the colors on Mr. Masterson's casket by the President of Argentina. She expressed to me her regret for Sergeant Markham's death and the wounds suffered by Special Agent Schneider. I'm afraid I was less than gracious to her. I had just come from the hospital, where Special Agent Schneider was lying in pain with her jaw wired shut, and sixty seconds before, I had walked past Sergeant Markham's casket.

"What I said to her, in effect, was that if she had been truthful, I thought Markham would still be alive and Schneider would not have been wounded."

"You called her a liar to her face, Charley?" Natalie Cohen asked in sad disbelief.

"Yes, ma'am. I'm afraid I did."

"And what was her reaction?" the President asked, softly.

"Not much at the time, sir, but just now, just before we came here, she came to me again, and said that now that she was in the United States, she could talk. She told me that her abductors wanted her to tell them where her brother is—"

"Her brother?" the President asked.

"Jean-Paul Lorimer, sir. He works for the United Nations in Paris. Mrs. Masterson said her abductors threatened to kill her children if she didn't tell them, and to kill the children and her family if she revealed any of this. And they murdered Mr. Masterson to prove they meant what they were saying."

"Sonofabitch!" the President of the United States said.

"Mr. President," Natalie Cohen said, "we've been trying to find Mr. Lorimer for several days without success. All we know is that he's not in his apartment and hasn't been in his office."

"Mrs. Masterson said she had no idea where her brother is," Castillo said.

"And why do you think, Major," Montvale asked, "that Mrs. Masterson chose to confide in you, rather than in, say, Ambassador Silvio or her friend the CIA station chief?"

"Probably because we had just landed in the United States," Castillo said.

"If I may, Mr. President?" Colonel Torine asked.

The President waved his permission.

"I was privy to the conversation between Major Castillo and Mrs. Masterson just now," Torine said. "And the reason she gave for her going to Major Castillo was because she believed what Mr. Darby had told her about Major Castillo."

"And that was?" Montvale asked.

"Apparently, sir," Torine replied, "Mr. Darby told Mrs. Masterson that he believes that Major Castillo is— this is just about verbatim from Mrs. Masterson—'one really tough sonofabitch, and just the guy you need in your corner when you're really in trouble.'"

The President cocked his head and smiled. "Well, for once I find myself in complete agreement with the opinion of a CIA station chief. That pretty much answer your question, Charles?"

"Yes, it does, Mr. President."

Castillo saw that General Naylor was quietly coughing behind his hand. From long experience, Castillo knew he did this when he wanted to conceal a smile.

When Castillo glanced at Secretary Hall, Hall winked at him and didn't bother to try to conceal his smile.

Up yours, Ambassador Montvale, you pompous sonofabitch! Charley thought, then caught himself.

There you go again, stupid!

If there's anybody you should try to get along with, it's Charles Montvale, the director of national intelligence.

You haven't been in his presence ten minutes and he's already decided—probably with justification—that C. G. Castillo is one arrogant little sonofabitch who needs to be cut down to size as quickly as possible.

The worst thing you can do to a guy like Montvale is humiliate him in the presence of his peers and the President of the United States. He's not going to forget or forgive that.

"Why do you think these people want the brother, Charley?" the President asked. "And who do you think they are?"

"I have no idea, Mr. President," Castillo confessed. "But I think talking to him—presuming I can find him—is the next thing I should do."

"And the UN says they don't know where he is, Natalie?" the President asked.

"We wanted to contact him when Mrs. Masterson was abducted, so that he could deal with the family, as their father, Ambassador Lorimer, has serious heart problems. Nothing. And all our embassy in Paris has been able to come up with is that his car is in his garage, his clothing is in his apartment, and it looks like he's just taken a trip or something. Apparently, he's pretty much his own boss, going wherever he wants, whenever he wants."

"These people have killed to show how much they want this fellow," the President said. "So his life is in danger. Are you going to tell the UN that? Would that get them off the dime?"

"Sir, I presume that the UN, in New York and Paris, knows of the Masterson murder."

"But not what Mrs. Masterson told Charley, right?"

"No, sir. I'll get on the horn right now to our UN ambassador and have him pass that on if you think I should."

"I wish you wouldn't," Castillo blurted.

"Why not?" Natalie Cohen asked curiously, not offended.

"I have a gut feeling it's the wrong thing to do."

The secretary of state looked at the President. His face was thoughtful.

"I'm about to make a point here, so pay attention," the President said. "We're going along with Castillo's gut feeling, not because I necessarily agree with it, but because I don't feel strongly enough about it to override him. And I am the only person who can—and from time to time will—override him. Okay?"

"Yes, sir," Dr. Cohen said.

"What are you going to do about the missing brother, Charley?"

"I'm going to go to Europe and see if I can find him."

"When?"

"As soon as I'm sure Mrs. Masterson and the children are safe, sir. I gave her my word she will be protected."

"And she will be," the President said. "Did you notice some of your Delta Force buddies out there, Charley?"

"Yes, sir, I did."

"The attorney general agreed with me that in this situation the use of troops to protect the Mastersons was justified. Obviously, there's a time limit. But for now, I'd say they're safe."

"Mrs. Masterson asked Special Agent Schneider to

find out about private security, sir. I'm going to see what I can do."

"That out of the way, you want to go to Europe as soon as possible?"

"Yes, sir."

"You want to ride to Washington with us? I suspect that you can get to Europe quicker from Washington than you can from Biloxi."

"Sir, I asked my cousin to bring the family's airplane here. I want to use that."

"Not an Air Force plane? A Gulfstream, maybe?"

"I think a civilian airplane would be better, sir. Less conspicuous."

"And very expensive to operate. What about that? Who's going to pay for that?"

"Sir, the last time we used it—in the 727 operation, flying it to Mexico and Costa Rica—it was leased to the Secret Service. I was hoping that could be done again."

The President looked at Secretary Hall. The Secret Service had become part of the Department of Homeland Security.

"Any problem there, Matt?"

"No, sir," Hall replied, and then added, "It's here, Charley. Fernando is in the hangar where we'll . . . hold the ceremony."

"Okay, then," the President said. "Anything else you need right now? Equipment, people?"

"It's a long list, sir."

The President signaled him to continue.

"I'd like to stop at Fort Bragg and pick up a Gray Fox

satellite radio, and an operator, and take that with us. And I'd like another installed at the Nebraska Avenue complex, and a third to be sent to the embassy in Argentina with an operator."

"That will pose no problem, will it, General Naylor?" the President asked.

"None, sir. I'll get right on the horn to General Mc-Nab."

"Anything else, Charley?"

"Yes, sir. I'd like to borrow one of Colonel Torine's pilots, one with over-the-ocean experience. I've never flown across an ocean by myself."

"Shouldn't be a problem, should it, Colonel?"

"Unfortunately it is, sir," Torine said. "Until this moment, Mr. President, I had no idea Major Castillo was not entirely satisfied with my flying skills. I am crushed and humiliated beyond words."

"You mean you want to fly his airplane?" the President asked, smiling.

"Very much, sir."

"So ordered," the President said.

"Thanks," Castillo said to Torine.

The President looked at his watch.

"Well, we're out of time. I've got to change my shirt. While I'm doing that, you can finish your shopping list."

He walked out of the conference room.

Castillo felt Montvale's cold eyes on him.

"So what else can we do for you, Major?" he asked, with emphasis on the "Major."

Castillo looked at the secretary of state.

"I'm going to need some help with my passports, ma'am."

"Passports, plural?" Montvale asked.

"I went to Argentina on my German passport—"

"I beg your pardon?" Montvale interrupted.

"Major Castillo has dual citizenship, Mr. Ambassador," General Naylor said, suddenly and pointedly. "Sometimes, he uses his German nationality—very effectively—when he's on a covert assignment."

Did he come to my aid as loving Uncle Allan?

Or because Montvale's attitude toward me got under his skin?

Maybe, probably both. In one of his many lectures before I went to West Point, he told me to never forget that being given rank does not carry with it the right to jump on those of junior rank, especially in the presence of others.

Which of course I did when I gave that Old Guard lieutenant hell with Corporal Lester Bradley, USMC, standing there with both ears open.

Which proves of course that I am not nearly as good an officer as I like to pretend I am.

"Go on, please, Major," Naylor said.

"General, Gossinger is on Argentine immigration records—"

"Gossinger?" Montvale interrupted. "Who's Gossinger?"

This time the secretary of state came to Castillo's aid.

"Charles," she said, "perhaps we could let Major Castillo finish at least one sentence before we start asking questions?"

Montvale, for a second, glared at her. But then he apparently considered that Natalie Cohen, as secretary of state, was not only the most senior officer of the Presidential Cabinet—and thus the presiding officer of this ad hoc meeting of members of the cabinet—but a close personal friend of the President, and therefore was not to be crossed.

"Pardon me, Major," Montvale said. "Please continue."

"The Argentines have a record of Gossinger entering the country, Dr. Cohen," Castillo said. "There was no immigration check as we left. Which was lucky for me, since I didn't have to produce an American passport, which didn't have an entry stamp, or the German passport, which would have blown that cover. So, according to the books, Gossinger is still in Argentina, and I'd like to get him out."

"I get the picture," she said. "I suggest we issue you a new American passport, which will obviously have no immigration stamps in it at all, and then have the CIA put an exit stamp on your German passport. Their documents section is very good at that sort of thing." She looked at Montvale. "Wouldn't you agree, Charles?"

"That would seem to be the solution," Montvale said.

"We'll need a passport photo," Dr. Cohen said.

"There's some in my desk in the Nebraska complex," Castillo said.

"Charley, if you'll give me both passports before we leave here," Secretary Hall said, "I'll have Joel Isaacson pick up the passport photo, and then run everything through Foggy Bottom and Langley. He knows all the right people in both places." He turned to Montvale. "That sound all right to you, Charles?"

"Whatever is the most efficient means of accomplishing what has to be done, of course."

"Would you like me to call DCI Powell, Charles, and tell him what we need, or would you prefer to do that yourself?" Natalie Cohen asked.

"I'll call him," Montvale said.

"Anything else, Charley?" she asked.

"Yes, ma'am, one more thing. There's an FBI agent attached to the embassy in Montevideo. David William Yung, Jr. He was sent to Buenos Aires when Mrs. Masterson was abducted as someone with kidnapping experience."

"What about him?" Montvale asked.

"He seemed to be unusually interested in me, for one thing," Castillo said.

"I would be, too, if I were an FBI agent and a young Army major was placed in overall charge of a situation like that," Montvale said.

Castillo looked at both Cohen and Hall and saw in their eyes that they had taken his meaning.

"And second," Castillo went on, "a usually reliable source, a former senior FBI official, who knows Special Agent Yung, told me he doesn't believe Yung is really doing what he says he's doing, looking into money laundering."

"In my experience, the FBI does not confide in outsiders," Montvale said. "Just who told you—"

The door opened.

Joel Isaacson put his head in.

"Excuse me," he said. "The President would like Mr. Castillo to join him."

"And I would like to know what Yung is really doing," Charley said, very quickly.

The secretary of state nodded at him. The secretary of Homeland Security gave him a thumbs-up.

Castillo got up quickly and started for the door.

"Charley," Hall called. "Your source is your friend from Vienna, right?"

"Yes, sir."

"Well, he has proven reliable in the past, hasn't he?" Hall said.

"Yes, sir, he has," Castillo said, and went through the door.

Isaacson pulled the door closed.

"He didn't answer my question, did he?" Montvale said.

"The President sent for him, Charles," Hall said.

"I'm not accustomed to having junior officers not answering questions I put to them, and, frankly, I don't like it," Montvale said.

"Charles," the secretary of state said. "May I say something?"

"Of course."

"The impression this meeting left on me is that the President made it clear that he places in Major Castillo a trust that you and I might not share—"

"I picked up on that," Montvale said, just a bit righteously sarcastic.

"The impression this meeting left on me, Charles," Secretary Hall said, "is that the President made it absolutely clear that Charley Castillo is answerable only to him. Or did I get that wrong?"

Montvale looked at the secretary of state for help. When it was not forthcoming, he stood up.

"I'd like to freshen up before we go to the ceremony. God alone knows how long we'll be standing out there in the heat and humidity for that."

[TWO]
The Presidential Suite
Aboard Air Force One
Keesler Air Force Base
Biloxi, Mississippi
2105 25 July 2005

"Charley," Supervisory Special Agent Isaacson said, as he put his hand on the door to the presidential suite, "Tom McGuire brought a bag for you."

"Containing, I desperately hope, some summer clothes."

"It does. And a .45. I had to clear the bag aboard, which meant I had to see what was in it."

"Where is it?"

"In there," Isaacson said, pointing to a door next to the entrance to the presidential suite. "It's the medical office. If the president lets you go in time, you could probably get out of those winter clothes. It's going to be hot as hell in that hangar."

"You will get your reward in heaven, Joel Isaacson."

Isaacson smiled, then opened the door to the presidential suite.

Castillo could see what was obviously the President's private office. It contained an angled desk with a high-backed red leather chair bearing the presidential seal in gold facing aft, two armchairs facing the desk, and a credenza behind the desk.

"Mr. President," Isaacson called. "Major Castillo is here."

"Come on in, Charley," the President called. "I'm in the bedroom. Straight through to the front."

When Charley made his way all the way forward, he found the President of the United States supporting himself with one hand on a chest of drawers as he fed his right leg through his trousers. There were two single beds in the small area, on one of which lay the suit the President had just taken off, and on the other, the jacket to the suit he was now putting on.

"God, you're going to be hot in that," the President said, as he stuffed his shirt in his trousers.

"Tom McGuire brought a summer suit for me, sir."

"Well, as soon as we're finished here, you better put it on. Quickly. God and the presidential protection detail wait for no man, including the President."

"Yes, sir."

"This won't take long. First, a quick question. What's Mrs. Masterson like?"

"Very tall and elegant. Very intelligent."

"Is she going to weep, maybe get hysterical?"

"I doubt that very much, Mr. President."

"Thank God for that. Okay. What I didn't say in the conference room was that in order to keep you out of the sight of the eyes in the White House, I want you to avoid going there as much as possible."

"Yes, sir."

"I also told Matt Hall privately that he'll be your conduit to me. A three-man loop, in other words. If he's for some reason not available, the switchboard has been told to put you through to me, and there will be an any time, any area White House pass for you in the guard shack closest to the OEOB at all times. Just identify yourself, and they'll pass you."

"Yes, sir."

"Natalie Cohen isn't happy with the finding, but she'll go along with it. The director of the FBI and the DCI are going to like it less than Natalie does, but I don't think they'll fight it. Charles Montvale loathes the finding. I understand why. I suspect that he will be searching for your failures, so that he can bring them to my attention. I'm going to speak privately to him. If he poses problems, tell Matt Hall. Or me."

"Yes, sir."

"And how do you think General Naylor regards the finding?" the President asked.

"Sir, I think his reaction is much like mine."

"Which is?"

"That you have given a lot of responsibility and a lot of authority to a very junior officer."

"Not without a good deal of thought, Charley. Not without a good deal of thought. Now go change your clothes."

[THREE]
Keesler Air Force Base
Biloxi, Mississippi
2120 25 July 2005

Jake Torine was waiting at the foot of the stairs to Air Force One when Charley Castillo came down them. They could see the Globemaster III was now backed up against the open doors of a huge hangar and that the hangar was really crowded.

Outside the hangar, and just inside it, held back by rope barriers and lines of airmen facing them, was a huge crowd of spectators.

Farther inside the hangar, what looked like a company of Air Force airmen was formed on one side of the cavernous space. Across from them was a U.S. Marine Corps band. A reviewing stand, with a lectern bearing the presidential seal, was in the rear of the hangar facing outward. The rear of the stand held maybe fifty American flags—*of course there're fifty; one for each state*—on either side of the presidential flag.

Next to the presidential flag were those of the secretary of state, the secretary of Homeland Security, and one that had to be the brand-new flag of the director of national intelligence. Flanking that were the flags of the Army, Navy, Air Force, Marine Corps, and Coast Guard, and maybe a dozen personal flags of the general and flag officers of the armed forces—*the red one with four stars is Naylor's*—present for the ceremony, most of whom were already on the platform.

Standing at Parade Rest in front of the reviewing

stand was a ten-man squad of Marines in dress uniforms and a second squad composed of two men from each of the armed services, each under the command of a crisply uniformed lieutenant.

And in front of the reviewing stand were two black-draped catafalques ready to receive the caskets.

Well, that's a nice touch. They're going to put Markham beside Masterson.

"Very impressive," Torine said, as the Secret Service Yukon stopped beside the Globemaster.

"The White House billed this as a major foreign policy speech," the Secret Service agent driving the Yukon said.

The proof of that was the unruly sea of television cameramen, still photographers, and what had become known as "print journalists" held back by barriers and more airmen on both sides of the reviewing stand.

Castillo and Torine got out of the Yukon and found themselves facing four soldiers wearing green berets and armed with Car 4s.

"I'm Colonel Torine, the aircraft commander—" Torine began.

"You are armed, sir," one of the Special Forces soldiers said to Castillo. It was an accusation.

Well, so much for trying to conceal a .45 under a seersucker jacket.

"Yes, I am."

"You can pass him, Sergeant," a voice behind them said. "Not only is he the man, he's one of us."

Castillo turned to see a very short, totally bald man wearing a tweed jacket that didn't come close to fitting around his barrel chest. He was cradling a Madsen sub-machine gun in his arm.

"Hello, Vic," Castillo said, offering his hand to CWO-5 Victor D'Allessando, Special Forces, USA, Retired.

"Just like old times, Charley," D'Allessando said. "You get yourself in the deep doo-doo, and McNab sends me to haul you out."

"You're running this?"

D'Allessando motioned for Torine and Charley to step over to a spot in the shadow of the Globemaster's wing where he could speak without being overheard. "Yeah, I am," he said.

"Boy, am I glad to hear that!" Castillo exclaimed. "What have you got?"

"Twenty-four shooters, mostly Delta, and a few guys from Gray Fox."

"I saw Sergeant Orson," Castillo said. "Actually, Colonel Torine saw him. Oh, hell, excuse me. Colonel, this is an old buddy of mine, Vic D'Allessando. I thought you'd know each other."

"Why do I think you're not wearing your green beret, Vic?" Torine said with a smile.

"I hung the fucker up, Colonel, after twenty-seven years. They medically retired me as a CWO-5. Now I'm a goddamn double-dipping civilian. GS-15, assimilated full fucking bird colonel."

"Who runs the stockade at Fort Bragg," Castillo said.

"I know it well," Torine said, smiling.

"Now I know who you are, Colonel," D'Allessando said. "You're the Air Commando who we used to fly our 727—"

"Almost correct," Torine replied. "*Former* Air Commando. When they made *me* a full fucking colonel, they paroled me from the stockade and put me behind a desk."

". . . from which McNab rescued you when Charley was looking for that stolen 727. You went with Charley to Costa Rica and flew it back to the States after Charley and some of my guys stole it back from the bad guys."

"Guilty," Torine said.

"And he's in on this operation, Vic," Castillo said.

"Welcome aboard," D'Allessando said, smiling and offering his hand.

"What have you got going, Vic?"

"In detail? Or just the highlights?"

"In detail."

"Okay. Naylor called McNab and told him that your boss, Hall, had called him and said the President wanted either Delta or Gray Fox or both to make sure nothing else happened to the Mastersons when they got here. I almost had to tie McNab down to keep him from coming here himself."

Castillo and Torine chuckled.

"So we saddled up. Like I said, twenty-four shooters, mostly Delta but with four guys from Gray Fox. We got two Black Hawks and two Little Birds from the 160th. Both Little Birds are gunships—we can move everybody on the Black Hawks, but you never know when you're going to have to pop somebody. Then we came here.

"The guy running things is Masterson's father. Big tall drink of water. The widow's father—they call him 'the ambassador,' which I guess he was—is a little guy who almost went out with a heart attack. So they're try-ing to keep him in the dark as much as possible.

"Masterson's father has a great big farm not far from here. No airstrip, but no problem with the choppers. They're going to bury Masterson in a cemetery on the farm, after a mass in a little Catholic church in a little dorf called De Lisle, right outside the farm property. They wanted to have a big deal with the funeral, but the old man—Masterson's father—told them no way.

"What's going to happen here, after the President does his thing, is take the body out to the farm in a hearse. Funeral's by invitation only, but they expect maybe three hundred people at the cemetery."

"Can you handle that many people?"

"I'm not going to have to. The old man mobilized the Mississippi State Police. There's about fifty of them, under a lieutenant colonel. And the head man, a colonel—tough bastard—is here as a friend of the family. So's the governor. Plus of course the sheriff and all his deputies."

"You don't see any problems in protecting the family?"

"No," D'Allessando said flatly. "But it would help, Charley, if I knew who popped Masterson and why, and why they may try to pop the widow and the family."

"I'll tell you what I know, Vic. It's not much. I have no idea who these people are. None. All I know is that it has something to do with Mrs. Masterson's brother. She—just now, after we landed here—told me that the people who grabbed her in Buenos Aires want her to tell them where her brother is, and promised to kill her chil-dren and family."

"And she didn't tell them?"

"She doesn't know where he is. He works for the UN in Paris, but we can't find him."

"Interesting."

"She said they killed Masterson to make the point that they meant what they said."

"And you have no idea why they want the brother?"

"No. All I know is they shot Masterson with Israeli-made nine-millimeter cartridges, and killed the Marine sergeant driving my car—and wounded a female Secret Service agent in the car—by sticking one of those through the window and emptying the magazine, also loaded with Israeli-made nine-millimeters."

"With a Madsen?"

Castillo nodded.

"How do you know that?"

"I think Sergeant Markham saw it coming, and as he tried to move out of the way, pushed the window-up button. It was automatic, and caught the Madsen. It was still in the window when I got there."

"That's interesting, too. There's not too many Madsens around. And that's all you know?"

"And I just now learned, in a sixty-second conversation with Mrs. Masterson, about Masterson getting whacked to make the point that they want the brother at any cost."

"Somebody's going to have to talk to her some more," D'Allessando said.

"I know. I don't know how much time there will be now, but that's why I'm here."

"Who's in charge?"

"I am."

"I mean, now that they're in the States. And after the funeral?"

"I am, Vic."

"No shit?"

"The President just told me."

"That's stretching your envelope some, isn't it, Charley?"

"Understatement of the year," Castillo replied. "I'd like to introduce you to Mrs. Masterson, Vic. See if you can reassure her that she's safe now."

"I want to meet her, too," D'Allessando said. "Now?"

Castillo nodded.

D'Allessando spoke to a lapel microphone Castillo had not noticed.

"Three coming through the side door," he announced.

[FOUR]

Lieutenant Colonel McElroy, the aide to the commander in chief, was standing at the foot of the steps to the passenger compartment of the Globemaster.

"Sir," he said, when he saw Castillo and the others coming, "the Masterson family is alone up there."

"My name is Castillo. Would you please go up and tell Mrs. Masterson I'd like a brief word with her?"

"Sir, Mrs. Masterson asked that the family not be disturbed."

"Do it, Colonel," Colonel Torine ordered.

"Yes, sir," Lieutenant Colonel McElroy said, and started up the stairs.

Castillo looked down the cargo compartment of the Globemaster. Corporal Lester Bradley, now wearing his dress blue uniform, was standing almost at attention while talking to a Marine captain.

Castillo walked to them.

"You look very spiffy, Corporal," Castillo said.

"Thank you, sir."

"Captain, what's Corporal Bradley's role in the ceremony?"

"May I ask who you are, sir?"

"My name is Castillo."

"Phrased another way, Captain," Colonel Torine added, "he's the man."

The captain looked at them curiously, and then replied to Torine: "Sir, immediately after the ceremony, when the sergeant's remains are taken from the hangar, the corporal will meet up with the cask—"

"Captain," Castillo interrupted. "I told the gunny in Buenos Aires that Corporal Bradley will accompany Sergeant Markham's remains all the way home. I'm sure he passed that on to Sergeant Markham's buddies. I want that to happen. Make room for him in the ceremony."

"Sir, I'm not sure that will be poss—"

"Do it, Captain," Colonel Torine ordered flatly.

The captain considered that just long enough for it to be perceptible, then said, "Aye, aye, sir."

"Thank you," Castillo said. "I'll see you later, Bradley."

"Yes, sir."

Castillo saw Mrs. Masterson coming down the stairway and hurried forward.

"I'm glad you're here, Mr. Castillo. My father is here, and the less he knows about the threats made, the better. He has a heart condition."

"I understand," Castillo said. "Mrs. Masterson, this is Mr. D'Allessando. Have you ever heard of Delta Force?"

"There was a terrible movie," she said. "You mean there's really something like that?"

"Yes, ma'am, there is. The real Delta Force is made up of the best of Special Forces. They're not much like what you see in the movies, but they are really professional. Mr. D'Allessando has been associated with Delta for a long time, and he's brought twenty-four men here with him to make sure you and your family are all right."

"That's very reassuring," she said. "I'm really pleased to meet you, Mr. D'Allessando."

"I'm really sorry about your husband, ma'am," he said. "That shouldn't have happened."

"Thank you," she said.

Castillo saw a very tall, very slim man in an elegant double-breasted dark suit coming down the stairs.

My God, he looks just like Masterson! The only difference is the white hair and that absolutely immaculate pencil-line mustache.

The man walked up to them and smiled.

"Dad," Betsy Masterson said, "this is Mr. Castillo and

Mr. D'Allessando. Gentlemen, my father-in-law, Winslow Masterson."

"How do you do?" Masterson asked, offering his hand. "May I ask which of you is Mr. Castillo?"

"I am, sir."

"I was actually about to go looking for you, sir, when it somewhat belatedly occurred to me that it was likely you were asking for a word with my daughter-in-law."

That accent is not what you expect to hear from a Mississippian, a farmer, or a black Mississippi farmer, or any combination thereof. What the hell is it?

"May I be of some service, sir?" Castillo asked.

"First, let me express my appreciation for everything you have done for my daughter-in-law—"

"Sir, that's absolutely unneces—"

"Pray let me continue, sir."

"Pardon me, sir."

"And then let me inquire of you as a government official—I spoke with Colonel McElroy, who had absolutely no idea what I was talking about—why, in a situation like this, with all the resources of the government presumably at your disposal, you have been unable to make contact with Jean-Paul Lorimer?"

Betsy Masterson and Castillo exchanged glances.

"Sir . . ." Castillo began.

"Mrs. Masterson's father, Ambassador Lorimer, is quite upset, Mr. Castillo. And if I may say so, understandably so. He has a certain physical condition and should not be under stress."

"Dad—" Betsy Masterson said.

"Please permit Mr. Castillo to answer the question, if he desires to do so."

"Sir, there are problems locating Mr. Lorimer. Mrs. Masterson is aware of them. . . ."

"Indeed?" Masterson asked, and looked at his daughter-in-law.

"I didn't want to get into it with my father listening."

Masterson nodded.

"I'd really like to explain much of this to you, sir," Castillo said, "but this, I suggest, is neither the time nor the place to do so."

"He's right, Dad," Betsy Masterson offered.

"Well, I need to know what's going on as soon as possible," Masterson said. "And at the plantation, your parents will be there, and it would be impossible to exclude them without . . ." He paused, visibly in thought, then nodded in obvious agreement with what he had thought of.

"Mr. Castillo, it was of course my intention to ask you to stay with us at the plantation."

"I wouldn't want to intrude, sir," Castillo protested.

Masterson dismissed that with a wave of his hand.

"But is there some reason you have to go there immediately after this?" Masterson inquired, gesturing toward the activities in the hangar. "Would my daughter-in-law and the children and of course the Lorimers be safe, in your judgment, if you weren't personally there for an hour or so?"

"Yes, sir, I'm sure they would be. In addition to the state police you already have, Mr. D'Allessando and his men—"

"You're thinking of the Belle Visage," Betsy Masterson said.

"And what do you think of me thinking of the Belle Visage?" Masterson asked.

"That'd do it, Dad," she said. "No one would disturb you there."

"Then it's settled. What we'll do as the cortege heads for the plantation, Mr. Castillo, is go to the Belle Visage. We can have our little talk in private and then go out to the plantation. You can ride with me. How does that sound?"

"Sir, I don't know what the Belle Visage is."

"It's a gambling hell on the coast. There's a place there where we will not be disturbed."

"Whatever you say, sir. But there is one other problem. I have to establish contact with my cousin."

"Your *cousin*? May I inquire what that's all about?"

"Excuse me," Torine said, "but I just heard the band play 'Hail to the Chief.'"

"Charley, I can handle things until you get to the . . . *plantation*," Vic D'Allessando said, as they saw Lieutenant Colonel McElroy walking up to them. "Colonel, you want to come with me or go with Charley?"

"Charley?" Torine asked, seeking guidance.

"I'll see you at the plantation," Castillo said.

"You stay here, my dear," Winslow Masterson said. "I'll go get the children and your parents." He started for the stairs, then stopped and turned. "If you are seen with me, Mr. Castillo, there might be interest that at the moment neither of us wants. Can you get to the Belle Visage by yourself?"

"Yes, sir."

"Well, then, I'll see you there," Winslow Masterson said, and started again for the stairs.

Castillo looked at D'Allessando. "You have wheels, Vic?"

"Not to spare, Charley."

"You have the Secret Service guy on your radio?"

D'Allessando nodded.

"Tell him that I need a Yukon here, right now, for I don't know how long."

"You can do that?"

"You can do that and we'll see what happens."

D'Allessando tilted his head slightly.

"You on, Ogilvie?" he said.

Mrs. Masterson looked at him with great curiosity.

"He's got a radio under there," Castillo explained.

"Mr. Castillo wants a Yukon at the Globemaster right now," D'Allessando said. There was a pause. "All he told me was to tell you he wants a Yukon here, now."

D'Allessando straightened up and announced, "On the way, Charley."

"Now tell them to find Fernando Lopez—he's my cousin, he's in the VIP section, and they know it—and bring him here."

D'Allessando bent his head again and repeated the order, and then said, "They'll do it."

Betsy Masterson's eyes met Castillo's.

"My father-in-law is just like Jack, isn't he?"

"Yes, ma'am, I was thinking the same thing."

"I guess it's the genes," she said.

[FIVE]

Estancia Shangri-La
Tacuarembó Province
República Oriental del Uruguay
2355 25 July 2005

Jean-Paul Bertrand watched the ceremonies taking place at Keesler Air Force Base on CNN.

They are really making a show of it, he thought, with somewhat grudging admiration. And then he thought, *That's precisely what it is, a show. Jack gets himself shot, and they're acting as if he were the secretary of state, and all he was was chief of mission in a third-rate embassy.*

The President arranged the show for his own agenda.

Jean-Paul got to watch not only Betsy and the kids this time but his father and mother as well. There was a camera long shot of the family walking behind the casket as it was slowly marched off the airplane.

Daddy looks fine, old but fine; not as one would expect of someone who nearly died of a heart attack. Mom must have her hands full with him. Jack's father looks just like Jack. And so does the older boy. What the hell is his name? Do they call him "Junior" or "the Third"?

The cameras were trained, too, on the reviewing stand as the family took their places beside the President. The President not only kissed Betsy but put his arms around her in a compassionate hug.

If that's not for the purpose of putting the ignorant masses who voted for him in a receptive state of mind for what he's going to say, then what is it for?

The secretary of state also embraced Betsy and kissed her, then did the same to Ambassador and Mrs. Lorimer and then the kids.

Daddy at least had the dignity to look a little offended.

God, how I loathe that arrogant little bitch! She's nearly as bad as the President!

"My fellow Americans," the President began, and Jean-Paul Bertrand almost switched the television off then, but curiosity stayed his hand.

"I come here tonight bearing two messages.

"One is from you.

"The American people offer their profound condolences to the families of J. Winslow Masterson and Sergeant Roger Markham, USMC, who gave their lives in the service of the United States.

"The second message is from me," the President went on. "It is to those who committed the cowardly murders of these two good men.

"I say to you that this outrage will not go unpunished. I have ordered . . ."

Jean-Paul Bertrand switched off the television.

It would have been nice to see more of the family, but if the price to do that is looking at that man while he mouths such nonsense, it is simply too high.

XIII

[ONE]
Penthouse C
The Belle Vista Casino & Resort
U.S. Highway 90 ("The Magic Mile")
Biloxi, Mississippi
2230 25 July 2005

When the dark blue, nearly black, GMC Yukon XL pulled up in the brilliantly lit drive of the hotel, the driver's door was opened by a doorman in what looked like the uniform of an admiral in the Imperial Russian Navy.

"Welcome to the Belle Vista Casino and Resort," he announced. "How may I be of service?"

"You can tell me where I can park this thing," the driver said.

"We have valet parking, sir."

"No," the driver said, and showed the doorman his Secret Service credentials. "I keep control of the vehicle. And I need it close, in case it's required in a hurry."

"Oh," the doorman said. "Is one of you gentlemen Mr. Costello?"

"My name is Castillo," Charley said, from the backseat.

"And you are Mr. Masterson's guest, sir?"

"Uh-huh."

"Welcome to the Belle Vista Casino and Resort, Mr. *Castillo*," the doorman said and opened the rear door. "Mr. Threadgill, the manager on duty, will be here momentarily."

Castillo and Fernando Lopez got out of the Yukon.

Fernando Lopez was an enormous man—six-foot-three, two hundred thirty pounds—with a full head of dark black hair and a swarthy complexion. He was wearing a dark blue suit, a crisp blue shirt with a white collar, a red-striped tie, and black ostrich-hide Western boots.

"If you want to get a cup of coffee or something," Castillo said to the driver, "I think this will probably take about an hour."

The Secret Service agent nodded but didn't say anything.

A tall, thin, elegantly dressed man in his late forties walked up to them.

"Mr. Castillo?" he asked and, when Charley nodded, put out his hand. "Welcome to the Belle Vista Casino and Resort, Mr. Castillo. My name is Edward Threadgill, and I am the manager on duty. If you'll follow me, please?"

He led them through the lobby. In a lounge to one side, three enormous television screens showed Air Force One taxiing toward a runway.

He stopped before an elevator, somewhat dramatically flashed a plastic card, and then demonstrated how the card operated the elevator door. He then presented the card to Castillo.

"He'll need one of those, too," Castillo said.

"Certainly," Mr. Threadgill announced, produced another plastic card, and handed it to Fernando. "There you are, sir. And you are, sir?"

"My name is Lopez," Fernando said.

"Welcome to the Belle Vista Casino and Resort, Mr. Lopez."

"Thank you."

Threadgill bowed them onto the elevator.

The elevator ascended, then its doors opened on a large foyer. Threadgill led them to one of the four doors opening off it, ran the plastic card through another reading device, and then bowed them through the door.

Penthouse C was a large, elegantly furnished suite of rooms. Threadgill threw a switch, and curtains swished open, revealing a wall of floor-to-ceiling windows offering what in daylight would be a stunning view of the Gulf of Mexico, the sugar-white sandy beach, and the highway running along the coast. Now, a few lights twinkled out on the water and U.S. 90 was an intermittent stream of red lights going west, white lights going east.

There was a basket of fruit on a coffee table, and beside it a cooler holding two bottles of champagne.

"If you need anything, gentlemen," Threadgill said, "there are buttons in every room which will summon the floor waiter. There is of course twenty-four/seven room service."

"Thank you very much," Castillo said.

"Is there anything else, or may I leave you?"

"I can't think of anything, thank you very much," Castillo said.

Fernando Lopez waited until the door closed after

Threadgill, and then said, "Knowing you as I do, Gringo, I'm sure there is some very simple reason why we are here in a suite normally reserved for really heavily losing baccarat players."

"Baccarat players?" Castillo asked.

"Yeah, this place is world headquarters for people who want to drop a couple of hundred thousand playing baccarat. You didn't know?"

Castillo shook his head.

"So what are we doing here?" Fernando asked.

"Thank you for not asking in the truck," Castillo said.

"That's the answer?"

"Masterson's father and I have to talk. We can't do that at his place—which he calls the plantation—because the widow's father has a bad ticker, and we don't want to upset him. He sent me here."

"What do you have to talk about? Wait. I'll rephrase that interrogatory: What the fuck is going on?"

"So I don't have to repeat everything twice, can you wait until he gets here? He should be here any minute, and I need a drink."

"Okay. I could use a little belt myself," Fernando said.

"What did that guy say about a floor-waiter button?"

"There has to be a bar in here," Fernando said.

He walked to a panel mounted on the wall and started pushing buttons. One of them caused a section of the paneled wall to move, revealing a small but well-stocked bar.

"Eureka, the gold!"

• • •

They had just enough time to fix the drinks and touch glasses when Winslow Masterson walked into the suite.

"I couldn't get away as quickly as I had hoped," he said. "But they were ready for you?"

"Yes, sir," Castillo said. "I took the liberty of . . ."

"You're my guests," Masterson shut him off with a gentle wave of his hand. "And a drink seems entirely appropriate at this time."

He went to the bar and poured himself a drink from the bottle of Famous Grouse that Fernando had used.

"The economics of this place has always fascinated me," Masterson said. "God only knows how much it costs them to maintain something like this, and since they are obviously not in the business of being a friend to man, there has to be a profit motive. It would therefore seem to follow that their hospitality is offered only to those who have—or are likely to lose—an enormous amount of money at the tables. Where do such people—and so many of them—come from?"

"I was thinking just about the same thing, sir," Fernando said.

"Excuse me, sir, for my breach of courtesy. I am Winslow Masterson."

"My name is Lopez, sir. Fernando Lopez."

"And you're a Westerner, Mr. Lopez. May I say I admire your boots?"

"Thank you, sir. Texan. San Antonio," Fernando said.

Masterson drained his drink and made another.

"Mr. Castillo tells me you're cousins," Masterson said.

"Yes, sir."

"Years ago," Masterson offered, "I had some business dealings with a delightful chap in San Antonio, who had your Christian name, Mr. Lopez, and your surname, Mr. Castillo. I don't suppose . . ."

"You may be talking about my—our—grandfather, sir," Charley said.

"Did your grandfather have a magnificent Santa Gertruda bull named 'Lyndon J.'?"

"Grandpa was not an admirer of President Johnson," Fernando said, "and Lyndon J., even as a calf, produced amazing amounts of droppings, so when it came to naming the calf for registering . . ."

"So your grandfather told me," Masterson chuckled. "What is it they say about a small world?"

He's making small talk, Charley thought. *He's delaying hearing what he knows he won't like to hear.*

What do I do? Bring him back to earth, so I can go out to his farm?

No. Fuck it. Vic's out there. The Mastersons are safe.

We just brought his son home in a flag-draped casket.

Let him do whatever he wants to do.

"I was distressed to learn he had passed," Masterson said. "My deepest condolences to you and your family."

Then he turned and walked to the plate-glass windows and looked out at the twinkling lights on the gulf.

A very long moment later, with his back to them, Masterson said, "Gambling has been going on here on this coast for centuries. Did you know that?"

"No, sir," Charley said, "I didn't."

"No, sir," Fernando added.

"The very first gamblers were the freebooters, the pirates, who plied their profession here," Masterson went on. "They had the custom of raffling off the more comely of the females they had removed, together with other valuable property, from vessels they intercepted entering or leaving the Mississippi River."

"I didn't know that," Fernando said.

"It is, I suspect, why my wife is a bit vague when discussing our ancestors. It is one thing to take some pride in them having been free men of color in New Orleans, before the war of cessation, and quite something else to acknowledge how they achieved that status."

"Excuse me?" Fernando asked.

Masterson took a long sip of his drink, and continued: "After the Battle of New Orleans, Jean Laffite was pardoned for his services. As were his officers and men. Most of them stayed in Louisiana, but some of them, including a notorious scoundrel, Captain Alois Hamele, and his son, Captain Francois Hamele, originally from Haiti, and before that of course from Africa, came here, where the land was cheaper and there were a number of bays and coves where ships not wishing to pass their cargoes through customs could unload.

"Captain—they used the French term, *maître,* in those days—Hamele and his son—commonly known as the *fils de le Maître*—decided, upon hearing that Jean Laffite had returned to his sinful ways, and knowing that the authorities would almost surely come looking for other pardoned freebooters, that a change of name was probably—"

"I know where you're going," Charley said. "Son of the Master, right? Masterson?"

Winslow Masterson slowly turned from the window, smiled, and nodded.

"Over the years," he went on, "the Masterson family acquired rather extensive land holdings in this area. Some of it was splendid farmland; some was in timber, and some, like the land on which this splendiferous gambling hell is built, was essentially useless swamp."

"And now," Fernando said, smiling, "I think I know where you're going."

"Perhaps," Masterson said, smiling.

"About fifteen years ago, some gentlemen from Las Vegas came to see me about acquiring this property. I suspect, perhaps unkindly, that they were disappointed when they found that I was not plowing my land walking barefoot behind a mule."

Castillo and Fernando chuckled.

"And I know they were disappointed when I told them I wasn't interested in selling the property. I didn't tell them that not only do I dislike selling property, but in this case my wife had also weighed in. She truly believes that proprietors of gambling hells grow rich on the poor.

"But it is true, I suppose, that everyone has their price, and in this case, the Las Vegas people finally met mine. An absurd, from my standpoint, amount of money. And this apartment, in perpetuity, together with what they term 'full maintenance,' which means I never am billed for anything. I suspect they still entertain hope I will come here, have too much of this stuff"—he raised his glass—"and go downstairs and lose it all back to them shooting dice."

Castillo and Lopez laughed.

"Primarily, I use it to house people who come to see me who I would rather not have in my home," Masterson said, and took a sip of his scotch. After a moment, he added, "My wife has never been in the building."

Masterson looked between them for a moment, then drained his glass. He put the glass carefully on the bar and turned to face Castillo.

"Very well," he said. "Enough of that. Please tell me, Mr. Castillo, who abducted my daughter-in-law and murdered my son, and why. And what I can do to avenge his death."

"Yes, sir," Castillo said. "I'll tell you what I know, which isn't very much. When the President heard that Mrs. Masterson was missing in what appeared to be a kidnapping, he sent me to Buenos Aires. . . ."

"And you have no idea whatsoever who these people are?" Masterson asked, when Castillo had finished.

"No, sir. I do not. Obviously, it has something to do with Mr. Lorimer. So I'm going to start by trying to find him. If there's anything, anything at all, you can tell me that you think might help . . ."

Masterson nodded thoughtfully.

"There is a subculture here, Mr. Castillo, of affluent Negroes who can trace their ancestry back to the free men of color. It is simply a matter of our being more comfortable with each other than we are with other people."

"We Texicans have something like that in San Antonio," Fernando said.

Masterson considered that, and said, "Yes, I daresay

you would. Your grandfather mentioned in passing that he had ancestors on both sides who died at the Alamo fighting the Mexicans. I don't know about Texas, but here ours is a rather small community. We're primarily Roman Catholic. We send our daughters to the nuns in New Orleans for their high school education, and our sons to the brothers at Saint Stanislaus here in Mississippi for theirs.

"My son went to Saint Stanislaus as I did, and my father did, and my grandfather. So did Jean-Paul Lorimer, as did his father, and—I believe—his grandfather. Jack's mother and Jean-Paul's mother had known each other in the Blessed Heart of Jesus School in New Orleans, and then gone to Spring Hill College in Mobile. It was thus inevitable that Jack would meet Betsy and that they became sweethearts when they were in their teens.

"Surprising most of us, the romance continued after Jack went off to Notre Dame on a basketball scholarship. They were married, against the wishes of both families, two weeks after Jack graduated. Our sole objections were that Betsy had not completed her degree—she's a year younger than Jack—and that they were too young. Their argument, to which we finally acquiesced, was they would be separated again by his professional athletic career."

He paused and smiled. "Betsy, I strongly suspect, was fully aware of the tales of the off-court activities of the Celtics, and was determined that she would not lose Jack to some adoring—what's the phrase?—'basketball groupie.' If Jack was going to Boston, so was she."

Fernando and Castillo chuckled.

"And then, of course, Jack's career ended prematurely

when he was struck by the beer truck. I hoped he would come home to work the plantation. He said he would the day I announced my retirement, and not before.

"The ambassador suggested he take the entrance examination for the foreign service, and we all thought this was a splendid idea. The world, as they say, is growing smaller every day, and by the time I was ready to retire, Jack would be fluent in more languages than French and English, and the fruits of their union would have been exposed to experiences they would not have if they went to the nuns and brothers here.

"And, with one exception, until this outrage occurred, their lives were going as well as my wife and I, and Ambassador and Mrs. Lorimer, could have wished. That exception was the unpleasantness that developed between Jack and Jean-Paul Lorimer."

Castillo, about to take a sip of his drink, stopped. "Over what?" he asked.

"At first, we thought it was differing political views, but on second thought, we realized that it almost certainly was more than that. It went back to their days at Saint Stanislaus, and had other causes." Masterson paused. "What I'm doing is what my wife would call 'airing the dirty family linen.' But you said 'anything at all.' Should I continue?"

"Yes, sir, please," Castillo said.

"Shortly after Jack joined the foreign service, he was posted to Paris. My wife and I went to see them. They had an apartment on the Quai Anatole France. . . . Do you know Paris, Mr. Castillo?"

"Yes, sir."

"I can find my way from the Arch of Triumph to the Place de la Concorde without a guide," Fernando said.

"Facing the River Seine from the Place de la Concorde," Masterson said, "just across the river is a row of apartment buildings on the Quai Anatole France. Do you know where I mean?"

"Yes, sir," Fernando said.

"The high-rent district," Castillo said.

Masterson nodded. "And Jack and Betsy—who was very pregnant—were ensconced in an upper-floor apartment in one of the more expensive buildings on the Quai Anatole France. He was so junior in the foreign service that government quarters were not made available to him; they paid a rental allowance instead, and you were supposed to find yourself someplace to live.

"What Jack and Betsy found was a lovely apartment, from which one could see the Bateaux-Mouches on the Seine, the Place de la Concorde . . . and it was priced accordingly.

"I questioned Jack about the wisdom of his flaunting his affluence. His response was that everyone knew of that incredible settlement he'd been given, and that it would be hypocrisy to pretend they were not extremely well-off. Later in his career he became more discreet.

"In any event, he and Betsy gave a party for us. Jean-Paul Lorimer was also in Paris. He had resigned from the State Department some months before—later I learned that was shortly after he learned Jack would be sent to Paris—and joined the UN. When my wife learned that he had not been invited to the party because he and Jack had had words, my wife prevailed upon Betsy to include him.

"I don't think Jean-Paul had been in the apartment ten minutes before he said something that Jack construed as anti-American. It quickly became ugly, very ugly. Betsy was in tears. Cutting that short, Jack threw him—literally threw him—out of the apartment. As far as I know, that's the last time they ever saw one another.

"At first we thought it was a question of their political differences—Jack's mother always said that Jack was more chauvinistically patriotic than Patrick Henry—but on reflection, we realized that it went back as far as Saint Stanislaus."

"I don't think I follow you, sir," Castillo said.

"The green-eyed monster, Mr. Castillo. Jealousy," Masterson said. "Jean-Paul is three years older than Jack. Saint Stanislaus's football team leaves something to be desired, but they have always had a first-rate basketball team. Jean-Paul didn't earn a place on the team until he was a senior. Jack made it as a ninth-grader. They played together, in other words. Jack immediately became the star. The Celtics—and others—made their first offers to him when he was still at Saint Stanislaus, and they were not doing so as their contribution to affirmative action.

"And then came the scholarship to Notre Dame. Jean-Paul went to Spring Hill, where he didn't attempt varsity sports, and where his academic career was unspectacular. Jack's skill on the basketball court, on the other hand, gave a new meaning to the term 'Black Irish,' and academically he did well enough to earn a Phi Beta Kappa key.

"Then came his contract for all that money from the Celtics, and shortly thereafter he was struck by the beer truck. The enormous settlement he received from that exacerbated, my wife and I came to realize, the resentment Jean-Paul—but not, I hasten to add, his father and mother—harbored for our being far better off than the Lorimers.

"Jean-Paul followed his father into the foreign service. His initial assignment was to Liberia. When Jack went into the foreign service, his first assignment was Paris. I later learned that he believed I had something to do with that. I did not, if I have to say so.

"Jean-Paul resigned from the foreign service and joined the United Nations and was assigned to Paris. Where he found Jack and Betsy in the apartment on the Quai Anatole France."

"Wow!" Castillo said.

"That said, Mr. Castillo," Masterson went on, "I cannot believe that Jean-Paul could possibly have anything to do with Jack's murder. Nor can I imagine Jean-Paul being involved in anything illegal. He is one of those people who go through life trying to bend the rules to their advantage, but who simply don't have the courage, if that's the word, to break them."

"Maybe drugs are involved?" Fernando said. "That's a murderous business."

"I find that impossible to accept, even as a remote possibility, Mr. Lopez," Masterson said. "Might it have something to do with our involvement in Iraq?"

"I don't think that's likely, sir," Castillo said.

"Giving my imagination free rein," Masterson asked,

"could it be that Jean-Paul has somehow annoyed the Israelis? Their intelligence agency . . . Mossad? Something like that?"

"Mossad," Castillo confirmed. "Formally, the Institute for Intelligence and Special Tasks."

"Mossad has a certain reputation for ruthlessness," Masterson finished.

"Maybe," Castillo blurted. He collected his thoughts. "All the shooters—of Mr. Masterson, Sergeant Markham, and Special Agent Schneider—were firing Israeli-manufactured nine-millimeter ammunition."

He heard himself. *Jesus, motormouth, why did you say that?*

"I shouldn't have said that," he said quickly. "My brain isn't functioning. All that proves is that Israel manufactures a lot of ammunition. It's unlikely that Mossad Special Task shooters would use traceable ammunition on a job like this."

"Probably not," Masterson agreed. "But now that I think about it, I don't think that Israeli involvement in this should be dismissed out of hand."

"On the other hand," Castillo went on thoughtfully, "since so much Israeli ammo is around, so readily available, maybe Mossad would use it. Why not?"

"Which appears to point right back to Jean-Paul Lorimer and his connections with the French," Masterson said, "as the key to this."

"Yes, sir, it looks that way. With a little bit of luck, I should be in Paris before our embassy closes tomorrow. Not that the embassy being closed matters. The CIA station chief will just have to give up his *cinq à sept*."

Masterson chuckled. "You have been in Paris, haven't you?"

"Yes, sir."

"What the hell is a sank . . . whatever you said?" Fernando asked.

"You could call it 'recreation on the way home from the office,'" Castillo said, and Masterson chuckled again. "It means *five to seven*. Something like a noonie in the United States."

Fernando shook his head. Masterson chuckled again.

"How well did you know my son, Mr. Castillo?"

"Not well," Castillo said. "But I liked what I saw."

"And that explains your enthusiasm to find these people?"

"That's part of it, sir. The other part is personal. I also really want to find the people who shot Special Agent Schneider and Sergeant Markham."

"Do you think the rest of the government is going to share your enthusiasm? Or will this just fade into memory?"

"I can't speak to enthusiasm, sir, but I expect cooperation."

"I thought perhaps other, higher priorities might be involved," Masterson said. "Or perhaps that when you turn over the rock, there will be worms some might wish had remained concealed. Perhaps in the national interest."

"When I was on Air Force One with the President just now, Mr. Masterson, he ordered Ambassador Montvale, the director of national intelligence, and the secretary of state to give me anything I asked for, and I intend to ask the CIA for everything they have on Lorimer. And I'm going to ask the FBI and the DIA and the DEA, the state department's bureau of intelligence and research, and the post office and the department of agriculture and anybody else I think might possibly have a line on him."

"Would a reward for information, as substantial as necessary, and offered either publicly or privately, be of any use, do you think?"

"I don't think that will be necessary, sir."

"Please keep it in mind, Mr. Castillo, that if something . . ."

"I appreciate that, sir, and I will."

"Is there anything else you'd be willing to tell me?"

"I can't think of anything else, sir."

"Then perhaps we should go out to the plantation before our being missing really attracts attention."

"Sir, about the plantation," Castillo said. "I'd really like to get out of here first thing in the morning, and we have to think about getting Fernando back to San Antonio—"

"Fernando's not going back to San Antonio," Fernando interrupted. "Fernando's always wanted to go to Paris in the middle of the summer. Somebody once told Fernando you can't find a Frenchman in Paris in July. Just think, all that beauty and no Frenchmen."

Masterson chuckled. "You sound like my son, Mr. Lopez." He turned to Castillo. "I really wish you would spend the night at the plantation, if for no other reason than I think Betsy will be pleased to see that I share her confidence in you."

Jesus H. Christ!

"I can only hope, sir, that her, and your, confidence in me is justified."

Which almost certainly won't be.

[TWO]
Pope Air Force Base, North Carolina
0715 26 July 2005

"Pope approach control, Lear Five-Zero-Seven-Five," Colonel Jake Torine called into his throat mike.

"Lear Five-Zero-Seven-Five, Pope."

"Pope, Seven-Five. Do you have us on radar?"

"Affirmative, Seven-Five."

"Estimate Pope in seven minutes. Approach and landing clearance, please."

"Lear Five-Zero-Seven-Five, be advised Pope is closed to civilian traffic."

Colonel Torine turned to Major C. G. Castillo, who was in the left seat.

"What now, O Captain, my captain?" he asked.

"I thought we'd be cleared," Castillo said.

"Always check," Torine said. "Write that down, Charley."

"You guys aren't very good at things like this, are you?" Fernando Lopez, who was kneeling between the seats, asked innocently, earning him the finger from Major Castillo.

Colonel Torine switched to TRANSMIT.

"Pope, Seven-Five has been cleared to land at Pope. Verify by contacting Lieutenant General McNab at Special Operations Command."

"Seven-Five, we have no record of clearance—"

"And while you're doing that, give us approach and landing clearance, please. This is Colonel Jacob Torine, USAF. Acknowledge."

It proved impossible for the airfield officer of the day, Major Peter Dennis, USAF, to immediately find anyone at the Air Force base who could confirm or deny that Lear Five-Zero-Seven-Five had permission to land. Neither could he immediately establish contact with General McNab.

With great reluctance, but seeing no other alternative, Major Dennis telephoned Major General Oscar J. Winters, USAF, Pope's commanding general, at his quarters, where the general was having his breakfast, and explained what had happened.

Major General Winters was fully aware that paragraph one of the mission statement of Pope Air Force Base stated in effect that Pope was there to provide support to Fort Bragg and the major Army units stationed thereon. Furthermore, he knew that Lieutenant General Bruce J. McNab, U.S. Army, was wearing the hats of both the commanding general, XVIII Airborne Corps, and the commanding general, U.S. Army Special Operations Command, and thus also had command control of the 82nd Airborne Division (which was under XVIII Airborne Corps) and the U.S. Army Special Warfare School (which was under the Special Operations Command).

He was also aware of General "Scotty" McNab's well-earned reputation for unorthodoxy, and of his legendary temper. And there was, General Winters knew, an Air Force officer, a colonel, named Jacob Torine. Why Torine would be flying a civilian Bombardier/Learjet 45XR Winters had no idea, except that Torine had spent much of his career as an Air Commando, and Air Commandos were about as well known for unorthodoxy as were members of the Army's Special Forces.

Wise major generals, Air Force or Army, make every effort not to unreasonably antagonize lieutenant generals of their own or any other service.

General Winters instructed Major Dennis to grant Lear Five-Zero-Seven-Five permission to land, but with the caveat that it be ordered to hold on the taxiway, where two Security Forces Humvees armed with .50 caliber machine guns should meet it prepared to take it under fire in case the sleek and glistening white civilian jet should turn out to be some sort of flying Trojan horse.

"I'll be right there, Major," General Winters said.

On the way to Base Operations in his Air Force blue Dodge Caravan, General Winters managed to get General McNab on his cellular phone.

"General McNab," he said, "we have just learned that a civilian Learjet is about to land at Pope, piloted by someone who says he is Colonel Jacob Torine, USAF, and that you can verify he has permission to land. I am on my way to the field."

General McNab's reply was succinct: "Well, I guess I better do the same. Thank you, Oscar. See you there."

• • •

The Bombardier/Learjet 45XR had been sitting on the taxiway near the threshold of the active runway for about ten minutes when both Lieutenant General Mc-Nab and Major General Winters personally appeared there.

General McNab led the way, standing up in the front seat of an Army Humvee. He was a small, muscular, ruddy-faced man sporting a flowing red mustache. He was wearing a desert camouflage uniform, aviator sunglasses, and a green beret. General Winters followed in his Caravan. He was wearing a class A uniform.

When the Humvee stopped thirty feet from the Lear, General McNab jumped nimbly to the ground and walked up to the Lear, where he, hands on hips, looked up at the cockpit with all the arrogant confidence of General George S. Patton. A very large and muscular captain, similarly uniformed, got out of the Humvee and took up a position immediately behind General McNab.

Major General Winters and Major Dennis got out of the Caravan and walked up beside Lieutenant General McNab and the Green Beret captain.

The Lear's door unfolded, and Colonel Torine and Major Castillo, each wearing a suit and tie, deplaned. Both saluted crisply, which reassured Major Dennis, who reasoned if they weren't military they would not have done so.

"Good morning, sir," Torine and Castillo said, almost in concert.

General Winters returned the salute crisply. General

McNab returned it with a casual gesture in the direction of his head.

"I must confess, Oscar," General McNab said, "that these two are well known to me, and that the really ugly one is indeed Colonel Jake Torine."

McNab looked at Torine, and said, "I knew they wouldn't let an old man like you fly big airplanes much longer." He looked at Castillo. "And Major Castillo, daring to show his face at my door again."

General McNab turned to General Winters.

"Whenever I think that Captain Walsh is the worst aide-de-camp I have ever had, Oscar, I think of Major Castillo in that role and realize I am wrong. Castillo earned that appellation in perpetuity."

Captain Walsh smiled, and shook his head.

"As to why there is no record of their aircraft being granted permission to land here, I have no idea. I was notified by CentCom that they were coming. I am forced to conclude that either CentCom or the Air Force fucked things up again, as both are lamentably famous for doing."

"I'll look into it, General," Winters said.

"If I may offer advice without giving offense, Oscar, let sleeping dogs lie."

"No offense taken, General."

"Would it be possible for you to drag that airplane somewhere where it will be more convenient for them to get back in it after we've had some breakfast?"

"Certainly, sir. Colonel, do you need fuel?"

"No, sir. We're all right," Torine said.

"Castillo, once again demonstrating his remarkable

ability to arrive at the wrong time, did so by arriving here just as Walsh and I finished our wake-up five-mile trot around Smoke Bomb Hill," General McNab said. "I require sustenance immediately after my morning five-miler. Otherwise, my wife accuses, I become ill-mannered."

"I understand, General," Winters said.

Fernando appeared at the Lear's door.

"Can I get off now without being blown away?" he asked.

"Aha," McNab said. "Unless I err, the owner of the airplane. You may not believe this, Oscar, but he was once a fairly competent captain of armor."

"How are you, General?" Fernando asked.

"Very well, Fernando, for an old man, with all these terrible responsibilities heavily weighing upon my overburdened shoulders. Could you use some sustenance?"

"Yes, sir, I could."

"I'll have it towed to Base Ops," General Winters said.

"Thank you, sir," Torine said.

"Thank you, Oscar," General McNab said, and gestured to Castillo, Torine, and Lopez that they should get into the Humvee.

There was still a small line waiting to be fed at what the Army now called the "dining facility"—formerly "mess hall"—of the 1st Battalion, 504th Parachute Infantry Regiment when McNab's Humvee pulled up outside. Everyone in the Humvee piled out and went to the end of the line.

One of the principles of leadership Castillo had

learned while he had been Second Lieutenant Castillo, aide-de-camp to Brigadier General McNab, was that the quality of food served was one of the most important factors in troop morale, and that a very good way to ensure that high-quality food was served at all times was for senior officers to drop in unannounced at a randomly selected mess hall and eat what was being served to the privates.

General McNab took out his wallet and paid for breakfast for everybody but his driver, an unmarried sergeant living in barracks who was not drawing a rations and quarters allowance, and they went through the line watched by a visibly nervous mess sergeant, who was aware both of McNab's legendary temper and that it was often triggered when food did not measure up to his expectations.

The food—and there was a wide array of choices—was good. McNab waited until they were through, poured himself another cup of coffee, and then handed Castillo a sheet of Teletype paper.

"If you have trouble with the big words, Charley, I will be happy to explain them to you," he said.

Castillo took the message and read it.

```
TOP SECRET-PRESIDENTIAL
OPERATIONAL IMMEDIATE

0205 27 JULY 2005

FROM: COMMANDER IN CHIEF
```

CENTCOM

MACDILL AF BASE

TAMPA FLA

TO: COMMANDING GENERAL

XVIII AIRBORNE CORPS/SPECIAL

OPERATIONS COMMAND

FORT BRAGG NC

EYES ONLY LT GEN B. J. MCNAB

COPIES TO:

SECDEFENSE WASHINGTON DC

EYES ONLY SEC BEIDERMAN

SECSTATE WASHINGTON DC

EYES ONLY SEC COHEN

SECHOMELANDSEC WASHINGTON DC

EYES ONLY SEC HALL

DIR OF NATIONAL INTEL

WASHINGTON DC

EYES ONLY DIR MONTVALE

1. CONFIRMING VERBAL ORDERS OF THE PRESI-
DENT TO THE UNDERSIGNED 26 JULY 2005 AND
TELECON BETWEEN GEN NAYLOR AND LT GEN MC-
NAB 2305 26 JULY 2005.

2. BY DIRECTION OF THE PRESIDENT:

(A) COMMANDING GENERAL XVIII AIRBORNE
CORPS/SPECIAL OPERATIONS COMMAND WILL IM-
MEDIATELY MAKE AVAILABLE SUCH PERSONNEL

AND EQUIPMENT AS MAY BE REQUESTED BY C. G.
CASTILLO, CHIEF, OFFICE OF ORGANIZATIONAL
ANALYSIS, DEPARTMENT OF HOMELAND SECURITY.

(B) ANY INABILITY TO PROVIDE SUCH PERSON-
NEL OR EQUIPMENT WILL BE IMMEDIATELY RE-
PORTED TO CINC CENTCOM EYES ONLY GEN
NAYLOR BY THE MOST EXPEDITIOUS MEANS,
PREFERABLY SECURE TELEPHONE.

NAYLOR, GENERAL, US ARMY
  CINC CENTCOM

TOP SECRET–PRESIDENTIAL

Castillo handed the message to Torine, who read it and then handed it back to McNab, who folded it and put it in his pocket.

"So tell me, Chief," McNab said, "what are you requesting besides the three radios, and operators therefor, that General Naylor mentioned last night?"

"That's about it, sir," Castillo replied.

"I have two more questions, Chief," McNab said, "if I may dare to ask them."

"Ask away, sir."

"Thank you, Chief. One, when do I get Vic D'Allessando and my twenty-four shooters back from Mississippi? General Naylor said that decision is up to you."

"Sir, just as soon as other security arrangements can be made to protect the Mastersons. I'm working on that now."

"Will it count as another question, Chief, if I ask you where you're going to get those security arrangements?"

"As soon as I get to Washington, sir, I'm going to call China Post and see who's available."

"What the hell is that?" Fernando asked.

"Some allege, Fernando," McNab explained, "that China Post Number One in Exile of the American Legion—your cousin and I are members—functions as an employment bureau for former and/or retired special operators seeking more or less honest civilian employment." He turned to Castillo. "If you'd like, Charley— excuse me, *Chief*—I'll give China Post a heads-up call and tell them you'll be calling."

"That'd be great, sir. Thank you very much."

"It would probably help if I could assure them the compensation would be in line with their skills."

"Money is not a problem, sir."

McNab nodded.

"Question two," he went on. "What the hell is going on?"

"Yesterday, sir, immediately upon landing, Mrs. Masterson told me the villains who abducted her and murdered Mr. Masterson . . ."

"So you're going to try to find this Lorimer fellow?" McNab asked, when Castillo had finished.

"Yes, sir. With a little bit of luck, we'll be in Paris late this afternoon."

McNab was silent for a moment, visibly thinking.

"You want to take two radios and operators with you, right?"

"Yes, sir."

"Al?" McNab said to Captain Walsh.

"Sir, they'll be at Base Ops by the time we get back over there," Captain Walsh replied.

"The best we could do about the radio for Buenos Aires is to get the operator on the 2310 American Airlines flight out of Miami tonight. That'll put him there at 0620 their time tomorrow morning. The radio itself posed a problem. I didn't want to send it through their customs, and not only because I wasn't sure we could get it through their customs, so I called Secretary Cohen, when she was still on Air Force One on her way back to Washington. She promised to have someone in Miami slap the appropriate diplomatic stickers on it to whisk it through customs unopened—it's addressed to the ambassador—but that may not go as smoothly as we like. I don't have a lot of faith in the State Department."

"Again, when I get to Washington, I'll call down there and give the ambassador a heads-up that it's coming."

"He's all right? He knows what you're up to, and won't leak it?"

"He's first class, and Alex Darby—remember him?"

"The CIA station chief in Zaranj?"

Castillo nodded. "He's down there. I didn't remember him, but he remembered me. He's a good man. He'll know how to get the radio through customs and what to do with it."

"Is there anybody else you can use down there if you need shooters?" McNab asked, and then, when he saw the surprised look on Castillo's face, went on. "We can get people in there, Charley, black, but if you need them in a hurry, we'll have to infiltrate them by air. That means either with our C-22 suitably decked out as an Air Paraguay or something 727—and that's a *long* haul for that airplane—or with a Globemaster III, which has the range, but would be harder to hide."

"I haven't even thought of shooters down there," Castillo confessed. "I don't see where I'm going to need them. But if something came up, yeah, there's people I could use. There's a Secret Service guy, and a DEA agent. In a pinch, I could probably use some of the Marine guards."

"To play it safe, what if I send another crate down there under diplomatic cover? Weapons, night-vision goggles, some flash-bangs, et cetera? Enough for, say, six shooters?"

"Yes, sir. That would be a very good idea. I'm really embarrassed I didn't think about that."

"Even though you studied at the feet of the master, Charley, the master didn't really expect you to be perfect," McNab said.

"Colonel," Castillo asked, turning to Torine, "how would the weight of what the general's talking about affect our cross-the-drink flight?"

Torine considered the question carefully.

"That's a crate weighing about, ballpark, what? Three hundred pounds?"

"The stuff is in the crate in two duffels," Captain Walsh furnished. "Total weight three hundred twenty pounds. Not much ammunition; we figured you could get some there. Knock off twenty pounds for the crate, we're right at three hundred."

"Another three hundred pounds gross isn't going to change much, Charley," Torine said.

"What about somebody getting curious about what's on the Lear?"

"Customs very seldom checks what a plane is carrying until you try to get it off the plane," Torine replied.

"You want to take the goodies with you now?" Mc-Nab asked.

"No, sir. I was thinking about it, but I don't think it would be a good idea. I don't think the risk of getting caught with half a dozen Car 4s is worth it."

"Okay, so that goes diplomatic," McNab said. "Anything else?"

"No, sir. Not that I can think of."

"Okay," McNab said. "That's the way we'll do it." He turned to Captain Walsh. "Go fetch the mess sergeant."

The mess sergeant appeared almost immediately.

McNab stood up. Everybody followed suit.

"Yes, sir?" the sergeant said, trying not to appear nervous. "Was everything all right, sir?"

"You look like you've been around the Army awhile. . . ." McNab began.

"Yes, sir. I'm working on sixteen years."

"I want a straight answer. Do you like it better with all these civilians doing what GI cooks and KPs used to do? Or do you miss the old days?"

"General, I really think the food is better now. But I sometimes wish I could eat some of these civilians a new asshole, like I could with cooks and KPs in the old Army."

"Sergeant, we all yearn for the old Army," McNab said. "But that was a first-class breakfast you just served us, and you can take pride in it."

"Yes, sir. Thank you, sir."

"Okay," McNab said, offered the sergeant his hand, and then turned to the others. "Okay, you clowns, get your asses out of low gear and get in the goddamn truck!" He turned back to the mess sergeant. "Oh, I really miss the old Army!"

The mess sergeant—now known as the dining facility supervisor—smiled broadly and followed them out of the dining facility.

[THREE]
Near Richmond, Virginia
0840 26 July 2005

"Washington Center," Fernando Lopez—who was now in the right seat—said into his throat microphone. "Lear Five-Zero-Seven-Five for direct Reagan National. We have special clearance Six-Dash-A-Dash-Two-Seven. Estimate Reagan in one zero minutes."

"Lear Zero-Seven-Five, you are cleared to Reagan Airport. Begin descent to five thousand feet at this time. Contact Reagan approach control on 122.7 at this time."

"Thank you, Washington Center," Fernando said, and switched frequencies. "Reagan approach control, Lear Five-Zero-Seven-Five."

"Zero-Seven-Five, Reagan. We have you on radar. Maintain current heading, airspeed, and rate of descent. Report when at five thousand feet."

"Reagan, Zero-Seven-Five understands maintain airspeed, heading, and rate of descent, reporting when at five thousand."

Fernando turned to Torine, who was in the pilot's seat—Castillo was now kneeling between them—and announced, "Now that, gentlemen, is the way a real pilot does it. He calls somebody important in Washington and makes sure he has a landing clearance before he takes off, thus ensuring—"

"Lear Zero-Seven-Five, Reagan approach control."

"What now?" Fernando wondered aloud.

"We have a saying in the Air Force, Fernando," Torine said. "Counteth not thy chickens until the eggs hatcheth."

"Reagan, Zero-Seven-Five," Fernando replied after keying the TRANSMIT button.

"Zero-Seven-Five, in-flight advisory. Be advised that U.S. Air Force C-37A Tail Number Zero-Four-Seven—that's a Gulfstream—entered United States airspace at one five past the hour."

Castillo had a sudden mental image of Special Agent Schneider wrapped in white sheets and bandages lying on the hospital configuration bed in the Gulfstream. His throat was suddenly tight and his eyes watered. He turned so that no one would see.

"Reagan," Fernando said. "Zero-Seven-Five acknowledges in-flight advisory. Furthermore, Zero-Seven-Five is at five thousand. I have the field in sight."

"Lear Zero-Seven-Five, change to Reagan tower, 119.1, at this time."

"Lear Zero-Seven-Five, roger."

Fernando switched frequencies. "Reagan tower, Lear Zero-Seven-Five, over."

"Reagan National clears Lear Zero-Seven-Five as number two to land, after the Delta 737 on Final."

XIV

[ONE]
Office of the Secretary
Department of Homeland Security
Nebraska Avenue Complex
Washington, D.C.
0925 26 July 2005

Major H. Richard Miller, Jr., was sitting behind Major C. G. Castillo's desk when Castillo, Torine, and Lopez walked in. Miller was wearing civilian clothing, a single-breasted, nearly black suit. His left leg was encased in a thick white cast from his toes to well past his knee. His toes peeked out the bottom of the cast, which was resting on the desk.

"Forgive me for not rising," Miller said. "I honestly try to be humble, but it is very difficult for someone of my accomplishments."

Castillo shook his head. "How's the leg?"

"Let me ask you a question first," Miller said. "Dare I

hope to have the honor of serving in some humble capacity within the Office of Organizational Analysis?"

"Why not?" Castillo replied.

"In that case, Chief," Miller said, "how does it look? As if I am about to run the four-hundred-meter hurdles?"

"What we should do, Colonel," Castillo said to Torine, "is hold him down and paint those ugly toenails flaming red, and then listen to him trying to explain that he really likes girls."

"Speaking of the gentle sex," Miller said, "Jack Britton called from MacDill about ten minutes ago. He said the Gulfstream was about to take off for Philadelphia about five minutes ago. Quote, Betty is resting comfortably, and the pilot estimates Philadelphia at eleven-thirty, end quote."

Miller saw Castillo's face, and when he spoke again, his tone of voice was that of a concerned friend. "I'm really sorry about that, Charley."

Castillo nodded.

"I told Tom McGuire," Miller went on, "and he's arranging for the aircraft to be met by a suitable Secret Service delegation."

Castillo nodded again, then asked, "How'd you hear about the Office of Organizational Analysis?"

"Secretary Hall showed it to me and Mrs. Forbison when we came in this morning," Miller said, then looked at Torine and added, "He said you'd been drafted, Colonel . . ."

"Given temporary duty, actually," Torine said.

". . . but he didn't say anything about you, Fernando.

How much about Charley's new exalted status do you know?"

"Consider him in. All the way," Castillo ordered.

"Can you do that?" Miller asked.

"There's a story that when General Donovan started the OSS—before he was General Donovan, when he was a civilian they called him 'colonel' because he'd been one in the First World War—he was paid a dollar a year. So hand Fernando a dollar and consider him on the payroll. I think I can do that."

"According to Hall, you can do just about anything you want to," Miller said. "So that makes"—he counted on his fingers—"three of us. You, the Texan, and me. Anybody else?"

Castillo turned to Torine and said, "We were talking about shooters in Argentina with General McNab. Jack Britton would make a good one."

Torine nodded his agreement.

"Where's Joel?"

"With Hall at the White House."

"Tom McGuire?"

"On his way here from Langley with your . . . *modified* . . . German passport. He also has your new American passport."

"When he gets here, I'll ask him if . . ." He stopped as Mrs. Agnes Forbison walked into the room.

The somewhat plump executive assistant to the secretary of Homeland Security walked up to Castillo and put her arms around him.

"I'm so sorry about Betty Schneider," she said. "Did

Dick tell you she's on the way to Philadelphia?"

"Just now."

"What were you going to ask the boss?" she asked, as she turned to smile at Torine and Fernando.

"I'm going to ask *Tom* if I can have Jack Britton. I'd like to send him back to Buenos Aires as soon as possible."

"You mean for the Office of Organizational Analysis?"

Castillo nodded.

"If you ask Tom, he will ask Joel. Joel will probably say yes, but if he doesn't, you'll go to the boss, who I know will give him to you. So consider it done."

"Okay, that's four," Miller said.

"I can think of two more people you could really use," Mrs. Forbison said.

"Who?"

"Tom, for one."

"I don't think that Tom would like taking orders from me," Castillo replied, "or that Hall would go along with that."

Mrs. Forbison seemed to be collecting her thoughts, and it was a moment before she responded.

"Charley," she said, "you need to learn to make better use of soft intel sources, and executive assistants such as myself are as good as it gets. Tom confided in me that he would really like to be in on this. Among your arguments for getting him—and there are many—is that you really need someone who knows his way around the dark alleys of federal law enforcement. He told me that, too."

Charley raised an eyebrow, both impressed at her

ability to have her finger on the pulse of the department and disappointed in himself at having forgotten that she had her finger on said pulse. "Okay, I'll ask. I'd love to have Tom. And all Hall can say is no. Or probably 'hell, no.'"

"Let me handle the boss," Mrs. Forbison said.

"Good luck. Who else?"

"Me."

Castillo looked at her in genuine surprise.

"Why would you want to do that?"

"Well, you know how busy I am here keeping the furniture polished against the remote possibility that the secretary will bring somebody here to dazzle him with his elegant official office. We both know—more important, the boss knows—that Mary-Ellen really runs things for him and that he doesn't need both of us doing the same thing."

Castillo smiled at her.

Mrs. Mary-Ellen Kensington, a GS-15 like Mrs. Agnes Forbison who also carried the title of executive assistant to the secretary of Homeland Security, maintained Hall's small and unpretentious suite of offices in the Old Executive Office Building, near the White House. Hall spent most of his time there. He and the President were close personal friends, and the President liked to have him at hand when he wanted him.

"Mrs. Kellenhamp," Mrs. Forbison went on, "can supervise the furniture polishing as well as I can, and bringing her out here would also get her out of Mary-Ellen's hair."

Mrs. Louise Kellenhamp, a GS-13 who carried the title of deputy executive assistant, worked in the OEOB performing mostly secretarial-type duties.

"You've given this some thought, haven't you?" Castillo asked.

"From the moment I realized the boss, whether he wanted to or not, was going to have to have his own intelligence people. And now that we have, thanks to the President, this 'clandestine and covert' Office of Organizational Analysis hiding in the Department of Homeland Security, it seems to me that you're really going to need someone who knows her way around official Washington. And how to push paper around."

"What do we do with him?" Castillo asked, nodding toward Major H. Richard Miller, Jr. "Send him back to Walter Reed?"

"Eventually, he'll get out of that cast," Mrs. Forbison said. "And if he behaves himself, he can try to make himself useful around here until he does."

"God spare us all from conniving bureaucrats," Miller said piously.

"You know I'm right, Charley," Mrs. Forbison said.

"You think you can talk the boss into this?" Castillo said.

"Consider it done," she said. "The next time the subject comes up, act pleasantly surprised when the boss says 'I've had an idea, Charley, I'd like to run past you.'"

"Mrs. Forbison, you're marvelous," Castillo said.

"I know," she replied. "Now that that's settled, Chief, what's on our agenda this morning?"

"I brought a satellite radio, and an operator, from

Fort Bragg. Like we did when we were hunting the stolen 727, the dish has to go on the roof, and the operator's going to need a place to live," Castillo said.

"Dick," Mrs. Forbison said, "if you'll take care of the operator, I'll deal with the building engineer. His delicate feelings were bruised the last time the chief put that thing on the roof."

"Yes, ma'am," Miller replied, smiling.

"And I need the passports," Castillo said.

"They're on the way," Mrs. Forbison said. "Tom's handling that."

"And I have to call Ambassador Silvio or Alex Darby—preferably both—on a secure line." He looked at Miller. "McNab is sending equipment for six shooters down there. I want to make sure it doesn't get lost."

"You'll have to use the one on my desk for that," Mrs. Forbison said. "I ordered one for you this morning, but it won't be in until later today."

"You ordered one for me?" Castillo asked, surprised.

"You're now on the White House circuit, didn't you know?"

"No, ma'am, I didn't."

"Well, you are. Anything else?"

"We'll need someplace to stay in Paris. The Crillon, if we can get in."

"Fancy," Mrs. Forbison said.

"And right next door to the embassy. Have them bill it to Gossinger. Four rooms."

"Let's talk about that," Mrs. Forbison said. "You, I can put on orders. The colonel, presumably, is already on orders?"

"Yes, ma'am," Colonel Torine said.

"But what about the other operator and Fernando?"

"I'll pick up the bill for the operator," Castillo said. "Then he can pocket the per diem check he gets from Fort Bragg. And I'll pick up Fernando's bill, too."

"If we hire him as a temporary contract employee . . . maybe as an aircraft pilot . . . I can cut orders on him, too."

"Mrs. Forbison, at the risk of repeating myself, you're wonderful," Castillo said.

"At the risk of repeating myself, Chief, I know. But you're going to have to start calling me Agnes."

He looked at her but didn't immediately reply.

"Please don't tell me—I already know—that I'm *nearly* old enough to be your mother. But you have just become a bureaucratic heavy, Chief, and bureaucratic heavies call their executive assistants by their first names."

"Whatever you say . . . Agnes," Castillo said, and then asked, "What do I do about Secretary Hall?"

"He said that he'd like you, if possible, to come by the OEOB before you leave."

"I'll do it."

Thirty minutes later, after having spoken with both Ambassador Silvio and Alex Darby; after being informed that the Hotel Crillon would be expecting all of them; after having received his new American passport and his German passport now bearing a departure stamp from the Republic of Argentina; and after having talked to

Tom McGuire long enough to be convinced that McGuire really wanted to become a member of the Office of Organizational Analysis and was going to have no problems working under a man ten years his junior, Castillo shook hands with Dick Miller and then went to Mrs. Forbison's office to say goodbye to her.

She gave him a quick hug and a kiss on the cheek and told him to be careful. He and Torine and Fernando were waiting for the elevator when Mrs. Forbison put her head in the corridor.

"Call for you, Chief."

"If you keep calling me chief, we're back to Mrs. Forbison. Who is it?"

"Somebody who wants to talk about Jean-Paul."

"Jean-Paul Lorimer?"

"All he said was Jean-Paul, Charley."

Castillo went into Mrs. Forbison's office and picked up the telephone.

"Castillo."

"You'll have to remember to turn your cellular on," Howard Kennedy said.

"Jesus, it's in my briefcase."

"Then it wouldn't matter, would it, if it's on or off?"

"What's up, Howard?"

"You have really opened a can of truly poisonous worms with that pal of yours, the one you asked me to find."

"What kind of poisonous worms?"

"The kind I have been absolutely forbidden to talk about on the telephone," Kennedy said.

"That bad?"

"Worse than that bad. Where can we meet?"

"Where are you?"

"Answer the question."

"As soon as I can go by the hotel and pack some clothes, and after a stop at Hall's coffee shop on Pennsylvania Avenue, I'm going to get on an airplane for Paris."

"What flight?"

"Air San Antonio, flight seventeen."

"Oh, really? Anybody I know coming with you?"

"The same crew we had in Cozumel. You know both of them."

"Interesting. And where will you be staying in Paris?"

"The Crillon."

"Lovely hotel. Unfortunately, too close for me to some former associates of mine who work close by."

Christ, I forgot to tell, or remind, Tom McGuire to find out what Special Agent Yung of the FBI is really doing in Montevideo! Castillo thought, then said, "What do you suggest?"

"When did you say you're leaving?"

"As soon as we can."

"You can't make it nonstop in that airplane, can you?"

"No. We're going to have to refuel at Gander, Newfoundland, and Shannon, Ireland. I figure it's going to take us, factoring in two one-hour fuel stops, about ten hours."

"Well, it's nearly half past four in Paris," Kennedy said. "If you get off the ground in an hour, that would make it half past five. Five plus ten is three o'clock in the morning. Figure another hour at least to get through customs and immigration, to get to the Crillon from Le Bourget . . . Is that where you're headed, Le Bourget?"

"Yeah," Castillo said.

"It will be five o'clock when you get to the hotel from Le Bourget. Factor in another hour for delays, call it six. See you in the morning, Charley. We really do need to talk."

There was a change in the background noise, and Castillo realized that Kennedy had hung up.

[TWO]
Old Executive Office Building
Seventeenth Street and
** Pennsylvania Avenue, NW**
Washington, D.C.
1120 26 July 2005

"The President told me you'd had a little chat," the Honorable Matthew Hall, secretary of the Department of Homeland Security, said. "You have any questions about that?"

"One big one," Castillo replied. "The soldier in me is uncomfortable not understanding my chain of command."

"The simple answer to that is that you answer to the President directly," Hall said. "But I think I know what you're asking. And proving that I'm learning to be a Washington bureaucrat, let me answer obliquely. When he came up with that finding, I wondered why I had been taken out of the loop. Then I realized I had not been. It all goes to deniability. I can now honestly answer, if someone asks, and someone inevitably will, either as a shot-in-the-dark fishing expedition or because this comes out, what's my relationship to you, that we have none. You don't work for me.

"Similarly, if someone asks the President's chief of staff what he knows about C. G. Castillo or the Office of Organizational Analysis, he can honestly say he doesn't know anything about it. If we get caught—which is a real possibility—we can hide behind the President's finding.

"The further you distance the Office of Organizational Analysis from the President, the better. That's why he's hiding it in Homeland Security. As far as you working for him directly, there's a lot of captains through colonels—the aides, the guys who carry the football, for example—who work for him directly, and if some enterprising reporter sniffs you out, you can answer the same way they are instructed to. 'Sorry, my duties in the White House are classified. You'll have to ask the White House.' Still with me?"

"Sir, what I was really asking was how much of what I'm doing do I tell him. Or you."

"As far as 'or me' is concerned: Whatever you tell me I will tell the President *when I think I should, and only then.* The President is not interested in the means, just the end. That's what puts me back in the loop. I will tell him only those things which may require some action on his part—I'm thinking of 'Hell no, we can't do that; tell him to stop.'" He paused, then asked, "You understand?"

"Yes, sir."

"Okay. Now is there anything you need?"

"Just one thing I can think of, sir. I asked Tom McGuire to do it for me, but I'm not sure—don't misunderstand this, I have a profound admiration for his abilities—that he'll be able to do it."

"You have 'a profound admiration for his abilities'?" Hall asked.

"Yes, sir."

"How would you like to have Tom working for you?"

"Is that possible, sir?"

"Joel suggested he would be very useful to you. I agree. Should I ask Tom?"

"I'd really like to have him, sir," Castillo said, and thought, *I have just proved that I, too, am learning to be a Washington bureaucrat. Those answers were, without being out-and-out lies, certainly designed to mislead. I already know Tom wants to work for me and that it's possible.*

"Okay, I will. Now what don't you think Tom will be able to do?"

"Find out what FBI agent Yung is really doing in Montevideo. If he's doing something covertly, they're not going to tell Tom."

"What makes you think he's not doing what he says he is?"

"I don't think you want to know, sir."

"Ah, you're learning," Hall said. "Has this guy got a first name?"

"David William, sir. Junior."

Hall pushed the speakerphone button on his telephone.

"Mary-Ellen, will you get me Director Schmidt on a secure line, please?"

"Right away, Mr. Secretary," Mary-Ellen Kensington said.

He pushed the button again and looked at Castillo.

"I know the DCI knows about the finding; he called me first thing this morning to feel me out about it. I don't think Schmidt has seen it yet. This is one-upmanship, Charley. A dirty game we all have to learn to play."

The speaker came alive with Mrs. Kensington's voice:

"Director Schmidt is on one, Mr. Secretary, the line is secure."

Hall pushed the speakerphone button again.

"Good morning, Mark," Hall said cordially. "How are you?"

"What can I do for you, Matt?"

"You've seen the Presidential Finding vis-à-vis the Masterson assassination, right?" Hall asked, ignoring Schmidt's abruptness.

"As a matter of fact, no."

"Well, hell. That makes this a little difficult, Mark. Obviously I can't talk about it if you haven't seen it. So forget I mentioned it. Just take this as a routine request for information. If you don't mind a suggestion, you might ask the attorney general what's new."

"What sort of information do you need, Matt?" Schmidt said, his voice betraying his annoyance.

"Would it be easier for you if I called the attorney general? I don't want to put you on a spot."

"What information do you need, Matt?"

"You have an agent in the embassy in Montevideo.

David William Yung, Junior. He's supposed to be working on money laundering. What I need to know is what he's really doing down there."

"What makes you so sure he's not doing what he says he's doing?"

"We're back to that area I can't talk about," Hall said. "Are you sure you don't want me to go to the attorney general with this? I know he's in the loop, and I'm surprised that you're not."

"I'll look into it, Matt," Schmidt said, "and get back to you."

"I need this information yesterday, Mark," Hall said. "So I have to ask, how long do you think it will take for you to get back to me?"

"I'll get back to you just as soon as I can. Probably this morning."

"I appreciate that, Mark. Thank you."

"Anytime, Matt."

Hall pushed the button, breaking the connection.

"See how it's done?" he asked. "I'll bet you two dollars to a doughnut that Schmidt is already trying to get the attorney general on the horn. The attorney general will tell him about the finding, and that he has to go along with it. Which will also make the point that I knew about it before he did, suggesting he's not as important as he likes to think he is."

"It's childish, isn't it?"

"Absolutely, but that's the way things work," Hall said. "Now that I've annoyed him, is there anybody else you'd like me to annoy?"

"Sir, when he calls back, could you ask him to contact the FBI people in Paris—and in Vienna, come to think of it—and ask them to give me whatever I need?"

"I will *tell* him that the chief of the Office of Organizational Analysis wants to make sure they know that when they are contacted, they will make any information they have on any subject available to him, and that they will probably be contacted by a man named Castillo." He paused, and then went on. "And I will contact Ambassador Montvale and tell him to do essentially the same thing vis-à-vis his CIA station chiefs in Paris and Vienna. And Montevideo, too, if you'd like."

"Thank you. It would probably be a good idea when you speak with Director Schmidt to ask him to tell the FBI in Montevideo to give me what I ask for."

Hall nodded his agreement.

"Anything else, Charley?"

"I can't think of anything else, sir."

"Let me run this past you," Hall said. "You're going to need someone to handle your paperwork, someone who knows her way around Washington. What would you think about me asking Agnes Forbison if she'd like to work with you?"

"I could really use her."

"I'll have a word with her as soon as I can," Hall said.

[THREE]
Over Wilmington, Delaware
1225 26 July 2005

They had been in the air only a few minutes when Castillo sensed the Lear had changed altitude from climbing-to-cruise-altitude to descent. There was only one reason he could think of for that; they were about to land.

Oh, shit, that's all I need! Red lights blinking on the panel! The goddamn bird is broke!

He got out of his seat, walked to the cockpit, and dropped to his knees between the pilot's and copilot's seats.

"What's going on?"

Fernando, who was in the left seat, looked over his shoulder.

"Please return to your seat, sir, and don't interfere with the flight crew in the performance of their duties."

"What's wrong with the goddamn airplane?"

Colonel Torine took pity on him.

"You really didn't want to go to Paris without saying goodbye to your girlfriend, did you, Charley?"

Castillo didn't reply.

"Does it make any real difference if we get to Paris at four in the morning, or five?" Torine went on. "I'll top off the tanks, get us something to eat en route, get the weather, and file the flight plan to Gander while the Secret Service runs you back and forth to the hospital."

When Castillo didn't reply to that, either, at least partially because he didn't trust himself to speak with the enormous lump in his throat, Torine went on: "Tom McGuire called and set it up."

Castillo laid a hand on Torine's shoulder, and then got off his knees and went back to his seat.

[FOUR]

Department of Oral and Maxillofacial Surgery
Fifth Floor, Silverstein Pavilion
Hospital of the University of Pennsylvania
3400 Spruce Street
Philadelphia, Pennsylvania
1340 26 July 2005

As the Secret Service Yukon pulled up outside the hospital, the agent sitting beside the driver spoke into the microphone under his lapel.

"Don Juan arriving."

Fernando chuckled. Castillo gave him the finger. He wondered, now that he had been given a hell of a lot of power, if it would be enough to have the Secret Service change the code name Joel Isaacson had given him when he'd gone to work for Secretary Hall.

The Secret Service agent led them to the elevator bank, waved them inside, and then said, "Fifth floor, Mr. Castillo. We'll be right here."

A tall, stocky woman—visibly some kind of Latin—was standing in the lobby of the fifth floor when the elevator door opened. Her hair was drawn tight against her skull, and Castillo could see the flesh-colored speaker in her ear. He could also see a bulge on her left hip that was almost certainly a handgun.

"This way, please, Mr. Castillo. Special Agent Schneider has been put in five-twenty-seven."

"Muchas gracias," Castillo said. *"Muy amable de su parte."*

It wasn't hard to find room 527. There were two law enforcement officers sitting in folding chairs on either side of the door. One was wearing the motorcyclist's boots and other special uniform items of the Philadelphia Police Department's elite highway patrol. The other was a large and burly man in civilian clothing with the telltale ear speaker of the Secret Service in his ear.

As Castillo got close to the room, both of them stood.

Castillo glanced to his left and saw a glass-walled waiting room. There were more than a half dozen people in it. Castillo recognized three of them as Philadelphia police officers: Chief Inspector Fritz Kramer, the commander of the counterterrorism bureau; Captain Frank O'Brien, who headed the intelligence and organized crime unit and for whom Betty Schneider had worked as a sergeant; and Lieutenant Frank Schneider of the highway patrol, who was Betty's big and, it could be reasonably argued, somewhat overprotective brother.

There were also a couple who Castillo decided were Betty's parents, a clergyman, and several other people.

Well, what the hell did you expect? That it would be just the two of you?

He had what he realized was the vain hope that no one in the waiting room would see him.

The Secret Service agent at the door said, "Special Agent Schneider is in X-ray, Mr. Castillo. She should be back any moment. There's a waiting room. . . ." He pointed.

"Any reason we can't wait in there?"

"No, sir."

Castillo and Fernando entered the room. The bed was mussed, but Castillo could see no other sign that Betty had been in the room.

And I didn't see Jack Britton in that waiting room. Where the hell is he?

He walked to the window and looked out into an interior courtyard, and turned only when he sensed the door to the room was opening.

Betty was wheeled in on a gurney. She didn't see Castillo until the technicians had moved her from the gurney onto the bed and moved out of the way.

Then she raised her hand and almost moaned, "Oh, Charley!" through her wired-shut jaws.

Castillo went to the bed and took her raised hand, and kissed it, and then bent over and kissed her very gently on the forehead. Then they just looked at each other.

Thirty seconds or so later, he took a chance that his voice would work.

"Wiener schnitzel, baby," he said.

Betty smiled at him.

"If you don't mind, Costello, our mother wants to see her!" Lieutenant Frank Schneider said behind him.

Castillo turned.

Standing behind Betty's brother was the couple Charley presumed were the parents. Behind them were the clergyman and another man.

"What's the matter with you, Francis?" Betty's mother snapped. "Can't you see the way she's looking at him?"

"I'm sorry," Castillo said.

Reluctantly, Betty let go of his hand.

Betty's mother touched Castillo's cheek, and stepped around him to the bed.

Betty's father eyed him icily.

Castillo walked out of the room, followed by Fernando, and a moment later by Lieutenant Schneider.

Did he leave because he wanted his mother and father and the minister to be alone with Betty? Or did his mother tell him to get out?

"Costello!" Lieutenant Schneider said.

Castillo turned. Schneider walked very close to him and asked, "You remember one time I promised to break both your legs?"

Both the highway patrolman and the Secret Service agent guarding Betty's door were now on their feet.

"The name is Castillo," Charley said evenly. "And, yes, I seem to remember something like that."

"I knew you were bad news the minute I laid eyes on you," Schneider said. "She's in there because of you."

Castillo nodded slightly. "Guilty."

"If you ever show your face around her again, I swear I'll break both your legs and then tear off your arms and shove them up your ass!"

Castillo didn't reply.

Fernando took a couple of steps closer. "Let me tell you something, Shorty," he said, aware that "Shorty" was relative. Lieutenant Schneider, at six-feet-one, was at least two inches shorter—and maybe forty pounds lighter—than Fernando Lopez.

"Butt out, lardass!" Lieutenant Schneider said.

"That's enough, Lieutenant!" Chief Inspector Kramer barked. "Back off! Now!"

"What I was about to tell the lieutenant," Fernando said, matter-of-factly, "is that the way it is in our family, anyone wanting to get at Charley has to get past me first."

"Don't pour gas on a fire," Chief Inspector Kramer said. "Ask any fireman. Both of you shut up."

Castillo chuckled.

"You open your mouth once more, Schneider, and I'll order you out of here. Capische?"

Schneider nodded.

"Say 'Yes, sir,' Lieutenant!"

"Yes, sir," Schneider said, reluctantly.

"Charley, I need to talk to you," Kramer said. "And O'Brien wants to know what's going on, too. If I order our gorilla to wait at that end of the corridor"—he pointed—"can you get your gorilla to wait down there?" He pointed in the other direction.

Castillo looked at Frank Schneider. "I think you have a right to hear what I'm going to tell the chief," he said. "Can you behave?"

Lieutenant Schneider nodded curtly.

"Say 'yes' or 'no,' goddammit, Schneider," Kramer snapped.

"Okay, okay," Lieutenant Schneider said.

"We can use the waiting room," Kramer said, and pushed the door open.

• • •

"Well, Frank, what do you think?" Chief Inspector Kramer inquired of Captain O'Brien when Castillo had finished.

"A lot of cocaine comes here from Argentina," O'Brien said.

"I didn't know that," Fernando said.

"They fly it from Colombia to Bolivia or Paraguay—sometimes direct to Paraguay—and then get it into Argentina," O'Brien explained. "And then they mule it to Miami from Buenos Aires. The Argentine drug cops—they call them SIDE—are smart. Instead of arresting the critters, they let them get on a plane, and then call our DEA guys down there. The DEA in Miami meets the airplane. That way the cocaine gets stopped, and we have to pay to try the critters and the cost of keeping them in the slam for fifteen to twenty."

"SIDE does more than drugs, Captain," Castillo said. "It's the Argentine FBI, CIA, and DEA under one roof."

"I didn't know that," O'Brien said. "What I'm thinking is that the drug guys—here, there, everywhere—do this kind of casual whacking. Anybody they think might be in the way of anything, anybody they think may have seen or heard something, gets whacked. Including members of their family."

"I'm not saying you're wrong," Castillo said. "But that didn't come up down there, either from a DEA guy I know, who would have told me, or from the head of SIDE."

"What did they think was going on?"

"They had no idea," Castillo said. "All we know—and I didn't know this in Argentina—is that somebody wants to get their hands on Jean-Paul Lorimer, and is perfectly willing to kill anybody to do that."

"We had a job here in Philadelphia a couple of years ago," Kramer said. "Drugs shipped from . . . where, Frank?"

"Senegal," O'Brien furnished.

"From Senegal to their UN Mission in New York. With diplomatic immunity. What happened was . . . out of school?"

Castillo nodded.

"Our dogs—not K-9, but the drug sniffers, those little spaniels or whatever—sniffed the cocaine in freight handling. We couldn't get a warrant to open the boxes, of course, but I happened to be down there looking for explosives and one of the boxes happened to get knocked over. Not much damage, but put enough of a crack in the box for me to be able to stick one of those meat-basting hypodermic needles . . . You know what I mean? They have great big needles?"

Castillo nodded again.

". . . into the box and come out with a white powder that tested to be really high-grade coke. So we called in the DEA. Who called in the FBI and customs and the State Department. It got to be a real Chinese fire drill. The State Department didn't believe the white power had just dribbled out of the box; they as much as accused us of violating diplomatic immunity. They were afraid the Senegalese ambassador would be pissed and give an anti-American speech to the general assembly.

"What finally happened was that the shipment was passed through customs. Then the FBI brought in the New York City cops, told them what we knew, and the New York cops put some heavy surveillance on the Senegalese mission, and they finally caught one of their diplomats . . . he was number two, right, Frank?"

"Number three. Deputy chief of mission," O'Brien corrected him.

". . . in the midst of a five-kilo sale to a guy in the Plaza Hotel. All they could do was charge the buyer with conspiracy to traffic. They couldn't even hold the Senegalese. He had diplomatic immunity. The State Department wouldn't even ask for the UN to send him home. They said they couldn't because they 'had knowledge of the legally highly questionable manner in which the alleged facts triggering the investigation had been conducted.'

"This really pissed off the New York cops, so wherever, *wherever* the Senegalese diplomat went for the next couple of months he had at least two cops sitting on him. And then one day, he had enough, went out to Kennedy, and got on an airplane and went home."

"Jesus Christ!" Fernando exploded.

"So when you find this guy you're looking for, Charley, maybe you better keep the drug angle in mind," Kramer said.

"I will," Castillo said.

"How do you rate the threat against Sergeant . . . sorry, *Special Agent* Schneider?" Kramer asked.

"I don't think these bastards were after her; they were

either after me or anybody—like a Secret Service agent—to make their point to Mrs. Masterson. So I don't think there's much of a threat here. Having said—"

"You sonofabitch!" Lieutenant Schneider interrupted. "You really don't—"

"Out!" Chief Kramer exploded. "Out of here, Schneider! Right goddamn now!"

"Let him stay until I finish," Castillo said evenly.

Kramer raised an eyebrow, stared at Schneider, then sighed and nodded.

"Having said that," Castillo went on, "I'm going to keep Secret Service protection on her until I get the bastards that shot her. The agents are pretty good at protecting people."

"So are we," Chief Kramer said. "And as far as you're concerned, Schneider, when you come to visit your sister and you see detectives from Dignitary Protection sitting on her beside the Secret Service, instead of Highway, you think long and hard about why I decided to do that. Now get out of here. Wait by the elevator. I'm not through with you."

"How about keeping him in here while I go say goodbye to her?" Castillo asked. "I really have to get out of here right now."

Kramer nodded. "Sit there, Lieutenant Schneider," he ordered, pointing to a vinyl-upholstered couch. "And if you get off that couch before I tell you you can, I'll have you up on charges."

Kramer waited until Lieutenant Schneider angrily threw himself onto the couch and then put out his hand to Castillo.

"Let me know what I can do to help."

"Thanks, Fritz," Castillo said, and walked out of the waiting room.

Special Agent Jack Britton was standing by Betty's door.

"I only heard you were coming here forty-five minutes ago, Charley. I called Miller and—"

"I'm glad you're here, Jack," Castillo said. "I'm headed for Paris and what I'd like you—"

"Miller told me," Britton interrupted. "Everything. Thanks for keeping me on this."

"I need you, Jack."

"I'm on an American Airlines flight from Miami to Buenos Aires at eleven something tonight."

"Go to the Four Seasons, and then get in touch with Tony Santini."

"I'll do it."

Castillo pushed open the door to Betty's room. Her mother and father were standing on either side of the bed. Her father gave him another icy look, and when he did, her mother looked over her shoulder and saw Castillo.

"Charley's here, honey," her mother said. "Dad and I will be right outside."

"Thank you, Mrs. Schneider," Castillo said softly. He offered his hand. "We haven't been formally introduced, and I'm very sorry it had to be under such conditions."

Betty's mother took his hand in both of hers, made a soft smile, then turned for the door.

Her father shook his head, walked wordlessly to the

door, and held it open for his wife, then followed her
through it.

Castillo went to the bed and took Betty's hand.

With great difficulty, Betty asked, "The Mastersons?
Okay?"

"They've got twenty-four Delta shooters and half of
the Mississippi state police sitting on them."

"Delta?"

"Special Forces guys."

She was surprised to hear that and asked with her eyes
for an explanation.

"Long story, baby. Not important. But the Mastersons are safe. The key to this is her brother. Right after
we landed in Mississippi, she told me the bad guys really
want her brother. She doesn't know where he is. So I'm
on my way to Paris to find him. He should know who
these bastards are."

"Can you do that?"

"Find him, you mean? I'm going to try hard."

"Just go to Paris?"

*Jesus Christ, I have to go through the classified business,
even with her!*

"Baby, this is Top Secret–Presidential, which means
you can't tell anybody, even your family."

Especially your goddamn brother.

She nodded, but her eyes asked for an explanation.

"The President, in what they call a finding, set up a
covert unit to find the people who did this. He gave it to
me, together with all the authority I need to do whatever
has to be done."

Her eyebrows showed that she was impressed.

"I'll make sure they keep you up to speed on what's happening. But you have to keep it to yourself."

"Will they tell me?"

"Special Agent Schneider, you are now assigned to the Office of Organizational Analysis, which is the cover for this," Castillo said. "I'm the chief. You'll be told."

"I wish I could go with you."

Jesus, she's not thinking of us holding hands as we take the elevator to the top of the Eiffel Tower. Or sitting in the Deux Magots on the Left Bank. She wants to go as a cop.

"Me, too."

"Be careful, Charley."

"Wiener schnitzel, baby. I have to go."

He bent over, kissed her very gently on the lips, and looked into her eyes for a long moment.

Then she shrugged, squeezed his hand, and motioned with her head toward the door.

As he and Fernando got on the elevator, he heard the Latin Secret Service agent talk to her lapel microphone.

"Don Juan coming down."

[FIVE]
Hôtel de Crillon
10 Place de la Concorde
Paris, France
0525 27 July 2005

Paris was just starting to wake up when they landed. There had been little traffic on the way in from Le Bourget, and the Place de la Concorde had been nearly empty of vehicles and pedestrians.

"I think the best thing to do is grab some sack time," Castillo announced as they registered. "What about leaving a call for half past ten?"

"Good idea," Torine said.

Castillo knew the problem was going to be jet lag. Their body clocks thought it was midnight, not half past five in the morning.

They weren't really tired, or even particularly sleepy, despite the time they had been up and the distances they had traveled since getting up almost twenty-four hours before at the Masterson plantation in Mississippi. For one thing, that had been only eighteen hours ago in real time. Paris time was six hours ahead of Mississippi.

For another, they'd shared the piloting between them, from Philadelphia to Gander, Newfoundland, and then to Shannon, Ireland, and finally Le Bourget. The "off-duty" pilot—a role each had played—had nothing to do but doze, and the Lear's seats in the main cabin, which folded back to near horizontal, had made dozing easy. It was as if they'd gotten up early and taken several naps before midnight.

The temptation was to take a quick shower, grab a quick breakfast, and then rouse the Paris CIA station chief from his bed and get to work finding Jean-Paul Lorimer. The smart thing to do was to take a quick shower and go to bed, sleeping as long as possible. When sleep proved impossible, with a little bit of luck, the body clock might be fooled, and it would be something like getting up fresh and ready to do a full day's work.

Castillo tipped the bellman and then looked around his suite. The heavy curtain across the windows of his bedroom was permitting a crack of light. He went to it and impulsively pushed it aside far enough to look out. He had a view of the Place de la Concorde and the bridge across the River Seine.

Then he pulled the curtain closed, took fresh linen from his bag, and started to undress. He was down to his Jockey shorts when the telephone rang.

"Hello?"

"Five minutes, in front of the hotel," Howard Kennedy said. "I'm in a black Mercedes."

"I expected no less of you," Castillo replied, even though halfway through the sentence he realized Kennedy had hung up.

Ten minutes later—having decided that his need for a shave and a shower was more important than jumping to obey Kennedy's curt orders—Castillo walked across the empty lobby and out onto the Place de la Concorde.

There was no Mercedes in sight.

Not to worry. Kennedy might be pissed, but he wants to see me, and badly. He's not about to drive off, never to return.

Castillo turned right and walked toward the U.S. embassy. He had just reached the fence, where he was able to see the American flag flying in the courtyard, when he heard the squeal of tires.

He turned and saw a black Mercedes S600 sedan in front of the Crillon. The headlights flashed. Castillo walked—purposely slowly—back to it.

The front passenger window was down, but the door

remained closed. Castillo leaned down, put his hands on the opening, and looked inside.

"Hello, handsome," he said to Kennedy, who was sitting behind the wheel. "Looking for a little action?"

"Goddamn you, Charley, get in the fucking car!"

Castillo opened the door and got in. Kennedy, with another squeal of tires, took off and then turned right onto the Champs-Elysées.

"Where are we going, Howard?"

"Unless you know someplace we can talk without being overheard, we're just going to drive around."

"You think my room in the Crillon is bugged?"

"I don't know for sure that it's not."

"Why all the concern?"

"How much do you know about Lorimer?"

"A little more than I knew when I first talked to you," Castillo replied. "There are people looking for him. They killed Masterson to make the point that they are willing to kill to find him."

"And do you know who these people are?"

"No. That's why I'm hunting Lorimer."

"Would it surprise you that some Russians are doing the same?"

"Nothing would surprise me."

"Or some Germans?"

"Same answer."

"Or some French? Or some former members of Saddam Hussein's regime? Or, for that matter, some people from Houston, Texas?"

"Get to the point, please, Howard. I'm not good at riddles."

"Your friend Lorimer was a bagman—maybe the head bagman—for that noble program called Oil for Food. Which means that he knows who got paid off. That's enough for any of the aforementioned people to take the appropriate steps to make him dead."

"Give me a minute to think that over."

A traffic cop stepped into the street and with a shrill burst from his whistle and an arrogant wave of his stiff arm stopped traffic. Kennedy, with a heavy foot, brought the Mercedes to a stop at the crosswalk. As Castillo watched the trickle of early-morning commuters making their way to cafés and then to work, he considered how Kennedy might—or might not—be trying to play him.

"In addition to his knowing too much, Charley, there are those who think he skimmed the payoff money. To the tune of some—depending on who you talk to— twelve to sixteen million dollars."

"Jesus!"

"Yeah, Jesus. And one more little item. This gets uncomfortably close to Alex."

"How Alex?"

"How do you think you move that kind of money around? By wire transfer? By UPS?"

"You tell me."

"One hundred thousand U.S. dollars fresh from the mint comes in a neatly wrapped plastic package about so big," Kennedy said, taking his hands off the wheel to demonstrate the size. He could have been mimicking a stubby shoe box.

The traffic cop blew another burst of his whistle and waved traffic forward.

"And Alex moves freight, right?" Castillo said. "No questions asked?"

"You don't really expect me to answer that, do you?"

"So why are you telling me what you did?"

"Alex thinks you're a lot smarter than I do," Kennedy said. "He thinks it's possible you'll find this sonofabitch before anybody else does, and that you'll share that information with him."

"Tell Alex, sorry, no. I want this sonofabitch alive, not with a beauty mark in the center of his forehead."

"Why? So he can tell you who's after him?"

"Exactly."

"You really are a virgin, aren't you? These people are untouchable. Believe me."

"The answer is no, Howard. Tell Alex that."

"I told him that's what you would probably decide," Kennedy said.

They were now almost to the Arc de Triomphe de L'etoile. Kennedy made an abrupt left turn onto Rue Pierre Charron and stopped.

"Get out, Charley. Conversation over."

Without another word, Castillo got out of the car. Kennedy drove quickly off.

Castillo walked back to the Champs-Elysées, and then down it, toward the Crillon.

XV

[ONE]
Suite 301
Hôtel de Crillon
10 Place de la Concorde
Paris, France
0730 27 July 2005

There was a knock at the door, and Castillo, still chewing on a piece of toast, stood up from the breakfast table and went to open the door.

A nondescript man in his late fifties—maybe a little older—was standing there in a somewhat rumpled suit.

"Mr. Castillo?"

"Right. You're Mr. Delchamps?"

The man nodded.

"Come on in. Would you like some breakfast?"

"No, thanks."

"Maybe some coffee?"

Delchamps shook his head, and looked at Fernando and Torine.

"I wasn't told about anybody else," Delchamps said.

"This is Colonel Torine and Mr. Lopez," Castillo said. "And this is Mr. Edgar Delchamps, the CIA station chief."

"Not only wasn't I told about anyone else, but, Mr.

Castillo, as you may or may not know, the identity of the CIA station chief, whoever that might be, is classified."

"Not a problem, Mr. Delchamps. Both the colonel and Mr. Lopez have the necessary clearances."

"How do I know that?"

"Someone from the office of the director of national intelligence was supposed to have given you a heads-up about what we're doing here."

"Someone did. But only your name was mentioned."

"It looks to me that there is some sort of a communications problem," Castillo said. "Before we go any further with this, why don't we go next door to the embassy, get on a secure line to the director of national intelligence, and clear this up?"

"It's half past one in the morning in Washington," Delchamps said.

"I know. But I don't have time to waste playing the classified game with you, Mr. Delchamps."

"Maybe later," Delchamps said. "I was told you were interested in a man named Jean-Paul Lorimer. What do you want to know about him?"

"Everything you know about him."

"The phrase used was 'tell him anything you think you should,'" Delchamps said.

"Then there is a communications problem between Ambassador Montvale and whoever you spoke with," Castillo said. "What he was supposed to tell you was to tell me whatever I wanted to know, and what I want to know is everything."

"It was Montvale who called me," Delchamps said.

"And the phraseology he used was you were to tell me what 'you think you should'?"

"That's what he said."

"In that case, Mr. Delchamps, when we go next door and get on the secure phone, we're going to talk to the President, and you are going to tell him what Ambassador Montvale told you."

Delchamps didn't reply.

"For what it's worth, Mr. Delchamps," Colonel Torine said, "I was with Mr. Castillo—on Air Force One—when the President told Ambassador Montvale that Mr. Castillo was to have anything he asked for."

"Why should I believe that?" Delchamps asked.

"No reason," Torine said. "Except it's the truth."

Delchamps considered that for a moment, then said, "Fuck it."

"Excuse me?" Castillo said.

"I said 'fuck it.' Don't tell me you never heard that phrase before. Montvale said you're really an Army officer. A major."

"Guilty."

"Who was given more authority than he clearly will be able to handle, and won't have it long."

"That sonofabitch!" Torine exploded.

"Yeah," Delchamps said.

"You're going to have to go to the President, Charley," Torine said.

"Before you do that, let me tell you where I'm coming from," Delchamps said. "And we'll see how this plays out."

"Go ahead," Castillo said.

"I've been in this business a long time," Delchamps said. "Long enough to be able to retire tomorrow, if I want to. I have been around long enough to see a lot of hard work blown—and, for that matter, people killed—because some hotshot with political power and a personal agenda stuck his nose in what was being developed and blew it. I've been working on this scum Lorimer for a long time, years. And it hasn't been easy."

"How so?" Castillo asked.

"Have you got any clue what he's been up to?"

"Yeah," Castillo said, "he's a bagman, maybe the most important bagman, in the Iraqi oil-for-food scheme."

Castillo saw the surprise on Torine's and Fernando's faces. He had not told them what Kennedy had told him, only that they had met and Kennedy didn't know where Lorimer was.

"The skinny is, as you know," Castillo said, "that the French wanted to ease the sanctions on Hussein but the United States—and the Brits—said hell no. So in its infinite wisdom, the UN security council, in 1996, stepped in with Oil for Food, saying it would keep the Iraqi people alive. It in fact provided Saddam a way to reward his friendly Frogs and Russians and other crooks. Oil allocations totaled some sixty-five billion dollars by the time the United States bagged Baghdad—and with. it the program—in 2003. There's plenty to skim off sixty-five thousand million dollars, and Lorimer was there holding the bag and taking names."

"You want to tell me where you got that about

Lorimer being the bagman?" Delchamps asked. It was close to a challenge.

"No."

"I'll ask you again, later," Delchamps said. "Maybe you'll change your mind."

"Anything is possible," Castillo said.

"Okay, for the sake of argument, he's been *the* most important bagman. He knows maybe fifty percent of the people—maybe more—who've been paid off, how much they've been paid off, how, and when. And what for. Some of these people are in the UN, high up in the UN. Therefore, the UN is not interested in having this come out.

"Some of those paid off are French. The French have an interesting law that says the President of France cannot be investigated while he's holding that office. And the Deuxième Bureau—you know what that is?"

Castillo nodded.

"They regard the agency as a greater threat to La Belle France than the Schutzstaffel ever was, and cooperate accordingly. That's made looking into this difficult."

"I can see where it would," Castillo said.

"Same thing for the Germans," Delchamps went on. "I've still got some friends on the other side of the Rhine—I did some time in Berlin and Vienna in the good old days of the Cold War—and they've fed me some stuff, together with the friendly advice to watch my back as some very important Germans were involved and don't want it to come out.

"There were a lot of Russians involved, too. A lot of the cash we found in Saddam Hussein's closets got there on airplanes owned by a legendary Russian businessman by the name of Aleksandr Pevsner. You ever hear that name?"

"I've heard it," Castillo said.

"He runs sort of a covert FedEx courier service for people who want to ship things around the world without anybody knowing about it. Going off on a tangent with Pevsner, about a month ago I was told—all the station chiefs were told—not to look into anything that sonofabitch was doing without the specific approval of Langley in each case."

"Pevsner was involved with the oil-for-food business?" Castillo asked.

"Not directly, as far as I've been able to figure out. What he did was move the money around—like so much freight—and I suspect that a lot of stuff Saddam Hussein wasn't supposed to get got to Baghdad on his airplanes."

Torine's eyes met Castillo's for a moment.

"Which brings us to the Americans," Delchamps went on. "We had several enterprising businessmen in Houston who were in the oil-for-food racket up to their eyeballs. Forgive me if I sound cynical, but it has been my experience that when rich oil guys make large contributions to politicians, the politicians lend sympathetic ears to them when, for example, they want the agency and the FBI, etcetera, to lay off another businessman, like, for example, this guy Pevsner."

Delchamps paused.

"Can I change my mind about the coffee?"

"Absolutely," Castillo said, and picked up the coffee pitcher.

Delchamps took the cup, added sugar, and stirred it for a moment.

"So there I was, a couple of days ago, when this Lorimer business came up."

"I don't think I follow you," Castillo said.

"The Secret Service guy here is a pal of mine. You know, two old dinosaurs in a forest of young, politically correct State Department flits. Some pal of his called him up and asked him to find Lorimer, and he came to me because he knew I was working on him."

He took a sip of coffee, and then went on: "I knew it was going to go bad, even before the ambassador called me in and asked about Lorimer. He'd had a call from . . . Whatsername, Cohen, the secretary of state herself."

"*Natalie* Cohen," Castillo furnished.

"Feisty little broad," Delchamps said. "I like her. Anyway, there I was, about to really bag the little bastard, when somebody blows the whistle on the whole thing."

"You want to explain that?"

"My somewhat cynical makeup made me suspect that somebody in Langley had a big mouth and told somebody in Foggy Bottom that I was about to finish my report on Lorimer. There are people in Foggy Bottom who deeply regret the current feelings of ill will between the Frogs and the United States—and between some senators investigating the oil-for-food scam and the UN—and think it would be just dreadful if we exacerbated those unfortunate situations by suggesting we had information that the Frogs—all the way up to Chirac, and maybe him, too—were involved, and that the bagman was a UN diplomat."

"You thought they were going to kill your report?" Castillo asked.

"Bury it," Delchamps said. "The way Lorimer was buried. If he was lucky."

"Excuse me?" Castillo said.

"It's possible, of course, that he's in Moscow, or maybe Berlin, telling all he knows about who got paid off besides the Russians or Germans. Knowing where the other guys' bodies are buried is a very useful diplomatic tool. It keeps them from talking about where yours are."

"You're suggesting that Lorimer has been killed?" Castillo asked.

"He was lucky if he was killed quick—in other words, just to shut him up. If somebody wanted to know what he knew . . . They did a real job on his pal, a Lebanese named Henri Douchon, in Vienna. To encourage him to answer questions, they pulled two of his fingernails, and half a dozen of his teeth. Then they cut his throat."

"When was this?" Castillo asked.

"A couple of weeks ago."

"When was the last time anybody saw Lorimer?" Castillo asked.

"Going by his American Express charges, he flew to Vienna on the twelfth of this month. The same day, he bought—or somebody bought using his AmEx card—a train ticket from Vienna here. I don't know if he ever used it; it might be something to throw off anybody looking for him. But he might have come back here. Just don't know. A scenario that occurs to me is that he was grabbed when he went to see his pal Douchon. Then they took him somewhere to ask him questions, or didn't. Following either possibility, they cut him up in little pieces and dropped him into the beautiful Blue Danube. Or he came back here, where they grabbed him, and after he answered their questions, what was left of him was dropped into the Seine."

"Have you considered he might be in hiding?" Castillo asked.

"Sure. Don't think so. My guess is that he's dead. These are very nasty people who wouldn't think twice before they took him out."

"I heard he might have been skimming from the pay-off money," Castillo said.

"Could be. I doubt it. He was paid well, of course, but I can't find any trace of big money."

"And you think you would have been able to?"

Delchamps nodded confidently.

"I even got into his apartment," he said. "He had some really nice stuff, antiques, paintings, etcetera. More than he could afford on what the UN paid him, but a lot less, I think, than he would have had had he been stupid enough to try to steal from these guys."

"Okay," Castillo said. "Thanks. But one more question: If, for the sake of argument, he were hiding, where would you guess that would be?"

"In a closet somewhere," Delchamps said. "Or under a bed. Jean-Paul Lorimer was a wimp. He didn't have the balls to be a criminal."

"You knew him?"

"I saw him around. I'm the cultural attaché at the embassy. I can put the opera, et cetera, on the expense account. And I get invited to all the parties. The Corps Diplomatique loves to have Americans around so they can tell us how we're fucking up the world." He paused. "Okay, that's what I know. Anything you think I missed?"

"I'd like to see all your files on Lorimer," Castillo said.

"So they can disappear into the black hole?"

"Photocopies would do. That way you'd still have the originals."

"You're not asking for the originals?"

Castillo shook his head. "Photocopies would be fine. How long would it take you to make copies?"

"Which you would then turn over to Montvale—or somebody in the agency, maybe—so they could message me to 'immediately transfer by courier the originals of the documents listed below and certify destruction of any copies thereof'?"

"I don't have to give Montvale anything," Castillo said, "and right now I can't think of anything I want to give him. And as far as the agency is concerned, I am on Langley's Fuck the Bastard If Possible list. I want the copies for me."

Delchamps inclined his head, obviously in thought. Then he took another sip of his coffee. Finally, he leaned back in his chair and lit a small cigar.

"Odd that you should ask about photocopies of my files on Lorimer, Mr. Castillo. By a strange coincidence, I spent most of the afternoon and early evening yesterday, starting right after Ambassador Montvale called me, making photocopies of them. At the time, I was thinking of retiring and writing a book, *What the CIA Didn't Want to Get Out About Oil for Food.*"

"What about the 'my lips are sealed forever plus three weeks' statement you signed? You could get your tail in a crack doing something like that."

"You ever run into a guy named Billy Waugh?"

Castillo nodded.

"I thought you might have," Delchamps said. "Billy wrote a book called *I Had Osama bin Laden in My Sights and the Wimps at Langley Wouldn't Let Me Terminate Him*—or something like that—and nothing ever happened to Billy."

"They were probably afraid that Billy would write another one, *CIA Assholes I Have Known,*" Castillo said.

Delchamps chuckled. "I thought about that," he said. "And I figured they'd probably come to the same conclusion about me."

He pushed himself out of the chair and held his hand out with his thumb and index finger held wide apart. "It makes a stack about this big," he said. "I'll go next door and get them."

"Thanks," Castillo said. "One more question. Why did you change your mind? About telling me anything?"

"Straight answer?"

"Please."

"Like I said, I'm a dinosaur. I've been doing this a long time. When I was a kid, starting out in Berlin, we had guys there who had been in the second war, Jedburghs, people like that. I even knew Bill Colby. One of them told me if you couldn't look into a man's eyes and size him up you'd better find something else to do. He was right. You—the three of you—have all got the right look."

Delchamps nodded at Fernando and Torine and walked out of the room.

When the door had closed, Fernando said, "So Lorimer's dead. So now what, Gringo?"

"We don't know that he's dead," Castillo said. "From what Delchamps said, if Lorimer was grabbed, it was around the twelfth of this month. They didn't even abduct Mrs. Masterson until the twentieth, or blow Masterson away until the morning of the twenty-third. That's several days. I think they would have heard, in that time, if somebody had blown Lorimer away."

"Okay," Fernando said. "Same question. What now?"

"Go get Sergeant Kranz out of bed," Castillo said. "Tell him to get packed."

Sergeant First Class Seymour Kranz, a Delta/Gray Fox communicator, had been one of the two communicators they'd picked up—together with their satellite communications equipment—at Fort Bragg. Colonel Torine had told Kranz he had been chosen to go with them to Europe, rather than the other communicator, who had set up at the Nebraska Avenue Complex, because Torine devoutly believed that when flying across an ocean every pound counted. Kranz was barely over the Army's height and weight minimums. The real reason was that Kranz had been with Torine and Castillo when they were searching for the stolen 727 and proved that you don't have to be six feet tall and weigh two hundred pounds to be a first-rate special operator.

"Where are we going?" Torine asked.

"We're going to see my uncle Otto," Castillo said, and walked to the couch and sat down and picked up the telephone on the coffee table in front of it.

[TWO]
Executive Offices
Die Fulda *Tages Zeitung*
Fulda, Hesse, Germany
0805 27 July 2005

Frau Gertrud Schröeder was a stocky—but by no means fat, or even chubby—sixty-year-old Hessian who wore her gray hair done up in a bun. She had been employed by the *Tages Zeitung* since she was twenty, and had always worked for the same man, Otto Göerner.

Otto Göerner had joined the firm shortly after he graduated from Philipps University in Marburg an der Lahn, in part because he was Wilhelm von und zu Gossinger's best friend. Wilhelm was the son and heir apparent to Herman Wilhelm von und zu Gossinger, the managing director and just about sole stockholder in Gossinger Beteiligungsgesellschaft, G.m.b.H.

When Gertrud joined the Gossinger firm, it had been a medium-sized corporation, not nearly as large as it had been before World War II, or was now. The firm's prewar holdings in Hungary and what had become East Germany—timber, farms, newspapers, breweries, and other businesses—had been confiscated by the communist East German and Hungarian governments.

By 1981, Otto Göerner had risen in the corporate hierarchy to become Herman Wilhelm von und zu

Gossinger's—the Old Man's—assistant. The title did not reflect his true importance. He was the *de facto* number two man. But clearly stating this would have been awkward. Wilhelm von und zu Gossinger was supposed to be number two in the family firm.

It had been Gertrud's very privately held opinion at the time that the issue would be resolved when Otto married Frau Erika von und zu Gossinger. Frau Erika had never married; she was called "frau" out of respect for the family's sensitivities. As a very young girl, Erika had made a mistake, with an American aviator of all people, the result of which was a boy, Christened Karl Wilhelm von und zu Gossinger. At the time, no one knew where the father was. Gertrud knew the Old Man could have found him if he wanted to, and concluded the Old Man had decided that no father at all was better, for the time being, than an American who might get his hands on Gossinger money.

The time being, in Gertrud's judgment, meant until the Old Man could arrange a marriage between his daughter and his assistant. He—everyone—knew that Otto Göerner was extraordinarily fond of Frau Erika and Little Karlchen, and that the Old Man thought Göerner would be both a good husband to Erika and a good father to his only grandson, whom he adored.

And once they were married, of course, it would be entirely appropriate for Otto Göerner, now a member of the family, to hold any position within the family firm.

The issue was resolved that year—but not in the way Gertrud hoped—when a tire blew on Wilhelm von und zu Gossinger's Mercedes as he and his father were on their way home from Kassel. The police estimated the car was traveling in excess of 220 kilometers per hour when it crashed through the guardrails of a bridge on the A7 Autobahn and fell ninety meters into the ravine below.

That meant that Frau Erika became just about the sole stockholder of Gossinger Beteiligungsgesellschaft, G.m.b.H. What shares she did not now own were in a trust fund the Old Man had set up for Karlchen, who was then twelve. As expected, Otto Göerner became the managing director of the firm. Frau Gertrud believed it was now simply a matter of waiting for an appropriate period of time of mourning—say, six months—to pass before Frau Erika married Otto.

That didn't happen, either. Frau Erika was diagnosed with terminal pancreatic cancer. She turned to the U.S. Army to find Little Karlchen's father. He was located in the National Cemetery in San Antonio, Texas, under a tombstone on which was carved a representation of the Medal of Honor.

His family was located, too, and to Frau Gertrud it seemed that the Gossinger empire was about to pass into the hands of a Texas family of Mexican extraction, and that Poor Little Karlchen was about to be moved from the family mansion—*Haus im Wald*—in Bad Hersfeld to an adobe shack on the Texas desert, where his newly found grandfather would doze in the sun with his sombrero over his eyes as flies buzzed around him.

That didn't happen, either. Less than twenty-four hours after she learned that her son had left a love child behind him in Germany, Doña Alicia Castillo was at the door of the House in Woods, where she told Frau Erika she had come to take care of her and the boy. She was shortly followed by Don Fernando Castillo, her husband, Little Karlchen's grandfather, and President and chief executive officer of Castillo Enterprises, Inc. When Gertrud turned to *Standard & Poor's* to see exactly what that was, she learned that Castillo Enterprises, Inc., was a privately held corporation with estimated assets worth approximately 2.3 times those of Gossinger Beteiligungsgesellschaft, G.m.b.H.

Two weeks before Frau Erika died, Don Fernando Castillo took Little Karlchen, now renamed Carlos Guillermo Castillo, to Texas, and left "for the time being, until I can get a handle on what's what" Otto Göerner as managing director of Gossinger Beteiligungsgesellschaft, G.m.b.H.

"For the time being" lasted until C. G. Castillo came into his inheritance at twenty-one—shortly before he graduated from the U.S. Military Academy at West Point. One of his first official acts in his role as sole stockholder of Gossinger Beteiligungsgesellschaft, G.m.b.H., was to negotiate a lifelong contract with Otto Göerner to serve as managing director. It provided for an annual salary and a percentage of the profits.

"*Guten morgen*, Gertrud," Otto Göerner said as he walked into his office. He was a tall, heavyset, ruddy-faced man who many people thought was a Bavarian.

"Karlchen just called," Frau Schröeder said.

"Why didn't you tell him to call me in the car?"

"He's coming here. Him and Fernando and two others."

"He say why?"

"He said he wants to show you—at the *Haus im Wald*—a new satellite phone he says you'll probably want to buy for all our foreign correspondents."

"Gott!"

"We got a charge for him and three others for last night at the Crillon," Frau Schröeder announced.

It was Frau Schröeder's custom, as her first or second order of business, to daily check the charges Karl W. Gossinger had made against his *Tages Zeitung* American Express card. It let the both of them know where he was.

"The one in Paris?"

She nodded. "And he still has rooms—maybe just one—in the Four Seasons in Buenos Aires."

"I wonder what our Karlchen is up to?"

"You could ask him."

"We've been over this before, Gertrud. If I ask him something, I'm likely to get an answer that I really don't want to hear."

Gertrud didn't reply.

"A new satellite phone? What the hell is that all about?" Göerner asked.

"Since you're not going to ask him, we'll probably never know," she said.

"Did he say when he's—when *they* are coming?"

"Today."

"He say what flight they'll be on? And can I make it to Rhine-Main in time to meet it?"

"He said they have Fernando's airplane, and are going to Leipzig-Halle."

"They flew across the Atlantic in that little jet?"

"Is that one of those questions you really don't want the answer to?"

"Another one is 'why Leipzig?' The last I heard, Frankfurt is much closer to Paris."

"We never know what our Karlchen is up to, do we?"

"*Really* up to," Göerner said. "As opposed to what he says he is. So when do they get to Leipzig?"

"He said it would probably take them an hour and a half to get out of Paris, and that it's a little more than an hour's flight to Leipzig-Halle. That was ten minutes ago, so they should arrive between ten-thirty and eleven."

"If I leave right now, and drive very dangerously, I *might* be able to meet them."

"Can you get them all in your car?" she asked.

"Probably not," he said. "If they have much luggage, no. We'll just have to rent a car at the airport."

"Or I could drive over there in my car."

"Why would you want to do that?"

"The last time he was in here, I had maybe two whole minutes alone with him."

"Don't let me forget to call my wife and tell her they're coming," Göerner said.

[THREE]
Flughafen Leipzig-Halle
1040 27 July 2005

"My God!" Castillo greeted Göerner and Schröeder. "Who's minding the store?"

He kissed Frau Schröeder wetly on the forehead.

"Ach, Karlchen!" she said.

"Where's your friends?" Göerner asked.

"Going through immigration. We Germans can't be too careful about what Americans we let into the country, you know."

"I don't think that's very funny, Karl," Göerner said.

"Neither do I," Castillo said. "But the facts are that as a good German, I got waved through, and my friends are being very carefully examined by the authorities."

"Just who are your friends?"

"One is an Air Force colonel and the other is a Special Forces sergeant."

"I won't ask you what they're doing here because I don't think you would tell me the truth, and even if you did, I don't think I would want to know."

"I'll tell you. We are looking into the oil-for-food scandal."

"We already have people on that story."

"And I want to talk to them, especially the guy who covered the murder of M'sieu Douchon in Vienna. And I want to hear more about what the *Alte Marburgers* were saying about sanctuary—"

"I don't think we should have this conversation here, Karl, do you?" Göerner interrupted.

"Probably not. We can have it in the car on the way to Bad Hersfeld," Castillo said. He turned to Frau Schröeder. "I don't think you want to be involved in this, *Tante* Gertrud."

She put both hands on his cheeks and looked into his eyes.

"I wish to God you weren't involved in this,

Karlchen," she said. "But since you are, don't you dare try to exclude me."

Fernando Lopez walked up. He wrapped an arm around Frau Schröeder's shoulders, kissed her on the cheek, and said, "Still taking care of ol' Whatsisname, are you, Frau Gertrud?"

"Somebody has to," she said. "Your grandmother is well, I hope?"

"Very well, thank you. If she knew I was going to make this grand tour of Europe, I'm sure she would have sent her love."

"How are you, Fernando?" Otto asked.

"I don't know, Otto," Fernando said. "I have the uncomfortable feeling that I have just become a file in some vast, Teutonically thorough database of suspicious people."

Neither Otto nor Gertrud responded.

Colonel Torine and Sergeant Kranz—who was towing an enormous hard-sided suitcase behind him—walked up to them a moment later.

"Everything okay, Seymour?" Castillo asked.

"Yes, sir. The authorities, who tried hard, failed to find any explosives or controlled substances in my luggage."

"Seymour, this is Mr. Göerner, who has been trying to straighten me out since I was in diapers, and this is Frau Schröeder, who keeps him on the straight and narrow."

"How do you do?" Kranz said.

"Herr Gossinger tells me you're in the Army, Herr Kranz?" Frau Schröeder asked, dubiously.

Kranz looked at Castillo, who nodded, before replying.

"Not exactly, ma'am," Kranz said in German. "I'm Special Forces."

"You mean," she asked, "with the beret, the green beret?"

"Yes, ma'am," Kranz said, "with the beret."

"How very interesting," she said. "And you speak German."

"Yes, ma'am. Most of us speak a couple of languages."

"And this is Colonel Jake Torine, of the Air Force," Castillo said.

"If you're responsible for keeping Karl—Charley—on the straight and narrow, Colonel, you have my profound sympathy," Göerner said.

"I think of him as the cross I have to bear as a righteous man," Torine said.

"Me, too," Göerner said.

[FOUR]
Haus im Wald
Near Bad Hersfeld
Kreis Hersfeld-Rotenburg
Hesse, Germany
1310 27 July 2005

Frau Helena Göerner, a svelte blonde who was a Bavarian but who didn't look as if she would be comfortable in an embroidered dirndl and with her hair braided into pigtails, had lunch waiting for them when they arrived at *Haus im Wald*.

"Welcome home, Karl," she said in English, offering him her cheek to kiss as if he were a very distant relative entitled to the privilege. Then she did the same to Fernando.

"Doña Alicia, Maria, and your adorable children are doing well, I trust, Fernando?"

"Very well, thank you, Helena," Fernando replied. "And *your* rug rats? How and where are they?"

Castillo and Otto chuckled.

"Our children are here, but I wasn't sure if it would be appropriate for them to have luncheon with us."

"Helena, you have to remember that your rug rats are my godchildren," Castillo said. "Bring 'em on!"

"Absolutely," Fernando chimed in. "The more rug rats, the better."

Frau Göerner, forcing a smile, turned to a maid wearing a crisp white cap and apron.

"Ilse, will you bring the children to the dining room, please?" she said, adding to everyone else, "I'll join you there."

She walked out of the foyer.

"Do you two have to do your best to destroy my happy marriage?" Otto asked. He didn't seem to be really annoyed with them.

"The both of you should be ashamed of yourselves," Frau Gertrud said, but she didn't seem very annoyed, either.

"I somehow got the feeling our hostess does not like my godchildren referred to as her rug rats," Castillo said to Torine and Kranz. "I will introduce . . ."

"You sensed that, did you?" Göerner asked, sarcastically.

". . . you two to her when she gets her Bavarian temper under control." He pointed to a door. "That's the elevator. The athletically inclined can use the stairs."

"When he was about nine or ten," Otto said, "Karl used to go to the stables, collect the cats—five, six, more—and load them on the elevator. His grandfather, who wouldn't let Karlchen use the elevator, and who hated cats, would summon the elevator, and when the door opened they'd all rush out into his bedroom. You could hear the Old Man in Fulda."

"He was a wicked little boy," Frau Gertrud said, smiling fondly. "Who looked like an angel."

"Is that a 'what the hell is this?' look on your face, Jake?" Castillo asked Torine, and then went on without waiting for an answer. "I was born in this house. I lived here until I was twelve." Castillo saw the look on Kranz's face, and went on: "Long story, Seymour. I'll brief you later. Let's go up to the dining room and have a beer. In a manner of speaking, I make it myself."

"If Helena offers champagne, Karl," Göerner said firmly, "you will drink it."

"*Jawohl,*" Castillo said, smiling. He clicked his heels, and waved everybody onto the elevator. It was a tight fit, but they all managed to get on.

The dining room was an enormous room on the third floor. One wall was covered with a huge, heavy curtain. Castillo walked to it, found a switch, and tripped it. The curtains opened, revealing floor-to-ceiling plate-glass windows offering a vista of gently rolling farmlands.

"Nice view," Torine said.

"Come here," Castillo said, "and Professor Castillo will offer a lecture on fairly recent military history."

Another maid in crisp white cap and apron appeared with a tray holding champagne stems. Castillo, Torine, and Kranz were taking glasses from the tray when Helena appeared.

"Ah, our hostess," Castillo said. "You'll have to forgive my bad manners, Helena. This is Colonel Jacob Torine of the U.S. Air Force, and Mr. Kranz of AFC Electronics of Las Vegas, Nevada, who is going to demonstrate the satellite telephone I'm going to recommend to Otto that he buy for the *Tages Zeitung*'s correspondents. Gentlemen, our hostess, Frau Helena Göerner."

Helena had her temper under control and was charming.

"You have a lovely home, Frau Göerner," Torine said. "The view is spectacular."

"Yes, it is, isn't it?"

"I was about to deliver a little lecture about the land, Helena. May I go on?"

"Of course," she said, with a hint of a smile and a visible lack of enthusiasm.

"If you will look halfway across that glorious field of corn," Castillo said, pointing, "you will see a strip perhaps seventy-five meters wide where the growth isn't nearly as luxurious as the rest."

"Yeah," Torine said, curiously, having spotted what Castillo had pointed out.

"At one time, as difficult as it might be to believe in

this time of peace and love for our fellow man, that strip was sewn with mines, about half of them Bouncing Betties. They were placed there by the East German authorities—"

"That was the East German–West German border?" Torine interrupted.

"Yes, it was. May I continue?"

"Of course. Excuse me."

"The mines were placed there by the East Germans to keep the West Germans from rushing over there to take advantage of the manifold benefits of communism," Castillo went on.

"Karlchen, be careful!" Frau Gertrud ordered.

"And just this side of the still-polluted soil there used to be a road on which members of the U.S. Army used to patrol. . . . This is really marvelous champagne, Helena! Might I have another?"

"Yes, of course," Helena said, and snapped her fingers impatiently at the maid, who hurried up with her tray.

Castillo took an appreciative swallow and went on: "As I was saying, there was a road on which valiant Americans of the Eleventh and Fourteenth Armored Cavalry Regiments patrolled to keep the West Germans from escaping into East Germany.

"One of those heroic young Americans was someone you both know. Second Lieutenant Allan Naylor came here just about straight from West Point, after pausing only long enough to take a bride and the basic officer's course at Fort Knox—"

"Naylor was here?" Torine asked. "Fascinating."

"As a second john, and later as a major," Castillo confirmed. "And he learned, of course, the legend of the *Haus im Wald*."

"Karl!" Göerner warned. Castillo ignored him.

"Would you like to hear the legend?" Castillo asked innocently.

Torine was silent.

"I would," Kranz said.

"Well, the legend was that in this house, which was known to the stalwart troopers of the Eleventh and Fourteenth as 'the Castle,' there lived a blond fair maiden princess who was ferociously guarded by her father, the king, also known as 'the Old Man.' He didn't keep the fair maiden in chains or anything like that, but he did do his best to keep her away from the Americans, who, as any Frenchman and many Germans will happily tell you, are bent on destroying culture around the world."

"Don't you think that's enough?" Göerner asked.

"I'm almost finished, Otto," Castillo said.

"I don't think you're being funny anymore, Karl," Otto said.

"Then don't laugh," Castillo said. "Well, one day, inevitably, I suppose, the inevitable happened. An American knight in shining armor rode up. Actually he was flying in the left seat of a Dog Model Huey. He set it down right there, on the cobblestones next to the stable."

He pointed.

"He had several things going for him. He was an Army aviator, for one thing, and everybody knows they possess a certain pizzazz. Most important, he was a Texican. As Fernando will tell you, handsome young Texicans send out vibes that women simply cannot resist. And such was the case here.

"He looked up at the mansion and saw the beautiful princess. She saw him. Their eyes locked. There was the sound of violins. The earth shook. Fireworks filled the sky. A choir of angels sang *Ich liebe dich* and other such tunes. And about nine months later they had a beautiful boy child who stands here before you."

"Oh, Karlchen!" Frau Gertrud said, emotionally.

"Your father was an Army aviator?" Kranz asked. "Where is he now?"

"He didn't make it back from Vietnam," Castillo said, evenly.

"I'm sorry."

"Yeah, me, too," Castillo said. "Lecture over. I hope you took notes, as there will be a written exam."

"Why don't we sit down?" Helena said.

"Is that a true story, *Onkel* Karl?" a very young voice inquired.

It showed on Helena Göerner's face that she had not been aware her children had been standing in the door and really didn't like it that they had.

"Ah, my favorite godchildren," Castillo said. "Yeah, Willi, that's a true story."

Castillo walked to the door and embraced, one at a time, two boys, one ten and the other twelve.

The twelve-year-old asked, "What's Vietnam?"

"A terrible place a long way from here," Castillo said. "Changing the subject, Seymour, what time is it in Washington?"

"About half past six," Kranz replied.

"And how long is it going to take you to set up?"

"That depends on where you want it."

"How about next to the stable? Where the knight in shining armor once touched down?"

"Ten minutes. You planning to leave it there?"

"Not for long," Castillo said. "So why don't we have lunch, then while I have a little talk with Otto, you have it up and running by oh-eight-hundred Washington time?"

"Can do."

[FIVE]

"A marvelous lunch, Helena. Thank you," Castillo said.

"I'm glad you liked it, Karl," she said.

Castillo motioned to one of the maids for more coffee. When she had poured it, he said, *"Danke schön,"* and turned to Göerner. "So tell us, Otto, what you heard at the fund-raiser in Marburg about the boys moving money to Argentina," Castillo said.

Göerner didn't reply.

"You said two things, Otto, that caught my attention. You said what caught your attention was they said something about, 'Ha, ha, Der Führer was the first to come up with that idea. . . .'"

Helena flashed him a cold look. "I don't think the children should hear this," she said.

"Your call, of course, Helena," Castillo said. "But when I was even younger than the boys, my grandfather, at this very table, told me all about the evils the National

Socialist German Workers Party—more popularly known as the Nazis—had brought to our fair land. He thought it was important that I knew about it as early as possible."

Her face tightened and grew white.

"You remember, Otto, don't you?" Castillo went on. "The Old Man, sitting where you are now sitting; you and *Onkel* Willi and my mother sitting over there, and me sitting where Willi is. . . ."

"I remember, Karl," Göerner said.

Helena stood up and threw her napkin on the table.

"Come on, boys," she said.

"You don't have to stay, *Liebchen*," Otto said. "But the boys will."

She locked eyes with him, and then walked out of the room.

Göerner looked at Castillo.

"Your mother used to say, you know, that the one thing you really inherited from the Old Man was his complete lack of tact," he said.

Castillo nodded, and then said, "You said you thought the money they were moving was from Oil for Food."

Göerner nodded.

"Let me tell you where I'm coming from, Karl," he said. "When you were being a smart-ass before, with 'the legend of the castle,' it started me thinking. You were right. Your grandfather didn't like Americans, and if the Old Man were alive today, he probably would like them even less. But then I realized that if he were still here, and knew what's going on, and an American intelligence officer—not you, not his grandson, any American intelligence officer he thought he could trust—came to him and asked about this, he would have told him everything he knew.

"And you're right, Karl, I am sitting in the Old Man's chair. And in this chair, I have always tried to do what the Old Man would do. You understand me? That's why we're talking about what we never said out loud before, what you really are; that's why I'm going to tell you what I know, and that's why I wanted the boys to hear this. The Old Man was right about that, too. You're never too young to learn what a lousy world we're living in."

"I understand, Otto," Castillo said.

"Some of this I know myself," Göerner began, "but most of it comes from Eric Kocian—"

"Who?"

"He's the editor of the *Budapester Neue Zeitung*," Göerner said. He looked at Torine. "That's one of ours, which is to say, one of Charley's. Charley did tell you, didn't he, that he's the owner of Gossinger Beteiligungsgesellschaft, G.m.b.H.? That's the holding company for everything."

"No, he didn't," Torine said. He looked at Castillo and added, "It probably just slipped his mind."

"Okay, Eric is an old man. Well into his seventies. He's half Hungarian and half Viennese. He was an eighteen-year-old *Gefreite*—corporal—in the Old Man's regiment in Stalingrad. They were really seriously wounded, which turned out to be a good thing for them. They were evacuated on the same plane; they didn't wind up in Siberia for a decade or so after the surrender at Stalingrad.

"After the war, Eric came here—Vienna was nothing but rubble; what was left of his family had been killed the day the Americans tried to bomb the *Hauptbahnhof* and missed and destroyed Saint Stephen's Cathedral—and he really didn't have anyplace else to go. The Old Man put him to work on the farm, and then on the *Tages Zeitung* when he could start that up again. And then when the Old Man got the *Wiener Tages Zeitung* up and running, Eric went to Vienna. He was managing editor, about to retire, when we got the *Budapester Zeitung* presses back from the communists. Eric came to me when he heard I was thinking of selling the plant, and asked that he be allowed to try to get the *Zeitung* up and running again.

"I didn't think that would work, but I knew the Old Man wouldn't have told him no, so I agreed. We renamed it the *Budapester Neue Zeitung* and he started it up. It worked. It's the largest German-language newspaper in Hungary, and is actually a competitor of the *Wiener Tages Zeitung* in Slovakia, the Czech Republic, and Eastern Austria."

"He's the guy who did the story on the Lebanese, what's his name, Douchon, who was murdered in Vienna?" Castillo asked.

"The first story was written by one of our men on the *Wiener Tages Zeitung*. When Eric saw it on our wire, he had serious doubts about it. So he went to Vienna himself, where of course he knew everybody, especially the senior police, and they told him that it wasn't a . . ." Göerner stopped and looked uncomfortably at his sons for a moment and then went on: ". . . a case of one more Middle Eastern homosexual being murdered by his blond Viennese boyfriend, as our man had hinted, but most likely by people who wanted to shut Douchon's mouth so that he wouldn't be talking about Oil for Food.

"Eric had already been looking into the oil-for-food story, and it fit what he'd dug up himself. So he came to me—came here; he didn't trust the telephone—and told me about it, and said he really wanted to go into it.

"I told him he was liable to get himself killed, and he responded, 'At my age, what a good way to go out, on a big story.' So I told him no, I'd assign people to the story, and then he said, 'Okay, then I retire. I'm going to do this story.' "

"Did he retire?"

"Of course not," Göerner said.

"I want to talk to him. Tomorrow."

"I'll have to go with you," Göerner said. "Like most people around here, Kocian thinks you're squandering the Old Man's money while pretending to be our Washington correspondent. He actually pointed out to me the striking similarities between a story we published under your byline and a piece that appeared in the *American Conservative* magazine. I forget what it was, but you certainly didn't spend a lot of time paraphrasing that story."

"I'll try to be more careful in the future," Castillo said.

Göerner nodded.

"Your original question, Karl, was about money being hidden, or washed, in South America, especially Argentina."

"Yes, it was."

"I've always been fascinated with that, and so was your grandfather. The Nazis didn't think it up. They weren't that clever. It actually started after the First World War and the Versailles Convention. The French and the English, you will recall, got German East Africa as reparations. As well as just about everything that could be taken out of Germany proper."

Göerner paused, then asked, "This is going to be a rather long lecture. You sure you want me to go on?"

"I don't know about Charley," Torine said, "but yes, please."

"Go on, Otto, please," Castillo said.

"As bad as the Geneva Convention was—and I'm one of those people who think it made Hitler's coming to power and thus World War Two inevitable—it did not confiscate outright the holdings of individual Germans, or Hungarians, or anyone else, in what had been German East Africa. It simply changed the colonial government from German to French and English; people still owned their farms and businesses and whatever.

"Then the French and English levied taxes on the farms, businesses, etcetera, which they had every legal right to do. The problem was that the taxes had to be paid now in French francs and English pounds. The German mark was worthless. There was no way a German landholder could come up with enough francs or pounds to pay his taxes. The properties were then confiscated for nonpayment of taxes and sold at auction in francs or pounds to the highest bidders, most of whom happened to be Frenchmen and Englishmen."

"Dirty pool," Torine said.

"Of questionable morality, perhaps, but perfectly legal," Göerner went on. "The only people who did not lose their property were a lucky few—including some of your Hungarian kin, Karl—who for one reason or another had gold on deposit in South Africa. The South Africans hated the English and the French, and closed their eyes when the gold that Germans held in their banks was transferred to either some friendly South African or Swiss bank.

"Then, when the tax auctions were held, lo and behold, some of the bidders were Swiss and South African, who were able to buy francs and pounds at very favorable rates with their gold, and be in a position to outbid the French and the English who had come to the auctions looking for a real bargain.

"That's how your *Nagynéni* Olga, Karl—"

"Excuse me?" Torine interrupted.

"My Hungarian aunt Olga," Castillo furnished. "She lived with us here, until I was what, Otto, about seven or eight?"

"You were eight when Olga died," Göerner said. "Anyway, because they had gold in South Africa, Olga and her husband, who was then still alive, managed to not only hang on to their former German East African property, but to buy at auction the Gossinger holdings, which otherwise would have gone to some undeserving Frenchman or Englishman.

"After World War Two, the communists in Hungary, of course, confiscated everything she owned there, but when the Old Man finally got her out of Hungary, she still held title to the African properties. She left it to the

Old Man when she died. He held it until he decided that Kenya was not really going to become the African paradise the new black leaders said it was going to be after independence."

"I never heard any of this before," Castillo confessed.

"All you had to do was ask, Karl," Göerner said. "The importance about all of this is that people learned the lesson. They understood that it was prudent to have hard currency out of whatever country they lived in. This proved a boon to the Swiss banking industry, who instituted the numbered account and really strict banking secrecy laws.

"The trick was to get the money out of your country without letting your government know. This generally required that you have a friend in the country where you wanted to hide your nest egg. For many Germans, a place where you could find German friends—in some cases, relatives—was in Argentina. In the thirties, people are prone to forget, Argentina had the largest gold reserves in the world."

"Were we involved in this?" Castillo asked.

"Yes, we were," Göerner said. "What your great-grandfather, and then your grandfather, did was begin to buy our newsprint from Argentina."

"I don't follow that," Castillo confessed.

"Newspapers consume vast quantities of newsprint," Göerner said. "Therefore no one was surprised when Gossinger Beteiligungsgesellschaft, G.m.b.H., began to buy newsprint from Argentina, where it was cheaper than newsprint from Denmark or Norway, and even cheaper than newsprint from the United States and

Canada. And the government didn't understand at first just how cheap it was."

"I don't understand that, either," Castillo said.

"Let's say newsprint from Denmark was so much a ton, say fifty dollars. Use that for the purposes of illustration; I have no idea what it was back then. And forty dollars a ton from the United States or Canada. And thirty from Argentina. Without raising any interest at all, the Dresdenerbank would transfer, say, three thousand dollars to the Bank of Argentina in payment for one hundred tons of newsprint. Bill rendered and paid. End of transaction. But actually, the newsprint cost twenty-five hundred. Which meant, for every one-hundred-ton transaction, there was five hundred dollars left over that could be quietly squirreled away in a bank account."

"We did this?" Castillo asked, incredulously.

"We did it. Mercedes-Benz did it. MAN diesel did it. Seimens did it. And I can't think of a brewery of any size, including ours, that didn't do it." He paused. "Where did you think the money came from for the economic miracle that saw Germany rise, phoenix-like, from the rubble we were in 1945?"

"I thought it was the Marshall Plan," Torine said. "And hard work on the part of Germany."

"All of the above, Colonel," Göerner said. "The Marshall Plan kept us fed and out of the hands of the Soviet Union. And repatriated nest eggs permitted us to have the raw material we Germans needed to go to work."

"Are we still doing this?" Castillo asked.

"Your grandfather thought Juan D. Perón was as dangerous as Hitler. We moved our nest egg from Argentina before you were born."

"So why are these good old boys from Marburg sending oil-for-food money there?"

"I'm about to get to that, but that's a two-part story, and one that will take some time. And I heard you tell Mr. Kranz that you wanted to demonstrate your miraculous telephone."

"Yeah, I have to get on the horn."

"We can get into this later," Göerner said.

[SIX]

"I lied, Otto," Castillo said. They were standing in the shade of the eaves of the stable, leaning on the wall, watching as Kranz set up the radio. A small circular dish pointed at the heavens. There was a control panel that resembled a small laptop computer to which had been added several rows of colored LEDs.

Helena had disappeared with the boys. Castillo wondered if she was protecting them from their godfather or whether Otto had subtly signaled her to take them away from something they probably would be better off not seeing.

"Why am I not surprised?" Otto asked.

"You can't really buy one of these. AFC makes some great stuff for the civilian market, but these aren't available."

"What's so fancy about this one?" Otto asked.

"All green, sir," Kranz said.

"Encrypted voice, right?" Castillo asked.

Kranz handed him a telephone handset, a small black one that looked like it belonged hanging on a *Reduced to $79.90* fax machine at Radio Shack.

"Encrypted voice all green, sir."

"I'm not going to need cans?" Castillo asked.

"With the signal I've got, I can put it on the speakerphone."

"Do it," Castillo ordered, and handed him the handset.

"Encrypted speakerphone green, sir," Kranz announced a moment later.

"Dick?" Castillo asked conversationally.

Castillo's voice was then converted to digital electronic pulses, encrypted, reduced to a message lasting just a few milliseconds, transmitted to satellite 22,300 miles above the earth, relayed to another satellite, and then relayed to the dish sitting on the roof at the Nebraska Avenue Complex. There, the "burst" was expanded, decrypted, and fed to the handset Major H. Richard Miller, Jr., was holding to his ear.

A just-perceptible delayed moment later, Miller's voice—having gone through the same series of events—came over the loudspeaker next to the stable near Bad Hersfeld: "Hey, Charley!"

"Where the hell have you been? We've been calling you for hours."

"You went up twelve seconds ago," Miller said.

"Anybody there with you?"

"Secretary Hall, Agnes, and Tom."

"Have you got signal strength for speakerphone?"

A moment later, another male voice said, "Encrypted speakerphone green," and a moment after that came the voice of Secretary of Homeland Security Hall. "How's that, Charley?"

"Loud and clear, sir."

"Tell me what you've got, Charley, and then I'll give you the good news," Hall said.

"Lorimer was a bagman in the oil-for-food thing," Castillo said. "A whole lot of people want him dead, both for what he knows and for skimming a lot of money—maybe sixteen million U.S.—from the players."

"You're saying he's dead?"

"The CIA guy in Paris thinks he is. I'm not at all sure. I'm going looking for him."

"Where?"

"There's a man in Budapest I want to talk to. He may have some ideas."

"Where are you?"

"In Bad Hersfeld. We're going to Budapest first thing in the morning."

"I knew you weren't in Paris," Hall said. "Ambassador Montvale told me. That's the good news."

"What?"

"He said he had some information for you, and wondered where you were. I told him."

"What's the information?"

"He seemed a little reluctant to share that with me," Hall said dryly. "And I thought it would probably be easier for him to give it to you—perhaps you would share it with me—than for me to go to the President."

"When is he going to share it with me?" Castillo asked. His eyes met Torine's. Torine disgustedly threw up his hands in a "what now?" gesture.

"When he called to tell me you were not at the Crillon, he asked me to put him in touch with you whenever you checked in. I told him I would. You want to talk to him?"

"What choice do I have?"

"Not much, Charley. But it's your call."

"How do I do that?"

"We're wired into the White House net. Just say the word."

"I wish you could eavesdrop, sir."

"If you don't tell me to get off the speakerphone . . ."

"Thank you."

Miller's voice went into the heavens and back: "Bring the White House switchboard into the loop."

"Switchboard."

"C. G. Castillo for Ambassador Montvale. I will need a secure line."

"One moment, please."

"Director Montvale's office."

"I have Mr. C. G. Castillo on a secure line for Director Montvale."

"One moment, please."

. . .

"Charles Montvale here. Is that you, Major?"

"Yes, sir. Good morning, sir."

"This line is secure, right?"

"So I have been informed, sir."

"I have made inquiries vis-à-vis the FBI agent Yung, in Montevideo, Major."

"Thank you, sir."

"An interesting situation, Major. The attorney general tells me that Yung has been seconded to the State Department on a mission with the highest possible security clearance. What he's doing is so secret, I am informed, that neither the director of the FBI nor the attorney general knows what he is doing."

"That's very interesting, sir."

"And there is more, Major. When I asked the director of the State Department's bureau of intelligence and research, he told me that he was unable to discuss Agent Yung's activities with me without the specific permission of the secretary of state."

"Even more interesting, sir."

"Apparently Secretary Cohen neglected to inform the appropriate people of the President's finding."

"Have you had the opportunity to discuss this with Secretary Cohen, sir?"

"This is where this situation becomes really interesting, Major. Yes, I have. She says that she has no knowledge whatever of Agent Yung beyond what she heard in our conversation aboard Air Force One. She assures me, however, that as soon as she gets to Singapore, she will take the appropriate steps to get to the root of the matter."

"She's on her way to Singapore, sir?"

"Apparently. And she did not choose to share with me her reasons for not making use of the communications system aboard her aircraft."

"Sometimes it doesn't work, sir."

"I suppose that's true. In any event, Major, I regret not being able to be of greater service."

"I understand the problem, sir. Thank you for your effort."

"This will, I am sure, be resolved shortly. When it is, Major, I will get back to you. As you might imagine, my own curiosity is now aroused."

"Thank you, sir."

There was a very clear click, and Castillo realized he was no longer speaking with the director of national intelligence.

And then Secretary Hall's voice came back from space.

"Charley, I have absolutely no idea what's going on. I suggest we wait until we see what Montvale can get out of Natalie."

"Yes, sir."

"Let me know what you find out in Budapest."

"Yes, sir, I will."

"Anything else we can do for you?"

"Dick, you still there?"

"Yes, sir, Chief."

"Will you send some flowers to the hospital for me, please?"

"That's a done deed, Chief," Agnes Forbison said. "She should have them by now."

"Thank you very much, Agnes."

"I like her, too, Charley."

"Is that about it?" Miller asked. "Break it down, Mr. Secretary?"

"Break it down," Hall ordered.

As he watched Kranz close the laptop, Göerner asked, "Who are you sending flowers to, Karl?"

"One of my agents was shot in Buenos Aires," Castillo said.

"That's bullshit, Otto," Fernando said. "One of his agents was shot, but it's anything but the professionally platonic relationship he's trying to foist off on you."

"You sonofabitch!" Castillo said.

"Ye shall know the truth and the truth shall make you free," Fernando responded. "Her name is Betty Schneider, Otto, and the two of them are like lovesick teenagers."

"Wunderbar!" Otto said.

XVI

When they walked up to the registration desk of the hotel, the manager on duty said that Herr Göerner had a call, and led him around the corner of the marble desk to a bank of house telephones.

Castillo watched him impatiently.

Göerner returned after a minute wearing a wide smile.

"That was Eric Kocian," he announced, "and what we're going to do now is go to our rooms, put on our robes, and visit the baths."

"I don't have time for a swim or a steam bath," Castillo said. "I came here to see this man Kocian."

"To accomplish the latter, Karl, I'm afraid you must do the former."

"What the hell are you talking about?"

"In a way I'm looking forward to this," Göerner said, smiling. "What is that line, 'What happens when the irresistible force meets the unmovable object'? I think we are about to see."

"Are you going to explain that? Or keep talking in riddles with a smug smile on your face?"

"Eric has the habit at this time of day of visiting the baths," Göerner said. "He suggested that we could talk there. The alternative is to meet him for lunch at the Kárpátia at half past one. That's on Ferenciek tere, in the—"

"I know where it is," Castillo cut him off. "Jesus Christ!"

Wrapped in thick white terry cloth robes, their feet in slippers, and their genitals contained in small—and, Castillo was convinced, transparent-when-wet—cotton swimming pouches, Castillo, Göerner, Fernando, Torine, and Kranz entered the thermal baths of the hotel.

"Fancy," Sergeant Kranz said. "Looks like something from ancient Rome."

"It was intended to look like ancient Rome," Göerner said. "They say there has been a thermal bath here for centuries."

"Where's Kocian?" Castillo asked.

"About halfway down the pool," Göerner said. "See the man with the float?"

There were perhaps fifteen people in the water, their individual conversations unintelligible as the hard acoustics of water and tile created a sort of deep-toned white noise. Halfway down the steaming pool, in water reaching almost to his neck, a head covered with luxuriant silver hair was almost hidden behind a floating table. On the table were a metal pitcher, an ashtray, several newspapers and magazines, two books, and a cellular telephone.

The man was looking at them without expression, his jaws clamped around a large, black cigar.

"What do we do, just jump in and swim up to him?" Castillo asked.

"It would be more polite if you slowly lowered yourself into the water and *waded* to him," Otto said. "This is a bath, Karl, not a swimming pool."

Göerner tossed his robe on a marble bench, slid out of his slippers, and went slowly into the pool by a flight of underwater stairs.

I never thought I would be a prude, Castillo thought, *but the only word to describe Otto with his privates in that tiny jockstrap is "obscene."*

When Otto reached the bottom of the stairs, he was in water just over his waist.

Well, at least his crotch and far-from-athletic buttocks are now concealed from public view.

Castillo shook his head, quickly tossed his robe on a marble bench, and very quickly went down the stairs into the water and then waded across the pool after Göerner.

Fernando, Torine, and Kranz took off their robes, looked at each other, shook their heads, and then, as if someone had barked "Ready! Run! Dive!" took running dives into the water.

The bushy white eyebrows on Eric Kocian's ruddy, jowly face rose in amazement at this display of bad manners.

"Good morning, Eric," Göerner said, when he'd waded close.

"*Grüss Gott, Otto,*" Kocian replied in a thick Viennese accent.

"This is Karl Gossinger, Eric," Göerner said. "Do you remember him?"

"The distinguished Washington correspondent of the *Tages Zeitung*? That Karl Gossinger?"

"*Guten morgen, Herr Kocian,*" Charley said.

"I was fond of your mother and your grandfather," Kocian said. "I never thought much of your uncle Willi. You look a lot like Willi."

"Thank you for sharing that with me," Castillo said in German and then switched to Viennese gutter dialect. "Can we cut the bullshit, Herr Kocian? I don't have time to play games with you."

"I'm crushed," Kocian said. "I know you have time to play games with Otto and our readers."

"Excuse me?"

A hand came out of the water and a pointing finger dripped water on one of the magazines. It was *The American Conservative*.

"There's a reason for that," Castillo said.

"It's easier to steal someone else's story than to write your own?"

"There's a reason for that," Castillo repeated.

"I'd love to know what it is," Kocian said.

"Because being the Washington correspondent for the *Tages Zeitung* is a cover for what I really do," Charley said.

"Which is?"

"I'm an Army officer."

Kocian considered that long enough to puff twice on his cigar.

"An Army *intelligence* officer, you mean?" he asked.

Castillo nodded.

Kocian looked at Otto Göerner, who nodded.

"You'll have to forgive me, Herr Gossinger. I'm an old man, my brain is slowing down, and for the life of me I can't understand why an American Army intelligence officer would confess that. To anyone, much less a real journalist."

"Because Otto has led me to believe we're on the same side."

"The same side of what, Mr. Intelligence Officer?"

"I'm after the people who are willing to kill to keep it from getting out that they've profited from the oil-for-food arrangement. Isn't that what you're doing?"

"You told him that, did you, Otto?" Kocian asked.

Göerner nodded.

"And what are you going to do if you learn who these people are?"

Castillo didn't immediately reply. He looked around and saw that they had an interested audience in Torine, Fernando, and Kranz.

Kranz may, just may, understand the Viennese patois. But Torine and Fernando don't. All they see is that the old guy and I are sparring, and not very politely.

"I'm unable to believe the U.S. government doesn't already know who they are," Kocian went on. "And that there are political considerations involved that have kept it from coming out."

"We don't know who murdered our chief of mission

in Buenos Aires, a very nice young Marine sergeant, and seriously wounded one of my agents."

"Okay. Let's talk about that. If you find out who these people are, then what?"

"I'll deal with them."

" 'Vengeance is mine, saith the Lord,' Herr Gossinger."

"My orders are to deal with them."

"Your orders from who?"

"Someone who remembers that the Bible also says, 'An eye for an eye, and a tooth for a tooth.' "

"Someone with the authority to give an order like that?"

Castillo nodded.

"And what will happen when, say, your secretary of state or, for that matter, your President learns—as they inevitably will—that someone has given you these orders?"

"That's not going to be a problem, Herr Kocian."

"You're not afraid that you and whoever gave you this order will not be—what's that wonderful American phrase?—'hung out to twist in the wind'?"

"No, I'm not."

"You will excuse me, Herr Gossinger, if I think you are being naïve," Kocian said. "Junior intelligence officers—and you're not old enough to be anything but a junior intelligence officer—are expendable."

"So what?" Castillo said.

"I was very fond of your grandfather and your mother. I don't want it on my conscience that I was in any way responsible for Little Karlchen being left hanging out twisting in the wind or, more likely, being strapped into a chair with his throat cut after his teeth were extracted with pliers."

"Why don't you let me worry about that?" Castillo said.

"I just told you, I was very fond of your mother and your grandfather."

"Eric, I'm as concerned as you are that Karl may be hurt, even murdered," Otto Göerner said, in the Viennese patois. "But I have reason to believe that he won't be left hanging in the breeze."

"What reason?"

"Otto," Castillo said. "Stop right there."

"What reason, Otto?" Kocian pursued.

"I know who gave him his orders."

"Otto, goddammit!" Castillo said.

"He told you who did, or you *know*?"

"Let me put it this way, Eric," Göerner said. "I *know* he's not as junior an intelligence officer as you might think he is; quite the opposite."

"Are you going to tell me how you *know* that?"

"Not unless Karl tells me I can," Göerner said.

"And are you, Herr Gossinger, going to give Herr Göerner permission to tell me?"

"No," Castillo said. Then he chuckled.

"What's funny, Herr Gossinger?" Kocian asked, politely.

"If I told you that, Herr Kocian, I would have to kill you."

Kranz laughed.

"I'm only kidding, Herr Kocian," Castillo said. "That's a special operations joke."

Kocian met Castillo's eyes for a long moment. Then he shrugged and said, almost sadly, "I'd be more comfortable, Karl, if I was sure you were not kidding."

Castillo didn't reply.

"All right. May God forgive me, but all right," Eric Kocian said. "I will tell you what I know. Come with me."

He started to wade toward the side of the pool, pushing the floating table before him. When he reached the side, he carefully put his cigar in the ashtray, then moved the ashtray to the low-tiled coping surrounding the pool. He did the same thing with his cellular telephone, the metal pitcher, the newspapers, and the copy of the *American Conservative*. Then he pushed the floating table away into the center of the pool and with surprising agility hoisted himself out of the pool and sat with his feet dangling into the water.

Out of the water, Kocian looked his age. The flesh on his arms and chest and legs sagged. His jockstrap was almost hidden by a roll of flesh that sagged down from his abdomen. There were angry scars on his upper shoulder, his abdomen, and his left leg.

"You speak German," Kocian said to Kranz. "I could tell."

"Yes, sir, I do."

"These two don't," he said, gesturing at Fernando and Torine. "You want all these people to hear what I have to say, Karl?"

"Bitte," Castillo said.

"Then I will speak English," Kocian said in English. "Very softly, because speaking English in here will attract attention." He switched back to German and pointed at

Kranz. "In each of those cubicles," he went on, point-ing, "there is a bucket and a water glass or two. Go get two buckets and six—no, eight—glasses, and bring them here."

Kranz hoisted himself out of the pool.

He then switched to English and quietly ordered, "The rest of you get out, and lay close to me—there are towels in the cubicles—and if you have something to say, say it very softly."

In a minute, after two trips to the dressing cubicles lining one wall of the pool, Kranz had arranged on the tile coping two white buckets, capable of holding per-haps a gallon each, and eight water glasses about six inches high, and everybody was sitting or lying on thick white towels on the tiled floor beside the pool.

"This," Kocian said softly, splashing his feet in the pool, "is the nearly limitless pool of oil under Iraq. It was controlled—owned—by Saddam Hussein. When Hus-sein was quote President of Iraq end quote, he was more of an absolute ruler than the king of Arabia.

"He had many vices, including greed, which did him in. He wasn't satisfied with what he had. He wanted the oil which lay under the sands of Kuwait . . . down there."

He pointed.

"If Hussein had not invaded Kuwait, we almost cer-tainly would not be sitting here today, but he did.

"This bothered the Americans, and even some mem-bers of the United Nations. Some say the Americans rushed to defend poor little Kuwait because they be-lieved that Saddam Hussein was naughty, and needed to have his wrist slapped. Others suggest that they were afraid Saddam also had his eyes on the oil under Arabia . . . over there . . . which was and is essential to the American economy.

"Whatever the reasons, there was a war. Iraq lost. Some of you may remember that."

"We were all there, Herr Kocian," Castillo said. "Can we get to the end of the history lesson?"

"I'm surprised that no one has taught you, Karl, that those who do not understand history are doomed to repeat it," Kocian said. "Would you like me to go on?"

"Sorry," Castillo said.

"It was not a total victory," Kocian resumed. "President Bush the First decided he did not need to occupy Baghdad to win the war. Ten years later, President Bush the Second decided that it would take American flags flying over Saddam Hussein's castles to win *that* war.

"At the end of the first Iraqi war, to make Saddam Hussein live up to what he promised to do at the armistice, and of course did not do, the Americans got the UN to place an embargo on the sale of Iraqi oil. That meant Iraq would have no money from the sale of their oil.

"France and Russia primarily, with some other nations, were suddenly deeply concerned with the helpless women and children of Iraq. Without some income to buy food, the French and the Russians cried, Iraqi babies would starve. Without medicine and medical supplies for Iraqi hospitals, Iraqi women and the elderly would die in agony.

"Oil for Food was born. Iraq would be permitted to

sell enough of its oil to buy food and medicine. The United Nations would monitor the sale of the oil, and ensure that nothing entered Iraq that wasn't food or medicine.

"United Nations inspectors were stationed—primarily at Basra on the Persian Gulf . . . down there . . . and in other places—to count the barrels of oil—the allocations—that would be shipped out for sale, and to make sure that nothing was shipped into Iraq that wasn't supposed to be."

Kocian examined the two buckets Kranz had fetched for him.

He dipped the larger bucket in the pool and hauled it out.

"This is how much oil it would take to buy food and medicine. You will notice that when I took it out, it did not noticeably lower the level of the water in the pool."

He leaned forward, took his cigar from the ashtray, relit it, puffed on it, examined the coal, took another puff, and went on.

"Saddam found himself sitting on—swimming in?—a sea of black stuff that was worthless to him, but considered black gold by the rest of the world. All he had to do was figure some way to get it out of Iraq, past the wall the UN had set up."

He tapped the tiled coping.

"First, he tried diplomacy. He would get the UN to relax or remove the embargo. To do this, he would have to have important friends in the UN. How does one acquire friends? Give them something. He arranged to have the oil allocations assigned to people he thought might become his friends. Many of these were French and Russians, but there were others, too.

"To keep this simple, what he did was arrange—by bribing a UN official—for his oil allocations to come into the hands of these people at prices lower than the going price for crude oil. Say, fifty cents a barrel lower. Fifty cents a barrel becomes a lot of money when one is dealing in terms of, say, two million barrels of oil—one tanker full of oil.

"All these people had to do to turn a quick profit of a million dollars was sign over their allocation of two million barrels of oil-for-food oil to someone else. Saddam also let it be known that if he were permitted to export more oil, there would be more millions—many more millions—of dollars coming into the hands of those who caused the UN to relax the embargo.

"He also made friends by not complaining when the medicine shipped into Iraq for the poor Iraqi children and women had a high price. Aspirin at five dollars a pill, for example. Flour at twenty dollars a kilo. *Und so weiter.*

"Now to do this, of course, he had to have friends among the UN officials who were checking to see that he didn't get anything he wasn't supposed to have. How to make these friends? Give them something. What did he have to give? This black stuff that was worthless to him anyway. How was he going to get it to them? Bribe the UN official checking the outgoing oil. If he happened to be looking the other way when, say, a hundred thousand barrels of oil was mistakenly pumped into a tanker hauling off the legitimate oil-for-food allocation, he could expect to have party or parties unknown drop off a package of crisp brand-new U.S. one-hundred-dollar bills at his grandmother's apartment."

He picked up the water bucket and poured from it into four of the water glasses. Then he picked up one of the water-filled glasses and moved it down the tile coping.

"This one goes to the UN official who happened to be looking the other way when the tanker was overloaded," he said.

He picked up a second of the water-filled glasses, moved it down the tile coping, and explained, "And this one goes to the UN official who sees nothing suspicious about five-dollar-a-pill aspirin, or twenty-dollar-a-kilo flour, and authorizes the bill therefore to be paid."

He picked up the two remaining water-filled glasses and moved them to a narrow shelf on the pool side of the tile coping. "And these two, now converted to packages of crisp one-hundred-dollar bills, go back across the border to Saddam, where they are thus available to build palaces for his sons and to bribe other people.

"You will notice, again, that filling the glasses did not appreciably lower the level of water in the bucket."

He paused, looked at everybody for a moment, and then filled the remaining water glasses.

"There are many refineries in Iraq," Kocian went on, "capable of producing far more gasoline, for example, than Iraq needs. What to do with this?"

He picked up two of the glasses and leaned forward to where Torine was lying on the tiles, and set them down by one of Torine's elbows.

"You are now Jordan," Kocian said. "Jordanians don't hate Americans as much as most other Arab countries, possibly because the widow of the late king was the daughter of an American general. And America tends to look less critically at Jordan than it does at other Arab countries. In any event, Jordan has a need for gasoline. There is no pipeline or port, but Iraq has many twenty-thousand-gallon tanker trucks. How to get it across the border? Bribe somebody."

He slid the water glasses from Torine's elbow to his waist, and picked up one of them. He moved it inside the tile coping. "This one, now miraculously converted to dollars, goes back to Iraq."

"Jesus!" Castillo said.

"Now, there were certain logistical problems to be solved, as well," Kocian went on. "Saddam wanted certain things—his sons, for example, liked Mercedes sports cars and *Hustler* magazine—which he could not legally import into Iraq. You may notice I am not even talking about war matériel, aircraft parts, etcetera, which is another story in itself. So, how to do this?

"Bribe a UN inspector into finding nothing suspicious, say, that an X-ray machine intended for an Iraqi hospital came from the Mercedes-Benz plant in Stuttgart. Or that a crate labeled 'Medical Publications' actually was full of pornographic videotapes.

"Saddam Hussein International Airport in Baghdad saw a lot of cargo airplanes—many of them owned by a Russian by the name of Aleksandr Pevsner—flying in things like hospital X-ray machines from the Mercedes-Benz plant—"

"Tell me about Pevsner, please, Herr Kocian," Castillo said.

"Tell you what about him?"

"How deep was he in the oil-for-food business?"

"He made a lot of money."

"He was one of those bribed?"

"We're playing semantic games here," Kocian said. "Did somebody hand him some money and say, 'Please defy the UN sanctions and airlift this Mercedes in an X-ray crate to Baghdad?' No. Did he carry an X-ray machine to Baghdad without looking to see what the crate really held? Yes. Did he charge twice or three times—five times—the standard rate for flying X-ray machines to Baghdad? Yes. Did he look to see if a case of ten million aspirin pills really contained aspirin instead of, for example, ten million dollars in U.S. currency? No. Was he bribed? That would be an opinion. Was he paid in cash? Yes. Was the cash he got from Saddam Hussein cash that had come into Saddam's hands for oil that he exported that he wasn't supposed to export? Almost certainly; where else would Saddam have gotten it? Can I prove any of this? No."

"Interesting," Torine said.

"What's your interest in Aleksandr Pevsner, Karl?" Kocian asked.

"The name has come up in conversation," Castillo said. "How were all these bribes paid, Herr Kocian, do you know?"

"In oil or cash, I told you."

"No. I mean, for example, you mentioned that a party or parties unknown would hand somebody's grandmother a stack of cash. Who was that party unknown? Who actually made the payoffs?"

"There was an elaborate system set up to do that," Kocian said. "What's your American name, Karl? 'Charles'?"

"Carlos," Castillo said. "That's Spanish for Karl and Charles."

"Yes, of course. Well, you're going to love this, *Carlos*."

"Love what?"

"When this business began to grow, and it became inconvenient to pass money through banks, laundering it, etcetera, Saddam began looking around for a paymaster. He needed someone, preferably an official of some sort, ideally a diplomat, who traveled around the area, and whose baggage would not be subject to search. The only people who did that routinely were members of the UN. So they started looking around the UN people they already had on the payroll, and they weren't very impressed. Finally they found their man in Paris, working for the UN. He was a UN bureaucrat, not a bona fide diplomat. He worked for—"

"The European Directorate of InterAgency Coordination, something like that?" Castillo interrupted.

"He was the chief of the European Directorate of InterAgency Coordination," Kocian said, looking at him strangely. "Which entitled him to a UN diplomatic passport. The passport—which, in addition to getting you through customs and immigration without getting your bags searched, exempts you from both local taxes and taxes in your homeland—is a prize passed out to deserving middle-level UN bureaucrats."

"What does the European Directorate of InterAgency

Coordination do, Herr Kocian?" Castillo asked. "I've always wondered."

"I don't really know," Kocian said. "From what I have seen of the UN, probably nothing useful. But this fellow had for ten, fifteen years been running all over Europe and the Near East and the United States, doing his interagency coordination, whatever that might be.

"He had other things going for him. He wasn't married, so there would be no wife boasting about what her husband was doing; and he wasn't homosexual, so there would be no boyfriend doing the same. And he wasn't very well paid. Even tax exempt, and taking into consideration his travel and representation allowances, his salary wasn't very much.

"But most important, he was not only American, which would keep the Americans off his scent, but he was an anti-American American. Possibly because he was black. Maybe not. But his being black was something else that would keep the Americans from looking too closely at him."

"And his name is Jean-Paul Lorimer," Castillo said. "And I want to know where he is."

"Just to satisfy an old man's curiosity, Karl, how long have you Americans known about Lorimer?"

"Not long. Where is he, Herr Kocian?"

"Possibly out there," Kocian said, gesturing toward the stained-glass windows lining two walls of the baths.

"You mean in Budapest?"

"I meant in the Danube," Kocian said. "Or possibly in the Seine."

"What makes you so sure he's dead?"

"Or possibly in a cell somewhere, where they are asking him for names, so there will be fewer witnesses around. But if I had to bet, I'd bet on one of the two rivers."

"What was his connection with Henri Douchon?"

"Ah, now I know why you came to see me. Otto told you about him."

"That's part of it. What about Douchon?"

"He was one of Lorimer's assistant paymasters," Kocian said. "He handled Lebanon, Egypt, Cyprus, and Turkey . . . maybe some other places, but that's all I've been able to confirm."

"Who killed him?"

"If I had to bet, I'd say either the French or the Egyptians. Possibly the Germans, or maybe even the Turks. I just don't know, but I'd bet on the French or the Egyptians."

"And you think the same people killed Lorimer?"

"The list of people who wanted to silence Lorimer includes all of the above, plus Russians, Syrians, Iranians. . . . It's a long list, Herr Gossinger."

"You don't think Lorimer would be in hiding somewhere?" Castillo asked.

"I think he might have tried to hide, after he saw what they had done to M'sieu Douchon."

"And you're sure he knew about that?"

"An old friend of mine in Vienna showed me photos of Lorimer entering and leaving Douchon's apartment in Vienna. They were taken *after* someone had pulled his teeth and carved him up. After that, Mr. Lorimer disappeared. It could be, of course, that he was taken bodily into heaven, but I think it far more likely that someone besides the Austrian *Geheimpolizei* were keeping an eye on that Cobenzlgasse apartment to see if Lorimer might show up, and they grabbed him."

"We know that somebody bought a train ticket to Paris on his UN American Express card," Castillo said. "Let's say it was Lorimer himself. They didn't grab him in Vienna, in other words. Let's say they didn't grab him in Paris, either. If he saw what happened to Douchon, he was watching his back. Let's say he got on the train, and didn't go to Paris because he thought they might be looking for him there. So, say he got off the train in Munich. Or didn't even get on the train to Paris. He could have bought a ticket to Paris on his credit card, then bought another for cash to . . . anywhere. Maybe even to Budapest."

"That's possible, of course," Kocian said. "But I don't think you're going to be able to find him."

"If he was going to hide—and why wouldn't he have thought of having someplace to hide if something went wrong?—where do you think he might have gone?"

"Anywhere," Kocian said. "The south of France. Lebanon. Maybe even the United States. Anywhere. Who knows?"

"You didn't mention South America," Castillo said. "Argentina or—"

Castillo stopped in midsentence, surprised when Kocian flashed Otto Göerner an angry look. This caused Kocian to look at him.

"Why not South America?" Castillo pursued.

Yeah. Why not? Did these bastards abduct Mrs. Master-

son in Buenos Aires and murder her husband in South
America because when they couldn't find Lorimer here,
they figured he might be in South America, and if his sister
was there, she would probably know where he was? Or that
he was there because she was?

"Otto, have you been talking to our Little Karlchen
about South America?" Kocian inquired sarcastically.

"Some," Göerner admitted. "Not in this context."

"In what context?"

"I told him of your suspicions—my suspicions, too—
that some of this oil-for-food money in Germany might
find its way over there."

"*Might* find its way over there?" Kocian snapped.
"The sun *might* come up tomorrow."

"You want to tell me about that, Herr Kocian?"
Castillo asked.

"No."

"But you will, right?"

"No."

"Kranz, get out the pliers," Castillo said. "We're going to do a little dentistry."

"Karl, that's not funny!" Otto Göerner said.

"What's funny, Otto," Kocian said, seriously, "is that
I'm not really sure he's kidding. I said something before
about him looking like Willi. His eyes right now make
him look very much like the Old Man. When the Old
Man looked at you with that look in his eyes, you knew
he was determined to get what he wanted."

"What I really want is to find Jean-Paul Lorimer,"
Castillo said.

"And what I really want is to burn the greedy bastards

in Germany who were involved in slimy profits from Oil for Food," Kocian said. "I'm close to having proof they won't be able to deny. And I don't want anyone—you—rushing over there and letting them know I'm getting close and giving them a chance—"

"I'm not interested in greedy German bastards unless I find out they're responsible for the death of Masterson and Sergeant Markham," Castillo said.

"Are we back to vengeance?"

"I'm back to following my orders," Castillo said.

"You heard that a lot at the Nuremberg Nazi trials," Kocian said. " 'All I was doing was following my orders.' "

"They said that to justify the murder of innocent people," Castillo replied. "These bastards are neither innocent nor helpless."

Kocian nodded. "That's true." He looked into Castillo's eyes. "You never told me exactly what your orders are."

"I'm to find the people responsible for the murders and render them harmless," Castillo said.

" 'Render them harmless'? Is that the same as 'terminate with extreme prejudice'?" Kocian asked. "Isn't that the euphemism for assassination you Americans used in Vietnam?"

"My orders are to 'find them and render them harmless,' " Castillo repeated. "The idea is to make it clear that there are certain things you can't get away with."

"And that sounds like vengeance to me. So what does that make you, the agent of the Lord?"

"No. Not of the Lord. It doesn't say *'Gott Mit Uns'* on my uniform buckle."

Kocian nodded at him. "Touché," he said, and then looked at Göerner. "There's a lot of the Old Man in him, isn't there?"

"Yes," Göerner said, simply. "There is."

"Your grandfather was a man of his word," Kocian said. "When he told you something, you could trust him. Are you that way, Karl?"

"I like to think of myself as an officer and a gentleman, if that's what you mean."

"That's what I mean," Kocian said. "What I'm going to do, Karl, if you give me your word you won't turn it over to the CIA, or anyone in your government, is give you the names of Germans I believe have both profited from Oil for Food and are now trying to hide that money in Argentina, Brazil, Paraguay . . . all over the southern tip of South America. If you can use this information to find Lorimer, fine. But you give me your word you won't use it for anything else."

"You have my word."

"And that you won't tell anyone where you got it."

"Agreed."

"And that these gentlemen will be similarly bound by our agreement."

"Agreed. When do I get the names?"

"Once I get to the office, it will take me an hour or more to go through what I have. I want to make sure in my own mind that if you have to render any of these people harmless—that's a much nicer phrase than 'terminate with extreme prejudice,' isn't it?—that they really deserve such treatment."

"Fair enough."

"And I don't want you—especially Otto—coming to the office and making people curious. So why don't you meet me at the Kárpátia at noon? You know where it is, Otto."

Göerner nodded.

"And so do I," Castillo said. "Not far from the American embassy."

Kocian nodded. "We can have a nice lunch," he said and, not without effort, got to his feet. Then, grunting, he bent over and picked up his ashtray, his cellular telephone, and the books and magazines.

Then he waddled down the tiled floor of the bath and disappeared through a door.

"You got more out of him, Karl," Otto Göerner said, thoughtfully, "than I thought you would. I can only hope that's a good thing. What he didn't say was that these people would torture and kill him without thinking twice about it if they knew he knows as much as he does. And unless you're very careful with those names, they will learn he does."

Castillo nodded but didn't reply. Then he stood up.

"Let's get out of here," he said, wrapping a towel around his waist. "I want to get on the horn."

[TWO]
The Embassy of the United States of America
Szabadság tér 12
Budapest, Hungary
1105 28 July 2005

Otto Göerner touched Castillo's arm as they started to get out of the taxi in front of the American embassy, a seven-story century-old mansion.

"You're not going to need me in there, are you?" Göerner asked.

"No."

"And it might even be a bit awkward, no?"

"I'll handle it," Castillo said.

"Why don't I keep the cab, go to the Kárpátia, get us a table, get myself a cup of coffee . . ."

"Okay, Otto. This won't take long. We'll see you there," Castillo said, and he and the others got out of the taxi. As Castillo watched it drive away, Sergeant Seymour Kranz touched his arm.

"Major, what the hell is that?" he asked, pointing.

Castillo looked. In the park facing the embassy was a statue of a man in uniform with his hands folded behind his back.

"It's a statue, Seymour. Budapest is full of them. They even have a section of the Berlin Wall around here somewhere."

"That's an old-timey American uniform," Kranz said.

"I'll be damned, I think he's right," Colonel Torine said.

Castillo looked again and asked, "What time is it in Washington, Seymour?"

Kranz consulted his watch and reported, "Oh-four-oh-five, sir."

"Since it won't make much difference to whoever we get out of bed whether it is oh-four-oh-five or oh-four-ten, let us go and broaden our cultural horizons by examining the statue," Castillo said. "Why the hell would there be a statue of an American officer in a park in Budapest?"

They walked to the statue. It was indeed of an American, wearing a World War I–era uniform of riding boots and breeches. He looked as if he were examining the embassy and found it wanting.

There was a bronze plaque with a legend in English beneath it. Kranz read it aloud: "Harry Hill Bandholtz, Brigadier General, U.S. Army. 'I simply carried out the instructions of my Government, as I understood them, as an officer and a gentleman of the United States Army.'"

"I wonder what the hell that's all about?" Fernando said.

"I wonder what the instructions he carried out were to get him a statue?" Kranz asked.

"Gentlemen," Castillo said, "fellow history buffs. Perhaps there is a public information officer in the embassy who can enlighten us all. Shall we see?"

There might have been a public information officer at the embassy, but they never got to meet him.

They encountered first a Marine guard, a buck sergeant, who politely but firmly told them there was no way they could see the ambassador without an appointment.

Colonel Torine produced his Air Force identification.

"Sergeant, you get the defense attaché on the phone, or down here, and do it now."

The Marine guard examined the photo ID carefully, and then picked up his telephone.

"There is a USAF colonel here who wants to talk to a defense attaché," he announced, and then handed the telephone to Torine.

"This is Colonel Jacob Torine, USAF. Are you the defense attaché, Captain?" Brief pause. "Then get him on the goddamned horn, or down here, and right goddamn now!"

An Army lieutenant colonel appeared.

"Colonel Torine?" he asked.

"Right."

"I'm Lieutenant Colonel Martín, sir. I'm the Army attaché. May I see your identification, please, sir?"

Torine produced his identification again.

"How may I help you, Colonel?"

"We would like to see either the ambassador or the chief of mission," Torine said.

"May I ask why?"

"No, goddammit, you may not!" Torine exploded.

"Jake!" Castillo said, warningly. "Colonel, what we need to do is get into the White House switchboard on a secure line."

"And you are, sir?"

"My name is Castillo. I'm with the Secret Service."

He showed Lieutenant Colonel Martín his credentials.

"This is very unusual," Lieutenant Colonel Martín said.

"I'm prepared to explain it to the ambassador or the chief of mission," Castillo said.

"One moment, please," Lieutenant Colonel Martín said, and motioned for the Marine guard to slide him the telephone. He punched in a number. "This is Colonel Martín. We have an Air Force colonel here, I've checked his ID, who wants to be connected to the White House switchboard. Can we do that?"

There was a reply.

Lieutenant Colonel Martín turned to Colonel Torine.

"He said that you have to be authorized to connect to the White House switchboard. Do you have that authorization?"

"I do," Torine said.

"Excuse me, sir. But how do I know that?"

Torine threw up his hands in disgust.

"That was your commo room?" Castillo asked.

Lieutenant Colonel Martín nodded.

"Is it tied into the White House switchboard?"

"To the State Department switchboard."

"Tell him to get the State Department switchboard operator. Tell her, or him, as the case may be, that C. G. Castillo wants to talk to the secretary of state, and that if she is not available, to be connected to the White House switchboard."

"You want to talk to the secretary of state, Mr. Costello?"

"It's Castillo. See that you get that right when you call."

"Sir, it's four o'clock in the morning in Washington."

"So I have been told."

"Just one moment, please," Lieutenant Colonel Martín said, and took his hand off the mouthpiece of the telephone. "Mr. Costello—"

"Castillo. Castillo. With an 'a' and an 'i,'" Castillo said.

"Mr. *Castello* wonders if it would be possible for you to contact the State Department switchboard and ask . . . see if they will take his call for the secretary of state." Martín turned to Charley. "The office of the secretary, Mr. Castello, or Secretary Cohen personally?"

"Castillo with an 'i,'" Castillo responded. "Secretary Cohen personally."

"Secretary of State Cohen personally," Lieutenant Colonel Martín parroted. He put his hand over the mouthpiece again. "It'll be just a moment."

A moment later, he announced: "They will take your call, Mr. *Castillo*, but Secretary Cohen is not available. She's in Singapore."

"What time is it in Singapore, Seymour?"

"Jesus, Major, I don't know," Sergeant Kranz confessed.

It was apparent to Castillo that Lieutenant Colonel Martín had picked up on Seymour's use of his rank.

"I don't think this is a secure line, is it, Colonel?" Castillo said. "I need a secure line."

"Yes, of course," Lieutenant Colonel Martín said, and thought that over. "If you'll give the sergeant your identity documents, gentlemen, he'll give you a visitor's badge and I'll escort you to a room with a secure telephone."

They were in the process of handing over their documents when a tall, rather distinguished-looking man walked through the door, smiled, and said, "Good morning."

"Good morning, Mr. Ambassador," Lieutenant Colonel Martín said.

"You're the ambassador?" Castillo asked.

"Yes, as a matter of fact, I am," the ambassador said. "And you are?"

"He's from the Secret Service, Mr. Ambassador," Lieutenant Colonel Martín offered helpfully.

"Really?"

"And he wants to talk to the secretary of state, sir, personally."

"Indeed?" the ambassador said, and went to the counter and examined the identification documents.

"You did tell Mr. Castillo that the secretary of state isn't here, didn't you, Colonel?" the ambassador asked.

"Actually, she's in Singapore," Castillo said.

"Is she indeed?" the ambassador said. "Would you mind telling me what this is about, Mr. Castillo?"

"I will tell you, sir. But I suggest this isn't the place to do that, sir."

"Well, then, why don't we go to my office and we'll see if we can get to the bottom of this."

"Thank you very much, sir," Castillo said.

"I knew Jack Masterson," the ambassador said. "He was a good man."

"Yes, sir, he was."

"You're in Budapest, so there's obviously a Hungarian connection. Are you going to tell me what that is?"

"I was running down a source of information, sir. There is no Hungarian connection I know of to Mr. Masterson's murder."

The ambassador considered that a moment, then pointed at a telephone on his desk. "Help yourself, Mr. Castillo."

"Thank you, sir." He picked it up and punched the "O" key.

"My name is Castillo. Would you get me the state department switchboard on a secure line, please?"

"Sir, I'll have to have someone authorize that."

Castillo pushed the SPEAKERPHONE button. "Mr. Ambassador, I'm going to need your authorization."

"It's okay," the ambassador said, raising his voice.

Castillo started to push the SPEAKERPHONE button again to shut it off but changed his mind.

"One moment, please," the embassy operator said.

"State Department."

"This line is secure?"

"Yes, sir."

"My name is C. G. Castillo. Can you patch me through to the secretary, please?"

"No, sir. The secretary is out of the country, and the secure voice link is down."

"Okay. Put me through to the White House switchboard, please."

"White House."

"C. G. Castillo on a secure line for the secretary of state, please."

"Her voice link is down, Mr. Castillo. We have a secure teletypewriter link. You'll have to dictate what—"

"Before we try that, put me through to Secretary Hall's office in the Nebraska Complex, please."

"Secretary Hall's office or your office, Mr. Castillo?"

"Okay, my office."

There was the sound of the phone ringing twice.

"Mr. Castillo's line. Mr. Miller speaking."

"What are you doing there at four o'clock in the morning?"

"I had them move a cot in. It's a long ride back and forth to your apartment in the back of a Yukon. I was starting to feel like a dummy in a disaster exercise. Where are you?"

"Budapest."

"Montvale wants to talk to you. So does the boss. And we have a mysterious message from your pal Natalie. The encrypted voice link on her plane is down, and so is the one in the embassy in Singapore. Heads are going to roll about that."

"Read me the message. Maybe I won't have to talk to Montvale."

"Okay. You going to write this down, or do you just want to hear it?"

"Just read it."

"Okay. 'Top Secret–Presidential. From SecState to SecHomeSec. Start Please convey following personal to C.G. by most expeditious means. Charley, believe me, I didn't know Yung was working for me until an hour ago. I have spoken with Ambassador Silvio in Buenos Aires and Ambassador McGrory in Montevideo and told both to tell Yung he is to put himself and whatever intelligence he has developed at your disposal. That's all I felt safe in doing as there is something wrong with the secure voice link on both the plane and in the embassy, believe it or not. Let me know what else I can do. Best personal regards. Natalie. End Personal message from SecState.' "

"Got it, Dick."

"Who the hell is Yung?"

"He's an FBI agent in Montevideo."

"And he's working for Cohen? What's that all about?"

"I don't know. And I guess I won't find out until we get to Buenos Aires."

"When are you going there?"

"Just as soon as we have lunch."

"Will that little airplane make it across the South Atlantic?"

"God, I hope so. Dick, wait until we're out of here—say, nine your time—and then tell Secretary Hall I called and have Secretary Cohen's message. I don't want to wake him or Ambassador Montvale at four in the morning. And send one to Secretary Cohen, quote Got it. Many thanks. Charley, end quote. And send one to Ambassador Silvio saying we're on our way and will be there however long it takes to get there. We should be wheels-up out of here in no more than two or three hours."

"The Gray Fox radio link is up and running in Buenos Aires. Should I use that?"

"Absolutely."

"Anything else, Charley?"

"Get your filthy rotten smelly cast off my desk."

"Go fuck yourself. I say that with all possible respect. Watch your back, buddy."

"I will. Break it down, please."

"After eavesdropping on your conversation, Mr. Castillo," the ambassador said, "I don't really know much more about what you're doing than I did before, except I now have no question about your right to use my secure voice link."

"Thank you very much for the use of it, sir."

"It should go without saying that I really hope you can find whoever murdered Jack Masterson. Is there anything I can do, anything at all?"

"I can't think of anything, sir," Castillo said. "Except one thing. Who was the American officer whose statue is across the street?"

The ambassador chuckled. "You saw that, did you?" he asked, rhetorically. "Brigadier General Harry Hill Bandholtz was sent here in 1919 to be the American on the Inter-Allied Control Commission which was supervising the disengagement of Romanian troops from Hungary.

"The Romanians thought disengagement meant they could help themselves to the Transylvanian treasures in the National Museum. General Bandholtz didn't think that was right. So, on October 5, 1919, he showed up at the museum, alone, and armed only with his riding crop, ran the Romanians off like Christ chasing the moneylenders out of the temple. He must have been one hell of a man."

"Obviously."

"And when they asked him why, he said something to

the effect that he was only obeying his orders as he understood them as an officer and a gentleman. You don't hear that phrase much anymore, do you, 'an officer and a gentleman'?"

"Mr. Ambassador," Torine said, "oddly enough, I heard it earlier today."

"Said seriously, or mockingly?"

"Very seriously, sir," Torine said. "Spoken by an officer and a gentleman."

"The Hungarians loved Bandholtz and had the statue cast," the ambassador went on. "They set it up in 1936. The Hungarian fascists and the Nazis didn't bother it, but when the Russians were here, right after the war—before they let us reopen the embassy—they took it down and away 'for repair.' We heard about it, of course, from the Swiss, who were supposed to be guarding the embassy property. We were actually in the process of having another made when we learned that the Hungarians had stolen it from the scrap yard, and were concealing it so it could be put back up when the Russians left. The Russians left, and General Bandholtz is back on his pedestal."

"Mr. Ambassador, that's a great story, and I'm really glad I asked. But now, sir, with our profound thanks, we won't take any more of your time," Castillo said.

"Where are you going now, to the airport?"

"First to the Kárpátia, sir, then to the Gellért to check out, and then to the airport."

"I'll get you one of our cars," the ambassador said, and reached for a telephone. "Then I can tell myself I at least did something to help."

[THREE]
Kárpátia
Ferenciek tere, 7–8
Budapest, Hungary
1215 28 July 2005

Otto Göerner and Eric Kocian were already mostly through what looked like liter-sized glasses of beer when Castillo and the others came into the restaurant. And the moment they sat down, a plump waiter with a luxuriant mustache showed up with a tray full of the enormous beer glasses.

"None for those two, thank you just the same," Castillo said in Hungarian, pointing to Torine and Fernando. "They're driving."

Göerner and Kocian chuckled.

"Are you going to tell us what you just said about us?" Fernando challenged.

"No booze, you're flying," Castillo said.

"And what about you?"

"I'll be doing the flight planning. I can do that with a little beer in my system."

"I'll do the flight planning, thank you just the same, Major," Torine said, and slid Castillo's beer away from him, picked it up, took a healthy swallow, sighed appreciatively, and added, "As an officer and a gentleman, I'm sure you're aware that Rank Hath Its Privileges."

"Well, in that case, I guess there's nothing for me to do but eat," Castillo said. "What do you recommend, Herr Kocian?"

Kocian reached into his pocket and handed Castillo a

business-sized envelope. It was stuffed with paper.

"I would only give this to a friend," he said. "You may therefore call me Eric."

"Thank you very much, *Eric*," Castillo said, putting the envelope in his inside jacket pocket. "Seymour, you can put the pliers back in the tool kit. Dentistry is apparently not going to be necessary."

"*Ach Gott*, Karl!" Göerner said.

"You're aware, I'm sure, Karl, that the Hungarians taught the Machiavellians all they knew about poisoning people?" Kocian asked.

"And with that in mind, Eric, what do you recommend? *Gulyás* lightly laced with arsenic?"

"Wiener schnitzel," Kocian said. "The Kárpátia serves the best Wiener schnitzel in the world."

"Better than in Vienna?"

"Actually, you can get better *Hungarische gulyás* in Vienna than you can here," Kocian said. "Things are not always what they seem, Karl. Do you know what the people in Hamburg call what you call a frankfurter?"

Castillo shook his head, then asked, "A frankfurter?"

"Right. And what do the people in Frankfurt call what you and the Hamburgers call a frankfurter?"

"Don't tell me—a hamburger?"

"A sausage," Kocian said. "And what do the Hamburgers call chopped and fried beef?"

"I know they don't call it a frankfurter."

"They call it fried chopped beef unless they don't fry it, and instead serve it raw, in which case it becomes steak tartar."

"Actually, Eric, I have a real fondness for Wiener

schnitzel. Do you suppose you could have the kitchen make up a dozen of them, and wrap them in foil so that we can take them with us on the plane?"

"Won't they go bad?"

"There's a little kitchen on the plane, with a freezer. The only thing in it right now is a bottle of beer and Colonel Torine's Viagra."

"Oh, Jesus Christ!" Torine said.

"My friend Karl," Eric Kocian said, "inasmuch as this is all going on Otto's American Express card, you can have anything your greedy little heart desires."

"In that case, a dozen Wiener schnitzels," Castillo said. "Plus one for my lunch, of course. I really love Wiener schnitzel."

XVII

[ONE]
**Approaching Aeropuerto Internacional Jorge
    Newbery
Buenos Aires, Argentina
0535 29 July 2005**

Castillo was flying. The night was clear and he could see the glow of the lights of Buenos Aires as he began his descent. As he dropped lower, the lights became more distinct. What had looked like a single orange line pointing at the city became a double line, and he could see headlights moving along what he now recognized as Route 8 and the Acceso Norte leading from Pilar to the city.

It had been quite a trip. The Lear was fast—its long-range cruise speed was three-quarters the speed of sound—but it was not intended or designed for flying across oceans. It had been necessary to make refueling stops within the limitations of the aircraft's range, about 1,900 nautical miles. The first leg—about 1,500 nautical miles—had been a three-and-a-half-hour flight from Budapest to Casablanca, Morocco. After refueling, they had flown 1,250 nautical miles in a bit under three hours to Dakar, Senegal, on the extreme west coast of the African continent.

From Dakar, it had been a four-hour, 1,750-nautical-mile flight, the longest leg, southwest across the Atlantic Ocean to Recife, Brazil. This had been the iffy leg. There are no alternative airfields in the Atlantic Ocean on which to land when fuel is running low. They had approached the Point of No Return with their fingers crossed, but there had been no extraordinary headwinds or other problems to slow them, and Torine, who was then flying in the left seat, had made the decision to go on. What could have been a real problem just hadn't materialized.

Recife apparently was not accustomed to either refueling small private jets or providing food at half past two in the morning, and it had taken them an hour and a half to get both. But with that exception, they had been able to land, refuel, check the weather, and file flight plans in remarkably little time everywhere else.

From Recife they had flown south to São Paulo—

1,150 nautical miles in just under two and a half hours—and then begun the last leg, to Buenos Aires, which would be a just-over-two-hour flight covering 896 nautical miles.

Alex Pevsner's down there, Castillo thought, *and I have a gut feeling I'm going to need him. And by now, Howard Kennedy has told him that I'm not going to point him in Jean-Paul Lorimer's direction so he can give him a beauty mark in the center of his forehead. That will be a problem, one that I'll have to think about later. Right now I'm too tired to make difficult decisions.*

Castillo pushed the TRANSMIT lever.

"Jorge Newbery, Lear Five-Zero-Seven-Five. I am forty kilometers north at five thousand feet. Request approach and landing."

"Lear Five-Zero-Seven-Five," Jorge Newbery ground control ordered, "at the end of the active, turn right, and proceed to parking area in front of the Jet-Aire hangar. Customs and immigration will meet your aircraft."

"Seven-Five understands right at the threshold, taxi to Jet-Aire parking area," Castillo replied. "Wait for customs and immigration."

As he approached the Jet-Aire hangar a ground handler in white coveralls came out and, with illuminated wands, directed him to park beside an Aero Commander.

When Castillo had finished the shutdown procedures, he took a closer look at the Aero Commander. If the light, high-wing twin wasn't derelict, it was close. The fabric-covered portions of the rear stabilizer assembly were missing or visibly decayed. The tire on the left landing gear was flat. The left engine nacelle was missing.

"I know just how that Commander feels," Castillo said to Colonel Torine, who was in the right seat. "Old, battered, and worn out."

Torine looked at the Aero Commander and chuckled.

"It has been a rather long ride, hasn't it?" Torine replied, in something of an understatement, as he unfastened his harness.

"And here comes what looks like the local officialdom," Fernando said from the aisle behind them.

Castillo saw two Ford F-150 pickup trucks with Grimes lights flashing from their roofs approaching them. Two uniformed men got out of the first, and a man in civilian clothing out of the second.

"The civilian is SIDE," Castillo said. "I don't know his name, but I saw him somewhere."

He unfastened his harness and stood.

When Castillo went down the stairs to the tarmac, he saw both that the SIDE agent's eyebrows had risen when he saw him, and that he immediately had taken out a cellular telephone.

Well, this time I'm arriving as C. G. Castillo, carrying a brand-new passport with no stamps on it at all.

When the SIDE agent came to the Lear, he gave no sign that he had recognized Castillo, even after he had examined his passport. The customs and immigration procedures were polite but thorough. The aircraft and their luggage were submitted to testing for drugs and explosives, which might or might not have been standard procedure for civil aircraft arriving from outside the country. Castillo was glad that he hadn't brought any weapons from Fort Bragg.

No questions were raised about Kranz's "satellite telephone antenna," which might or might not have been because Castillo had asked them if it would be safe to leave it on the aircraft while they were in Buenos Aires. Neither did the "laptop"—which actually controlled the radio and held the encryption system—cause any unusual interest. It had been designed to look like a typical laptop computer.

The customs officer did, however, unfold the aluminum foil in which the Wiener schnitzel in the freezer was wrapped. It might have been idle curiosity or he might have been looking for a package of cocaine.

"What is this?" he asked.

"Wiener schnitzel," Castillo told him. "Sort of a veal *milanesa*."

And if you hadn't gone in there and found it, I probably would have forgotten it, and with the juice turned off, when I finally remembered it, it would have been rotten Wiener schnitzel.

"I think I'd better take that with me," Castillo said as the customs officer started to put it back in the freezer. He put it into his laptop briefcase.

"Enjoy your stay in Argentina, gentlemen," the customs officer said.

"We'll certainly try," Castillo said.

[TWO]
El Presidente de la Rua Suite
The Four Seasons Hotel
Cerrito 1433
Buenos Aires, Argentina
0605 29 July 2005

A sleepy-eyed Special Agent Jack Britton answered the door in his underwear.

"That was a quick European tour," he said, offering his hand.

"The last two hotels we were in, we didn't even get to muss the beds," Castillo said. "Except Kranz, of course. He's smarter than we are. Whenever he's not eating, he's sleeping."

"I'm Kranz," Kranz said.

"He's our communicator," Castillo said.

"Jack Britton," Britton said as he shook Kranz's hand. "I'm impressed with your buddy Kensington. He's got that fantastic radio set up in his room. All he has to do is open the drapes and the window, and we're talking to Dick Miller."

"That's great," Castillo said. "Even if it may require yet another shuffling of living arrangements."

"I'm in your bed. . . ." Britton said.

Yeah, you are, and I don't like to think of anyone else sleeping in the bed where Betty and I were.

"Not for long," Castillo said. "When I told the desk I needed more rooms, they told me this suite is expandable. So I took a three-room expansion. But I forgot about Sergeant Kensington."

"I can bunk with Kensington, Major," Kranz said. "Not a problem."

"Dibs on that bed," Fernando said, pointing through the door at the huge bed in the master bedroom from which Britton had just risen.

"Like hell; that's mine. I'm now the chief, and you're just a lousy airplane pilot, in any interpretation of that term you may wish to apply."

Fernando, shaking his head and smiling, gave him the finger.

Castillo walked to the telephone and picked up the handset and punched the FRONT DESK key on the base.

"I'm going to need one more room," he said. "And send up several large pots of coffee." He hung up and turned to Britton. "Did Tony Santini get you a cellular phone?"

Britton nodded. "Me and Kensington."

"With his number and Darby's on them?"

Britton nodded again.

"May I have it, please?" Castillo asked.

Britton went into the master bedroom.

"You're going to get Santini out of bed at this unholy hour?" Torine asked.

"Santini and Ricardo Solez and Alex Darby, and then as soon as one of them tells me how to get him on the phone, Special Agent Yung in Montevideo."

"I am awed by this very early morning display of energy," Torine said.

"Jake," Castillo said, very seriously, "if Jean-Paul Lorimer is here, and I have a gut feeling he is, I want to find him before anyone else does."

"Point taken," Torine replied. "I wasn't thinking. Sorry, Charley."

Britton, now wearing trousers but no shirt and still barefoot, came back into the room and handed Castillo a cellular telephone.

"Santini's on two," he announced. "And Darby on three."

"And Ricardo Solez?"

"After you left, he went back to drugs," Britton said. "I don't have a number for him."

"I've got his home number," Fernando said.

"Yeah, that's right, Don Fernando, you would have it," Castillo said, not very pleasantly. "Well, get on the phone, call him, tell him to call in to the embassy that he'll be late, and to come over here. And because you'll be on an unsecure cell, figure out some way without using my name to tell him not to tell anyone I'm back."

"Is that a secret?" Fernando asked.

"For the time being," Castillo said, and punched autodial button two on Britton's cellular. Then he said, "Shit!" and pushed the END button. He went to the minibar in one of the cabinets, took the ice trays from it, and in their place put the foil-wrapped Wiener schnitzel. Then he pushed the cellular's autodial button two again.

Tony Santini arrived first.

"Looks like old home week," he said when he saw everybody. "Welcome back to Gaucholand. I guess you got something in Europe?"

"I'll have to remember to tell Tom McGuire to button his lip," Castillo said.

"Tom and I go back a long way, Charley. But while we're on the subject of what Tom told me, where do I go to enlist?"

"Excuse me?"

"I hadn't planned to make this pitch with anybody listening, but what the hell. I'll eventually go home, but they'll never assign me to the presidential protection detail again. Falling off a limo bumper is just about as bad as goosing the first lady. People aren't supposed to snicker when the motorcade rolls by. From what Tom told me about what you're going to be doing, that'll be at least as interesting. How about it?"

Do I have the authority to just say, "Yes, sure"?

I do until someone—and that means the President— tells me I don't.

"Welcome aboard, Tony," Castillo said. "That's presuming someone important doesn't say 'Not only no, but hell no you can't have Santini.'"

"We'll worry about that when it happens. From what Tom told me, I don't think it will. So what's up?"

"You have a look at the package from Fort Bragg?"

Santini nodded. "Very impressive weaponry," he said. "And black jumpsuits. And those face masks! This may be an indelicate question, but who are we going to whack?"

"The answer to that is Top Secret–Presidential, Tony," Castillo said, seriously.

"Okay," Santini said, his voice now serious. "Understood."

"My orders are to locate and render harmless the people who murdered Masterson and Markham."

"It's about time we started playing by their rules," Santini said after a moment.

"The President apparently has made that decision," Castillo said.

"Now all we have to do is find them, huh? How do we do that?"

"You remember Mrs. Masterson's brother, the UN guy we couldn't find to tell him about Masterson?"

Santini nodded.

"It seems he was the head bagman for the oil-for-food payoffs," Castillo said. "He went missing—probably from Vienna—immediately after he found one of his assistants dead of a slit throat in Vienna. Nasty. Before they killed him, they pulled several of his teeth with a pair of pliers.

"The CIA guy in Paris and my source in Vienna think Lorimer is probably in the Seine or the Danube. I don't."

"Why not?"

"Wait until you hear this. When we landed in Mississippi, Mrs. Masterson told me the reason she was abducted was because they thought she would know where her brother was. They killed Masterson to show her how serious they were about wanting to know; the Masterson kids would be next. And I think they whacked Sergeant Markham and almost whacked Schneider to show her they could get to whoever they wanted to."

"I had a gut feeling at the time they were after you," Santini said. "It was your car."

"That thought has run through my mind," Castillo said.

"She didn't know where he was? Or she figured her kids were more important? Which?"

"She didn't know," Castillo said.

A knock at the door announced the arrival of Alex Darby.

"Why do I feel I'm late for the party?" Darby asked, and then looked at Fernando and Kranz.

"Fernando Lopez, Seymour Kranz, Alex Darby," Castillo said.

"And these gentlemen are?" Darby asked.

"Mr. Lopez is an airplane pilot under contract to the Office of Organizational Analysis," Castillo said.

"To the what?"

"The Office of Organizational Analysis. You don't know what that is?"

"Never heard of it," Darby confessed.

"I'm surprised. It's in the Department of Homeland Security."

"I told you, Charley, I never heard of it," Darby said.

Using my miraculous powers to judge a man's thoughts by looking into his eyes, I deduce that Darby really doesn't know.

"There's been a Presidential Finding, Alex," Castillo said. "A clandestine and covert organization charged with finding and rendering harmless those responsible for Masterson's and Markham's murders has been set up within the Department of Homeland Security."

"And who was put in charge of this It's About Goddamn Time for Payback organization? And why didn't I hear about it?"

Torine pointed at Castillo and said, "Say hello to the chief, Alex."

"The answer asks more questions than it answers," Darby said, "starting with why didn't I hear about it?"

"I just told you about it," Castillo said.

"And who's Kranz?"

"He's our communicator."

"There's a rumor floating around that there's already a special communicator down here," Darby said.

"Now there's two. They call that redundancy."

"I'm getting the feeling you know who these bastards are," Darby said. "And I would really like to help you render them harmless."

"We don't know who they are," Castillo said. "But there's a guy I think is here who can probably tell us."

"Who?"

"Jean-Paul Lorimer."

"I thought they couldn't find him in Paris. What's he got to do with this? He's here?"

"I think so. Somewhere here in the Southern Cone. What he has to do with it is that he was the bagman for Oil for Food. Not only did he skim a large sum—sixteen million, according to one source—from the bribe money, but he knows who got how much, when, and what for. That's what the whole thing was about. The people who want his mouth permanently closed—and their money back—really want to find him."

"That sounds pretty far-fetched, Charley. Lorimer—I

told you I met him—is a typical UN bureaucrat. I can't imagine him being involved in something like that. Where'd you get it?"

"I got the fact that people are looking for him from Mrs. Masterson. They kidnapped her because they thought she would know where he is. I think they believed her when she said she didn't. But they think he'll contact her. They told her that they'll kill her children if she does find out where he is and doesn't tell them. Masterson was blown away to make the point that they will kill to get what they want."

"You got that from Betsy Masterson?"

Castillo nodded.

"Why didn't she tell me?"

"She didn't tell me until we landed in the States. Her primary concern was protecting the children, and God knows she had reason not to feel secure in Argentina. I guess when she saw the Globemaster surrounded by Delta Force shooters she felt secure enough to tell me."

"Does she know why these people are looking for Lorimer?"

"If you mean, did she know he was the oil-for-food bagman, I don't think so. If she knew, she would have told her husband, and I don't think there's any question that Masterson would have blown the whistle on him."

"And he would have," Darby said. "So how are you going to find Lorimer?"

"I don't know. But the first thing I have to do is talk to Yung."

"The FBI guy in Montevideo? What's he got to do with this?"

"I don't know. But I do know he's not looking for money laundering, as he says he is . . ."

"How do you know that?" Darby challenged.

". . . and that he's working for the State Department, not the FBI."

"I don't understand that."

"Neither do I, but I got that from Natalie Cohen. Who has told Ambassador Silvio and Ambassador What-sisname in Montevideo . . ."

"McGrory," Darby furnished.

". . . to tell him to, quote, put himself and whatever intelligence he has developed, end quote, at my disposal."

"She didn't tell you what he's doing?"

"She's in Singapore—or was—and believe it or not the secure voice links in both her airplane and the embassy were fucked up."

"You want to try to talk to her from the embassy?"

"What I want to do is talk to Yung."

"Here or in Montevideo?"

"Montevideo is where his files are going to be," Castillo said. "I want a look at them. How's the best way to get to Montevideo?"

"Starting about now, there's Austral flights from Jorge Newbery every hour or so. You want me to go with you?"

"What I'd like for you to do is show Lorimer's picture to everybody in the embassy—your people, the DEA, the military people—and see if it rings a bell. Don't tell them why we're looking."

"You have a picture?"

The CIA guy in Paris gave me two. I have them in my briefcase," Castillo said. "If I give you one, can you get me twenty copies of it?"

"No problem," Darby said.

"Do you have a safe house?"

"A safe apartment not far from here, and a safe house in Mayerling. That's a country club out in Pilar."

"Mayerling?" Castillo asked.

"Yeah. Mayerling. Upscale gated community where the guards at the gate have Uzis."

"Mayerling?" Castillo repeated.

"Is there something I don't know, Charley?" Darby asked.

"My mind is flying off at a tangent," Castillo said. "Let's suppose you're an Austrian, and you have some money you're not supposed to have from Oil for Food, and you manage to get the money laundered here in Argentina, and you're looking for an investment—"

"What the hell are you talking about?"

"I've got an envelope in my briefcase stuffed with names of Germans and Austrians who have—what's the phrase?—'ill-gotten gains' from Oil for Food that they've moved here."

"Really?"

"Yeah, really."

"Are you going to give it to me?"

"No. Sorry. I gave my word as an officer and a gentleman that I wouldn't give it to anybody in the CIA or other agency of the U.S. government.

"Now, let me finish what I was saying: So you're an

Austrian and looking for a sound investment for your now thoroughly washed ill-gotten gains. Where to put it? Eureka! I know. Real estate. I will build an upscale country club and sell expensive houses to rich people wanting to escape crowded Buenos Aires. All I need is a romantic name, with overtones of aristocratic class. So what will I call it? Mayerling! That's what I'll call it, Mayerling! Ain't *nothing* no more classic than Mayerling! I'll have everybody in Argentina who traces his ancestry back to the glorious days of Franz Josef and the Austro-Hungarian empire standing in line to throw money at me so they can say, 'I live in Mayerling.'"

"What the hell are you talking about? What the hell is Mayerling?"

"Alex, for someone in your line of work, your ignorance of history is shocking," Castillo said solemnly. "You don't know about Mayerling?"

"No, goddammit, I don't."

"Once upon a time—in 1889—one version has it, Crown Prince Rudolph, who would on the death of his father, Franz Josef, become king and emperor of the Austro-Hungarian empire, was called in by Daddy and told to divest himself of his mistress.

"Crown Prince Rudolph was thirty-one. His mistress was a sixteen-year-old tootsie, the Baroness Maria Vetsera. The relationship was embarrassing to the throne and had to be ended, Daddy said.

"Rudolph took Maria to his hunting lodge, which was called Mayerling, to break the bad news to her. After talking it over, they decided that since (a) Rudolph could not disobey his father the emperor and (b) that life was not worth living without each other, there was only one solution, and they took it. Rudolph popped Maria with his Steyr automatic and then popped himself in the temple.

"He was given a state funeral, and the entire Austro-Hungarian empire went into an official state of mourning. Maria's body was sent back to her village.

"The other version, according to Otto Göerner, who got it from my aunt Olga—she was actually my grand-aunt—who was Hungarian and moved in high social circles, was that Franz Josef really didn't give a damn who Rudolph was diddling—ol' Franz Josef's own mistress lived with him in Schönbrunn palace—but was really annoyed when he found out that Rudy was in serious conversations with some Hungarians vis-à-vis what we now call regime change. Rudy wanted to be king and emperor now, not when the old guy finally kicked off.

"According to that version, Franz Josef had Rudolph popped while he was fooling around with Maria in his hunting lodge, which, if I didn't happen to mention this before, was called Mayerling.

"The result of Rudy's sudden demise at Mayerling was that his cousin, Franz Josef's nephew, Archduke Franz Ferdinand, became heir to the throne. On 28 June 1914, in Sarajevo, a Serbian anarchist tossed a bomb into his car, mortally wounding poor Franz Ferdinand.

"Franz Josef simply couldn't put up with having his heir whacked, so he declared war on Serbia, and World War One was off and running. And it all started in Mayerling. I'm really surprised you didn't know this, Alex."

"Jesus, Charley, you're amazing," Darby said. "You're not really suggesting there's a connection with this country club and oil-for-food money?"

"Far be it from me to suggest anything to an old spook like you, Alex, but if I were in your shoes, I'd have a good close look at it. Truth is stranger than fiction. There's a reason they call your country club Mayerling. And you are looking for foreign-laundered money, right?"

"The trouble with you, you sonofabitch, is when you come off the wall like this, half the time you're right," Darby said.

"Actually, it's closer to seventy-five percent of the time," Castillo said. "Now tell me, do you think you can smuggle the stuff I had sent from Bragg past the Uzi-armed guards at Mayerling?"

"No problem," Darby said.

"How about moving it out there while I talk to Yung? You said something about airplanes to Montevideo every hour on the hour?"

"Yeah, but if you don't want me to go with you—"

"I thought I'd take Jack. He's an ex-cop."

"You and Britton had better take Tony with you."

"Okay. Why?"

"Because he has a diplomatic passport and is accredited both here and in Uruguay. They're not going to search him for weapons."

Darby opened his briefcase and took out two Beretta 9mm semiautomatics, opened their actions, and handed them to Charley.

"Thanks, Alex," Castillo said.

"Buenos Aires cellulars work in Montevideo—and some other places over there," Darby said, and went back into his briefcase.

"I've got two cellulars," Tony Santini said. "And also a couple of Berettas."

"Spread them as far as they'll go," Castillo ordered. "And then, Alex, can you take care of those who need either a pistol or a phone or both?"

Darby nodded. "You're going to need wheels, too," he said. "But to get them for you, Ambassador Silvio will have to know you're here."

"I sent word that we were coming," Castillo said. "But I'm not going to tell him any more than I have to about what we're going to do. He's a good guy, and I want him to be able to honestly say he knew nothing about it."

" 'It' covers a lot of territory, Charley," Darby said.

"That's because, right now, I don't know what's going to happen," Castillo said. "How do we get to Jorge Newbery?"

"I've got a car," Santini said.

"With CD tags?" Darby asked.

Santini shook his head.

"Then take mine. That way you can park right in front."

[THREE]
Aeropuerto Internacional General C. L. Berisso
Carrasco, Montevideo
República Oriental del Uruguay
0710 29 July 2005

There had been a parking area for perhaps thirty cars reserved for the Corps Diplomatique against one wall of the Jorge Newbery passenger terminal and fifteen minutes after Santini parked Darby's embassy BMW they were aboard Austral flight 311, Boeing 737 nonstop service to Montevideo.

Immigration formalities for leaving the Republic of Argentina and entering the Republic of Uruguay had been simple. Castillo saw that Argentine and Uruguayan nationals simply had to show their national identity cards. He made a mental note to see if the friendly folks at Langley could make him one.

As foreigners, Castillo and Britton had to go through formal procedures. These consisted of submitting their passports to an Argentine immigration officer, who exposed them to a computer reader. He then applied the EXIT stamp in the appropriate spot, and then handed the passport to the Uruguayan official sitting next to him. The passport was again exposed to a computer reader, stamped with an ENTER stamp, and then handed back to the traveler. There would be no immigration formalities when they actually got off the airplane in Uruguay.

Airport security had come next. It consisted primarily of walking past two police officers, who didn't show

much interest in any of them. The carry-on baggage
X-ray machine wasn't even turned on.

*Even granting that Austral flight 311 really is a flying
commuter bus, and that the possibility of Muslim terrorists
taking over the aircraft and diving it into the, say, Daim-
lerChrysler building in downtown Buenos Aires is admit-
tedly slim,* Castillo thought, as a stewardess handed him a
copy of *La Nación, the airport security check of boarding
passengers was still a little lax.*

The flight itself, from wheels-up to a somewhat hard
landing, took about twenty-six minutes.

Once in the terminal building, there were signs in
Spanish and English offering travelers their choice of
NOTHING TO DECLARE and PAY CUSTOMS CHARGES lanes.
Castillo did not see officials of any kind in either lane.

Special Agent David William Yung, Jr., of the FBI was
waiting for them in the airport lobby.

*I'm going to have to remember I don't like this son-
ofabitch.*

"Hello again, Yung," Castillo greeted him. "It was
good of you to meet us."

"Mr. Darby suggested it would be best," Yung said,
ignoring Castillo's outstretched hand.

Well, fuck you, Yung!

"You remember Mr. Santini, I'm sure," Castillo said.
"I'm not sure about Mr. Britton."

"I saw him when I was in Buenos Aires," Yung said.

"Pleased to meet you, too," Britton said cheerfully,
with a broad smile. "It's always a pleasure to work with
the FBI."

Castillo and Santini smiled. Yung didn't.

"Where would you like to go, Mr. Castillo?" Yung asked.

"Where are your files?"

"I have some in my office in the embassy and some in my apartment," Yung said. "I don't know what you're after."

"I'm looking for an American. He works for the UN. His name is Jean-Paul Lorimer."

Yung shook his head, indicating he'd never heard of him.

Or doesn't want to give me what he has.

"Which is closer? Your apartment or the embassy?"

"My apartment."

"Then why don't we go there? After we stop someplace for breakfast?"

"You didn't eat before you came over?"

"Yeah, sure I did. But it was so long a flight, I'm hungry again."

"My car's out here," Yung said, and walked out of the terminal.

He walked so quickly he was soon out of earshot.

"Charley," Britton asked, "why do I think that guy doesn't like you?"

"You're perceptive?"

They found an open restaurant not far from the beach.

"Why is the Atlantic Ocean so dirty?" Britton asked.

"That's not the Atlantic Ocean, that's the Río de la Plata," Castillo told him.

"That's a river?"

"The mouth of the 'River of Silver' is a hundred-plus miles wide. The Blue Danube isn't blue, and the River of Silver is muddy. The Atlantic starts about sixty miles north of here. There's a resort there called Punta del Este. Point of the East. Pretty classy. The water there is blue."

"Very handy to launder money," Santini said.

"Yeah," Castillo said, thoughtfully.

"How do they do that, launder money?" Britton asked.

"One way is through the casinos," Santini said. "There's a bunch of them there. Hell, there's one right here in Carrasco, a Marriott, and a couple more downtown. The biggest one in Punta del Este is the Conrad, named after, and I think owned by, Hilton. The way it works is that you slip the casino a bunch of cash. Then they let you win, say, ninety percent of it. You declare your gambling winnings, pay taxes on it, and your money is now laundered."

"You're telling me that Marriott and Hilton are laundering money?" Britton asked, incredulously.

"Marriott and Hilton, no," Santini said. "There's generally at least one legal attaché—which is what they call FBI agents in the diplomatic world—on their premises. Marriott and Hilton are thus reminded of their patriotic duty not to launder money. The locally owned casinos are where it's done. Isn't that so, Yung?"

"If you say so," Special Agent Yung said. He turned to Castillo. "When do you want to see Ambassador McGrory?"

"I don't need to see him," Castillo said.

"He wants to see you."

"I don't need to see him, at least not today."

"He wants to see you."

"So you said."

"You are aware, aren't you, Mr. Castillo, that the ambassador is the man in charge of all U.S. government activities in the country to which he is accredited?"

"So I've heard," Castillo said. "We'll talk about this when we have some privacy."

Yung didn't reply.

Yung had a spacious, top-floor apartment in a three-story building on the Rambla, the waterfront highway between Carrasco and Montevideo, to the south.

Yung waved them, not very graciously, into chairs in the living room.

"All right, Mr. Castillo, what can I do for you? I'm sure you'll understand that I am obliged to report to Ambassador McGrory what may be discussed."

"Special Agent Yung," Castillo said icily, "I am now going to show you my credentials identifying me as a supervisory agent of the United States Secret Service."

He got out of his chair and held his credentials in front of Yung, who examined them and then nodded.

"Are you satisfied that I am Supervisory Special Agent Carlos G. Castillo of the United States Secret Service, Special Agent Yung?"

"I'm satisfied," Yung said.

"These gentlemen, Special Agents Anthony J. Santini

and John M. Britton of the Secret Service, will now show you their credentials. When you are satisfied they are who I am telling you they are, please say so."

Santini and then Britton got out of their chairs, walked to Yung, showed him their credentials, waited until he nodded, and then went back to their chairs.

"Are you satisfied, Special Agent Yung, that we are all who I am telling you we are?"

"I'm satisfied. Are you going to tell me what—"

"Gentlemen," Castillo interrupted him. "I want you to make note that at zero-eight-one-zero hours, local time, 29 July 2005, in his residence in Carrasco, Uruguay, we identified ourselves to Special Agent Yung as members of the U.S. Secret Service by showing him our credentials, and he acknowledged their validity."

Santini and Britton nodded.

"Special Agent Yung, what I am about to tell you is classified as Top Secret–Presidential. The unauthorized disclosure of any of this information to any person not authorized by the President, or myself, to have access to this material, and that specifically includes Ambassador McGrory, is a felony under the United States Code. Do you understand all that I have said?"

"You're telling me I can't report this to Ambassador McGrory? Frankly, Castillo, I don't believe you have that authority."

"In the vernacular, Special Agent Yung, I don't give a flying fuck what you believe or don't believe. The question was whether or not you understood what I said to you."

"I understood it."

"Good. I now inform you that I am the chief of the Office of Organizational Analysis—"

"The what?"

". . . which is a covert and clandestine organization set up in a Presidential Finding within the Department of Homeland Security and is charged with locating the assassins of J. Winslow Masterson and Sergeant Roger Markham, USMC, and rendering them harmless. Do you understand that?"

"That sounds as if you plan to . . . kill them."

"The question was, do you understand what I have just said?"

"There's nothing wrong with my hearing."

"To carry out this mission, it is necessary for us to find one Jean-Paul Lorimer, an American citizen employed by the UN, who I have reason to believe is somewhere in this area."

"I told you before, I never heard of him."

"Aware of my mission, the secretary of state, for whom you work, has relayed through either or both Ambassadors McGrory and Silvio her orders to you to place yourself and whatever information you may have at my disposal. You have received those orders, have you not?"

"Ambassador McGrory told me that you were going to come to me, and that I was to cooperate with you as much as possible," Yung said. "And that if you came to me directly, instead of through the embassy, I was to tell you he wanted to see you. Immediately."

"With the implication that you didn't have to cooperate with me unless he knew what this is about? And until he gave his permission?"

"For Christ's sake, Castillo, he's the ambassador."

"Tony, see if you can get Ambassador Silvio on your cellular," Castillo ordered.

"I work for Ambassador McGrory, not Silvio," Yung said.

"No, you don't. You work for the State Department's bureau of intelligence and research. Doing something so secret that the secretary of state didn't know about it until the day before yesterday," Castillo said.

Castillo could see a flicker of surprise on Yung's face.

"Did you tell McGrory what you're really doing down here?"

Yung didn't reply.

"Okay, that explains a lot. You didn't tell McGrory what you're really doing, so he thinks you're just one more legal attaché working for him. Right?"

"I've got the ambassador, Charley," Santini said.

"That was quick," Castillo said as he reached for the telephone.

"The miracle of modern communications," Santini said.

"Good morning, Mr. Ambassador. I'm on a cellular, so we're going to have to be careful what we're saying. I'm in Montevideo—actually, Carrasco—with Special Agent Yung. What I hope you'll be willing to do is relay the message from our friend Natalie to Yung. When the other fellow did that, it got a little garbled, and he's annoyed that I'm walking on his grass without his permission."

Ambassador Silvio replied briefly.

"Thank you, sir. I hope to see you shortly," Castillo said, and handed Yung the telephone.

"Special Agent Yung, Mr. Ambassador," Yung said.

He had the cellular to his ear for thirty seconds, and then he said, "Yes, sir, that's perfectly clear. That's not exactly the way I received the message here."

Ambassador Silvio said something else.

"Yes, sir," Yung said. "I understand, sir. Thank you very much, sir. Do you want to speak with Mr. Castillo again, sir?"

The ambassador apparently did not wish to again speak with Castillo. Yung ended the call and handed the cellular to Santini.

Yung smiled wryly at Castillo.

"After the ambassador relayed Secretary Cohen's message," he added, "he said, 'For purposes of clarification, Mr. Castillo has permission from the highest possible authority not only to walk on anybody's grass he wants but to sow it with salt if that's what he chooses to do.'"

Castillo chuckled and smiled and said, "Okay. You satisfied?"

Yung nodded.

"So what are you actually doing here? I know it's not looking for money launderers."

"You don't know?"

"No, I don't. But you're going to tell me, right?"

Yung nodded. "Actually, it has something to do with money laundering. But not to develop a case against money launderers."

"I don't think I follow you."

"How much do you know about the UN oil-for-food business?"

"A hell of a lot more now than I did a week ago," Castillo said. "What about it?"

"An astonishing number of people all over Europe and the Middle East—for that matter, all over the world—made a lot of money from that operation. Primarily Frenchmen—some very highly placed Frenchmen—and Germans. And Russians. It's an incredible amount of money, and like the Nazis in World War Two, they decided that South America, primarily the Southern Cone, is the place to hide it.

"The director of the bureau of intelligence and research started to build dossiers on these people even before the Second Desert War. Using his own people, I mean. And it got out. There's a lot of one-worlders, UN lovers, in the State Department. They think that leaking things is their patriotic duty. So he, quote, called off, end quote, the investigation. And then he went to the director of the FBI—they were both FBI agents as young men—and explained the situation and asked for help. And here I am."

"I heard you were a hotshot," Castillo said.

"Who told you that?"

"The same guy who told me whatever you were doing here it wasn't looking for money launderers."

"Howard Kennedy," Yung said.

"Who?"

"I know you're pals," Yung said.

"I never heard that name in my entire life until just now," Castillo said. "Cross my heart and hope to die."

"Yeah, sure. Well, if you should ever happen to meet somebody with that name, give him my regards," Yung said. "When we were young, innocent, and naïve, we really thought we could protect society from the barbarians. Had a lot of fun, for a while, doing it. And then Howard decided he'd rather be a barbarian. It paid better, and it wasn't nearly as frustrating. Sometimes I think I should have changed sides when he did."

"So tell me about these dossiers you're building," Castillo said.

"Well, there's fourteen FBI agents, including me, here looking at money laundering. As one of them, I have access to what's developed. They're looking for drug money, primarily—and there's a hell of a lot of that—which means they're looking for Colombians and Mexicans, mostly. And Americans, of course. When they come across some European moving a lot of money around here, they check with the DEA, the treasury department, whoever, to see if there's a drug connection or an American connection of some kind. If there isn't, they let it drop." He paused, then added, "And I pick it up."

"And do what with it?"

"What my boss wants is proof—photocopies—of bank records; who deposited how much and when; records of who bought an estancia or a car dealership or a million-dollar villa in Punta del Este. I don't really know what he thinks anybody will do with it. He still has stars in his eyes. Expose the bad guys and the world will be a better place. I can't see that happening."

"Yes, you can," Castillo said. "You've still got stars in

your eyes, too. Otherwise, you'd have changed sides when your friend—what was his name?—did."

"And what about you, Castillo? No stars in your eyes? How did you get involved in something like this? I know what 'render them harmless' really means."

"I am simply carrying out the instructions of my government, as I understand them, as an officer and a gentleman of the United States Army."

"Oh, shit!" Yung chuckled. "Yeah, that's right. You are an Army officer, aren't you? A major. Back to my question, how did an Army officer get involved in something like this?"

"I just told you," Castillo said. "Where are your files?"

"Here. I can't leave them in the embassy. Another price I pay for being a secret hotshot, to use Kennedy's words, is that my fellow FBI agents think I'm either stupid or lazy or both. I don't turn in half the work they do."

"If you're working on something like this, I'm surprised you can turn in any work at all," Castillo said. "Can I see the files?"

"Reluctantly," Yung said. "I don't want it getting out what I've been doing here. Who else is going to know what's in my files? Even that I have them?"

"Would you believe me if I say no one?"

"Why should I?"

"I'll make a deal with you," Castillo said. "I'll show you mine if you show me yours. And that will be our little secret."

"What's in your files?"

"The names of people—Germans, French, and

Russians—who are reliably reported to have made money on Oil for Food and probably are sending it over here. I promised my source I would not turn them over to the CIA or the FBI or anybody. And I won't. But maybe it would help if you took a look at them, maybe make a match with somebody you've got a dossier on. That might help us find this bastard Lorimer."

"What's your interest in Lorimer?"

"He was the head bagman for Oil for Food. He knows who got how much, and when, and what for. And if I find him, I think I can convince him to point me in the direction of whoever whacked Masterson and Markham. Lorimer is who I'm really after."

"Never heard of him," Yung said. "Sorry."

"And I have to find him before the bad guys do. They want to make sure he doesn't talk. They already whacked one of his guys in Vienna. Deal?"

"Why not?" Yung said. "Where's your list?"

"In my briefcase," Castillo said, and picked it up from the floor and placed it on a coffee table. Yung pushed himself out of his chair and walked to the table as Castillo opened the briefcase.

"Well, I can save you time about him," Yung said.

"Excuse me?"

"Bertrand," Yung said. "The guy in the picture."

"This picture?" Castillo asked and held it up. "You know this guy?"

"His name is Bertrand," Yung said. "He's a Lebanese antiquities dealer."

"A Lebanese antiques dealer?"

"*Antiques* are old furniture, things like that," Yung

clarified. "*Antiquities* are things boosted from King Tut's tomb, things like that. Really old stuff. And Bertrand's very good at it, makes a lot of money. I learned a lot from him."

"About *antiquities*?"

"About how to have money in a bank and not worry about getting it back out. You do know, don't you, why people don't use Argentina much to launder and/or hide money?"

"No. But I wondered why there were so many FBI agents in Montevideo and zero in Argentina."

"Because this is where the money is laundered and hidden," Yung said. "Argentina used to be the place, but a couple years ago, just before Argentina defaulted on its government bonds, the government decided to help themselves to the dollars in everybody's bank accounts. The peso on one Sunday was worth one U.S. dollar. On Monday morning, the government announced the 'pesification of the dollar.' All dollar deposits in Argentine banks were converted to pesos at a rate of one-point-three pesos per dollar. In other words, if you had a hundred dollars on Sunday, on Monday you had a hundred thirty pesos. Now, if you wanted dollars, you had to buy them, and the rate was five to the dollar. In other words, your hundred-dollar deposit was now worth twenty-six. A lot of people—including a lot of honest ones—took a hell of a bath. The Argentines blamed it on the IMF, who had loaned them the money they couldn't, didn't want to, repay."

"Fascinating!"

"Their argument was pure Argentine. It was like some

guy on a thousand-a-month salary buying a Cadillac with no money down. Then, when it comes time to make the monthly payment, he says, 'Not only am I not gonna make the payment, but I'm gonna keep the Caddy, too, because you should have known I couldn't afford to pay for it.' "

"You're serious, aren't you?" Castillo asked.

"Absolutely. The banking system took a hell of a beating. The Scotia Bank—one of Canada's biggest; they'd been doing business in Argentina for more than a century—just took their losses and pulled out. For a while it looked like CitiBank and Bank of Boston were going to take *their* losses and leave, too, but they finally decided to stay."

"How did this affect the antiquities dealer? Bertrand?"

"Well, first of all, he was smart enough to have his money here—a lot of money; the last time I looked it was a little over sixteen million, U.S.—and not across the river. And then he's got an interesting deal with the banks."

"What kind of a deal?"

"This is pretty complicated. . . ."

"Make it simple for me," Castillo said.

"Okay. He doesn't *deposit* his money in his banks. He *loans* it to them, just like he was another bank. Banks are always borrowing money from each other, so nobody notices one more loan. They don't pay Bertrand what they have to pay other banks, so they're happy. And he's happy because he has their note, callable on demand. Or he can endorse the bank's promissory note over to somebody—anybody—else, an individual or another bank. You see how it works? Like a super cashier's check."

"I'm not sure," Castillo admitted. "How is he sure the banks will come up with the money when he says, 'Pay me'?"

"Because he's taken out insurance that they will," Yung said, just a little smugly. "He gets it either from the bank or the insurance company. It costs him a little money, sure, but his money is safe."

"What if somebody steals the promissory notes?"

"Unless he signs them, they're just pieces of paper."

"You know a lot about this guy, don't you, Yung?"

"I've been keeping my eye on him ever since I came down here."

"You know something about his personal habits? Where he lives?"

"He's got an estancia—he calls it 'Shangri-La'—in Tacuarembó Province, and a fancy condominium in Punta del Este. He doesn't use the condo much because, getting to his personal habits, he likes the young girls—very young girls—he has at Shangri-La."

"There's one thing you don't know about this guy, Yung," Castillo said.

"And what's that?"

"His real name is Jean-Paul Lorimer."

Yung looked at Castillo incredulously, and then smiled. "You're kidding!"

Castillo shook his head. "Uh-uh. Can you show me where Shangri-La is on a map?"

XVIII

Alex Darby—notified by the guards at the gate that his guests were arriving—was waiting at the door of the large, stucco house when Castillo, Britton, and Santini drove up.

"Come on in," he said. "Have any trouble finding it?"

"Just followed the signs," Castillo said. " 'Our Little House'? Isn't that a little cutesy-poo for a safe house, Alex?" He looked around the foyer and the well-furnished living room. "And fancy. What's this place costing the agency?"

"There are safe houses and safe houses, Charley. This is a safe house, but not the agency's. I own it. I stole it."

"You own it?"

Darby didn't reply.

"Come on in, and we'll have some coffee. Unless you want something stronger?"

"I would love something very strong, but not now," Castillo said as they followed Darby into the living room and sat down around a coffee table.

"Get this, Charley," Darby said, and pointed under the coffee table.

Castillo saw him push a floor-mounted button with his shoe.

There was a faint tinkle of a bell, and a moment later a middle-aged woman in a maid's uniform appeared.

"Yes, sir?"

"Juanita, will you bring us some coffee, please?" Darby asked. "And some pastries?"

"Yes, sir."

"Very classy," Castillo said. "You said you own this place? Correction, you said you stole it."

"Both," Darby said. "What do you think a place like this is worth?"

"Half a million, anyway. Probably more, a lot more, with the panache of Mayerling attached."

"You heard what happened here a couple of years ago, the 'pesification'?"

"Special Agent Yung delivered a lecture on that just now in Carrasco."

"I'd been here a couple of months when that happened. Nobody had any dollars anymore. The government had just converted them to pesos, at a third—a fourth—of what they had been worth before. People were desperate for dollars; the bottom fell out of the real estate market. I paid a hundred and seventy-five grand for this."

"You did steal it," Castillo said. "And you live here?"

"I rent it to Cisco Systems. They pay me twelve thousand a month so the guy who runs things for them in the Southern Cone has a nice place to live, reflecting the prestige of Cisco Systems to the natives. He lets me use it when I need it."

He saw the look on Castillo's and Santini's faces. "You know what Cisco Systems does, right?"

"Data transfer? Something to do with the Internet?"

"Largest operators in both. Can you imagine how much goes over their nets that would be of interest to me?"

"This guy is undercover with the agency?"

"No. But he's a retired Signal Corps colonel. He used to work for IntelSat. From time to time he tells me things he's found interesting. And from time to time—like now—I ask him if I can borrow the place to get out of the city for a couple of days. Cisco maintains an apartment in the Alvear Plaza for visiting executives. So he and his wife stay at the Alvear for a couple of days, do the restaurants, go to the Colon, etcetera."

"Nice deal!"

"It's now all paid for, so the rent goes in my pocket." He paused, smiled, and chuckled. "Which came to the attention of the counterintelligence people in Langley. I guess the Riggs Bank felt it their patriotic duty to tell them I was depositing a lot more money than I should be on what the agency pays me. So they investigated. They came down here and spent three weeks investigating."

"And?"

"I'd already told my boss what I was doing. His reaction was jealousy, not disapproval. So when they triumphantly laid on his desk their report that the guy in Buenos Aires was in the real estate business, he said, 'I know.'"

Castillo chuckled.

"And it's like we're queer, Charley, to answer that question before you ask it. The Cisco guy doesn't ask, and I don't tell."

"You're a lot smarter than you look, Alex," Castillo said.

"So what did you find out from the FBI guy in Montevideo?"

Castillo didn't answer the question, but asked one: "What time is Ambassador Silvio coming?"

"I didn't know how quickly you could get here, so I told him three. Everybody will be here at three. Is that okay?"

"That's fine," Castillo said. "I've got an errand to run. I'm sure I can be back by then. While I'm gone, Tony and Jack can tell you what happened with that sonofabitch in Montevideo."

"I thought maybe you'd be pals after he was told to make nice," Darby said.

"Not quite. And I'm going to need some maps, topographic maps, of Tacuarembó Province, Uruguay. The more detailed, the better. And of the terrain on a reasonably straight-line route from here to there."

"Why do I think you're planning a helicopter flight?"

Castillo didn't answer that question, either.

"And, to go on my errand, I'm going to need a car without CD tags."

"Our host has a Mercedes SUV he lets me use. It comes with a driver."

"I don't want the driver," Castillo said. "Just the car."

The maid came in, pushing a cart with a silver coffee service.

"By the time you finish the coffee, I'll have the keys to the Mercedes."

"I don't have time for coffee, Alex," Castillo said, and stood up.

[TWO]
Buena Vista Country Club
Pilar, Buenos Aires Province, Argentina
1345 29 July 2005

Castillo braked to a stop at the heavy, yellow-striped barrier pole, and with some difficulty finally found the window control switch and lowered the window.

The guard eyed him suspiciously but didn't speak.

"I'm here to see Mr. Pevsner."

"I'm sorry, sir. But there's no one here by that name."

"Get on the phone and tell Mr. Pevsner his friend from Vienna is here."

The guard opened his mouth.

"Get on the phone and tell Mr. Pevsner his friend from Vienna is here," Castillo repeated. "That is not a friendly suggestion."

The guard stared at him for a moment, and then said, "Park over there, please, señor." He pointed to a three-car, nose-in parking area.

Castillo saw that another heavy steel barrier pole would keep people out of the country club until it was raised, and that a menacing-looking tire shredder would keep them from changing their minds about wanting to enter Buena Vista and backing out. The guard waited until Castillo had parked the Mercedes before he returned to the guard shack, and the moment the guard entered the shack, another came out, leaned against it, folded his arms on his chest, and stared at the car.

Castillo got out and waved and smiled at the guard, which seemed to confuse him. Castillo took out a small cigar and lit it.

Five minutes later, a Mercedes-Benz ML350 identical to Castillo's came through the gate, made a U-turn, and pulled in beside Castillo. Castillo had examined it carefully, but the windows were so heavily darkened that it wasn't until the door opened that Charley could see the driver, and then recognize him.

This doesn't give me a lot of time to figure out—even guess—what he's doing here.

"Alfredo! What a pleasant surprise!" Castillo said. "Fancy meeting you here."

"Mr. Pevsner had no idea that you were going to call, Karl," Colonel Alfredo Munz said. "You really should have called first."

"I will offer my apologies for my bad manners."

"I know he's going to be pleased to see you. Would you follow me, please?"

"How do you know that he'll be pleased to see me?"

"Because when I saw you puffing on your cigar, I called and told him who his friend from Vienna was, and he said, 'Wonderful. I really want to talk to him,'" Munz replied, snapped an order to the guards to raise the barrier, and got back in his Mercedes. By the time Castillo got behind the wheel, the barrier pole was already high in the air.

Aleksandr Pevsner, wearing riding breeches and boots and a heavy, red, turtleneck woolen sweater, was standing on the verandah of his house waiting for them.

"Charley, how good to see you!" he exclaimed, and embraced him in the Argentine manner.

"How are you, Alex?"

"If you had given the guards your name, I would have had them pass you in," he said. "All I heard was a 'friend from Vienna,' and I have many of those."

"I understand," Castillo said. "You thought it might be Henri Douchon, miraculously raised from the dead."

"Who? I have no idea what you're talking about, my friend."

"Okay," Castillo said, smiling.

"Come on in the house, we'll have a glass of wine. Have you had luncheon? Can I offer you something?"

"I had a small ham-and-cheese sandwich at the airport in Montevideo, and yes, you may offer me something. Thank you very much."

"Anna and the kids are at school. I have been at school. Horse school—"

"Equestrian, Alex," Castillo corrected him. "I keep telling you things, and you keep forgetting them."

"So you do. I was at *equestrian* school—I wonder, what's the etymology of that word? What's it got to do with horses?"

"It means horses, Alex. From the Latin *equus*," Castillo said.

"I keep forgetting how smart you are, Charley. At least most of the time."

"You mean you keep forgetting most of the time? Or that I'm smart only part of the time?"

"How about both? Anyway, I am just back from learning how to properly ride a horse, and I was about to have a *lomo* sandwich. May I offer you the same, or would you prefer something . . ."

"A *lomo* sandwich would be delightful, Alex."

"With wine or beer?"

"Beer, please. And coffee."

"Let's go in the breakfast room," Pevsner said, gesturing. "And would you mind if Alfredo joined us?"

"Not at all."

"I thought he would like to hear what you have come to tell me."

"What makes you think I've come to tell you anything?" Castillo asked.

Pevsner didn't answer. He gestured for them to sit at a round, glass-topped table, and then left, presumably to order their lunch.

"So how do you like working for Alex, Alfredo?"

"It pays much better than SIDE did," Munz replied. "How is your female agent?"

"Thank you for asking. She's a lot better than she could be. I saw her a few days ago in Philadelphia."

"And the Mastersons? Are they well? Safe?"

"They are being protected by twenty-four Delta Force shooters and half of the Mississippi gendarmeria."

"I saw your President on television," Munz said. "When he said 'this outrage will not go unpunished.'"

"I saw that, too."

"Would it be reasonable to assume that you're somehow involved with doing that for him?"

"Where would you get an idea like that?"

"Where would Alfredo get an idea like what?" Pevsner asked as he came back into the breakfast room.

"The U.S. President promised he would punish those responsible for what he called 'this outrage,' the murders of Masterson and the sergeant . . ."

"The sergeant's name was Markham," Castillo interrupted. "Sergeant Roger Markham."

". . . and I asked Karl if he was involved."

"And what did my friend Carlos say?"

"He asked me where I got an idea like that."

"Aha!" Pevsner said. "So if you're not involved in punishment, and you didn't come here to tell me something, to what do I owe the honor?"

"I came here to borrow your helicopter for a couple of days," Castillo said. "I just knew you'd be happy to loan it to me."

Pevsner's head snapped around to look at him.

After a moment, he said, "So he is alive and here."

"Who's alive and here?" Castillo asked.

"The man you asked Howard Kennedy to find for you."

"Did Howard find him?"

"You know he didn't, Carlos."

"The word on the street in Paris and elsewhere in the old country is that he's in either the Seine or the Danube.

Didn't Howard tell you that? What was his name again?"

"Jean-Paul Lorimer, as you damned well know," Pevsner said.

"You told me you'd never heard of him, when I asked you," Castillo said.

"Sometimes it's better not to know people's names," Pevsner replied. "I know who a lot of people are who do things. Sometimes I can't put a name to them. I just know what they do."

"That's interesting," Castillo said. "Can I take that as a 'Yes, I'll be happy to loan you my helicopter'?"

"Let me offer a hypothetical situation," Pevsner said. "Let's suppose someone came to you in Texas and said, 'I want to borrow a horse. I have an errand to run.' And you said, 'But it's raining and if I loan you my horse, you will get soaking wet, and maybe even get your death of cold and die. Why don't you let me run your errand for you?' Wouldn't that make more sense?"

"Not if your idea of an errand is to send someone to the beauty parlor to put an Indian beauty mark on his forehead. I told Howard, in Paris, to tell you I want this sonofabitch alive."

"To do what?"

"I want to hear him sing. You know, like a canary. I want him to tell me not only who he thinks whacked Masterson and Markham, but everything else he knows about who got what and when and what for in the . . . you know what, Alex. A series of business transactions involving food, medical supplies, and oil."

Pevsner stared at him coldly for a long moment.

"And just to satisfy my curiosity, how would you go

about making the canary sing?" Pevsner asked.

"You mean in case pulling his teeth with pliers didn't work?"

"Or the Chinese water torture."

"Well, first I would appeal to his sense of honesty and fair play. If that didn't work, then I would tell him I understood completely. And since I knew people were worried about him not being in Paris, I was going to send him back there. And there would be nothing to worry about the trip either, because I was going to give him enough Gamma Hydroxybutane so that when he woke up he was going to be in the Place de la Concorde. Chained naked in a sexually suggestive pose to one of the statues around the Obelisk of Luxor wearing lipstick and earrings and with a rose stuck up his ass."

"Oh, Charley!" Pevsner laughed. "What a wonderful picture! Unfortunately, I can't permit it."

"I'm not asking you for permission, Alex. All I want to do is borrow your helicopter for a day or two."

"You're not listening to me, Charley. I said I can't permit it. I have too much to lose if the canary sings."

"And you're not listening to me, Alex. You tend to forget what I tell you."

"I really don't want this to become unpleasant, Charley. I really like you, and you know that. I would be very unhappy—"

"Let me tell you how things really are, Alex."

"Okay, my friend, tell me how things really are."

"Right now, the pressure is off you because I went to the President and got it taken off. As far as I know—I was about to say 'correct me if I'm wrong,' but I don't think you would—your only connection with Oil for Food was to move things around in your airplanes. You didn't buy ten dollars' worth of aspirin and sell it to the Iraqis for ten thousand, and then kick back half to Saddam. Or anything like that. Right so far?"

Pevsner nodded, just perceptibly. "I'm a businessman, Charley. If people want me to airlift something somewhere, I'll do it."

"I understand. The point is, right now we have an understanding. You don't break any American laws and we don't come looking for you. The problem is that you're about to break an American law."

"What law would that be?"

"Interfering with an official investigation; obstructing justice."

Pevsner smiled.

"You're not suggesting that I would actually be charged with something like that? Come on, Charley."

"Oh, you wouldn't be charged with anything. But the arrangement would be broken, and the President would be free to really start helping Interpol in their so-far not very successful attempts to put the cuffs on you."

"As much as it pains me to even think of something like this, have you thought of what might happen to you before you could tell anybody anything?"

"You mean, maybe getting my throat cut? Or getting a beauty mark?"

"Those things seem to happen, Charley, to people who threaten me or, more important, the happiness of my family."

"You don't think I just walked in here cold, do you? If I'm not back where I'm expected within an hour—and it's a ten-minute drive—or I don't make a telephone call and say the right things, Ambassador Silvio will request an immediate meeting with the foreign minister. He will tell him he has just learned that Aleksandr Pevsner, who Interpol is searching so hard for, is living in the Buena Vista Country Club."

"What makes you so sure he doesn't already know?" Pevsner snapped.

"I wouldn't be at all surprised to learn that he does. But that's not the same thing as being told he does by the American ambassador, is it? And the Argentines seem, at those levels of the government, to solve embarrassing problems by throwing people to the wolves. Wouldn't you agree, Alfredo?"

Pevsner glared at him.

"Think it over, Alex," Castillo said. "Very carefully."

"Goddamn you, Charley," Pevsner said, more sadly than angrily.

"And fuck you, Alex. I say that in the friendliest possible way."

"What do you want to do with the helicopter?"

"You really don't want to know, do you?"

"Hypothetically?"

"Hypothetically, if I knew (a) where somebody I wanted to teach to sing was located—in a foreign country; and (b) I knew that other people were trying to make sure that he didn't sing, what I think I would do would be to get him back home to the good ol' USA as quickly and quietly as possible. A helicopter would be useful if someone was, hypothetically, of course, thinking of doing something like that."

"You just told me, you realize, that Lorimer is not living in Buenos Aires. Or any other city. You want the helicopter to move him from someplace in the country to an airport. An airport large enough to take a plane that could fly him out of the country. You didn't, by any chance, come all the way down here in that Lear you had in Cozumel?"

"I'd love to keep playing twenty-questions with you, Alex, but I have to be running along. Are you going to loan me your helicopter or not?"

"Goddamn you, Charley."

"You already said that. Nice to see you, Alex." Castillo stood up. "I'll have to pass on the *lomo* sandwich and the beer. Thanks anyway."

"Sit down, Charley," Pevsner said. "You can have the helicopter."

"Thank you."

"What do I tell the pilot? Have you thought this through?"

"Tell your pilot to fly it to Jorge Newbery by five o'clock this afternoon. Tell him to park it at Jet-Aire. Have him top off the tanks, leave the key under the pad in the pilot's seat, and take three days off."

"Who's going to fly it?"

"I will. And when I'm through with it, I'll take it back to Jorge Newbery, give you a call, and your pilot can pick it up."

Pevsner nodded. He looked at Munz, and after a moment added, "Take Alfredo with you. I'm sure he'll be useful."

"Absolutely not. But thank you just the same."

"Alfredo is not in the beauty spot business, if that's what you're thinking."

"But he could come back and tell you where we'd been, couldn't he?"

"If you'd already taken Lorimer out of the country, what difference would that make? What I'm thinking is that when it comes out—and it will—that you got to Lorimer before the other people looking for him did, it would be embarrassing for me if people knew you'd used my helicopter to kidnap him."

"Kidnap him? What a terrible thing to even think! What I'm thinking of, hypothetically, of course, is returning this poor, lost soul to the bosom of his loved ones."

"Of course. What I'm suggesting is that if something happened while you were carrying out this humanitarian mission of yours—officialdom asking questions you'd rather not answer, for example—Alfredo could deal with that better than you could."

Goddammit, he's right.

The question is, will Munz deal with the officialdom, or just wait for the opportunity to whack Lorimer?

Castillo looked at Munz.

"Are you wondering, Karl, if I have become an assassin for hire?" Munz asked.

"That occurred to me."

Munz met his eyes for a long moment.

"If I were in your place, I would wonder, too. The answer is no, I have not. I ask you to consider this: These people have changed my life, too. I bear—and my wife and my family shares—the shame of my being relieved and retired for incompetence. I would really like to find out who they are."

So you can pop them, Alfredo?

"I said the thought had occurred to me. It did, and I dismissed it," Castillo said.

Do I mean that? Or am I already wondering who I can trust to pop him the moment he looks like he's thinking of whacking Lorimer?

I guess I meant it.

But that doesn't mean I shouldn't seriously consider the selection of someone to pop him in case I'm wrong. Or prepare to do it myself.

"Thank you," Munz said.

"Why don't you tell your pilot to fly Alfredo to Jorge Newbery?" Castillo said. "That will make him less curious about what's going on."

Pevsner considered that and nodded.

The maid appeared with a tray laden with hard-crusted *lomo* sandwiches and a wine cooler filled with ice and beer bottles.

"Ah, our lunch," Pevsner said. Then he turned to Castillo. "Didn't you say something about having to call someone, Charley, to let them know you're with friends?"

"I was lying about that, Alex."

Pevsner looked at him, shook his head, and said, "You sonofabitch. I say that in the spirit of friendship and mutual trust, of course."

[THREE]
Nuestra Pequeña Casa
Mayerling Country Club
Pilar, Buenos Aires Province, Argentina
1505 29 July 2005

Ambassador Juan Manuel Silvio, Ph.D., ambassador extraordinary and plenipotentiary of the President of the United States of America to the Republic of Argentina, was sitting in the living room attired in blue jeans, battered health shoes, and a somewhat ratty-looking sweatshirt on which was the faded logo of Harvard University. He had a beer bottle in his hand.

"Good afternoon, sir," Castillo said.

"Good to see you again, Charley," the ambassador said, rising from his chair to offer his hand. "Do I detect curiosity on your face? Perhaps because of my attire?"

"If I may say so, sir, you're not your usual natty self."

"I'm glad you asked," Silvio said, as he sat down. "When Alex said you wanted to see me and here, rather than at the embassy, the problem then arose, 'How was I going to get out here without having my SIDE escort wonder what I was doing at Our Little House?'"

"So you ditched the SIDE escort?" Castillo said, smiling.

"In a manner worthy of James Bond," Silvio said. "I left the embassy, went to the residence, changed clothes, and went jogging. I led three SIDE stalwarts on a merry chase through the park until they were puffing with the exertion. Then I speeded up the pace until they were far behind. And then I just happened to see a car driven by one of Alex's men, who stopped and offered me a ride."

"Just happened to see it, huh? What they call a fortuitous happenstance?"

Silvio nodded. "I've always wanted to be the subject of an all-points bulletin," Silvio said. "I can just see my good friend the foreign minister somewhat incredulously asking, 'You're telling me you lost the American ambassador?'"

Castillo chuckled, then said, "Thank you for coming, sir."

"Thank you for asking me," Silvio said. "Or aren't you going to tell me what you've been doing? Or plan on doing?"

"Alex," Castillo said, "is there someplace here where the ambassador and I can have a couple of minutes alone?"

Darby pointed through the plate-glass windows toward a small, tile-roofed building in the garden.

"How about the quincho?" he asked. "There's even beer in a refrigerator out there."

"That will do very nicely," Castillo said.

Castillo helped himself to a bottle of Quilmes beer, and then offered one to Ambassador Silvio, who smiled and nodded and said, "Please."

When Castillo handed him the bottle, the ambassador settled himself in an upholstered armchair and looked at him expectantly.

"I don't think you want to know all of it, sir," Castillo said.

"Tell me what you think you can," Silvio said.

"Well, sir, the President was waiting for the Globe-master at Biloxi with a finding he had just made. . . ."

". . . And that's about it, sir," Castillo concluded twenty minutes later.

Silvio, obviously considering what he had heard, didn't reply for a moment.

"My Latin blood took over for a moment," he said. "The first thing I thought was sympathy for Betsy Masterson and Ambassador Lorimer. To learn that your brother and your son was not only involved in that slimy oil-for-food business, but—indirectly, perhaps, but certainly—responsible for the murder of your husband and son. And the murder of a very nice young Marine. And the wounding of . . ."

He stopped and looked at Castillo. "I'll understand if you'd rather not answer this. Is Dr. Lorimer on your list you intend to 'render harmless'?"

"What I intend to do with him, sir, is take him to the States. Alive."

Silvio nodded.

"I'm sure he could be a cornucopia of interesting information," he said. "But that won't keep Ambassador Lorimer and Betsy from having to learn what a despicable sonofabitch he is, will it?"

"Sir, I'm ashamed to say I never even thought about

that before. What I want Lorimer to do is point me in the direction of those who murdered Mr. Masterson. They're the ones I have been ordered to render harmless. Both Santini and Darby tell me the most likely scenario once I get him to the States is for him to be taken into the Witness Protection Program, which is run by the U.S. Marshal's service, in exchange for his cooperation."

Silvio grunted. "And if he doesn't choose to cooperate?"

"I think he will, sir. He knows that people are looking for him. And he'll understand, I think, that if we can find him, the people trying to find him to kill him—torture and kill him—can also find him. And I've had the fey notion that one thing I could tell him, to get him to cooperate, would be to threaten to take him back to Paris and turn him loose on the Place de la Concorde."

"After making sure *Le Monde, Le Figaro,* and *L'Humanité* are informed that the missing UN diplomat can be found there? I don't think that's a fey notion at all; that makes a good deal of sense."

"I didn't think about telling the newspapers," Castillo admitted.

"Is there anything I can do to help, Charley?"

"Would you be willing to call Ambassador McGrory and tell him the reason I didn't go to see him?"

"He wanted to see you?"

"He doesn't know what Yung is really doing in Montevideo . . ."

"And therefore feels he has the right to know what Yung is doing? Especially with you? What the telephone call from Secretary Cohen was really about?"

"Yes, sir. He told Yung if I went to Yung without going through the embassy first to tell me he wanted to see me immediately. I don't think he has to know about the finding. I'd like to leave him in a position where he can truthfully say he knew nothing about this. Either what I'm going to do, or what Yung has been doing."

"I understand. I'll call him as soon as I get back to the embassy."

"Thank you."

"He's going to be curious—from his standpoint, he has a right to know—what Yung's role in what you're going to do is going to be. Or, past tense, was. Can I tell him that after you're gone?"

"Yung's not going to have a role in what I'm going to do."

"Okay," Silvio responded. "That answers that, doesn't it?"

What's that look on Silvio's face mean?

That he doesn't believe Yung won't be involved?

That he's surprised that he won't be?

That he doesn't like me keeping McGrory, a fellow ambassador, in the dark, to pick up the pieces after I screw up?

"Sir . . . there was a look on your face. Did something I said make you uncomfortable?"

"I guess I don't have the poker face good diplomats are supposed to have," Silvio replied. "And I certainly have no expertise in your area. But I was surprised that you're not going to use Yung and then take him out of the country when you leave."

"Why?"

"Well, for one thing, won't his position with Ambassador McGrory be compromised? McGrory will soon learn that Yung wasn't what he believed him to be. And since you're not going to tell him that you're operating with the authority of a Presidential Finding, I'm sure he'll go to the State Department with that. I would, in his shoes. Absent a Presidential Finding, an ambassador is responsible for anything any government agency is doing in his country. And has veto power over any action proposed. He's not even going to know about this until it's over. He's going to be more than a little annoyed."

"Yes, sir. I know. What I'm trying to do is leave the ambassador in a position where he truthfully can deny any knowledge of what I plan to do. Or did."

"I understand. What I did was presume that you would take Yung with you, taking advantage of his expertise, and then take him out of the country when you left. And that, once your mission was accomplished, the secretary would tell Ambassador McGrory there were reasons for what had happened, and that she had decided it was best that he not be cognizant of those reasons. He wouldn't like it, but he would understand."

"And if I don't take Yung with me, and Yung obeys my orders to tell McGrory nothing—I threatened him with the felony provisions of violating Top Secret–Presidential material, so I think he would keep his mouth shut—McGrory would blow his top?"

"And a number of senior officials in the State Department who have no legitimate reason to know, would know that something had gone on in Uruguay . . ."

"And be curious and ask questions that shouldn't be asked," Castillo finished for him. "Which questions

would come to—be leaked to—the *Washington Post* and
the *New York Times* and other President-haters."

Silvio nodded.

"With all the ramifications of that," Castillo added.

"I'm sure you've thought of the risks involved,
Charley. I'm not trying to tell you your business."

"The truth is I didn't think about it all," Castillo confessed. "Mr. Ambassador, you just kept me from making
a stupid mistake. A serious mistake. Thank you." Then
he blurted, "You know what Ambassador Montvale said
about me?"

Silvio shook his head.

"Montvale said that I am someone 'who was given
more authority than he clearly will be able to handle.' It
looks like he's right on the money, doesn't it?"

"From what I've seen, Charley, you handle the authority you've been given very well."

"I'm so drunk with my authority that it never even
entered my mind to ask you what you thought about
what I'm going to do. Which means I just about blew
the investigation into the oil-for-food scandal out of the
water, and embarrassed the President personally. That
doesn't strike me as handling my authority well."

Silvio studied Castillo for a long moment, then asked,
"How much sleep have you had in the past few days?"

"It shows, huh?"

"It shows. If you really want my advice, get yourself
some rest."

Castillo considered that, took a sip of his beer, then
asked, "Can you recommend a quiet hotel near the airport in Montevideo?"

"As a matter of fact, I can. The airport's in Carrasco. There's a really nice hotel in Carrasco. The Belmont House. A little stiff on the pocketbook. But I was thinking you might get some rest today."

"So was I, sir. You think I could get a couple of rooms there for tonight? For two days? How would I get the number to call? I really don't want a record of me booking it through American Express."

Ambassador Silvio reached into the pocket of his frayed blue jeans, took out his telephone, and punched the appropriate buttons.

"Juan Manuel Silvio here," he said a moment later. "Please tell me that you'll be able to accommodate two friends of mine—separate rooms—for tonight and to-morrow night."

Thirty seconds later, he returned the cellular to his blue jeans.

"Done."

"Thank you very much."

"My pleasure. Anything else I can do?"

"Let me see if I can at least do this by myself," Castillo said, and took out his cellular and punched the appropriate buttons.

"I'm glad I caught you, Yung," he began.

"I'd offer to drive you to the airport," Ambassador Silvio said, "but I don't think that would be a very good idea inasmuch as I suspect there's a good many people in uniforms looking for a man in a Harvard sweatshirt and blue jeans."

Castillo smiled at him and chuckled.

"I meant what I said before about you keeping me from making a royal ass of myself, and more important, making the President look like one. *Muchas gracias, amigo*."

Silvio made a deprecating gesture with his hand.

"What time's your plane?" he asked. "Or are you taking the Lear? Or shouldn't I ask?"

"You can ask me anything you want to," Castillo said. "And I'll tell you everything I think I can."

"Okay. I will. How are things going so far? Just generally, if details may be inappropriate."

"The first thing that can go wrong with this operation is that when I get to Jorge Newbery at five o'clock, a helicopter I borrowed won't be there. Or it will be there and the man in it will shoot me. Or if it's there and he doesn't shoot me, it will be equipped with a pressure-sensitive detonator and a couple of pounds of Semtex, which will go bang when I pass through one thousand feet. Or if that doesn't happen, the engine will quit when I am equidistant over the Rio Plate between Jorge Newbery and Corrasco. Aside from that, everything's going swimmingly."

Silvio shook his head.

"That's today. The list of what can go wrong tomorrow is a little longer," Castillo said.

"You will be in my prayers, Charley," Silvio said softly.

Castillo nodded at him.

"I'd love another beer, but I'm driving," Charley said. "But there's no reason you can't."

[FOUR]
Belmont House
6512 Avenue Rivera Carrasco
Carrasco, Montevideo
República Oriental del Uruguay
1925 29 July 2005

"Nice place," Castillo said as they stood at the reception desk of the small, luxurious hotel. "Looks more like a club than a hotel."

"Fidel Castro thinks so," El Coronel Alfredro Munz (Retired) said with a smile. "This is where he always stays when he's in Uruguay."

"If you would like a drink, gentlemen," the desk clerk said as he returned Castillo's passport and American Express card and Munz's National Identity Card and handed them keys to their rooms, "I'll have the bellman take your bags to your rooms."

He gestured toward the interior of the building. Castillo saw a small, wood-paneled bar with leather-upholstered chairs at small tables.

"I think that's a splendid idea," Castillo said. "I'm expecting a visitor at seven-thirty. A Mr. Yung. Would you point him toward us, please?"

"Certainly, sir."

Castillo walked into the bar and sat at one of the tables. Munz followed him but did not sit down.

"Will I be in the way, Karl?" Munz asked.

"Does 'in for a penny, in for a pound' mean the same thing in Spanish that it does in English?"

"Only to someone who speaks English," Munz said.

"And we both do," Castillo said. "Sit down, Alfredo."

A young waiter in a white jacket appeared.

"Do you have Famous Grouse?" Castillo asked.

"Yes, sir."

"A double, please. Water and ice on the side."

"That sounds good," Munz said.

"Aren't you taking a chance, Karl?" Munz asked when the waiter had gone to fill their order.

"That I'll really get Famous Grouse, you mean?" Castillo asked innocently. "Instead of some locally distilled copy thereof?"

"You know what I mean," Munz said.

"I've learned that every once in a while, you have to take a chance," Castillo said. "I'm taking one on you not to interfere with this operation by either telling Alex about it until it's over or choking the canary before he can sing."

"When I went to work for Alex—"

"You mean full-time? After you were retired, in other words?"

Munz's face tightened. "When I was with SIDE I never gave Alex any information that in any way betrayed my duties or my country."

"Okay."

"I told Alex, before I went to work for him, that there were certain things I would not do," Munz said. "'Choking canaries,' as you put it, was among the things he understood I would not do."

"I'm sure Howard Kennedy made a deal very similar to yours," Castillo said. "But what I was wondering about, before I decided on 'in for a penny, in for a pound,' was whether or not the things you would not do included giving him information that might see my canary choked by somebody else."

"If you feel that way, why did you agree to my coming with you?" Munz asked icily.

"I agreed to your coming along *after* I decided that you're not the sort of man who could look at himself in the mirror after deciding that it would be morally justifiable to arrange for a canary to be choked, providing someone else did the choking."

Munz looked at him coldly but didn't reply.

"And because Alex was right," Castillo went on. "I think you're going to be useful. We're back to having to take a chance every once in a while."

"Like flying a single-engine helicopter across the River Plate? That was taking a chance, wasn't it? What if the engine had failed?"

"We would have drowned," Castillo said. "Unless you're a much better swimmer than I am."

Munz shook his head.

"The seats—like those on airliners—are flotation devices," Castillo said. "We might have had to float around in the river for a while, but I filed a flight plan, and if we hadn't showed up on time, they would have started looking for us. I don't like to take *foolish* chances, Alfredo, and don't."

The waiter appeared with a tray holding a bottle of Famous Grouse, glasses, a silver ice bucket, a silver water pitcher, and a pair of tongs. He was pouring whiskey into the glasses when Special Agent David William Yung, Jr., came into the bar. He was visibly surprised to see Alfredo Munz.

"Right on time," Castillo said, half-standing to offer Yung his hand. "You two know each other, right?"

"How are you, Colonel?"

"Mr. Yung," Munz said.

"I'm sure you're both wondering what happens next," Castillo said.

Their eyes reflected their interest.

"I'm going to have at least one more of these," Castillo said, raising his glass and taking a healthy swallow, "have some dinner, and go to bed." He paused and added, "A very wise friend pointed out to me that people who haven't had much sleep tend to make bad decisions. I haven't had much sleep, and I can't afford to make any more sloppy, much less bad, decisions. So just a question or two, Yung. What do you hear about visiting friends from Montevideo?"

"They'll be on the first Busquebus from BA. It gets here at about ten-thirty."

"And you found accommodations for them?"

"Yes, sir."

"You have those maps I asked you for?"

"Yes, sir."

"Are you going to have any trouble waking up in time to pick up Munz and me here at the hotel at, say, seven o'clock in the morning?"

"I'll be here, sir."

"Where are we going?" Munz said. "Can I ask?"

"Generally speaking, we are going to reconnoiter the

target. I'll be more specific in the morning." He paused. "I wonder where the restaurant is?"

"Right next to us," Munz said. "But it doesn't open until eight. In half an hour."

"Well, that'll give me time to finish this drink and have another," Castillo said.

He saw how they were both looking at him.

"What I'm doing now is running on my reserves. When I'm doing that, I can't get to sleep unless I dilute the adrenaline, or whatever the hell it is, with substantial quantities of alcohol."

"I understand," Munz said.

"Mr. Castillo, can I speak to you privately for a moment?" Yung asked.

"It won't wait until the morning? I wasn't kidding. I'm in no shape to make decisions."

"It won't take a moment, sir."

"Alfredo, order me another one, please. I will be back directly," Castillo said and stood up.

He followed Yung out of the bar and through the lobby to the street.

"Okay, what?" Castillo asked.

"I know we got off on the wrong foot, Mr. Castillo— my fault . . ."

"Water over the dam," Castillo said.

"And I just wanted to say I'm grateful you're not cutting me out of this. I thought, when you went back to Buenos Aires this morning, that's what was going to happen. So thank you. I'll do my damnedest."

Castillo thought, unkindly:

Jesus H. Christ! He's acting like a high school kid, blub-

bering his gratitude to the coach for letting him back on the team after he got caught smoking in the boys' room. He thinks what's going to happen is some kind of a game.

So how do I handle this?

Castillo smiled at Special Agent Yung, then punched him on the shoulder.

"I'm glad you're going to be on the team, Yung," he said, hoping he sounded far more sincere than was the case.

XIX

[ONE]
Estancia Shangri-La
Tacuarembó Province
República Oriental del Uruguay
0855 30 July 2005

Jean-Paul Bertrand, patron of Estancia Shangri-La, naked under his silk Sulka dressing gown, his bare feet in soft brown unborn calfskin loafers, carefully pushed open the French door from his bedroom to the interior courtyard of his home.

He was carrying a cup of tea in his left hand, and when it was raining—as it was now—the damned door stuck and the tea would spill. It didn't matter if he slopped tea on the tile floors, of course, but getting tea on the light blue dressing gown was really distressful.

He had managed—not without a good deal of effort—to teach the laundress how he liked his shirts—lightly starched—and his linen, and how she should carefully wash his silk socks in cold water. But dry cleaning was an entirely different matter. There was no dry-cleaning establishment worthy of the name in Tacuarembó, which meant that *all* his dry cleaning had to be taken to Punta del Este. The place there charged an arm and a leg to dry-clean something, but at least it was returned clean, in one piece, and usually of the same color.

There were several problems with that, too, however. For one thing, he did not think it wise to go to his condominium in Punta del Este. People might be looking for him to show up there. And even if he could go—in, say, six months—the stains he got on anything here would by then be permanent.

Therefore, he opened the door very carefully, and was pleased with his foresight and care. The damn door did stick, but he didn't spill any tea on his dressing gown.

He sighed. It was drizzling. And from the appearance of the sky, it was going to drizzle all day. That happened often in winter.

What it meant was that he would be a prisoner in the house at least for today and tomorrow, and probably longer than that. The paths in the interior courtyard garden were paved with tile, and if he wanted to, he could pace back and forth—like a prisoner being allowed to exercise—for as long as he wanted. But leaving the house was out of the question. Walking on the grass was like walking on a wet sponge. Jean-Paul had ruined more than one pair of shoes like that.

And where the grass ended, there was mud. The only way to move through the mud was to wear calf-high rubber boots. The rubber hurt his feet, ruined his silk socks, and made his feet smell. And too frequently the boots became stuck in the mud, which meant that when he tried to take a step, his foot came out of the boot and wound up in the mud past the ankle—if he didn't fall down on his face in the mud. Or worse, on his back.

Jean-Paul heard the helicopter a long time before he finally saw it. While helicopters were certainly not common, he seemed to see more and more of them, even way out here in the country. He had learned that some of them were owned by people who used them to commute between Montevideo—or even Buenos Aires—and their estancias. That was especially true in the winter, when the goddamn persistent drizzle turned the roads into impassable quagmires. And some were used to take hunters from Montevideo or Buenos Aires to the duck-shooting areas.

There was a lot of that, too. Well-to-do American and European hunters had discovered the wild fowl of Uruguay. He had even heard that the Vice President of the United States had shot Perdiz over dogs—whatever that meant—on an estancia owned by a Uruguayan lawyer not far from Shangri-La.

In the summer, there were frequent overflights of Shangri-La by helicopters taking people from Argentina and Brazil to Punta del Este. Jean-Paul had toyed with the idea of getting one for himself. Having one would solve the problem of getting back and forth to Punta del Este. It was a dreadfully long drive on narrow highways. And he now could easily afford one.

But a helicopter would draw attention to him, and it was a little too soon to be attracting attention. The helicopter, like a good many other things, would just have to wait until everyone forgot Jean-Paul Lorimer.

The sound of the helicopter grew louder and then—startling him—it suddenly appeared out of the drizzle, no more than several hundred feet in the air, and flashed overhead.

It was quickly gone, and then the sound of its engines and thrashing rotor blades grew dimmer and finally disappeared.

Jean-Paul Bertrand decided the pilot had somehow become lost and had flown close to the ground to find a road and reorient himself.

He tossed what was left of his tea onto a flower bed and went back into the house for a fresh cup.

[TWO]
Suite 735
Victoria Plaza Hotel
759 Plaza Independencia
Montevideo, Uruguay
1125 30 July 2005

Suite 735 was classified by the Radisson Victoria Plaza as a "hospitality" suite, intended for the use of businessmen who wished to entertain potential clients in privacy.

There was a bedroom with two king-sized beds, plus a large sitting room with a wet bar, a refrigerator, and a large table seating eight that was suitable for use as either a dining table or a conference table. An enormous Sony flat-screen television was mounted on one wall of the sitting room so that those sitting at the table could view sales presentations, HBO, or, for that matter, the XXX-rated video dramas that were available for a nominal fee.

When Castillo walked into the hospitality suite with Munz and Yung, there were ten people in the room: Colonel Jacob Torine; Special Agents Jack Britton and Tony Santini of the Secret Service; Special Agent Ricardo Solez of the Drug Enforcement Administration; Mr. Alex Darby, the commercial attaché of the U.S. embassy in Buenos Aires; Mr. Fernando Lopez; Sergeants First Class Robert Kensington and Seymour Kranz of Delta Force; Corporal Lester Bradley of the United States Marine Corps; and someone—a mild-looking man in his early thirties—Castillo had never seen before.

Castillo walked directly to Darby, took him by the arm, led him into the bathroom, closed the door, and somewhat indelicately demanded, "What the fuck is Bradley doing here? And who the fuck is the other guy?"

Darby made a time-out gesture with his hands, then went and opened the door.

"Bob, will you come in here a moment, please?"

The mild-looking man came into the bathroom and closed the door after him.

"Bob, this is Mr. Castillo," Darby said. "Charley, Bob—Robert—Howell."

"How do you do?" Bob Howell extended his hand.

Castillo did not reply; instead he looked questioningly at Darby.

"Bob is the cultural attaché of the U.S. embassy here in Montevideo," Darby said.

"The head spook, you mean?" Castillo asked.

Darby nodded. "Tell Mr. Castillo what you told me when you called yesterday, Bob."

Howell nodded.

"I received a telephone call on a secure line from Ambassador Montvale. . . ."

What? Castillo thought. *Jesus Christ! Is that sonofabitch Montvale trying to micromanage me?*

"He first informed me that what he was to tell me was classified Top Secret–Presidential," Howell said, "and that no one in the embassy here was authorized access, including the ambassador. Then he told me he had reason to believe you were in Buenos Aires. I was to make contact with you immediately—he suggested Mr. Darby would probably know how to do that—and place myself and my assets at your absolute disposal." He paused. "So I called Alex."

"What else did Montvale have to say?"

"That's it, sir."

"He didn't tell you to check back with him? Let him know how things were going?"

Howell shook his head. "Nothing like that."

"And how much did you tell Mr. Howell, Alex?" Castillo asked.

"Only that I would be here this morning, and we would need a secure, discreet place to meet with maybe a dozen people."

"So I arranged for this, Mr. Castillo," Howell said. "I've used it before. I came earlier and swept it."

"And I asked him to stay to see what you wanted to do," Darby said. "This is his country, Charley. He knows it."

Castillo nodded.

"And what about Corporal Bradley? Did Montvale call him, too?"

"Can Howell hear this?"

Castillo thought that over for a moment, then offered Howell his hand.

"Welcome to Castillo's traveling circus, Mr. Howell," Castillo said. "This operation is authorized by a Presidential Finding. The classification is Top Secret–Presidential. What we're going to do is take a man, an American citizen named Jean-Paul Lorimer, who is here in Uruguay—more or less legally—as Jean-Paul Bertrand, on a Lebanese passport, from his estancia in Tacuarembó Province to the States. Whether or not he's enthusiastic about being repatriated, and without going through the usual immigration departure procedures. Getting the picture?"

Howell nodded. "Can I ask what this guy's done?"

"He has been a very naughty boy," Castillo said. "There are people who would like to see him dead. So we have to do this before they get to him."

"Okay," Howell said.

Castillo turned to Darby. "Okay, Alex. What about Bradley? What's he doing here?"

"Well, you wanted two hundred gallons of fuel for the helicopter," Darby said. "The question—this is before I got the call from Bob, you understand—was where to get it without having questions asked. That meant I'd have to get it in Argentina. Getting the fuel was no problem; getting it over here was. I knew you didn't want questions raised around the embassy, either. The embassy routinely trucks stuff over here, but I thought there might be questions asked if I tried to get on the Busquebus with four fifty-five-gallon barrels of jet fuel—plus the other stuff—in the back of a pickup truck.

"So that meant it would have to be driven over here. That's a long drive, all the way up to Gualeguaychú, across the bridge over the Río Uruguay into Uruguay, and then all the way down here. But I didn't think there would be many questions asked at the border if there were CD plates on the truck.

"Better yet, on a Yukon being driven by a Marine guard. They often make freight runs over here by road, so I knew they had a Yukon. So I called the gunny and told him you needed a quiet favor. I needed to take four drums of fuel and some other stuff to you in Uruguay. Would it fit in his Yukon and would he loan it—and a driver—to you?

"For some reason—maybe your charming personality—the gunny likes you. So he said, 'Sure, and for a driver, guess who's standing right here in my office, just back from the States?'"

"Corporal Lester Bradley, my stalwart Marine bodyguard," Castillo said, shaking his head.

"Who had already heard more than he should," Darby said. "I figured it was better to use him than go through the hassle—"

"Yeah, and what the hell, I just might need a body-guard," Castillo said. "Okay, let's go look at the home movies."

Sergeant Seymour Kranz was sitting at one side of the table. A laptop computer was in front of him. There was a rat's nest of cables attaching the computer to a small video camera, to a small color inkjet printer, and to the control panel of the Sony television on the wall.

"Please don't tell me that the Minicam batteries were dead, or that Yung forgot to take the cover off the lens," Castillo said.

"No, sir," Sergeant Seymour Kranz replied. "It worked better than I would have thought."

"And we're set up, right, so I can push the right button—which you will show me—and can make stills as we watch it?"

"Yes, sir," Kranz said, handing Castillo the control as Castillo sat down beside him. "And it's already loaded into the computer, so you can send it to Washington or Bragg if you want to."

"Let's hold off on that," Castillo said, and then: "Okay, guys. Here's the tape we shot of the target this morning. I could only make one low-level pass over the house itself, so I'm sure I missed something important. Make a note of what else you would like to see. When I drop Kranz off up there this afternoon, I'll have another shot at it." He paused. "Are we going to have to turn the lights off to see this? Well, let's find out."

The huge television screen began to show the

Uruguayan countryside, and then approached a city.

"That's the town of Tacuarembó. Not much of a town. The road to the estancia is at the top right of the picture. A quarter of a mile or so out of town, the paving stops. The roads, according to the maps, are 'improved,' which means anything from paved with stone to mud. We better count on mud; this is the rainy season."

"Now there's Estancia Shangri-La itself. Shot through the soup from about twenty-five hundred feet. I think— I hope—the stuff Yung shot when I made the low-level pass will give us a hell of a lot more detail. But you can see the house. Notice the interior courtyard, and the outbuildings."

"Now this is the road leading away from Shangri-La. In other words, farther away from Tacuarembó. What I was looking for was a place where we could set up Kranz's radio today. And tomorrow, where we could form up, and where I can leave the chopper while we're making the snatch. I went five miles or so in this direction and didn't find one. It all looked like swamp—maybe because of the rain—or it was full of rocks or trees, or both."

"So I went over here. *Much* closer to where we're going. You can't tell it from the air, but the maps show that it's a hundred or so feet higher than the buildings at the estancia. I'm sure I can get in there without being seen, and I don't think anyone will be able to tell the difference between a chopper flying overhead and me landing. And . . . where the hell is it? There it is. A field without rocks or trees, and it looks as if it drains pretty well."

"And here, a half mile, give or take, from the field is another 'improved' road. You have to go all the way back to Tacuarembó to get on it. But that's what, Bradley, you're going to have to take to get to it. You'll take Ricardo Solez with you. I don't know what the hell to do about the damned CD plates on the Yukon. . . ."

He stopped the video and looked at Darby.

"The Yukon now has Argentine plates on it, Charley," Alex Darby said. "And Argentine documents in the glove compartment."

"How less suspicious will the Argentine plates make it—?" Castillo heard a whirring noise, and realized the printer was already printing the stills.

"Not as unsuspicious as Uruguayan plates," Darby admitted. "But I just couldn't put my hands on Uruguayan plates on such short notice. And anyway, Uruguayan plates have the province on them. You can't tell where an Argentine vehicle is from from the plates."

"Okay," Castillo said. "Bradley, keep your mouth shut if you get stopped or anything. Ricardo's Texican, speaks pretty good *porteño* Spanish, can probably pass for a Uruguayan, and probably can get away with explaining you as his anemic cousin."

"Yes, sir."

"The way we're going to do this is that you're going to drive the Yukon to Tacuarembó as soon as this meeting breaks up. It's about two hundred twenty miles, so figure five hours, six if the roads are bad, but it's a real highway as far as Tacuarembó—I flew up it this morning—so we may get lucky. If you leave here by twelve-thirty, that should put you in the city by six-thirty at the latest. There will still be some light until about half past five. The priority, obviously, is to get the fuel and weapons up there safely, even if that takes you until midnight. Having said that, the sooner you get there, the better. Understand?"

"Yes, sir," Corporal Bradley said. "Highest road speed consistent with safety."

"And share the driving," Castillo ordered, and thought, *At least Ricardo will be driving half the time.* "Change over every hour."

"Yes, sir," Bradley almost barked.

You're being unfair. He may look like an escapee from the high school cheerleading squad, but he did get the Yukon here, didn't he? And the fuel and weapons past the border guards?

"In the best of all possible worlds," Castillo continued, "you would get to Tacuarembó at, say, quarter to five, even a little earlier. That would give you time to find the right road out of town, and then to find the field. You'll have a map. Getting from the road to the field is the problem. Reconnoiter it on foot, make sure, operative word *sure*, that you won't get the truck stuck in the mud. If we get really lucky and you can drive to the field, dump the fuel barrels and the pump. Not the weapons. Just the fuel and the pump. And then go find the Hotel Carlos Gardel in Tacuarembó. It shouldn't be hard; it's the only one. Decide for yourself if you want to take the chance of leaving the weapons in the Yukon or taking them and the other stuff into the hotel."

"You don't want us to just stay in the field overnight?" Solez asked.

"If some gaucho rides up on the fuel, he might figure someone left it there to fuel a tractor or something. He would get curious to find two guys in a Yukon."

"Okay."

"If you can't get the Yukon in there, we'll just have to land the chopper on the road in the morning and refuel it there."

"Why do you have to refuel it at all?" Britton asked. "I mean, you went up there and back—"

"Because I'm going directly to Jorge Newbery from Shangri-La," Castillo explained. "To do that I'm going to need a full load of fuel. Torine and Fernando are going to stay here—the Lear is—until they get word that we have Lorimer in the bag. We should know whether that worked by, say, twenty-one hundred tomorrow night. When—if—they get the word, they immediately go wheels-up to Jorge Newbery.

"The next morning—I'm going to have to wait until it's light to take off—I'm going to fly nap of the earth, under, I devoutly hope, any radar. I don't want to try that in the dark with the equipment on the Ranger."

He looked at Munz.

"Tell Alex that whoever sold him the avionics on that chopper screwed him. And that, in the spirit of friendship, I'll send him a list of what he should have."

"Somebody cheated Alex?" Munz said. "That wasn't smart, was it?"

"Who's Alex?" Darby asked.

"You don't want to know," Castillo said.

"And if things don't go well, Charley?" Torine asked.

"We'll have to play that by ear," Castillo said. "Maybe stay one day and try it again. Or abort this operation and think of something else."

Torine nodded.

"If it works, and you go to Buenos Aires, check out of the Four Seasons."

"Check everybody out?" Torine asked.

"Britton, me, and you and Fernando," Castillo said. "Kranz and Kensington will have to stay here long enough to get the weapons, the gear, and the radios back to Buenos Aires. And then get with Darby and Santini and get it to the States through the embassy. So they'll need rooms for a day or two. Then they'll go back to Bragg commercial. Is getting them tickets going to be a problem, Alex?"

Darby shook his head.

"Good. Okay, Fernando and Torine will go to Jorge Newbery, check the weather, file a flight plan, etcetera, and be ready to go the minute I get there in the Ranger with Lorimer and Yung and Munz. That's where you come in, *mi coronel*—Alex said you'd be helpful—"

"Who the hell is Alex?" Darby asked again. Castillo ignored the question.

"If I'm able to reason with Lorimer," he went on, "that is, convince him the only way he's going to stay alive is by going with me, fine. He may even have his American and UN passports in his safe. If he gives me trouble, if I have to put him to sleep—Yung, a man of many unexpected talents, tells me he'll have no trouble getting into his safe—I think we can count on his Lebanese passport for sure. But if he is knocked out, how do we get him through immigration and into the Lear?"

"I can arrange that," Munz said. "No problem."

"And I just come back to Montevideo, right?" Yung asked.

"No. You're going to the States with us," Castillo said.

"What about my investigation, my files? I'd really like to stay here."

"This is not open for debate, Yung," Castillo said. "You're going with us. Your cover as just one more FBI agent will be blown with the ambassador the moment he hears what happened. So this afternoon, pack a bag with enough clothes for a couple of days and give it to Fernando. A small bag."

"What the hell happens to my files?"

"You are tenacious, aren't you?" Castillo said sharply. "But that is, in fact, a good question. Mr. Howell, this afternoon—when you go with him to his apartment—Mr. Yung is going to give you some files, which, as of this moment, are classified Top Secret–Presidential. You will find someplace to keep them until I decide how to get them to the States. Maybe in the hands of a diplomatic courier."

"And what happens to my files in the States?"

"Whatever the President decides to do with them."

"Which means they disappear down the black hole of diplomacy?"

"I just changed my mind," Castillo said. "Colonel Torine, will you go with Howell and Yung to Yung's apartment and take possession of Yung's files? That way, we can take them home with us."

Torine gave him a thumbs-up signal.

Castillo nodded. "The subject is closed, Yung. You understand?"

Yung exhaled in resigned disgust.

"Okay," Castillo said. "Now to the assault team. Those two"—he pointed to Kranz and Kensington—"have some very rudimentary skills in that area. So they'll be on it. But that means they won't be on the radios. You can set them up, can't you, so all someone has to do is turn them on and talk?"

"No problem, sir," Sergeant Kensington said.

"One goes with us. That leaves the question of where to set up the other one. Here? Can you just aim the antenna out the window, the way you did in the Four Seasons?"

"I think so, sir. I'll have to try it."

"Okay, but if Miller, or anyone else in the States, tries to talk to you, it fails, right? I don't want anybody trying to micromanage this operation."

"Got it, sir," Kensington said.

"How big is the antenna?" Howell asked.

"A little larger than a satellite TV antenna," Kensington answered. "Eighteen, twenty inches in diameter."

"There's a backyard at my house," Howell said. "Fenced in. Would that work?"

"Where's your house?" Castillo asked.

"In Carrasco, not far from Yung's apartment."

"Okay, you are now our base station radio operator. Kensington will go with you, set it up, and show you how it works."

Both men nodded.

"Jack Britton, who knows how to operate a Car 4, and I know is pretty good at running around in the dark, gets suited up. Tony, you want to go?"

"Absolutely."

"I would like to volunteer, sir," Corporal Lester Bradley said. "I have never fired the Car 4, but I shot Expert at Parris Island with the M-16, and with the Beretta, and in Iraq I was the designated marksman of my fireteam. I used a bolt-action 7.62×51mm sniper's rifle for that, sir. Essentially a Remington Model 700 modified for Marine Corps use, sir."

"You were a sniper in Iraq?" Sergeant Kranz asked incredulously.

"We don't have snipers in the Corps, Sergeant. But the better shots are issued a sniper's rifle and are assigned as 'designated marksmen.'"

"We have a Remington, right?" Castillo asked.

"I do, sir," Kranz said.

"Well, Lester," Castillo said, "you're just the man I've been looking for. What you're going to do is take Sergeant Kranz's rifle, make yourself a suitably camouflaged firing/observation position . . . We have binoculars, too, right, Kranz?"

Kranz nodded. "And the night-vision goggles. The new ones, the really good ones."

"Make sure that Corporal Bradley knows how to use them," Castillo ordered. "He's going to guard the Ranger while we're at the house."

"Sir, since it's Sergeant Kranz's rifle," Bradley said, "maybe he'd prefer to guard the helicopter, and I could go on the assault team."

"In special operations, Bradley," Castillo said, very seriously, "we operate on the principle of the round peg in the round hole, not personal desire. Sergeant Kranz is not the best man to guard the chopper. You are."

"Aye, aye, sir," Bradley responded with not much enthusiasm.

"Ricardo, you want to go with us?" Castillo asked. "I realize you haven't had much training in things like this."

Please say no. If anything goes wrong, you'll be the first one to take a hit. And I really don't want to have to tell Abuela about that. That would be even worse than having to tell your father.

"Nothing like this, I suppose," the young DEA agent said. "But I have had training."

"The DEA school . . . is there such a thing?"

"Yeah, and that's tough. But what I meant was that when I was at A and M, in the Corps, I went through the Ranger Course at Benning and Hurlburt Field one summer. Don Fernando can tell you that's rough. Yeah. I really want to go. Don't worry about me."

"Okay. You're on."

He glanced at Fernando and saw that Fernando's eyes were on him. Castillo shrugged slightly. Fernando tipped his head slightly.

He's thinking exactly what I'm thinking.

It's one of those things. It has to be.

"That makes seven on your assault team, right?" Darby asked. "Plus Bradley at the helicopter. That's eight. You have enough black suits, weapons, night goggles, etcetera?"

"Where do you get eight?"

Darby ticked them off on his fingers: "Kranz, Kensington, Yung, Britton, Santini, Solez, Munz, and you." He held his hands up, with five fingers on his left hand and three on his right extended. "That's eight. When I took those bags from Fort Bragg out to the house, I counted equipment for six-shooters."

"That's the trouble with you agency people," Castillo said, with a smile. "You assemble a few facts and immediately draw the wrong conclusion. Or usually, conclusions, plural."

Darby rearranged his extended hands and gave him the finger. Twice.

"What Colonel Munz and you and I are going to do, Alex, is drive sedately up to the door of Shangri-La in a car."

"You're just going to drive up in a car? Where, question one, is the car coming from?"

"Howell will rent it for us this afternoon from Hertz at the airport. He will use his credit card, thus keeping your name off the books."

"I have a car that you can use, Mr. Castillo," Howell said. "A five-year-old, powder blue Peugeot."

"Better yet," Castillo said, "things are going so well, I'm waiting for that famous other shoe to drop. Would your car be the sort of car used by Uruguayan bureau-crats on official business, Mr. Howell?"

Howell nodded. "That's why I bought what I did, actually."

"Alex, you will drive Mr. Howell's five-year-old, pow-der blue Peugeot to Tacuarembó early tomorrow after-noon; there's no sense you being there any sooner than, say, half past five or six. . . ."

"And when I get there, then what?"

"Go to the Hotel Carlos Gardel. If it doesn't have a bar, it has to have a place you can have a cup of coffee. Munz and I will meet you there, say, at eight or eight-thirty. We will be wearing suits and trying to look as much as possible like Uruguayan bureaucrats. Don't rec-ognize us. Finish your coffee and leave. Go to the car. We'll find it. It's powder blue, right? That should make it easy to find."

"And then?"

"We drive out to Shangri-La, quickly flash our badges to whoever answers the door. Eventually, we will get to Mr. Bertrand, who will be informed that there seems to be some irregularity with his passport, and might we have a look at it?

"If this goes as I hope it will, Lorimer will open his safe—saving Yung the difficulty of blowing it open—to get either his Lebanese passport or money to bribe us with, probably both. Once the safe is open, Munz will put handcuffs on him, and I will begin to explain to him what happens next, and the wisdom of his cooperating. Once we get that far, you, who will have been waiting patiently outside, will drive the powder blue car back to Montevideo.

"Anybody around, seeing the car leaving, will presume we're in it," Castillo went on. "As soon as they see you leave, while Britton, Yung, and Solez are cutting the telephone line and/or any cables leading to any transmitter antennas, Kranz and Kensington will come into the house, put plastic cuffs on anybody in the house, and make sure there's nobody lurking around who can cause trouble. They will then go outside to make sure there are no visitors, or that we're warned if there are. Ricardo, Britton, and Yung, who should be in the house by then, will herd everyone we've cuffed into a bedroom, where they will be attached to the furniture with more plastic cuffs.

"When that's been done, leaving Ricardo to watch those cuffed, Britton and Yung will start to search the house for anything interesting that Lorimer didn't choose to put in the safe.

"That's in Munz's area of expertise, too, so he'll help with that. I'll sit on Lorimer.

"Just before dawn, we take Lorimer out of the house and head for the helicopter. By the time we get there, there will be enough light to take off. The way I figure it, we'll have anywhere from a half hour to an hour before those cuffed manage to get loose, or someone comes in to make breakfast, or whatever, and discover Jean-Paul has been kidnapped by—this is important—Spanish-speaking people, two of whom look like cops/businessmen/bureaucrats and the rest like those people one sees in thriller movies. Those balaclava masks really scare people."

Darby thought the scenario over carefully.

"You don't need permission to speak, you know, Alex," Castillo said after a very long thirty seconds.

"Jesus, Charley," Darby said, smiling, "this might just work."

"And nobody gets hurt," Castillo said. "I want everybody to keep that in mind. This is not an assault. The only man at Lorimer's estancia who deserves to die is Lorimer, and unfortunately I need the sonofabitch alive. The primary purpose of the black suits and the balaclava masks and all the weapons is to scare everybody into behaving while we're there. And the masks will make everybody hard to describe to the local gendarmes when they finally show up and start asking questions."

"At what time do you want me to chauffeur you and Munz out there?" Darby asked.

"Probably about nine o'clock. At that time, there probably won't be more than two or three servants in the house. Plus, maybe, his tootsie. Anyway, Kranz and Kensington will have kept an eye on the place for at least an hour before we get there, and if it doesn't look right, one or the other of them will wave us off at the driveway.

"If that happens, we may wait until later. Midnight, for example, and forget the bureaucratic business, just drive up in the Yukon, bust in, grab Lorimer, bust open the safe, and get the hell out of there. We can hide in the field where the chopper is. Or maybe just get in the chopper and go."

"I think the first scenario will work," Darby said.

"Jesus, I hope so," Castillo said. "Okay, we'll get to the rest of the tape. Make notes of what we're missing, and I'll try to get what I missed this afternoon."

He pushed a button on the control and the videotape began to play.

"This is where we followed the road Bradley's going to use into Tacuarembó. I didn't see anything extraordinary about it, but take a real good look, Bradley."

"Okay. Here we are over the field again. I didn't see one, but there has to be a road, a path, into it. Look for it, Bradley. Don't just drive over the field. We can't afford to have the Yukon stuck in the middle of the field when the sun comes up. I'm glad I thought of that. If Bradley gets the Yukon stuck, he will be shot, and his carcass left in the Yukon, which will be then torched by Ricardo. Ricardo, make sure that Kranz gives you a couple of thermite grenades and shows you how to use them before you drive up there. One for the engine compartment, the other on one of the barrels of fuel."

"I've seen a thermite grenade before," Solez said.

"Okay, here we are. I'm about to make the low-level pass over the main house at Shangri-La."

• • •

"Jesus, there's somebody in the interior courtyard."

He stopped the tape.

"Gentlemen, there is Mr. Jean-Paul Bertrand, aka Lorimer. Apparently having a wake-me-up cup of coffee in his garden."

[THREE]
Estancia Shangri-La
Tacuarembó Province
República Oriental del Uruguay
2110 31 July 2005

Jean-Paul Bertrand was not only dining alone, but he had prepared the meal himself.

There were several reasons. For one, he was bored. For another, his cook's idea of a gourmet meal was to throw something—usually beef, sometimes pork, and less often chicken—on the wood-fired *parrilla* grill, char it, and then serve it with either mashed potatoes or what they called here *papas fritas*, and a sliced tomato salad. Wrapping a potato in aluminum foil and baking it apparently overtaxed her culinary skills.

There were some marvelous chefs in Uruguay, but not in Tacuarembó. And, of course, he had to stay in Tacuarembó for the time being. Jean-Paul had come to believe that the northern Italian kitchen—which is what the good restaurants in Montevideo and Punta del Este served—was, in fact, as hard as this was to accept, actually a bit superior to that of the French.

Tonight, with Anna-Maria, the cook, watching—and, he dared hope, perhaps learning—he had prepared

Châteaubriand. First, after putting on a chef's apron, he had gotten a knife really sharp and then trimmed all the fat and sinew from a *lomo*. A *lomo* was the entire tenderloin of beef. A tenderloin that would cost forty—or more—euros in Paris was available here as a *lomo* for the equivalent of nine or ten. And it was magnificent beef. Then he first cut a ten-inch section from it and set it aside.

The remainder of the tenderloin he carefully cut into bite-sized pieces. Tomorrow, or the day after, he would make *boeuf bourguignonne* with the remaining meat.

He rubbed the ten-inch length of tenderloin with a garlic clove, salt, and pepper, and set it aside while he prepared the vegetables. The green beans were marvelous as is, but the carrots were the size of his wrist and he had to slice them into finger-sized pieces before he could use them. He put the steamer on so that he could steam the beans, the potatoes, a half dozen stalks of celery, and a dozen large white mushrooms.

He told Anna-Maria to open a bottle of the cabernet sauvignon. Just open it. Not decant it. And leave it here in the kitchen for the time being.

Then he sliced another dozen and a half white mushrooms very thin, vertically, and then sautéed them in a pan until they were about half cooked. Then he added a tablespoon of flour and stirred it into the mushrooms until it was no longer visible. Next came a cup of the very good local merlot. With the gas as low as it would go, he stirred patiently until the sauce formed. Only then did he add a touch of garlic and basil and salt and pepper.

He went to the *parrilla* outside the kitchen and carefully arranged the coals under the grill, testing to see if he had the proper heat with his hand. When he was satisfied, he laid the tenderloin on the hot steel grid.

When he went back in the kitchen, the cabernet sauvignon was on the table, with a glass. He poured and took an appreciative sip.

Maria came into the kitchen from the outside. Jean-Paul could tell from the young face of his current companion in the bed that she was afraid he was angry with her. He had told her he wanted to read while dining, and she should find something to eat by herself. The truth was, not only did her manners leave a good deal to be desired, but setting a fine meal before her made him think of the phrase, "Casting pearls before swine." If it wasn't charred black on the outside and raw inside, Maria eyed it with great suspicion and only ate whatever it was to please him.

Maria and Anna-Maria watched as he examined the mushroom mixture, and then added a half cup more of the merlot, and loaded the vegetables into the steamer. He had then gone back to the *parrilla* and turned the tenderloin.

Then he went back into the kitchen, had another sip of the cabernet, and told Anna-Maria to set the table for one, with the candles in the candelabra lit. Then he told Maria to go to his bedroom and to bring his reading glasses and the book with the red jacket that was on the bedside table, and put both on the dining room table.

Then he went back to the *parrilla* again, turned the tenderloin again—it was browning nicely—and went back into the kitchen. The sauce was now *almost* of the right consistency—the merlot had been reduced just enough—so he turned off the gas under it.

Then he tested the vegetables in the steamer with a fork, and with the same result. Another five minutes and everything would be done at just about the same time. He looked at his watch, then sipped the cabernet until the five minutes had passed.

Then he took a meat thermometer from a drawer and went to the *parrilla*. He turned the tenderloin again, then inserted the meat thermometer into it. The dial showed 140 degrees Fahrenheit.

He then removed the tenderloin from the grill to a plate and took it back in the kitchen. There he rolled it onto a large oblong platter, and then placed the first plate over it.

He tested the mushroom sauce one last time, added a touch of salt, and then closed the lid again.

Then he went to the steamer and carefully removed half of the vegetables, arranging them neatly to one side of the platter.

He ran the knife against the steel again until it felt right, then took the tenderloin and put it on a cutting board. He sliced the entire piece into pinkie-finger-thick slices, and then skillfully lifted them all at once and laid them in the center of the platter.

He used the knife blade to carefully push the vegetables already on the platter against the tenderloin. Then he arranged the vegetables remaining in the steamer against the other side of the tenderloin. When that was done, he placed the knife blade on the tenderloin and pushed, so that the slices were displaced and lying on one another.

Then he went to the mushroom sauce pan, picked it up, and dribbled an inch-wide path of sauce on top of the slices.

"Anna-Maria," he announced. "This is called a Châteaubriand."

"*Sí, señor.*"

"Put this sauce in a sauce bowl," he said. "And then serve the Châteaubriand. I will take the wine and glass with me."

"*Sí, señor.*"

"Do you want me to come sit with you?" Maria asked.

"No, dear. Thank you just the same. Why don't you have a bath? I'll be in shortly."

He picked up the bottle of cabernet sauvignon and his glass and went into the dining room and sat down at the table.

Anna-Maria came in with the platter.

"I will need some bread, please. The hard-crusted rolls. And butter. And, of course, salt and pepper. And don't forget the sauce."

When Anna-Maria had delivered everything, he checked to see that everything he needed was present.

"Thank you, Anna-Maria," he said. "You may go. I do not wish to be disturbed."

"*Sí, señor,*" Anna-Maria said, and left the dining room.

Three minutes later, she was back.

Jean-Paul was annoyed. He had told her he did not wish to be disturbed, and he had had just barely time enough to move a couple of slices of the beef—and it looked and smelled marvelous—to his plate, and here she was, back.

"I told you, Anna-Maria, that I didn't wish to be disturbed."

"Excuse me, señor. But there are two men here . . . officials."

"Officials? What kind of officials?"

"Officials, señor. From the government. They have badges."

What the hell?

"And they wish to see you, señor."

Jean-Paul rose angrily from the table, threw his napkin on it, and marched to the front door.

Two men were standing there.

"May I help you, gentlemen?"

"Are you Señor Jean-Paul Bertrand?"

"Yes, I am. And who are you?"

"I am Assistant Chief Inspector Muller of the Immigration Service," the larger of the two said. "And this is Inspector O'Fallon."

He held out his credentials.

"We are very sorry to trouble you, señor," Chief Inspector Muller said. "And at this hour of the night. And we do apologize, sir."

"What is it?"

"Do you have your passport, Señor Bertrand?"

"Yes, of course I do."

"You're sure, señor?"

"Yes, of course I'm sure. Why do you ask?"

"Señor Bertrand, as you may know, our immigration records are now computerized."

"So I've heard."

"This afternoon, Señor Bertrand, according to the computer, you attempted to enter Uruguay on a Varig flight from Río de Janeiro."

"That's absurd!"

"The computer also says that you entered Uruguay some time ago, and have never left."

"That's true."

"What we suspect, Señor Bertrand, is that the other Señor Bertrand, who is being held in custody, is not really who he says he is. That his passport is either a forgery, or that he has somehow come into possession of your passport."

Assistant Chief Inspector Muller gave Jean-Paul Bertrand time to think this over, and then went on. "One or the other is true, Señor Bertrand. And the question can be simply answered. If you have your passport, then the other is a forgery. And the other Señor Bertrand will be dealt with accordingly. On the other hand, if your passport has somehow been . . . misplaced . . . It happens, señor. If it has been misplaced into the hands of the other Señor Bertrand, then he will be dealt with accordingly. I cannot believe that a gentleman of your reputation and standing would loan his passport—"

"I certainly would not!" Jean-Paul proclaimed righteously. "My passport is—or should be—in my safe. I'll get it for you."

"Thank you very much, señor."

"May I offer you a cup of coffee, something to drink, while I get it?"

"No, thank you, señor," Inspector O'Fallon said. "We're on duty."

"I'll be right with you," Jean-Paul Bertrand said. "My safe is in my office, in the rear of the house."

"Thank you, señor," Assistant Chief Inspector Muller said.

"The sitting room is in here," Jean Paul said. "If you'll wait there? Are you sure I cannot offer you anything?"

"Thank you just the same, señor," Muller said.

The safe was bolted both to an interior wall and to the floor. Jean-Paul had learned that when he was looking for something in it, it was much easier just to sit on the floor than to bend over and try to look inside. He had done so now.

He had a hell of a time finding the damned passport, but finally did.

A forged passport, I understand. But one with my name on it? What's that all about?

Oh, of course. In case someone checks, there is a valid passport in the name of Jean-Paul Bertrand.

Oh, God, is this incident going to be in the newspapers?

He heard a sound, and looked over his shoulder.

The younger one, Inspector O'Fallon, was standing behind him.

What the hell is he doing in here?

"Inspector O'Fallon, isn't it?" Jean-Paul asked.

"No, not really," Castillo said, in English.

"I beg your pardon?"

"You know how it is, Lorimer. Sometimes people use other names. Will you hand me the passport and stand up, please?"

"What's going on here?"

Castillo snatched the passport from Lorimer's hand as he stepped over him and pushed the safe door open more widely.

Jean-Paul scurried backward on the floor and ran into a set of legs.

Then he felt himself being hauled to his feet.

"Put your hands behind you, please," the man who had said he was Assistant Chief Inspector Muller ordered.

Jean-Paul did as he was told.

He looked around his office.

Muller was doing something with his wrists.

Jean-Paul took a closer look at the face of the man who had said he was Inspector O'Fallon but had just now called him Lorimer, in American English.

But then something else caught his eye.

There was a face at the window, and it looked as if whoever stood there was trying to break the window with something.

The last thing Jean-Paul Lorimer, Ph.D., saw in this world, before two 9mm bullets struck him in the mouth and forehead, was the breaking glass of the window and an orange flash.

Castillo reacted to the sound of the breaking glass and the burst of submachine fire instinctively. He dropped to

the ground, scurried behind the desk, and reached for
the Beretta he was carrying in the small of his back.

What the fuck?

*This desk is going to be about as much protection against
a 9mm as a Kleenex.*

There was the sound of more firing outside. He recognized the characteristic chatter of a Car 4. More than
one Car 4. And then the sharper crack of a 7.62.

*Didn't I hear a 7.62 just before the goddamn subma-
chine gun went off?*

He saw a cord running across the floor to the desk.

If they can't see you, they can't shoot you.

Unless they spray the room with a submachine gun.

What the hell!

He jerked on the cord and a lamp on Lorimer's desk
crashed to the floor. But didn't go out.

Sonofabitch!

There was the sound of another 7.62mm round going
off, and of voices shouting something unintelligible, and
then several more bursts from Car 4s.

Castillo reeled in the lamp, finally found the switch,
and turned it off. The room was now dark.

Castillo got to his knees, then took a running dive
from behind the desk toward the corner. No one shot at
him. He found the wall with his hands and pushed himself into the corner. He waited for a moment to give his
eyes a chance to adjust to the darkness. To turn the lamp
off, he had had to find the switch, which was a push device in the bulb socket, which meant that he'd had the
light from a clear-glass sixty-watt bulb right in his eyes.

Finally, he could make out the outline of the windows, and raised the Beretta in both hands to aim at it.

"Alfredo?" he called.

"I'm hit," Munz called back. "I don't know how bad. I have Lorimer's brains all over me."

There was another burst of Car 4 fire, this one farther away.

And then Sergeant Kensington's voice. "Anybody alive in there?"

"Only the good guys," Castillo called back.

There was the sound of a door being kicked open. And then a hand holding a flashlight appeared in the door and the light swept the room.

Then Kensington came into the room with Corporal Lester Bradley on his heels, sniper rifle at the ready.

"Get that goddamn light out of my eyes," Castillo ordered. "There's a lamp on the floor behind the desk."

Kensington found the light and turned it on, and then walked to where Castillo was getting to his feet. He waited until Castillo was fully up, then said, "These cocksuckers, whoever the fuck they were, got past Kranz. Can you believe that?"

"Is he all right?"

"They garroted him, Major," Kensington said.

"Oh, shit!"

Castillo walked to the desk again, looked at the exploded head of Jean-Paul Lorimer, and then at the blood oozing from the chest of El Coronel Alfredo Munz, and said, "Oh, shit!" again.

[FOUR]
Estancia Shangri-La
Tacuarembó Province
República Oriental del Uruguay
2225 31 July 2005

"You're going to be all right, Colonel," Sergeant Robert Kensington said to Munz, who rested just about where he had fallen behind Lorimer's desk. "There's some muscle damage that's going to take some time to heal, and you're going to hurt like hell for a long time every time you move—for that matter, breathe. I can take the bullet out now, if you'd like."

"I think I'll wait until I get to a hospital," Munz said.

"Your call, Alfredo," Castillo said. "But how are you going to explain the wound? And if Kensington says he can get it out, he can."

"No offense, but that looks to me like a job for a surgeon."

"Kensington has removed more bullets and other projectiles than most surgeons," Castillo said. "Before he decided he'd rather shoot people than treat them for social disease, he was an A-Team medic. Which meant . . . what's that line, Kensington?"

"That I was 'qualified to perform any medical procedure other than opening the cranial cavity,' " Kensington quoted. "I can numb that, give you a happy pill, and clean it up and get the bullet out. It would be better for you than waiting—the sooner you clean up a wound like that, the better—and that'd keep you from answering questions at a hospital. But what are you going to tell your wife?"

"Lie, Alfredo," Castillo said. "Tell her you were shot by a jealous husband."

"What she's going to think is that I was cleaning my pistol and it went off, and I'm embarrassed," Munz said. "But I'd rather deal with that than answer official questions. How long will I be out?"

"You won't be out long, but you'll be in la-la land for a couple of hours."

"Okay, do it," Munz said.

"Well, let's get you to your feet and onto something flat where there's some light," Kensington said. He looked at Castillo, and between them they got Munz to his feet.

"There's a big table in the dining room that ought to work," Kensington said. "It looks like everybody got here just in time for dinner. There's a plate of good-looking roast beef on it. And a bottle of wine."

"Okay on the beef," Castillo said. "Nix on the wine. We have to figure out what to do next and get out of here."

"Major, who the fuck are these bad guys?" Kensington asked.

"I really don't know. Yung is searching the bodies to see what he can find out. I don't even know what happened."

"Well, they're pros, whoever they are. Maybe Russians? Krantz was no amateur, and they got him. With a fucking garrote. That means they had to (a) spot him, and (b) sneak up on him. A lot of people have tried that on Seymour and never got away with it."

"Spetsnaz?" Castillo said. "If this were anywhere in Europe, I'd say maybe, even probably. But here? I just don't know. We'll take the garrote and whatever else Yung comes up with and see if we can learn something."

When they got to the dining room, Kensington held Munz up while Castillo moved the Châteaubriand, the sauce pitcher, the bread tray, and the wine to a sideboard. Then he sat him down on the table.

"Tell me, physician," Munz said. "What would the effect of wine be on this happy pill you're about to give me?"

Kensington went to the sideboard and picked it up. "Cabernet sauvignon," he said. "There is a strong body of medical opinion which suggests this is indicated in a procedure of this nature. You want a glass?"

"Yes, please," Munz said.

Kensington poured wine in the glass and handed it to Munz.

"Take these with it," he said, putting two white gel capsules on the table. "And when you start to feel a little woozy—it usually takes about a minute—just lie down. I'm a little surprised you're not in pain."

"What makes you think I'm not?" Munz asked as he tossed the capsules into his mouth and then picked up the wineglass.

"You won't be out for long," Kensington said.

"What happened out there, physician?" Munz asked.

"The first thing I knew that anything was wrong was when I heard the Remington go off. And God forgive me, what I thought then was that the goddamn kid was playing with the rifle and it went off. So I ran around the side of the building to chew him a new asshole. And that's when I saw the two guys. One of them was on the ground and the other was pointing a Madsen at me—"

"A Madsen?" Castillo asked.

"Yeah. That mean something?"

"It might," Castillo said.

"And I had just decided, *Oh, shit, he's got me,* when another 7.62 round went off. Down he went. Two shots from the kid. Both in the head. The little sonofabitch can shoot. He saved my ass. And yours, too. The first one he popped was the guy who stuck his Madsen into the office window. Bradley told me he waited until he was sure what he was up to before he popped him."

"He was supposed to be guarding the goddamn chopper!" Castillo said.

"And aren't you glad, Major, that he didn't understand that order?" Kensington said. "And then things got a little exciting. There were six of them in all. Five at the house, and the one who garroted Kranz. Kranz managed to get his boot knife into him. When we found Kranz, that one died trying to escape."

"That wasn't smart, Kensington."

"Yeah, I know. But Seymour and I went way back, and I didn't think."

"I am starting to feel a little strange," Munz said.

"Let me help you lie down," Kensington said.

Kensington gently lifted Munz's eyelid and shined a small flashlight into it.

"Okay, he's out. He'll probably be out for thirty minutes. But he's a big sonofabitch, and I have no idea what his threshold of pain is, so he may start to wake up when I'm working on him. I want you to be prepared to hold him down—lie on top of him, whatever's necessary—if he starts to move. Okay?"

"Got it," Castillo said.

"And now, before I lay out my surgical instruments, you may help me scrub."

"How do I do that?"

Kensington handed him an aerosol can.

"Spray this crap all over my hands. It's advertised as better than a good scrub with surgical soap. It fucks up your hands, but what the hell?"

Castillo sprayed a foaming, pale orange substance over Kensington's hands from the aerosol can, and then watched as Kensington pulled on rubber gloves.

Then Kensington came up with a thin black plastic envelope. He tore it open. Inside was a small set of surgeon's tools.

"No offense, Major," Kensington said, "but if you feel yourself getting a little woozy when I start to cut, for Christ's sake, sit down on the floor and put your head between your knees. The last thing we need is you cracking your head open on the table. You have to get us the fuck out of here."

"No identification whatever," Special Agent David William Yung of the FBI reported to Castillo forty minutes later. "No labels in the clothing, and I'm almost sure they're manufactured locally, or at least available here, so there's nothing there. I fingerprinted the bodies, and took enough blood to do a good DNA. But a DNA is good only when you have something to compare it to. Sorry. They came in cars from Enterprise Rent-A-Car, the airport office. We can run those credit cards, but if these people are as professional as it looks, that'll be a dead end, too. Sorry."

"That's what Kensington said. They're pros. So what did we expect?"

"Four Caucasian, two black. I took pictures, of course, but . . ."

"Okay. Thanks."

"That's the bad news. The good news is an address book from the safe, and these." He wagged a dozen sheets of what looked like stock certificates.

"What are those?"

"These are the certificates of loan. Fifteen point seven million U.S. dollars' worth. Of course, since Lorimer didn't sign them, they can't be cashed, but it proves he has all the money in the banks. Maybe some bank officers can be talked into telling us what they know about Lorimer's activities."

"On the other hand, once they learn he's dead, they'll deny their existence, and they're fifteen point seven million ahead."

"Yeah," Yung agreed.

Corporal Lester Bradley, USMC, came into the kitchen.

"Sergeant Kensington said he's ready to mount up anytime you give the word, sir. The colonel is on his feet."

"Bradley, I owe you. You saved my tail and Colonel Munz's."

"Just doing my job, sir."

"Tell Sergeant Kensington to get the show on the road, Bradley."

"Yes, sir."

[FIVE]
The Oval Office
The White House
1600 Pennsylvania Avenue, NW
Washington, D.C.
1825 1 August 2005

The President of the United States was behind his desk. Across the room, Ambassador Charles W. Montvale was sitting next to Secretary of State Natalie Cohen on one of two facing couches. Secretary of Homeland Security Matthew Hall was on the other couch.

Major C. G. Castillo, who was in civilian clothing, was nonetheless standing before the President's desk at a position close to "At Ease."

Or, Secretary Hall thought, *like a kid standing in front of the headmaster's desk, waiting for the ax to fall.*

For the past ten minutes, Castillo had been delivering his report of what had happened since he had last seen the President in Biloxi, when the President had issued his Presidential Finding aboard Air Force One.

"And so we landed at MacDill, Mr. President," Castillo concluded, "where we turned over Sergeant Kranz's remains to Central Command, and then we came here, arriving at oh-nine-thirty. I took everyone involved to my apartment and told them nothing was to be said to anyone about anything until I had made my report, and that they were to remain there until I got back to them."

"Colonel Torine, too?" the President of the United States asked. "And your cousin, too? How did they respond to your placing them in what amounts to house arrest?"

"Colonel Torine knows how things are done, sir. I didn't *order* him. . . . And Fernando, my cousin, understands the situation, sir."

"And that's about it, Castillo?" the President asked.

"Yes, sir. Except to say, Mr. President, how deeply I regret the loss of Sergeant Kranz, and how deeply I regret having failed in the mission you assigned."

The President did not immediately respond. He looked into Castillo's eyes a moment as he considered that statement, then said, "How do you figure that you have failed, Castillo?"

"Well, sir, the bottom line is that I am no closer to finding the people who murdered Mr. Masterson and Sergeant Markham than I was before I went looking for Mr. Lorimer. Mr. Lorimer is now dead, and we'll never know what he might have told us if I hadn't botched his . . ."

"Repatriation?" the President offered.

"Yes, sir. And Sergeant Kranz is dead. I failed you, sir."

"Charles," the President said, "what about the long-term damage resulting from Major Castillo's failure? Just off the top of your head?"

"Mr. President, I don't see it as a failure," Secretary Hall spoke up.

"The director of national intelligence has the floor, Mr. Secretary. Pray let him continue," the President said, coldly.

"Actually, Mr. President, neither do I," Montvale said. "Actually, when I have a moment to think about it, quite the opposite."

"You heard him," the President pursued. "This man Lorimer is dead. We have no proof that Natalie can take to the UN that he was involved in the oil-for-food scandal or anything else. And Castillo himself admits that he's no closer to finding out who killed Masterson and the sergeant than he ever was. Isn't that failure?"

"Mr. President, if I may," Montvale said cautiously. "Let me point out what I think the major—and that small, valiant band of men he had with him—has accomplished."

"What would that be?"

"If we accept the premise that Mr. Lorimer was involved in something sordid, and the proof of that, I submit, is that he sequestered some sixteen million dollars . . ."

Montvale looked to Castillo for help.

"Fifteen point seven, sir," Castillo offered.

". . . Close enough for Washington. Some sixteen million U.S. dollars in Uruguay, and that parties unknown tracked him down to Uruguay and murdered him to keep him from talking. After they abducted Mrs. Masterson and later murdered her husband."

"So what, Charles?" the President demanded.

"I don't seem to be expressing myself very well, Mr. President," Montvale said. "Let me put it this way. These people, whoever they are, now know we're onto them. They have no idea what the major may have learned before he went to South America; they have no idea how much Lorimer may have told him before they were able to murder him. If they hoped to obtain the contents of Lorimer's safe, they failed. And they don't know what it did or did not contain, so they will presume the worst, and that it is now in our possession. Or, possibly worse, in the possession of parties unknown. They sent their assassins in to murder Lorimer, and what we, what the major and his band, gave them was six dead assassins and an empty safe. And now that we know we're onto them, God only knows how soon it will be before someone comes to us . . ."

"And rats on the rats, you mean?" the President asked.

"Yes, sir, that's precisely what I mean. And I'm not talking only about identifying the Masterson murderers—I think it very likely that the major has already 'rendered them harmless'—but the people who ordered the murders. The masterminds of the oil-for-food scandal, those who have profited from it. Sir, in my judgment, the major has not failed. He has rendered the country a great service, and is to be commended."

"You ever hear, Charles, that great minds run on similar paths? I had just about come to the same conclusion. But one question, Charles: What should we do with the sixteen million dollars? Tell the UN it's there and let them worry about getting it back?"

"Actually, sir, I had an off-the-top-of-my-head thought about that money. According to the major, all it takes is Lorimer's signature on those documents, whatever they're called, that the major brought back from the hideaway to have that money transferred anywhere."

"But Lorimer's dead," the President said.

"They have some very talented people over in Langley, if the President takes my meaning."

"You mean, forge a dead man's signature and steal the money? For what purpose?"

"Mr. President, I admit that when I first learned what you were asking the major to do, I was something less than enthusiastic. But I was wrong, and I admit it. A small unit like the major's can obviously be very valuable in this new world war. And if sixteen million dollars were available to it, sixteen million untraceable dollars . . ."

"I take your point, Charles," the President said. "But I'm going to ask you to stop thinking off the top of your head."

"Sir?"

"The next thing you're likely to suggest is that Charley—and that's his name, Charles, not 'the major'—move the Office of Organizational Analysis into the office of the director of national intelligence. And that's not going to happen. Charley works for me, period, not open for comment."

Secretary Hall had a sudden coughing spasm. His face grew red.

Ambassador Montvale did not seem to suspect that Secretary Hall might be concealing a hearty laugh.

"Natalie, do you have anything to say before I send Charley out of here to take, with my profound thanks, a couple of weeks off? After he lets everybody in his apartment go, of course."

"I was thinking about Ambassador Lorimer, sir. He's ill, and it will devastate him to learn what his son has been up to."

"Jesus, I hadn't thought about that," the President said. "Charley, what about it?"

"Sir, Mr. Lorimer is missing in Paris," Charley said. "The man who died in Shangri-La was Jean-Paul Bertrand, a Lebanese. I don't think anyone will be anxious to reveal who Bertrand really was. And I don't think we have to, or should."

"What about his sister?" Natalie Cohen asked. "Should she be told?"

"I think so, yes," Charley said. "I haven't thought this through, but I have been thinking that the one thing I could tell Mrs. Masterson that would put her mind at rest about the threats to her children would be that I knew her brother was dead, and with his death, these bastards . . . excuse me . . . had no more interest in her or her children."

"And if she asks how you know, under what circumstances?" the President asked.

"That's what I haven't thought through, sir."

"You don't want to tell her what a despicable sonofabitch he was, is that it?"

"I suspect she knows, sir. But it's classified Top Secret–Presidential."

"Would anyone have objections to my authorizing Charley to deal with the Masterson family in any way he deems best, including the divulgence of classified material?"

"Splendid idea, Mr. President," Ambassador Montvale said.

"Do it soon, Charley. Please," Natalie Cohen said.

"Yes, ma'am."

The President stood up and came around the desk and offered Castillo his hand.

"Thank you, Charley. Good job. Go home and get some rest. And then think where you can discreetly hide sixteen million dollars until you need it."

[SIX]
Room 527
Fifth Floor, Silverstein Pavilion
Hospital of the University of Pennsylvania
3400 Spruce Street
Philadelphia, Pennsylvania
2135 1 August 2005

"Hey, baby! I'm home."

"Oh, Charley!"

"How are you doing?"

"Look at me. My face looks like somebody attacked me with a baseball bat."

"You look beautiful. Can I kiss you?"

"You're sure you want to?"

"I'm sure I want to."

Five minutes later, they stopped.

She smiled at him.

"What I was afraid you were going to do was come back from Europe, and walk in here and start that stupid Wiener schnitzel nonsense again. I like it better when you just say you love me."

"Oh, shit. I forgot."

"Forgot what?"

He went into his briefcase and came out with an aluminum foil–wrapped package.

"What's that?"

"Wiener schnitzel, the real thing. Except that this comes from Budapest, not Vienna. You get the best Hungarian *gulyás* in Vienna, but the best Wiener schnitzel comes from Budapest. Understand?"

She didn't reply. She simply took his hand and held it against her cheek. He saw that she was crying, but he knew it wasn't because she was unhappy.

AFTERWORD

One of the characters in this book was a Special Forces medic.

The Special Forces Association tries hard to keep up with former Green Berets. Sadly, this includes regularly publishing brief notices of their passing, giving their name, rank, where they served, as what, the highest medal (if any) for valor they were awarded, and the cause and date of their death. One such will appear for a Special Forces medic who died as I was finishing this book. It will read something like this:

WALTON, John. Sergeant. Vietnam. Medic. Silver Star. While piloting experimental aircraft. 27 June 2005.

In the case of Sergeant Walton, other obituaries published in newspapers around the world—often on the front page—were much longer, and made reference to the fact that he earned the Silver Star—the nation's third-highest award for valor—by saving the lives of fellow soldiers under fire.

And reported that the Wal-Mart executive, and son of the founder of Wal-Mart, died the eleventh-richest man in the world, with a fortune of $18.2 billion.

W.E.B. Griffin is the author of the bestselling Brotherhood of War, Corps, Badge of Honor, Men at War, Honor Bound, and Presidential Agent series. He has been invested into the orders of St. George of the U.S. Armor Association and St. Andrew of the U.S. Army Aviation Association; is a life member of the U.S. Special Operations Association; and is a member of Gaston-Lee Post 5660 of the Veterans of Foreign Wars, China Post #1 in Exile of the American Legion, and the Police Chiefs Association of Southeast Pennsylvania, South New Jersey, and Delaware. He has been named an honorary life member of the U.S. Army Otter & Caribou Association, the U.S. Army Special Forces Association, the U.S. Marine Corps Raider Association, and the USMC Combat Correspondents Association. Visit his website at www.webgriffin.com.

Penguin Group (USA) Inc.
is proud to present

GREAT READS—GUARANTEED

**We are so confident you will love
this book that we are offering a
100% money-back guarantee!**

If you are not 100% satisfied with
this publication, Penguin Group (USA) Inc.
will refund your money!
Simply return the book before
March 2, 2007 for a full refund.

**With a guarantee like this one,
you have nothing to lose!**